FALLING FOR THE ENEMY

THE COMPLETE SERIES

Falling for the Enemy

A PARANORMAL WHY CHOOSE COMPLETE SERIES

LUNA PIERCE

Editing by Cruel Ink Editing
Proofing by Tiffany Hernandez
First Edition 2025
ASIN (ebook)
ISBN 978-1-957238-23-4 (Hardback)
ISBN 978-1-957238-29-6 (Paperback)

Stolen by Monsters

FALLING FOR THE ENEMY (BOOK ONE)

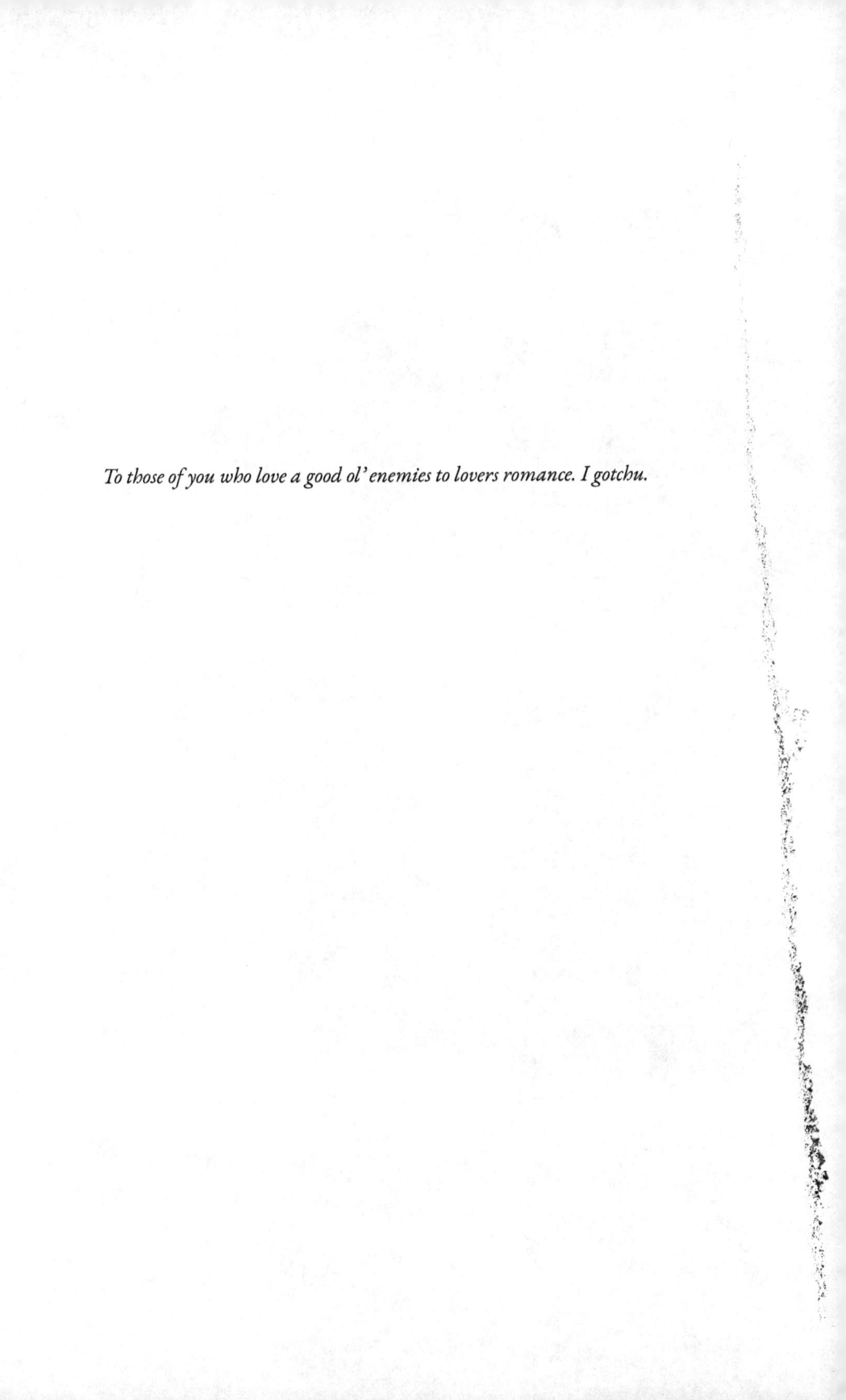

To those of you who love a good ol' enemies to lovers romance. I gotchu.

Wren

Warm and thick blood trickles out of my nose and gurgles its way up my throat and into my mouth.

I lay there, face down, silent, and motionless on the cold, hard, dirty floor.

I don't dare open my eyes. According to the pain coursing through my body, I'm convinced that I've fractured multiple bones.

I'm not sure I could move if I wanted to.

I was once a feared assassin, and now I'm a broken mess scattered at the base of these stairs in an old, abandoned building on the outskirts of a run-down town.

I wait for death—slow and cruel in her sadistic manner. But she takes her time, taunting me from the sweet release only she could bring.

"Is she alive?" A male voice whispers.

"I...I don't think so," the other person responds.

His tone is smooth and angelic with something resembling concern weaved in.

One of the men approaches, so close I can smell the sweet scent of honey on his breath. Such a contrast to the dirt and decay of this end of the forgotten city.

But there's nothing sweet about him. I'm in enemy territory and this can only mean one thing—he's come to finish me off.

I did something I never do; I made a mistake...a slip up that cost me everything. And now, not only did I miss my target, but I'm going to meet the same fate that was intended for him.

If only death would stop playing games and hurry up and take me from this disgusting place and save me from whatever torture I'm about to endure.

Despite my best efforts to play dead, I choke on the red metallic mess coating my mouth.

One of the people gasps. Or maybe it was both. I can't be certain with the ringing in my ears and throbbing in my head.

Cool hands find their way under my frame, gently tilting me to the side.

I keep my eyes shut. There's no need to witness what will happen next.

I'm no stranger to gore but being on the receiving end of it is never any fun.

Unless it's consensual, then that's a different story entirely.

I stifle a curse that rolls off my tongue and wince at the new wave of pain coursing through me at the change in positions.

Why couldn't they just leave me there to die alone, semi-peacefully?

Haven't they already done enough damage?

I know better than to expect anything different out of their kind. Vile, demented creatures who do nothing but torment and taint our world with their bloodlust and desire to take what is not theirs. They kill without cause, wiping out entire villages and leaving no innocent spared. It's those like me who are tasked to eliminate them in an attempt to even the playing field and protect the balance. The demons and their bringers are the evil that must be purged from our world.

I have trained for this position my entire life. And I have worked tirelessly the last four years to wipe out every target I've been assigned. Up until today, I have had a complete success rate, killing more of them than I can count and saving many lives in the process.

I rose through the ranks swiftly, becoming the acclaimed *Furla Ain* only two years into my post.

Most feared assassin.

My name is respected, carries great terror, and is something I take immense pride in.

What a disgrace I am, my limp body being carried out of here by the enemy.

Everything hurts. Every inch this creature takes is another blip of sharp pain, dull pain, fierce pain.

I clench my jaw, desperately trying to disassociate myself from the agony and somehow, it only brings more.

How I'm still alive is a mystery in itself. I should be dead from the injuries alone, and yet, here I am, writhing through the torment.

Don't get me wrong, in any other situation I'd be grateful...but knowing I'm in bad company means the suffering has only just begun. Whatever they have in store for me will be much worse than the trauma I've already experienced.

"Wes, what are you doing?" The one guy asks the other.

His core tightens along with his grip on me. "I don't know."

"We...we aren't taking her, are we?"

"We can't leave her there."

"Since when?" The person shuffles closer.

"Let it go, Dash. We'll talk about it at home."

Home? He's taking me to where they live? This can't be good. I must do something, anything.

I wiggle under his grip, doing everything I can to garner the strength to move.

Maybe if I free myself, I can drop to the ground and my injuries will finally deliver me to death's front door.

His hold on me remains tight and unwavering.

I force my eyes open despite their swollen nature and settle my sights on the thing I'm pressed against. A creature resembling a man, the one I had laid my gaze on earlier. When I made the simple and careless mistake of faltering.

Chiseled jawline, pointed nose, thick and bushy eyebrows. If he were of my kind, he'd be attractive, but he's not. His blood is tainted. His demonic nature is prevalent in the glowing red orbs of his eyes and pulsing energy he exudes. A trait that hunters like myself are capable of seeing thanks to the additional lens we were gifted with when we became of age. It allows us an advantage in our hunts to find our targets with ease. A talent that I have refined these past few years to become the best possible assassin I could be.

I suck in a breath, choking on the copper-tasting liquid caked on the inside of my mouth and throat.

The thing holding me tilts his head down and peers into my eyes. "Sleep." His voice is solid, stern, penetrating. It's powerful and commanding and somehow has total control over me.

My dreams are filled with endless recollections of my failure playing on repeat. Each one of them ends the same, with me being captured by the enemy and tortured until my warrior body finally gives out.

Killing me quickly would be too much of a gift that they would never be willing to give me. No, they want it slow and agonizing. Their joy comes from inflicting pain on others and draining the lifeforce gradually from their victims.

At least, when I kill their kind, I'm swift and merciful, ending their lives before they know what hit them. My job is to eliminate, not drag the process out. I don't take pleasure in murdering them—I take it in protecting my kind and eliminating any threat they may bring.

Some would say those go hand in hand.

I don't kill for fun. I kill because I must. Because it's what I'm good at. Because it's the only way for us to survive.

I was never going to be one of those girls who stayed home and made children. Who coddled their babies and tended to their partner's needs. Don't get me wrong, it's probably an equally difficult job, it just wasn't what I was designed to do.

Not when danger was always one step away.

I made that decision at the ripe age of three when my birth mother was brutally slaughtered, and I hid like a coward under the floorboards of the shack we lived in. There was nothing she could do to protect me, and the same could be said the other way around. Our home was set on fire and the smoke had almost gotten to me by the time I crawled my way out and ran as fast as I could to the neighboring town.

I was a child, and at that moment, I knew all I needed to know about the brutalities of this world and what I must do to protect myself, and those around me. I wouldn't take the same path as the other girls my age—no, I would spend every single day training to become a fearless hunter, because that was the only option I saw in my mind. I would not allow myself to succumb to that same fate. I would not be helpless and fall victim to the demon bringers and the vile creatures they unleashed on us.

I would make it my life's mission to vanquish every last one of them.

And now, here I fucking am, reliving an endless nightmare of all the things I did wrong to end up where I am today. Beaten, bloodied, and close to death with those I hate the most.

My entire body aches—dull and sharp all at once. I suck in a breath of the stale air and wiggle my fingers, then my toes.

Yep, I'm very much alive, despite how fucking terrible I feel. And being able to move just that little bit means I'm not completely broken beyond repair.

Not that it matters, I'll never make it out of here alive, not if these brutal beasts have anything to do with it.

The scent of beeswax and rosemary tickles my nose. A healing salve.

I blink a few times, adjusting my eyes to the dimly lit room I've been put in, but don't bother moving. Not yet. I must take things slow and assess my surroundings before acting too irrationally. Hightailing out of here is a given, but I must be smart about it. I'm in no condition to take on two demons, especially the one who refused to let me die in that building. If he wanted me here, it was for some twisted game, and I refuse to play into his hand. If my survival stands any chance, I have to be strategic.

I sigh and scan the space. Not like I have much of a future if I make it out alive anyway. Dravin and Parla will have my head for the mess I created. Not eliminating my targets and getting taken is a huge no-no, along with the handful of casualties and weapons that were lost. I'm valuable to them, and they would rather I die at their hands than that of a demon. If my soul is captured by anyone other than the committee, it will mean an entire shitstorm for my people.

My essence is too precious for anyone other than the right people to get their hands on.

That's the thing with us warriors—our souls become more powerful with each demon life we end, their power diminishing and transferring over to us. There's more magic behind it than I'll ever begin to understand, but the moral of the story is—don't get caught. Not everyone knows this fancy little detail, but those that do are incredibly dangerous. Consuming a seasoned warrior's soul can do irreparable damage to what we've spent centuries working toward.

I should have died back in that building, alone, with no one around, and my soul to vanish into the abyss, never to be used as a power source by any other living creature. Instead, I'm here, going to die at the hands of the very man I was set out to kill.

Man...I shouldn't even refer to him that way. He's part man, part demon. A walking disgrace and a reminder of the life I lost all those years ago. He may not be directly responsible for my mother's death, but he might as well have shoved his fist into her chest and ripped her heart out himself. I can't look at a single demon without imagining it being them that ended her that fateful day. Or think that maybe they're the reason my father never came home. I never learned what happened to him, but I can only assume his death was caused by the evil creatures I wish to rid from our realm.

"You're awake," a soft voice says.

My heart goes wild, but I do my best to calm it. I will not lose control, not yet.

"Here." He stands from his spot in the corner and brings over a small cup.

How did I not notice he was sitting over there? I can smell the demon in the other room, but nothing of this one. No, he smells of cedar and lavender mixed with sweat.

I grip at the small cot I'm lying on and shove myself to where I'm sitting upright. My head spins and I continue to blink to clear my sights. I'm dizzier than I should be. Like there's a poison in my veins rendering me weak and unable to act normally.

My gaze settles on my left leg, and the two wooden slats on both sides. Dirty fabric is tied around the top and bottom, securing it in place.

Why would they try to help me when they're only going to end my life eventually?

"Here," he says again. "Drink."

I lift a shaky hand and take the offering from him, watching his bright eyes shine through the murky room. I tilt it sideways and dump the contents on the floor, not caring about it splattering onto his shoes.

There's no way in hell I'd consume whatever that was and he's a fool for ever thinking I would.

"Ah, man. Really?" He snatches the cup from me, but instead of getting mad and hitting me like I expect, he walks back over to the small table with the pitcher and pours more of the liquid into the cup. "I get it, really, I do. You don't trust easily. But listen..." He steps over and kneels beside me, tipping the thing up to his lips. "Look." He takes a sip and swallows. "See."

I narrow my gaze at him, desperately trying to sense his aura. It doesn't add up. There's nothing demonic about him. He's also not one of me. And if that's the case, that means he's...human? We don't have those here though. Not in this realm. It's incredibly uncommon, if not rare for that to happen. The realms were closed off ages ago, and the chances of their kind surviving here are slim to none.

There's no possible way he could have made it through on his own.

I shouldn't, but I open my mouth anyway. "What are you?"

He continues to extend his hand, offering me the cup. "I'm Dash."

"What's a *dash*?"

"No, that's my name." He sighs and glances at the cup. "You should really drink this. You'll heal quicker if you do."

Why does he care if I heal or not?

I study his frame, sizing him up to determine whether I could overpower him in my current state. I've taken down larger beasts, telling me that the chances here are likely, but not knowing what waits for me outside this small room has me hesitant on acting just yet. I must be smart, cautious, mindful. All the things I was not when I hesitated and messed things up terribly.

"Why?" I eye the cup and then him.

His features are soft, not at all like the hardened exterior of the *thing* that carried me to my confinement. Thick, red hair, and kind eyes. Which can only mean he's good at this whole pretending to care act he's putting on.

Maybe they're going for the good guy bad guy thing to fuck with my head.

"Well, staying hydrated is important, obviously," Dash says. "And if you don't take care of your body, it will hinder its ability to bounce back from situations such as these."

Is he really explaining to me the importance of water? "That's not what I meant."

"What then?" He tilts his head slightly, a genuine confusion settling onto his handsome face.

"Nothing." I take the cup from him because regardless of his intentions, he's telling the truth. I need whatever strength I can recoup if I stand any chance of breaking free of my captors.

"Don't drink it so—"

But it's too late, I down it all in three swigs, a bit of the liquid trickling down onto my tattered but still intact armor.

My stomach immediately gurgles but I ignore it and assess the rest of my body.

I should be worse off than this. I was close to death when they took me, but now, I'm somehow remotely healed of a handful of the injuries I had obtained. That doesn't make any sense. None of this does. Why am I not already dead?

The door to the room bursts open and I do my best not to flinch at the sudden arrival. Instinctually, I reach for a weapon, but come up empty-handed. I grab the cup I had sat beside me and grip it in my hand. Anything can be a weapon if you try hard enough.

The intruder scoffs. "What do you intend on doing with that?" He leans into the doorframe and crosses his arms over his chest. His muscles bulge the dark fabric of the shirt he's wearing. He's more man than a beast at this point, but I can still sense his demonic nature.

I clench my jaw and imagine the many things I'd like to do to him. All of them ending in his death.

That's what I've trained for my entire life. Kill the demons and their bringers that have corrupted our realm with their impure and ruthless bloodline.

Many, many years ago, our realm was compromised by the demon bringers. A portal to the hell dimensions was opened and their kind was brought over to feast on the souls of all that called Prania their home.

A war ensued that went on for ages—finally resulting in triumph over the demons. The portals were closed off permanently, allowing no travel to and from our realm to any other. All that remained of their kind went into hiding, only to come out every so often to feast on the innocent when the opportunity presented itself. The more they consumed, the more powerful they became.

It is up to those with specialized skills like me to eradicate them before they can gain enough power to reopen another portal and unleash havoc on our realm once again.

Each of my kind they kill, the greater the chances of that happening. Especially when our power from killing them is transferred over if they consume our soul.

I cannot permit that to happen.

Another door opens, from outside this room. The man in the doorway flits his gaze at the source of the sound but remains firmly planted a few feet away from me.

I smell the thing immediately—the demon's heavy aroma filling the air at a quick pace.

His blood must be entirely made up of darkness if his scent is that potent.

Now there are three of them I must overpower if I intend to make it out of here.

It's not an impossible task, but my injuries will make it a difficult and interesting one.

"You brought a fucking hunter here?" The monster growls and tries to push past the other demon in the doorway. "Let me in there, I'll rip its flesh off and savor every last bite."

Yeah, it's safe to say things are about to get even more interesting.

CHAPTER 2

Bo

I hate hunters.

Warriors.

Assassins.

Demon slayers.

Whatever the fuck you want to call them, they're all garbage and I'd like to end every single one of them.

Preferably slowly, and as painfully as possible. You get what I'm putting down, right?

They kill us and I kill them.

I shove Wes and grip at his arm, trying to pry him out of my way. "What the fuck is wrong with you?"

He stands there, taking up the space and not budging to let me through. "Bocephus."

"You're really pissing me off, Wes."

"What's new?" He slams his hand into my shoulder and knocks me back. "A minute of your time before you dismember our newest arrival?"

I breathe in deeply and exhale, steadying my gaze on him. "Fine." I crane my neck to look past him. "How come Dash gets to be in there?"

Wes runs his fingers over his jaw. "Because Dash is harmless." He pokes me. "You, on the other hand, need to learn a little restraint."

I throw my hands up and take a step back. If they want restraint, they'll get it. For now.

"Sit." Wes points at our eating table in the front room.

I comply, only because I know if I give him a bit of what he wants, it'll get me closer to ripping that hunter apart with my razor-sharp teeth. Oh, what a tasty snack it will be.

"Wipe that murderous look off your face, too, while you're at it." Wes crosses his arms over his chest.

"What, is it your new plaything or something?"

"*She* could be the leverage we need."

"*She?*" I stiffen and glance toward where we just came from. I didn't notice *what* it was, only that it was the enemy. There aren't many female hunters, and in my time spent in this realm, I've only encountered one other. I didn't get the privilege of ending it, but she died that day all the same. One less hunter is a win in my book.

And considering there's one sitting in the other room, it's only a matter of moments before I end its life, too. *Her* life.

"Your ass stays firmly planted in that chair if you know what's good for you." Wes draws my attention back to his stupid face.

"You better get to that part where you explain what's going on or I'm going to go in there and finish it off." My skin crawls at the idea of it being in such close proximity and not being able to wrap my hands around its throat until the life leaves its body.

They all deserve to die, especially the one in the other room. I can smell the stench of her kills lingering from her body despite her feeble attempt to cover them with magic. When you've been around as long as I have, those tricks no longer have the same impact they do on others.

"You want her back, don't you?"

At this, he steals my attention fully. "What kind of question is that? You know I do."

"Then let's use her."

"How?" She'll kill us the second she gets the chance.

"She's skilled, potentially the fiercest hunter I've come across in all my years." It's almost like Wes is bragging about her.

"Your point?" Because all he's doing is making me want to end her life even more.

"Her life is of value to them. We can barter her, get our people back."

I sigh and rub my temple. "That will never work."

Wes slams his fist on the table, splintering the weak wood surface. "Damn it, it has to."

I study his face, wondering why he's so hellbent on doing the impossible. It's hard enough to survive, let alone go against their kind in the way he's speaking. Going directly to them is suicide, and it has been for everyone with demon blood who's remotely tried it. Prania is ruled and governed by *them* and only them. They answer to no one, especially our kind. We'll be executed on the spot, and that's if we make it there without being killed.

"Why her, Wes? What's different about her than any other hunter we've encountered?"

Wes shifts in his seat, a tell that he's hiding something. We all are, but for once, it's something new I'm unfamiliar with.

"Spit it out." The beast in me stirs, wanting to end this conversation and drain the hunter of its lifeforce, ridding her of any opportunity to kill a demon ever again.

"It's nothing," Wes lies. "Nothing other than the break we've been waiting for. A possibility we didn't think we'd ever get."

"It's never going to work. It's been years, Wes. The chances of them—"

He cuts me off. "Don't talk like that."

"What? For being realistic in managing my expectations? Something you're clearly unable to do." I clench my fist and dig my nails into my palm. The pain slices through me, my own venom stinging my skin. "And you think bringing a fucking hunter into our home is a good idea? You're going to get us all killed. Is that what you want?"

Wes lowers his head, and for a second, I almost feel sorry for him, but that's not an emotion I'm capable of feeling. "No."

"You have a week to figure this shit out, otherwise I'm gutting her." Oh, the satisfaction that would bring me.

Dash mutters something from the other room but I can't quite make it out.

The female appears in the doorway, and for a split second, I'm completely taken by surprise at her features. Dark hair spilling over her shoulders. Plush, pink lips that are cracked and swollen. A deep greenish purple bruise covering most of her face. Blood speckles her cheeks and somehow brings out the golden hue of her eyes. Her porcelain skin is dusted with dried remains of her injuries and potentially her victims. Thick armor covers her body and despite it being worse for wear, it hugs her like a well-fitted glove.

I've never seen a hunter so...

I shake my head. No. I will not allow myself to fall prey to whatever allure she exudes. She is the enemy, and she will remain that until I end her myself. But for now, I will give Wes the satisfaction of thinking he's in control of this situation.

Still, though, there's one thing I absolutely must do. And so, I stand, rushing across the space before anyone can stop me, and spin her toward me. Her scent mixes with mine, her frail figure weakened from the injuries she's still healing from.

I swipe at her hair, moving it from her shoulder, and sink my fangs into her flesh. Her blood pools into my mouth, a decadent flavor, more delicious than anything I've ever tasted.

She wiggles under my grasp, but I continue sucking and enjoying the heavenly surprise of her blood that gushes into my mouth and down my hungry throat.

A fire burns through the clothing covering my shoulder, and latches itself onto my skin in the shape of a hand. It's enough to send me back to reality, the one where Wes is screaming at me to stop, his radiant power melting the skin off my back while he pries this *female* from my grasp.

With her eyes closed, her body goes limp and falls into Dash's arms.

Wes shoves me with a force more powerful than anything he's used on me in the past. A rage unlike any other consuming him—something that makes no fucking sense at all.

She's just a hunter.

"What the fuck is wrong with you?" Wes growls, his other self partially showing through. His eyes glow fiery red. The hand he had touched me with, still a flame flickering along his skin. His own fangs exposed and ready to tear me apart.

I lean against the wall he pushed me into and wipe at my bottom lip with my thumb, licking the remains of her blood off it and allowing the high to consume me. "I was doing you a fucking favor."

"By sucking her dry?" His other fist ignites into a flame and his whole aura borderline engulfs, too.

When has he ever been this concerned about killing a hunter?

"No, you psychotic mutt. By *marking* her." I kick off the wall and point to her body, still being held by the pathetic human we keep around. "She gets too far away from me and that thing will go off like a beacon alerting every demon around to her presence."

"You put a fucking target on her back?" Wes's dark nature doesn't dim down at all.

"I mean, technically it was her neck, but yeah."

Wes acts quicker than I can react, gripping me around my throat and scorching me with his touch. "I'll show you a fucking mark."

"Guys, stop," Dash calls out from his spot hovering near the ground. Somehow, he stands, her body still in his grasp but now he's cradling her.

I've always thought he was a weakling, but he lifted her without wavering whatsoever.

He carries her body out of sight, back into the room she once was in.

Wes turns toward me and points his flaming finger. "You touch her again; I'll fucking kill you myself."

I roll my eyes. "I'd like to see that."

We're a similar height and stature—tall and wide, but with layers of muscle that allow us to crush our victims with ease. There's no telling whose beast is stronger, which makes me uncertain how I would fare if we went head-to-head. It's possible mine would crush his, but considering I've never seen his at full capacity, it's difficult to know with certainty. I might be a cocky shifter, but as much as I enjoy killing, I prefer to live, too. Still, I'd love for the chance to kick his ass.

"Don't test me, Bo." He growls low and shoves me one last time before leaving me there in the hallway.

If I didn't know better, I'd think he had feelings for this hunter, but I do, and there's no way he'd ever be stupid enough to care for the enemy. Either way, he's going to get us all killed with his foolishness.

CHAPTER 3

Wren

I wake feeling worse than I did earlier.

My fingers skim the soft, raised spot on my neck. I wince and steady the anger that builds as I recall the cause of the new wound.

That fucking demon bit me.

"You going to run out of here again?" Dash quips from his spot in the corner.

I sit up and scoot myself against the wall. "Maybe." I swallow the dry lump in my throat and desperately wish for another cup of the water he had offered me earlier. And maybe something of substance to put in my stomach, and a healer to tend to my injuries.

I'd take my weapons, too. One to shove into each of their chests, straight through their hearts to end their lives with more grace than they intend on showing me.

"Are you thirsty?" Dash rubs his eyes and yawns.

"No."

"You're probably not hungry either, or in pain." He stands and walks to the door, turning once he's at the threshold. "Don't move."

And if I do?

Not that I intend on finding out, I'm too tired and worn out to protest. I must gain my strength if I'm going to make it out of here. I snuck past him once before, but the demon in the other room overpowered me with ease. There's no way I'd make it in my current weakened state.

In need of a stretch, I stand, doing my best to stay upright despite the brace on my leg and the dizziness that ensues from being vertical. I hurt everywhere but it will only get worse if I continue to sit still. There's no telling the damage my body has undertaken, especially now that I have demon venom laced in my veins.

I waddle over to where Dash was sitting and run my finger along the small table. Various herbs and salves are haphazardly placed about with no real order to any of them. I pick up one of the cylinders of brown mixture and bring it to my nose, inhaling the strangely familiar scent.

"Old family recipe." He hesitates and adds, "Not mine, but someone else's." Dash plucks it out of my hand and sets it on the table. "I thought I told you not to move."

I cautiously look him over while reading his energy. "I'm not much for following orders."

"Here." He raises his arm, revealing a banana held in his grasp. "Eat this."

Narrowing my gaze, I don't bother taking it.

Dash sighs and peels back the layers of the thing. He nibbles off a small section and holds it out toward me. "Now will you eat it?"

My stomach growls, giving away any chance I had at pretending I didn't want to eat.

"Why are you trying to feed me?" I carefully pluck the banana from his hand without touching him and hobble around to the other side of the table. I bite a chunk of it and force myself to savor the meal, uncertain when my next will be.

There's no telling what kind of torture they have in mind for me. The whole not knowing might possibly be the worst of all. I expected it to start already—either by way of beatings or some kind of physical abuse. Waterboarding, branding, asphyxiation. Maybe they're going for a slow, agonizing, psychological torment. If I'm being honest, I think I prefer the former. It's more predictable and easier to navigate. Whatever is happening now, I'm at a complete fucking loss.

"You won't heal if you don't eat," Dash says very matter-of-factly.

I swallow the mouthful and side-eye him. "And why does it matter if I'm healed?"

He starts to speak but is cut off by a figure appearing in the doorway.

My body tenses immediately, my hunter nature sensing the threat all too late. My injuries are weakening me from the most basic of my skills and that alone is going to guarantee my demise.

"Fraternizing with the enemy, I see." It's the man-beast that brought me here.

"She needs her strength," Dash tells him.

I can only imagine what for, given my history with these types of creatures.

Dash I'm unsure of, but the *thing* in the door, he's up to no good.

"I'm sure you've already noticed, but the bite on your neck." He points to his own skin. "Has infected you with demon's venom."

I continue to eat the rest of the banana Dash had given me and pretend I'm not bothered by what he has to say. It's nothing that a bit of rest won't rid from my system soon enough.

"And since Bo is an alpha."

Those six words halt my heart.

My eyes widen and I do everything in my power to remain calm. "You're lying."

"Why would I lie to you?"

I shift my gaze to the human in the room.

Dash nods gently, a sincereness about his gesture, almost like he feels sorry for what happened. "It's true."

"What is this, some sick fucking game to you?" I steady my body against the wall and frantically search for anything other than this banana peel to arm myself with.

The monster raises his hand out toward me, and although he's across the room, I shrink away from him.

"Don't touch me."

His jaw tenses and he exhales dramatically. "It doesn't have to be like this."

"Why don't you just kill me and get it over with?" I blurt out at them, hoping like hell one of them will take me up on the offer and not realize the weight my soul carries. If I've made it this far, maybe they're unaware of the power it yields.

"We're not going to *kill* you." Dash looks to my captor. "Wes, tell her we don't mean her harm."

"I wanted to end your life the second I sensed your presence." Someone approaches from behind Wes—my radar confirming it's the monster who marked me. He nudges Wes out of the way, trying to get around him.

Wes holds his place but allows him to step into my line of sight.

The creature is as tall as Wes, similar in build, but with a darker aura about him. *Pure evil*, my intuition tells me.

Long black hair pulled partially back, matching onyx eyes, and a jawline that must have been carved by the angels before he was discarded into hell. He brushes his tongue against his teeth, exposing his fangs to me. A grin settles on his face like he knows exactly what he's doing. Taunting me.

"Enough, Bo." Wes elbows him in the chest. "You're not making this any easier."

"Easier?" I laugh. There is no humor in this moment, not with three of my enemies holding me captive, no doubt planning something particularly evil.

If only I had killed them first when I had the opportunity. I'll never make that mistake again. I sealed my own fate when I faltered. I allowed *something* to distract me. Something I'll never quite make sense of no matter how many times I run it through my head. A strange flutter that filled my chest—a stirring, like something was awakening within me. A pointless nothing that would no doubt get me killed by the *thing* that caused it.

Now, I look at that same face that sparked that feeling and am struck with the realization that I was mistaken.

He side-eyes Bo and speaks. "You're not getting inside this room, not after what you did. So stop fucking trying to push past me." A guttural growl escapes him. "You cannot overpower me."

Dash slowly approaches me, a small cup in his hand. "Here."

I don't take my gaze off the men in the doorway as I slide the cup from Dash's hand and down the contents. I shouldn't trust him this easily, but he's given me no reason not to—other than aiding in my captivity. At every possible opportunity, he's shown me kindness and maybe if I play into that, I can use him to get free of these other two.

"Thanks," I tell him.

Dash points toward the bed. "You should sit, elevate that leg." He snaps his fingers like he suddenly remembered something and turns toward the table filled with various concoctions.

I watch him out of my peripheral while I continue to stare at the beasts in the doorway.

In my current condition, there's no way I could fight either of them, let alone both. Especially knowing that Bo is an alpha. That means his powers are stronger than I anticipated, possibly the fiercest demon I've come across. And here he is, having marked me and standing only a few feet away, practically foaming at the mouth to finish me off.

Legends say that being marked by an alpha is a surefire way to get killed, because the only way for it to not send out a glaring beacon to other demons, is to stay close to the one who bit you. But when the one who bit you is the sick fuck who wants you dead, there is no making it out alive. His venom might not kill me, but he will. And if I manage to get away, any demon within the surrounding villages will be on my ass the second I break free.

Maybe that's a reality I'll have to accept—that a target will forever be on my head, or well, neck. I guess it'll make my job easier, the demons coming to me instead of me having to go to them. Not knowing which targets are coming my way though, sure does complicate things.

I typically try to be thorough with my research, figure out my enemy's strengths and weaknesses before going after them. It's one of the things that ensure my success rate. On rare occasions I hunt on a whim, it's usually prompted by a short notice order given by my authorities.

This last mission confirms my dislike of not being prepared.

I will do what I do best and figure my way out of this, though. I will strategize and use any resource I can to free myself, even if I have to start with the sweet red-headed human fumbling through the miscellaneous vials.

"Ah, there it is." He plucks a small dark-colored bottle and pours some of the contents into the cap. "Drink this."

What's with him constantly trying to feed me things?

Without asking, he sips a tiny amount and refills it. "Not trying to poison you. It's a healing tonic to speed up your natural healing process."

I make note of the way the bottle looks for future reference. I'll down the whole thing if it means getting better sooner and regaining my strength. I'd love to try my hand at fighting these two beasts and adding them to the souls I've consumed to rid them from this realm.

An alpha would no doubt fuel me in a way I could never imagine, making me an unstoppable force in the face of my enemies. Maybe then I could eliminate the filth from our world and give my people a fighting chance at truly being free.

Dash plucks the empty cap from my hand and secures it back on the bottle, tucking it in with the others it was surrounded with. He smirks, a bit pleased with himself—either from not having to convince me to consume the liquid or at having come up with the idea of the use of the tonic.

"Are you going to tell her, or shall we stand around all day gawking at the revolting bitch?" Bo leans against what little of the doorframe that Wes allows him to have.

"Language," Wes snaps at him.

Bo exhales dramatically. "She is rather revolting, there's no denying that."

I glare at him and imagine ripping his tongue out and shoving it down his throat.

"Tell me what?" I settle onto the bed, scooting myself up to the wall and bringing my injured leg up onto the sad excuse of a mattress.

It could be worse, I remind myself.

My thoughts float through countless scenarios of what Wes could possibly say next, all of which end terribly for me. Regardless, if they're going to confide in me their plan, it could help me maneuver my way out of it. I won't deny them of that error in judgment. Their loss will be my gain.

"We'd like to discuss your release." Wes seems uncomfortable with these words, giving away a falseness to them that I'm not sure he realizes he's exuding.

I snort, crossing my arms over my chest. The movement sends spikes of pain through my body that I choose to ignore. I'm covered in bruises and abrasions from head to toe, just rubbing my skin against my clothing is uncomfortable. "Go on."

Fat fucking chance they're going to free me, but I'll entertain whatever this is considering I have nothing else to do at the moment while my body rebounds from the brutal beating it took.

"We have people at Rock Bridge. You're going to help us get them. If you succeed, we go our separate ways." Wes continues to stiff-arm the doorway to disallow Bo from getting through.

An alpha being subdued is a strange sight to witness.

Wes is clearly the one in charge, but why? Shouldn't Bo be the one calling the shots? How did that power dynamic switch from what the natural order should be?

Unless...

I swallow and will my hunter nature to come to the surface and examine Wes for what type of demon he is. My skills fail me, unable to read through his tainted aura. He's a demon, there's no doubt about that, but if he's able to dominate an alpha, he must be something powerful.

Is that why my superiors tasked me to kill him?

I was told he was some low-level grunt, nothing special. An easy target. All I got was his whereabouts and the order to kill on sight. No one warned me of the magnitude of his power. Only that he must be eliminated.

They withheld vital information. Details that absolutely should have been disclosed.

"Are you listening?" Wes snaps his fingers.

I bob my head up and down. "Yeah."

"Then what did I just say?" Wes clenches his jaw and huffs, clearly annoyed by my lack of paying attention.

It's not my fault this entire situation is incredibly distracting. Between my injuries, my captivity, the demon venom coursing through me, and the puzzle I've yet to solve, my mind is going wild at trying to focus on any one thing.

I stare at him, unable to form a proper response. Truthfully, I have no fucking clue what he said. It couldn't be more important than figuring out what kind of demon he is.

Bo shakes his head. "Bitch isn't even listening."

I'm on my feet in an instant, despite the two boards strapped around my leg hindering me from moving how I typically do. "Why don't you come in here and say that again?" I rush over but Dash quite literally dashes over and steps in front of me.

I breathe in his human scent and push up against his warm non-demonic body.

How could someone so...*innocent* be in cahoots with these two hellish creatures?

Wes holds Bo back from bursting into the room, his hands glowing red as they pierce Bo's flesh. "If I have to remind you one more fucking time about your language."

Bo snarls at him. "You'll what? Huh." Bo squirms under Wes's grip. "Get your fucking hands off me."

Wes breathes and a billow of smoke comes rolling out, fire trickles behind it, and nips at Bo's hardened face.

Bo winces and ducks from being struck again by the flame. "What the fuck, Wes?"

Fire ripples on Wes's hands and out his mouth. He could be a witch, but no, I'd be able to sense that. His nature is too demonic. Dragon shifter? No, those have been extinct for quite some time, and he shows no other features alluding to that.

I rack my brain for what other demons have this ability, coming up short every time I think I find a lead to follow.

What could he be? And why am I so hellbent on figuring it out? He's powerful, that's a given. But maybe if I discover what he is, I can unearth his weaknesses, too —getting me one step closer to freedom.

Bo is a demon, clear as day. His blood is purely evil, nothing else about him. He's an alpha of his kind, making him that much more of a threat. Alphas are usually immune to a plethora of the typical demon weaknesses—lamb's blood, sugar, angel's feathers. Alphas have few flaws, and they're usually personal to the beast. I was once told that an alpha's ultimate downfall is its heart. Like, they have one of those. At least, not in the capacity of loving a damn thing other than killing my kind.

Dash continues to guide me away from the two idiots at the door. "You really should rest." He pauses, his hands gripping my shoulders. "I don't know your name." His brows furrow with the loss of not knowing that one word. He peers down at me, waiting for some kind of response.

His recent kindness is the only reason I open my mouth. "Wren."

"Wren," he repeats, trying it out for himself. He grins. "I like that."

I ignore the sense of satisfaction I feel rush over me at his smile. My injuries and the demon venom must be messing with my system, making me susceptible to his charm.

"Wren," another person mutters.

I glance around Dash to see Wes finally let go of Bo. They both gawk at me like I just grew a horn out of my forehead.

"What?" I ask them.

Bo waves his hand at the smoke billowing from his melted flesh, but remains in place, not coming forward despite Wes no longer blocking his path.

I hobble over to the bed and plop onto the mattress. The minimal exertion wasted almost every ounce of strength I had. I am no longer the strong and capable warrior I once was. I have been weakened, subdued, and poisoned—my power at an all-time low in the worst possible situation.

I want nothing more than to escape this hell, but how will I manage that if I can't even walk across the room without overexerting myself? Is it the injuries? The venom? A different infection in my body I'm unaware of? Has Dash been using his soft nature to lure me in and trick me into consuming something that would keep me weak?

"I said..." Wes clears his throat. "That if you help us, we can cure the marking."

I blink up at him, his words piercing through my soul.

Cure?

That's not possible. There is no such thing for an alpha bite, other than death itself.

"You're lying," I tell him.

"I'm not."

"Why would I believe you?"

"I give you my word." Wes stands firmly in place, like his serious nature will somehow convince me he's telling the truth.

"Your word means nothing to me." I narrow my gaze at him.

He shifts slightly, almost flinching at my declaration. "These people, they're important to us. You might not care about them, but I do, and I wouldn't risk their life on that."

I desperately try to read him, not just with my hunter skills, but with everything I have. If it weren't for his demonic nature, perhaps I'd feel sorry for him. He seems genuinely concerned about whoever it is he wants to rescue. Maybe he is being truthful about the cure. But if that's the case, why have I never heard of such a thing in all my years?

I bite at the inside of my lip and recall my earlier thoughts, of not being informed that Wes was anything other than the fierce creature he is, dominating an alpha with ease. If that major detail was so easily omitted, what else have I not been told? Is it possible there is a cure after all? And if that's the case, wouldn't I be a fool for not doing whatever I can to get it?

Even if that means going against every single instinct I have and teaming up with the things I hate the most.

CHAPTER 4

Wren

No one has ever made it out of Rock Bridge alive.

Demons are taken there, tortured for information of the whereabouts of others, and slaughtered once they are of no further use.

It's the worst place for a demon to go. Not that they deserve any special treatment considering their existence is a plague I wish to rid from our realm.

Some low-level demons might get put to work at other locations, but Rock Bridge is a death sentence for anyone with demon blood.

I keep those details to myself though, because if I confess that to the men holding me captive, I might never get that cure they're bartering with. If it even exists. On the off chance that it does, maybe if I actually help them, they'll sympathize and follow through with their end of the bargain. If I want to be free of the mark lighting me up like a beacon to other demonic creatures, I have to at least try.

Countless things are going against me here. The wounds on my body. The lack of proper hydration and nutrition. The stress and fatigue I've undertaken. The venom flowing in my veins. The broken leg. The concussion. The fact that Dravin and Parla are no doubt sending out a team to either recover my soul or chop my head off for failing a mission. The hotheaded demon who marked me and wants nothing more than to end my life in the same capacity I want to end his. The beast that is more powerful than his comrade, one I can't quite figure out. I could go on and on, the odds continually being stacked against me.

At least there's Dash—the thoughtful and kind human who doesn't fit in at all here. It's hard to hate him when he's as soft as he is. An anomaly to this sick and twisted world we live in. Trusting him is dangerous, but I use it to my advantage; the more I grow lax to his presence, the more I can learn about the situation to gain an upper hand.

"I brought you something to eat." Dash steps into the room with a plate in his grasp. Resting on top is a large chunk of bread and a few pieces of cheese. "I'm sorry it's not much, we haven't made a supply run in a while."

I wonder where they typically get their resources from, but I don't bother asking. I don't want to hear the stories of the villages they must ransack and pillage to fuel their demonic ways.

Despite my sudden distaste for his offering, I take it anyway knowing if I don't nourish my body, I won't get better.

I plop a slice of the cheese into my mouth and lean against the wall. "Thanks." I finish chewing before speaking again. "How did you end up with those two?" I point toward the doorway where at least one of them is keeping put around the corner. Their energy floats toward me and when I suck in a breath, I grow familiar with the darkness.

If I'm not mistaken, that would be Wes in the other room, not Bo. Bo's scent is more pungent.

Dash sits in the chair at the small table in the corner. "Well, there's not much to the story, really." He scratches at his chin. "I woke up in the forest to them poking me with a stick. I guess they both thought I was dead." Dash shrugs. "I have no memory prior to that. Not of my name, where I came from, my family, nothing."

I chew another bite of the cheese and wait for him to continue.

"I had no idea who they were, but they refused to leave me out there. They took me in, let me tag along with them in the hopes that I would regain my memory and find my way home. Days went by, then weeks turned into months, into years. I never did piece anything together, and by the time I realized I wouldn't, there was no point in separating from them. It's..." He glances toward the door. "Too dangerous out there for someone like me. I don't have any powers, I'm just...me."

Two demons adopting a human—what a strange thing to witness. If I hadn't heard the story directly from his mouth, I'm not sure I ever would have believed it. And even now, part of me still doubts the validity of it all. Demons are cruel, brutal, violent—why would they spare this meager person's life? Not to mention, the liability he is to them, the weakness and weight of having to fend for someone who cannot fend for himself.

And to think that it's Wes and Bo, an alpha and...something else much more powerful. They should have ripped apart Dash on sight, eaten his flesh, and desecrated his body in their natural demonic ways.

Dash continues, "They trained me in combat, so I'm not completely useless, but I still stand no chance with the creatures of this world. And despite their extensive help, we haven't met any others like me in all our time together."

"They tried to find your family?" Another detail that surprises me. Perhaps they were just doing what they could to get Dash out of their hair without feeling guilty about it.

Demons don't feel guilt.

"For a while, yes. It was a fruitless labor though. And a risky one. I finally insisted that we stop and accept the fact that I was forsaken, abandoned, or just plain alone, whatever you want to call it. No one was coming for me, and there was no one out there expecting me to come home."

"You have Wes and Bo, you're not alone." I suddenly find myself trying to ease his sadness.

Dash smiles without showing his teeth and nods. "Yeah, you're right."

Shuffling in the other room draws my attention, and not a few moments later, Wes appears in the door. I ignore the immediate stir in my chest at the sight of him, and shove it down and away. Is it a warning? My natural instincts telling me to choose fight or flight if I want to survive? Whatever that is, I cannot afford to allow it to distract me.

He leans against the doorframe; a post he typically holds each time he somewhat enters this space. He doesn't come inside but maintains a distance. Something about it sets me on edge.

Wes looks me straight in the eyes. "Have you had adequate time to think over my proposition?"

I'm not sure there are enough seconds that could tick by that would prepare me for making a deal with the enemy. Never in a million years did I think my life would squander to this, but here I am, at his mercy, an alpha marker on my neck and no way out.

A week ago, I was at my peak, slaughtering anyone who dared cross me. I was strong and powerful and feared. Now...well, now I feel like a damn fool.

"I have," I tell him.

"And?" Wes stands straight, crossing his arms over his chest. His face hardens in anticipation.

"You're sure there's a cure?" I ask him, despite knowing he could lie to me.

Wes nods. "Yes. On my life."

Something I'm not so sure he realizes I don't care much for.

That unfamiliar thing in my core flutters again at that thought. Something inside me does not agree with my mind. So that's not a warning sign after all? Or maybe it's letting me know that I need him alive if I stand a chance. He does seem to be the only thing holding Bo at bay from ripping out my throat. And in my weakened state, I sort of need that assistance. I've got Dash on my side, what's the harm of doing the same with Wes until I can come up with an actual plan to break free. Even if they get me a cure, there's no telling if they'll follow through with letting me go. Hell, I wouldn't if I were them. I'd kill me on the spot before I had a chance to kill them.

"Okay."

"Okay?" Wes drops his arms to the side and hesitantly inches forward.

I sense Dash's gaze flitting between the both of us.

Wes takes a few steps into the room, closing that barrier of distance between us. He extends his hand. "Then it's a deal?"

I stand and hobble toward the beast towering over me. His outstretched hand is massive compared to mine, and yet, I grip it anyway and firmly shake it, fully ignoring the strange sensation now coursing through me.

I've only ever touched a demon either during or right after I killed them. Never casually and this...intimately. What I expected to be repulsive and degrading, felt nothing different than that of shaking the hand of an associate. And like I already noted, aside from his aura, he appears similar to that of a man.

A rather attractive one, a little voice in my head tells me.

I push that ridiculous idea away.

"Can we have a moment alone?" He asks me while still touching me.

My mouth parts slightly, his request catching me off guard. "Um."

"I wish you no harm," he assures me. Glancing over his shoulder, he looks to Dash. "I don't need long."

Dash sighs and stands from his spot at the table. "You better not hurt her."

"What good would that do me?" Wes mutters before turning toward me. "Sit."

I do so without argument, surprising myself at how obedient I was to such a creature. Is that part of his gimmick? Mind control? That can't be true, otherwise, Bo would have been more receptive to Wes's commands without Wes needing to use brute force. Unless Bo can break free of the compulsion because of his alpha abilities. The variables are seemingly endless.

Wes kneels in front of me and studies my boarded-up leg. He hovers his hand just along the surface and shifts his attention up at me. "May I?"

I swallow and reposition myself. "What are you going to do?"

"I wish you no harm."

"You said that already, but that doesn't answer my question." My heart steadily gallops a bit more intensely at how close he is to my body. I do a quick scan of the room, my instincts trying to locate a weapon. I could rip the sheets off this bed, wrap them around his throat and choke him to death. Smother him with the thin and sad excuse for a pillow I've been using. Or perhaps rip one of the boards from my leg and smack him over the head with it.

A strong part of me runs numerous scenarios through my head, but a little voice floats in and tells me to do the impossible—trust him.

"I'm going to help you." Wes stares up at me through his thick lashes.

"How? Why?"

He breathes in and exhales slowly. "Wren..."

The sound of my name on his lips is something...completely unexpected.

"Fine." What do I have to lose? I'm already at his mercy. He could easily end my life in the blink of an eye at this proximity and the current state of my body.

Wes averts his gaze to my leg and lowers his head to where it's only inches away. His lips move but I cannot make out the words he's muttering against my injury. Slowly, he brings one hand up to untie the fabric at the top of the contraption, and the other to gently hold onto my ankle.

My eyes remain on him the entire time.

A cooling sensation fills the area he's whispering to, followed by a warm rush.

He continues to remove the thing from my leg and discards it to the side. "This is going to be painful, but it won't last, okay?"

Is this it? The moment he ends it all? Why go through the trouble of putting on a show? Is he weirdly ritualistic?

Still, I nod approval. "Okay."

He speaks to my leg once more through the armor of my bottoms. A snap rings out and I stifle a groan that forces its way up my chest. He wasn't wrong—that was brutal, but he was telling the truth when he said it wouldn't last, because within a few seconds, the ache I've felt for days dissipates into a dull and tolerable throb.

"How did you...?" I reach down and run my hands over my leg, wincing at how tender it remains to the touch but reveling in the no longer broken bone.

Does that explain why I am healed of most of the ailments I sustained? That it wasn't my body that did the repairs, but this beast before me?

Wes hesitates with his hand still resting on my lower thigh, almost like he's trying to make sense of the whole situation himself. He stands and dusts off his sides despite having nothing there to swipe away.

Is he nervous? Embarrassed? What strange behavior is this that he's displaying and why can't I figure it out?

He reaches for me. "Try to apply some weight to it."

I pause, too, but decide to take him up on his offer. I slide my hand into his and permit him to assist me in getting vertical. Cautiously, I maintain the majority of my weight on the other side, while slowly testing out the renewed limb.

Wes keeps his grip on me, watching me attentively.

I stand straighter as I challenge my leg to do its job. When it succeeds, I let go of him and take a step, then another. A few moments prior I could barely walk without being in pain, and now...I'm practically my old self. "This is incredible."

Wes grins. "Take it easy, killer. It's not fully—"

One too many steps in, a blip of discomfort shocks me, twisting my ankle and sending me falling face-first into...

Wes stops me from hitting the ground, my body landing smack dab into his chest. He softens the blow and wraps his arms around me, lifting me from the floor and into his arms. My mind is taken back to when he carried me to this place, my beaten and bloody body limp in his arms. I thought I was a goner then. Hell, maybe I still am. His breath is warm against my face, as is his frame pressed against my side.

"I'm fine."

Wes gently lays me onto the small bed and steps away. "I should have warned you; these things take time."

"Everything okay in here?" Dash pokes his head into the room. He frowns and steps inside. "What did you do to her leg?"

I scoot off the side, lowering my legs to rest against the floor of this small room. "He fixed it." I glance up at Wes, a bit of pink floating to the surface of his cheeks.

"It was nothing, I just set it in place." Wes rubs his neck and for a split second, I see him not as the beast that he is, but the humble man who showed me a gentle kindness.

It's only a moment before I realize it's for his own selfish reasons. He didn't offer me aid until he was sure that I would help him with his plan to rescue the other demons from Rock Bridge. An impossible task but if anyone could pull it off, it would be me. That is if they're not already dead. The likelihood of that being extremely high given the way history typically plays out. I've never heard of a single demon ever making it longer than a week in that place, let alone however long his kind has been there.

I've also never known of a demon to go to such lengths for another. They're typically lone creatures, not often teaming up with any outside their species. These three are not only a complete abnormality, but the fact that they're going after others, that's unheard of.

Are those that they're attempting to rescue family? Friends? Part of their pack? Perhaps lovers? Or maybe they're powerful demons who can aid in reigniting the war that was over a long time ago. No matter the answer, I cannot allow them to fully succeed. I will do my part to get the cure, but then, I will have to end all their lives. That's the only way to ensure the safety of this world.

For now, I will play along.

CHAPTER 5

Wes

"What the fuck is wrong with you?" Bo throws a rock at me, but I catch it and drop it to the ground.

"Nothing. Why don't you fuck off?"

We continue through the woods, carrying the meager supplies we were able to acquire on a quick run. It's becoming more difficult for us to scavenge without drawing attention from hunters. The fewer of us that there are in existence, the more targeted their searches are for us. Every step we take is a glaring signal of our whereabouts.

Just like the mark that's lighting up Wren's neck.

My inner beast stirs at the anger of Bo's careless actions. I understand why he did it, but he could have at least consulted with me first. Not like Bo has ever done that in the past. I shouldn't have expected anything different now.

Bo had stayed within range of the cabin while I went out to gather provisions. He was close enough to hear a distress call but not far enough away that his distance would have activated Wren's marker.

Leaving her behind without protection was unsettling. Both because I wasn't there to provide it, and because I shouldn't feel that way at all.

She is a hunter. The worst kind of beast. She kills without regard and is the reason my kind has gone nearly extinct in this realm. According to rumors, I'm the last one standing, not only making me more powerful than an alpha, but of all alphas combined. It also makes the bounty on my head incredibly high. Prior to Prania being shut off from the other realms, my species was already diminishing in numbers. I wouldn't at all be surprised to find that I am alone in this world.

Perhaps that's why I relate to Dash and his situation. He's in our realm when he should be on earth with the rest of his kind. He is human. A mere mortal who has no recollection of who he is, or where he came from. There is no hope for either of us, given escaping this realm is impossible. We are doomed with a fate of fighting for our lives until we finally meet our end. Some days that reality is harder to stomach than others.

"What, are you attracted to her or something?" Bo continues to pry when he should keep his mouth shut.

Again, an unrealistic expectation for such a foul-mouthed bastard.

"That would be blasphemy," I tell him, because it's fully the truth.

A hunter and a demon. There could be no such thing. And yet, that doesn't stop my inner self from nearly bursting through the surface every time he catches a whiff of her scent. He wants her, and there's nearly nothing I can do to stop him. I am abundantly full of strength, but it is thanks to him, and he makes sure to remind me of that every second I spend denying his desire. I've never had to fight harder at withstanding his pull and I grow weary of how much longer I can keep his animalistic instincts at bay. His lust for her is misplaced, unnatural, and surely going to get us all killed.

Hell, it's the reason she's alive right now. If it were any other hunter, he would have let her die. I would have let her die. But the second I locked eyes with her, it was like I awoke from a lifetime slumber and fresh air was breathed into my lungs. I couldn't leave her there, not to bleed out and fade into nothing. No, I had to save her, and part of me is unsure whether that was me or my beast who made that decision. Perhaps it was both of us in tandem.

Something I will never admit out loud, especially to Bo. He'd never understand. Not when the only thing on his mind is killing anything that remotely smells of hunter. The fact that he showed restraint when marking her was baffling on its own. I was sure he would have drained her on the spot.

The second I saw her walk through that doorway, my heart nearly leaped from my chest. But upon seeing him grab hold of her and sink his fangs into her neck, I've never felt a rage quite like I did in that moment. I wanted to rip him apart. I wanted to end his life but in the most brutal way possible. How dare he think that he could touch her. He had been my partner for many years and despite our differences, up until that moment, I saw him as an equal. The second he laid a finger on her that completely changed. I had to restrain myself from killing him although the beast in me wanted nothing more. I could not give in to that temptation. But I did have to stop him.

I took great comfort in letting my beast rise to the surface and inflict pain on him. Although that fiery touch would have been nothing compared to the wrath he would've seen if he would've hurt her more seriously.

"It would be, yes. But that doesn't seem to be stopping you." Bo side steps a fallen log and continues along the path back to our sanctuary. The one spelled to repel hunters from pinpointing our location. It's not a permanent solution but it does the job for now. There's no telling how long until they find us and put an end to this incessant suffering of constantly being on edge and looking over our shoulders for the endless bitch that is our demise.

"You know nothing," I tell him.

"I know enough. And I'm no fool, Wes. You've got the hots for the hunter." Bo laughs and adjusts the bag hung over his shoulder. "Not that I blame you, she is one fine specimen."

My beast reacts before I can, grabbing Bo by the neck and slamming him into a nearby tree. A fire ignites on my skin scorching everything that it touches, Bo included. "You will *not* talk about her that way."

Bo grins from ear to ear despite the flaming touch lighting him up. "Just admit it and I'll stop."

I clench my jaw and grip him tighter. "I will do no such thing."

His flesh bubbles under my touch. My other self begs to turn the heat up, but I keep it at bay. I don't wish to kill him. Not yet, at least. My beast on the other hand wants to end him for speaking of her.

Bo shrugs. "Then neither will I."

"I could kill you right here, right now." I squeeze his neck.

"You won't." He continues to smile through the torment of my touch. "You need me."

"I need no one."

"Keep telling yourself that."

My senses alert me to a sound in the close distance. I focus my attention on it, a momentary distraction that Bo uses to his advantage as he frees himself from my hold and punches me across the face.

I bring my flameless but smoking hand to my cheek. "You fucking asshole."

"Oh, I'm the bad guy? You're the one unleashing your fucking beast on me." He picks up the bags and storms off, not saying another word the rest of the way.

We arrive at the cabin and I outstretch my arm to stop him. I pause to listen to her laughter float through the space and out to my ear, a soothing lullaby to my aching soul. How completely fucking wrong of me to get relief from such a thing.

Bo shoves me off him. "I won't hurt your precious hunter." He glances over his shoulder on his way up the small porch. "But that doesn't mean I won't eye fuck her."

My beast lets out a growl, my entire body engulfing into a roaring fire that I quickly disengage. "Simmer down," I tell it. "You're being irrational."

Another groan bubbles out of my chest as if to challenge my command.

I suck in a deep breath and ground myself. "She is not yours; you need to realize that. The sooner you do, the easier this will all be."

My beast stirs, my heart aching with the words I spoke. It pains us both, but the truth of the matter is, she is a hunter. She is a means to an end. She will only be around long enough to serve her purpose and then we will go our separate ways, so long as she doesn't go against her word and kill all of us first.

It's not what I want; it's not what my beast wants, but it's what must be done.

I waste no more time stewing in the yard and follow Bo into the small place we currently call home. It's not much. A one-bedroom shack hidden in the thick of the forest with an outdoor bathroom. There's a stream close enough for us to gather water from, that of which we must boil over the fire if we intend on bathing. It wasn't always like this. We once lived like royalty, with running water and ample food sources. But now we are fugitives in a land we cannot escape, fighting for our lives every single day. It's only a matter of time until we are caught but until then I will do everything in my power to stay alive. My beast does not give in easily and neither do I.

I step across the creaky threshold and into the front room that also triples as our kitchen and dining room. Two small couches line both walls in the corner. The place where we sleep when given the chance. We used to take turns, or well, fight over the bedroom, but with Wren here, it's only obvious to allow her to stay in there. And with no window attached, unless she got wickedly creative, there's no way for her to escape without us realizing.

My beast tugs me toward her, demanding that I get closer and at least confirm she is still okay. I hate how helpless I feel as his longing for her seeps its way into my own soul. It's difficult to differentiate where the origin of the desire comes from when I want her just as badly. Of all the females he could have taken a liking to he had to choose the worst possible one. Why are we both equally as fucking stupid? To yearn for a woman we can never have.

Says you, my beast taunts. *She will be mine.*

"Shut up," I blurt out loud.

Bo tosses the empty bag onto the floor and glares at me. "I didn't say anything."

For once, he actually did have his mouth shut.

"Not you." I run my hands through my hair. How am I going to go along with this plan when my beast is so unruly?

Bo sighs and crosses his arms. "That mutt trying to overpower you?"

"I don't need your smart-ass mouth, Bo." What I need is to see her and reassure my disobedient beast that she hasn't disappeared.

Isn't her scent alone enough? Or the sensation of her near proximity? Clearly, he can tell she's near the same way I can. But that's not sufficient for such a greedy creature. He's not used to being told he can't have something. He takes what he wants, when he wants. Perhaps denying him is only fueling his desire that much more. Maybe if I satiate those cravings he will calm the fuck down.

I go the rest of the way into the house and step into the doorway. I maintain my distance, afraid that if I give him too much, he will overpower me and claim her fully. He's already made it clear that she will be his, but if he marks her, similar to what Bo did, there's no stopping him from following her wherever she may go. I cannot allow him that authority. Not when being with her would only get us killed.

I risked too much when I offered to heal her. It's one thing to mend her wounds when she's unconscious, but feeling her golden stare on me while awake, it was a dangerous thing to do. When she fell, I considered letting her fall to the floor just to not touch her and give him the satisfaction. I couldn't though—my own pull to her overrode that rational thought and swept in to whisk her to safety.

I should hate her. I want to hate her. But it's something I find myself unable to do.

She stiffens when I arrive, the carelessness she exudes when in Dash's presence alone being replaced by the hatred she no doubt feels toward me. I don't blame her. She was born and raised with a delusional mindset that anyone with demon blood was the enemy. She was taught to hate us, to want us dead. Typically, the females of her kind are the homemakers, not the hunters. Which only reinforces the idea that she chose this path due to some heavy influence that caused her to hate us that much more. Whatever her reasoning, it still doesn't justify eradicating us completely from this realm. Some of us were just innocent bystanders caught up in the remnants of a war from long ago. Some of us are simply trying to survive until we can find a way out of this hell.

Have I killed my fair share of hunters? Absolutely. But I did so because I had to. It was me or them, the choice a simple one. It goes without saying that I have ended the same number, if not more, of demon lives with the exact reasoning. As with any species, there are bad apples. And with each of them waging a war against one another, it's only natural they would have an immense hatred for each other. I once called Prania home, but I wish to rid myself of this realm and find refuge elsewhere and perhaps live a life where I am not constantly fearing whether I would see the light of the next day.

I won't do so until we get our people back though. I've been searching for countless years for a way out for me and my own, only to have that halted when a ruthless hunter broke us apart. Each passing day, the chance of getting them back dwindled, but when my beast locked its sights on Wren, I felt that flicker of hope reignite in my soul. Perhaps we could both get what we wanted after all. Him, a chance to be near her, and me, the return of my people. *Our* people. Me and Bo. We both lost someone that day and I will stop at nothing to get them back, even if that means trusting the one who sees me as their enemy.

"Did you find what I was asking for?" Dash stands from his chair and walks toward me.

Wren scoots further away from me and leans against the farthest wall.

"I did." I tilt my head in the direction I came. "It's in the kitchen."

"Cool." He slaps my shoulder and steps around me. "Thanks, Wes."

Despite the small size of the house and the people just in the other room, it dawns on me that she and I are now alone. A welcomed thing for my beast.

"You going to stand there and stare?" Wren mouths off.

My beast stirs at her feistiness and recalls watching her eliminate three demons with absolute ease prior to her locking her eyes on us. A feat not taken lightly given her size and stature. She is small but she is lethal. It was that momentary exchange that caused her to waver, allowing her enemy the upper hand. I watched in terror as six other demons descended upon her, attacking her from all directions. Something she might have been able to overcome had I not been there and forced her to stutter. I felt her soul the second I walked into that place. The sensation rattling through me was completely foreign and yet so fucking familiar. My beast had no doubts that she was the one.

I rose from my spot across that old, abandoned building and single-handedly ripped apart all but one of the creatures that took her down. I would have finished the last of them too, had Bo not chased him off and made a game out of hunting him.

"Maybe," I finally say. "Is that an issue?"

Wren blinks up at me like she's analyzing my every movement. "It's a bit creepy, if you ask me."

Go toward her, the voice in my head commands.

"Do you mind?" I point at the chair Dash typically sits in. Perhaps that will suffice both of us without giving in too much.

She narrows her gaze. "You're holding me captive, yet asking permission to sit in your own home?"

"Shall I take that as a no?" I continue to lean in the doorframe and study her as she does the same to me.

"By all means..." She motions for me to come inside.

I lower myself onto the stiff chair and rest my arm on the table, scanning the strewn about contents to avoid looking at her.

"Is there something I can help you with? Or are you just here for guard duty?"

I drag my gaze from the herbs and potions to meet hers. I stare for only a moment and somehow it feels like an eternity, my soul igniting with a blaze unlike anything I could have imagined. What is wrong with me? Why her? Of all the women in this realm, it had to be a hunter? Internally, I curse at my beast for choosing her over anyone else. *Fucking fool.*

"No, I..." I don't typically find myself at a loss for words. I may be a man of few of them, but this, this feeling of helplessness and confusion at the situation is over-whelming. "I thought we could discuss how to move forward." There we go, think logistics and strategy. That will be a nice distraction.

For you, not me, my beast scoffs.

She hesitates before nodding. "Yes, that would be wise." Wren scoots herself to the edge of the bed and reaches to pick up the cup on the floor. She brings it to her lips and drinks some of the water.

I don't mean to, but I watch her intensely as if every movement is a work of art.

I bite at the inside of my cheek, drawing blood and allowing the sensation to snap me out of my stupor. It's only mildly successful.

I can't stay away; my beast won't allow it. And I can't be near, otherwise my mind turns into a pile of fucking mush. How is it possible that I am quite literally the most commanding of my kind in this realm but in her presence, I am completely powerless? What a complete contradiction. And if she knew it...well, I'd be a goner no doubt.

"Well, then, what's the plan?" Wren sets the cup back in its place but remains on the edge of the mattress. Her still weakened body hanging over and calling mine toward her.

No, I will my other half to understand. *She would never want us; you need to get that through your thick skull.*

These thoughts and feelings are not mine alone.

He's right. I'm just as guilty for this absurd obsession as he is.

But it's not like I can back out now. I must follow through with this plan, otherwise Bo will never remove the mark and we may never rescue our people. It's best for us all if we get this done as soon as possible and go our separate ways.

I won't allow that, he growls.

You have to, we don't have another choice in the matter.

"Wes, hello?" Wren waves her dainty hand in the air. "Are you purposely ignoring me or what?"

"No, my apologies. I have quite a bit on my mind at the moment." I provide her with what little of the truth I can. After all, I cannot lie to her, not when my beast has set his sights on her. I'll have to get creative with the words I use so I don't give her too much of the upper hand. At the end of the day, she would still betray us given the chance and I will not permit my beast to put us in danger that way.

"Is everything all right?"

I'm surprised by her question, caught off guard by it, actually. So much that I do that thing where I just stare at her for far too long. I can only imagine how absolutely insane I must appear to be from her perspective.

Bo stomps into the room, his sudden appearance stealing both of our attention. He plops onto the bed next to Wren and leans against the wall. "Sup?"

She and I stand at the same time, stepping toward each other. I shove her behind me and steady the fiery rage coursing through me.

"Oh, chill out." Bo raises his hands in the air. "I'm only having a seat. Would you rather I take that one?" He points to the chair I was in. "And you can sit here." He pats the bed, a bit of dust scattering from the dirty blanket.

I'm not sure which is worse, having Bo close to her, or allowing my beast the pleasure of being that near. I can somewhat control both of them, but I'd rather take my chance with the internal idiot I've spent my entire life with.

I grip Wren's hand, taking note when she doesn't flinch or jerk away. Pulling her toward the bed, I smooth out the blanket and offer her a seat before settling in next to her. I keep my guard up and my beast at bay. He purrs with satisfaction at the close proximity.

"Now that you two love birds have settled in..." Bo leans into his chair and props his legs up on the table, crossing them and his arms behind his head.

I ignore his comment but not the slight shift that Wren makes.

Bo snatches a small splinter of wood from the table and picks his teeth with it. "Breckenridge will be our first stop. We leave in the morning."

Wren interjects immediately. "That's demon territory."

"Yeah, and we're demons. What's your point, Birdie?" Bo doesn't bother looking at her, instead he uses that same splinter to scrape under his nails.

"Birdie?"

"Mmhm. Thought of it myself. What do you think?" He's taunting her. He's taunting me. He's taunting my beast. And he's doing a damn good job at it.

I choose to disregard his attempt and focus on the task at hand. Tilting my head toward her, I explain. "It's a safe spot for our kind. That will be our first destination on our way to Rock Bridge."

"But I'm a hunter. They'll kill me on the spot."

Over my dead body, my beast growls.

A bit of his groan rumbles in my chest, giving away more than I'd prefer to show.

Bo laughs and plops his feet onto the floor. "Fucking told you."

"Told him what?" Wren looks between us, confusion furrowing her brow.

Her questioning cannot persist if I stand any chance of ignoring the truth. "The beacon on your neck will also provide a mask to hide your true identity. They will see you as one of them, not of the enemy."

She shakes her head. "I don't think you understand. I'm Furla Ain, people know who I am."

My chest tightens. I knew she was feared, but I had no idea she claimed this title.

Me, the most powerful demon—her, the deadliest demon assassin.

"Now that," Bo chuckles. "Is fucking hilarious."

Wren rises to her feet, advancing on Bo. She kicks him in the shin. "What, because I'm a girl? Because I'm small." She grabs blindly at the table, snatching a wooden spoon and holding it to Bo's neck. "I've ended bigger and stronger demons than you."

Bo smiles from ear to ear and steps into the thing at his throat, towering over her when he says, "Do it, then you'll be marked forever."

I shove myself between them, pushing their chests with my open palm to separate them. My skin brushes against hers, my beast salivating in response. I drop my hand from her body and look at the instigator. "Can you be serious for one fucking minute?"

He raises a brow. "Sure." Bo tilts his head around me to focus on Wren. "It's not because you're female at all. It's because Wes—"

I clench his throat and permit my powers to flow through and scorch his skin. Cutting off his airway and ability to speak, I thrust him into the wall and raise my arm until his rather large body is dangling above the floor. "Do you wish to die? Is that it?" I grip tighter, my touch melting his demonic flesh that had already been healed from my previous assault.

"Wes," a dainty voice calls at me from behind. She places her soft but calloused hand on my shoulder. "Let him go."

I drop Bo immediately, my beast submitting to her request. Oh the power she already has over me without even knowing it.

Bo clutches his neck and gasps for air. "Fuck, Wes. Are you out of your mind?"

When it comes to her, there's no denying that. Everything I've done since I laid my sights on her has been insane. And I can't imagine that that will change.

CHAPTER 6

Wren

I shouldn't find it surprising that my captors are keeping secrets from me and yet I am growing incredibly curious about what it is that they are withholding. It's like some inside joke that they refuse to let me in on. It makes sense for them to have those, but it seems directly related to me and that detail alone makes me want to be in on it, too. Especially if it could be the difference of whether or not I make it out of here alive.

Wes is weirdly protective of me. I can sense his tension rise each time Bo is near. And considering Bo wants nothing more than to end my life, I can understand the threat that he poses. I am potentially the only chance they have of getting their people back—if they're not already dead. Wes wanting to keep me alive is the obvious choice if they want their plan to work.

But shouldn't Bo want the same?

Why is he so insistent on taunting the hell out of Wes in the process?

"Breckenridge." I tug at Wes to provide some kind of distance between the two of them.

He turns toward me, his eyes glowing red and his aura showing brighter than I've ever seen. It's almost...

No. I shake my head and rid myself of the thought. I will not allow his allure to consume me. He is a demon. A monster. The enemy.

As if noticing my mindset change, he blinks and the glow disappears, revealing a seemingly normal gaze.

"I didn't mean to frighten you." His demeanor softens.

Is that what he thinks that was? Fear? And if it was, why would it matter either way?

"You didn't," I assure him. There isn't much I'm afraid of anyway. I've pretty much seen the worst of the worst. Battled demons of all sorts. Ogres, Burners, Flapping Mitts, mutts from all the hell dimensions, shifters of many different variations, you name it, if it's lived in this realm, I've probably killed one or two if not more of them. I wouldn't be surprised if I'm the reason Bo ascended to alpha. Wes on the other hand, I'm still unsure what he is. I've yet to come across anything similar to him, convincing me that he may be the only one of his kind.

Is that even possible?

Would I have known about such an unusual species?

Shouldn't Dravin and Parla have warned me of such a thing?

Did they not have any knowledge of his rarity either? Or did they simply not tell me to keep it a secret. To keep others from finding out and potentially stealing his power source.

If his energy got into the wrong hands, it could be devastating to everything we've worked toward to regain control over our nation.

"You're a sick fuck." Bo's neck begins to heal before my eyes, his skin repairing itself and the charred remains littering the floor at his feet. He shifts his gaze to my leg. "You healed her leg, didn't you? Isn't it fucking obvious, Wes?"

What is he talking about?

"She would be of no use to us while injured, Bo. You know this."

A knock sounds at the door. "You two want to maybe stop acting like children?" Dash continues into the room, stopping right beside me. "You good?" His blue eyes look me over.

"Yeah." Leave it to the weakest in the space to be the most level headed.

"Are you interested in a shower? Surely you'd like to get clean prior to heading out tomorrow?"

Bathing hadn't even crossed my mind, but now that it has, my clothes suddenly become itchy and uncomfortable. I glance down at my dirt and blood-covered body, noting how terrible I must smell. "That would be preferable."

Perhaps freshening up will provide me with a renewed sense of self given the rather peculiar situation I've gotten myself wrapped up in.

Dash and I leave Bo and Wes behind to stew in their petty dispute. Whatever is going on between them is not a concern of mine. It's clear I'm involved somehow, but there's no sense in getting worked up about it if they refuse to tell me.

We step into the space that I had made it to when I had escaped the room I was being held captive in. It leads directly into a cluttered, open area with a small kitchen, a tiny table, and tattered couches. There are no other doors aside from the one leading to the porch and there is only a single window above the sink basin in the kitchen. I had thought I was being held in squalor, when in reality, they had given me the only bedroom in the house while they made do with the couches and hard floor of what they call their living room.

This is how they live? It's no wonder they're miserable.

When we reach the front door, Wes appears in a flash, slamming his hand into the thing to stop us from exiting. He looks directly at me. "Do not run."

I had no intentions of doing so, not knowing where I am or what would happen when I get too far away from Bo. He had gone out on a supply run and with each bit of distance he put between us, I could feel the mark growing warmer. I was told he wouldn't go far enough to set the beacon off, but even with that much space, the thing became uncomfortable to bear. It wasn't painful, just a reminder that I was no longer free to do as I wanted without consequence.

But even knowing I didn't intend on leaving, Wes's command solidifies that within me. Another sign that I am losing control over my free will. And to a freaking demon.

What has my life come to?

"She won't," Dash tells him, for me. "Now move your arm."

Wes huffs but ends up complying. He reaches for the knob and opens it for us. "Don't be long."

Wes is aware he has authority over me, because why else would he be comfortable in letting me go outside this place with a human who I could easily overpower and escape from?

In all my experience, I've never come across a demon who could possess such power over a hunter. Does that make me weak? Incompetent? A disgrace to my kind?

Dash guides me through the door, onto the dilapidated porch, and around the side of the shack they call home. The air is comfortable, not too warm, not too cold, but it's thick with fog and the lingering smoke from the surrounding villages that have been burnt to the ground.

Without drawing too much attention to myself I skim the vicinity with my gaze, looking for any kind of identifying factor. Somehow, it all looks the same. Overgrown trees billowing with weeping greenery that fades into a shit-colored brown. Paths leading from each direction of the home show no clear sign of which way they come and go. There's no telling where we are, at least I've never been here before. But if Breckenridge is our first stop that must mean we're close to there. A location I don't venture often to, and perhaps the reason why they chose it, because I would be unfamiliar with the territory and the likelihood of me escaping would diminish considering the number of demons in a demon-infested area. Leaving their sight would be foolish of me given the glaring beacon on my neck that would attract every single demon around.

"I took the pleasure of heating the water for you." Dash points to the wood-slatted area.

I peek my head around the corner and study the outdoor shower. Dark stone covers the ground and vines twirl up and between the wooden walls. It might not be much, but it very well could be the nicest part of this thing they call home. If it weren't for the smog lining the air and the demons holding me captive, this wouldn't be an entirely unenjoyable experience.

Dash comes to my side. "That lever over there, just pull it down when you're undressed and ready. Don't tug it all the way, only slightly, and you'll have to do it every minute or so to keep it flowing. It's nothing special but you should get about ten minutes out of it. There's soap down there." He grazes his hand against my lower back before exiting the space. "I'll be, uh, out here." He nods and closes the gate to the shower, leaving me alone in the decent-sized space.

I step in further and sit on my ass, reaching down to unbuckle my boots. I slide each of them off, setting them out of the way, and stand to unbutton my armored pants. The material is thick and clunky with various compartments for hidden weapons. Each of which has been robbed from my possession by my captors. Each time I graze an empty spot, a sigh of disappointment leaves me. How dare they be thorough at their jobs.

I peel my bottoms off, wincing at each unhealed wound still left on my body. I'm in rough shape, but nothing compared to a few days ago. I would have bled out on that dirt-covered floor had they not decided to spare me. Although, they may be only prolonging the inevitable. I drop my pants with my boots and go to work unbuckling my top. I pry it from my filth-covered body and revel in the weightlessness of not carrying the brunt of such armor. I feel exposed, vulnerable, but in the moment, completely free. As free as a captive person can be, given the circumstances.

Stepping out of my undergarments, I undress completely and turn toward the overhead contraption. I reach for the lever Dash had told me about, coming up short when I stand on my tiptoes.

Fuck. I guess that's what happens when you try to wash in some seven-foot-something demon's shower. Dash is significantly shorter than Wes and Bo, but for a human, he's still exceedingly tall. Me, on the other hand, I was not blessed in the height department. Although, it has served me well in sneaking in and out of rather tight and confined locations.

"Um, Dash," I call out.

"Yes? Is everything okay?" Dash responds with a bit of concern lining his tone.

"I'm afraid I can't reach the lever." I stand taller and attempt one more time to no avail. "Can you get it for me?"

"You want me to...come into the shower with you?"

I yank open the door, revealing myself in nothing but my birthday suit. "Don't be modest. You've seen other naked women before."

Dash's mouth drops open. "Wren, you're...you're nude." He glances down for the quickest second and covers his eyes.

"Do you shower with your clothes on?" I ask him while tugging his arm and dragging him into the space with me.

"No, but I..."

I grip his shoulders and turn him so his back is to me and toward the lever I cannot reach. "There. Sorry, I didn't mean to offend you. I should have asked before exposing myself to you."

"I mean, I'm not mad about it." Dash reaches up and pulls the thing, the warm water beginning to flow down and trickling over my bare body. He steps out of the way of the stream but keeps his back to me. "It was unexpected is all."

"Such a gentleman." I run my right hand over my left arm and rub at the dried dirt and blood caking my skin. "Unlike your friends."

He nods. "They're not all bad. Well, Wes isn't. Bo is questionable."

By that I'm not at all surprised.

"Can you hand me that soap?" I close my eyes and submerge myself under the stream, soaking my hair in the process.

"Yeah, of course." Dash leans down to get it and reaches back to give it to me. "Does that hurt?"

I laugh. "Which one?"

He glances over his shoulder, a look of pity on his freckled face. "All of them?"

"A little, some more than others." I lather my hands and scrub at my face. The small cut on my lip reopens and blood from the wound trickles down my chin and mixes with the dirty water from my body. "Shit."

"You okay?" He tilts his head to the side but doesn't look.

"Nothing I can't handle."

I use the same soap for my hair that I do my body, but it works all the same, ridding most of the gunk from my dark locks. I snatch my belongings and bring them under the water with me. I give them a solid scrub, rinsing and tossing them over the side of the shower to air out while I make quick but effective work of cleaning myself the best I can given the accommodations. When I'm somewhat satisfied with my personal hygiene, I stand there, unmoving and allowing the water to crash over me. "I'm done."

Dash stands on his toes to look over the shower. "You have some water left if you want it."

"What about you? Do you need to bathe?"

He chuckles. "Are you implying that I stink?"

I shouldn't, but I place my damp hand on his shoulder. "No."

What the fuck am I doing? And why does it seem so wrong yet so right?

Dash's body stiffens and then relaxes. "Wren." My name is just a whisper on his lips.

In these few days, he's done nothing but try to make me feel comfortable despite my confinement. We've shared stories, laughs, and have broken bread together. He's attempted to gain my trust and has been an unlikely friend and companion. I'd be lying if I said I wasn't drawn to his innocence, his candor, his ordinary nature. No, that's a lie—Dash is not ordinary, he is a rarity to this world, perhaps more so than the alpha and unknown creature inside the very building this shower is attached to.

He turns around slowly, cautious with his gaze as he keeps it at eye level with mine. "Your lip..." Dash hovers his hand next to my face.

I lean into his inviting touch. "It's nothing."

Dash trails his fingers along my cheek and down my neck. He runs his thumb over my collarbone and rests his palm on my shoulder. "Wren, you owe me nothing."

"We're running out of water." I glance up at the slowed trickle of liquid.

Dash reaches to tug the lever and renew the stream, then immediately steps into it, pressing his mouth to mine and parting my lips with his tongue.

I moan against him and press my wet body to his clothed one.

His hands roam my frame, settling on my lower back and my neck. Dash tugs me into him and kisses me with a feverish intensity. "I..." He breaks away, his breath ragged. "I haven't been with a woman since..."

I stop my advancement and look him directly in the eyes. "I'm so sorry, I didn't mean to force myself on you. I thought—" I pause and shake my head. "I shouldn't have assumed."

Dash smiles. "No, trust me, I *want* to. You're the most beautiful woman I've ever laid my eyes on. It's just..." His expression changes. "I have no idea what I'm doing."

"We can stop." I wipe his dampened red hair off his brow. I don't want this to be a bad experience for him, even if it's my last chance to be intimate with a man before I trek across this forsaken land to a fate that will likely end in my demise.

"Do you want me?" He swallows in anticipation.

I nod. "I do." I latch onto the hem of his shirt and pull the thing over his head.

He grins again and melts his mouth onto mine, his hand wrapping around my waist and lifting me off the stone-covered ground.

I secure my legs around him, ignoring all the little aches and pains of the injuries still healing on my body. The pleasure of his touch is everything I need to distract myself from the overwhelming shit show that has consumed my life.

Dash presses my body against the wooden wall of the shower and continues to taste my tongue with his. With my leg still wrapped around him and my arms around his neck, he reaches down to undo his pants and drag them over his growing erection. "Are you sure?" he asks me.

I answer him by sliding my hand down and stroking his thick length.

Dash sighs and cups my breast, pinching my nipple between his fingers.

The water trickles onto us, keeping us from getting too cold as the temperature grows chillier in the approaching nighttime.

"I want you," he moans into my mouth.

I glide him into place and whimper when his cock penetrates my eager hole.

"Is that okay?" Dash fills me with caution, treating me far too delicately than he should.

"Yes. Is it okay for you?" I pivot my body up and down the best I can from this position.

Dash exhales and smirks. "More than okay." He tightens his grip on my waist with one arm and extends the other to hold onto the shower wall. He's surprisingly strong despite being a meager human. He thrusts inside of me like he knows exactly what he's doing. His muscle memory doing him justice despite him having no recollection of being with a woman.

He skims my neck with his lips, sucking on my neck and biting the soft skin.

I tighten around him, my climax growing nearer sooner than I expected. I guess it's been a while since I've been intimate with another, too, and my desire for affection was higher than I realized. I don't get much downtime in my profession, leaving minimal opportunities for basic needs to be met. Plus, it's not often I'm held captive by three incredibly attractive men. If only two of them weren't the enemy, then things here could have gotten much more interesting.

Dash rests his forehead on mine but continues rocking his hips up and down. "Does that feel good?"

Something about his genuine consideration turns me on even more. "Yes," I moan.

He picks up his pace, slamming me into the shower wall. His hot breath floats across my shoulder, his teeth nipping the skin. "Fuck."

I come undone, my body spiraling into a whirlwind of pleasure and temporarily transporting me to somewhere far away from here, where it's only me and him, no demons, no other hunters, no obligations, or threat to our safety. All my pain is erased, and I become one with the pleasure.

"Wren, that was..."

"Put me down," I whisper into his mouth.

He gently lowers me to the shower floor, his cock gliding out of me in the process.

I grasp it in my hand, swirling my grip around his lust-soaked rod and stroking him.

Dash leans down, placing his lips on mine, his heavy breaths mixing between every passionate kiss. His tongue trails the cut on my lip as he clutches both sides of my face in his palms, running his fingers up and into my damp hair.

His cock hardens and he rocks himself into my hand, his climax following in an explosive burst.

I stroke him until I'm sure he's finished and nudge our bodies toward the slowed stream of water.

A perma-grin cakes itself on Dash's handsome face. "That was hot." He presses his lips gently to my forehead and reaches for the lever to pull down the remains of our water supply. It might not be much, but it'll be enough to wash the sex off us.

My gaze lingers to his back, my jaw clenching at the sight of scars that litter his beautiful skin. I extend my hand but don't touch him. It seems a more personal thing than something you discuss with a random hookup.

"They were there from *before*." Dash catches the shift in my attention and chooses to answer me anyway. "I had no idea until Bo blurted it out one day when I was changing."

"You don't remember how they happened?"

Dash pulls me into the water, lathering the soap and gently cleaning my stomach. "Nope. And I'm kind of glad I don't."

I glance up at him. "You know we can't tell them about this, right?"

His smile fades and he nods. "Yeah."

I graze his cheek with my knuckles. "It can be our little secret."

"Will you promise me something?" Dash tucks my hair behind my ear.

"Maybe, what is it?"

"When the time comes for you to betray us, will you at least warn me?" He sighs and lowers his voice. "I won't try to stop you; I just want to know if it'll be the last time I see you."

"I..."

The door to the shower creaks open and a throat clears. "How cute." Bo leans against the wooden wall and looks me up and down. "When's my turn?"

"In your fucking dreams." I don't bother concealing my body. He's already gotten a peek, might as well give him something to ingrain into his memory since that's all he'll ever have of my body.

Bo shrugs. "In due time, Birdie. I have no doubt you'll be begging for it in the future."

Dash grabs his shirt and covers my front with it. "Seriously, Bo? Do you have to be so vulgar?"

"I'm the vulgar one? You're fucking the enemy." He snorts. "Wait until Wes finds out. His mutt will tear you apart."

Keeping me alive is one thing, but why would Wes care if I had sex with Dash? That doesn't screw with his plan at all. If anything, it benefits him.

Dash steps into his pants and I drag my clothes off the side of the shower. They're still moist but I didn't exactly expect them to be dry by the time I was finished. I toss Dash his shirt and slide my garments onto my body anyway. As much as I'm enjoying teasing Bo with something he'll never have, I'd rather feel the thick armor weighing my body down than be without it. A sort of protective blanket I've grown fond of over the years, saving me from death more times than I can count.

"Tell him then, I dare you." I buckle the top of my shirt in place. "Go ahead. We'll wait here. If he's going to react the way you're implying, he'll end your life first just for being the messenger." I slide my feet into my boots. "Or are you afraid of him? Is that it? Because he's clearly more powerful than you, that much is obvious."

"You bitch." Bo grits his teeth and then snarls, exposing his fangs at me. "I should have sucked the life out of you when I had the chance."

I approach him, pausing to pat his shoulder as I pass. "You're right, you should have." I walk away, leaving him behind to stew at my truthful accusations. He's well aware that Wes is the dominant one in their little trio, and for some unknown reason, he's overly protective of me. It wasn't until Bo confirmed that a moment ago that I realized that fully.

Now I just have to figure out how to use that to my advantage.

CHAPTER 7

Wes

Wren storms into our cabin like she owns the place and goes straight past me and into the bedroom. Dash follows close behind and disappears into the room with her.

Their scent intermingles together, creating an aroma that turns my stomach and stirs my beast.

Calm down, I tell him. *They walked by in tandem, that's all that was.*

A small part of me knows better but refuses to acknowledge the overpowering thought.

Bo slams the door shut, stealing my attention from my spiraling mindset.

"What's wrong with you?" I ask him,

He stalks to the kitchen and rips off a chunk of bread. "Nothing."

Bo is typically pissed about something, so his behavior isn't entirely surprising. But paired with how Dash and Wren entered, it has my suspicions growing. Did he do something to her? Is he the reason Dash and Wren ignored me and went directly into the room? Bo has attempted on numerous occasions to attack her, did he do so again?

"If you touched her…" My hand hardens into a fist at my side, the heat already bubbling to the surface.

"Me?" Bo laughs. "You think *I* would fornicate with that disgrace? Even I have standards, Wes." He obnoxiously chews the bread, swallowing it down with a gulp of water from the cup near him.

"I thought you did pretty well." Wren's voice echoes through the small space to meet my ears.

I tilt my head, cracking my neck and exhaling. Turning on my heel, I stomp the few feet across our tiny home and barge into the room Dash and Wren are occupying. "Out," I spit at him.

Dash stops fumbling with the vials in his hands and wide eye stares at me.

I partially expected to walk in here and find them *together*, but I was wrong. They're in their typical positions. Dash at the table and Wren sitting on the bed. Am I being overly paranoid for no reason? My beast and his claim of her getting the best of both of us?

"What the fuck?" Wren rises to her feet immediately. "What's your problem?"

"You." I whip my head toward her and furiously point at the bed. "Sit."

She complies, not because she wants to, but because my beast commanded it. A power he has over only one type of being—one I don't wish to acknowledge. It can't be true. She can't be. I won't allow it.

You have no control over such things, my beast reminds me.

"Wes," Dash mutters. "Don't you—"

"No." I cut him off. "We leave in the morning. Go pack the rest of our supplies."

Dash runs his hand through his hair, and that's when I notice it's damp. Similar to that of Wren's. I suck in a breath, hoping like hell I can maintain the reigns over the beast threatening to rip him apart. I care for Dash. Like a friend. Like a brother. I do not wish him dead. It would go against everything I believe in. I do not kill the innocent.

He is not innocent, the voice demands.

"Now!" A growl escapes me and fire ripples up my chest and out my mouth.

Dash flits his gaze at Wren one last time before exiting the room and leaving the two of us alone.

"What's gotten into you?" She repositions herself on the mattress.

I could ask her the same question, but I won't. I cannot afford to hear the truth, not when my beast is so hellbent on taking what belongs to him. What should not be his that he insists on claiming. What a hopeless fool we both are.

I step into the doorway and lean my back against it. Crossing my arms over my chest, I stare forward and away. I cannot stand to look at her right now—not if I don't want to fall completely apart. There is too much on the line for such things to happen.

When I spared her life, I never expected any of this to happen. I knew in my soul that I couldn't allow her to die but I didn't realize the magnitude of what would follow. I'm still not even sure if I do.

"What, so you're not going to talk to me?" She's annoyed and I can't say that I blame her.

I've been acting like an irrational fool from the second I laid my eyes on her. I never should have allowed any of this to happen, but my beast refused to let me walk away from her. I am supposed to be brutal, fearless, in complete and utter control. But here I am losing my goddamn mind over a female I know nothing about other than the fact that she wants to end my life and eradicate all demons from this realm. Why would my beast decide that she was worthy of his admiration?

You know why.

"You're going to stand there all night? Brooding in silence?" Wren continues to pry, to try to get me to say anything.

But there is nothing that can be said to make sense of any of this. Not to her. Not to me.

I must focus on the task at hand. Getting through the night and the next few days as we embark on this seemingly impossible journey to rescue our people from Rock Bridge. I will leverage her to my advantage and then, when we are finished, I will sever our ties and get as far away from her as possible. Once I have done that, I will continue searching for a way out of this dreaded realm. Then, I will be worlds apart and can end this profane connection.

You will do no such thing.

Wait and see.

"Fine." Wren huffs and pats the thin pillow on the bed.

I steal a glance at her out of the corner of my eye, and watch as she attempts to get comfortable on the rather stiff and rough mattress. I stay firmly in place at my post, fully prepared to stand here all night if I have to. I will not permit Dash or Bo to enter this room without my consent.

I spend my time studying the wood frame of the doorway across from me. I count the splinters blistering off the poorly built structure to distract myself from the irregular breathing of the woman only a few feet away. No matter what I consume myself with I cannot detach my thoughts from her. There's this visceral desire to know her, to enter her mind and discover every inch of her soul that she has never shared with another. My beast argues that he already has this knowledge but that would be impossible, completely improbable, given we only just encountered her a few days ago. He insists he's known her his whole existence. One soul that was split in two and dropped into beings that would eventually reunite one day. If that's the case, the universe really has it out for me by making my mate a fucking hunter. More specifically the one with the highest acclaimed title. And if my beast were correct in his ramblings, wouldn't Wren know those too? He must be mistaken and the sooner I get him to realize that, the better.

Still, it doesn't stop the intense urge I have to gravitate toward her. To protect her. To shield her from any harm that comes her way and defend her honor. If only there were a way to shut this off. To no longer feel these feelings and think these thoughts. It serves me no purpose since she will never be mine.

Seconds turn into minutes. The time ticking by at both an impossibly quick and painfully slow pace. Part of me wants to pause it, to stand here in her presence until the end of days. I would accept the small gift of this nearness even if it meant nothing more. But with that thought, I realize I cannot keep her forever, and the sooner day breaks, the closer the realness of detaching myself from this horribly toxic situation.

Both Bo and Dash quit stirring and eventually claim the available sleep spaces as their own, drifting off into the last comfortable slumber I assume they will have for a while. There's no telling what the coming days will bring. We have a plan, but it's shotty at best.

Wren whimpers. The softness of her cry pivoting my body toward her. I squint, scanning her petite shape through the darkness and searching for any sign of harm.

She's on her side, facing the wall, her back toward the room. Her knees pulled to her chest and her body trembling.

An ache rumbles in my core at the very sight of her distress.

Her hand clenches the bedding and her body twitches.

My feet betray me, taking silent steps toward her. I kneel next to her and hold my breath as I watch the goosebumps on her flesh prickle. Carefully, I rest the back of my hand against her bare skin. She's ice-cold to the touch.

I latch onto the measly blanket at the foot of the bed and drape it over her body in hopes that she will warm soon, and the quivering of her body will stop. I rest against the wall next to the bed and wait for it to take effect. Those seconds turn into minutes. All of which does nothing to rid her of her discomfort. I grow tired of watching her struggle, her body still reeling from the injuries and no doubt the shock of her current situation. Going to bed with damp hair did her no favors, either.

Get in with her, my beast commands.

Instead of following through with his order, I sit back along the edge and reach my hand toward her. I allow my power to come to the surface, warming my skin without catching it ablaze. I place it under the blanket and hope that it will be enough to help regulate her temperature.

She stirs and for a second, I'm afraid she will wake and catch me this close to her. That she will ask me questions that I shouldn't answer. I do not want to lie to her... I cannot lie to her. Telling her the truth would only complicate things much worse than they already are.

Wren flips over to face me, and I freeze. She throws her arm over mine, the coolness of her skin desperate for the warmth of mine. I don't dare move, not yet, not while she's teetering on the brink of consciousness.

She nestles her head against the pillow and tugs my arm toward her, clutching it to her chest. Her damp armor hints as to why she cannot get warm. Between her wet hair and clothes, to the pathetic accommodations I've given her, she's had no fighting chance.

I increase my heat level without harming her and will her shakes to dissolve. Ignoring my beast's desire to climb in and press my body to hers, I do what I can to make her comfortable while maintaining somewhat of a distance. Although, my skin pressed to her bare chest is not much space at all. My beast and I revel in the temporary pleasure it brings us.

I study her breathing, noting each irregularity and quiver that leaves her. Minute's pass and it evens out, her body relaxing to the warmth that mine provides. She clings to me, reminding me just how dainty she is compared to my stature. It's a strange reality that this small being is as powerful and feared as she is in our world.

She doesn't let go of my arm and I don't pry it away. Perhaps I'm being selfish in wanting to hold onto this moment a bit longer. The calm before the storm I can only imagine will come raging down on us in the coming days.

I lay my head to the side, relaxing as I bring her the smallest amount of peace. I get lost in the steady rise and fall of her chest and ignore the intrusive thoughts that follow. I don't want to imagine her and Dash being together—it's a vision I cannot stomach. I refuse the truth of it no matter how real it may be. His scent still mixed with hers in a way that could only be from...

Kill him, my beast growls.

You'll wake her, stop.

The selfish bastard shuts up, knowing that if we disturb her, this might end all too soon.

CHAPTER 8

Wren

I wake to find Wes slung over the side of the bed, his warm hand resting on my forearm. I pull myself away from him while watching his motionless face. From this close, I can examine every freckle and scar littering his skin—the long, wispy lashes that line his eyes, and the plushness of his lips.

It should feel wrong to have him this near, but instead, it's strangely comforting.

Enemy, I remind myself.

What could have possibly provoked him to choose such a sleep position anyway? Because he refused to let me out of his sight? So he would be sure he'd wake if I stirred and wanted to sneak out? Regardless of the reasoning, it appears absurdly uncomfortable. His neck twisted to the side; his large frame contorted as he clings to stay upright.

Has he been that way long?

A small part of me wants to stay here and watch him sleep. There's something oddly mesmerizing about being this close to someone so off-limits. I've snuck up on demons in the past. I've slit their throats while they slumbered, but I never stopped to admire one as they slept, caught up in their peculiar beauty. That type of thing is forbidden. Taboo. Against our basic hunter nature.

I poke Wes gently on the cheek.

His eyes flicker open, slow at first, but then, as if realizing that he shouldn't be here, he jumps to his feet, wiping at his chin.

"Were you drooling?" I ask him with a smile.

He shakes his head. "No, of course not. My apologies, I must have dozed off."

"Mmhm. And was there a reason as to why you insisted on sleeping on the side of my bed?" I hop off the edge, in the space between him and my mattress, and adjust the buckles on my top, making sure they're snug in place.

"You were..." He pauses momentarily. "Cold."

I stop what I'm doing and hesitate before fully looking up at him. "Cold?" I narrow my gaze at him.

"Yes." He holds his hand up and his skin begins glowing. "Built-in heater."

I recall my slumber, trying desperately to go to sleep when I was annoyed at Wes for posting up at my door. It's one thing when he does it outside the room, but he made it a point to make it known he was keeping guard. And the way he treated Dash was unacceptable. Between my aggravation with him, and the wet clothes I wore to bed, it was rather difficult to get comfortable enough to rest. It took me what felt like forever until I dozed off, only to have night terrors and a chill I couldn't seem to shake.

I briefly dreamt of a fire, warm and inviting. I was wrapped in a thick, heavy blanket that cloaked me from the frost nipping at my body. I clung to it and refused to let go, for once feeling like I had found a safe place to rest my head.

And this whole time, that was *Wes* that brought on that comfort? What the actual fuck?

"Oh," is all I can manage to say.

Wes clears his throat and rubs at his neck. "I..." He points to the open door. "Should get my things ready so we can head out."

I nod. "Yeah, obviously." I'd do the same, but it's not exactly like I have any of my own stuff here. I'll have to rely on whatever they bring to serve us on this journey. One that will no doubt end in all of us dead. There's no way in hell they could ever get what they want and get away with it. Not when the number of hunters far outweigh the demons. But, despite the odds being against us, I have to try, otherwise I'll never get them to tell me how to cure this beacon on my neck. And right now, that's all I care about.

Wes awkwardly goes to leave the room when Dash approaches.

"I need to get supplies." He motions toward the table full of his herbs and salves.

Wes sighs. "Be quick."

"Sure thing." Dash steps around him and into the room. "Hey," he shyly says as he comes closer.

"Is there anything I can do to help?" I approach and stand there a bit out of place, unsure of what the heck I'm supposed to be doing.

Dash scans the contents of the disorganized table. "Do you see the mugwort anywhere?"

I grab the vial of familiar-looking leaves and extend it toward him. "Here."

Dash smiles and takes it from me, securing it into the satchel at his side. "What about Satan's breath?"

"I'm afraid I don't know what that one looks like." Still, I look through and try to locate it.

"Ah. Here it is." He plucks one with a dark reddish powder inside and places it with the others, the bottles gently clanging against one another. Dash snatches a few more and then scratches at his chin. "What am I forgetting?"

"What about that feverfew?" I nod to a small bottle with tiny white flowers that have a round, yellow center.

"Good call." He takes it without a second thought and lets out a breath. "That should do."

I skim the remains in search of the healing tonic he had given me prior, only to find that it's missing. He must have already placed it into his bag, meaning that maybe I can commandeer it from him later and down the rest of it in hopes I can recuperate quicker. I'll need all the strength I can muster if I'm going to get through the next few days. I'm not sure how effective the tonic is considering nothing about my stay here has been normal. I shouldn't even be standing as it is, given the injuries I sustained. Between whatever magic Wes did on my leg, and that of the tonic, I've bounced back far better than I could have imagined in the short amount of time. Why stop here though? I'd rather be at full capacity in the company of these men, especially when it's likely they'll turn on me at any moment.

"You jealous?" I overhear Bo say from the main area of their small house.

A mild growl fills the space next, and when I step out of the bedroom, I smile at Bo's hands raised in the air in front of him.

Any chance of that sick bastard being put in his place is a win in my book.

Bo latches his sights onto me and winks. "And there she is."

I ignore the way Wes's entire body seems to stiffen at my arrival. He turns slowly, glancing over his shoulder. "Here." He holds a satchel in my direction. "Your supplies."

Continuing to disregard their obnoxious masculinity, I march over and pluck the thing from his hand, pulling it open and rummaging through the meager contents. "Is this a joke?"

I blink up at him.

Bo slides a long dagger off the counter and secures it in the sheath on his waistband.

"You trust *him* with a weapon but all I get is *this*?" A few rations and something that could be used as either a blanket or a pillow. I guess I'll have to decide which is more important when the time comes.

Wes stands there firmly in place. "I barely trust you with that."

He twitches slightly, almost like he doesn't believe his words fully. But if that's the case, why am I only equipped with the very barest of essentials?

Bo chuckles. "What, Birdie, you don't think we can protect you?" He wraps his arm around Wes's shoulder.

Wes immediately shrugs him off. "Don't touch me."

"I don't need anyone to protect me," I say through gritted teeth.

"Mmhm, well, if I'm not mistaken, you're alive because of us." Bo steps toward me. He brings his index finger to my chin, tapping it gently. "I'd be grateful if I were you." His warm breath lingers against my cheek.

I glare up at him. "I'd kill myself if I were *you*."

Bo grins. "Those are fighting words."

I steady my mind and assess numerous scenarios. I could grab the knife from his waistband and shove it between a soft spot in his ribs in hopes of penetrating something vital enough to kill him. I could slit his throat with it, but considering how tall he is, he could snatch it from me in time, and then use it on me. If I manage to pull off the first option, I'd have to act swiftly and end Wes's life, too. But from this position and his control over me, I'm not sure if I could gain the upper hand. And then, well, there's Dash I'd have to deal with. Could I bring myself to harm someone so...Dash? It's not his fault he got wrapped up in the wrong crowd. It could have easily been hunters who found and influenced him to join their cause instead.

As far as I know, the only thing Dash has done wrong is keep terrible company.

Does that mean he deserves to die?

"Can you two give it a rest?" Wes shoves his arm between me and Bo and nudges us apart, ending any chance I had at seizing that microscopic opportunity.

The odds weren't exactly in my favor anyway. Given I'm spending the next few days with these idiots, there has to be another that has a higher probability of success.

Not to mention, Bo holds the key to ridding my neck of his mark, so maybe I shouldn't be so hasty in ending his life just yet. Couldn't it have been Wes that marked me instead, leaving me the freedom to purge this realm of the demonic scum that is Bo?

"You know...I'm really enjoying this." Bo goes back to the counter to retrieve the rest of his belongings.

"Yeah, that much I'm aware, dumbass." Wes throws his bag over his shoulder and settles his sights on me. "You're not getting a weapon; not right now. You won't need it."

"Marching me into enemy territory unarmed makes all the sense. Why don't you just kill me and get it over with?" I've gone into battle with less before, but that didn't mean I wouldn't, at the very least, *try* not to be so vulnerable.

Dash appears from the tiny living room, his own bag secured to his body. "They've kept me alive, even when I had no idea how to fight. Put a little faith in them for the time being."

Wes steps toward the door, gripping the handle and tugging it open. "With Bo's venom flowing through your veins, you'll smell like him, not like you. They won't see you as the enemy."

An easy way for me to pick a few of them off and gain a little strength.

"Don't draw attention to yourself," Wes continues. "Most demons are too narrow-minded and egotistical to notice anyone other than their own reflection."

He's not wrong there. Demons are arrogant as can be.

Bo reeks of textbook demonic behavior. Wes on the other hand...he's unlike anything I've ever come across. Confident, but not quite cocky. And not only did he save me, but he took Dash in, too. Hell, even Bo gets a brownie point for helping Dash stay alive despite it not benefiting him in some way.

I step through the threshold of their cabin and out onto the creaky porch. The brisk morning air nips my cheeks and soaks its way into my lungs with each breath.

Structures often bring safety, but nature, nature provides freedom. Just this little bit gives me hope that maybe I'll make it out of this nightmare after all.

Bo shoves past me, nudging my shoulder and reminding me of his revolting existence.

"Excuse you." I dust off the spot he touched me and straighten my armor.

Dash comes around my side and offers me a weak smile, then glances up at Wes, who takes his place in front of us.

Wes clears his throat. "Our first stop is Breckenridge. We should arrive by dusk if we don't encounter any trouble. Stay alert, stay close, and do not try to run." His gaze bores into me with his last few words.

Their meaning seeping its way into my chest and rooting itself within me.

My lips part and the intent of asking him what the fuck kind of power he has over me is right on the tip of my tongue. But I keep the thought to myself, because if I'm right, Bo and Dash have no idea that he can do this. And if Bo finds out, there's no telling what he'll expect Wes to do with that authority. Instead, I'll bide my time until I can question Wes without Bo's prying ears and eyes.

What's bizarre is that Wes could have already abused this ability, but he hasn't. He's only used it on a few rare occasions. What could he possibly gain from sparingly compelling me? Does he think I don't know he can do this? That I can't feel his words root their way into my core and lock onto my free will? Maybe he's trying not to be obvious so he can use the skill more effectively at another time? Clearly, *he's* aware he's doing it, right? Does it consume an excess of his energy? Or use some kind of power of his that he doesn't want to dwindle? There must be a reason why he's not mistreating this influence over me. It might just take me a bit longer to figure it out.

"I won't," I finally mutter to assure these three that I will follow along for the time being. It serves me no purpose in running now, not when I'm still weak, have no idea where I am, and have a glaring alpha marker on my neck. Not *glaring* glaring. It's barely noticeable if you don't go looking for it. My hair pretty much covers it up to the unknowing eye. But the second Bo and I get close to that boundary point, the thing will go off like a beacon for any demon in the close vicinity, alerting them to a tasty meal.

I'd prefer not to be eaten by anyone, let alone a repulsive monster. And most definitely not one that is keen to the information of a warrior soul's yielding power if consumed. I don't want to be the reason the realms are reopened and more of their kind contaminate our home. Prania is still recovering from the war of the realms and can't afford the damage another war would no doubt cause.

"Scout ahead." Wes nods toward an area that looks vaguely the same as each direction I turn.

It must be some kind of illusion spell, which is no doubt what protects them from hunters finding their cabin.

I'll add casting abilities to the list of things they can do. That, or they're in cahoots with a witch or warlock. I wouldn't be surprised. At this point, if Wes and Bo sprouted wings and flew away, it wouldn't be that alarming. Most of the witches went underground though, quite literally. With their blood lingering on both the light and dark scale depending on the magic they cast, it puts them somewhere in the middle between both sides. Most hunters see them as traitors though and will kill on sight without even hearing them out. The little bit of darkness is one less demonic being in our realm. I've taken out my fair share, but they were on the far end of the spectrum, worshiping at least one of the Princes of Hell.

Their beliefs didn't matter to me though. I kill who I'm tasked to kill. I don't ask questions. I do my job and up until a few days ago, I was damn good at it.

That's not to say there have never been issues. I've had my hands full with beastly opponents in the past, but there hasn't been a single target I haven't been capable of eliminating. I've spent weeks pursuing jobs, days in battle, and fought fierce demons. Sometimes one after another. And these two here, their fate has been sealed. They will join their place with the others once I find an opportunity to redeem myself of this failed mission.

Dash

I'm fairly certain Wes hates me.

Bo has never really liked me, and I don't think that will ever change. I'm okay with that. He tolerates me. He helps keep me alive. For what reason, I'm not entirely sure, but I accept his assistance and occasional disregard either way.

Wes, on the other hand, has always been kind to me. Warm. Inviting. Never cold and shut off like Bo.

Bo acts like he doesn't have a heart, and I wouldn't be all that surprised if it were a true statement. That perhaps he has something else fueling his lifeforce. Stale bread and ale are the only two things he seems to get excited about. Well, that, and killing. Hunters, demons, witches, fae, vampires, werewolves—you name it, Bo will slaughter it. He doesn't really discriminate. Basically, if it looks at him wrong, it's fair game.

Luckily for me, I've managed to not piss Bo off enough for him to end my life. And up until recently, I thought Wes would be the person to reinforce that belief that I wasn't on the menu for dinner.

Now, Wes can barely meet my gaze, and the few times he does, he suppresses a snarl that rises from his chest. His beast is mad. No, his beast is furious. But why? Because I slept with Wren? She's a hunter, why would any of them care? If anything, they should be grateful that she doesn't hate at least one of us. I'm not convinced she won't butcher us the first chance she gets, but if she does, maybe the little bit of a relationship I've formed with her will aid in my ability to reason with her. It's wishful thinking, that much I'm aware of.

I've spent enough time with Bo to know that those carnal desires are often impossible to turn off. And despite Bo and Wren hating each other, they're more alike than they think.

They are both passionate about their beliefs. And they are determined to kill anyone that crosses them. Unfortunately for them, they're at far ends of the spectrum, naturally wanting nothing more than to rip each other's throats out.

Wes is brutal, too, but he's rational. He doesn't kill just to kill the way Bo and Wren do. He does it to survive. He's able to separate his distaste for Wren's kind enough to not go seeking them out. He actually tries to avoid hunters at all costs unless necessary. And if it weren't for the distress call that we overheard that day, he wouldn't have rushed to that dodgy side of town and did what he could to save a few demons who got caught in the crossfire.

I wasn't there to witness the fight firsthand, but I could barely believe my own eyes when I saw him pick her nearly lifeless body off the ground and bring her back to the cabin. I should have realized then that she was something to him, but in all my time with these two guys, I never would have imagined that kind of connection happening with a hunter.

It goes against their fundamental nature.

I may not have a vast knowledge of this world with my limited memory, but I know enough to know that kind of thing is off-limits—let alone highly unlikely.

I didn't mean to overstep by having sex with her. And a large part of me doesn't regret it at all. I have no recollection of being with a woman in any capacity and given how dangerous this life is, I didn't realize I was missing it until I saw her. From that very first moment, I was drawn to her. Something about how in this dark and gloomy existence, there was this brightness she exuded, regardless of her title. She might be Furla Ain, but she's still Wren.

A strong but damaged, delicate flower.

Maybe it was from seeing something so deadly be so incredibly vulnerable. It was like that veil was lifted and I could finally view her not as a hunter but as a woman.

I've never had those immediate desires to kill the way Wes and Bo do. The way everyone else in this dreaded realm does. I've never really fit in. That much has always been obvious. But I still hung onto the hope that maybe not everybody wanted to kill each other. Or at the very least there could be some good in the seemingly endless darkness.

Somehow, I knew deep down that she wasn't all bad. I clung to that, and put faith in the fact that if I showed her a little kindness, she might reciprocate. That she was probably just doing the same thing Wes and Bo were doing—surviving. She was fighting for what she believed in and what she was taught. I don't blame her for being the way she is and if anything, I applaud how she embraces it with such a truly admirable tenacity. She became the greatest of her kind. Similar to that of Wes and Bo.

Which leads me back to the topic at hand—how was I supposed to know Wes's beast felt the way he did when it's completely unheard of?

It's not exactly like he informed us. Maybe Bo would back off if he knew what she meant to Wes. Maybe I wouldn't have had sex with her if he simply communicated a bit better.

I sigh, because that would mean I wouldn't have experienced her tight and wet...

Bo slaps my arm and drags my attention from the growing erection in my pants. "We're going to take a break over here."

"Right. Yeah." I nod and blink to try to erase the image of her petite body from my mind. Following the three of them to the fallen logs, I pull the bag off my shoulder and claim a free spot.

"Do I even want to ask what you were lost in thought about?" Bo slides in next to me.

I swallow, briefly glancing over at the oblivious Wren and Wes across from us. "No. Probably not."

"I could guess." Bo breaks off a chunk of cheese and passes the larger hunk to me.

"I'd rather you didn't." I repeat his motion and give the rest to Wes, who breaks off his share and offers Wren the remains.

She takes it without saying anything and bites off a corner, chewing the mouthful slowly and scanning the forest behind me. Wren swallows and glances over her shoulder. "Any idea how far out we are?"

"Another two hours or so." Wes extends his canteen toward her and waits while she takes a long swig and returns it to him. He drinks some and then puts the thing back into his bag. "We've made decent time." He tilts his head toward the sky but when he lowers it, his eyes glow red, his beast rising to the surface.

"What is it?" I ask him, knowing damn well trouble is no doubt about to follow.

Wes brings his index finger gently to his lips and gazes at each one of us.

Bo whispers. "How many?" His ears perk at trying to figure out the answer himself.

"At least four," Wren answers. She closes her eyes for a moment and draws in a breath before opening, only now, a sly grin is on her beautiful face. "Make that six; more incoming."

Wes nods and Bo tips his head in some unspoken agreement.

Wren scans the ground and slowly latches onto a stick that's near her. She grips it in her hand and sets the rest of her cheese off to the side.

In the blink of an eye, shadows appear from every direction, various shapes and sizes, all hurtling toward us.

"Get behind me," Bo yells at me.

Wes repeats the same words to Wren, attempting to shove her body out of the line of fire.

"Fat fucking chance." She darts around him and shoves the blunt end of the stick right into the neck of an oncoming demon.

Wes exhales a puff of literal smoke. "You're going to get yourself killed." His beast growls and rises to the surface, his body glowing and flames nipping at the surface of every inch of him. He turns on his heel and snatches a dagger mid-air as it's flying toward his head and tosses it to Wren. "Don't make me regret this." He rushes over and snaps the neck of the mangy half-wolf-looking thing that threw the weapon at him.

I keep my back to Bo, my gaze wide and flickering in each direction. Bodies drop all around me despite my lack of participation in the battle.

"Uhh, little help here," Bo groans from behind me.

Four demons ascend on him, two of them launching themselves into the air.

Bo jumps out of the way in time and the monsters land on all fours, their bodies morphing into a vicious canine of sorts. Bo extends his arm and slices at the closest one with his razor-sharp talons. The beast yelps and black blood oozes out of the wound. The thing falls over on its side whimpering in pain.

One of the remaining three latches its sights on me and advances. I steady myself and step backward, hoping that I can draw the attention away from Bo long enough he can finish the other two off. This one remains unshifted, yet no less terrifying.

"Come and get me, you disgusting mutt," I yell at it.

Mid being attacked, Bo lets out a chuckle. "Good one."

Gripping the handle of the knife in my grasp, I wait for the opportunity to strike. I may not have supernatural abilities like my companions, but I do have one advantage—I'm often underestimated. Sure, it might not seem like much, but it almost always results in my attackers letting their guard down and exposing some kind of weakness.

I stop when my heel brushes up against something sturdy. I glance at the tree behind me and steady myself on it as I wait for the monster to continue to advance on me. I note its languid steps and cocky grin. The mostly man, part beast, licks at its exposed fangs and scratches just under one of the horns protruding out of his forehead. It's like he's going on a leisurely afternoon stroll through the woods and that's exactly how I want him to act. I want him to think this is going to be easy.

Shifting my vision past him, I spot Wren on top of a demon, thrusting her dagger in and out of his chest, and Wes blasting waves of flames at a group that comes toward him. Bo struggles with the beast-man and beast creature that are still on him, but it isn't nothing he can't handle. I've seen him battle an entire swarm of hybrid vampires and come out on top.

The thing approaching me smirks. "You think your friends are coming to save you? That's cute."

No, but that's what I want him to assume.

I swallow, painting on my best acting face. It doesn't take much. Regardless of my sly puppy dog act, I really am shaking on the inside. "Oh, it speaks."

"I'm going to enjoy this..." The beast steps directly in front of me and throws his fist up on the tree beside my head. He breathes in deeply and inhales my scent.

The split second he closes his eyes to savor the aroma, I slide my partially hidden knife out and use all my might to shove it directly into the spot just under his armpit.

His dark orange eyes widen and blood trickles from his mouth. He stumbles, and I yank out the serrated blade and move out of his path as he clutches the tree.

Satisfaction rolls over me at having duped such a fierce creature. I am merely a pathetic human in this realm, and I have somehow managed to stay alive this long. Granted, I owe many thanks to Bo and Wes, but they taught me well.

With a smile on my face, I turn toward the action, the feeling is immediately drained out of me as I see a terrible sight unfold.

Dagger clutched in her grasp and ready to be thrown in the direction of Bo and the man he's still wrestling with. The two guys tumble and kick up dust, snapping their jaws while they hold each other back. Demon blood pools on the ground around them and I'm not sure who it's coming from. Although, if Bo is having this much trouble, I can only imagine he's injured in some capacity.

My eyes go wide, and I dig in my heels and take off in a sprint toward the two. Life seems to get stuck in slow motion as I frantically try to get there in time and stop what's about to happen. But it's no use, I'll never make it there before her dagger does.

I watch as it soars through the air, my heart aching in my chest and wishing like hell I had supernatural speed to rush over and snatch it mid-air. I scream but it doesn't matter. Wes is fighting his own battle and could never make it in time either.

Wren is using Wes's distraction and the perfect opportunity to eliminate Bo. I can't say I blame her, given how poorly he's treated her, but not only is he the only thing that can cure her alpha bite, he's not so bad once you get to know him. I'd even go so far to say he's a decent guy. A bit murderous, obviously.

The blade makes a dull thud upon impact and the guys both stop moving and fall on top of one another. Between the dust floating through the thick air and the tears welling up in my eyes, I can't make out a damn thing until I skid to a halt beside them.

A loud groan fills the space and I firmly grip the knife in my own hand, ready to end another demon's life to end this nonsense.

One of the bloodied bodies is shoved to the side and the other struggles to sit up.

My breath hitches when I realize it's Bo emerging from the chaos, dirt and demon gore caked on his entire body.

"Fuck, man." He laughs and slides the dagger Wren had thrown out of the beast and rises to his feet. Bo tosses the thing to Wren as she approaches. "About damn time."

Wren catches it with ease and smiles. "You wouldn't stop flopping around long enough for me to get a clear shot."

Wes jogs over to join us, a look of surprise no doubt matching the one on my face.

Bo raises his hand toward her. "High five," he says when she doesn't seem to understand.

She slaps his palm and then points at his leg. "You're injured." A slight hint of concern lines her features.

She and Bo both turn toward me.

Bo speaks first, "What's with the look?"

I blink at him and then at her.

"Are you okay?" She asks while her gaze scans my body.

Wes interjects. "The dagger, Wren." He holds out his hand and clenches his jaw.

"What?" She tilts her head in his direction.

"The dagger, I won't repeat myself." Wes lets out a low grumble.

"Are you fucking serious?" She points to Bo. "I just saved his ass."

She did. Which is somehow more surprising than when I thought she was going to kill him the first chance she got. I wanted to hope and believe there was good in her, so why am I shocked the moment that becomes a reality? Wes seems to be thinking the same thing. Or at least, some version of it. He doesn't trust her, that much is certain. Wasn't this all his idea after all?

"I have to agree with Birdie on this one." Bo steadies himself on his good leg.

"This isn't up for debate." Wes continues to hover his hand there in place. "Give it to me, or I will take it from you. The choice is yours."

As much as I think it would make for an interesting fight, I don't want to see either one of them hurt, especially inflicted by each other.

"Whatever." Wren surprises me once more and gives Wes the dagger. She's feisty enough that I thought for sure she would have chosen the more complicated route.

"Seriously? Giving up so easily, Birdie?" Bo stumbles and falls to the ground. "Whoa."

The three of us that remain drop down with him.

"I don't feel so hot." Bo's head spins and he blinks repeatedly.

"It's a claw," Wren declares. She tears at his pant leg to expose the wound. "See that, it must have broken off in there and is just continually poisoning you." She nods to the body she had thrown the dagger into. "What is that?"

Wes grips the man-beast's shoulder and flips it onto its back. "Drakka."

"Are you sure?" She cranes her neck to get a better view of the fallen demon.

"Positive," Wes says with a hint of annoyance in his voice.

"Okay." Wren exhales. "Does anyone have a knife that doesn't have demon guts all over it? I need to get this thing out before it continues to burrow its way into his leg."

Bo slips a clean blade from his side and gives it to her. "Will this work?"

She nods and turns toward me. "I need you two to hold him down." She focuses on Bo for a second. "This is going to hurt."

Bo grins. "Give me your worst."

Wes latches onto Bo's thigh and I grip Bo's ankle, both of us holding him in place like she asked.

"Once I get this thing out, I'll need your flame, Wes." She eyes him briefly and goes to work, wasting no more time by digging the sharp end of the blade into the swollen flesh.

Dark blood seeps out and Bo flinches only the smallest amount.

I glance up at his stoic face. He's a better man than me for tolerating this so well.

Wren continues digging the knife into his leg for another second before shoving her thumb and index finger into the opening and rooting around.

"Oh yeah, that's the spot," Bo grumbles.

"Why do I get the feeling you're weirdly enjoying this?" Wren counters with her fingers digging around his wound. "Got it." She seems to latch onto something and yanks it out through the slit and holds it in front of her for a moment, then tosses it to the side. Picking up the knife, she looks to Wes. "Flame, please."

He complies, snatching the blade from her and blasting it with a wave of fire.

Wren clutches the glowing thing and presses it against Bo's oozing cut. It sizzles and smoke rolls off his flesh.

"Ah, fuck me," Bo grits his teeth.

"You wish." Wren finishes applying pressure to the wound and stands, wiping the blade on her pant leg. "Here." She extends its handle first to Wes, who takes it and gives it back to a rising Bo.

"Well, that was fun." Bo shakes some of the dirt off himself and applies a bit of pressure to his injured leg.

"You okay?" I ask him, because what the hell else am I supposed to say in a moment like this.

"Mmhm. My body should heal itself soon now that the toxin is out of my system. I knew something was fucking wrong when I didn't recover immediately. Fucking Drakka are an abomination."

"I could say the same thing about you." Wren winks at him and strolls over to our makeshift campsite. She rummages through the wreckage and points to something. Snatching it off a rock, she grins. "There you are." Wren bites into the remains of her cheese and comes back over. "What?" She looks between us. "No sense in being wasteful."

I shift to peer at all the dead bodies around us and can't help but wonder what my life entailed prior to losing my memory. Was I surrounded by death and destruction? My muscle memory kicked in when I was intimate with Wren, but it never has when I've been in battle. Does that mean my existence before this was free of such things? Or was I fighting to live every day of that time, too? Will I ever know the truth about who I am or where I came from? Why has no one ever come looking for me? Maybe not knowing is better, but that doesn't make the questions stop coming.

CHAPTER 10

Wren

We make it to the outskirts of Breckenridge without any other major issues.

There was the mild dispute of Wes not wanting to give me privacy so I could take a leak, and then him being dramatic when Dash offered to stand guard. Bo volunteered, too, to get Wes to shut up, but there's no way I'm letting him anywhere near me with my pants down.

Sure, I saved his life, but he is the only thing that can rid me of this damn alpha marker.

Did the idea of soaring that dagger into his chest cross my mind? Watching in what I can only imagine would have been pure bliss as the blade pierced his heart? Ab-so-fucking-lutely.

But I'm not a complete fucking idiot.

I have to keep reminding myself to be strategic if I want out of this alive.

And the added satisfaction of Bo giving me a split moment of respect when I rescued his ass was definitely a solid trade-off.

Ultimately, I was able to piss by myself, using the leverage that I did, in fact, save the unruly demon, and that if I wanted to escape, I would have when they were all distracted. If I didn't have the mark on my neck, I undeniably would have taken that out when it presented itself. Although, I'm not sure they'd give me the amount of leash that I currently have if I didn't have the constant reminder that I cannot leave permanently on my body.

I'm at their mercy for the time being and we all are aware of that.

And yet, it came as a complete shock to Dash that I spared Bo's life.

I shouldn't be surprised he was concerned for his friend, especially after asking me to let him know when, not if, I would betray them. I guess he knew the time was coming at some point and thought that it was then. I never did promise him one way or the other and it's not exactly like I owe him anything. But somehow it stings a little that he actually thought I would go through with it like that.

"We're not going to just waltz up there are we?" I reach out and stop Wes from going any further.

His serious gaze trails down to my hand on his arm and up to meet mine. For a split second, his demeanor hardens and softens and hardens again, like there's some internal conflict going on that I'm unaware of the details.

"Sure thing, Birdie." Bo slaps me on the back.

The commotion from inside the local establishments floats out toward us in our covered area right on the edge of town. Now, we're hidden by a vast forest, but the second we step through this tree line, we're exposed to anyone within an eyesight distance. We're no doubt already in range of any supernatural who might be intrigued by our presence, regardless of the natural concealment we've journeyed through all day.

"There shouldn't be any issue if you don't bring attention to yourself." Wes runs his hand through his thick hair. "That thing on your neck makes you blend in with the rest of us."

"And that's supposed to put me at ease? You do remember who I am, right? That might not mean much to you three...but I have a reputation."

"What do you expect me to do then, Wren?" Wes sighs heavily. "Would you like me to announce to everyone who you are and say you're under our captivity? Risk every demon in the surrounding area finding out where you are, and maybe inform them of that mark on your neck?"

"I mean, no. I was thinking more along the lines of throwing a shirt or something over this." I point to the thick, black armor hugging my body tightly. "Doesn't it look a little obvious?"

Without meeting their gaze, I'm certain each one of their eyes goes directly to my cleavage. I don't blame them—it was sort of an open invitation.

"Here." Bo grips the hem of his shirt and tugs it over his head, exposing his chiseled exterior.

I do my best not to study the many lines and curves covering his frame. We are still enemies after all, and I can't afford to see him in any other light.

Bo tosses the dirt and blood-covered thing straight into my face.

I catch it and glare at him. "Really?"

He shrugs. "You asked for it."

"Better?" Wes asks before turning to look through the brush at the small village we've arrived at.

I make the mistake of sniffing the garment as I drag it over my head. "This reeks."

"You want these, too?" Bo latches onto his waistband and unbuttons his pants.

Wes growls at him. "Don't even think about it."

Bo sighs and secures them back in place. "Your loss."

"Don't speak to anyone." Wes looks me straight in the eyes, doing that thing he does so well, tightening that control he has over me.

Fucking bastard.

I open my mouth, but the words don't come. Are you kidding me? His stupid power trip included him, too? What am I supposed to do if there's an issue? Or if I actually *need* to say something? He should really be more specific with his stupid commands.

Whatever.

If that's what he wants, then that's what he'll get.

I break away from them and march my way through the trees, waiting for the idiots to follow. They catch up within a second, Wes and Bo jumping ahead of me and Dash trailing us. I glance over my shoulder and take in the solemn expression on his face.

Demons of many shapes, sizes, and variations loiter about, none of them giving us a second look. Maybe this plan will work after all. A small group of partially shifted werewolves congregate near the entrance to an establishment a few doors down. Dark fae flutter past us, the wind from their wings floating across my cheeks. The scent of so many demonic creatures fills my chest and the need to slaughter every one of them rises to an uncomfortable level.

A wendigo stomps by, flicking up dirt with its every step. The creature's arms are stained red with the blood of its kills. The same substance drips off its chin and the antlers protruding from its skull exposed head. I've never seen one this up close and personal, considering the only time I interact with demons of this caliber is when I'm tasked to eliminate them.

"Kinda creepy, right?" Dash whispers in my ear.

I start to speak, but the words don't come. Instead, I offer him what I think is an acknowledging toothless smile and nod in agreement.

I'm not sure I'd categorize the beast as creepy, as much as I would disgusting and repulsive. But I can't exactly say that, considering Wes had taken my voice from me.

"This way." The asshole points.

I guess I should specify that I'm referring to Wes.

One could easily confuse him and Bo, but with Wes's current behavior, Bo is shining in a much brighter light. I still hate the bastard, but the race for which I dislike more is becoming a closer one by the minute.

I follow Wes up a set of creaky stairs leading to a small tavern. Noise billows out, but not the way it does from all the others we've passed. Hopefully he purposefully chose one with less potential prying eyes.

Wes holds the door open for me and I step inside the quaint establishment, a bit hesitant to go any further into enemy territory. Not a single being glances in our direction.

Bo comes from around me and makes his entrance known. "Tommy," he shouts at the barkeep. He makes his way over and slams his fist on the counter. "Two pitchers of your finest ale and stew for four. Don't forget the bread."

The old man with grey lining not only the thick hair on his head, but his bushy eyebrows and beard, too. "We only have one ale, Bo, you know this." He pauses and perks up one of those brows. "Four?" His lazy gaze trails the direction Bo came from, and stops when he lands on me. "A lady friend?"

I swallow and clench my jaw in hopes of hiding any bubbling up nerves at being in a place like this. Wes nudges me, and Dash places his hand on the small of my back to guide me over to where Bo is standing.

Bo throws his arm over my shoulder. "She's with me."

"Is that so?" The man grins.

"Birdie, meet Tommy, Tommy, this is Birdie."

"The pleasure is all mine."

I force another pleasant smile and nod, not saying anything because not only do I not want to, but because I can't.

Wes slides a few coins across the wooden surface. "We'll be over there." He points to an empty booth in the corner and leans in. "Know where I can find Frank?"

"Mmhm." Tommy nods. "Evening, Dash, you doing okay?"

Dash reaches over the counter and shakes Tommy's hand. "I'm still kicking, that's about as much as I can ask for. You?"

"Me, too, my boy, me, too."

Bo leads me away from the bar and through the not-so-crowded seating area.

If only I had supernatural hearing so I could listen in on what Wes and Tommy are chatting about where we left them. Who's Frank? And what does he have to do with our plan? Unease rises up within me at not knowing what this other person might entail. I was just starting to figure these three out, and now there's going to be someone else? What if they know who I am and the weight that my soul carries in terms of power?

We pass a table with three mediocre demons. Low-level grunts that I could take out with my eyes closed and my hands tied behind my back. They lack most common knowledge and quite a few brain cells, making them predictable and easy to kill.

One of them flits their gaze up at me as we go by. His muddy brown eyes do a double-take, and he turns to get a better look, drawing unwanted attention my way.

I slide into the booth, my back against the wall, and Bo climbs in next to me, his large frame taking up a considerable amount of space. His leg bumps into mine and I scowl at him.

Dash settles in across from us and cups his head in his hands on the table, his elbows resting on the uneven top.

Something is bothering him, more so than usual. Part of me wants to ask him, to figure out what it is, and see if I can help, but even if I decided to, it's not like I could. Wes has made damn sure of that.

I cast him a glare and watch him disappear around the side of the bar, through a swinging door. I don't enjoy this not knowing thing.

I eavesdrop on the conversation of the men in the bar, doing my best to pick up any useful information I can obtain.

"I wouldn't mess with him," one of the drunken demons slurs.

The other scoffs. "You're afraid of *that*?"

"You haven't heard?"

I peek over at them and watch as the horned demon leans in closer to the other. I strain to listen to his words.

"Rumor has it, he's a..."

The third friend of theirs slams a pitcher of thick, dark liquid onto the table, sloshing it over the edges and disrupting the man from finishing his statement.

Who was he talking about? Bo? Wes? Dash? Clearly, it was one of them. Are these demons familiar with who they are? What they are? Further proof that if they've made such a name for themselves, they are surely the enemy.

I lean against the booth and cross my arms over my chest, waiting for when we can get the hell out of here. This is no place for a hunter. Not when every instinct in my body screams at me to end the life of all the demons in here. Oh, the power I would gain from that, and the less they would have to reopen the gates of the demon realms and unleash more of their kind in Prania.

The pathetic demon who made it a point to crane his neck at me a second ago has repositioned himself in his chair to have a partial view of us. His not-so-obvious attempt to keep an eye on me sets my nerves on edge even more.

Does he recognize me? Does he know who I am? Is this entire plan about to come unraveled because these fucking idiots thought it was a good idea to bring me to a disgraceful town full of their kind? How did they ever assume no one would recognize my face when I've spent my entire life training for the title I've earned?

I may be overreacting. Despite being Furla Ain, I do pride myself on not allowing my targets to get away, meaning word of me only comes through the whispers of hear-say, not first-hand experience. Unless someone managed to slip away without my knowledge, how would these three half-drunk demons know who I am?

Either way, the incessant dimwit who keeps looking my way needs to stop before I do the thing my hunter instincts are telling me to do—snap this fool's neck.

CHAPTER 11

Wren

A short, younger boy drops two pitchers onto our table, the contents overflowing and spilling over the sides. "Sorry," he blurts out and reaches into the apron around his waist to pull out a rag. He makes quick work of cleaning it up, his head lowered the whole time. He scurries away for a moment and returns with four mugs.

"Thanks," Dash tells the kid.

Bo wastes no time filling all but one and giving me and Dash ours. He downs the contents of his own in a solid guzzle, and refills it to the brim. "That's good ale." Bo leans back and throws his arm across the back of our side of the booth.

I eye the cup in front of me, then Dash, who is sipping his. Sighing, I pick the thing up and press it to my lips. I taste the golden liquid, letting the coldness of it melt in my mouth and slide its way down my throat. It's better than I expect, with its oak and molasses flavor. I gulp down a bit more and wipe the residue off my lips.

"Good, huh?" Bo raises his dark brow at me.

I nod, given that's all I can do.

The boy returns with a plate of bread and cheese, setting it onto our table and walking away like he can't disappear quickly enough.

Bo digs in immediately, ripping off hunks of each and putting some in front of me and Dash, then himself. For such an egotistical demon, he sure is considerate at times. I'll add that to the list of things that don't really make sense.

I scan the crowd for anything out of the ordinary. And by ordinary, I don't mean the countless demons surrounding me. That stupid guy at the table we passed still continues to flit his gaze my way every so often. If I had fangs, I'd expose them and growl at him in an attempt to get him to stop fucking staring.

Bo tilts his head toward me, then follows my line of sight.

The man plays it off like nothing was going on, and carries on talking to his tablemates.

"Is he bothering you?" Bo asks me.

I shake my head and bite into the firm and salty cheese, chewing it with purpose and following it up with a mouthful of bread. I wash it down with the ale and wonder how much longer we'll be in this hell hole.

Wes is nowhere to be found since he vanished through the door in the far corner in his search for a man named Frank.

I'd ask Bo and Dash what that was all about, but, well, I can't. This whole not being able to talk thing is a real buzzkill.

Speaking of...I swallow the rest of my ale and slide the mug over to Bo.

He refills it without a word and does the same to his own.

"Do you think we could—" Dash begins but stops when the guy with a staring problem scrapes his chair across the floor loudly.

I study the demon's plump form as he stands, and hold my breath in hopes that he doesn't do what I think he's about to.

But the universe is a real bitch, so she sends the guy waltzing in our direction.

I'd mutter the word, *fuck*, if I were allowed.

"What do we have here?" The guy nods toward me.

"None of your business," Bo replies.

"Mmhmm." The guy rubs his bearded chin. "I was thinking..."

Bo stands from his spot, his frame towering over this asshole.

This is where I clarify that it's not Wes. He's still an asshole, as is Bo, but not the asshole I'm referring to at the moment. I should consider calling them asshole one, asshole two, and so on.

"Maybe thinking isn't your strong suit." Bo steps out of the booth and forces the guy to take a step back.

"Come on, man. There's enough to go around."

He better not be referring to me.

"I'll wait my turn." The bastard licks his lips and winks at me.

At this, Dash joins in, rising to his feet and placing his human hands on the man's shoulders. "That's enough."

The man shrugs him off and shoves him. "Don't touch me."

This little bit of interaction causes the other two men this guy was sitting with to stand. The taller of the duo tilts his head, cracking his neck and then his knuckles.

I never understood the point in doing that. Is it supposed to be intimidating? All it shows me is that you're too old and have joint issues.

The shortest of the three, a bald demon with nubbed horns and glowing dark green eyes calls out to his friend. "You good, Storm?"

Storm? What kind of name is that?

Bo steps closer to Storm, again, and comes close to bumping him with his bare chest. He's taunting him, that much is sure. He's giving him the chance to concede, but making his dominance known.

Men and their masculinity.

I stay firmly rooted in the booth, sipping my ale and watching this unfold. I'm pissed, and ready to rip every single one of their throats out, but for the time being, I'm going to let this play out a bit more. Storm will probably cower back to his table and resume being a creep from afar, and Dash and Bo will return to their drinks while we wait for Wes to reappear with, hopefully, some insight to where he went and who this Frank fellow is.

I couldn't be more wrong though. Storm has the audacity to shove Bo, but not before igniting some kind of electrical spark shit that floats off his hands.

Bo growls upon impact and reacts by palming the man's head and slamming it into our table.

Dash's eyes go wide and he ducks to avoid an empty mug flying at his head from across the way, no doubt thrown by one of Storm's buds.

I pour myself some more ale and gulp it down while Bo kicks the shit out of Storm.

He snarls, the beast shifter part of him rising to the surface. Long, sharp claws extend from each fingertip and thick, black scales pop up all over him. A self-made armor I was unaware he possessed. I'll lock that detail away in my mental bank of useful info.

"All over some slut," Storm slurs from his spot on the floor.

I sigh and roll my eyes. Slut? Really? That's what we're going with?

The tingling of the alcohol floats through my body, lightening my mood but somehow empowering me to get off my ass and climb my way out of the booth. There's no way I'm going to miss out on this action, not when it's finally getting good.

I grip Dash's collar and pull him behind me, nestling him into the corner of the bar.

Four completely new demons appear from who knows where and attack Bo, dragging his attention away from Storm. He stumbles only slightly and regains his footing, ducking to kick the legs out from under one and punching his fist through the chest of another. He rips the demon's black heart out and squeezes until it turns to mush.

Storm lays at my feet, whimpering and bleeding out. If only I were the one to have done that to him. I guess carnage inflicted on his peers will have to suffice.

I latch onto one of the demons after Bo and thrust him to the side.

"Fucking bitch," the vampire-like creature spits.

I'll show him a bitch.

I spin on my left leg, circling my body and putting all my force into kicking him square in the jaw with my right foot.

He stumbles into a table, breaking it with his fall, and clutches his face. The demon spits a darkly discolored substance onto the floor. "I'll kill you for that."

I cup my fingers and motion for him to bring it, a devious grin no doubt caked on my face. This is the shit I live for.

He heaves his body at me, and despite his supernatural speed, I hop out of the way in time, sending him into an empty space, causing his frustration to rise even more.

I can't help but laugh at the pathetic attempt to subdue me.

"Oh, you think this is funny, do you?" He raises his upper lip, snarling and exposing his fangs, a bit of his own blood spattering out. His gaze flits to something behind me, and he dips his head barely enough to signal to whoever must be joining us.

Grabbing a knife off a nearby table, I secure it in my hand and spin out of his path once more. I shove a chair at him and scan to see who the newcomer might be.

Another demon, not one of these two, blasts me with a chair, pieces of the wooden thing splintering and flying all around. I stifle a groan at the impact and rotate quickly, shoving the blade into the creature's calf.

It cries out and drops to the floor, clutching the gushing wound left when I yank the blade out. I jerk my arm back and plunge the knife into its chest and dodge another chair from my vampire fight partner.

The thing explodes and I catch a rather large chunk of it as it flies past my head. I rise to my feet, sizing up both opponents and smirking at their failed attacks.

The entire tavern has erupted in chaos. Demons fight demons for no reason other than because they can. What started as a dispute at our table became a full brawl for the sake of drawing blood. I can't say I disagree with their ways, regardless of how senseless they may be. Especially when it's this damn fun.

Two more of their kind rush over behind them, making it a four-on-one battle.

I scan the floor, looking for other possible weapons and ways for me to get creative with ending their lives.

Bo's baggy shirt hangs from me like a loose nightgown, more blood speckled on it now than when he tossed it to me. Not that I imagine he'll mind—he's sort of disgusting either way. Something about it is incredibly infuriating, too.

Dash drops to my side and I almost stake him with the wood in my fist. His eyes go wide.

I want to say sorry, that I thought he was one of them, but the spell Wes has on me is still too strong.

The four vampires jump on us with haste, two on Dash, two on me.

Fuck. Not what I had bargained for. It was fine when it was my battle, but now that Dash is involved...

I latch onto mine while Dash uppercuts the fang-toothed creature in his grasp, its venomous teeth clanging together and its head snapping up violently. He ducks out of the way from the other one, sending a jab up its chin, too.

I blink a couple times, not sure if I'm seeing this correctly. That was a solid punch for a human, let alone on something with supernatural strength. Maybe Dash isn't so helpless after all.

"Are you fucking kidding me?" Wes calls out. He slams his fist into the face of a man who swings at him first, knocking the guy to the floor with a thud. He shoves two more on his way into the anarchy.

Hissing draws my attention from the filthy bloodsuckers chomping at the bit to drain me.

Impatient little shits. I hike my leg up, kneeing the vamp straight in the groin, buckling him over. With the reinforced padding and armored additions to my clothing, there's no type of man that wouldn't hurt—demon or not.

"Bitch," the thing blurts out while clutching its groin.

Quickly, I grip a fistful of his hair and hold him in place, taking that same knee and jolting it up into his face this time.

The other vampire, clearly shocked at my ability to battle them with ease, stutters before deciding that grabbing my arm is the best idea. Exposing his fangs, he sinks them into the soft flesh, his venom stinging my skin and sending a burning sensation up into my chest.

He immediately withdraws, coughing and hacking up the blood he just drew. He drops to his knees, alongside his partner who is still trying to regain his composure.

I've been bit by various creatures in the past, can't say I've ever had that reaction.

The thing writhes in pain and claws at my ankle.

I kick it away, the same moment something tackles me from behind, knocking me to the ground.

This is usually where I mutter a few colorful words.

"Wren," Dash cries out from somewhere.

I crane my head to make sure he's okay, but the weight of the beast is too much. My body aches under the pressure, the air escaping my lungs and my chest unable to rise and refill. If I don't get this thing off me soon, it's going to fucking suffocate me. Sure would be nice to, I don't know, maybe ask for a little fucking assistance from the folks I came here with.

I've never had help before though, so why would I expect anything different here?

Hot breath nips at my neck and saliva dribbles out onto my cheek.

Did this thing just tackle me and fucking pass out?

That's when it dawns on me—the mass, the nasty breath, the motionless weight of it—this *thing* is a scurni. And yes, it did, in fact, just take a nap on my rather small frame.

The ogre-type creature might be large and strong, but it has goat-like tendencies where they faint when overexerted. Meaning, the chances of it crushing me are pretty high if I can't get it off before I run out of air.

I wiggle with all my might to press my palm flat against the debris-covered ground and strain to get this thing to budge. Pain shoots up my arm from the place that vampire had bitten me.

Great. Not only am I not operating at full strength, but that bite is hindering what little of my power still remains. The lack of air no doubt making the entire situation even worse. If it weren't for the armor encasing my body and holding the brunt of this beast's mass, I'd already be dead. And I will be soon if I don't figure this out.

Maybe dying isn't so bad. I mean, the likelihood of me making it out of the next few days is pretty slim, given the control Wes has over me and the mark on my neck left by the idiot who most definitely wants me dead. If it's not them that end my life, or the countless demons we'll encounter on our way, the guards at Rock Bridge will make a solid attempt at killing all of us on sight. If this first outing is any indication of the shitstorm we're bound to face, I'd wager to say none of us make it out alive.

But when have I ever gone down without a fight? And to die at the hands, or well, the massive weight of a scurni—doesn't seem like a very worthy death for an acclaimed warrior.

So, I do what I always do, I dig my heels in and don't give up.

One minute of self-pity is enough for this week.

I ignore the shooting pain in my arm and push again, rocking the beast ever so gently. Its weight heaves down on me with each movement, and the soft crunching coming from my armor alerts me to the ticking clock that remains. My gear can only hold on for so long, and then I'm a goner for sure. Without its assistance, this scurni will smash me like a bug.

I blink through my clouded vision and search for anything that can be of use. I spot the metal leg of a nearby booth, welding securely into the floor. I reach for it, the cracking growing louder by the second. The battle between moving too quickly and not slow enough is a fine line I'm barely hanging onto.

My ears pop and are unable to make out the commotion around us. I have no idea if the vampires killed Dash, or if Wes and Bo are faring well in this fight. For all I know, they've finished and are sitting at the bar chugging their ale and toasting to finally getting rid of me for good. Maybe they're taking bets on how long until this thing flattens me like a pancake.

I extend my hand, my fingertips grazing the cold metal. I clench my jaw and muster all my willpower to go a little further. I wrap my aching grip around the thing and pull with everything I have.

The beast groans and shifts its position just enough to give me the chance to free part of my torso, the weight of it crushing the bottom half of my body.

"One, two, pull," someone shouts.

The beast's body rocks, and I free myself completely. My chest heaves with the ability to finally expand without the crushing weight of the ogre. But, with each breath, another sharp pain spikes through me. If it's not one thing, it's another. Regardless of the new source of agony, I latch onto the discarded blade under the booth and bring myself to my feet.

The scurni hitting the floor rattles the old tavern and sends a shiver up my spine.

"Holy shit, Wren," Dash rushes over to me, his hands hovering over my body as frantically as his gaze. "Are you...are you okay?"

I swallow and blink to clear my vision, settling my sights on Wes and Bo behind him.

Bo drops to his knee and drives a knife into the chest of the vampire who bit me, pulling it out and repeating the motion three times. Overkill for sure, but still satisfying all the same.

"We need to get out of here." Wes rushes over and grips my elbow.

I yank it away from him and stifle a wince at the swift motion. My entire body aches, from the top of my head to the tip of my toes. I guess that's what happens when a giant fucking beast takes a nap on top of you.

Couldn't that have happened to Bo instead? Not the smallest member of our little group.

"We can assess your wounds later, right now, we need to leave." Wes nods toward the door he disappeared through earlier. "This way."

Keeping the blade I had found only a moment ago, I cling it to my side and follow him through the remains of the fallen. Whimpers float through the space but I don't bother taking inventory of the casualties. I'm not too stupid to know I need to get the hell out of here.

"There," someone shouts. "The hunter is right there."

Fuck.

CHAPTER 12

Wes

Wren is in pain—I can feel it in my soul.

The second I scanned that tavern and couldn't find her, the world felt like it slipped from my grasp. My beast slaughtered every demon in our path between us and her. I had caught a glance of a sliver of her hair under that hideous ogre and immediately thought the worst. Bo helped me lift that thing off her, and the whole time, I feared that she was dead—that I had lost her forever.

The blasphemy of my emotions grows out of control with each passing moment. Even if she cannot be mine, the idea that I caused her death would be something I could not live with. Every moment she spends in our captivity is one more that I put her in danger. But we're all in too deep now. Bridges have been crossed that cannot be taken again and the only way we can go is forward.

Bo has marked her and he's made it known that he will not rid her of it until she follows through with her end of the bargain. A deal that puts all our lives at risk.

He won't even tell me the details—just that it can be done. I'm putting my faith in him that he's telling the truth, because if he isn't, that means I lied to Wren, and given her connection to my beast, that's a serious offense.

"Wes, hello, you fucking idiot." Bo shoves me and points toward the door we just ran through. "Catch the building on fire."

My gaze trails over Wren, then Dash, and Bo, confirming they're all on this side with me. I draw in a long breath and allow the heat to bubble to the surface, my skin warming and my hands glowing brighter and brighter. I thrust two fistfuls of flames at the tavern and scream a wave of inferno, making it impossible for anyone to safely pass through the way we came.

"Run," I yell once I've finished.

They all comply, not a word coming from any of them.

A few moments of our labored breaths pass, and I follow Bo into a cave-like dwelling on the side of a hill.

"We need a plan," he admits.

Wren, knife in her left hand, makes a fist with her right and slams it across my cheek. She drops the blade into the dirt and shoves me with what little strength she has left.

"What the fuck?" I rub my jaw.

Bo leans against the entrance and raises his shoulder when I glance at him.

Dash tries to reach out to her, but she shrugs him off and gives him a death stare.

Turning back to me, she grunts and points to her mouth.

"What?" I furrow my brow, and then my stomach sinks—the mystery unraveling in my mind. "You can speak."

"I fucking hate you."

My beast and I wince. "I'm aware." I would hate me, too. What a fucking fool I am for abusing the very power I didn't want to abuse. I didn't mean for the control I have over her to be so fucking literal. I just didn't want her to draw attention to herself in that tavern, not take away her ability to speak permanently. It's no wonder she didn't scream for help under the weight of that ogre.

That thought alone rips my heart in two.

"If you ever fucking do that again..." Wren clenches her jaw. "I will slit your throat while you're sleeping."

"I...I didn't mean to..."

"You knew exactly what you were doing." She turns towards the other guys. "I know a place. It's not far from here."

I shake my head. "No. Not happening."

"Why?" She barely faces me.

"Because I don't trust you."

"Great," she blurts out. "Because I don't trust you either. But I don't intend on sitting out here in the open just waiting for who knows how many demons are after us. Do you have a better idea?"

"I'm with Birdie." Bo surprisingly adds in while keeping his gaze trained outside the pathetic covering. "No sense in letting them gain on us."

That traitorous demon is really starting to piss me off.

"You're bleeding," Dash says to Wren, reaching for her arm.

She pulls away. "I'm fine."

What little trust she had in Dash seems to have been erased, too. We're not even a full day into this journey and shit has already massively hit the fan. The whole point in going to Breckenridge was to secure transport to Rock Bridge. Prior to finding Frank, the guy who was going to help with transportation, the brawl broke out at the tavern. Meaning, not only did the plan fail, but now we have demons aware we're traveling with a hunter, and they're hot on our asses.

"Let me see it." I step toward her, knowing damn well that I can fix the problem with a few simple words. A skill only capable of being used in our *unique* situation.

She glares up at me. "Don't you fucking touch me."

"Ouch," Bo mutters.

"I can at least..." Dash pulls off his backpack and unzips it.

"I'm fine," Wren snaps at us. "How many times do I have to tell you? I'm fucking fine." She snatches the knife she discarded and walks over to where Bo is standing. "We're leaving, you can come or don't, I don't care either way."

"But..." My statement falls flat when they leave.

How did I go from being in charge to being left behind? This was all supposed to be my plan, and now she's calling the shots. Someone who Bo wanted to slaughter, is leading him to who knows fucking where. And he's a willing participant.

After a few minutes, Dash falls back to walk alongside me.

If I weren't seeing it for myself, I'd never believe that Wren and Bo would be shoulder to shoulder, chatting like they weren't on opposite sides of a war.

Is he doing this to get at me? So I'll admit the truth about what happened? The reality that I refuse to believe myself. The one my beast keeps taunting me with every chance he gets.

"What's up with that?" Dash tips his head toward the same sight I'm struggling with.

I shrug and scan the surrounding area to make sure we're not being followed. "I don't know."

"Hey..." He lowers his voice. "Can we talk?"

I side-eye him. "About what?"

Dash scratches at his neck, clearly uncomfortable about whatever it is that's on his mind.

My beast stirs at the very idea of it all.

"Not now, Dash." I swallow down the rage that builds up.

"I..." He flits his gaze at her then at me. "I didn't know."

"Didn't know what?"

"That you...your beast..."

"It's not what you think," I snap at him. "You're mistaken." A blip of fire puffs out of my mouth and zips past Dash's face.

He ducks out of the way but not before it singes a bit of his hair. "Christ, Wes, you could have hit me with that."

"I'm sorry," I cover my mouth and shake my head. "I didn't mean to." I really didn't.

Dash sighs and walks away, muttering with each step. "I was just trying to apologize."

I'm left alone once more and wish I could separate myself from the intense emotions threatening to tear me apart. It's enough that I feel the way I do about Wren, but to let it come between me and my friends, that's another. I'd never hurt Dash on purpose. Bo, on the other hand, yeah, I'd cause him pain every day of the week, but because he can take it, and has supernatural healing powers. And obviously, because he deserves it. He's an asshole—an arrogant and self-centered demon.

And right now, he has a better relationship with Wren than I do.

How the fuck is any of this possible?

When my beast locked its sights on her and refused to leave her behind in that building, I knew I had to come up with a plan. I would use the excuse that she could help us get our people back and in exchange, I could help her stay alive. The thought of the alternative was not an option. I would not allow her to die. I guess I didn't exactly think the entire thing through. I was a fool to assume I could control my beastly side. That in this entire lifetime spent with him, I had gained some kind of authority.

No, the moment he claimed her, I was a goner.

Not only does he want her, but he needs her, like the breath in his fucking lungs. The breath in mine—because he and I are one and the same. And for every bit of desire he has for her, so do I. That longing to be near her, to brush the hair from her face, to take away all her pain and give her everything she could ever ask for —I need that as much as he does. I shouldn't, he shouldn't, but we do, and there's not a damn thing I can do to change it.

The universe already decided it long before I had any say in the matter.

My fated mate—a fucking demon hunter.

CHAPTER 13

Wren

I hurt all over. Each step is a heavy rippling wave of pain coursing through me, but every inch brings me a little closer to a temporary haven.

One of my safe houses, tucked in the woods, warded similarly to how the guys had their cabin, only with running water and more than a deflated cot to sleep in. It isn't much, but it will provide us some shelter to regroup and figure out our next move.

I'm running on pure adrenaline at this point—a mixture of the high from the demon fight and the anger I have toward Wes.

How dare he compel me not to speak. And then pout like a baby when I say I don't trust him. Why should I? Not when he doesn't bother giving me the same courtesy. I could have run on numerous occasions, and yet I haven't. I could have killed every one of them, and yet, they're all still standing, even thanks to me saving their asses. I'm bringing them to a place I seek refuge, which is absolutely not something I ever thought I'd do, considering they're quite literally the enemy, and still, that's not enough.

Doesn't he realize that I intend on holding up my end of the deal? I need the cure of the alpha bite, and the only way to get it is to see this thing through. Unless they change their mind, or I find out they're lying, I'm very much getting them to Rock Bridge.

The puncture wounds on my forearm burn, no doubt having some kind of weird reaction to the alpha venom that was already in my system. I can only imagine that's what caused the vampire to stop and vomit up my blood. Between that and the giant who nearly crushed me to death, I grow weary of how much longer I have before my body decides it's going to give out. I want to stop, catch my breath, and rest a little, but if I succumb to the darkness tugging at my consciousness, there's no telling what kind of trouble Wes will get us into.

"It's just…" I point through the thick brush. "Up ahead."

"You sure it's safe?" Bo asks me.

"Promise," I reply, the word barely a whisper on my lips.

"You okay?" Bo slows his pace to match mine. "You don't look so good."

"For hating me, you sure do care a lot."

Bo rolls his dark eyes, but there's a bit of playfulness there that's new. He shoves a large branch aside and lets me walk ahead of him.

The murky night sky barely provides enough light to see where we're going, but home calls to me like the beacon on my neck does to demons. We're so close I can almost smell the lavender hanging in my kitchen and the eucalyptus in my shower.

I dig my heels in to climb up the final incline to my sanctuary. My foot catches on a rock, twisting my ankle and sending me backward.

Bo steadies me with his hand on my lower back. "Not trying to cop a feel."

"Uh huh, sure." I regain my footing, desperately ignoring the new blip of pain. Hasn't my body already had enough for one day?

"You good?" Bo asks when I don't continue.

Dizziness takes hold and it's everything I can do to stay upright.

"What's going on up there?" Wes asks from his spot in the back.

"I'm fine," I tell them. The same two words I've used over and over couldn't be further from the truth. I feel like shit. Like I've been crushed by a giant ogre and bitten by a vampire, and then hiked through the forest for a couple hours.

Oh wait, I have.

Bo steps up and cowers beside me. He takes one look at my face and then turns his back to me, still in the crouched position. "Climb on."

I blink at his bare skin. "What?"

He reaches behind, grabbing my hand and tugging me toward him. "Hop on, Birdie."

He can't be serious.

"I'm serious, get on. Hurry up before I change my mind." He brings my hand onto his shoulder and pulls me up with ease.

I reposition myself and wrap my arms around his neck, and my legs around his waist. Warmth flows through me at the close contact and my body thanks me for the reprieve. "You better not drop me."

Bo chuckles. "Don't tempt me."

"What the…" Wes mutters.

"She hurt her ankle, calm your tits, beast boy." Bo strolls up the hill at a much quicker pace than I was walking with ease, alerting me that I was holding us up from getting to safety.

We arrive at the top and I point the direction I want Bo to go.

"Uh, Birdie, are you sure you know where you're going?" Bo hesitantly walks toward what he assumes is nothing. "You're not delusional, are you? Wes is going to have my ass if he was right all along."

I mutter the incantation to myself to give the guys the same view that I have.

"Oh." Bo tenses for a second at the sudden change in scenery, and then briskly continues.

One of the perks I have from being a hunter—my safe houses are spelled so no one can access them without my consent. The few words I whispered give these three that ability. Here's to hoping I don't come to regret that decision.

"You can let me down now," I tell Bo once we're within a few yards of the porch.

He remains in motion, not stopping until he arrives at the small house. He turns and sets me down onto the wooden exterior.

I hobble over to the door, relief flooding through me when I grip the handle. It's only temporary, but it feels good to be somewhere familiar. Somewhere safe.

"Damn, Birdie, this place is nice." Bo climbs up behind me, pressing his arm above me and leaning against the side of the building. His scent floats down to me, and for the first time since we've met, I'm not utterly repulsed by it.

My head spins, the mixture of his venom and the vampires running through my veins does me no favors.

I stumble and reach for anything to steady myself.

"Whoa there." Bo places his large hand on my back.

Wes growls and hops onto the porch with us. He pulls Bo away. "Why are you so handsy all of a sudden? Did you forget you want her dead?"

"You're acting like children." I turn, but too quickly, causing my vision to blur that much more. I fall forward, everything going black as hands from each direction catch me from hitting the ground.

***

I wake sometime later, abruptly, sitting straight up and gasping for breath. I blink a few times, taking in the sights of my bare bedroom. I clutch my chest, my gaze trailing down to see that the puncture wound on my arm is gone, and the blood has been wiped away.

Wes, no doubt, doing the thing I asked him not to.

Burning wood crackles from the fireplace in the corner, and a small piece breaks off and falls to the side, a bit of smoke billowing up and away. The darkness of night through the window means I haven't been asleep too long.

The ache in my body tells me that Wes only healed *some* of my wounds, not all of them. Probably in his attempt to keep me weak and under his thumb. That bastard.

Hushed whispers bring my attention outside my closed-off room. I hold my breath and strain to hear what it is they think they're being secretive about.

"I told you, Wes, there is one." Bo pauses. "But you'll never let it happen."

"Why? Tell me what it is, and I'll decide for myself." Wes replies.

"Your mutt can't handle it."

"Don't act like you know what you're talking about."

"I see the way you look at her. It's obvious to everyone but you, and you're the idiot trying to ignore what nature has already commanded."

What the fuck is he talking about?

"I said *tell me*." A quiet but guttural growl follows Wes's words.

"See, right there. Why else would you be so defensive of a hunter if you weren't—."

"If you so much as finish that sentence, I will set you on fire."

"You're only continuing to convince me of what I already know."

I rack my brain to try to figure out what it is that they could be referring to. Wes has been nothing but evasive and weird since I met him, despite him randomly saving my life. Still, none of what they're saying adds up.

"Don't worry, once I tell her how the cure works," Bo adds, "she'll run for the hills. No way she'll go through with it either."

That's what this is all about? The fucking cure? The thing I've been using as motivation to go along with this entire stupid plan. The only reason I'm entertaining their idiocracy is something Bo is convinced I'll never do anyway.

Then what's the fucking point? Why risk my life to save more of their kind if there's nothing in it for me? I should have known these demons would bring me only disappointment and regret.

The firelight reflects off the knife sitting next to me on my bed, leading to countless ideas that pop across my mind. I could go out there, slice each one of their throats and be done with it. I could consume their souls and become a stronger version of myself, more powerful than ever before with their rare and mysterious energy. I could use it to slit my own throat and end the torment that will no doubt haunt me for the rest of my existence.

Instead, I grip the handle of the knife and carefully creep out of my bed, paying special attention to every creak I may cause. I tiptoe across the small space and as quietly as possible, lift the hatch on the window and tug it open. I eye the door and when I'm certain they haven't heard a peep, I climb out the opening and jump onto the ground. My feet land with a soft thud on the grassy surface and without another thought, I take off through the forest behind my house.

It's not much of a plan, and with the beacon on my neck, I can't imagine I'll get far, but considering I've been stuck with these fucking assholes for days, I need a moment to myself to process what the fuck I'm going to do with this new information.

I breathe in the night air and allow it to soak into my lungs. A light fog litters the ground and provides for an eerie yet calming stroll. Glancing over my shoulder, I exhale as the building grows smaller with each step away from it. My heart constricts at the sudden emptiness I feel without them around. What a strange immediate thought.

This whole time I've been dying to get away, and now that I am, I find myself unsure of quite literally everything. Maybe it's the mark on my neck causing me not to think clearly, or perhaps Wes has me under some kind of mind control spell again.

Either way, nothing makes sense at all.

Why wouldn't I take the cure? What could possibly be so fucking bad that I would refuse to do it? That Wes and his *mutt*, as Bo calls it, would disallow it from happening. Wes is the one who used the cure as a bargaining chip; why wouldn't he be a little more confident he could follow through with his end of the deal? Unless he never intended on delivering on his promise.

All of that aside, I still haven't figured out the answers to any of the other questions nagging at me. Like why my superiors failed to mention that Wes was anything other than some random demon. They played it off like he would be an easy target, and here I am, days into being around him and I'm no closer to determining what kind of powerful creature he is. Not to mention the fact that he's buds with an alpha and has taken a human under his wing to care for. None of that is typical demon behavior and goes against everything I've ever been told and conditioned to believe.

Why would they withhold vital information that could easily put my life in danger?

I get that I'm a soldier in this war, but I was under the impression I was valued and respected enough to get that kind of insider information.

No, I'm just a disposable grunt doing the work they aren't willing to do.

My neck burns the further I get away from Bo. That stupid fucking marker getting close to alerting any nearby demon of my whereabouts. I sigh, stopping my impromptu walk, and lean against a large tree. The ache in my ribs throbs through me at the pressure of my back on the hard surface.

Couldn't Wes have just healed those, too? Or maybe he wasn't aware of them since they're not visible. I guess I could give him a few brownie points for not looking where he shouldn't be while I'm unconscious.

A familiar sensation flutters in my chest. My warrior alert system kicking in. Something that's been on the fritz since these three came into my life. I disregard it at first. But it lingers there unwilling to dissipate.

A scream follows, making its way through the forest and slamming me in the gut.

An all too human sound.

Not wasting another second, I kick off the trunk of the tree and take off into a sprint. I push my legs harder to move quickly over the patchy terrain. I hop over a fallen log and burst straight through a bush, not a care in the world about the briars that plunge themselves into my flesh or the rippling of pain from my broken and bruised ribs.

The closer I get, the deeper the thought that I won't make it there in time. I push myself harder, drawing the blade from where I had sheathed in my waistband as I run onto a boulder, leaping through the air and landing within arm's reach of a demon. I shove the knife into its back, yanking it out in one swift motion, and turn to the others.

My fears are confirmed when my eyes settle on Dash, being held captive by a wendigo easily twice his size. The one from the fucking tavern.

Dash screams again, but the thing shoves its filthy hand over his mouth to muffle the sound.

Anger rises up within me. A possessiveness I will add to the list of things I cannot explain.

A swarm of darkness appears from the trees behind the wendigo. Partially shifted wolves, drakka, and beasts I cannot identify rush past them and unleash themselves on me.

I steady my footing and eye each of them, only one weapon in my grasp and a dozen demons that need to die.

The first, a vampire-looking thing, uses its supernatural speed to advance on me, but not before I pivot and shove the knife into its heart. Another two try their luck, only to meet the same fate. I spin and duck and use every single fight I've been in and ounce of training I've ever received to allow my body to do what it does best —destroy.

In the blur of the chaos, two dominant figures appear, one glowing bright red, engulfing everything he sets his sights on into flames, and the other, snapping neck after neck.

A sense of hope reverberates through me.

But we all know, hope is a fickle bitch.

I shift toward the wendigo holding onto Dash, ready to take matters into my own hands. But instead of releasing him and fighting someone on his own level, he does the unthinkable.

With a solid and swift motion, the ungodly beast places a hand on the front and back of Dash's head, his ginger locks flowing through the demon's fingers as his neck is abruptly snapped.

For a split moment, Dash and I lock eyes, a million words unspoken between us. And like the life is being sucked from the both of us, his limp body drops to the cold, hard ground.

"No!" I scream, but it's no use. The worst has already happened.

And there is not a damn thing I can do about it.

Dash is dead, and it's all my fault.

CHAPTER 14

Wren

The wendigo takes my momentary surprise as its excuse to retreat into the shadows of night. Fighting me was one thing, but upon Wes and Bo arriving, it knew the chances of it surviving were slim to none.

I scuttle across the ground over to where Dash's body remains.

Unmoving. Unresponsive. Dead.

I brush the golden locks from his forehead. "No," I whisper. This can't be happening.

Out of the corner of my eye, I spot Wes and Bo finishing off the last of the wolves that stuck around. I hop up and rush over to them.

"Heal him," I yell at Wes. "Do something."

He shakes his head, his brows furrowed. "It doesn't work like that."

"Why?" I point to my leg and then my arm. "You did it for me. Do it for him." I reach for his arm and tug at him.

He yanks himself free. "Wren, stop."

Bo crouches next to Dash's lifeless body and runs his fingers over Dash's eyes to close his lids. "He's gone."

"No." I refuse to believe that. Because if I do, then I'll have to come to terms with the fact that it was my fault. That Dash is dead because of me. And that's not a reality I'm ready to face just yet. I drop to the ground and lightly smack Dash's expressionless face. "Wake up, Dash. Come on, wake up." I pinch his nose and open his mouth, breathing what life I have into him and hoping like hell it works. Pressing my hands into a ball, I push on his chest, pumping him the way I was taught all those years ago when I was a child. If only I had paid more attention, I'd be more confident in knowing what I was doing. I simply go through the motions as best as I can remember. "Dash, please."

Minutes pass of my failed attempt at bringing him back. Wes and Bo remain quiet while they watch me with pity. I don't even know why I do it, knowing in my gut that his injuries are far more serious than breathing life back into him.

Unwilling tears roll down my cheeks at the loss of a man I barely knew, but knew well enough that he didn't deserve what this life gave him. This world. It was far too cruel for someone like Dash.

"There has to be something," I mutter.

Bo kneels next to me and places his hand on my shoulder. "Wren, he's gone."

My name, he used my name. Which can only mean that he's not trying to tease me, or play coy, he wants me to understand that this innocent man is truly dead.

I blink up at Wes. "Why can't you heal him? Tell me." I stand and wipe at my cheeks. "And why won't I take the cure?" I look between Wes and Bo, desperate for answers to any of my questions.

When they don't speak, I raise my voice. "I deserve the truth."

Bo scratches his neck and glances at Wes. "Dude, you should take the lead on this one."

Wes runs his hand through his hair. "I...I don't know where to start."

"What's the point then? Huh? If you won't tell me. What reason could you possibly have to keep things from me? Have I not proven myself trustworthy? I agreed to this fucking mission, and I've let you recklessly endanger all of our lives, and for what?"

"You wouldn't understand." Wes averts his gaze.

I step toward him and shove his chest. "Then make me understand." I turn toward Bo, pointing my finger at him. "You're just as guilty so knock that smug look off your face." I yank the knife tucked into his waistband out. "Fine, if you two don't want to talk." I flip the blade so it presses into the exposed skin right near my heart.

Both of them lurch forward but I anticipate it and match their stride the opposite way. "Don't you fucking come any closer." I push the blade in, drawing a bit of blood that trickles down my breast. "If you won't give me answers..."

I never really anticipated my death coming at my own hands but with the way things have been going lately, I don't think I'm at all surprised. Who better to end my life than myself? At least I will go down on my own terms. Not because of some demon.

I'm exhausted. Both mentally and physically. I'm not a quitter—I just don't really want to go on. I mean, what's the fucking point when quite literally nothing makes sense? My entire life hinges upon lies and deception and I find it difficult to know what to believe in. What to trust. It's hard to put faith in my own thoughts when even they betray me.

I glance down at my feet, where Dash's body remains.

"Wren, can you..." Wes pleads.

How does he not realize he holds all the cards right now? If he would be honest with me, maybe I'd put down the knife.

A crackling sound comes from Dash, stealing my attention from Wes's concern-riddled face. It's strange really, to witness two incredibly powerful creatures actually show worry at my dramatic display. Why would they care if I end my life or not?

Oh, wait, they can't continue to use me as leverage. That's why.

Dash's lifeless body starts to smoke, then catches fire.

Panicked, I look at Wes, but there is no sign of his beast side showing through. And if Wes didn't cause the fire, then what did?

Dash burns for an agonizing second, his entire body going up in flames.

"Is that supposed to happen to humans in this realm?" I watch in horror as Dash disappears in the blaze.

The flames burn out and a solid shell encases where he once was.

"I don't...I don't think so." Wes appears at my side.

Bo snatches the knife from my slack hand, offering me an apologetic shrug at having seized the distracted opportunity. He returns his attention to Dash with the rest of us.

The hardened tomb-like thing cracks and a hand reaches through.

Dash—unharmed, and somehow alive breaks through the surface, the encasement breaking all around him.

"How is this possible? You're...you were..." But my words continue to fail me.

"A phoenix," Bo declares, reaching down to help Dash to his feet. "My boy is a fucking phoenix."

It's no wonder I couldn't sense a demonic aura on Dash—because he has none. His magic is pure, untainted, and unlike anything I've ever come across. In all my years, I've never heard of a phoenix being in our realm. And if I'm not mistaken, their kind is almost completely extinct, making the story of why no one came for Dash all that much more credible.

Without thinking, I wrap my arms around Dash's neck and pull him to me.

Too damn slowly, he latches onto my waist and picks me off the ground.

"I thought you were dead." I weep into his neck.

He breathes me in and squeezes me tightly. "I think I was."

Dash sets me to the ground, and I study him over, not a scratch or ginger hair out of place. Just that adorable grin and those baby blue eyes.

"What did I miss?" He asks us.

Bo is the first to speak up, because why wouldn't he want to hear himself talk? "Birdie here was about to off herself."

I narrow my gaze and glare at him.

"What? Why?" Dash scans all around us, no doubt taking in all the dead demon bodies around us.

Bo shrugs. "Must really be into that whole Romeo and Juliet thing."

"What's the last thing you remember?" Wes ignores Bo's remarks and focuses on Dash.

Dash puts his finger to his chin. "I...um...I came out here." He looks to me. "To find you." Then he motions to the massacre. "And I'm pretty sure that big scary thing from the tavern was here. You know, that beast with the antlers and the skull and stuff." He shakes his head. "Creepy son of a bitch."

"Wendigo," the rest of us say in unison.

"Yeah, that." He scans the crowd again. "Um…"

"It got away," I tell him. I should have gone after it, but I was a bit more concerned with Dash being dead. Mark my words, one way or another, I will hunt it down and make it suffer for what it put us all through.

I shift my focus to these men around me. Wes—the enigma who is more powerful than Bo, the alpha of alphas, and Dash, a complete rarity to the supernatural world—a freaking phoenix who rises from its own ashes upon its death. All three are unheard of, and here I am, in the presence of each one of them.

"We can worry about that later," Wes says. "We shouldn't stay out here in the open much longer."

I take a step but then realize none of the things I asked were answered. I glue my feet in place. "I'm not moving until *someone* tells me *something*."

Dash widens his stare. "Um." He glances between us. "I'm a phoenix?" He draws out the last word and squints a bit.

I let out an exasperated breath. "Not you." I pat his shoulder and let the gratefulness of his continued existence calm me.

Bo points to Wes. "He's in love with you."

I swallow, then blink a few times. "I'm sorry, *what*?" Crossing my arms over my chest, I wait for some kind of explanation. Is this some ruse to get me to stop asking questions? I jut out my hip. "Is this true?" I stare directly at Wes, whose face reddens, but not because of his beastly abilities.

"I fucking knew it," Dash adds.

"Knew what?" Why can't these guys just fucking answer me?

"That's why your beast has been pissed at me. Because I slept with her." Dash nods his head like all the pieces are starting to fall into place.

Must be fucking nice not being in the dark.

I slap his arm lightly. "A little discretion, if you will."

A growl ripples out of Wes and a burst of fire follows the sound.

I grab Dash out of the line of fire but not before the flame licks at my skin.

"What the fuck, Wes." Bo shoves Wes with force, knocking him off his feet. "You could have hurt her."

"Um, hello?" I point to my blistered arm and then press my hand to it even though that's probably not the ideal thing to do. "And what do you care? Don't you want me dead anyway?"

Dash steps in front of me like he's going to protect me.

I smile at the thoughtful and misplaced gesture.

"Don't you think if I wanted you dead, that you'd already be dead?" Bo rolls his eyes.

"This is all your fault," Wes slams his palms into Bo, pushing him the same way Bo had done to him. "If you hadn't started that fucking fight at the tavern, we wouldn't be in this mess."

"Well, *excuse me* for defending her fucking honor," Bo blurts out.

All three of us gawk at him.

"What?" He throws his hands up. "The dude was out of line. He had it coming."

"Wait, you're telling me you beat the shit out of that demon because he was *hitting* on me?" Am I hearing this correctly or did Bo actually do a gentlemanly thing?

"He said he'd wait his turn, as if you were some piece of meat to go around." Bo continues to surprise me with each word.

"Oh," Wes mumbles. He extends his hand. "Well, then. Thank you."

"Thank you?" I retort. "You're *thanking* him?"

The two of them shake hands and a sort of unspoken understanding falls between them.

I shake my head. "Whatever." I storm off, heading back in the direction of my house. One thing is for sure, we shouldn't be out here any longer. There's no sense in waiting for more demons to attack us while we're all still reeling from our last battle. At least my place is warded from that kind of thing while we regroup.

And regroup is definitely what we need to do after *all* that just happened.

I stomp my feet each step of the way, the guys hot on my trail as they follow me without saying anything. Of course they won't. They're all about keeping secrets and being weirdos who I'll never seem to understand.

My body continues to ache, and now my head decides to join in on the fun from the tears I had shed at thinking Dash had died. My forearm stings from the burn of Wes's flame, and my mouth feels like it's full of cotton. I need a damn drink —a stiff one, that's for sure.

I burst through the threshold of my house, the door open upon my arrival, no doubt a result of Wes and Bo rushing out at hearing the same scream I had heard from Dash. I go straight to my kitchen, and pull a bottle of the strongest whiskey I have available off the top shelf. I pour myself a thick helping of it, and down the contents in one fell swoop.

The guys hover inside, but near the exit, looking all like they might flee at the slightest confrontation.

"You." I point to Wes. "You are going to get us all killed if you don't get yourself under control. And that thing, I know you know what I'm talking about. If you do it again, I will fucking castrate you."

Wes swallows roughly and nods. "I understand."

"You." I turn my attention to Bo. "Is there a cure or not? Don't fucking lie to me."

"There is." Bo steps into the kitchen and takes the bottle from my hand and pours himself a glass. "But you're not going to like it."

I glance up at him. "Do any of you have to die?"

"What?" Bo scrunches his brows together. "No. Of course not."

"Okay, well whatever it is. I'm sure it'll be fine. We can cross that bridge when we get there."

"You." I focus on Dash.

"Yes, ma'am?"

"Try not to die again, that was unpleasant."

Dash blushes and rubs at his neck. "You care if I die?"

"Is it not obvious?"

"I just…" He tugs at his bottom lip with his teeth. "I wasn't sure. I sort of misjudged you and thought you were going to kill Bo, you know, with the whole knife throwing thing."

"Hell, even I wasn't totally convinced I wasn't going to kill him, until I didn't." I look over at the arrogant asshole who is currently downing all my booze.

From the moment I saw him—sensed him—I wanted to end his life. It was the hunter nature kicking in like it always has. I see the enemy, I eliminate it. And Bo, he is very much the enemy in every sense of the term. But strangely enough, he's grown on me. How? I have no fucking idea. Maybe it's the subtle kindness he exudes, like making sure Dash stays behind him during battle, breaking off chunks of bread for us before allowing himself the pleasure of indulging, and fighting off that ignorant demon who insisted on insulting me. I recall the satisfaction on his face when he smashed that vampire's heart in his hand, and stabbing the one who had bitten me, and the high-five he gave me when we tag-teamed destroying those demons together. Or maybe it was the innocent piggyback ride when I twisted my ankle.

It's a collective of things, really, all adding up to the fact that I don't hate him as much as I once did.

Plus, I mean, if we're being honest, he's a total smoke show with that bad boy dark vibe about him and his rock-hard, chiseled body. He even has the long, jet-black hair totally working in his favor thing going on. His looks alone are a convincing argument to keep him around.

"So, you're not mad at me?" Dash asks while hesitantly stepping closer.

"No." I shake my head and extend my refilled cup to him. "You want a drink?"

Wes does that thing he always does, growls a bit from his chest.

"Okay, *that*. Whatever *that* was. Has to stop." I glare at him.

He clears his throat. "I'm sorry, I didn't mean to."

"Then who did? Explain to me what's happening so I understand." When he doesn't say a word, I press my hand to Bo's shoulder. "Does this make you angry?" I mouth to Bo, "Just go with it."

He grins and winks at me, grabbing me by the waist and tugging me toward him. "With pleasure," Bo whispers into my ear.

I turn, pressing my ass up against Bo and reaching for Dash, who goes along with the plan without a second thought.

Dash cups my face in his palms and runs his thumb along my cheek, his gaze trailing down to my lips. "May I?"

I reply by pressing my mouth to his, but we're soon interrupted by the fiery inferno that engulfs Wes upon our embrace.

"Shit, fuck." Wes flings his arms like he's trying to put himself out. "I…" He continues to shake them.

I can't help but laugh at the sight of such a commanding beast struggling to gain control of his power. "You better put that out before you burn my house down."

Wes sighs and a blip of fire rolls out of his mouth. "I'm fucking trying."

I step away from Bo and Dash and approach Wes. "Hey," I say softly.

He meets my gaze, and there's something painful about the way he looks at me. A struggle I'm not sure I could ever understand hidden behind his eyes. "I never asked for this."

"Asked for what?" I continue toward him as his flames die down.

"Careful, Birdie," Bo calls out from behind me.

I ignore his warning, knowing damn well I was ready to drive a knife through my heart not too long ago because of their lack of answers. What's the worst that could happen now? Wes catches me on fire? I could think of worse ways to die.

I glance over my shoulder. "Could you two give us a minute?"

They nod and shuffle out of the room, through the front door.

"We'll be right out here if you need us," Bo mumbles on his way out.

I reach for Wes, his hand glowing and then returning to normal. "Come." I lead him into the small sitting area and drag him onto the couch beside me. Maybe if I get him more comfortable, he'll spill whatever it is that's going on with him.

Wes stiffly complies, his body facing away from me. "This isn't a good idea."

I grab his knee and pivot him in my direction while pulling my own legs onto the couch.

"Why?" I prop my arm up on the back of the couch and rest my head on it.

His gaze shifts to where he had burnt me.

"I'm fine, really." Between all the other injuries I've sustained the past few days, that one is just a small drop in the barrel.

"Okay, if you won't talk, then I will. Correct me if I'm wrong." I clear my throat. "So, I was ordered to kill you, obviously. And I majorly failed at that. Which isn't something I ever do, making this an entirely new situation for me. Instead of you letting me die there alone, or finishing me off, you bring me back to your place, and nurse me back to moderate health, and then decide I'll be useful to you in this mission of saving your friends from Rock Bridge. But here's the thing I'm unsure of. Did the idea to use me come before or after you saved me from that building?" I leave out the part about why I didn't succeed in killing him. That, the moment I locked eyes with him across that building, something fluttered in my chest that I haven't been able to make sense of no matter how hard I try. Something I've continued to ignore each time he's near.

Wes clenches his jaw.

I continue, "You show signs of jealousy when Bo or Dash get close to me. You have been a jerk to Dash since you realized we had sex. And your entire body was set on fire a few minutes ago. Bo blurted out that you're in love with me, but that doesn't really add up considering aside from the time you kept me from freezing to death in my sleep, you do pretty much everything you can to stay away from me, like I have the fucking plague."

Finally, his lips part. "I don't think you have the plague."

"Then what, are you into Bo or Dash, and you don't want me near them?"

His dark eyes go wide. "You think I'm...?" Wes shakes his head and chuckles. "No."

"Then what? Why do you refuse to tell me the truth?"

"Because I can't change it, no matter how hard I try. And if I say it out loud, then..."

"Change what?"

"Fate."

I blink at him, still not following where he's going with this. What does fate have to do with anything?

"My hound..." Wes takes a steady breath in and then meets my gaze. "Has claimed you as his mate."

Finally, it's my turn to be speechless.

His *hound*? Mate? How is that possible? I'm a hunter. Why would he want me out of everyone else he could choose from?

"Say something, please." Wes swallows like it causes him pain.

"I didn't expect that." But it makes sense of the way he's acted. And the sensation rippling through my chest when I saw him. It wasn't *just* his hound that felt the connection, but me, too. I've never heard of such a thing happening to a hunter before.

Something he had said sticks out in my head. It takes the shape of an ugly insecurity rooting in place.

"Wait, you...you don't want it? The fated mate bond?"

He said it himself that he can't change it, meaning that he would if he could. He's definitely done what he can to refrain from acting upon it. Is he repulsed that his hound would pick me?

"It's unnatural." Wes points to me. "You're a hunter." And then to himself. "And I'm...your target."

I nod slowly and lower my gaze. "I understand."

Wes reaches forward and tips my chin up. "I didn't say I didn't want it."

I ask the question I shouldn't. "Then what do you want?"

He sighs and skims the side of my cheek with his knuckles. "You."

That simple word is enough validation to give me an overwhelming amount of confidence and send me climbing across the couch and onto his lap. I straddle his legs and press my palms to his broad chest.

"What are you doing?" He stares at me with wild eyes.

"Shut up and kiss me."

His hardened expression softens, and he runs his hands up my neck and weaves his fingers into my hair, tugging me down and pressing my mouth to his. There's nothing gentle about it, just a purely passionate moment that took entirely too long to come to fruition.

Wes's warm tongue skims itself along mine and a low groan rumbles out of his chest.

I grip my fingers in his thick, dark hair, and run my nails against his scalp. My body melts into his, becoming this over clothed unit that can't seem to get close enough. I've never lusted for a being more in my entire life, and a month ago, if someone would have told me who it would be with, I'd slit their throat just for making such a wild and outlandish statement. Now, I can't imagine it any other way.

The front door bursts open and Wes pulls himself free from my kiss, apparently having more self-control than I do.

"Sorry to break up what looks like a great time," Bo apologizes. "But there's howling outside, which probably means we shouldn't be out there as the welcome party to whatever demons are searching for us."

"Right, yeah." I climb off Wes and pat my, no doubt, unruly hair down. I wipe at my moistened lips and fight the urge to say fuck it all and climb back on top of Wes, not a care in the world who might bear witness to us both finally giving in to our carnal desires.

CHAPTER 15

Bo

"We need a plan." I honestly can't believe the words out of my own mouth.

When am I ever the fucking logical one?

I'm used to living my life on the run, constantly wondering where my next meal might come from or who's plotting to try their hand at killing me.

But now, everything has changed.

I should've realized it sooner. Like the moment I acted on impulse and tasted her decadent blood in my mouth, or when the craving for death nearly overcame me when that demon wouldn't leave her alone. The satisfaction of blasting my fist through that vampire's chest and ripping out its heart should have alerted me to the shift in dynamic, but I was just as much an ignorant fool as the rest of us. None of that matters though if we don't stay alive.

A wendigo has set its sights on us, and has no intention of letting us go until we're dead.

And the tricky thing about those creatures is, even if we manage to kill the bastard, he's already shared the intention with his many followers, making survival in this realm that much more difficult.

Fucking yay.

If things weren't hard enough with the hunters, now the demons are after us, too.

"A plan." Wren adjusts her armor. "Get inside." She mutters something under her breath. "I've spelled the house to be concealed from anyone other than us. But there's no telling how long it will hold if they have a witch on their side."

Wes clears his throat and straightens up on the couch.

From the smug look on his face, he must have finally told her the fucking truth. That his hound has a perma-boner for her. And if I'm not mistaken, the news must have been well received since I caught her straddling him in a pretty heated make-out session. I could smell her lust before I stepped foot through the front door.

Maybe shit will be less awkward now that the truth is out.

Either way, his bond to her is unimportant in the grand scheme of things.

"Someone want to tell me why this feels much more dire than it typically does?" Dash glances between us for answers. "I mean, don't get me wrong, I'm getting used to this way of life, but this feels...I don't know...bigger."

"Wendigos don't like to lose," I tell him. "I'm assuming when they found out she was a hunter back at the tavern, the dude volunteered to take us out. Since he was unsuccessful, and we ran him off, he's probably recruited all of his little minions to assist in finishing the job."

Dash nods. "So, it's like, personal."

"Yep. And he'll stop at nothing to make sure it happens."

"Cool."

"It's nothing we can't handle." Wren strolls over to the kitchen and stands on her tiptoes to reach into a cabinet. She pulls out a loaf of bread and sets it on the counter, then pulls out a large platter and plops the bread onto it. Digging through her fridge, she drags out a few hunks of cheese. She snatches an apple out of the wicker basket, sniffs it, and takes a bite. Satisfied, she places three more on the tray and carries it over. "Eat."

I study her every move and wonder where she gets all that confidence from. She's tiny, and somehow, manages to kick major ass.

Wren breaks off a chunk of the bread and tosses it to me. "I said eat."

I catch it and grin. A girl who knows the way to my heart is through my stomach. Is there anything she isn't capable of?

And that's if she even considered me that way. There's no denying shit has been rocky between us from the start. The whole being complete enemies and all, and the numerous times I've threatened her life, and the mark I put on her neck like the arrogant asshole I am. I wouldn't like me if I were her.

"Demon zones are off-limits then." Wren settles into her spot on the couch.

Dash follows her over and sits in the chair next to her, while Wes remains disheveled and flustered.

I drag a chair from the dining table over and flip it to sit in it backward. I rest my arm on the back of it and chew the bread she gave me. "Obviously. Why? What did you have in mind?"

"What if we try a different approach?" Wren reaches for the apple she had already taken a bite of and nibbles off another piece of it. She wipes at her lip with her thumb and sucks the juice off.

Fuck. That was hot.

"Like what?" Wes snaps out of his stupor and goes into strategy mode, something I find myself struggling with at the moment.

It's easy to get distracted with Wren looking the way she does.

And the recollection of her ass pressed up against my groin while she was trying to make Wes jealous was pure fucking bliss.

"Do you trust me?" She flits her gaze between me and him.

"Of course," Dash answers for us, even though I don't think she was considering him as part of the equation. That idiot has been wrapped around her finger since she abruptly stepped foot into our lives.

And that lucky bastard has already gotten a taste of what it's like to be with her.

"The shortest route between here and Rock Bridge is hunter territory. It's a straight shot that will lead us right there with minimal chance of them following us. They'd have to circle around unless they're willing to go headfirst into the danger zone. I know the terrain like the back of my hand. From there, I have another safe house that's not too far where we can regroup and figure out what to do next once we rescue your people."

She's still willing to see our plan through, after everything that's happened?

"Unless you want to go your separate way," she adds.

"What?" Wes blurts out. "No." A growl escapes him. "Sorry." He clears his throat. "I mean, not yet, not until…"

But he doesn't finish, and I'm certain it's because he doesn't ever want to let her go.

A feeling I can only imagine is mutual between all of us.

"How do you plan on pulling this off, Birdie?"

"That parts easy. I've taken prisoners there before. This would be no different. These people trust my word, and if I have you in *my* captivity, they'll believe whatever it is I have to say."

That's right. She's their Furla Ain.

If anyone was going to pull this off, it would be her. But there's still the possibility that she's bluffing and scheming to walk us directly to our death. Why go through the trouble of faking these relationships with us though? Seems a bit too fucking elaborate if you ask me. But I guess that's my hopeful thinking at desperately wanting this all to be true. Her liking us, not her plotting our demise.

"And once we get to Rock Bridge?" Wes asks like he's actually considering her plan.

"I'm open to suggestions."

"Okay," is all he says.

"So, we're really doing this?" Dash takes a bite of his apple and leans back in his chair.

Wren's gaze meets mine, then Wes's. "I think so."

"Fuck it, I mean, what's the worst that could happen?" I reach across to snatch another chunk of the bread. If I'm going to my death, I'm sure as shit not doing it on an empty stomach.

CHAPTER 16

Wren

I must have really lost my goddamn mind.

Not only have I invited three incredibly rare and powerful creatures into my home but now I am a willing participant in an elaborate scheme to rescue more of their kind. And I'm not just doing it for the cure. Sure, that's an added bonus, but after everything I've been through with them these past few days, I'm not so sure that someone who associates with them deserves to be in a place like Rock Bridge.

A prison-type fortress where demons go and never return.

The likelihood of their friends still being alive is slim to none, but I at least have to try. Especially when I am potentially capable of pulling this off.

The plan is simple enough. I fake that they are my prisoners and march them straight through enemy territory. I've done it before. So why wouldn't it work now? And if they question what took me so long or where I was in my absence, I have them as an alibi. Capturing all three of them would be no easy feat, giving my plan that much more validity. It's almost foolproof, really.

But I'd be lying if I said there wasn't an uneasy feeling rising in the pit of my stomach at putting their lives in danger like that.

I've run countless other scenarios through my head and none of them have the probability of success that this one does. The wendigo that has set its sights on us and the demon army following its command raise too many variables if we opt to take any other route than the direct one. Not knowing how many demons are on its side really throws a wrench in determining the risk factor. But at the end of the day, my title carries enough weight that the hunters that we no doubt will cross shouldn't question my authority. At least, that's what I'm fucking counting on.

I'm swallowing the last bite of my apple when a log bursts through the window in my kitchen, shattering the glass and landing with a thud onto the floor.

"What the fuck?" I hop to my feet as Wes and Bo mirror my movement, Dash following closely behind.

"Guess they have a witch after all." Bo slides the knife out of his waistband and grips the handle firmly. "Weapons?"

"This way." I wave for them to come with me, ducking as another branch penetrates the same window, this one burning red hot with a flame.

Fucking assholes are going to burn my house down.

"They must not be able to get in, so they're trying to smoke us out," Wes announces on our way into my bedroom.

I rush over to the closet and press a panel on the back side. A compartment opens and I grip at the wooden slat to reveal my meager arsenal. It isn't much, but it's more than we were working with.

"Sick." Bo reaches for a compact crossbow. "I call dibs on this one."

"Grab whatever you can." I snatch a couple of my favorite blades first and secure them in place on my body. A person can never have enough knives. I slide out a sword and reach for the bag laying at my feet. The sound of chains clang from inside.

"What's that?" Wes asks me as he's stashing a blade into his waistband. His main weapon of choice is no doubt himself, considering he can set himself ablaze at a second's notice.

"Part of our ruse."

He tosses the strap over his shoulder and nods to the window I had escaped from when I overheard them whispering their secrets. "How far until we're in enemy territory?"

"Just on the other side of Wade Creek."

Another crashing commotion comes from the kitchen. They must be restricted to one area of the house if they haven't breached any other entry. The magical shield is partially in place, and if we're lucky, it'll hold long enough for us to get away.

Wes clutches my arm. "They're going to burn this place down. Is there anything you want to take with you?"

I stare up into his glowing eyes. "There's nothing here for me that can't be replaced."

Was this one of my favored safe houses? Yes, absolutely. But getting them out safely far exceeds any desire I have to keep this place standing.

"I'll go first." Bo reaches the window and grips at the base.

Wes stops him. "No, I can hold them off if they come."

"Will one of you fucking go?" I urge them.

Wes hops through and lands with a thud, glances around, and then reaches back in. "Come on." He drags Dash next, getting him safely outside my burning home. Smoke floats into my bedroom and flames nip at the doorway.

"You go first," I tell Bo, nudging him to the opening.

"Like hell, I will." Bo stands firmly in place.

"Go, you fucking stubborn idiot." I shove him. "Wes can heal me; he can't heal you." I guess it's one of the perks of being a fated mate of whatever Wes is. A mystery I've yet to uncover.

Hound, I recall him saying.

"One of you better hurry up before I come back in there and drag you out myself." Wes frantically looks behind him and back at us. "*Move.*"

Bo grunts and shoves his large self through the small space, not fitting quite as easily as Wes had despite their similar size. Bo's shoulders must be a bit wider than Wes's. Although this is not the opportune time to realize such a thing.

Smoke continues to fill the room, more so now that Bo is blocking it from getting outside. The fire consumes the doorway, snaking itself up the wall, and dances across the ceiling in a kind of beautiful display.

"Uh, Bo, think you could suck it in and hurry up?"

"I'm trying, Birdie," he groans. His body slides slowly, inching further in the direction he needs to be going.

I shove at his large frame and hold my breath as my eyes begin to burn. They water and I close them in a weak attempt to protect them from the fumes.

Bo slips out the window and my body slams into the frame.

I blink through the tears and cough at the tainted air I sucked in from the impact.

A hand latches onto my forearm and when I squint, it's Wes pulling me through the window.

"Fuck, are you okay?" Wes holds onto my shoulders to steady me.

I nod and wipe at my eyes. "Yep, I'm golden." I point to the tree line ahead. "This way." I take off in that direction and glance behind me to make sure they're following.

Wes trails me closely with Dash in his wake, and Bo leading up the rear. Bo nods at me and I pick up the pace, grateful for the fresh air to fill my lungs despite the pain each labored breath causes me. Those fucking ribs are still broken from being crushed by that massive ogre. My poor body would be stoked to go a day without being injured in some insanely stupid capacity. How I'm still functioning is a shock to even me.

The night sky breaks with the promise of morning quickly approaching.

I was hoping we would have gotten the opportunity to rest in the safety of my home before embarking on the last leg of this journey, and maybe tie up a few loose ends on our half-assed plan, but that wendigo seized the chance to push us out while we were still weak. Clever thinking on its behalf, really. The demon is aware that we're powerful together, and it stands a much better chance of beating us in a weakened state. I was naïve for thinking we could rest when such a vile creature had begun its pursuit.

What can I say, I haven't exactly been at the top of my game lately with all the shit that's gone down.

I haven't recovered fully from the first incident, let alone the many that have followed.

And with Bo's venom still coursing through me, my hunter abilities aren't functioning the way they should.

A war cry rings out behind us as the demons realize we've escaped through a blind spot in my magical concealment.

I push harder, but the spikes of pain make me lose steam quicker than I'd hope. I disassociate from it, shoving it into the furthest place in my mind, and kick my feet harder. Now is not the time to succumb to a little fucking discomfort. Not when we've already made it this far.

Something flutters in my peripheral and my instincts kick in all too late. The buzzing creature attacks, stinging me and moving on to another target. A swarm of the same kind follows and they all take turns assaulting whatever exposed flesh we have.

"We're almost there," I yell through the incessant high-pitched humming of the bee-like demonic creatures.

"What's stopping them from following us in?" Dash calls out from behind me.

"It's a one-way ticket," I pause to suck in a breath. "Only a hunter can get a demon out of sacred land. Can't you feel the barrier approaching?"

A loud roar rattles my ears, followed by the monstrous footsteps of a large creature.

I keep my eyes trained forward, not daring to turn around and look at what's pursuing us. Blisters and welts pop up all over my body and my face swells at being stung so many times. The stream, so close I can taste it, is our only chance of separating us from this torment.

The sound of flowing water soothes my soul, and the second I'm within range, I leap off the embankment and crash into the chilling liquid.

Another splash, followed by another. But the third doesn't come.

I frantically turn around, the current fighting me with every move. I scan the ridge, not waiting for the heads to appear from under the water to determine who didn't make it. My sights settle on a body almost completely covered in those hornets. I kick off the large rocks lining the stream and push toward the mound. Whoever it is, I refuse to leave them behind.

"Birdie, stop." Bo, water dripping over his long black locks, catches my hand and prevents me from going any further.

I try to yank free, but I can't. If he's here, that means it's either Dash or Wes out there in the danger zone. Just because Dash is a phoenix doesn't mean he should have to die because I can't save him. We know nothing about phoenixes. What if they only resurrect one time? Is that really a risk Bo is willing to take? Because it's not for me.

But my fears are erased when that mop of ginger hair gasps for air as he crashes through the surface of the water.

Another wave of terror flows through me when I realize Wes doesn't have that same skill that Dash does, and if he dies, it's possible he won't come back at all.

"Let go of me," I scream at Bo.

He shakes his head and latches onto me tighter. He nods toward the coast. "Just watch."

I look back to the sight of Wes being consumed by the buzzing beasts, my heart constricts at not being able to get to him. My lips part when the creatures start falling away, and in their place, a steaming orange light blasts through each crack until all of them drop to the ground and a blinding red emerges, flames completely dancing over Wes's exterior.

Slowly, he rises to his feet, setting fire to any leaves and grass he may touch. Flaming footprints remain with each step in his wake. He continues toward us and my mouth remains open in complete awe of how glorious his beastly side is.

Something I would have once found repulsive is now the most beautiful thing I've ever laid my eyes upon.

Wes drops into the water, his fire dwindling but still remaining like a protective shield. The closer he gets, the warmer the liquid becomes, until finally, he returns to his more human-looking self.

Bo releases me but I remain in place.

"Are you okay?" I mutter to Wes over the current rushing by.

He nods, his jaw clenched in a hard line.

I want to reach out to him, to pull him close and hold him tight and bask in his very existence, but there's no time for that when we're still dangerously near these demons. They might not be able to enter, but they can use their powers and weapons on us from this proximity.

Bo pulls Dash and the bag of chains up onto the bank on the other side of the stream. Marks litter both of them, but Bo's are vanishing from his own healing abilities.

I follow them out and shake my arms to rid myself of some of the excess water. I strain my hair and let out a breath. "There's a fountain up ahead, it will take care of this stuff." I motion to my face and look at Dash, who must be feeling like a hot bag of shit right now.

His eyes are nearly swollen shut, and his cheeks give off the impression that he's smuggling acorns in them.

"I can help you," Wes whispers.

But I shake my head, if Dash must suffer through this, then I will endure it with him.

We walk in silence to the spot I was referring to. The land grows quieter the further we go. The demons on our ass choosing not to pursue us in this demon-forsaken territory. At least one part of my plan has been a success, although getting here was a bit more stressful than I anticipated.

I cup the water from the fountain into my hand and splash it onto my face, showing them the magical effect it has. "See." I reach for Dash and rub some of the water onto his swollen arm and watch with him as the engorged skin goes back to how it once was.

"Wow," Dash whispers while dipping his arms completely into the fountain.

I savor the kid-like reaction and do the same, ridding myself of the painful blisters. It's not a moment later before we're both cleared of the stings.

"How did you know it would do that?" Dash stares at his forearm, turning it over and examining it from each direction.

I huff. "Not the first time I've been attacked by those stupid things." I recall one of the training sessions I had gone through when I was younger, where we encountered a smaller hive of those creatures and I was stung repeatedly on the face. I genuinely thought I was going to go blind until my instructor shoved my head into a fountain similar to this one on the far side of this territory. I sort of made it a point to track down the location of more of these just in case it happened again.

"Wes, Bo," Dash calls to the other guys. "You should try this."

Bo drops the bag of chains at my feet, ignoring Dash's amazement. "What's next, Birdie?"

I kneel and pry open the soaked top, reach in, and pull out a set of shackles. "These."

Bo takes them from me. "Kinky."

Leave it to him to say such a thing.

"Each of you, put a pair on." I give Wes and Dash theirs. "But don't clasp them." I tug out the long chain and secure it to their cuffs. "This is typically where I'd spell this to me, that way you can't get away, and it would diminish your power. But you aren't actually my prisoners, so we'll go ahead and skip that part."

"You're sure this is going to work?" Wes eyes me suspiciously.

No, not really, but I don't really see any other option available that doesn't immediately result in all our deaths.

"I've walked this path countless other times. I can't imagine this will be any different." It's not a lie, but I've never done it with three powerful beings that radiate so much demon energy that it's overwhelming. Any hunter in range will be alerted to the nearby threat and will no doubt want to come check it out for themselves.

I finish pretending to tie them up and toss the empty bag to the side. I sling the dagger over my shoulder and study the three of them. "I wouldn't make eye contact with any of the hunters if you can help it." I focus on Bo. "Do not draw attention to yourself."

Bo scrunches his bushy dark brows and points to his chest, his chain clanging from the motion. "Me?"

I tilt my head to the side and glare at him. "Yeah, you."

He rolls his eyes. "Whatever. I'll play along, don't worry."

Easier said than done when worry seems to be the one thing I'm excelling at.

"We need to get moving before someone comes looking for us. Once we've made it through the village, we'll have a moment to regroup before crossing into Rock Bridge. Until then, keep your mouths shut, please." I don't mean for it to come out as harsh as it does, but if they rile up a hunter, there's no telling what kind of trouble they'll get us all in. The safest bet is for them to remain quiet and not cause any unnecessary drama. Their presence alone will drum up enough of it.

The walk into the town is filled with nervous energy.

The guys obey me by not speaking, but it doesn't manage to settle my anxiousness at all. I've never deceived my people before, especially with something so blasphemous as marching three unheard of demons through their encampment. I've taken prisoners to Rock Bridge in the past, but nothing like this.

The air radiates of hunter power and I can't help but wonder if they can pick up on the mark Bo left on my neck.

Heads turn when I step into view, but I carry on the same way I have every other time. I silently thank my past self for being so thorough in the manner I conduct business. Despite being recognized immediately, my peers are aware I prefer to deliver my targets prior to fraternizing and recharging at their various establishments. Even then, I typically keep to myself and stick to the bare necessities to get me by.

I carry the lead of the thick chain in my left hand and march through the middle of the road with my dagger over my right shoulder. I glance behind me and confirm that all three men are following closely, but not too close, behind. Their postures slack, their gaze averted to the ground. They look defeated, but that's all part of the act.

"Well, well, well, what do we have here?" A voice calls out.

I continue walking as a man I can't recall the name of jogs up to us.

"Quite the load you have there, Furla Ain. Need assistance?"

I glare at the on-comer and respond how I would any other time. "Does it look like I need help?"

He throws his pudgy hands up in the air. "Meant no offense, miss." He scans the men and his eyes narrow. He rubs at his chin. "Haven't seen one quite like this before." He approaches Wes a little too closely.

"I wouldn't do that if I were you," I warn him.

"Oh," he says with a bit of surprise. "You're telling me." He reaches toward Wes and clicks the lock on his shackle in place. "That could have been bad." He moves toward Bo next.

I stop and in one swift motion, point my dagger at his chest. "Don't patronize the way I do my job. I didn't get this title for nothing." I dig the tip of the blade into his armor, piercing it with ease. "Move along before I make you regret speaking to me."

The man blinks and steps back cautiously. "Very well." He continues to backtrack until he turns around and scurries out of sight.

"Fucking bastard," I mutter under my breath. "We'll fix that later." I briefly glance at Wes's cuffs, which are now restricting his power.

He meets my gaze, and his glowing orbs tell me that he's not entirely powerless.

I grip the chains and tug the men behind me, hoping that another ignorant hunter doesn't try the same shit that one did. I catch glimpses of others as we pass by, but I don't pay any of them more than a lingering look.

A few minutes turn into what feels like a century of not knowing whether my acting is convincing enough. But why would these people assume anything other than the truth I'm giving them? How could I have become Furla Ain if I was anything other than a ruthless demon killer?

My hideous past is the one thing that's keeping this entire deception afloat.

It isn't until we're completely out of sight that I let out a breath and relax my shoulders. I go a little further into the thick forest between here and Rock Bridge, and guide the guys toward a set of trees.

"Wait here," I tell them. I point over to the path in the dirt. "I can get a better view from over there and see what we're working with." I shove my dagger toward Bo. "Hold this for me." I take off without another word, leaving them and the chains behind. Once I figure out how many guards are posted outside, we can come up with a plan of attack.

I rush over to the spot and cup my hand over my forehead to shield my eyes and get a better look. Three bodies pace the entrance of the fortress. It's possible we could eliminate them each and storm the place. But a subtle approach might be better. I could escort one of the guys in with me, tell the guards I'm delivering a prisoner, keeping true to the nature of my visit. Insisting that I have to bring the criminal directly to its holding cell, we could scout the other prisoners and find their people. I'd go in alone, but that would be a harder lie to sell.

A twig cracks behind me and when I turn, a familiar shape appears. Poker straight blonde hair, cut into an obnoxious bob, dressed head to toe in a dark blue pantsuit. Her serious expression slices through me like a knife.

"Parla," I mutter.

My fucking superior. One of them, at least. The eviler one of the two. Dravin looks the part, but he's a bit softer than Parla is. His bark is much feistier than his bite. Parla on the other hand, she's a fucking psychopath.

"Wren, darling." She smiles. "How lovely to see you. I was concerned when you hadn't checked in that you had fallen." She looks me up and down. "What a shame that would have been."

"Things were a bit more complicated than I anticipated." My words are nothing but the truth.

"Hmm, I see." She shifts her focus to the watch on her wrist as it lights up briefly.

I use the distraction to subtly hold my hand down and signal to the guys to stay in place. If they're witnessing this, they're no doubt chomping at the bit to make a move.

"Where are they?" Parla cranes her neck to peer all around us.

With her back to me, I press my finger gently to my lips and stare in the direction of my men. "I already delivered them," I lie.

She narrows her pensive gaze at me. "You were ordered to kill on sight. You never disobey an order."

"My apologies, ma'am." My heart thumps wildly.

"Well then." Parla looks me up and down. "You must be punished for your insubordination."

If she knows what I think she does, then she's under the impression I just brought in one of the most powerful demons in our realm. And that still warrants punishment? But I can't exactly say that, because that would show my awareness of the situation, too.

Parla latches onto my wrist before I can process what's happening. "Wren Oliver, I hereby sentence you to a term at Rock Bridge, effective immediately."

"What? No. You can't be serious." I try to break free of her, but her grip is too tight.

"Do not talk back to me." Parla winds up her other hand and smacks me across the face, knocking me to the ground.

I spit out blood and blink through the dusty dirt that flies up at me.

Shuffling of feet heightens my senses and when I look up, Wes is skidding to a halt in front of me. He mumbles a few words I can't decipher, and within seconds, I feel little layers of myself unlocking. My power comes back in full force, all the weakness I've had these last few days melts away until I'm almost completely returned to my hunter self.

Had he been suppressing my powers all along?

I shove the thought away because right now, none of that matters.

"Run, Wes, you have to run," I scream at him.

Parla laughs and mutters a spell. Sparks ignite from her fingertips and blast Wes in the chest, throwing him off balance.

"Stop it," I yell at her, jumping in the line of her attack. "Take me instead."

But whatever the magic is that she used renders both of us incapable of doing anything other than lay on the ground, writhing in agony, our arms outstretched toward each other, but not close enough to touch.

I stare into Wes's glowing eyes, the redness in them fading at not being able to access his other self.

"I'm sorry," he mouths to me.

She snaps her fingers together and a shadowy figure appears beside her. "Find the rest of them," she orders the creature.

My heart rips in half. She's already gotten me, and she's taken down Wes. I burst through a layer of pain to scream as loudly as I can muster, "Guys, run!"

I'm met with a blow to the head, the painful sight of Wes becoming a blur and everything fading away.

To be continued in Fighting for Monsters, the second book in the Falling for the Enemy series...

Fighting for Monsters

FALLING FOR THE ENEMY (BOOK TWO)

Who you were yesterday does not dictate who you can become tomorrow.

CHAPTER 1

Wren

The musty air assaults me with its vile and putrid stench. Piss, no doubt, and *other* bodily functions. The scent of blood lingers, and the coppery taste of it coats my mouth.

My head throbs and it takes all my strength to sit upright.

I blink through the darkness, and my eyes desperately scan for a sign, any indication of where I am.

But even with the absence of a flashing sign alerting me to my whereabouts, my gut knows either way. I'm in hell, or at least, a version of it in this realm.

A place that is inescapable.

Rock Bridge.

Once you step foot in here—as a prisoner—freedom becomes a thing of the past.

The weight of that hits much harder now that I'm on the opposite end of things for a change.

How many creatures have I brought here over the years? All have met the same tortured end—thanks to me.

I was proud. I was celebrated. And now, I am locked behind the same walls I once put those creatures behind; every ounce of my liberty stripped from me.

In one sheer moment, I have become nothing.

And for what?

My palm rests against my chest as the ache of a memory crashes over me.

Wes, helpless and writhing in agony, his arm outstretched toward mine, his lips muttering an apology that he never should have spoken. One I wish I could erase from history. If only I could have willed him to stay concealed with Bo and Dash.

Then he would be safe, and it would only be my life on the line.

I swallow the cruel reality of not knowing what fate has in store for him, and there not being a damn thing I can do about it. Not when I'm locked in this fucking cage.

Cold metal shackles clamp down on both of my wrists, hindering my ability to access any of the magic within my body.

I'd pry at them, but I know better than to expect them to come off without the key.

I might be powerless, but that doesn't mean I'm completely defenseless. I'm trained in combat and have a handful of skills that could never be stripped so easily.

Still, I'd rather be at full strength than thwarted by these magical restraints.

"Fuck," I mutter, rising to my feet.

Keeping my hands out in front of me, I feel along the brick wall, carefully skimming my fingers in search of anything to help familiarize myself with this place.

"Why is it so fucking dark in here?" I ask myself.

I've been in here a matter of hours, and I'm already acting like a crazy person.

I stop when I catch the sound of a dainty voice floating toward me.

"Hello?" I say into the darkness. "Is someone in here?"

"Shh," the person replies. "Down here."

I cower my aching body toward the source of the whispers.

"This way," she guides me.

I press my core flat against the concrete floor and fumble with the tiny opening separating our chambers. Small sturdy rods ensure that we both stay put in our isolated spaces.

"It's no use," she tells me. "Not like you'd do any better over here than in there."

I sigh and scoot onto my butt, pressing my side on the wall. "How long have you been here?"

The girl considers the question for a long moment before answering. "A while."

No doubt one of my kind that put her in that position.

With the suppression of my powers, I can't access my hunter radar to tell what she is, but if I had to guess, she seems no different than me. What could she have done to deserve being locked up like this?

A ripple of pain abruptly rushes through me. I gasp and clutch my hand over my torso to try to locate the source of the profound brutality. I stifle a moan and hunch over as another fierce lash strikes.

"Are you okay?" the girl asks.

"I...I don't know. Is this...?" I struggle to get out the last word before I'm struck again. "Normal?" I finally blurt out.

How can I be tortured without someone here doing it to me? Even magic has its bounds.

"You're alone, aren't you?"

I grip the wall and force myself to my feet. Reaching blindly, I throw my arms around the space, slamming them into the bricks but nothing else. I kick a bucket, knocking it over and sending it clattering. I push through the pain to verify that unless someone outmaneuvered me in complete silence, I am the only one in these confines.

Using my instincts to guide me back, I settle onto the floor near the opening between our cells. "What's with the fucking dark?"

"I think they do it to disorient us." The girl's metal chains clang as she repositions herself. "There's no pattern to when they blast us with light, but shield your eyes when it happens. It's bright as hell at first."

Hell, that's for damn sure. I've never been to the realm ruled by Balial or his brothers, but I can only imagine the similarities given the stories I've been told.

I double over, muttering obscenities as another round of pain strikes my core.

Fingers, cold and small, wrap themselves around my forearm.

Startled, I want to pull away, but the agony keeps me rooted in place. I allow the stranger to comfort me because I can't exactly do much of anything else.

A moment passes along with the discomfort, and the girl pulls her hand back through the small opening.

"Why did you do that?" I ask her.

The girl inhales deeply and lets out a hasty breath. "Us girls have to stick together."

She doesn't even know me and she's already shown me extreme kindness. If she was aware of the truth, she probably wouldn't want anything to do with me. I am the enemy after all. Especially in a place like this, when it's because of me and my kind that these people are here.

People. At the end of the day, they're no different than me, not if you really think about it. All of us fighting to stay alive—killing each other to survive. It's no wonder this realm has gone to complete shit when its main agenda is war.

My usual distaste for their kind doesn't come, only continually reinforcing my newfound understanding that maybe I've had it wrong all along. I've spent my entire life waging an unwinnable war, and for what? To be stabbed in the back the second I disobey an order.

Turning to the wall, I mutter, "What's your name?"

She hesitates, quite like how she did when I questioned how long she had been here. "You promise you won't tell anyone?"

The mark on my neck burns, a permanent reminder of a life I will never know.

"I promise." And although we've only just met, I mean those two words. I've never been the trusting kind, but where has that ever gotten me?

"Franny," she finally confides in me.

"Franny," I repeat. "My name is Wren, and one way or another, I will get us out of here."

How? I have no fucking clue, but I refuse to die in this shithole.

A soft double knock sounds from her room.

"Quick, shut your eyes," Franny urges me.

I comply, the light blasting my face a second later. The heat of it scorches my face and slowly dims down into a tolerable warmth, which continues to fade.

"You should be safe to open them now."

"How did you know?" An uneasy suspicion rises within me.

She does that thing where she wavers again, no doubt wondering if she can put her trust in me. "There's a guard...he tries to warn me sometimes."

Perhaps we could use that to our advantage.

I allow my eyes to adjust to the yellowish illumination in my cell. It's exactly how I imagined. Four solid brick walls with one heavily armored door posted across from me. An identical small opening connects each room to the next at the base of the floor and wall. There's a grated drain in the middle of the room with a slope coming off each corner. The only luxury in here, the bucket I had kicked over, sits haphazardly in the place it landed.

I scan the ceiling, squinting through the light but not finding anything noteworthy.

Sighing, I hobble over to the door and examine its solid nature. I skim my fingers along every inch of it, pushing and poking and wishing for even the smallest weakness.

Commotion from outside my room sparks my interest, and I do what I can to peer through a small crack on the hinge of the door.

My heart stutters, my mouth gapes open, and my sights settle on the last face I saw before being brought here.

Wes. Beaten and bloodied, worse than he was then.

I pound my fist against the cold, hard surface and scream. "What did you do to him?"

But it's no use, the guards dragging his body don't give a shit about me or what I have to say. Instead, they continue on their path, opening the cell next to mine and throwing Wes inside.

His body lands with a thud on the floor, followed by a groan that escapes him.

I drop onto my chest and scamper toward the small opening between our rooms. "Wes," I whisper. I painfully shove my hand through the bars, my skin scraping against the surface, and reach with intense desperation toward him. "Wes," I repeat. "I'm here." But what good will that do him? I'm the reason he's in this mess in the first place.

It's my fault. All of this is my fault.

Wes shifts toward me like he finally realizes who's calling out to him. He inches his weakened frame in my direction.

My breath catches at witnessing him this weak. How could they have done this to such a powerful being?

He extends his hand, his fingers barely grazing mine as he collapses in place.

I shove myself further through the meager opening, ignoring the sound filling my room. Metal creaking, voices that follow. None of it is as important as making sure he knows I'm here, that I'm sorry, that I would do anything to make this right.

But that time never comes.

My ankles are gripped by strong hands, and I'm yanked away from the opening, my flesh torn away from the abrupt motion against the bars.

I immediately flip onto my back, drag my knee to my chest, and kick the guard directly in the stomach, knocking him from his feet. I hop onto my own and slam my fist into the throat of the other nameless guard.

"Fucking bitch," he blurts out while clutching himself.

A smile creeps across my face as another guard enters my cell. This one with a long metal rod that sizzles with energy.

Fuck.

He jabs the thing into my side before I can jump out of the way.

My vision blurs and my body rattles with the electricity now surging into me.

"I will make you pay for this," I say through gasping breaths once the jolts pass through me.

I will make them *all* pay.

CHAPTER 2

Bo

"I can't just fucking sit here and do nothing."

Dash glances behind him and then at me. "I'm not asking you to, but I'm pretty sure we can't help them if we're dead."

I narrow my gaze at him. "Don't be so sure of yourself, that's kind of your special talent."

"Great." Dash throws up his arms. "The only thing I'm good for is dying. How do you expect that to come in handy?"

I shrug. "We'll figure something out."

A branch breaks in the distance, drawing our attention in its direction.

We're stuck in enemy territory with no way out, and Wren and Wes have been beaten and brought to the worst possible place—Rock Bridge. A place that, in all my years, I've never heard of anyone making it out of alive. A place our people were taken to years ago. I sort of accepted the fact that I would never see them again, but now that Wes and Wren have met that same fate, it's not as easy to stomach.

It shouldn't bother me. She *is* the enemy after all; but deep down she's so much more than that. Not just to me, but to Wes and Dash, too. I can't explain it—and I'm not even sure I want to. But I cannot allow that place to consume her, too. Maybe it's the mark I left on her neck drawing me to her. Maybe it's because, from the moment I saw her, I haven't been able to get her off my mind. I thought it was the hatred that fueled my incessant thoughts. But now I'm not really sure of anything.

And as for Wes, well, he's been like a brother to me. I can't just let him rot in that place.

But how do I get him out—get her out—when it could be the most impossible thing ever?

"I don't think we're safe here," Dash whispers.

"No shit." I nudge his shoulder. "We have to keep moving."

Our distance from the place causes another issue. I marked Wren, and if the two of us are separated by much space, a beacon alerting demons that she's fresh for the taking will go off. And unless I'm heavily mistaken, she's surrounded by the likes of them in that hellhole.

I thought I was doing the right thing at the time—marking her in order to keep her close.

But it very well could be the thing that gets her killed.

How do I keep myself safe when doing so could risk her life?

"You're telling me you don't have any other powers?" I glance over at Dash as we run through the densely packed forest to find another spot to catch our breath and regroup.

Maybe eventually we'll come up with some kind of plan.

"I...I don't think so." Dash stays near my side.

I recall the time I've spent with him over the years and try to pinpoint anything that could be of use. He's not any good in battle, although on occasion he's held his own. There's nothing remarkable about winning a fight every now and then, though.

"A phoenix is a bird...you're telling me you can't fly?"

"Pretty sure you'd know if I could fly," Dash quips. He throws his arms out to the side. "Do you see any wings, Bo?"

Despite the running for our lives, I chuckle. "No, all I see is an idiot flapping his arms."

"I just found out what I am, cut me some slack."

He's right. I've had powers my entire life and still come across new skills from time to time. Hell, my species doesn't even have a name—one that I'm aware of, at least. All I know is that I'm an alpha, the last of my kind, which gives me a superior strength over pretty much all other demons. All of them except for Wes. His hound supersedes any power known in this realm.

And here he is, locked away like a fucking idiot. If he would have just stayed put, all three of us could have figured out how to rescue Wren together. Instead, Dash and I are left up shit's creek with no paddle to figure this mess out and try to stay alive in the process.

"We're going to have to circle closer," I tell Dash when I notice the tether connecting me to Wren tugs tighter.

"Why? What's wrong?"

What *isn't* wrong at this point? We're basically running around the same confined area and dodging random hunters. Hunters who will no doubt stop at nothing to either kill us or bring us in to potentially meet a much worse fate. But if I get inside those walls, maybe it'll give me a better chance of getting to Wren. Maybe I could free her and find a way to get myself and Wes out.

I shake my head. What am I thinking? That's a suicide mission. And yet, it's incredibly enticing. How did I go from wanting to rip her throat out to risking my own life for hers in a matter of a week? What the fuck is wrong with me?

Dash grips my shoulder and stops me in place. "Dude, talk to me." He slaps my face. "Snap out of it."

"What?" I huff.

"You've got that murderous look on your ugly mug. The one you get right before you do something stupid."

I deadpan. "I don't know what you're talking about."

"You care, and it's eating you alive." Dash surprises me with his bluntness.

I blink down at him. "Do not."

He runs his hand through his red hair. "I care about her, too, and Wes."

"Only because you slept with her," I mouth off.

Dash leans up against a tree and catches his breath. He grins and his cheeks redden. "You're jealous."

"Am not."

"Whatever. You don't have to admit it for it to be true." Dash pulls off his backpack and reaches in to pull out a hunk of bread. He bites off a piece of it and throws the rest at me. "And for the record, I cared about her before I had sex with her."

I chew the bread slowly and attempt to savor the dwindling rations we have. It won't be long until we'll have to start getting dangerously close to the hunters if we want to feed ourselves. We're already running on fumes, no sense in dwindling away completely if we want to be of use to Wes and Wren. It'll be a necessary risk if we intend on staying alive. Nothing we haven't done before, although usually we aren't stuck behind enemy lines with no chance of escaping.

I swallow the mouthful and keep my gaze trained on the distance. "Why?"

"You already know." Dash sighs. "She's special."

"I refuse to accept that." I plop my ass onto a fallen log and stretch my arms. "*Special*, seriously? You buy that?"

Dash seems to consider my words. "Yeah." He rubs the toe of his shoe into the ground. "It doesn't have to make sense if it *feels* right. Listen, nothing about my life adds up. Not why I have no memory, why I was left out here alone, how I came back from the dead. Questioning those things has only added to the heartache, so you better believe the first time something *truly* good comes along, I'm going to just roll with it." He pauses for a second. "Did she cast a spell on me? On us? Is she going to be our demise? I don't fucking know. But honestly, I don't care. Not if for the first time in my life, from what I can remember, I've felt something that resembles happiness. And you'd be lying if you said you didn't feel that connection with her, too. We already know Wes does. Maybe that's why you two found me instead of someone else. Maybe our fates were decided long ago, and we're just now lining the puzzle pieces into place. Or maybe I'm a fool who's drunk on the idea of possibilities that could never happen."

Every single word he speaks somehow makes complete and utter sense, despite it making none at all. I don't know how Wren has managed to wrap us all around her finger with such ease, but the idea of not ever seeing her again pains me in a way I can't begin to describe. I'm not meant to have *feelings* like this. I never have, and the more they fester, the angrier I get at not having control over them.

Dash smiles to himself. "There's no denying how great she is. She's funny, smart, strong as hell, and stunning. I've never met anyone like her in my limited time in this realm."

I exhale and tuck a strand of my black hair behind my ear. "Neither have I." And I've been alive a lot longer than Dash has, even with his memory problems making his experience much shorter.

"So, you admit it?" Dash raises a brow at me.

"That you're an idiot? Yeah." I throw a rock at him and stand, dusting my pants off.

"I see the way you look at her. How protective you are of her. That guy at the tavern. Any other instance you would have blown someone like him off..."

I scan the vicinity and try to pick up any nearby hunters that might be on our tails. "You're pushing it, Dash."

"But I'm not wrong."

I stretch my neck from side to side, cracking it with each movement. "She's infuriating."

And I can't get enough.

Dash swings his backpack over his shoulder and secures it in place. "She's the only woman who's ever stood her ground against you, and I think it drives you crazy."

I ignore how right he is and shift the focus of our conversation to more pressing matters. "We need to find shelter and wait out dusk. We can move more freely at night."

He may not have night vision, but I do, and we must take any advantage we can over the hunters.

CHAPTER 3
Wes

I grit my jaw and take every ounce of pain they unleash on me.

"You will talk, one way or another." The man slams his fist across my face.

My blood splatters against his shirt and trickles down onto the floor, along with everywhere else gravity demands. Down my chin, my neck, onto my chest.

Even if I wanted to talk, there's nothing of value I have to add. He's asking questions I don't have the answers to.

The guy yanks the collar of my shirt and tugs me toward him, despite the fact that I'm secured to this chair he's strapped me to. "Where is the rest of your kind?"

I glare up at him through my lashes. "Go to hell." I shouldn't, but I suck in a breath and spit in his face. There are no others, and there haven't been for as long as I can remember. I was orphaned from birth—my parents were killed by hunters, and I was left to die in my mother's womb. I should have died along with them, but I wasn't that lucky. No, I was cut out by a woman who would assume the maternal role and do her best to raise me as her own. I don't blame her for her kindness, but knowing the outcome of both of our fates, it may have served us both better if she let me perish that day.

"I can't wait until I get the order to gut you." The man wipes at the blood-covered spittle on his cheeks. "I will take great pleasure in making you suffer."

He isn't already doing so?

"Are we done here, or do you need to get your rocks off a little more?" I ask the sick fuck.

"Oh, I haven't even gotten started." The man draws back his fist, this time flipping something metal onto his knuckles.

"Enough," another guard calls out as he stalks into the room. He grabs my tormentor's shoulder and reels him back. "I said *enough*."

The newcomer is easily half the age of the arrogant brute but somehow has authority over him. It takes him a second to get the guy to snap into place, but once he does, he huffs and storms out of the room. The new guy watches him intensely, not taking his gaze off him until he's shut the door. Only then does he look down at me.

"What? You ready to take your turn?" I reposition my tied hands and straighten myself in the chair, preparing myself for whatever is to come next.

Instead, he walks around me and kneels. "I'm here to escort you back to your holding cell." He unlatches my cuffs from the chair but keeps them secured behind me.

I consider the possibilities. Could I break one of my wrists and maneuver my hands to the frontal position before he could stop me? Or perhaps shove him with brute force and knock him down and attempt to locate the key to my magical restraint? Then I could finally unleash my hound on him and the rest of this wretched place.

Countless scenarios run through my mind, but all of them end up with eventual failure. There's no telling what kind of magical hold this place has on me; no telling the number of guards posted outside this door or along my path to freedom. The simple fact that I haven't had any contact with my hound since stepping foot in this place is enough to cause me to tread lightly. In all my life I've never been this separated from him. His typical obnoxious and annoying banter has been replaced with a sort of shadow...a ghost where he once was. It's unfamiliar and completely foreign, and I'd be lying if I said it wasn't alarming. Did he distance himself to keep us both safe? To keep our identity concealed? Is it possible that this prison did something terrible to him? What could've caused my other self to disappear?

What kind of twisted hell hole is this place?

"Where did they take the girl?" I ask, knowing damn well I shouldn't. The question burns through me and forces itself out of my mouth.

The guard pauses on our way to the door. He leans in a little closer like he's about to tell me a secret.

I hold my breath in anticipation, a million different outcomes that will wreck me all the same. Even with my hound's absence, my desire for her remains unchanged. If anything, it's heightened now that she somewhat reciprocated my feelings back at her place—kissing me with an intensity to spark a forest fire. And the idea of her being put through the same torment they're inflicting on me, or something worse...

"They're trying to get you to crack," he finally tells me.

"Crack?"

"They want to know where the rest of your kind are."

Again, with the shit I can't help them with.

He continues, "Once they realize one way or another, they'll be done with both of you. If I were you, I'd stop being so convincing that you don't know anything."

"Why are you telling me this?" I scan his features, noting how weirdly soft and sincere they are. He reminds me a bit of Dash and how innocent he is on the surface. Or well, as a whole—that guy is the best of us all. So very human, despite him being a rarity to this world. A fucking phoenix.

The man opens his mouth to speak but the handle on the door wobbles and creaks. He stutters for a second and mutters, "Follow my lead."

The thick metal door opens and another guard, wearing the same generic black uniform as the others, appears on the other side. "Oh, didn't realize this one was occupied." He averts his gaze to the floor once his eyes lock onto the badges pinned to the lapel of the man holding my cuffed arms. "Sir," he adds.

"Out of my way," the guy commands while tugging me with him. He yanks on my arm and shoves me through the doorway.

The other guy steps aside and keeps his head down the whole time.

I steal a glance at his strange obedience as we round the corner into an empty corridor.

The man loosens his grip on me once we're out of sight. "I'm not like the rest of them."

"I've gathered that," I whisper quiet enough that he can still hear me.

"There are other guards posted in your hallway, so you need to play along."

"What's your name?" I ask him before we've gone too far.

He slows his walk for a split second to say, "Everest, but you must never call me by it."

Just like he mentioned, two chattering guards are down the next pathway. The duo immediately stand alert and shut their mouths, scampering to look as on-duty as possible.

I avoid meeting their glares and stay focused on the cobbled stone of the floor below my feet.

One of them clears their throat, "Do you need assistance, sir?"

Everest tugs on my arm. "I've already broken this one for the day." He nods toward my door. "Open that and step away."

The little bitch boy runs ahead to comply with the order and then goes back to his post.

Everest stops us in front of the open door and fumbles with my cuffs, freeing my hands from behind my back. The metal shackles remain on my wrists, suppressing my magic, but it's a welcomed relief not to have them tied in such an uncomfortable position. Especially during the pathetic attempts that guard used to *break* me.

"I'm going to shove you," he mumbles quietly.

With his warning, I dramatically fall into the holding cell, dropping onto my knees with a grunt, performing this strange role play with a man I know next to nothing about. I can use any help I can get, no matter where it comes from. My only concern is that he's playing me like a fool.

The metal scrapes against the floor as the door shuts behind me, sealing me into my confinement. I wait until it's latched in place to lift myself up and hurry over to the tiny opening between cells.

"Wren," I whisper into the hole. I press my bloodied face on the concrete and frantically try to peer into the last place I saw her.

My heart aches when my eyes continue to scan the emptiness on the other side of this wall. Her touch is like a fever dream that has me concerned I made the whole thing up as some sort of coping mechanism. It's been at least a day since she called out to me and reached her dainty hand through and grazed her fingers against mine. It took all my strength to drag myself closer to her, but by the time I made it there, I was too late. Someone had come into her room and viciously yanked her away from me.

She had screamed and called out but there was nothing I could do. I slammed my fists into the wall until my knuckles and hands were coated with blood and plasma and dirt. The pain was nothing compared to what I felt inside...at what I continue to feel at having put her in this position. I never meant for any of this to happen. The whole reason I saved her from that abandoned warehouse was because I couldn't fathom watching her die. My soul wouldn't allow it. But little did my soul know, everything that would follow would only continue to put her in danger, and it would all be my fault.

I could've saved her and let her go. Why did I have to bring her back to our home? A home full of her enemies. Why did I have to be selfish? Why did I refuse to see any other alternative other than keeping her nearby? Why did I continue to keep her powers at bay knowing what a dangerous world we live in? I was too much of a coward. Too afraid that she would leave given the chance. My selfishness is what got us in this mess. And I can only imagine the shit Dash and Bo are going through trying to figure out how the hell to get out of this enemy territory.

I've doomed us all.

Even my hound.

Because of something the fucking fates decided long ago.

I settle against the uncomfortable hardness of the wall that's separating me from where Wren once was. I sigh, looking my hands over front to back. The healing process is considerably much slower than it typically is. It's almost as though these magical restraints have left me as nothing more than a shell of a weak and fragile human. Everything aches. I'm not sure there's an inch of me that doesn't have something wrong with it. I'm used to pain, quite fond of it, actually. I'm just not accustomed to it lingering in this capacity. Although, I am grateful for its constant reminder of how badly I royally fucked things up. I deserve no less than this torment. My only wish is that she's safe from whatever this place has in store for us. I would allow someone to slowly rip my skin from my body if it meant getting her out of here.

Everest told me that they would do anything they could to get me to crack. Unfortunately, there's nothing to give. I have no information to exchange for her freedom. I could give them something false to buy us some time, but how long would that last? And would the punishment that would follow be worth it?

He seems to have authority here, maybe I could cut a deal with him to set her free. Or maybe he's just playing a really solid game of good cop/bad cop to trick me into telling him whatever these sick fucks want to know.

I lean my head against the wall and draw in a breath. My torso aches with each inch it expands.

"You in there?" I mutter to no one other than myself. My hound refuses to answer and I'm not convinced it's because he can't...maybe he just won't.

CHAPTER 4

Wren

"Wes," I plead while gripping his hand tighter.

He's on his side, his blood-covered face toward the small opening between our rooms.

I stare intently and wait for the steady rise and fall of his chest. I don't dare exhale until I see the smallest movement, denying my fear that the worst has happened.

I lay on my own side while keeping my hand shoved through the bars and loosen my hold on him. I keep it there but decide to stop trying to wake him. It must have been difficult for him to fall asleep given the conditions—he should rest while he can.

Studying the cuts littering what I can make out of his body, I grow concerned about his lack of healing. Usually, those types of things would have fixed themselves by now, but instead, he looks terrible. Dark lines crease his brow and dirt and dried blood touch nearly every inch of his skin. A purple bruise covers his cheek, and his lip is split on the bottom.

What are these assholes doing to him?

I bring my finger to my own mouth, skimming it over the fresh wound that still oozes blood. They worked me over pretty well, too, but I won't be broken that easily. Physical torture is nothing I'm unfamiliar with. I was trained to withstand this kind of torment.

Sighing, I wiggle my hand under Wes's and cup his large palm. I close my eyes and allow this temporary moment to comfort me. I can't say I've been in worse situations than this, but I've escaped death enough times to know I need to gain my strength if I want to make it out of this one, too.

I don't dream, and I'm not entirely sure I fall asleep at all. Perhaps I was stuck in that sort of in-between of consciousness. Either way, my attention clings to the cracked voice of the man across from me.

"Wren," he breathes. "Is that really you?"

As if I'm what, a figment of his imagination?

"In the flesh." I blink my vision straight and take in the sight of his beautiful and tortured face. "You look like shit."

Somehow, this garners a grin out of him. "Thanks, so do you."

I stay on my side, my arm outstretched through the meager opening. I squeeze his hand despite the incredibly uncomfortable position I'm in. Tingles float from my fingertips up to my shoulder. "Why aren't you healing?" I ask him.

His smile fades and he shakes his head. "I don't know." Wes wiggles his wrist. "Must be these."

"I'm sorry," we both say at the very same time.

Our brows furrow, almost like we're mimicking each other's expressions.

He runs his thumb along the outside of the wound on my hand. "You have nothing to be sorry for."

"I'm the reason we're in this mess." If I would have come up with a better plan this wouldn't have happened. If I wouldn't have underestimated how vicious my superiors were maybe I would've anticipated this. Maybe if I didn't work for the fucking bad guy.

This whole time I thought I was on the right side of the war. But now I'm not so sure. I was always taught that demons and their bringers were the evil in this world. From my current position, it kind of looks like I was wrong. That's not to say that demons aren't bad, it's just that...maybe hunters are getting more credit than they deserve.

"You're joking, right?" Wes stares through the opening at me. "Everything leading up to this moment was my fault. What happened at that warehouse. Bringing you to my home. Allowing Bo to mark you and pretending I did any of this for any reason other than the most obvious one."

I swallow down the lump of emotions bubbling up. "You did it for your people. To get them back."

Wes steadies his gaze. "You don't get it, do you? I did it for *you*. Because I'm selfish and couldn't stand to let you go."

"You know nothing about me," I say, like it'll somehow convince him otherwise.

"That's what I kept telling myself. But I knew deep down, in a visceral way, that I would follow you to the ends of this world and whatever comes next. My hound made damn sure I knew that, too."

"And what does he have to say now?"

His jaw clenches and his nostrils flare slightly while he averts his gaze. "I don't know."

"He's having second thoughts?" I try to make sense of what he's saying.

"No."

"Then what do you mean?"

"I..." Wes chews at the inside of his lip.

It suddenly dawns on me. Wes isn't healing. His powers are suppressed. I haven't seen the glowing red orbs of his eyes since we got here. Not a trace of his fiery energy. "He's gone?"

"I'm not sure where he is."

"How is that even possible?" I know this place has control over our magic, but never in my wildest dreams would I have imagined they'd be capable of blocking such a commanding beast.

"I'm sorry I can't heal you." Wes flashes his gaze to the cut on my hand. He brings it closer to him and presses his lips along the edge. "You don't deserve this."

"It's kind of funny," I find myself saying.

"What?"

I grin at him. "This." I give his hand a gentle squeeze. "I thought you hated my guts a week ago. I mean, hell, *I* hated *your* guts a week ago. I wanted to kill you...and Bo." I shrug and add, "Dash a little bit."

"And that's funny to you?" Wes raises a brow.

"You were so hot and cold; I couldn't get a read on you to save my life. No pun intended." I wink despite being unsure if he can see it. "Now it's like the floodgates have been opened and you're kissing my boo-boos and actually telling me how you feel."

"I guess I don't have anything to lose at this point...other than you."

And what do I have to lose?

Him. Dash. Bo.

I've already lost everything else that mattered to me—stripped away in the blink of an eye when my cunt of a boss decided to turn on me.

"What are we going to do?" I grip his hand tighter.

"The same thing we always do." He stares me directly in the eyes.

I finish his train of thought, "Survive."

Wes nods. "We need some time to heal, garner our strength."

The lights shut off without warning, everything going pitch black. I struggle to see through the darkness but keep my hold on Wes.

"I'm still here," he reassures me.

"There's a girl," I whisper. "In the cell next to me. She seems nice. She gave me a warning when they were turning the lights back on." I leave out the part where I was having phantom pains for no fucking reason.

Wes shifts a bit closer. "How did she know?"

"A guard." I keep my voice as quiet as I can.

"I think I met him." Wes lays on his side fully and rests my hand on his cheek. He brushes his lips against my skin again, sending a spike of pleasure up my arm, comforting me in the slightest. "Tell me about this girl."

I swallow and consider the promise I made her, and the one my soul had already made with Wes. Whether I acknowledge it or not, the connection he and I have runs both ways. I knew it from that first moment of seeing him, when that fluttering sensation had rattled in my chest and caused me to falter. I should have wiped that warehouse clean and killed every demon in there, but instead, I let that moment distract me and set my life on an entirely new course.

I settle on the things that I can confide in him without betraying the girl. "She was nice."

"You mentioned that already."

"She sounded young, maybe a few years younger than me. Alluded that she had been here for a while. We didn't really talk much, but she told me there's no pattern to when they turn the lights on and off, and that they do it to fuck with us. It's easy to get disoriented when you lose track of the time. One minute they were off, and the next she urged me to shut my eyes, and a split second later, they were on."

Wes's body stiffens. "Was her name Jade?"

"No." Who's Jade? One of the people they were coming here to rescue? A previous lover? A family member? A friend?

He relaxes. "Oh."

But I don't ask him any of the questions that float into my mind, not when I'm afraid to know the answers to them. The thought of him belonging to anyone else weirdly unsettles my core. I've never been one for jealousy—the possessiveness feeling unfamiliar as it takes hold.

I avoid my train of thought. "What about you? Is there another cell on the other side?"

"Yes, but I'm not sure who's in it, or if there is anyone at all. They haven't made contact." He pauses and adds, "I can't imagine this is the most social of places."

"Will you distract me?" I mutter. Between the awkward position I'm in, both physically in this cage and overall in my life, and the countless other worries running through my head, I could use the tiny break.

"Are you in pain?" Wes repositions himself toward me.

"No."

He doesn't question my intentions anymore, instead, he asks something else. "What's your favorite color?"

A smile creeps across my face. "Red, what about you?"

"Blue, definitely blue. Like the sky, before our world turned to complete shit. Your eyes, that exact shade." His voice cracks a little. "What kind of red?"

I hadn't really put too much thought into it when he asked. Red was sort of a knee-jerk reaction to the inquiry. But now, I can't help imagining the glow of his irises, the flickers of flames that dance across his skin, the heat from his body and the inferno that engulfs him. I'm not entirely sure if red has always been my favorite, or if I had finally seen the color for all that it was when I witnessed him embody it. How do I articulate that though, without sounding like a fucking crazy person? And how do I choose just one when he is all of them? "Every variation, really," I finally say. To avoid any further probing, I initiate another round with him. "What's your biggest pet peeve?"

Wes exhales before answering. "Bo."

I let out a soft chuckle. "Mine, too."

"No, really, everything he does irritates me. The way he chews, his arrogant attitude, even how he sleeps. Have you heard him snore?"

"Can't say I've had the privilege."

"I don't recommend it. It'll keep you up all night." Wes presses his lips to my hand, almost like a habit he doesn't even realize he's formed.

What once would have repulsed me is a sensation I can't get enough of.

"Why keep him around then? If you dislike him so much."

"He's family." A solemn tone settles in his voice and despite not being able to see his face, I can picture the seriousness of his expression. "Both Wes and Dash."

"I never knew your kind could be so sentimental." A total truth at hearing his admission.

"There's a lot you don't know about us. That your kind refuses to acknowledge in their attempt to justify the eradication."

Nearly no time has passed since I made the life-altering mistake back at that warehouse, and already I've recognized the brutal reality that I've been conditioned to hate something I know next to nothing about. I should have died that day, but instead of meeting a cruel fate at the hands of three ruthless beings, I was tended to and nursed back to life. Part of me understands why Wes did it, due to the primal bond we share, but what did Dash or Bo have to gain from showing me kindness?

That alone is the first major wake-up call beating me over the head and planting little seeds of doubt in literally everything I believe in.

Add in the fact that each of them possesses a rare power that is unheard of in our realm, and you've already got a recipe for *what the fuck is going on.*

"Tell me more, then? I want to know everything." Because how else will I make sense of any of this without the facts.

"I will, I promise. Just not in here."

Not when it's unclear who might be listening in on our conversation. It's possible that we truly are alone, but risking any crucial details would be careless.

"We've probably already said too much," Wes says the words quietly in his attempt to shield them from prying ears.

"Will you keep talking? For a little bit? Doesn't have to be about anything in particular." The simple cadence of his voice is a salve to my aching soul.

"What's the most embarrassing thing you've ever done?"

"So, we're back to this game?" I grin and let my eyes close as I try to get more comfortable.

"I figure if I'm going to profess my love for you, the least we could do is get to know each other first." Wes kisses my hand again.

"And what better time than now."

"Mmhm."

I draw in a breath, ignoring the random spikes of pain throughout my battered body, and recall a memory to share. "Back when I was still in training, I was once woken up in the middle of the night to a simulation. I ran out and made the quickest time of all the recruits."

"I don't exactly see what's embarrassing about that. If anything, after watching you fight, I'm not at all surprised."

"I—um…I was naked."

Wes laughs faintly. "Wow, okay, yeah, I get it now."

"It was mortifying. My superiors were there overseeing the examination. My peers laughed and ended up being reprimanded, which made them even angrier at me. Originally for beating them, but beating them nude, and then them being docked points for finding the humor in it. Only made the whole *fitting-in* thing that much more difficult."

"Fitting in is overrated."

"Says the guy with two best friends. Growing up was lonely."

"I'm sorry; I didn't mean it like that." As if recalling a memory of his own, his tone softens, "I know what it's like being alone."

"What about you? What's your embarrassing tale?" I ask because I'd do anything to shift the direction of this conversation.

"Well," he says, considering his response. "It doesn't involve me being naked."

I shake my head and wait for him to continue.

"Do you speak Bravlavian?"

"Not fluently, no. Only a few words. Why?"

"I was once in a tavern predominantly filled with Bravlav's. Hell, even the barkeep was. And as any respectable patron would do, I tried to adapt to their language since I was under the impression I had picked up enough over the years. Seemed like a considerate thing. Anyway, I went to the bar the same way I always do and ordered a pitcher of ale for the table. It wasn't until everyone within an earshot distance around me came to an abrupt silence, followed by Bo clasping onto my shoulders, nearly dying from laughter, that I realized something must have been lost in translation. Apparently, instead of asking for a pitcher of ale, I requested a bucket of semen."

A laugh bubbles out of my own chest and I take my free hand to clasp it over my mouth to suppress the noise. "Okay," I muster through the giggles. "You might have beaten me on this one." Just the very idea of Wes, a fierce whatever he is, stone-faced serious and asking some man for something so absurd is enough to make me temporarily forget my worries.

"Talk about mortifying," he resumes. "I felt like such an idiot. And the guys didn't let me live that one down for months. They still bring it up from time to time just to fuck with me."

"I can't say I blame them." I inch closer to the wall separating us and reposition the weight of my body pressing down on my shoulder. It's not much relief, but enough to keep my arm from falling completely asleep.

"Great, now you won't let me forget it either."

"Never," I tell him playfully. "My turn to ask a question."

"After that one, I don't know how much more I'm willing to share." Wes runs the tip of his nose along the side of my hand.

"If you could travel anywhere, where would you go?"

"Easy, Arthlia."

His response is strangely unexpected, and it takes me a moment to process he's even said it at all.

"You'd want to go to Earth? With the humans?"

"There are magical beings there, too," he tells me. "I've heard it's peaceful, nothing like what we face in this wretched realm."

I've never considered the alternative of living or even existing in any place other than my homeland. I've always fought to protect it and have done everything I could to make it better, safer. But what if my efforts have all been wasted? What if it was all for nothing? I've only further caused more of a divide, and I'm not sure today is any different than before I was even born. What's the point in fighting a war that will never be won? Especially when I doubt the side I'm on.

But with that startling realization, I grow aware that nothing is ever really what it seems. And the Earth realm could be just as dangerous as here in Prania. Monsters come in many shapes and sizes and some hide as people you may trust; authority figures you've looked up to your whole life. A month ago, I thought the demons were the only monsters plaguing this dimension, but now I find myself wanting to fight for them, not against them.

And on the off chance that what Wes is saying is true, our realm was sealed off decades ago, and travel to another is literally impossible.

For the sake of Wes's morale, I choose to go along with him anyway. "Sounds lovely."

For a split moment, possibilities linger between us, perhaps even a little hope that maybe one day we can escape from this nightmare. But dreams are simply that, flickering and temporary and always just out of grasp.

I'm reminded of that when the sound of metal scrapes against the stone floor. The door to Wes's chamber opens and there isn't a damn thing I can do about it.

In the time it takes me to blink, Wes is ripped away from me. My fingers claw desperately at the stale air filling the space where he once was. I strain to reach further through the small, grated section between our cells, and my flesh tears a bit more with each labored movement.

"Stop!" I yell out, but it's no use.

He's gone.

CHAPTER 5

Wren

It's bizarre to care about someone else. Not to mention that very someone being the enemy. A monster I was told to fear. A demon I was instructed to kill.

I've always been on my own. And that's been okay. I've had ambitions. I've had goals and tasks and targets to eliminate. I was busy doing what I thought was right. Too distracted by my thirst for revenge to ever consider allowing feelings to develop. My entire life I've felt like an outsider in almost every situation. So, I took it upon myself to simply become the best. If I was going to be alone, at least I would be known for something.

I trained. I fought. I advanced my skills at every chance that presented itself.

I never questioned what I was doing or why I was doing it. My mother was killed by the vile creatures I was ordered to eliminate. That was as much proof as I needed to validate my actions.

But with each passing second of Wes being gone, and Dash and Bo out there on their own, no doubt struggling to stay alive, I'm reminded of just how very wrong I might have been.

I wince as another phantom pain strikes my chest; a rippling over my back like a whip slicing through my skin. I press my fingers to my shoulder expecting there to be blood and a gaping wound. But neither are there. The injuries are not my own despite sharing the agony.

"Are you okay?" A delicate voice whispers through the space between our rooms.

"Mmhm," I mutter through clenched teeth.

I'm no stranger to violence, but this is an entirely new experience.

"What's happening to you?" she asks me.

"I...I don't know." Is this some kind of magical abuse? A fresh take on torturing

I've never heard of in all my years? What else are these sadists doing within the walls of this prison? And for what possible gain?

"You should try to get some sleep," Franny suggests.

"Has this ever happened to you?" I lean my head against the barrier between us and let the weight of my body fall into it.

"No." She lets out a breath. "Although, this place has no shortage of tricks up its sleeve."

"I just hope he's okay." The words leave my mouth before I can catch them. I don't mean to say this out loud, but my worries have transformed into something I can barely maintain.

Between the poor conditions, the injuries, and the heaviness of the entire situation, I find my mind slipping in a way that I never could have imagined. I thought I was stronger than this. More capable. I've been through extreme situations numerous times but for once it's not just me on the line, and that hurts in a way that no physical pain can.

My thoughts go wild at the possibilities. The endless things that could happen to these three men who put their trust in me. I marched them to their demise. And now they're trapped because of me. Dash and Bo might as well be locked in cells here with us considering they have no way of escaping hunter territory without someone on the inside helping them out. If I was a betting woman, I'd wager the likelihood of them finding a demon sympathizer slim to none.

Franny shuffles from her spot on the other side of the wall. "If it's any consolation, it's rare they actually kill anyone."

I consider her words, allow them to be processed, then analyze them again. I blink through the yellow light in my cell, my gaze darting to and from, but not really settling on any one thing in particular.

"What do you mean?" I ask her. "How can you be so sure?"

"I told you, I've been here for a while, as have a lot of others." She hesitates before adding, "I can *sense* when death is near."

I swallow the realization of what she is. "You're a…" But I don't finish my statement because she and I already know.

She's a banshee.

Another rarity in our world. A female who can sense impending demise. One whose screams can shatter glass and slice through a person like the sharpest of blades. A powerful and incredible creature who is often underestimated. Banshees are rumored to have descended from the fae and in some lore, are known to be immortal.

Two weeks ago, I would have killed her without thinking twice, but now, all I want to do is ask questions and learn more about her. I curse this situation, but without it, I'm not sure I ever would have woken up from the lifelong slumber I've been in—killing anything that smelled demonic.

That familiar scraping sound floats from Franny's cell into mine—her door being opened.

The guard steps closer into the room. "Making friends with a hunter, are we?"

"A hunter?" she blurts out.

Metal pings on the floor, followed by the door shutting.

My own door moves next, and the man drops a tray inside and kicks at it with his dirty boot. "Traitor," he slurs before disappearing behind the thing keeping me locked in here.

"It's not what you think," I tell my cellmate.

Franny sniffs in twice. "You smell like a demon, I don't understand."

I could lie, tell her that I am, and use Bo's mark as a way to maintain this unlikely alliance, but that would be deceitful and if she found out, there's no telling the damage it would do.

My gaze falls to the grayish-looking pile of sludge on the tray that was brought in. The cup of liquid tipped over on its side, the meager contents spilling onto the filthy floor. My stomach betrays me with a growl, and it's then that I realize how fucking parched I am. I struggle to swallow the sandpaper coating my tongue and focus on the wall. If I stand any chance of breaking out of this torture chamber, I can't lose the one alliance I was trying to build.

"I *was* a hunter, but I'm not anymore," I begin to explain.

She cuts me off, her voice coated in disappointment, "Once a hunter, always a hunter."

"Things have changed, *I've* changed." Despite my dehydration, unwanted tears fill my eyes.

I am not weak. I will not cry. I am stronger than this.

But how can I remain this gallant force when my entire life has been nothing but a lie?

I've taken lives—too many to count, and for what?

And now I'm having an internal existential crisis when I should be pulling up my bootstraps and figuring out how to get out of this fucking mess.

No—I won't let this place break me—not like this.

So, I do the thing I probably shouldn't, tell her the truth. "I was marked by a demon."

"An alpha," she mutters.

"Yes," I confirm. "I'd be lying if I said we didn't start off as enemies, but it quickly became more than that. I..." Recalling the memory of that arrogant demon who pushed every one of my buttons, my heart constricts at the involuntary feelings that have developed. I never meant for it to grow into what it has, but as much as I try to deny that Bo and I share anything in common, we're actually more alike than we thought. And when you're taught to hate each other, the lack of bullshit pleasantries really shows you what kind of person someone is. It's almost like there's a mutual respect because you don't get a muddled-down version, you get the real them. Through that lack of false pretenses, I was able to see Bo more clearly.

"You're telling me you fell in love with a demon?" Franny drags the tray in her cell toward her.

"No," I blurt out. "It's not that."

"Mmhm, okay. You're falling for the enemy. Same thing."

I follow suit and bring the pathetic platter closer, careful not to spill the rest of the water even more. I tip the cup to my mouth and let a few drops fall onto my tongue. There's no telling if any of this is drugged, but starving to death isn't a great choice, either. I'll take my chances in an attempt to replenish my strength, at least for the time being. If only Wes could heal me with his words like he's done in the past, I'd snap the neck of the next person who walked into this room and free anyone I could on my way to freedom.

Another blast of pain strikes my back unexpectedly. I grit my teeth, exhaling through my nose, as I wait for another to come. Glancing toward the empty cell beside me, I worry about what Wes might be experiencing. I take small comfort in knowing that Franny hasn't anticipated an upcoming death, but things could change in the blink of an eye, the last couple of weeks of my life have proven exactly that.

"The alpha," Franny says between scraping some of her sludge into her mouth. "Is he your other cellmate?"

"No," I tell her.

"But you're worried about him, too?"

I breathe in deeply and consider her question and the hidden implications behind it. Do I care for the alpha? Of course. But do I also care for the infuriating man who shares a mate bond with me? Without a doubt. And then there's Dash, who surprised every one of us by dying and bursting into flames, only to be reborn again. My heart was torn to shreds when I thought he was gone—that I was responsible for his death. Not that it's any less true, but witnessing him come back to life was a second chance I never imagined I'd get with him.

From then on out, I've wanted to protect him, to prevent something like that from happening again, but here we are, me and Wes locked up with a one-way ticket to Hell, and Dash and Bo no doubt following suit at any given time.

Do I tell Franny all of that though? No, because what good would it do other than give out more vital information that I should probably keep tucked away. Still, she deserves some part of the truth. "Yes," I respond because there's no denying that I am worried about Wes.

"Interesting." She places her bowl onto her tray and pushes it across the floor. "You should eat while you can. Sometimes they come back in and take it before we get a chance."

"Thank you." I spoon some of the gross mixture into my mouth and swallow it without another thought.

"What for?"

"Choosing to still talk to me, to give me advice on how to survive in here."

Franny repositions herself on the other side of the wall. "I guess I would want someone to do the same for me." She hesitates before adding, "But that doesn't mean I trust you."

"Good," I reassure her. "Don't."

Franny chuckles, whatever she's about to say cut off by the creaking of the door to her cell opening.

"Up," a guy commands. "I said *up*, bitch."

I press my palm against the cold stone between us and wish I could knock it down and punch the asshole who insulted her. "Don't fucking touch her!" I yell in their direction.

My words fall flat as the man gets his way. And now I'm left here, once again all alone, wondering when it'll be my turn to be taken.

"Wren," a deep but quiet voice calls out to me.

I blink my eyes open and rise from the dirt-covered concrete floor, dusting off my legs and tucking my hair behind my ears.

"Wren," they whisper to me again, only this time with haggard breaths. "I need you."

Is this another trick? A figment of my imagination? My mind finally losing it once and for all?

"Wes?" I tiptoe closer to the space he's been held captive in. "Are you okay?"

But instead of him responding, it's the man from a moment ago. "He needs your help."

There's something strange about the way the sound is coming more from my own head than in the other room. It doesn't quite make sense at all.

"Don't you hurt him," I tell whoever might be over there. A threat lingering on each word.

Silence fills the space and I hold my breath in anticipation of whatever comes next.

Finally, the melancholy man continues, "You're the only one who can save him."

"I..." An ache fills my chest. "I don't know how." The door to my room is sealed shut, and I have no doubt his is, too. And even if I *could* get through both barriers and fight off anyone who might try to stop me, I don't have healing powers.

"You must try."

His statement is followed by the sudden clank of metal being turned. The guard I expect to enter my room never comes. Instead, only the sound of my wild heart fills the air. I stare for a long moment at the thing keeping me locked in here. With cautious steps, I move toward it. My pulse thumps in my ears as I grow more uncertain of this entire situation. I place my hand carefully on the lever and hold my breath as it gives under my weight.

To my utter disbelief, the door creaks open.

A million different scenarios cross my mind, all of them ending in more questions than answers. A sinking in my gut tells me I have to get to him, that I must use this opportunity to do what the voice instructed me to. I'm not quite sure why I trust it so blindly, but I'm convinced it wouldn't steer me wrong.

Poking my head through the opening, I study the eerie hallway. Not a soul in sight—demon or guard. I creep further, the hair on my skin raising in anticipation of a threat I cannot determine just yet. I stay close to the interior wall and slink my body along the rough surface.

This is all too good to be true, and I'm damn well aware of that. My main priority is to get to Wes, beyond that I'll figure out after.

My breath catches when I spot the slight opening in his cell. I swallow down the mystery of who unlocked both of our chambers and file it in the *what the fuck is going on* folder for later.

My entire body tenses as I press my hand against the door and push it ajar enough for me to slip inside. A second passes before my eyes adjust, and when they do, my reaction is more urgent. The space seems to expand with each passing second it takes me to reach him.

Wes, collapsed in the corner of the room, blood coating his body.

"Oh no, no, no," I babble while dropping to my knees next to him. "Please be alive, don't be dead." I grip his face in my palms and tilt it toward me. Rubbing my thumbs on his cheeks, I silently pray to the gods, to the angels, to anyone who might be listening. *Please let him live.* He can't be dead. Not like this.

Each moment drags on and I'm reminded of watching Dash be killed right in front of me. The snap of his neck, the thud of his body hitting the ground, the pain ripping through my chest. The wound that was mended when Dash resurrected is now torn apart and gushing at the seams. I was lucky to get him back, but what if luck isn't on my side this time? What if when Wes dies, that's it? What if he's gone from this world forever?

My stomach turns as nausea rises. I blink and a flash of my vision takes me back to when I was only a small child, ignorant to the dangers of the world. My dad was gone, fighting in a war that was impossible to win, and my mom was murdered as I cowered and hid from the monsters that took everything from me. They burned down my home and left me with nothing but a thirst for revenge that would never be satiated. I've spent the rest of my life trying to feed that hunger. To kill every single demon I could. But what if the things I think are monsters aren't the ones I should fear after all?

What if the true villains of this story are my own kind?

A flutter of hope returns as my fated mate's eyelids twitch, and finally part ways, gifting me with his life.

"Wren?" he struggles to speak.

"I'm here, I'm right here," I reassure him.

His blood speckled cheeks turn up slightly and he raises his arm toward my face. He rests his palm gently on my cheek. "You are, aren't you?"

"Wes," I breathe into him. "We have to go. I have to get you out of here." But before I can convince him further, the door I had left cracked open is shut, the metal jangling is an unfortunate indicator that we're now locked in place.

"Come here." Wes grips my waist and, despite his tattered exterior, manages to drag me onto his lap.

If we're going to be trapped in this hellhole, at least we're together.

"What did they do to you?" I ask him.

"Nothing I can't handle." Wes wraps his arms around me and holds me close. He rests his head in the crook of my neck.

I flinch when my own arms graze his back. I wiggle from his grasp to take a better look. The torn fabric from his shirt intermingles with the ripped flesh struggling to heal. The wounds cover the span of his trunk, some of them much deeper than the rest. A familiar sensation lingers along my own skin, a ghost of the phantom pain I had experienced earlier.

Is something like that even possible? Could I have been feeling what Wes was while they were torturing him? I've never heard of such a thing in all my life. But at this point, why would I be surprised that he and I would share that kind of bond?

"I'm fine, really." Wes steadies my shoulders and returns me to his lap.

"Wes." I fix my gaze on him. "I thought you were dead when I came in here."

His hard demeanor relaxes. "I was resting, that's all. I didn't mean to worry you."

"I can't wait until these cuffs are off and you can go back to not being able to lie to me."

"You noticed that, did you?" He smiles through his pain until his brows furrow. "Wait, how did you get in here?" Wes tilts his head to look around me, toward the door.

This is the part where I could do the same, withhold the truth. But is that really the best course of action? Secrets will only no doubt get us killed. And if we're going to die, what's the point in keeping things from each other? The things that might make a difference in whether we live or die.

I choose to follow my gut. "I have to tell you something, but it's going to sound crazy."

"I'm sure it can't get any crazier than this." He motions into the space at nothing in particular.

"I...I heard a voice. It told me you needed help. I questioned it, but then the door to my cell unlocked, and when I went into the hall, no one was there. I came straight here, and your chamber was open, too. That's when I saw you lying there." My voice trails off with the memory of his seemingly lifeless body.

"Hey." He tips my chin up and stares into my eyes. That usual glowing red is replaced with a dull crimson, another reminder of how much they've stolen from him here. "I'm sorry you thought I was dead, but I'm not, okay? That must have been triggering for you. I'll do my best to appear more alive from here on out."

I sigh and shake my head. Even in such terrible circumstances, he's able to soften my resolve. "Is it supposed to feel like this?"

"What?" He tucks my wild hair behind my ear.

"A fated bond."

Wes swallows and stiffens slightly. "Don't worry about all that."

I narrow my gaze. "I'm as in this as you are, buddy."

"Buddy?" he laughs. "Don't be concerned about the bond, Wren. That's between me and my hound. It shouldn't affect you in any way...other than both of us being a little possessive over you." Wes tugs me closer. "Or maybe a lot—we can't exactly control it."

"And you think I can?" I bite at my bottom lip.

At this very subtle movement, the atmosphere shifts and desire swirls around us.

"What are you saying?" Wes eyes my mouth briefly.

"It's not only you, *or* your hound, Wes."

"That's impossible."

"It's safe to say this world has proven anything is possible. That I'm just as much your fated mate, as you are mine." I have to prove it to him, to get him to understand. "I could feel when they were hurting you. Those marks on your back, the strikes across your face. I felt that, too. What else would possibly explain that?"

He opens his mouth, but I cut him off.

"That voice I heard, the one telling me to come to you. That I had to save you. It took me until now to realize it, but...Wes...I think it was your hound. You said you haven't heard from him, but what if whatever ties us together allows for that contact? There's no way that would be possible if this were only one-sided. You have to believe that."

His dull eyes glisten with all the things still unspoken between us. "Wren, I..." He cups both of my cheeks in his hands, the span of them encompassing nearly my whole face. "I really want to kiss you right now."

"What's stopping you?"

And after what could have been a lifetime ago since the two touched, he presses his warm lips against mine, our mouths desperate to reconnect with one another and confirm the truth of this link.

I move, either by his hands that guide me, or by the natural manner in which my body pleads to be closer to him. The reasoning doesn't matter. My main concern is discovering the shape we make together. Straddling his waist, his growing erection presses into my bottom.

Wes swirls his tongue over mine and lets out an animalistic but suppressed moan.

I allow him to deepen the kiss and grind myself on top of him. I ache in an entirely different way than I did an hour ago. Every bit of pain and suffering is replaced with the longing I have for him. Should we be discussing a way out of here? Probably. But with the likelihood of us both dying being so fucking high, why not enjoy ourselves a little while we have the chance?

He breaks away and trails his lips down my chin and onto the base of my neck, over my collarbone. "Wren, we..."

Pleasure cascades over me at his touch—a pure heaven while trapped here in this hell.

Digging my fingers into his hair, I moan and tilt my head for him to get a better angle. I wrench at my armored top and wish for the first time in my life that it weren't in the way between a demon and my skin. Finally, I pull it to the side and expose part of my chest to him.

He immediately takes my breast into his hand, massaging it and teasing my nipple with his teeth. I nearly explode from the contact and the ever-rising urge to feel him inside of me. The craving shifts from a want to a need and consumes my every thought.

With my hand still twirled through his luscious locks, and a carnal desperation to taste him on my tongue, I yank him away with the intent of kissing him again. I expect to find his drab gaze, but instead, I'm met with the simmering glow of that recognizable red.

"Wes," I mutter while the revelation courses through me.

His hound side reacting to us being together means that maybe we might actually make it out of here alive.

But before I can tell him that, ice-cold water is thrown onto my face.

When I open my eyes, I'm not with Wes at all, not even in his room. I'm in mine, laying in the corner up against the wall, a guard standing above me with an empty bucket.

"Wake up, bitch." The man kicks my leg and then reaches down, gripping me by the collar and yanking me onto my feet.

"Don't fucking touch me," I spit at him.

He wastes no time in reacting, taking his pail and slamming it into my face.

The room spins but I regain my footing. My blood splatters onto the floor and the man's shoes.

"Great, now I'm contaminated."

I glare up at the tall and stocky older man. There's nothing special about him. Not his standard-issue haircut, clothing, or the privileged arrogance seeping from every inch of him.

What a fucking waste of oxygen.

I damn well know I shouldn't, but fueled by my rage to put this man in his place, I suck in a breath and spit the blood that had pooled in my mouth onto his ugly face.

I smile as he turns red, both from his own anger and my generous decoration.

His attention momentarily flashes behind me and alerts me of a newcomer to our little party.

I duck and spin, avoiding the man who entered the space, but what I didn't expect was the third asshole jabbing me with a fucking cattle prod.

The jolt drops me to my knees, placing me right in the way of the first guy's fist.

What a bunch of cowards needing three of them to take down *one* girl.

I brace myself and wipe at my nose, pushing off the floor and searing my gaze at each of them. "Is that all you fucking got?" I spit onto the bucket guy's shoes again, making sure to really leave a mark.

"When we get done with you, you're going to wish you were fucking dead."

That threat is the last thing I hear before the man with the prod reels up his leg and kicks me square in the chest. I slam into the hard wall behind me, and my entire world turns black.

CHAPTER 6

Dash

It would be really cool if my only superpower wasn't dying.

I mean, what the heck am I supposed to do with that? Die? How does that help anyone? I guess that means there's less risk. So, I can be the one going head first into danger, because if I do die, I'll just come back to life. But when literally everyone else has *supernatural* abilities, dying over and over again seems kind of pointless. It's not like I can *die* someone to death.

I'm sort of an okay fighter, and demons really love to underestimate my ability to fend for myself. I can't say I blame them though. I'm puny compared to them. In their eyes, I'm a pathetic human trying to blend into a world where I don't belong. On occasion, I'm able to kick a little ass and stay alive.

Luckily, Bo and Wes, two incredibly powerful creatures, took me under their metaphorical wings. Although, I wouldn't be surprised if either one of them sprouted the feather-covered things and took off into flight, considering this entire realm continues to amaze me.

Despite what everyone thinks of demons, they've had my back from day one, and I've never questioned that. But now, now one of them has been taken hostage, along with a woman I'm falling for at the light of speed. Damn it, the light of speed. No! SPEED OF LIGHT.

GET IT TOGETHER, DASH.

Every time I think of her my brain turns to mush. My palms get all sweaty, and my heart races. Partly because of how freaking lucky I am that she gave me the time of day, but mostly because I'm concerned that I'll never see her again. And unlike me, Wren is not a phoenix. If she dies, she's gone for good, and I'm not sure there's a world I ever want to live in without her.

I know what you're thinking—heck, I'm thinking it myself. Something along the lines of, "Whoa there, slow down, man. You've only just met the female."

141

But, Wren? She's not your average lady. No, she's fire and ice, sweet and savory, and brains and brawn, all mixed up into one. She's fierce, brave, and stubborn-headed as all get out, but there's this unspoken passion behind everything she does. Foolish, most definitely, but her tenacity is inspiring, and I cannot help but be drawn to how damn captivating she is. For the first time since I woke up in this realm with no recollection of who I am—I feel alive. I feel seen.

"Are you talking to yourself?" Bo smacks my shoulder and continues on his path through these thickly covered woods.

"Don't you?"

He turns toward me, raising a brow and then focusing forward again. "You fucking with me?"

"Probably." Maybe I should take a chapter out of Bo's book and disassociate from my thoughts and feelings until they bubble up into an uncontrollable rage.

Seems like a total dude thing to do.

I'll pass.

"Where are we going, anyway?" I ask him.

We've been on the move for days now, crisscrossing and zig-zagging our path in every kind of direction, not going the same way twice out of fear that our scent might get picked up and followed. And on the chance that it does, the erratic pattern will hopefully send them on a wild goose chase.

Our supplies are dwindling fast and if we don't find a way to replenish them soon, Bo's hunger will no doubt get the best of him. Which isn't saying much because that man prides himself in being as bad as possible.

"I can smell some hunters up ahead." Bo points his long arm in front of him.

I reach out and latch onto his shoulder. "Hey."

He yanks free of my grasp but pauses. "What?"

"I have a serious question." I'm not sure why it never dawned on me until now.

Bo sighs and rolls his eyes. "No, Dash, I'm not attracted to you."

I narrow my gaze at him and chuckle. "Okay for one, I don't buy that. And for two, that's not what I was going to ask. But you're going to think it's weird, so hear me out."

Bo crosses his arms over his chest and waits for me to continue. "Fine," he huffs out. "What is it?" He takes a few cautious peeks in the direction we were heading and then behind him.

"Can you smell me?" I stare at him and motion toward my body.

"I'm going to stab you."

"You said you would listen."

"I can listen and stab at the same time."

"Seriously, Bo, smell me. What do I smell like?"

"Stop saying the word 'smell' so much. *That* is weird."

I pull the blade from its sheathed spot in my waistband. "Fine, my turn. Now I'm the one going to do the stabbing."

Bo laughs but remains arms crossed. "What're you going to do with that thing? Tease me with a good time?"

I grip the handle and swipe it in the air between us, rustling the hair spilling onto his shoulder.

He narrows his gaze and bobs his head up and down. "Okay then, this could get fun."

But when I move the knife the next time, he reaches out, and in a split second, he's disarmed me and turned the blade around to point it at my chest. "You might be a phoenix, Dash, but that doesn't mean I won't kill you."

"Fine, whatever. Do I *smell* like a phoenix though?" I wiggle under his grasp. "Let go of me, you buffoon."

He complies, flipping the knife around to hold it by the sharp end and give it back to me. "No, dumbass. You don't *smell* like a phoenix. What's this all about?"

"It was something you said. You can smell the hunters. And they can smell you, right?"

"I swear to my maker, if you say smell one more time." Bo rubs his temple and exhales dramatically.

"This conversation would be over a heck of a lot quicker if you would cooperate."

Bo glances around us, always on alert for a potential threat. He's much better at this survival thing than I am. "You are correct. I guess you could say we have a natural scent. Them and us. And it is detectable to the trained tracker, yes. Most hunters are skilled at it, like it's part of their training protocol. Most demons are too stupid to sharpen theirs. And now that I've answered you, care to tell me why you're asking about something I assumed you already knew?"

"I did, but hear me out. I don't have a scent either way."

"I'm still missing your point. Can you just spell it out already so we can get this show on the road?" Bo extends his arm and uses the other to pull it in a deep stretch in front of his chest while he waits on me to continue.

"I can sneak in undetected," I say confidently.

Bo stops moving. "Where?"

I point to where we were heading. "Food, big guy."

He scrunches up his face like he's deep in thought. "I don't know, man. This is probably where Wes would tell us it's not worth the risk and come up with some other plan."

I widen my eyes and peer into the empty space around us. "But Wes isn't here. And considering the position he's currently in, perhaps we should reassess who's the boss around here."

Bo scoffs. "He isn't *the boss*."

"Is too, you basically just said it yourself."

"We're a team. That's much different than there being *one* leader. Just because I consider his input doesn't mean he's the top dog."

I let out a chuckle. "I see what you did there."

"Besides, you know damn well Wren will have my ass for putting your life in danger any more than it already is." Bo rifles through his bag to come up empty.

Through the silence of the eerie forest around us, I can make out the grumble of his belly.

"I think your stomach speaks for both of us."

He tosses the bag over his shoulder and starts walking away from me. "It's your funeral," he quietly calls back.

"Aw, I'll never get one of those." I take off after him.

Bo shoves me playfully. "Don't tempt me, I'll get creative enough to find a way for you to permanently die."

The rest of the walk is quiet, aside from the dirt giving way under our tired feet and the occasional branch falling in the distance. It isn't until we're nearly upon the hunters that the tune of their voices begins to carry toward us.

Bo gets us as close as possible without drawing unwanted attention and allows us to remain concealed.

We huddle behind a large tree surrounded by lush shrubbery and assess the situation.

Three buildings fill the space, and a few bodies walk to and from. Nothing major, but considering we're trapped in enemy territory, we cannot afford to have this many hunters aware of our whereabouts.

It's equal parts shocking and strange that we haven't already been found and captured, thrown into the hell Wren and Wes have gotten themselves wrapped up in. Word of us hasn't traveled the way I assumed it would, which only raises more questions. Why would they be keeping that a secret?

"That one," Bo points to the building on the far left. "That's where they're eating." He hovers his finger to the other end. "That looks like their lodging."

"What's the one across the way?" I whisper.

"Supplies, I'm guessing. Maybe an infirmary." Bo side-eyes me. "Food and water are our priority. Don't get any ideas."

"Me? I didn't say anything. I was just curious." I might be a phoenix who can resurrect, but I can still get injured. As can a certain woman we're all pining after. It wouldn't hurt to grab some of that stuff on the off chance we figure out a way to free her from Rock Bridge.

"Wes can heal Birdie."

I crane my neck to look at him. "Who's the weird one now? Stop reading my mind."

"I'm not. You just have a terrible poker face."

"What's poker?"

"I sometimes forget you were born not too long ago. It's a card game, requires strategy and a hefty dose of luck."

"Teach me sometime?"

"Sure." He slaps my shoulder in a way that makes me think he's only trying to shut me up. "I guess we have forever now that you're never-ending and all."

I take a deep breath. "Is that the case? I don't know anything about being a phoenix. I get unlimited lives?"

"Uh, maybe that's a question for someone else. How about you try not to die in the meantime."

"Deal." I focus on the hunters up ahead. "Wait, you're immortal?"

Bo nods stiffly. "Something like that."

"Hmph. Cool. What about Wes?"

"Wes is sort of an enigma." He shrugs.

But where does that leave Wren in the mix of all of this? Will there be a day when no amount of safety precautions can erase the natural progression of her life? I'm destined to just continue living for...ever? It's no wonder I have no family— they're probably all dead.

"If I get any closer, they'll be able to pick up my scent." Bo pulls a knife from seemingly out of nowhere. "Here, it's smaller than yours; easier to handle in close quarters. And if you need to cut anything, it has a wickedly sharp blade."

"Thanks," I tell him while taking the thing into my own hand. "It'll be fine, this will be easy. Don't worry about me."

"You reassuring yourself or me?" Bo steadies my shoulders and looks me square in the eye. "I'll be watching you the whole time, and I refuse to let you have all the fun if shit goes down."

My cheek turns up into a grin. "Mmhm. That's an awfully weird way of saying you care about me."

His gaze falls to the knife he handed me. "It's not too late for me to stab you."

"You're sweet, Bo, really. Such a softie." I pat his arm and step around him to find the path to the hunters.

Steadying my breath, I walk further away from the last being who was protecting me in this dangerous world. I glance back once to find that I can no longer spot him. A chill flutters up my spine. I've done risky shit before, and we've been apart in the past, but never when I've been marching headfirst into enemy territory with no chance of escaping. We're quite literally trapped in this secured portion of our world and the only person who can save us is trapped in an impenetrable prison. I'd live forever on the run like this if it meant she stayed alive, though. Only, there's no way of guaranteeing that—so the only thing me and Bo can do now is survive and then try to find a way to free her, to free Wes.

The ground crunches softly beneath my boots, a much-contrasted sound to that of my thudding heart. I scan the near vicinity, pretending like I'm Bo, and try to identify any potential threats. The few hunters walking to and from seem to be so consumed in their own missions that they don't even give much attention to each other, let alone me.

The rear of this mess hall gets closer and closer with every step I take toward it —the reality of this plan succeeding grows more likely by the moment. My chest warms with the possibility that maybe we aren't so screwed after all.

If it were Bo stalking into this camp, he'd be outed prior to anyone latching their sights on him. His scent is strong and powerful, at least that's what I'm told. He smells like musk and rain to me. He could use a wash more often than he settles on, but it's not a *demonic* scent. Me, on the other hand, I'm able to walk in undetected, which means we might finally have found our advantage.

I approach the mound of crates stacked near the building and quickly release my pack from over my shoulder. Popping the top on one of them, I'm assaulted in the best way ever by the aroma of bread. My cheek turns up into a grin knowing how happy this will make Bo, and the realization that maybe we won't starve to death out here. Oh, how fun would that be, dying over and over painfully and terribly.

I shove a few loaves into my bag and put the lid back in place. The less it looks like I was here, the better. I pry another off and revel at the sight of bright red apples. I waste no time placing some of them next to the commandeered bread. Moving onto another crate, I peer to check my surroundings. My heart races with the excitement and terror of this entire situation. My next discovery is lined with various meats, mostly that of the dried variety. My stomach grumbles its approval. I put the top on and decide to risk it by taking the whole thing.

Gripping the sides of the box, I stand and do my best to hide the triumphant emotions bubbling to the surface. If I can get out of here without getting caught, Bo and I will be eating good tonight, and for the foreseeable future. Maybe hope isn't as lost as we once thought it was.

I could kick myself in the ass for my optimism when the door to the back of the building flies open, and a man steps through it. The thing latches shut behind him, leaving the two of us out here alone.

"What are you doing?" His serious tone ripples through me.

His posture is stiff and rugged; his frame is easily a few inches taller than mine. The man is bigger, but the softness leads me to think it's not all muscle behind his clothing.

Don't panic, Dash, don't panic.

I swallow the immediate fear that consumes my entire body. "Following orders, sir."

The man raises a brow, assessing whether he should believe my cover story. His nostrils flare slightly, perhaps determining if I am friend or foe.

This is it, the moment my entire hasty plan falls apart. Endless possibilities run through my mind, all of them ending in my demise. At least Bo won't be slowed down by my dead weight—the only silver lining I can come up with while this man takes a freaking eternity to decide his next move.

He steps forward and I brace myself for impact. I'd reach for my knife, but that would be too obvious, too foolish at this point. I'd draw attention to our direction and that would only put Bo more at risk of being caught. The only way to give him a fighting chance of getting away will be to cause as little commotion as possible.

"Take this to B11." The guy plops the package in his grasp on top of the box I'm holding in my arms. The one I hadn't even noticed he was holding in the sheer terror of him appearing in front of me. "And when you're done." He nods toward the other building near us. "They could use another hand cleaning the weapons."

I unclench my jaw and tip my head in agreement, hoping the sweat trickling down my back doesn't spread to my face. "Yes, sir. Anything else, sir?" Because compliance very well could be the best course of action right now.

He lets my request linger between us for what feels like an eternity, causing me to second guess saying it. "No, that'll be all." He points to the package in my possession. "Make sure that gets to B11, son." He rotates to walk back in the direction he came.

"Sir?" I find myself saying.

He turns on his heel and waits for me to continue.

"I seem to have misplaced my canteen. Do you know where I can find a replacement?"

The stout man sighs and glances down at his side, pausing for a second before making an internal decision. He unlatches his own from the hook on his waistband. "Here. Do yourself a favor and try not to lose this one. *Others* won't be as kind as I am."

I reach out awkwardly from underneath the boxes in my arms, and take the thing from him, noting the weight of the liquid inside sloshing around.

Good, it's nearly full.

"Thank you, sir," I tell him as he nods stiffly and goes on his way.

I exhale slowly and blink down at the crates left untouched. I could gather more, give us a better chance of survival, but if I linger any longer, I'm only increasing the likelihood that I get caught. And what good will this risky mission have been if I fuck up like that? I must be smarter, more strategic, and get back with Bo sooner rather than later. I've already pushed my luck enough by interacting with this hunter.

When I'm positive the man is on the other side of the door he came from, I step away from the treasure. With my arms full of goods, I tiptoe and glance behind me, making a beeline for the forest-covered area Bo is hiding out in. If I can make it to the covered area, I can breathe easy knowing I secured provisions for us to get by.

Each step closer feels like another that I'm cheating death. I wait for someone to come and stop me, but it never happens. Inching nearer to the finish line, I grow more satisfied that my plan is working. I had my doubts, that's for sure, but something crazy had to be done if we stand any chance of living through this nightmare. What good are we to Wren and Wes if we wither away out here?

I cross over the thickly covered barrier shielding us from the prying eyes of the hunters at the camp below. I exhale and blink my vision clear as it adjusts to the dimmer light of the concealment. Pausing, I skim my surroundings, and wait for the broody and arrogant demon friend of mine to appear. I guess we hadn't talked this all the way through, but I sort of assumed he would greet me upon my arrival. I ignore the sinking pit in my gut and chalk it up to residual anxiety from my foolish scheme.

Continuing to move through the woods, I focus intently on the sounds of the area. It's not until I climb a little further that my vision confirms my fear before my hearing.

Bo, unmoving, lifeless on the ground. Shackles on his wrist, and a dagger pointed at him.

"Oh, it's just another hunter." The one man says to the other.

I drop the boxes and let the straps of my backpack slide over my shoulders and down my arms. The bag hits the ground with a thud, and apples roll out in the wake of the fall. I'm not even sure of the movements I make, but I find the knife Bo had given me gripped tightly in my hand.

Still thinking I'm on his side, the man holding the blade against Bo's throat smiles. "You want in on this, too?"

I don't say a word, I only continue to step toward this disturbing sight. Rage builds within me and overpowers my ability to function; instead, it takes control of my arm, raising it up, my opposite fist grabbing onto the hair on the man's head firmly to secure him in place as I drive the cold metal into his chest.

Wide-eyed and mouth gaped, the realization finally settles in. Blood overflows from his lips and he struggles to breathe through the liquid no doubt pooling in his lungs.

"What the fuck!" the other guy calls out.

I let the man in my grasp fall to the ground and slide the crimson-stained blade free of his torso. I allow the rage to guide me, to take the reins and steer me through.

I'm met with a blow to the face, throwing me off balance and onto all fours. I spit my own blood onto the dirt and glare up at the man who was planning to kill Bo. I've fought countless demons in the past, but only rarely a hunter. Their skills far surpass mine, but at least I don't have to worry about magic I cannot anticipate.

The guy acts irrationally, literally throwing himself toward me with his knife clasped in his hands.

I roll out of the way and laugh as he falls to the ground.

"What are you? A fucking sympathizer?" He regains himself while I do the same.

We both climb to our feet and face one another.

"You're scum, that's for sure." He spits onto the ground between us.

Are his words supposed to intimidate me? If anything, they only continue to fuel the metaphorical fire raging from within.

I don't reply, I only wait for him to strike. To make a mistake so I can end his life just like I did to his friend.

He does exactly what I expect, advances in haste.

I duck and slice my own blade at him, cutting through a thin layer of his pants. I repeat the motion back and forth rapidly and finally draw a bit of blood.

The man, about equal to my size, curses and stumbles back, his free hand reaching toward the new wounds on his shins. I use the opportunity to swipe at the dirt-covered ground and toss the debris into his face.

His palms go to cover his eyes but it's too late, the dust causes him to temporarily lose his vision.

I grin and advance on him in his moment of weakness, my knife gripped in my fist and the blade aimed at his heart.

Only, somehow, this man isn't as incapacitated as one would assume. The loss of his vision almost makes him more aware of his surroundings. His body pivots toward me and at the moment I'm about to strike him, he jumps out of the way. My own form stumbles from the misjudged target, and is met by a blow across the back, knocking the wind from my chest and my legs out from under me.

Shit.

I hit the ground hard, my hands desperate to absorb the impact and protect the rest of my body. The flesh on my palm stings, a painful reminder of what is at stake here. My life. Bo's life. And ultimately, the lives of Wren and Wes.

"What are you, anyway?" The man calls out from behind me. He sniffs the air aggressively. "His scent is strong, pungent...I get nothing on you." He kicks me square in the side and flips me onto my back.

I blink through the automatic tears that form in my eyes and frantically search for the knife that was lost in the fall. My fingers dig into the ground, scanning the surface all around me for any clue on where it might be.

In a flash, he climbs on top of me, straddling my waist and pinning me to the ground. His fist meets my jaw in a blast of pain that sends sparkling things dancing in my vision. He hits me again, and again, my face reacting immediately to the impact and swelling.

I do my best to block his blows, yet still, most of them are effective.

I buck but it's no use, I cannot dismount him for the life of me.

It's only a matter of time until he finishes me off and then returns to Bo to complete the slaughter. All of this because I was too weak to overpower a hunter. All of this because I am useless in this world.

The man strikes me once more.

A new fear rises within me. Not that of being killed, but of my phoenix powers activating after my death. I'll resurrect to find Bo murdered and there not being a damn thing I can do about it. He'll be dead and it'll be my fault.

A burst of renewed spirit and hope explodes inside of me when my fingers graze the cold surface of what I pray is my knife. I crane my arm to grab it, coming up short every time.

My attacker switches up his assault and latches his thick hands around my neck, squeezing and tightening them. "I don't care what you are, you're a fucking sympathizer."

His hold continues to cut off my oxygen supply and my vision blurs even more.

I begin to lose that momentary hope, but when he focuses on choking the life out of me, he rises off my waist, giving me the smallest ability to shift us a little.

Enough for my pleading fingers to dig and scrape and pull the knife within reach.

Consciousness threatens to drag me under with each passing second, but I know I must act, I have to get that fucking knife into my grasp.

The moment I latch onto it, I use every ounce of strength I have left to plunge the sharp end into the man's neck.

His grip loosens on me and his hands frantically move to the knife.

I shove him off me and cough as air fills my lungs.

If I've learned anything from my training with Bo and Wes, it's that sometimes, all it takes is one deadly move to end a fight. Our attacker might still be alive, but it's only a matter of moments before he bleeds out completely.

I scoot myself across the ground to Bo's side and search for any sign of life. His chest rises slowly and then falls, a small but powerful signal that he's still in there. I shake him and like he's just waking from a nap, his eyes open. "About time you wake up."

He sits up and rubs his temple. "What did I miss?" His gaze falls to my face. "You look like shit."

"I thought you were a fucking goner." I will my heart to slow down its pace.

"You can't get rid of me that easily." Bo grunts and rises to his feet, reaching for my hand to bring me to his level, too. He latches onto my shoulder and gives me a firm shake. "Plus, I still have to teach you how to play poker." Bo shakes the shackles latched on his wrists and glances at the fallen men. "I hope one of these fools has a key."

The man I left to bleed out gurgles his last breath and his body goes still.

"Ah man, you had all the fun without me." Bo strolls over and kicks the man onto his back. He rummages through his pockets in search of his freedom.

"Can't say it was much fun." I gently rub at my neck, wincing at the minimal contact on my skin. My entire body aches in some profoundly terrible way. I've had my ass kicked in the past, but this takes it to a new level. It's going to take me days— if not weeks—to recover from these injuries. "What happened to you, anyway? Since when do you fall so easily to two hunters?"

Bo finds what he's looking for and unlocks the cuffs on his wrists. He discards them on top of the man's lifeless body. "Well." He places his hands on his knees and shoves himself upright. "I saw that guy come out of the back of the building, so I started toward you." He motions to the bodies and says, "One of those idiots came out of nowhere. I thought it would be best to deal with him under the cover of the trees. His friend got the best of me and must have whacked me over the head. I don't remember anything after that."

"None of that is like you. It's sloppy."

Bo sighs heavily. "What can I say, I'm not on top of my game."

"You could have gotten yourself killed," I tell him.

Bo remains silent, almost like I struck a nerve somehow. He latches onto one of the men and tosses their body into an overgrown bush. Scanning the vicinity, he searches for another. He grabs the blade out of the guy's throat, wipes the blood onto his pants and once he finds his mark, he throws that man into the concealment of nature. "I'd rather burn their remains, but I don't want to draw any more unwanted attention to us."

As if suddenly remembering what this was all for, I walk over to the supplies I had dropped when I saw Bo in danger. I kneel and retrieve the apples that had scattered and toss the bag back over my shoulder, ignoring the pain that the thing awakens.

"We should get some distance between us and them." Bo comes to my side and grabs the crate, tucking it easily under his arm and securing the other package in the wide grip of his hand.

For the next hour or so, we do exactly that. We zig-zag, crisscross, and walk in silence until the swelling of my face becomes too difficult to see through. I blink and blink, but my lids grow to be small slits I can barely open.

I stop completely and blurt out, "You're going to have to kill me."

"Are you out of your mind?" Bo halts and turns toward me.

I point at myself from head to toe. "I'm worthless in this condition."

"You're worthless in any condition," Bo mouths off.

"No." I shake my head. "Not doing your sarcastic avoidance right now. I'm serious. If you won't do it, I will." I unsheathe the knife from my waistband. Somehow, the idea of killing myself is more unsettling than Bo doing it, but if he won't cooperate, I'll take things into my own hands. "Since when do you have an issue killing someone?"

Bo clenches his jaw and glares at the blade in my hand. "You will not," he growls.

I take a step away from him and grip the thing firmer. "I'm only slowing us down and you know that. I can hardly fucking see. Everything hurts. It'll take me too long to heal. And we cannot afford that kind of delay. We have an advantage, and we need to use it. You don't have a choice in this, Bo."

He matches the distance and then some, appearing right before me. "The hell if I do."

I aim the pointed side at my heart, hoping this is the most effective way to end my life.

Bo places his palm on top of mine and uses his other hand to support my back. "This better fucking work." His voice is strained as he meets my gaze.

Together, with no more argument, we plunge the knife into my chest.

"Thank you," I mutter while maintaining eye contact.

My only hope is that this plan actually works, and I didn't just force my best friend to murder me. Either way, I refuse to be dead weight.

Bo takes my body when I grow weak, and lowers me onto the ground. He holds me in his arms and as my eyes flutter closed, I almost think I see tears well in his. "You better not keep me waiting," he demands.

His words are the last thing I hear before the life leaves my body.

CHAPTER 7

Wren

"I don't understand why this isn't working," a man complains.

I keep my eyes shut and my body still in hopes that I can play pretend and listen in on their conversation. I'm tied firmly to a metal chair, it's not like I could go anywhere if I wanted to.

"You're weak, that's why." A woman replies. "I should have known you wouldn't be strong enough to do this."

The more she talks, the more familiar her voice sounds. Through the ringing in my head, I finally realize who it is.

Parla.

My fucking boss. The one who betrayed me and locked me in this torturous place. But if that's her, who is she arguing with?

"I'm sorry, ma'am. It's not without great effort."

Parla grabs onto my chin and tilts my head up at her. "I know you're awake."

I yank free of her grasp and finally take in the room. It's small, but bigger than that of my prior confinement. Similar brick walls and a sturdy door keeping us locked in here. A shiny tray perched atop a stand with various tools. Some are sharp and pointy, and some of the crystal variant. A few vials with no doubt an unfavorable concoction inside. They intend to use both magical and regular physical torture to get what they want out of me.

Good thing they trained me for this kind of thing.

"You want to stop running your mouth and get on with it." I nod toward the selection of devices she can choose between.

Parla folds her arms across her chest and looks down at me through her thick lashes. "It doesn't have to be this way."

"Oh, yeah?" I raise an unamused brow at her.

She's stalling because she knows this type of interrogation won't work on me.

"Tell me what I want to know, and I'll see to it that your sentence is reduced."

"Reduced?" I laugh. "To what? Life in prison? I'll pass."

"It could be worse. I can make it worse. Is that what you want?"

The man she was demeaning fidgets nervously in the corner of the room, hidden under the shadow cast across his face.

I stare directly at her. "There's nothing you can do to me that hasn't already been done."

Parla unfolds her arms and skims her finger along the edge of the tray. "I'm sure I could get creative."

A grin forms on my already beaten face. "I wish you would."

I didn't rise through the ranks as quickly as I did to claim the title of Furla Ain for nothing. No one handed me anything, I earned it through grit and determination. I became the best of the best. I trained harder than anyone else—put in more time and energy, more blood, sweat, and tears. I gave my soul to the cause because I thought that was the righteous path. Each passing second is a brutal reminder that I was wrong all along. Sure, demons and the like are plaguing our land, but so are the hunters, the purebloods. Both sides are only continuing to fuel the fire of this war.

I'm done being a pawn, a tool used for their advantage. They abused my thirst for vengeance, and I obeyed every order because I was desperate to make a difference. I did, though, that's without a doubt. I've killed countless demons and their bringers, most of them I consumed their essence, making myself that much stronger. Their residual power lingering within me, begging to be let loose. I hold it hostage with no way of setting it free.

"What magician are you working with?" Parla thoughtfully picks a black stone off the tray and holds it in her palm, examining it.

I sigh, unsure of the angle she's working here. Truthfully, I have no fucking clue what she's talking about. Does she mean the standard-issue witches we use for spelling our safehouses and getting various supplies from? What difference would it make? That person hasn't done anything wrong.

"Rollo," she calls out to the man in the corner.

He appears from the shadows, cowering and keeping his eyes trained on the floor. His old age trails from his snow-white hair to the thickly grooved wrinkles on his brow. His clothes are tattered and worn, his hands filthy. He's not wearing cuffs, but if I had to guess, he isn't here of his own free will.

"Ma'am?" Rollo doesn't look up.

Parla shoves the stone toward him. "You know what to do."

He complies without another word, taking the black rock and coming toward me.

I study him carefully but notice how Parla takes a cautious step back.

Rollo kneels between my restrained legs and lets out a long but quiet breath. He briefly glances up into my eyes and mouths, "I'm sorry."

I clench my jaw and nod stiffly, a silent gesture telling him it's okay, that he can do it.

It's not like either of us has any choice in the matter.

Rollo moves the hair from my right shoulder, exposing a bit of skin on my chest. He places the cold stone in the open space and mutters a few words. The stone heats up, and with whatever magical spell he spoke, becomes fixed to my body.

A strange sensation floats through me, like little roots taking hold.

This is probably the part where I should fear for my life, but all I feel is a rage that continues to build.

"Was the tether successful?" Parla questions him.

"Yes, ma'am." Rollo stands and moves to her side.

"Give her a taste." Parla grins with each word spoken like she's getting far more enjoyment out of this than she should.

Rollo dips his head even lower, like he's ashamed of being used this way.

That makes two of us.

With a small twist of the wrist, Rollo turns an invisible dial. Immediately, a dull pain consumes my entire body, making it difficult to pinpoint its exact location. You would think the source would stem from the rock adhered to my chest, but no, it's like a million different entry points all buzzing as one.

"More," Parla commands.

Another minor turn increases the voltage flowing through me, but still, I swallow it down and refuse to react. I glare directly at Parla to let her see how unaffected I am.

Does it hurt? Sure. But does she need to know that?

"I said more," she barks at him.

He hesitates despite the approval I had given him to do what she demands.

Parla grows impatient by his lack of enthusiasm and raises her arm, smacking him across the face. "Be of use or I will dispose of you and find someone who is."

I tug at my restraints, eager to bust out of them and choke her until her life leaves her body. "He's doing what you asked, you fucking bitch. It's not his fault I have a high pain tolerance."

Parla's arm twitches like she's considering hitting me, too. "Max capacity," she tells him.

"Ma'am."

She latches onto his shoulder and forces him to face her. "This is your last chance."

"Do it, Rollo. It's fine, really," I reassure him.

He meets my gaze briefly, tears welling in his dark brown eyes before he sinks his head toward the ground, turning his wrist.

The pain slowly increases like he's helping me build a tolerance to it instead of jamming it all into my system at once. Energy fills my veins, and every inch of my body comes alive in the worst way possible. I steady my breath and take it, desperately trying not to give her the reaction she so feverishly desires. My teeth chattering and the sweat building on my brow are the only sign that I'm suffering.

I'm brought back to that day at the warehouse, when I had locked eyes with Wes, our mate bond clicked into place and caused me to make a deadly mistake. I was overcome by demons and left for dead. I had numerous broken bones and wounds that would no doubt result in my death. I couldn't move. All I could do was become one with the agony that was consuming my entire being. I grew familiar with the torment, like it was an old friend I was getting reacquainted with. I accepted my fate.

Part of me was relieved that I would finally see an end to the anguish I carried with me every day since I had run out of that burning house when I was a child. Witnessing death, especially a brutal one, at such a young age changes you, and from that day forward, I was never the same. Nothing has ever been the same.

"Turn it off," Parla tells Rollo. She stalks toward me and grabs my chin, tilting it up to her. "I could listen to your screams all day long, but I have better things to do."

I blink through the sweat that trickled down my face. "I was screaming?"

She huffs. "Don't play dumb with me."

Dizziness threatens to take hold and nausea rises, but I swallow it down and steady my gaze on her. "Anyone ever tell you how boring you are?"

Her grip on my chin tightens. "Who are you working with?"

"I'm Furla Ain, I work for you, dumbass." I yank myself free of her grasp.

"Ms. Oliver." Parla sighs and changes her tactic. "There is a barrier in place, hindering extraction from your person. That block is impossible without magical assistance. So let me ask you again, what witch or warlock has performed this spell on you?"

I allow her accusation to sink in. Extraction? Block? Assistance? I've had no such thing done. How would I even give her the truth if I don't know it myself?

She crosses her arms again and eyes me carefully.

"I have no idea what you're talking about."

"Lies!" she yells, but then quickly composes herself. Parla dusts off invisible debris from her sides and straightens her shirt. "Rollo, max capacity."

He pauses again but with one fierce glare from Parla, he complies, turning the dial on my magical torture device.

My teeth chatter as heat rises within me. A total body electrical field ignites, and pain consumes me. My eyes water and sweat pools between my breasts and in the swell of my back. Hands and legs trembling, I allow it to overtake me, becoming one with the agony. I flip the switch, disassociating from the torment, and give my mind permission to wander, to take me away from this dreadful place. Screams fill the small room, and I drown them out, despite now knowing their source.

I play through the only few memories that bring me joy. Wes, sleeping uncomfortably next to me in his attempt to keep me warm through the night, his possessive and protective nature a characteristic I adore immensely. Dash, making sure I stayed hydrated when I was still considered the enemy, a bright light in this dark and gloomy world; his kindness is something I will cherish until my last breath. Bo, giving me a high-five when we battled together, the stubborn asshole with a subtle compassion he doesn't often let show.

The agony threatens to drag my attention toward it, but I dig in and steer it away. I will not be broken, not by this evil and sadistic bitch.

My chest tightens, bringing me closer to reality than I wish to be. Is this the point of no return? When the line is crossed and I succumb to the attempt to break me? There has to be a threshold, a point where my body can no longer go on—a point where it gives out completely. My will can handle so much, but my actual life-force, that's an area I'm unfamiliar with.

The dark stone fixed to my chest pulses, pumping more agonizing pain through me. The end grows near, and I embrace it, giving in to the sweet relief that it will bring. I don't know what will come in the afterlife, but it sure has to be better than this. My only regret is that I have lived my entire life for a hopeless cause. A soldier in an unwinnable war.

"What's happening?" Parla mutters to Rollo.

A scream ripples up and out of my chest, the sound so unfamiliar. My throat aches but it is nothing compared to the pain in the rest of my body.

I grip the arms of the chair and brace myself for what comes next.

Only, instead of death, it's something much more bizarre.

A bright white flash of light fills the room, blinding us all for a split moment. I blink through the illumination and try to find a source of the madness, but it all seems to be radiating from my torso.

I let out another uncontrollable ear-piercing shriek and in the wake of the shock wave, the rock causing my agony splits off from my body and flies across the room, nearly missing Parla and Rollo, and shattering to pieces.

Panting and attempting to slow my racing heart, I lean my head back and soak in the relief of being free of that thing. How it happened? I have no idea. It must have been a malfunction of some sort.

"That's impossible," Rollo whispers.

Parla grills Rollo. "Did you do this? Did you help her?"

"No, I...that's not how this works, ma'am. I cannot do such things."

"If I find out you're lying to me, I will make you suffer worse than this." Parla threatens him and then turns her attention to me. She stands above me, her expression littered with distaste for how this transpired. "You think this is funny, don't you?"

"Hilarious," I struggle to say.

She leans in close, placing both hands on the back of my chair. Steadying her gaze, she smirks. "You're going to find it humorous when I force you to kill your boyfriend and absorb his essence."

My heart stutters, and for the first time since I've been in this torture chamber, she finally strikes a nerve. "What?"

Parla tilts her head. "Oh, you think I don't know how powerful he is? I might not be able to extract your energy supply yet, but that doesn't mean I can't make you grow in power while I figure out how." She pauses to let that sink in. "In two days, when the moon is at its peak, you will end his life and there will be nothing you can do to stop it from happening."

She stands upright, a smug grin on her stupid face.

A new bout of nausea tumbles around in my stomach. Could what she's saying be true? Is she really going to make me kill Wes and consume his soul? I recall what Franny had said, about no one being killed in a long while, and that of Parla mentioning her having issues extracting power. Does that mean I'm the only one capable of absorbing demonic magic? Is *that* why she's always been so persistent that I do my missions alone, and gives me exceedingly powerful targets? She's been using me as her personal siphon all along and I was none the wiser.

Regardless of the reasoning, one thing is certain—Wes and I are in grave danger and I'm not at all convinced that one, or both, of us are going to make it out of this alive.

CHAPTER 8

Wes

My beloved is gone, and with her absence, I am helpless and riddled with despair.

I cannot free her of this hell. I have let her down.

My fated mate. The other half of my soul. The person I never thought I'd find, only I found her too late.

If I were honest with her from the start, maybe none of this would have happened. If I never came up with the stupid plan to use her, she would be safe. I could have told her the truth and accepted her rejection, saving us all from this nightmare. Bo could have been reasoned with. Surely he would understand the impossibly rare connection between the two of us. He wouldn't have marked her. She would have healed and left on her own accord, never to be seen again. She would have a future. But no, I was selfish, and now I've doomed her to a worse fate than being mated to a repulsive creature like me.

For that, I will forever be in mourning.

"Someone over there?" A gravelly voice calls through the small, grated opening between our cells.

I lift my head from the shared wall to Wren's empty chamber and look toward the other side but don't respond.

"I can hear you breathing," the man tells me.

I clear my throat. "I'll try to be quieter."

"I haven't had a cellmate in a long time." He pauses and for a moment, I think he's done speaking completely. "You must be powerful if they put you in there."

I let out a small chuckle. "That's doubtful." Glancing at the shackles on my wrist, I'm reminded once again of how powerless I am. Even my beast side has forsaken me.

"Just because they've suppressed your abilities doesn't mean they're any less there. No, they're simply lying dormant, ready to rise to the surface."

"Seems unlikely, but I appreciate the words of encouragement."

The man moves around in his room, perhaps finding a more comfortable way to engage with me. "May I ask?"

"I'd rather you didn't." There are very few who know the truth about what I am, and even then, I can't be certain I know much about myself at all. I was orphaned at an early age, my birth parents a mystery I've never solved. I was taken in by a kind woman who raised me and despite not sharing blood, she was my mother.

In the perpetual state of war our realm is in, there has been no opportunity to research, and even if there was, most demonic historical centers have been burned to the ground. Our history has gone up in flames, diminished to the burning embers and waning ash.

"I came to Prania to seek refuge," he confesses.

"Did you find what you were looking for?" There's no hiding the sarcasm in my inquiry.

He laughs bluntly. "In a way, yes. But what's that old saying, 'you trade in one set of problems for another'?"

"I can't imagine a reality where I would choose being here over anywhere else." Prania is home, but it is also a lost cause.

"After being here a few years, I can agree with you there."

I crane my neck toward the voice coming through the other side of my room. Did I hear him correctly? *A few years?* That can't be true. Prania has been closed off to any other realm for far longer than that. It's inescapable. No one comes in or out. The hunters made damn sure of that when they shut it off and started eradicating anyone but themselves.

I push myself up off the floor and weakly walk over to him. With a thud, I slide down the wall and resume my pitiful existence near this strange man. "How is that possible?"

"Which part?"

"How did you get here?"

He lets out a long breath. "Like I said, I was running from something. I called in a favor, hoping to travel to any realm other than my own. Little did I know that I'd end up here."

"A favor? With whom?"

"Someone more powerful than me. Although, I do wonder if I would have fared better had I stayed put."

I shouldn't entertain this conversation, but if what he's saying is true, that means it could actually be possible to escape this realm. That is, if we can find a way out of this prison. Something I've been searching for my entire life, right here just out of reach.

The man continues, "I've done a lot of thinking while locked in here. Reflecting on the things I've done in the past. Solitude will do that to a person."

"And what have you learned?"

He exhales again. "For one, it's okay to be wrong. To make bad decisions and regret them. To realize that maybe you were the villain after all." He repositions himself again. "I hurt a lot of people. I lied; I stole. I let even more down, and it was all for nothing. I thought I was taking back what was mine, but I was just being a bully. A selfish and inconsiderate power-hungry jackass."

Each of his words are layered with guilt and remorse, and if I had to guess, he means every one of them.

"I went through withdrawals when I came to this realm. It was painful. But it was a necessary purge I didn't know I desperately needed. I had gone so long with stolen power, that I felt uncomfortable with just my own. I was dependent on it, and I grew too familiar with what wasn't mine that I couldn't recognize the person I was without it. The longer I went without, the harder it became. And then all of a sudden, there was one day when it wasn't as difficult. With each passing day, I grew more okay with myself. That's when I realized the horrors of what I had done and what it cost me, and so many others.

"I want to make amends. To right my wrongs, but the time for that has passed."

A glimmer of hope sparks in my chest. "What makes you so sure?" First, it was the guard showing me a small kindness, and now my cellmate has information on how to get out of Prania. Either the fates are truly out to screw me over, or there might be some chance of surviving this.

"You alluded to it yourself about being powerless in here."

"Not if we work together." It's an unlikely alliance, but if it means getting out of here, I'd align with the devil himself. "You're a witch?"

"In my past life, yes."

I shake my head. "That isn't something you ever shake, sir."

"No need for the formalities, son. You can call me Tremont."

"Tremont," I repeat. "I'd shake your hand, but our accommodations don't exactly allow for it. I'm Wes."

"They are rather...confining, aren't they?" He laughs gently. "You call out a name in your sleep sometimes. Is that who's in the next cell?"

My chest tightens and if my hound were present, his possessiveness would rise to the surface. It's strange not having him constantly causing a commotion in my head, but my reflexes somehow know how he would react in most situations. "Yes," is all I respond.

He takes a long moment before saying anything else. "Wes?"

"Hm?" My eyes grow heavy as the exhaustion threatens to take hold. My wounds are healing much slower than normal, and the cuffs on my wrists prevent any of my powers from rising to the surface. Between the intermittent torturing and the lack of proper hydration and food, my body is fighting to perform at even a minimal capacity.

"This wing, the one we're in right now. It houses the prison's most profound creatures. They wouldn't have put you or her here if they didn't fear you. They're trying to break you. To get in your head. You mustn't allow that to happen."

That's easier said than done. I'm supposed to be this wrecking force and here I am, weak and struggling to stay alive. They've nearly made me mortal, and yet are treating me like a beast.

Why don't they just kill me and get it over with?

A loud creaking sounds from the cell next to me, snapping me out of my stupor and sending me scuttling across the floor to the other side.

"Wren," I plead with the once empty space.

A thud is followed by the door closing, and then the faint sniffling of my angel.

"Wren," I say again. "Are you okay?"

Shuffling ensues and then a dainty hand weaves its way through the grated area. "I'm okay."

Her skin is cold and clammy to the touch, and when I latch onto her completely, I notice she's trembling.

The door to Tremont's cell opens and by the sound of it, he's next in line for an afternoon of torment.

"What did they do to you?" I press myself on my side and desperately try to peer into her cell at her.

"Nothing I can't handle," she tells me with her eyes pinched closed and sweat coating her forehead.

Wren's black hair sticks to her cheeks and I wish for nothing more than to brush it away, to pull her to my chest and keep her safe from any harm that may come to her. To be the man she needs, that she deserves.

"I'm so sorry," I whisper while grazing my lips against her knuckles. I kiss every inch of her I can reach, apologizing with each one of them.

"Hey." She peers through her heavy lids. "We're in this together, okay?"

"Yeah." I should have anticipated this. I should have protected her. I should have done *something* to stop this from happening.

"Speaking of..." Wren opens her eyes wider. "I need in there."

An automatic grin forms on my face. "You and me both."

"No, I'm serious." She brings her other hand to her mouth to cover a nasty cough.

My breath hitches. "Is that blood?"

Wren blinks a few times and examines her hand. "That's nothing." She wipes it on her side and ignores my growing concern. "I have an idea, but we have to be in the same room."

"What is it? The idea?" Not that I'd say no to not having a wall separating us.

"I'd rather just try it, but we have to find a way. The guard, the one that we discussed, maybe we could convince him to give us a few minutes."

"I don't want to put you in any more danger."

She narrows her gaze at me. "I think the time for that has passed, don't you think? Desperate times call for desperate measures. And if I have to put a little faith in one of them, it's a risk I'm willing to take. Especially if it means the possibility of gaining any kind of advantage." She draws in a breath. "Besides, stop pretending like I can't defend myself. I understand that you feel that need, but I've been doing fine without you this long."

"And look where that got you." Before I allow the guilt to continue to sink in, I shift the topic of conversation. "I met my other cellmate."

"Yeah?"

I nod and lower my voice. "He's a witch. But get this...he's only been in Prania a few years."

"That's impossible."

"That's what I thought."

"You believe him?"

"He had a rather compelling story, and I can't for the life of me come up with a reason why he would lie about it."

"Wes, if that's true..."

"I know."

Her eyes dart back and forth like she's considering a million different possibilities. Finally, she stops and focuses on me. "Do you think they're okay?"

Dash and Bo.

The two of them have been in my thoughts almost as much as Wren. They're my family and there is no telling how dangerous things have been for them trapped inside enemy territory.

"Do you still feel him?" I flit my attention to the faded but still present mark on her neck.

Wren brings her fingers to it, skimming along the ridges. "I do," she whispers.

"If they've survived the initial fallout, I'm sure they'll be fine." My mind wanders to the close calls we've experienced together, none of them quite like this, but they never failed to survive then, so I have to hope they will do the same now. "And D...at least we can worry a little less about him now."

"That doesn't mean they aren't suffering." Her body tenses with each word. "Just because he *can* come back..."

"I know," I tell her. The idea of Dash dying over and over to stay alive isn't something any of us want to imagine. Luckily, he and Bo have each other, the same way Wren and I do.

We'll get through this—together.

Wren wiggles her hand back over to her side and pushes herself onto her butt. "We can't afford to waste any more time."

I grip at the grate between us. "You need to rest." Oh, what I would give to whisper a few words and give her reprieve from her injuries. Sure, it takes a strain on me, but I'd gladly endure it if it meant she was better. The fated mate bond we share allows me to control her, and with that, I can mend her wounds if I align my request correctly. By setting my intentions properly, I can absorb her pain with just a touch. I've abused these powers in the past, hindering her healing progress and even disallowing her from being able to speak. That one was a mistake on my behalf, which could have resulted in her death. I hate myself for continuing to put her in harm's way.

That's why I leapt out of those woods that day. I had been suppressing Wren's powers because I worried if she gained her full strength that she would leave us. I could have let her be taken and then work with the guys to figure out a way to save her, but I couldn't send her in here without her strength. She never would have made it through the first round of interrogation with my compulsion still intact. It put me in danger, and exposed the lie that she had told, but there was no way my beast would allow her to face this on her own. If she was going down, so were we.

Only, he isn't here to help us—and that alone is not something I anticipated.

"I'll rest when I'm dead." Wren rises to her feet and walks over to the other side of her cell.

I strain to see through the small barrier. She whispers something but I can't make it out. My enhanced hearing is also suffering now that I'm locked in here.

My heart picks up its pace, thudding wildly in my chest. I wish to be over there, right beside her, ready to throw myself in front of her if any danger comes her way. Even without my hound present, I'm still territorial and protective over her. That natural reaction coincides with being completely captivated by a person. I would do anything for her; give my life for her.

A couple minutes pass of hushed conversation, and Wren tears herself away from the wall but doesn't return to me. Instead, she goes toward her door, and taps on it gently. Once. Twice. Then three rapid but quiet knocks.

I stand, my hand pressed against the stone between us, my breath caught in anticipation of the unknown. What if she summons the wrong person? What if her plan blows up in her face and makes our situation somehow worse? If that's at all possible. My soul can't continue to bear the weight of seeing her abused and tortured when it knows with certainty that all of this is my fault.

Her lock turns slowly, grinding with each minimal rotation. The door groans open, and with it, I'm left wondering which outcome we're about to experience.

CHAPTER 9

Bo

I really love killing people.

I mean, I'm not kidding. There's something exciting about ending the life of someone who deserves it. Watching the light leave their eyes and knowing you were the one to snuff out their flame.

I've done it more times than I could count—not that the number would matter anyway.

But even knowing Dash will resurrect, the weight of his demise comes at no less of a gut punch. I shoved a knife into his heart and held him as he slumped to the ground and his body finally gave in to the injury.

And now, I watch over him with bated breath as I wait for him to come back.

I didn't want to assist him, but if he did it himself, he might have missed and caused himself more pain than necessary. He gave me no choice in the matter, and despite him having a compelling case for wanting to die, it still didn't make it any easier to go through with.

I've never been one to need or desire the company of others. I've grown fond of my time alone. I've sort of resented Wes for his insistence that we stick together, and that only grew when Dash came along. I've been bitter and callous toward them. I thought they were holding me back and contributing to the stresses of my existence.

I didn't realize how very wrong I was until Wes and Wren were taken, and Dash decided to end his own life, leaving me here without any of them to annoy me. Maybe, just maybe, I don't hate them as much as I thought I did.

Because why else would I be genuinely concerned that Dash might not resurrect?

If he doesn't, I might as well off myself, too. On the chance that Wes and Wren break out of Rock Bridge, they'll murder me for what I permitted Dash to do. And

I'm not entirely sure I would blame them. Dash is the one innocent in our little group of castaways, and we must protect him at all costs.

I keep an eye on our surroundings, noting every leaf that falls or gust of wind that floats by, stirring the branches of the trees. If one weren't running for their life, this dense forest might actually be considered peaceful. But like Wren's disarming beauty, what's under the surface is far more deadly.

I press my hand to my chest and close my eyes, conjuring the connection I have to her. It's difficult to access, but with great effort, I can faintly sense her—meaning she's still alive. Wes, I'm not so sure. But one of them is better than none, and just because I can only confirm her life, doesn't mean Wes is any less alive. It's hard to imagine a fierce beast like him being taken down without one hell of a fight—and with the two of them together, Rock Bridge doesn't know what it's messing with. Although, the sooner we can break into the place and free them, the better. There's no telling what kind of torment they're experiencing.

A guttural growl rumbles in my chest at imagining someone hurting Wren. I once wanted to end her life, and now, the thought of it drives me nearly mad.

I recall the warmth of her body as she pressed it against me when she was trying to make Wes angry. It was all an act, but still, it stirred things I've been fighting to suppress. It's one thing to *tolerate* a hunter, but it's another to...

My thoughts are halted by a crackling, and then a flicker of flame.

Relief washes over me as Dash's transformation begins. How would I have explained to Wes and Wren that I accidentally on purpose killed their sweet ginger?

It takes another moment before Dash's body completely catches fire. It burns bright and hot for another long minute, and then a solid encasement covers him. The dark smoke flutters up and through the trees, a signal that we should get out of here sooner rather than later. The hunters tracking us will surely pick up on any sign of life not sanctioned by their own authority. Especially when they realize there are dead bodies of their comrades stuffed in the bushes outside their encampment.

The shell cracks slowly, like Dash is taking his good ol' time.

I sigh and cross my arms. "Today," I tell him.

Watching him resurrect the first time was incredible, a gift from the universe when we needed it most, but now I'd rather him hurry up.

Finally, his hand bursts through the center and shoves away the debris. Dash rises to the seated position and dusts the excess off his shoulders.

"About time." I reach over and ruffle his head, knocking off a bit of the molt.

"It worked." He grins at me and holds his arms out to examine his injury-free body. "I feel great." Dash touches his face, and then his chest, where I had shoved a knife through it not too long ago.

I extend the thing to him, handle first. "Here."

"Right. Thanks." Dash stands, brushing himself off more before taking the knife from me and tucking it away on his person. Glancing down at the remaining embers of his transformation, he says, "Let's get out of here." He steps out of the debris and tosses the backpack over his shoulder. "I'm starving."

"Me too, bud, me too."

"You didn't eat?" He pauses and narrows his gaze at me.

"And miss the show?" I tuck the crate under my arm and grip the other parcel in my hand. Without lingering any longer, I take off away from our campsite.

"Aw, you were worried about me." Dash jogs to catch up.

"Was not." I huff.

"Admit it, you don't hate me as much as you let on."

I glare at him out of the corner of my eye. "I never said I hated you."

Dash breaks out into a shit-eating grin. "I knew it."

"We need to get out of here."

"Sure, change the subject." He nudges me with his elbow.

"Until we learn more about whatever your abilities are..." I look at him briefly. "We should probably hold off on resorting to death."

"What, you think it has a limit?"

I shrug and continue stalking further from the remains that could get us caught. "Nature always has a give and take. My powers don't come without restraint, some exchange to maintain the balance. Wes is no different. There's always a *price*."

"Oh." Dash looks to the ground, watching his feet with each step. A silence falls between us until his curiosity overtakes him. "Like what kind of price?"

My stomach grumbles, reminding me of one of the costs. "Energy."

"Energy?" he echoes.

"We all need substance to survive. Whether it be food, blood, or flesh. Each creature is different, but when you use your powers, you lose those reserves quicker, and they must be replenished. Sometimes, it's not so easily restored."

"What do you mean?"

I grip onto a small tree on the side of a ridge and lift myself over the edge, careful not to drop the packages that Dash risked his life for.

He grunts and struggles, but manages to maneuver himself up and over, too.

I close my eyes and breathe deeply, sensing our surroundings. The cool air floats through my chest and reassures me that we are far enough away to take a quick break.

"Are you okay?" Dash whispers at my side.

I peek through one lid at him. "We should eat."

Finding a few discarded logs to set our supplies on, we dig into the stolen goods. I rip the top off the crate and nearly salivate at the sight of meat. I yank out two equally sized dried hunks and extend one toward Dash. When he doesn't take it immediately, I turn to him, watching as he unzips his pack and fumbles with the contents.

My mouth literally drops open upon seeing the loaf of bread he pulls out.

With a giant grin on his face, he shoves it in my direction while taking his piece of protein.

I bring the thing to my nose, breathing in the fresh scent. Only one thing in this world smells better than bread...

My chest tightens at the idea of her being starved and tortured, and here I am, drooling over some carbs. Still, if I stand any chance of saving Wren and Wes, I have to fuel my reserves.

"Did I do good?" Dash chews his meat and leans against a tree.

I rip a small corner off the loaf and hand the rest to Dash. "I could pretty much kiss you over this." I lift the piece that I kept for myself. "But we should ration. There's no telling how long we'll be out here, and when we'll come across food again."

Dash nods, shoving the thing back into his bag and pulling out a bright red apple. "I got a few of these, too."

Setting my provisions to the side, I take the apple from him, gripping both sides and snapping the thing in two. I give him one half and keep the other, placing it with the glorious meal we've put together. If only we had some cheese to go with it.

Cheese.

Immediately, my mind assaults me with the memory of her, nibbling on a hunk of the salty substance, basically smiling and buzzing the same way I do with bread.

Dash interrupts my thoughts. "Can I ask you a question?"

"You just did."

Dash rolls his eyes. "You know what I mean."

"I'm waiting." I force myself to chew slowly and savor each bite of the bread.

"Why didn't you...*eat* those hunters? You know, like drain them of their blood the way you normally do."

I inhale deeply, considering my response. "We were in a hurry."

"We're always in a hurry, and that's never stopped you before."

Gritting my teeth, I glare at the questioning redhead. "It was different this time."

"Bo?"

"Yes, Dash?"

"Have you at all? Since..."

He doesn't have to say another word for me to comprehend his train of thought. Since I marked Wren; since I tasted her sweet essence; since I sank my teeth into her flesh, and everything changed. "No."

It's the first time I've truly acknowledged it, to myself, to anyone else. I've known all along that the course of my existence had altered that day, but I've done everything I could to evade whatever was set in motion. I kept to the ruse of hating her, of wanting to end her life, because that's how it should have been. Instead, I gravitated toward her, curious about the connection I felt for her. My hatred for her turned into pure rage for anyone who so much as glanced in her direction.

"Do you want to talk about it?" Dash pries a bit further.

"No." I shut him down. It's not like I'd know what to say anyway. I can't seem to make sense of any of this myself. I shouldn't feel the way I do for her, and yet, I find it all-consuming.

"We're going to get her back, Bo. I don't know how, but we will."

I sink my teeth into the flesh of the apple and ignore the unfamiliar concern that settles in my core. It's unlike anything I've ever known to worry about another.

Even as close as Wes and Dash have been to me, I've never felt quite like *this*. No, this is foreign, new, and a bit terrifying.

Eyeing that other package Dash had retrieved, I snatch it and tear open the side, desperate for something to distract me from my *feelings*. Blinking a few times, I allow my mind to catch up. Carefully, I pull one of the many small things out, tilting it around in my hand to take a better look.

"What is that?" Dash steps closer.

"Our saving grace." Or our demise, but I don't tell him that part.

One thing is certain though, I will do whatever it takes to make sure Dash's words ring true. We will save her if it's the last thing I do—even if that means I die in the process.

CHAPTER 10
Wren

I knock on the door just like Franny told me to, holding my breath in anticipation of the unknown. If I choose to do nothing, I'm a dead woman, so what's the harm in being bold and taking risks?

Wes's beast side came to me, told me that I have to act in order to save us both. He alluded that we must consummate our mate bond for Wes's powers to return. And without those, we stand no chance of making it out of here alive. We need every advantage we can get, even if that means trusting a stranger. In this case, trusting two. Franny seems genuine, but there's no telling if it's an act to let our guards down. I don't really know much about this guard, but Wes is slightly convinced he could potentially be an ally. Given his connection to Franny, I hope it's true.

The lock on my door creaks, and the latch is turned slowly.

I step out of its way and ready myself for a battle if need be. One way or another, I am going to get to Wes.

A man, perhaps a bit younger than me, looks through the opening. "Yes?"

I study the softness of his expression, the hint of concern lingering on his brow. His demeanor is nothing like the other guards—completely absent of that volatile hatred and thirst for inflicting pain. He shifts his gaze toward the hallway and then back at me.

If I were in better shape, I could easily overpower him. But I'm not, and that would only cause more chaos.

"I..." My voice cracks and I clear my throat. "I need a favor, please."

The man doesn't get angry, he doesn't shove in and beat me with his baton, he doesn't even seem irritated at my request.

"My authority is limited in here, miss."

"I just need five minutes, that's all I ask."

He raises his brow. "Of what, exactly?"

I force myself not to glance down at the knife at his waist. The urge to fight is strong, but I must be smarter, more strategic, if I want to get out of this mess. I tilt my head toward Wes's cell. "I need to see him."

He shakes his head but keeps his voice low. "No, not happening."

Tears well in my eyes, partially from the possibility of this plan failing, and from wanting to appeal to his empathetic side. "I don't think he has much longer. He's not healing from his injuries."

"It's too dangerous, if someone catches you in there, it's not only your head, it's mine, too." He tugs on the handle. "The risk is too high."

I shove my foot in the open space so he can't shut the door. "I just want to say goodbye, face to face. Please, I'm begging you."

I take his pause to run a few scenarios through my head. I could use what little strength I have to kick him in the chest, knocking him to the ground. If I don't render him unconscious, I'd have to kill him, because I couldn't gamble with him stopping me. I'd have to figure out which key unlocks Wes's door, and hope I could get in without drawing the attention of any other guards. And then there's the possibility that the mate bond doesn't ignite Wes's powers. But if it doesn't, at least we'll be together when we meet our demise, and that alone is enough to make all this worth it.

The man tilts his watch toward him. He clenches his jaw and lets out a breath. "You have two minutes, that's it, okay?"

Hope bursts throughout me. "Yes." I bob my head up and down. "Yes. Thank you."

He stiff-arms the door and stares directly into my eyes. "You follow my orders and do not run, deal?"

In another life, I would have lied, told him what he wanted to hear, and then turned on him the second the opportunity presented itself, but I can't afford to be that way, not when the variables are constantly changing. So instead, I tell him the truth, because that's all I can afford right now. "Deal."

I slither through the small opening and into the damp, empty hallway. My thoughts are taken back to the dream I had, only this time, the guard is guiding me along, not the hound. Together, we pause in front of Wes's chamber, my heart beating wildly in my chest for a million different reasons. My head goes fuzzy at the overwhelming nature of the endless outcomes that could come to fruition.

What if I'm wrong? What if this causes more harm than good? What if I've used up my one courtesy with this random guard? What if he gets caught and is taken to another post, leaving us with the rabid other men who would rather beat us than show us the slightest kindness? What if I ruin whatever Franny and this guard have because I was selfish in needing this time with Wes?

But, what if it's the difference between us surviving or not?

"Two minutes, the clock is ticking." The guard slides the key into Wes's lock and opens the door, moving me through the small space and closing it behind me.

I blink through the darkness to adjust my eyes and gasp when a large form completely consumes my body. I relax into him and wrap my arms tighter around his strong form. "Wes," I breathe.

He pulls away, gripping my face in his hands. His eyes dart back and forth to mine. "Are you fucking crazy?"

"We don't have long." I stand on my tiptoes and brush my lips against his.

Wes stiffens and hesitates, but gives in to my kiss, deepening it with a gentle intensity.

I tug him tighter, and he winces under my minimal force, reminding me exactly why I'm here. "Hey." I break from his mouth and stare at him. I trail my hands down to his waist and unbutton his pants.

"What are you doing?" His chest heaves from the labor he's already exerted.

"Do you trust me?" I ask him.

"With every fiber in my being."

I reach up and skim my hand over his battered face. "Then drop your pants and sit down against the wall."

Wes locks his eyes with mine and contemplates the severity of my request. For a split second, I'm convinced he's going to say no, to protest and persuade me to come to my senses. But despite my weakened condition and my frantic state, there's nothing more that I want than to be close to him. In our final moments, I consider that a gift from the universe—and a twisted cruelty by the fates.

Going to work on my own bottoms, I drag them over my ass, peeling them off my swollen and dirty body.

Wes watches me intensely as I stroll over to him, straddling his legs and kneeling over his lap. Just the minimal skin-to-skin contact is enough to send fireworks dancing across my flesh.

He shakes his head faintly. "You don't know what you're doing, Wren."

My name on his lips is another burst of pleasure in this torture chamber.

I graze my thumb over his bottom lip, tugging it down. "Yes, I do."

His erection pulses beneath me but he doesn't move otherwise. Wes remains still, allowing me to be the one in control.

If we were anywhere but here, I would take my time exploring his body, building us both up to magical bliss. I'd savor this experience with him.

His lips part and he sighs. "I wanted this to be somewhere romantic..."

"What's more romantic than life or death?" I force a smile, although I'm sure it comes out more pathetic than I intend. "Do you want this?" I ask him.

It's then that he finally raises his arm, hovering his hand beside my cheek, the width of his palm encasing the side of my face. "Only if you do."

I position myself closer, one arm wrapping around his neck, the other going between my legs to grip his shaft. I suppress my surprise by locking my mouth onto his. Our tongues dart out to dance with each other like long-lost lovers, moving in a way that would make you think we'd done this a million times before.

The room melts away and it's only me and Wes left behind.

No danger. No worries. No enemies.

Only, I'm not that fucking foolish.

I slide further, running the length of him over my slit. Without breaking from his kiss, I kneel taller and situate his cock at my entrance.

"Wren?" Wes breathes into my mouth. "There's no going back from this."

I pull his lip between my teeth. "I don't want to."

"The mate bond, I won't be able to resist it." His voice cracks with concern.

I tilt his neck up so he can meet my gaze. "That's the point." Not wasting another second, I push myself down, forcing his thickness inside of me. I fight the urge to drop my head back in both pain and pleasure and maintain my eye contact with him.

His lids flutter and his breath catches. "My love." And like he finally gives in to the temptation, he glides his hands over my thighs and grips onto my waist, digging his fingers into my skin and guiding me up and down.

My heart nearly leaps out of my chest when I catch a faint flicker of red spark in his eyes, but he shifts his focus before I confirm or deny.

"Keep looking at me," I urge him.

A light knock sounds on the door—a warning that our time is almost up.

"Wes, I need you to come for me."

"What?"

I tighten myself around his cock and increase the tempo, desperate to make sure this plan has any chance of succeeding. I don't know the intricacies of a mate bond, but I'd do anything to lock it in place.

"I want you to..."

But I cut him off before he can finish his statement. "This isn't about me right now, it's about you. It's about us. And what I want more than anything..." I press my mouth along his and try to persuade him with my kiss. "Is for you to come."

"Wren," he breathes.

I wrap my hand around the base of his neck, applying soft but firm pressure. "Do you want to please me?"

He nods while dragging one of his hands from my waist and placing it on top of mine, intensifying the force of my grasp. "Yes."

"Then make me yours, Wes, I'm begging you."

In a flash, I'm on my back and Wes is still between my legs. He keeps a hand under my head to protect it from the cold, hard floor, while the other is planted firmly to the side to keep the brunt of his weight off me. He could easily crush me if he wanted to—our bodies are drastically different in size in almost every way, and yet somehow, we fit perfectly together.

Wes closes his eyes and thrusts inside of me, his girth stretching me open.

My own body surprises me with what it's capable of taking.

"Wes." I dig my nails into his back and drag him closer and closer.

An explosion sounds in the distance, rattling the walls of our chamber, but it's no match to the eruption I feel building in my core.

Wes blinks up at me, flickers of red sparking his irises.

My mouth drops open and I gasp. "There you are," I whisper.

"Am I hurting you?" Wes pauses momentarily and the crimson begins to fade.

A tear betrays me by rolling down my cheek. "No." Because no amount of pain would ever *not* be worth this moment. "Keep going."

"Are you sure?"

"Wes, I swear to the fates, if you don't..."

Wes grins and crashes his lips onto mine, kissing me with an intensity unlike anything I've ever felt. His cock hardens and a moment later, he moans into my mouth, his orgasm finally crashing over him and into me. He slows his pace while he drags it out and stares into my eyes.

The glowing red orbs I thought I'd never see again glare back at me, sending me spiraling into my own climax. I pulsate around his shaft and my entire body trembles with the aftershock. Together, we ride out this temporary bliss until we're two euphoric bodies left here in this dirty cell.

Only now, Wes's beast side has joined us.

Wes presses a soft kiss on my lips and sits up, gently pulling himself out of me. "Fuck, Wren, you're bleeding."

I sit up on my elbows and revel in the surrealness of the fading moment. "What did you expect? You're built like a..."

He raises a brow. "Like a...?"

I shake my head and chuckle. "You'll have to ask me again when I'm not high on you."

Wes places his hand just along the outside of where he just wrecked. He mutters a few words and within seconds the pain subsides, and I'm left with nothing but pleasure.

"You did it." I fully sit upright. "You fucking did it."

But as I move closer, Wes stumbles a bit. "That took more out of me than it normally does."

"Wait." I catch up to the meaning behind his words. "It takes a toll on you when you heal me?"

Wes nods. "Usually it's manageable."

I climb to his side and hold his face in my hands. "No more, okay? Not until we're out of here, and we're far, far away. You use every bit of strength you have to tend to your own wounds."

His jaw clenches under my touch. "I can't do that."

I graze my thumb along his skin. "Yes, you can. Promise me, Wes."

His fiery gaze meets mine.

"Promise me," I repeat with more conviction.

"Please don't make me." Pain lingers in his voice.

"You have to," I insist. "You're our only chance of making it out of here. I need you to be strong for both of us."

Something I've never done before, give someone else the power to control whether I live or die. I've gone my entire life fighting my own battles, waging my own wars—but right now, I've conceded to this hauntingly beautiful man in front of me.

"Okay."

I grip his pants and toss them onto his lap and crane my neck to find where I had discarded my own. "That was more than two minutes, the guard must have gotten distracted by whatever that explosion was." I stand and slip into my leather bottoms, securing them in place. "But he gave us enough time to get the mate bond in place."

Wes doesn't respond as he finishes getting dressed.

"What aren't you telling me?" I ask him.

He leans against the wall, crossing his arms over his chest. He's trying to shut me out, but now that his powers are somewhat in place, I'd wager he can no longer lie to me. That's why he didn't want me to make him promise, because his word to me is something he cannot break.

The door to Wes's cell cracks open. "Time's up, you need to go."

Wes kicks off the hard surface and rushes over to me, his hands find my shoulders and guide me toward the opening. He leans down to kiss me, but I evade his lips.

"Wes?" My heart pounds wildly at the unknowns filling my mind.

"You can't get caught, Wren." He continues to move my stiff body.

"The mate bond..." It's the only thing I can think of that would make sense. Sex wasn't the only variable in consummating the link between us.

The guard latches onto my arm and tugs me through the opening. "We have to hurry."

"I'm sorry," Wes murmurs as the door closes us off from each other.

Anger and sadness and confusion consume me.

Was all of that for nothing? If I failed the mission, maybe we really are doomed after all.

Parla told me that I would have to kill Wes and consume his essence and I thought the only way to stop that from happening was to follow through with the dream I had of Wes's beast. To grant him the power to free us of this nightmare. Wouldn't his beast have told me if there was another step in the plan? Or what if I was woken up prior to getting to that part and I've been a fool this entire time thinking it would be *that* easy?

It's clear that *some* of his powers are back, but with how sporadic they came and went in those few moments, there's no telling how long they will stick around. My only hope is that it's long enough for Wes to heal, to become strong enough to at least save himself.

But the sinking pit in my stomach alerts me that hope is a useless thing.

CHAPTER 11

Wren

"What was that commotion?" I ask the guard before we reach my cell.

"Not sure yet. But you're lucky, it bought you a few extra minutes." He slides the key into my door and tugs me toward the opening. "Sector twelve is on high alert. Guard activity will no doubt be increased as soon as they clean that mess up. I'll do my best to stay positioned over here, but I cannot control where they send me." He flits his gaze toward the empty hallway and then back at me. "Get in."

Lucky. More like cursed.

"Why are you doing this? Being kind to me, to him?" I nod my head toward Franny's chamber. "To her?"

"Because good and evil are not what they want us to believe. Now hurry, before we both get caught." He nudges me through the threshold and shuts the door behind me. "I hope you got what you were after, because that can't happen again."

My heart rips in two at the weight of his words and the realness of the situation. I was convinced I would succeed, that my crazy and spur-of-the-moment plan would work. But with each passing second, the pit in my gut grows, reminding me that nothing in my life has ever been easy, so why would I expect it to start now? Doubt continues to creep in, and no matter how hard I try to fight it, it becomes all-consuming. I've always figured out how to get out of tight situations, but what if this is the one time my brain and brawn fail me for good? And for the first time in my life, it's not just my own ass on the line. It's Wes's. It's Bo's and Dash's. It's Franny's. People I never thought I'd have—taken too soon.

"Did it work?" A small voice calls out to me from the meager opening between our cells.

I exhale and make my way over to her, leaning against the wall and sliding down onto my ass. "I don't think so." I close my eyes and let the weight of my head fall back, bringing my knees forward and holding myself tightly.

"Wren…?"

"Yeah, kid?"

"I have a bad feeling."

"You and me both." My lids open in a flash. "Wait. Like a *feeling* feeling?" I lower my tone to a whisper. "A banshee one?"

"There's a burning under the surface of my skin. An itch in the back of my throat. A pulsing throb in my skull. An overwhelming sense of doom. I cannot shake it, and it only continues to grow in intensity." She pauses. "I don't know how I know this…but it's big."

"Big like a powerful demon big?"

"Maybe. I can't be sure."

"Wes," I breathe.

"What did you say?"

"Nothing." I shake my head. "Do your powers give you any insight on *when* it might happen?"

"No, not really. It's all muddled and being in here doesn't help matters. I'd venture to assume we don't have long."

Bringing my hands to my head, I rub my temples. It can't end like this; I won't allow it. I haven't fought and trained my entire life to die at the hands of the monsters who created me. I refuse to let Wes or Franny succumb to them either. I have to do fucking *something*.

Shuffling from across the room steals my attention. *Wes.* The fierce beast who holds more power than any other creature in this prison. "Wren," he calls out to me.

"Franny, I'm going to figure this out. I won't let you die in here." And because I need her to understand how serious I am, I add, "I promise."

"Don't make promises you can't keep, and regardless, you don't owe me anything."

At the end of the day, no one really owes anyone anything, but I have a lifetime of mistakes to make up for, and if I can begin by helping her, I'll do it without question. A month ago I would have been selfish and only focused on saving myself. Now, I'm sickened with the reality of that being no way to live.

"Will you keep me posted if anything changes?" I ask her.

"Of course."

I crawl from one side of my cell to the other to join Wes. Is it possible for a heart to break just from the thudding concern of not knowing how to fix the unfixable?

"I'm sorry," he blurts out as soon as I approach.

"How do we finalize it, Wes? You have to tell me, please." Because his beast side very well could be the only thing that has the potential of saving us all. Without it, we're a lost cause.

He remains quiet despite being the one that called me over here.

"Wes." I calm the rage that builds within me and focus on the severity of my next statement. "We don't have long. Something bad is going to happen, and I don't think I'm strong enough to fight."

"Let me heal you." His voice cracks with each word.

"No." It's not even an option in my mind. If Wes gives me some of his power, then he loses it for himself. Our best bet is to bank on Wes mending from his own injuries and conjuring his beast side. We need every ounce we can get and cannot afford for him to heal my measly injuries.

"Wren..."

"Damn it, Wes, you're not going to convince me otherwise." I fight the rage that builds within. "Do you not understand how careless you're being? Stop for a second and think logically. If you want to help me, you have to help yourself. That's the only way. So have a little chat with your beast side and tell him to step up his fucking game."

Another explosion sounds in the distance, this time a bit closer than earlier.

"If we're going to make it out of this, I need you to do everything you can to unleash your beast side." Never in my wildest dreams would I imagine that I'd be convincing a demon to embrace his demonic nature and truly desire it to happen.

Once upon a time, I hated all things demon. Am I still furious that they stole my family from me? Absolutely, but being lied to and conditioned to hate a species because of it pisses me off even more. They leveraged my hatred to fuel their agenda, whatever it may be. I've been used as a puppet, a soldier who was disposed of the second I deviated from their orders. I gave them my life. I fought and killed and did their bidding, and for what? Where has it gotten me? Nowhere but locked in prison with trust issues and a deep-seated thirst for getting revenge on who actually deserves it.

The demons of Prania are not the real monsters—the fucking administration running this place are. A bunch of hypocritical, power-hungry cunts.

That familiar sound of my door unlocking draws my attention toward it. Given it hasn't been long since I arrived, I don't startle, assuming it's our friendly guard coming to share an update on the random explosions causing chaos around us.

But I couldn't be any more wrong when I hear the voice of Dravin—Parla's partner and second in command. "Wren?" His voice is soft, calculated, and slightly comforting.

He's always been the more rational of the two. Which isn't exactly saying much considering Parla is a fucking lunatic dressed in pressed pantsuits.

I stand, my body going stiff as he enters my confinement.

He glances around, his gaze finally settling on me. Extending his hand, he says, "This is unacceptable. Come with me."

I stay firmly rooted in place. "What is this about?" I study his lazy posture and unkempt beard, the wisps of white giving away his older age.

"Our Furla Ain being held in a place like this is unspeakable." He motions once more. "Come."

With my arms crossed over my chest, I step toward him.

"Wren," Wes speaks through the grated barrier. "Don't fall for it. You're smarter than them."

I don't dare respond, because I don't want to give Dravin any more ammunition than he already has. Whatever he's up to, I will play along.

Dravin's expression softens when I approach, and he opens the door a bit further for both of us to fit through it. "This way, Ms. Oliver."

When I step into the hallway, the kind guard and I exchange a quick glance, but don't allow it to linger more than a second. I avert my gaze and walk alongside Dravin, past Wes's chamber and that of his other cellmates. I count the doors, making note of the locks on each of them and how far it takes to get from one end to the other. It's the little details that matter, the stuff people don't usually pay attention to. We round the corner and we're greeted by two more guards wearing standard-issue outfits, making them almost impossible to tell apart with their matching haircuts and arrogant demeanor. On a bad day, I could take down both of them, but it's the mystery lurking behind every corner that has me hesitant from acting just yet.

There's no telling how many more of them there are and the number of locks that stand in the way of our freedom.

"In here." Dravin places his hand on the small of my back and guides me to an open room.

I cringe at his touch and move to get away from him. The aroma is the first thing I notice, followed by the sight of fresh bread and large chunks of cheese sitting beside a steaming bowl of stew.

"You must be famished." Dravin strolls over and pulls out a chair from the small table and motions for me to sit.

I drag the thing from his grasp and scoot it in myself. "I've been hungrier."

Dravin strides over to the other side of the table, running his finger along the surface of it as he goes. He pulls out the only other chair and takes a seat. "May I?" He points to the chilled pitcher of water and nods toward the cup in front of me.

I eye him suspiciously and snatch the empty cup before he can pour anything in. I examine the inside, not seeing anything hidden within.

He chuckles. "I'd expect nothing less from you."

If they were going to poison me, they would have done it in the stew or various sides. I wouldn't so easily fall for the unsuspecting drink trick. I set the cup down, nudging it toward him in approval of his request, then turn my attention to the spread before me. They're probably assuming I would think they spiked my food, so it's possible they put the drugs in his, hoping I would swap the two. Meaning mine would be fine and his wouldn't be. But if they anticipated correctly, they might have guessed I'd do that, leaving the tainted food to actually be my own.

"What can I do to prove to you that the food is safe to eat?" Dravin sips his own drink and leans back in his chair.

"You could start by taking these off." I hold my hands up where the cuffs still remain on my wrists, suppressing any power that lingers inside of me.

"You know I can't do that."

"Can't or won't?" I raise a brow despite already knowing the answer.

Dravin picks up his spoon and points it at my bowl. "Eat, we have much to discuss, no sense of doing it on an empty stomach."

I let out a chuckle and reach for the glass he poured for me. "Right." I sip the cool liquid and revel in the satisfaction of tasting something so fresh. When his eyes are trained on something other than me, I cautiously steal glances around the room, desperately searching for anything that could prove useful in my future plan; I pray to a higher power that one will come to me.

"Fine, suit yourself." He breaks off a hunk of bread and raises it toward his mouth.

"Give me that," I interrupt him from continuing.

He blinks a few times as if processing the request. Latching onto the piece he had set back on the table, he holds it out to me.

I shake my head and nod to the one still in his grasp. "That one."

Dravin rolls his eyes and sighs, tossing the bread over to me. "Let me guess, you'd like my stew, too?"

Considering he hasn't taken a single bite of it yet, I'll pass on finding out the hard way if it was poisoned. As much as I'd love to chow down on every last bit of this food, it's not worth the risk. "Have at it." I push my own bowl toward him. My mouth nearly waters at the sight of the cheese, but I settle on the bit of bread I'm semi-certain is safe to consume.

I nibble at the edge and take my time with the bread. Guilt floats in and reminds me of Wes's and Franny's poor conditions. The only food we've been given has been stale leftovers that were barely edible, and no doubt tainted in one way or another. I only allow myself the pleasure of the bread as a means to gain any kind of strength in hopes of breaking out of here. Without Wes's healing powers, it's up to my own body to fend for itself. I've made it this many years on my own, what's a little longer?

"What do you want to talk about?" I grow impatient with the game he seems to be playing.

Dravin pats the corners of his mouth with his napkin. "Well. I do have quite a few questions. Curiosity really, and a few formalities."

"Like?" I bite off some of the bread and chew it slowly.

"Perhaps we should start at the beginning, where everything seems to get blurry."

"You mean when you and Parla groomed me to be a demon assassin and used my anger as a tool?"

Dravin feigns surprise. "If I'm remembering correctly, you came to us. You sought out our training programs, our expertise."

"I was a child." I slam my fist into the table.

Dravin flits his gaze behind me and lifts his hand to dismiss whoever is no doubt standing in wait to strike at a moment's notice. "We have many young recruits; you were no exception to that. You just happened to be the most gifted of them all."

"You used me."

He runs his hand through his beard. "I can see how you'd think that."

I narrow my gaze at him. "Think it? You're going to pretend it's not the truth? That your army isn't made up of orphaned kids who are full of rage and an insatiable hunger for revenge?"

"If that's what you choose to believe, there's no convincing you otherwise. You are a rather strong-willed woman."

I let out a quick and humorless laugh. "And that's the problem, now, isn't it? I'm no longer bending to your will, and that's become an issue for you." I circle my finger in the air. "And that's why you've locked me in here, because I'm not an asset anymore, I'm a fucking liability."

"Oh, Ms. Oliver, that is where you are mistaken. You are very much still an asset to our cause."

"Cause? Seriously? What the fuck does that even mean? What good could you possibly think you're doing here? Your main focus is to eradicate anyone who isn't like you. How are you okay with that?"

Dravin plops his elbow on the table and rests his head in his hand. "You're aware that not too long ago, you were fully supportive of our mission."

"Well, I changed my fucking mind."

"I see." He pauses briefly. "And that explains why instead of eliminating the target, you spread your legs to him instead."

"Are you fucking serious? *That's* what you think this is about?" I grit my teeth. "You think that lowly of me?"

"What else am I supposed to believe when our top hunter suddenly goes AWOL? Feel free to fill in the gaps for me if there's another version of the story."

"I almost died." The memory of that day comes floating in—flashes of the fight, locking eyes with Wes, not having any clue what the rattling in my chest was, and then being attacked and left for dead. "If it weren't for my *target*, I would have perished."

"So, one demon shows you the smallest kindness and you disregard everything you've worked toward your entire life?"

I open my mouth to speak, but I realize what he's doing. He's baiting me into admitting there are others. I'm playing right into his hand and if I'm not careful, I'll give away more than I should. "Maybe we could discuss that mission itself, how I was told it was routine, nothing out of the ordinary. You failed to mention it would be a challenge."

"I never once doubted your abilities, why put that in your head if it weren't necessary?"

"Are you missing the part where I almost died? Perhaps if I were better informed, none of this would have happened at all." Although, I'm glad everything has played out the way it has. Without this entire chain of events, I wouldn't have snapped out of my sheep-like mentality.

"And here you are, very much alive. It appears everything worked out the way it should have." Dravin brings his glass to his mouth and swallows some of the water before continuing. "We can fix this; get you back on track." He shifts his gaze around the room. "It doesn't have to be like this."

"Even if I were to agree, you know damn well that isn't true." I shake my head. "Parla would never allow that to happen."

"Perhaps if you provided her with some information, she'd be willing to forgive you of your wrongdoings."

I laugh again. "You're not serious, are you? You're as delusional as she is, as I once was. She's a monster, there's no convincing her of anything."

"I'll do everything in my power to prove you wrong." Dravin leans forward in his chair. "Tell me who you're working with."

I mimic his movement and narrow my gaze at him. "I don't know what you're talking about." The honest fucking truth. Parla was going on about some kind of spell blocking the extraction process, and I couldn't have been any more lost at what the hell she was talking about.

The only witches I've dealt with in the last few years have been those to spell my safehouses and maintain the integrity of keeping them concealed from both demons and hunters alike. My privacy has always been a priority and recent events have clarified the importance of that.

"You're making this harder than it has to be." Dravin plops a cube of cheese into his mouth and that alone makes me want to stab him in the throat with the spoon only inches away from my hand. "She won't stop until she gets what she wants. You're better off to just give in and forego whatever torture she has in store for you."

"Is that supposed to rattle me? To scare me into submission? There isn't a single thing either of you could do to me to make me help you ever again. I'd rather fucking die." I shove the rest of the bread into my mouth and savor the lingering warmth still locked within its tender insides.

"We don't want that to happen, Wren, none of us do."

I glare at him. "Because I'm too valuable, not because you care."

"You have this all wrong."

I reach for my cup, washing down the minimal substance I felt comfortable enough to consume. Standing, I set the cup down with force, the bit of water remaining sloshes over the sides. "No, you do. You're a fool if you think I'd ever make this easy for you. You want answers? Why don't you give me some? What's the end game here? What's *really* going on? You use the story of war to disguise the hidden agenda. You create fear to propagate the compliance of everyone involved, keeping us in the dark about the bigger picture."

Dravin steadies his gaze between me and whoever is behind me.

"Are you fucking done with this good cop/bad cop charade?" I shove the offering he had tried to win me over with toward him, spilling the contents all over the table. "I will not be a puppet any longer!" I yell at him.

A shadow approaches from behind but I anticipate it coming from a mile away.

Fucking amateurs.

I shove the blunt end of the handle of the spoon right into the attacker's eye socket, twisting it and yanking it free.

The man screams and reaches for his face, giving me the perfect opportunity to place my hands around his head and snap his neck. His body falls to the floor with a thud and another man just like him appears.

I duck to block his blow and kick at his legs, knocking them out from under him and sending him next to his fallen comrade. "This isn't personal," I tell him knowing it wasn't too long ago that I was just like him, a soldier doing whatever I was told. It's not his fault that he's ignorant to the truth. Still, I cannot allow him to live, not when his very existence threatens my chance of ever getting out of here.

"Fucking bitch," he mutters while trying to regain his footing.

I slam my fist into his face and straddle his chest, pinning him to the ground and landing blow after blow across his face.

His nose cracks and sends blood trickling down and into his mouth. It splatters onto my face, misting me like a ripened orange does when you break it open. He tries to wrangle free of me but is too surprised by my overpowering that he can't seem to find a way to buck me.

A sharp clicking of heels threatens to steal my focus. Parla's annoying voice follows. "Wren Oliver, you have been charged with aiding and abetting a criminal of the highest caliber. With attacking and killing our kind, and numerous other offenses. You are sentenced to live out your days in Rock Bridge, pending parole, given your cooperation."

I continue to hit this man. "I. Will. Not. Cooperate. With. You." Each word is another fist to his blood-soaked and swollen face. I don't even realize that he's stopped moving until something sharp is jabbed into my neck. "I will get out of here. You fucking watch."

An explosion rattles the building and small pieces of debris float down from the ceiling.

"We'll get answers out of you one way or another." And as the crippling realization that I've lost control consumes me, I'm taken under by whatever they injected into my veins.

Once again, making me believe that the end is finally near.

CHAPTER 12

Wren

My arms ache from the restraints holding them in place.

I draw in a breath and lift my heavy head. My eyes fight to open, but when they do, I wish they hadn't after all.

Wes. Standing in the center of the room with chains around his wrists and ankles securing him to the concrete floor. His tired gaze meets mine, and it's like a thousand knives take turns slicing through my heart.

Franny was right, death would be coming soon. And here I am, staring it in the face.

"Oh, good, you're awake." Parla approaches from the side, stopping a few feet away. She crosses her arms over her chest and juts out her hip. All attitude, all the time. She glares over her left shoulder and then nods toward me.

"Wait," I call out, unsure what the fuck I plan on saying next. Maybe if I stall them enough, *something* will happen. Perhaps a fucking miracle from the universe.

She blinks at me, clearly annoyed with having uttered a single word. "What?"

I look at Wes, and back at her. "Why are you doing this?" I take note of the rest of the room I can make out without being too obvious. Rollo, the old man who showed me kindness is avoiding us all and fiddling with his magical devices. A guard stands behind him, and there are at least two more posted up by the door.

Parla taps her pointed shoe against the floor. "You wouldn't understand."

"Enlighten me." Anything to prolong the inevitable while I run possible scenarios through my head. There has to be *something* we can do to get out of here. I gently tug at my wrists and grow weary of ever escaping the restraints. Wes seems impossibly bound, too, making this whole thing that much more difficult.

"I'm rather ambitious."

I study her otherwise beautiful face, noting the hard lines on her jaw and the sharp slope of her nose. I catch a slight twitch of her lip, like she's not quite being truthful. "And?"

Wes clears his throat. "Who hurt you?"

She rolls her eyes, but that alone is a giveaway that he struck a nerve. "No one."

"It was a demon, wasn't it?" He grips the chains and repositions his footing to focus on her.

Parla steps closer to me. "You think you love him, don't you? That he's in love with you?" She shakes her head. "They're incapable of such, and you know damn well it won't end well. I'm doing you a favor, Ms. Oliver. The sooner you're cut from his compulsion, the better. Although..." She swipes my hair off my shoulder and skims her fingers over the mark left behind by Bo. "There's no escaping that one. You're better off dead."

I shrug and try to evade her touch but it's nearly impossible tied to this chair. "You don't know what you're talking about. *One* of them hurt you, that doesn't make them all bad. That doesn't justify eradicating their whole species from our realm."

She dryly laughs. "Oh, you think I'm going to stop there?"

I process the severity of her statement. "You can't do that."

"Watch me." Her cheeks turn up into a devilish grin. "And you will help me do it."

"You're out of your mind."

"You have no choice." She pauses and looks me up and down. "You are making it rather difficult with that spell we can't seem to crack. But don't worry, we will break you one way or another."

"Why me? Why not another one of your many minions?"

"That is the ultimate question, isn't it?" She lets out a breath. "Must be tied to your lineage, but you're only one of the few who can actually survive after consuming a demon's essence. Most can only do a few months of it and then their weak little souls give out. You've been doing it since you came to us and we've been harvesting that power from you in batches, well, until a little over a year ago. That must have been when you found a witch to block us."

"You're giving me far more credit than I deserve. I didn't have a witch do anything to me."

Parla tips my chin up to look at her. "There's no sense in lying, we will figure it out."

But if what she's saying is true, why have they, all of a sudden, lost access to the demon energy remaining inside of me? I truly never have had a witch put a spell in place, so it had to have been done without my consent. Not that I'm upset about that, I'd just like to know what the hell is going on. Maybe if whoever did that would have told me back then what was happening, it would have saved me all this torment now.

"Why do you need all that power anyway, what do you plan on doing with it? Clearly, you don't *only* care about killing them; you want their energy, too."

"You are a curious little shit, aren't you?"

"If you're going to kill me, what's the harm in telling me what I'm going to die for?"

"Oh sweetheart, I have no intentions of ending your life. You're far too valuable to me alive." Her eyes bore into mine in a way that sends a chill down my spine. "But if you must know. The goal was always to reopen the borders."

My mouth falls open slightly. "What? I thought..."

She smirks and nods. "Because that's what we want you to think. That we're the reason it's in place. Otherwise, if our population believed it wasn't us, chaos would ensue. We keep the peace this way."

"The peace?" I laugh. "Having every single citizen afraid of the other is what you call peace? Pitting us against one another and justifying all the violence, and for what, your broken heart? News flash, *sweetheart*, you're not that important. People are betrayed every single day and they don't start wars over it.

"Do you not care about anyone other than yourself?" I nod toward Rollo, who appears to be practically crawling inside his own skin trying to escape this place. "Witches aren't even demons. What could he have possibly done to deserve this?"

"I don't have to explain myself to you." She motions to Rollo. "Now."

"You were fine with it a second ago, but now that I've struck a nerve you're done. It's almost like you *know* what you're doing is fucking wrong." I crane my neck to face the guards at the door. "Don't you see what she's making you do? This is *wrong*."

Parla grips my chin and yanks my head back around. "The demons and their bringers are the evil of this world, and they must be purged."

The same mantra I have told myself time and time again to justify all the killing I've done. There was a small part of me that felt it was wrong, but I clung to the image of my dead mother and childhood home burning to the ground to fuel the hatred I had for them. I slaughtered countless demons who were only trying to survive this hell that they were trapped into with no chance of escaping.

I suck in a breath and spit onto her polished and prim face. "Fuck you." I yank at the restraints around my wrists and block out the pain of my skin being torn under the pressure. My gaze meets Wes's, frantically hoping that his beast side will surface. "You have to do something, please."

He slowly shakes his head. "This is the only way."

"You can't possibly believe that." My heart shatters at seeing the defeat lining his features. How have they been able to break this unbreakable man?

Rollo kneels at my side. "I'm sorry," he whispers.

"No, whatever you're about to do, don't do it. You don't have to do it. I'll do anything else, just let him go."

Parla firmly grasps Rollo's shoulder. "Continue or I will find someone else to replace you." She trails her eyes from him to stare into mine. "First, you will end your boyfriend, and then, when the one who marked you comes for you, because there's no doubt in my mind that he will, you will kill him, too. And with that beacon on your neck finally fully engaged, you will become a magnet for every single creature left here in Prania. Once you have eliminated them all and I have broken the barrier, that's when the real fun will begin."

Rollo mutters an incantation and lightly holds onto my hand. Something flickers in my chest and no matter how hard I fight it, I feel him enter my core. He takes Parla's hand in his other one and I watch in horror as whatever evil plan she has in place unfolds before me.

"It's done," he says while standing and averting his gaze to the floor. He steps away and returns to his place in the corner of the room.

"Wiggle your right foot," Parla tells me.

I comply without a thought, moving the thing to and from.

"Okay, now your left hand."

I do as she commands, my stomach turning at the loss of control over my body.

An explosion shakes our room, this one sounding the closest of all the rest. I will whoever is causing that chaos to plant one in here and kill each one of us before Parla can possibly get her way. I'd rather be dead than give this bitch any more power than she's already stolen.

"Guard, her restraints." She turns her attention to me. "You will not move unless I tell you to."

Despite my internal struggle, I nod in agreement.

The young man unlocks the cuffs on both my ankles and my wrists, leaving me free to escape and snap each one of their necks. But no matter how hard I try, I cannot bring myself to act on my desires.

"Stand."

I rise to my feet. "Please, don't do this."

"Approach the demon."

My body betrays me, stepping closer to this man who I share a fated bond with.

"It's okay," he whispers. "Don't fight it. You must do as she says. You get to live this way."

"I don't want to live without you." My voice cracks alongside my heart with each spoken word.

"I'll always be with you." Wes sighs. "I'll be in the sun that warms your skin on a bright day; in that bite of cheese that you savor because it's your last; I'll meet you in your dreams and maybe then I can give you the life you deserved; I'll be the partner I never got to be in this lifetime. And when it's finally your time to cross over, I will find you in the next life. I will always find you; I promise."

Tears well in my eyes. "Why didn't it work?"

Wes raises his upper lip to expose his fangs. They glisten under the fluorescent lighting.

I lower my voice even quieter than it already was. "You have to mark me?"

He nods, shifting his focus to the bitch behind me who is whispering to either the guard or Rollo, I can't be sure from this angle.

"Mark me, Wes. Please, I'm begging you. Fucking do it."

Wes grips the chains holding him in place. "I can't. And even if I could, there's no telling if it would work. If I would be able to save you. If you comply, you'll live, that's the only thing I'm sure of, Wren. You have to do whatever she tells you to."

I shake my head. "No, I won't do it." I speak louder. "Can I hug him, please? Give me that, Parla. If you understand the loss of love at all, you'll at least let me say goodbye."

"I don't owe you a damn thing." She approaches my side and places a small but deadly dagger in my hands. "You will do nothing but what I command you, do you hear me?"

My mind urges me to drive the thing into her cold heart, but my body won't allow it. Here stand the two most powerful beings in this whole prison, both completely unable to access their powers.

"It's okay," Wes reassures me again. "I will love you either way."

I study the delicate yet rugged features of his face, the thickness of his brows, and the ever so gentle curve of his lashes. Lips that I've kissed far too few times, and eyes that I wish would glow as they stare into mine.

Where has his beast side gone and why has it chosen to abandon us? I thought he loved me, cared for me, wanted me. But all I can see is that he left me and Wes here when we needed him the most. Why convince me to secure the bond but leave out one major fucking detail?

"Parla, please." I plead with her one last time.

"Kill the monster."

I inch closer to Wes, the dagger poised between us, aimed at his chest. "I can't stop it..." Uncontrollable tears stream down my cheeks, but they're mine, not some creation of Parla's command.

Wes doesn't move back, he doesn't try to avoid the inevitable. He embraces it like a long-awaited hug from a loved one. He lowers his arms to the side, allowing me to advance on him with nothing getting in the way. His body softens in anticipation of the end. "I will find you."

"You promise?" I continue forward despite conjuring every ounce of strength I have to withstand her authority.

"With all my heart." Wes blinks and for a split second, there's a flicker of red that ignites in his eyes, but as quick as it appears, it's gone again.

Could the mate bond be in place enough that he's telling the truth? I'll never know, but I accept the comfort that I will see him eventually, one way or another. We will get our happily ever after in a different life.

Something stirs inside of me, but I'm afraid it might not be strong enough to overpower Parla. "I'm sorry." I collapse into him, shoving the weight of the dagger forward.

Parla triumphantly gasps from behind me, but I refuse to let her win that easily.

"Now, Wes!"

Without wasting a single precious fucking moment, his fangs pierce the flesh on the side of my neck. Pain and pleasure ignite under my skin and my eyes nearly roll back in my skull.

Wes's arms do what they can to hold me upright despite the chains hindering him from having a full range of motion. His moans vibrate my tender skin, and his touch warms my body.

Mark him, a voice rings through my mind. *Do it*, it calls out louder.

"Kill him," Parla screams at me.

But one of the commands is stronger than the other, so I comply, biting into the exposed part of his shoulder closest to me.

Wes tenses and groans, his temperature rising to the point it becomes painful to be this near him. But no amount of torment could be worse than killing my fated mate.

Blood pools in my mouth and I swallow the coppery liquid down. Once I'm certain I've done what I was supposed to do, I break away and meet his gaze.

His shock and surprise match mine, but I'm riddled with fear that I have done something terribly wrong. That this isn't what he wanted. I asked him to mark me, but he never asked me to mark him. I've done this against his will and what if he never forgives me for this blatant disregard for his autonomy.

Through clenched teeth, Wes mutters, "Get back."

"I'm sorry." A drop of his blood rolls down my chin. "I'm so sorry."

"I said *kill him*," Parla yells once more.

I turn on my heel, regaining control over my body with each movement. "No, you said to kill the monster." I twirl the blade in my grasp. "And the way I see it, you're the only one of those in this room."

Parla's eyes widen in horror at the sight before her.

The trained assassin she betrayed, stalking toward her with the knife she so foolishly gave.

"Do something!" She clumsily steps back and shakes Rollo. "Guards!"

As much as I want to slit her throat right now and get it over with, there's still the matter of Wes being tied to the chamber floor. I refuse to allow her to command these pathetic excuses for men to end his life while I'm distracted with her.

But to my continued surprise, Wes is no longer in the condition he was only seconds prior. No, his entire body burns red hot, flames attempting to flicker along his skin.

"Get back," he grunts again, his voice strained. "I don't want to hurt you."

A low and throaty rumble sounds from deep within him, and it's enough to cause Parla's minions to hesitate in advancing him. They're no doubt just as uncertain of what's about to happen as we all are.

"What are you waiting for?" she yells at them once more.

Two almost identical looking men spare a glance at each other and then advance. I shouldn't discard my only weapon, but without thinking twice, I reel my arm into position and send the blade soaring across the room and through the chest of the one closest to Wes.

Wes roars and I can't quite tell if he's in pain or simply frustrated. He wraps his burning hands around the chains attached to the floor and pulls with all his might. The concrete where the thing is anchored buckles but doesn't give yet.

Three more soldiers run into the room and that's when I fully comprehend how outnumbered we are in this place.

Will that stop me from fighting to the death? Absolutely-fucking-not.

I take off into a sprint toward them, sliding to the floor at the last second and knocking one of them onto the ground. I fumble with the knife tucked into his waistband and drag it out, shoving it rapidly into his torso. One down, many more to go.

Adrenaline pumps through my veins and for the first time in a long while, I feel right at fucking home.

A random guard latches onto the back of my head, snatching me by the hair and yanking me off his lifeless comrade. "Fucking bitch." He kicks me in the side and pulls his foot up to stomp on my head.

Little does he know, I've been in this position countless times before, and his carelessness is no match for my cunning. With the handle of the knife still poised in my grasp, I roll out from under his attack and drive the sharp end into his thigh, grinding it in place and fully fucking enjoying the sheer terror that devours him.

"Who's the bitch now?" I slide the blade out and rise to my feet. Grabbing a fistful of his hair, I tug his head back and make a clean cut straight across his neck.

Blood splatters onto my face and I smile as I shove him onto the floor to finish bleeding out. I skim my gaze over the men standing in wait, their natural instincts causing them to consider whether this battle is worth dying for. "Who's next?"

"Enough," a familiar voice calls out from behind me.

Dravin.

Over my shoulder I catch him muttering something to Parla.

Wes, still struggling with whatever transition he's going through, burns hotter with each passing second. The temperature of the room rises along with him, and I consider how much longer we can stay in here at this rate.

"What are you waiting for?" Parla screams at the men. "You're telling me you can't take down *one* girl?"

As if coming to a collective decision, they advance on me. I try to count them, but I lose track after seven blurred figures charge at me. I smirk, ready to accept my fate either way.

I swipe the blade through the air, hoping to make contact in some capacity. I duck to avoid a fist as I'm met with another kick to the chest. I grab onto the foot and circle, creating a diversion from the brunt of the attacks. I send that man into the throng of other men and get hit from behind with a violent burst of air. "What the fuck?" I blurt out through my ragged breath.

Parla's hand remains extended while the other is latched onto Rollo tightly while he mumbles something beside her. She's channeling his magic to try to win this fight. And if I'm not careful, she very well could.

It's one thing for her to use her pathetic soldiers and her own weak attempts to subdue me, but I'm no match to old magic. I could easily cast a knife through the air and end Rollo, eliminating her assistance, but despite him aiding in my torture, I know he's only doing it to save his own life. I can't fault him for trying to stay alive. Especially when he has shown moments of benevolence to me when given the opportunity.

A laugh bubbles out of my chest. "You're too much of a coward to fight your own battles."

She slams another burst of power into my chest, knocking me off-kilter and rattling my core. She rapid fires two more, then follows it up with some kind of paralytic magic, rendering me incapable of moving a single inch. "Your strength," she spits through her teeth. "Is only because of me. Don't you dare for a second question that."

The heat in the room rises.

She flits her attention toward Wes briefly and then to the men behind me. "Subdue her." When they hesitate, she adds, "Now!"

Dravin raises his hand to put them at ease. "I'll do it." He strolls across the room and pauses at my side. "Cuffs?" he asks a guard. Dravin kneels, his gaze meeting mine. "This could have been easy, Wren, but you always have to make things difficult." His clammy hand reaches out to grasp mine, securing the restraint on one of my wrists.

I inhale deeply, my jaw clenched tightly. My stare flicks to Parla, and then Dravin. I meet Wes's painfully fiery gaze and consider all the things we both could have done differently to end up anywhere but here.

"In another life," I whisper.

"What's that?" Dravin questions.

A sensation I've felt before flutters in my chest. Not from when I first saw Wes, but on another occasion. A quiet rumble starts low in my core, and rises to the top, like water shifting from a simmer to a soft boil. Only the more heat that it's exposed to, the greater the intensity it will become, spilling over the sides if not careful.

I wiggle my pinky, grateful for the smallest ounce of control it gifts me. But will it be enough when I'm this close to being bridled once again?

Dravin secures the other cuff in place, my heart dropping in response to the realization that this is all about to end and there will be nothing I can do to stop it. "It's better this way."

Wes roars loudly, garnering the attention of every remaining member alive in the room. He clutches his chains and pulls them straight from their concrete securement with minimal effort. With his legs still attached, he reaches to the nearest guard, latching onto him and dragging him toward him like a child's doll. The man's standard-issued uniform melts away at Wes's touch and he lets out a shrieking scream when his skin bubbles from the flame melting away his flesh. Wes sinks his mouth into the man's neck and rips his throat out, spitting it onto the floor and tossing the body aside. He grasps for more life forces to end but comes up short, another ear-shattering howl escaping him.

"There you are," I speak softly.

"Not happening," Parla cries. "Rollo, do something."

But as if he finally refuses to continue to aid her in this despicable act, he wiggles free of her hold and swipes a vial off the table. He pulls the cork, discarding it onto the floor without a care, and tips the thing back, swallowing the contents in one gulp. "No." He shakes his head and meets my gaze. "I'm sorry."

I struggle against the hold still keeping me in place, slowly breaking through it. A memory suddenly floats into my mind; Dash being held in place, his neck snapped in front of me, wishing like hell I could have reached him in time. I had caught his body as he collapsed to the ground, and my heart ripped apart knowing there was nothing I could do to bring him back to life. Our only saving grace was the fact that Dash's powers surfaced, gifting us with his life from his ashes.

But now, watching this man with thick wrinkles and endless gray hair, I know I couldn't possibly be that lucky twice in one lifetime.

He may not mean to me what Dash does, but it's still a life that doesn't deserve to die, especially not like this.

His shaking form hits the floor and Parla clutches her chest, her sights quickly moving from him to me.

I move faster than I ever have in my life and wrap the new chained cuffs on my wrists around Dravin's throat, using the weight of my body to fall back and pull with everything I can. My only regret is that I won't see the life leave his eyes when I end him for good. My trade-off is that I get to witness Parla's eyes nearly pop out of their sockets at her partner being murdered by the *girl* she thought she could screw over.

"You're next," I call out to her while waiting for Dravin to stop squirming under my authority.

She runs past me, shoving any guard she can toward us. "Do not let them escape."

An explosion shakes the walls and I have to press my eyes shut to protect them from the debris that flutters down from the ceiling.

When I open them, not only is she gone, but Wes is, too. His entire body is covered by guards attacking him in every direction. The fear I felt when I lost Dash floods through me and I can't get Dravin's heavy corpse off of me quick enough. I wiggle out from under him and shove his body aside, gasping for breath now that I'm free of his weight.

"Wes!" I scream through troubled lungfuls of air. Locating the first weapon I can find, I snatch an arm's length dagger from the man Wes had ripped apart. I latch onto one of Wes's attackers but instead of killing him swiftly, he pushes me and knocks me to the ground.

His face is lined with dread and his damp skin is ashy and pale. Instead of pursuing me, he takes off into a sprint out of the room, leaving us all behind.

I guess that's one way to eliminate the enemy. But it's also possible he's going to call in reinforcements, and there are only so many people I can take on at once.

Pressing my palm into the floor, I try to regain my footing again, my wrist aching under the pressure. It nearly gives out, but I grit through the pain and refuse to let it keep me down. "Wes," I cry into the crowd again.

The sound of knives slicing through flesh fills the space, along with grunts and groans caused by who fucking knows. Each moment that passes, I grow more concerned with the condition in which I will find him in after I kill every last one of these men.

Sweat beads on my forehead and trickles along my spine with the continued increase in temperature.

A roar so loud it rattles the chamber the same way the explosion had done earlier fills the space. I take pause, my heart pounding wildly in suspense for whatever will follow.

In a burst of red, the men surrounding Wes scatter, some of them quite literally flying through the air and slamming into the walls. One body slams into mine, knocking me down for what seems like the millionth time.

I stare in disbelief as Wes emerges from the chaos, his entire body a mixture of fire and smoke. His arms contort and he lets out a bellowing howl, his chin tilting toward the ceiling like he's in immense pain. I blink and his frame twists in an unnatural manner. I blink again and he's down on all fours, gasping for air and shoving his fist into the floor.

What is happening to him? Is all of this because I asked him to mark me? Because I marked him without his consent? What have I done?

I get my footing while I glance around at the fallen bodies, some whimpering and some completely still. None of them are a threat to us anymore—not in their condition. That's not to say more of them won't appear, though.

Our chance has finally come, and we need to act now if we intend on getting out of here. Parla escaped but there's no doubt in my mind that she's rallying every ounce of back-up she can to ensure we never leave this place.

I turn my focus back to Wes, but I struggle to make sense of what my sights have locked on. Black fur covers his face and lines the sides of his neck, claws protrude from his fingertips, and his hindquarters have...

I shake my head. *No, this can't be right.* I must have fallen hard and got knocked out.

But the more I stare, the more my disbelief evolves into complete and utter shock.

It's not until the man I'm fated to is no longer a man at all. He's a creature, standing on all fours, and yet he's nearly as tall as me, with onyx fur and flames dancing over his sleek coat. The only similarity between the two is those familiar glowing red eyes that I've yet to grow tired of seeing. I've come across werewolves and shifters of varying kinds in all my days, but never one of this caliber.

The details of the last few weeks rise to the surface, all pointing to an outcome I never expected. His control over Bo, the alpha of alphas. The occasions when the guys would slip up and mention the term *hound*. His sheer strength and almost impossibly rare brute force. The reason Parla was so fucking determined to get me to consume his essence, because it would be the most potent one in this realm— giving her immense power to do whatever she wished.

Wes is no man, he's a hellhound.

A myth to this world that I never imagined could be real.

Saliva drips from his exposed fangs and he slowly takes a step forward, the way a predator does before attacking their prey.

I place both hands in the air between us. "Wes, it's me."

I should be afraid, perhaps even run, but if this is what fate has decided, who am I to alter our course?

Wes

This has never happened to me.

None of it.

Not the immense pain, not the tethering between two forms, not the complete and total shift into my beast side.

I didn't even know it was possible.

I thought that was a myth—something made up in old fables that were an exaggeration of the truth. Some nighttime story told to children to lull them to sleep and ensure they stayed put in their beds.

But when every single bone in my body cracked and moved around, rearranging into something entirely different than I've been all my life, I knew.

I fucking told you, that arrogant voice in my head calls out. *Now, give me control.*

Never. I fight back. Because there's no telling what he'll do if I give him the reins.

Hunger, unlike anything I've ever experienced, threatens to consume my entire focus. For what exactly, I'm not sure. A burger, a human heart, maybe a piece of chocolate cake. I don't know, but I want it all.

Then, take it all, my beast suggests.

I ignore him and blink through the lids of my shifted form. I try to take in my shape, noting the fur covering my hind legs and side. My entire being is thickly covered in a black coat. Saliva drips out of my gaping mouth and as strange as this new body is, it's oddly freeing. It's strong, nimble, and full of energy, both a blessing and curse, considering I want nothing more than to run around in circles and chase my fucking tail. What a strange thing to desire.

We have time.

No, we don't. I cautiously move forward like a baby taking its first steps.

"Wes, it's me," Wren says with her hands outstretched.

I open my mouth to speak to her, but it comes out as a growl. I guess being in my shifted form doesn't exactly offer the best communication. I get closer, only to find that my continued presence seems to induce the fearful look gracing her features. The exposed teeth, heavy breathing, and salivating mouth don't help the situation either. Not to mention, despite being on all fours, I'm nearly looking her in the eyes.

Still, I hope that she trusts me enough to continue. I lower my head, inching closer to her until the top of my scruff rests against her still extended hand. I brace myself, unsure if she will accept me in this form. It's one thing for her to want to be with me when I'm mainly a man, but now, I'm all hound.

There's nothing wrong with us, my hound snaps at me.

Then why are you just as nervous as I am?

Things were already complicated when a demon was fated to a hunter—I can't imagine what must be going through her mind as that demon she had only just grown to accept has shifted into a blasphemous creature.

Wren's cool fingers weave their way through my fur, melting the tension in my bones like a hot knife on butter. I nestle into her touch and she responds by wrapping her arms around the base of my neck and hugging me tightly.

"I thought you were going to fucking eat me," she laughs into my side.

My own laugh comes out like another muffled growl. I really have to stop trying to do normal human things in this form.

How do I shift back? I question my hound, because the realization that I have no idea how to control the transformation suddenly hits me.

So soon?

I'm distracted by his arrogance and completely miss the threat incoming from Wren's flank. A man reaches for her, yanking her free of me and sending her into the hard floor. I act, not even hesitating, by pouncing on him and pinning his shaking body to the concrete. I latch my mouth around his jaw and rip the bottom half of his skull off. I toss it aside, the metallic of his blood bursting my tastebuds to life. My hound takes over, clawing his chest, making damn sure there's no way he could ever recover from his wounds.

He was already dead, you idiot, I tell him.

Don't lie, you're enjoying this as much as I am.

He overpowers me once more and rushes to another whimpering guard, latching onto his torso and flipping him over. The guard lets out a yell, but it's no use, neither I nor my hound intend on allowing him to live. Not after he threatened Wren's life.

Time becomes this bizarre passing thing, and each moment is now counted by the lives we manage to end together. We take turns clawing and biting and devouring our prey. The only reason we stop is because the last remaining heartbeat in the room is our beloved.

"Wes!" she screams. "Are you fucking in there? We have to go."

I nod, but knowing how everything else I do seems to be lost in translation, I have no idea what this actually looks like on her end.

I need to shift back into my other form, hound.

But we're just getting started.

I crane my head around and latch onto my arm, biting it with enough pressure to cause both of us pain. I sense the lack of control slip for a brief moment.

"This way!" Wren motions while running out of the room. She dodges the incoming attack of a guard and drives a knife into his side, yanking it out and kicking him off his feet. She glances back to make sure I'm following her, not phased at all about the man she just killed so easily.

Because she is like us.

Finally, I agree with my other side.

Wren may be small, she might be dainty and beautiful as a flower, but she's poison wrapped in a deceiving package and she is my perfect match.

Wind caresses my fur as the three of us rush down the corridor and enter the hallway of chambers that have kept us captive for far too long.

Everest's gaze meets Wren's, then goes wide when he locks his sights on me. He fumbles at his side to retrieve a weapon. "Holy shit, behind you."

Wren rushes in front of me to block his path. "It's Wes, he won't hurt you." She looks over her shoulder. "Right, Wes?"

I expose my teeth on accident, not quite in control of all the mannerisms of a hound, yet. And I'm not entirely sure the beast side of me wasn't doing that for show. I pause in front of Tremont's door, sniffing around the thing and trying to find some way to open it. I claw at the thick metal exterior, penetrating it but not enough.

I need to shift, you fucking idiot. You're wasting time, and if you ruin our chance of getting out of here, I'll lock you back in a cage for good.

A loud roar bellows up and out of my chest, followed by the crunching of bones. I scream as the pain settles into every inch of my body. Snapping, popping, cracking. Everything becomes a blur of red-hot scorching agony until I'm left in the fetal position, completely fucking naked and whining like a baby.

Get it together, it wasn't that bad.

My hound is a real asshole.

I blink a few times to adjust my eyes and get used to the newness of being in my original form. Cool hands hover along my skin once more, grounding me to the here and now. "Wren," I mutter.

"Are you okay?" Her steady blue gaze focuses on mine. "Here." She shoves the clothes I was once wearing on top of my exposed body. "I thought these might come in handy."

"Yeah," I croak. "Thanks." I slide the pants over my legs and toss the shirt over my head. I cup her cheek in my hand and skim my thumb along the soft edge of her skin. "We'll talk later, okay? When this is all over."

There are a million things I need to say to her, but they'll all have to wait. None of this will have mattered if we get caught again and lose the little bit of an advantage we've gained.

"Okay." Wren nods, standing up and extending her hand to me.

I latch onto it and she helps me to my feet. I wobble slightly but regain my footing. I've spent my entire life with these two legs and somehow, they feel entirely foreign.

Because your true form is as a hound.

"Shut up," I accidentally say out loud. I grip Wren's shoulder. "Not you, I'm sorry." I point to my chest. "The idiot that lives in here."

An explosion rattles the walls of the building and causes the three of us to brace ourselves and cover our heads.

"What the fuck is going on out there?" I ask Everest.

He shrugs, "I'm not sure. They don't tell us much, only that we must protect the integrity of keeping our prisoners locked away."

My gaze trails to Wren's neck, where a fresh set of fang marks are now at home next to the ones that Bo had left on her. "Can you still feel him?" I reach out and skim the scar that remains from his marking.

Wren presses her hand against mine and sighs. "Yeah."

"Good." That means Bo is still alive. And given nothing has changed with Dash's supernatural abilities, he should be, too. For the first time since knowing both of them, I worry more for Bo's well-being than Dash's, considering Dash can resurrect if he dies. Bo is fierce and nearly unstoppable, but he's still capable of being killed. Being trapped in enemy territory only guarantees that will eventually happen if nothing changes.

Gripping the handle of Tremont's door, I tug the thing and pound on it with my other hand. "You in there?" I slam my fist against the metal exterior and it rattles in response.

"Wes, is that you?" The older man calls out.

"I'm going to get you out of there, and then we need to run." I turn toward Wren and Everest. "We need to free as many prisoners as we can."

Wren nods and rushes over to where Everest is standing and fumbling with his key-filled chain to find the one to open Wren's cellmate's chamber.

I hike my leg up on the exterior of Tremont's door and channel every ounce of strength I can muster. The heat along my skin rises, flames flickering to the surface and gracing me with their presence. To anyone else, the temperature would be unbearable, but to me, it's a familiar friend I welcome to my side.

"Come on!" I groan as the door bends to my strength. I yank the thing free from its hinges and pry it open enough to allow a person to slide through.

Catching my breath, I run my fingers through my hair to swipe it out of my face. "Tremont." I nod toward Wren and Everest. "Go with them." I flit my attention to my fated mate. "I have to find my people. I'll catch up with you soon enough, I promise."

"Wes," Wren calls out. "No." She reaches her arm out to me. "I just got you back." She rushes past the man I just freed. "I'll go with you."

I shake my head. "It's too dangerous. I need you to get them out. I'll find you."

Everest drops the keys onto the ground and frantically retrieves them. "I can't find the fucking master key."

The longer it takes for him to free this girl, the more danger Wren is put in.

I exhale a puff of smoke and take things into my own hands. I walk over to him, nudging him out of the way. "Keep looking for it." I repeat the same thing I had done on Tremont's cell, positioning my leg on the outside of the frame, and digging in deep to garner my strength. A guttural bellow escapes me and I fall back as the door gives way. "There. Now all of you, *out*." I look to Wren. "That includes you."

The whole fucking reason I allowed Wren to risk her life at all was to attempt to save my people—we can't be this close and I not try to find them. This can't be all for nothing. It's not until I'm a few feet away that I glance over my shoulder and catch sight of the person who appears from the shadows of their captivity.

I stop dead in my tracks, my heart pounding wildly. Slowly, I turn toward this girl with dark brownish red hair and a glistening stare. "It's you," I gasp, my mind not quite wrapping itself around the reality of seeing her face again.

"It's me." Tears well in her eyes and roll down her cheeks.

"You two know each other?" Wren points between the two of us.

"*You* two know each other?" The feisty red-head quips back, motioning to me and Wren.

I close the space between us in an instant, my arms wrapping around the small frame of this girl I thought I'd never find. I breathe her in and spin her in a circle before gently putting her back on her own feet. Gripping each of her shoulders, I look her over. "You're okay, you're really okay?" Aside from growing the hell up, she's otherwise unharmed. A small scar lines her brow and dirt speckles her body. Her clothes are tattered and aged, but it's nothing a long shower and a pint of ale won't remedy.

She shoves me hard in the chest and slaps me across the face. "What took you so long?"

My heart aches at knowing she's been here all along and I hadn't figured out how to break in and save her. "Blame your brother."

Her gaze shifts behind me as if she's looking for a ghost. "Is he? He's alive."

I reach for Wren, my arm lingering in the air waiting for her. "According to the mark on her neck."

Wren appears at my side, her fingers sliding around mine, and her other hand wrapping around my forearm. "You're Bo's sister?"

Tremont clears his throat. "Listen, I don't mean to break up this family reunion, but we should get going."

"Not by blood," Jade tells Wren. "But close enough." She glances over at Everest. "Are you coming with us?"

Everest steadies his gaze on her, like he's trying to make sure she's aware of just how serious the words that are about to come out of his mouth are. "I'm not going anywhere without you."

I ignore the brotherly instincts that arise and decide that's a battle I will wage another day. "Where's..." But before I can finish my question, Jade bows her head and rocks it back and forth.

"I'm sorry, Wes."

I swallow down the pain that rises and the guilt that follows. If I had only been smarter, more strategic, quicker—I could have saved her, too. Now, the only mother I've ever known is another casualty in this endless war.

I came to terms with the loss of her a million times over, but with the finality of it sinking into place, the wound rips open deeper than before.

Everest holds a key between his fingers carefully, like he's afraid he might lose it forever if he lets go.

"Is that the master?" I ask him.

He nods in confirmation.

I draw in a breath and squeeze Wren's hand. "How do we get out of here?"

Everest goes into strategy mode. "Sector twelve took the biggest hit. We're a few sectors over. If we can make it past whatever guards are still holding their ground, we have a clear shot out of here."

"How many are there?" I ask despite being afraid to know the answer.

"If you mean guards, there's no telling on any given day. Sectors though...there are eighteen." He points to the faint number painted on the wall, telling us that we're in the very last one.

I do the math quickly in my head and glance down the corridor. "Are we clear?"

"Yes, the other two prisoners were downgraded upon your arrival."

"We have six sectors to empty between here and freedom." I look at each one of the people around me. "Are you ready to fight?"

"I was born ready," Wren chimes in immediately, a grin forming on her beautiful face.

Tremont holds his cuffed hands in the air. "I'm not much help without my powers."

"Can you do anything about that?" I glance at Everest and then down the hall in anticipation for whatever army Parla is no doubt forming to stop us.

"Not yet, but if you broke out of the interrogation room and left behind any bodies, there should be something on one of them to get the cuffs off."

"Jade, stay close." I ruffle the hair on her head, falling into the routine of annoying her the way I had done in the past.

"I don't go by that anymore. Not since..."

The years aren't the only thing that has changed. She's older now, more mature, but more weathered, too. She's been through hell and that little girl who would run around picking wildflowers and insisting on making Bo and I jewelry out of them is no longer. Her innocence has been stripped and that's something that can never be replaced. It wasn't just me that lost a mother figure, it was her, too. And where I had Bo and Dash to fill that void, she had no one. She was left here all alone to eventually fall to the same fate that Mother did.

"What should I call you then?" I wrap my arm around her shoulder and pull her close.

She looks up at me, her eyes still red and watery. "Maybe I could get used to Jade again."

An explosion shakes the building, and we huddle together, the men shielding the women from the brunt of the debris that falls from the ceiling.

"I think they're hitting every sector!" Everest shouts over the echoing of the boom.

"There they are!" A man yells from the end of the hallway, which doubles as our only way out.

"Stay behind me," I tell them while stepping in front. Lowering my head, I let my powers rise to the surface, growing comfortable with that welcoming flicker of flame that nips at my skin.

CHAPTER 14
Wren

I get as close to Wes as I can without getting burnt. "I'm only staying back here because I don't want you to set me on fire."

He stalks toward the guards, swatting away their pathetic attempts to subdue him with tranquilizers. He grips one of them by the throat and raises their body completely off the ground, no doubt crushing their windpipe and then tossing them aside. "Who's next?"

I grin and find a gap between him and the wall that I can squeeze through, readying the blade at my side and going to work at what I do best. *Fight*.

First, I was stolen by monsters, and now here I am, fighting for them.

I guess that's what happens when you fall in love with the enemy.

Wes acknowledges me by giving me some space to evade his heat.

The temperature really does grow rather rapidly in such tight quarters. Part of me wants to reach out and touch it. To embrace the fire that lives within him, but I know better than to think I could do it without consequence.

I drive my blade into a guard's leg, yanking it out and shoving it into the same man's neck. Blood spurts out and I move on to my next target, going through the motions like my body is running on autopilot. I duck an incoming blow, and then take another to the side, the wind escaping my lungs temporarily. I spin on my heel and push my next target off balance and into Wes's grasp.

He snaps his neck, burning the man's cheeks in the process. Wes wrings his hands to free himself of the dead guard's melted flesh.

I pause mid-plunge as I'm about to end another life, only to realize the guard I had latched onto is actually on our side. "Fucking hell, you're going to have to take that stupid fucking outfit off. I almost killed you."

I release him and glance around to the rest of them, counting the standing bodies and hoping we didn't suffer a loss.

A fallen man groans and Wes kneels beside him to finish him off.

"I'm Everest, by the way." He extends his hand toward me.

I wipe the blood of my victims on my leg and place my palm in his. "Sorry about that, Everest. I'm Wren."

He shrugs. "Honest mistake." Everest grips the center of his buttoned-up shirt and rips them to the side, the buttons popping off and littering the already messy floor, revealing a plain white tee underneath.

Franny, or well, Jade, helps him out of the sleeves and tosses the thing onto a dead man. They exchange a bashful glance like an innocent crush would.

"Interrogation room, then clearing out the sectors one at a time, moving as quickly as possible. Got it?" Wes stares at each of us, his gaze lingering on mine.

Watching him take control like this sends a rush straight to a place we don't have time to stop and rectify.

The second we get a chance to breathe, that's another story.

As if he recognizes the blaze that burns in my own stare, he hides a smirk and steps over a body, walking headfirst into the unknown.

"Can you fight at all?" I ask the old man just standing like a bump on a log, eyes wide and a bit terrified. I follow Wes's path and the rest take up the rear.

"With my magic, yes. I'm rather useless without it."

Wes simmers the fire burning on his exterior and glances over his shoulder at me.

I quicken my pace to catch up to him, comfort settling over me at being by his side. I've never been the type to fall in line behind a man and that isn't going to change just because my fated mate is some powerful and mighty creature. His authority and control are sexy, but there's a time and place for it, and it won't take away from everything I've built and earned on my own.

He keeps his voice low. "We're carrying the weight of three others, you're aware of that, right?"

I look up at him. "There will be casualties."

His gaze trails down my body and back up to meet mine. "Let me heal you, please."

I breathe in deeply and train my attention ahead of us. "I'm fine."

Truth is, no matter how skilled I am at fighting, Wes is still our best chance of making it out of here alive. He needs to be at one hundred percent, not just for himself, but for us, too. I refuse to weaken him and risk everything because of some minor injuries.

We step into the room where everything changed. The bodies of those Wes ripped to shreds still lie on the floor, their blood and innards soaking into the concrete.

"Rollo!" Tremont gasps and rushes over to the dead man.

I suppress my sorrow and rummage for anything that could be of use. I snatch a set of keys off a guard and hold them out to Everest. "Does this have a master, too?"

"Here." He gives the one in his hand to Fran—Jade—and looks the new one over. "It appears so."

I slide a knife from another dead body and tuck it into my waistband.

"These marks." Jade nudges a corpse with her shoe. "Are animalistic."

I continue to check for loot and ignore the secret that is not mine to share.

"About that…" Wes says after what feels like an eternity. "When we get out of here, we have a lot to discuss."

I observe Jade out of the corner of my eye, her brow raised at Wes.

"I'd say so." She lets out a long breath. "My brother marked a hunter, and you're fated to her."

"That's probably not the most surprising of it all."

"You're not going to tell me Dash is dead, are you? Because I've been avoiding asking this whole time, afraid you dropped the ball on him, too."

Another secret that isn't mine to confess.

I stand and grip her shoulder as I pass. "Dash is alive."

"I don't understand why he would do this…" Tremont stands from his spot near Rollo and wipes away a tear.

"Him," Everest points across the room. "That guy should have something to get those cuffs off."

Dravin.

"I've got this." Wes holds out his hand to stop me.

I don't protest because I'd rather not have to look at that bastard ever again if I can help it.

"He was kind to me," I tell Tremont. "Parla made him torture me. The first time, he attached this black pain device to my chest and I swear he compromised it because there was this burst of light and it quit working. She was using him to abuse me, and he refused to allow it to go on, that's why he took his own life." I point to the discarded vial he consumed. "He drank that before anyone could stop him."

Everest approaches with a small silver-looking rock. He reaches toward Tremont, taking one of his hands into his, and waves the thing over his cuff. It unlatches and falls to the floor with a clang.

Tremont gives him the other one and rubs at his wrists once they're finally free. "Thank you."

"How do you feel?" I study him carefully, wondering if he's going to turn and use his magic against us. My hand rests readily on the knife at my waist.

Tremont takes in his fallen friend and then those around us. "Like we need to get out of here."

"Two master keys?" I point to Everest and Jade.

They nod and hold them for us to see.

"You can rip the doors off the hinges." I flit from Wes over to Tremont. "We'll hold off any guards that come our way. Got it?"

Tremont turns his wrist over, a crackling of magic rising to the surface like he's manifesting electricity. "Got it."

A million uncertainties run through my mind but I push them all aside and focus on the few things I can control. Like getting us out of here alive.

"You'll want to hang onto this." Everest shoves the silver apparatus into Tremont's hand. "The demons will be cuffed, too."

I rush to the entrance of this room to join Wes at his side. "You ready for this?"

He stares back at me, his eyes glowing redder than I've ever seen before. "Let's get out of here."

A place that is known to be inescapable. A prison where demons go to rot, to be abused, to die. A one-way ticket to their demise, with no chance of ever seeing the light of day again. Only, they made a gigantic mistake thinking they could hold us captive without a fight. They may have held us for a little while against our will, but the time has come to unleash those they deem monsters.

We step into the smoke-filled corridor and I blink to adjust my eyes to the thickness of the air. Readying a knife in both of my fists, I walk at Wes's flank down the long windy hall. I count the footsteps behind me, noting the differences among them. Jade's and Everest's are almost in tandem, while Tremont's are staggered and hobbled like he has a slight limp.

I'm not entirely sold that we aren't making a mistake by allowing him to tag along, but what else were we supposed to do—leave him here?

We need every bit of help we can get if we want to make it out alive. Not just from this prison, but from this enemy territory we're trapped in. I'll be able to get us out using my hunter's mark, and then we'll be on the run for who knows how long until they catch up.

Parla will stop at nothing to make me pay for disrupting her evil plan and I have no doubt that she will spare no expense to track me down and suck the life out of me, along with every single demonic essence still lingering within my being.

"Incoming," Wes warns only a moment prior to my own senses kicking in.

"Sector seventeen," Everest adds from behind.

"Spread out." I motion for them to move out of the way. "Wes and I will take the lead. Tremont, you cover them. You two open whatever cells you can."

Wes claims the wall next to him, and I slide along the one at my side. I focus my breathing and channel my strength to carry me through. Each sector we clear is one step closer to our freedom. Something that was once so far out of reach, now taunting us with its proximity.

"Shh," a guard whispers to another. "I hear something."

"You're being fucking paranoid, Briggs. They escaped out of eighteen."

Little does he know, he's massively misinformed.

The two of us pop around the corner and grab each of them, Wes catching his victim on fire while I slit the throat of the other. It's cruel and inhumane, but we don't have the luxury of anything else.

"Get to work," I tell the others, eyeing the corridor as far as I can see. I spare Wes a glance. "That was easy, too easy."

He tips his head. "You're right." Gripping onto the cell door nearest him, he yanks the thing open. "You're free."

Everest unlocks his door while Jade fumbles with the latch on hers. Tremont approaches the small man with various horns protruding from the top of his skull that Wes had broken out.

"Your wrists, I can get those off."

With a hesitant but curious stare, the man squeezes out of the opening and holds his arms out to Tremont. He anxiously looks at the lot of us. "Wh-what's happening?"

A large woman with dull blue skin and a long trunk for a nose steps around Everest and hugs the man covered in feathers Jade had freed. "Are you okay?" She squeezes him tightly with tears in her eyes.

"We're getting out of here, that's what," I tell them. "You can stick with us or flee at the first opportunity, but you'll be stuck in their territory unless you can find a hunter to let you out."

The fact that I'm still considered one turns my stomach. I don't want to be associated with these people—even if it is only by blood.

"What can we do to help?" The woman steps toward me. "I'm Pippa, this is Lo."

The quiet other prisoner joins us. "I'm Landry." He rubs at his wrists, the same reaction everyone else has after finally getting those things off.

Not only are they uncomfortable, but they restrict our power by some kind of current it pushes into our body. The second we're no longer restrained by them, it's like that energy comes rushing back through us.

Mine has been on the fritz ever since I stepped foot in this place. Typically, I have certain abilities that come naturally, but whatever they did to me, it's rattled my core. I feel unsettled and foreign in my own skin. But given everything that's changed lately, I'm not at all surprised.

"We're escaping through twelve," I tell the newest members of our group. "And we're freeing every demon we can between here and there. Whatever you can do, whether it be fight alongside us, or help us explain to the prisoners what's going on. Just stay out of the line of fire and don't get killed."

Something I never thought I'd hear come out of my mouth—telling a demon *not* to die. The old me would be salivating at the thought of all these souls for the taking. That version of me is dead.

"We good?" I ask the group while realizing I've sort of put myself in charge here.

Wes steps to my side and presses his hand against my shoulder. "Ready when you are."

I draw in a long breath, giving myself a quick moment of reprieve in anticipation of what's waiting for us in the next sector. "Let's go." I motion for everyone to follow and take off into a sprint around the corner and down the corridor. With Wes at my side, I ask him, "Can you throw your fire?"

He nods and as if reading my mind, he increases his speed to get in front of me.

Like he's turning up the dial, his body flickers to life and flames dance over his skin, somehow not burning his clothes off. I stopped trying to understand the specifics of magic a long time ago. Still barefoot from his shift into hound form earlier, each step he takes leaves a soft trail of fire in his wake. It's kind of magnificent, really.

Wes plants his arms to his side, his fingertips pressed toward the floor. He ignites further, balls of fire forming in his palms. He throws the first one, causing chaos the second he rounds the corner into the next sector.

Men scream and cry out in pain, while others frantically try to regroup and attack the flaming man.

"Stay back unless you can fight!" I yell at my group.

I tally up the soldiers until I cannot keep track any longer and go to work eliminating them one by one. They duped us in the last sector by only having two guards. They tried to make us believe escaping would be easy in an attempt to get us to lower our inhibitions and fall victim to this ambush they planned. They massively underestimated how powerful we are both mentally and physically. I'm sure Parla thinks that her extensive torture and interrogation did a number on me, but that couldn't be further from the reality of this situation. All of their torture tactics fueled us to want to end each and every one of their lives *that* much more.

My only hope is that I'm the one who gets to drive a knife into her chest and watch the life leave her fucking eyes as she comprehends that I am the reason for her downfall.

Wes throws another ball of fire into the crowd, eliminating at least a half dozen guards. He glances over at me and goes back to snapping the neck of a man who approaches his side.

I kick a guy in the stomach and double him over, using the movement to slice his throat and turn my attention to another target.

Out of the corner of my eye, Everest punches a guard in the face and Tremont casts what appears to be a protective barrier around Jade so she can unlock a cell. I skim the bodies in an attempt to locate our other members in between jamming the sharp end of my blade into the people who stand between us and our freedom.

I spot Landry climbing up a pile of fallen men and then using his hands like suction cups, he slithers up the wall. He disappears through a crack in the ceiling that was probably formed by one of the various explosions lately. He may have abandoned us, but he's one less person I have to worry about keeping alive. He's made his own bed, and now he's on his own to figure out how to navigate this hell.

Kneeling to the ground, I spin in a circle and slice the knife through three different men's calves. They cry out and frantically search for the cause of their pain. I roll out of sight and thrust the knife into one of their chests.

Someone grabs a fistful of my hair from behind and yanks me off my center.

Always the fucking hair.

I reach up and latch onto the person's wrists to stifle their control over my body. Reeling my leg up, I throw the brunt of my force backward and slam my foot straight into their chest. The man heaves and loosens his grip enough that I can maneuver myself to face him. With his fingers desperately trying to cling to my head, I reach into my waistband to pull out a small knife and slice it against his forearm. I dig the blade deep, causing damage that he will bleed out from within minutes. He releases me completely and presses his other hand into the wound, stumbling and tripping over a lifeless body behind him.

"Fucking prick," I mutter once I'm free of him. I scan the floor for the first blade I had dropped when he attacked me, sighing when it's nowhere in sight.

A few bodies rush into me, knocking me down and pinning me under them. A flashback of that day I was lost under the scurni with Wes's power making me unable to speak trickles into my mind. I was furious with him for abusing his power that way, and when I was finally granted the ability to talk again, I gave him an earful for it. Hell, I may have even told him I hated him. In hindsight, I see the error in judgment he made, and realize he was only trying to keep me safe, despite using the absolute worst choice of words to do so. At that point, I still didn't know he had feelings for me, and he was doing everything he could to evade that part of him from rising to the surface. Maybe if we had embraced our connection sooner, we wouldn't be in this mess now.

I shove my palms into the concrete to gain some traction on my situation, wiggling my body to try to free myself of the dumbasses on top of me. My wrist gives out and launches a new steady ache throbbing down my forearm. I roll my eyes and let out a breath. I didn't make it this far to be smothered by some fucking guards.

"Wren!" a frantic voice calls out through the chaos.

"Under here!" I yell back, relieved at my ability to actually direct my savior to my whereabouts this time.

The load on my back lightens and the spots in my vision clear up with each body removed.

Once I'm uncovered, I use my non-injured hand to press up off the floor.

Wes helps me off the ground and tugs me to his body, squeezing me so tight I can barely fucking breathe.

"Wes," I mumble into him. "You're…"

He releases me, pressing his hands to my cheeks and scanning my face. "I thought I lost you."

"If I could stop almost being crushed to death, that would be great." I take a step but wince at the pain shooting up my leg. "Fuck," I blurt out, seeing the knife I was using earlier jammed into my thigh. "That's going to leave a bruise." I grip the handle and clench my jaw as I yank it free. Not allowing Wes to say a damn word, I glance up at him. "No, you cannot heal it, but you can use your flame to stop the bleeding."

A blast of light fills the space and a loud crashing sound follows. Whoever is bombing this place is getting dangerously close to where we are.

Wes shields me from the debris with his large body and uses his right hand to press his flaming finger against my exposed and bloody flesh. "You have to let me take care of you when we're done. I'm begging you."

I exhale deeply at having my skin melted together and pat his shoulder. "I'll think about it." I hobble over to a guard who has the upper hand on Everest and starting from the top of his back, I drag the knife in my grasp down to his waist. Immediately, he stops attacking Everest and screams out in agony. "You good?"

"Yeah, thanks." Everest pants and nods rapidly.

A demon with skin as black as night and a tail longer than its own body rushes past me, using said tail to penetrate a guard's throat and fling the man's frame off into the wall.

"Retreat!" One of the remaining guards calls out, not waiting for anyone else to follow as he takes off down the corridor leading him to the next sector.

The newest member of our group swirls his tail around his legs and picks him up into the air before he can get away.

"I like him, who's that?" I ask Jade from her spot behind me.

"That's Rudy. Pretty polite guy if I may say so myself."

I chuckle. "Seems like it." I watch with a grin as the last of the guards scuttle up and attempt to get away.

Rudy sinks his claws into one of the guards and rips a long strip of flesh off his throat. He obnoxiously chews the meat and drops the body.

"Could use some table manners," I add.

I take in the sight of my team assembling around me, a few fresh members in tow, relief flooding in at everyone appearing decently unharmed. "Only lost one, that's good." I point to the spot in the ceiling where Landry had escaped out. "If anyone wants to follow suit, now's your chance."

A small woman with scales covering her cheeks and slits for a nose blinks a few times, her many eyelids showing with the movement. She mumbles something incomprehensible and climbs the wall. Her hands suction to the surface the same way that Landry's had.

"We're sticking with you," Pippa chimes in.

I skim the gazes of the rest of the group, noting the subtle nods of each member.

"Rudy," I call out down the corridor. "You lead the way."

We take off after him, no doubt exhausted and ready for this to all be over, but growing in numbers, our chances of making it out of here rising along with the morale.

Wasting no time, we clear the next three sectors without issue. Their guards have pulled back and are nowhere to be found. Do they not realize we're releasing their prisoners along the way, which is only strengthening our defenses against them?

I keep bracing myself around every corner, expecting them to advance on us, but it never happens. Have they truly given up and accepted the fact that they cannot win this war? If Parla has any say in it, she'd let every one of them die if it meant a chance at stopping us.

We clear the sector with the faded thirteen painted on the wall and pause before the last leg of our journey. There have only been small openings to escape along the way, either in the ceiling or in places too difficult to squeeze through. According to Everest, the biggest breach is sector twelve, giving us all the opportunity to escape.

And if what he's saying is true, that's probably why the troops have been called back.

The likelihood of them rallying the brunt of their forces there is strong, meaning the worst of this battle is just around the next corner. But as I stand here, scanning the faces of these people, I'm struck with the realization that some things are worth fighting for—worth risking your life for. Their freedom is at the top of the list. They might have demonic blood running through their veins, but that doesn't make them any less deserving of their rights than anyone else in this realm. Parla claims that they are the evil of this world, and yet all I see are a group of terrified and tortured souls begging to be set free.

"Hey," Wes whispers while tucking a strand of my wild hair behind my ear. "In case I don't get the chance to say it..."

I shrug him off. "Nope, no goodbyes today, Romeo."

"That's not what I was going to tell you." He tugs me to his chest anyway. "I'm proud of you."

I hug him back briefly. "Be proud when we've made it out alive."

"Okay," he smiles down at me and presses his lips to my dirty forehead.

"You two make a cute couple." Jade nudges me with her elbow and then nods ahead of us. "They're going to try to ambush us, aren't they?"

I sense the nervous energy in the small space we're all crammed into. "Yes." I turn toward the crowd. "I want each of you to get out as soon as you can. Run for the forest and do not stop until you hit the barrier." I look to Everest. "You will go with them, get them out of here, you hear me?"

"What about you?" he asks me.

"I won't be far behind." I must see to it that every person in our group makes it to safety.

Pippa steps forward, a small group of demons gravitating toward her. "We'd like to continue on to the remaining sectors."

Tears well in my eyes but I blink them away. I've had a sinking feeling this entire time knowing we'd be leaving so many behind. I'd be lying if I said I wasn't conspiring to come up with some kind of plan to stay back and free them on my own, but with her help, and those volunteering to go with her, I can breathe a little easier. Still, I can't help but be consumed by the nagging selfishness of leaving them unprotected.

Rudy glides across the back of the crowd and takes his place with Pippa and her people. "I'll see this through." His voice is thick like tar.

"Thank you," I tell all of them.

Pippa steps toward me, enveloping me in her arms. "Bless you for not leaving us here." She gives me one final squeeze. "You are an angel."

If only she knew my past, if she could see the pile of bodies that would no doubt fill this very room and many more. She'd hate me. Hell, I hate myself enough for the both of us.

I focus on Everest. "You get them out, okay?"

He responds by inching closer to Jade, his body acting as a shield.

Collectively, our entire group moves down the final corridor into the unknown. We don't run, we don't charge, we save our energy for the battle ahead.

When we approach the last leg, Wes leaves my side to lead us. My soul begs to be up there with him, but my brain knows it's the most logical formation. I will be with him soon enough. Either in death or free of this place. Both are an oddly comforting reality. This life has been torturous, and I'm not sure there's anything I can do to redeem the actions of my old self. I am ashamed of the person I was. Not even death can purge me from my sins, though.

Wes's entire body ignites into a beautiful flame seconds before he shoves through the door separating us from the other side.

I rush behind him, knives staged in both hands, readying to fight our way out of this place. A battle cry floats its way up my chest but falls flat when I blink around the vast and empty area. A chill creeps up my spine and an uncomfortable pit grows in my stomach. I swallow down the unease and watch the rest of the group funnel in.

My attention falls to the gaping crater on the side of the building. Rubble is littered on the floor of the room and piled haphazardly outside. Dust and fog fill the air but there's not a person in sight.

"This doesn't feel right," I mutter under my breath.

Are they waiting for us to escape? Is the trap actually outside these walls instead of in this confined room? What angle could Parla possibly be playing right now, and why have I not figured it out yet?

Wes tilts his hand upward and conjures a ball of fire in his hand. He glances over at me. "I hope this doesn't work." He throws the flaming thing into seemingly nothing, erupting the room into chaos.

Screams follow his attack and a few people who aren't immediately killed from the fireball flail their arms and frantically pat at them to extinguish themselves.

The barrier keeping the guards invisible flickers, showing some of them, then all of them.

My heart stutters at the sheer number of men standing around us, blocking our path to freedom.

I walked these people straight into a trap and now here we are, outnumbered and completely surrounded by people who wish nothing but to kill us.

CHAPTER 15
Wren

I drive the knife in my right hand into a man's chest and yank it out quickly, moving on to my next target. Dodging a baton from a guard, I spin on my heel and crouch, shoving the sharp end of the blade into another guard's thigh.

His screams are a comfort to my soul—one less person standing in our way.

I'm kicked from behind and flipped around.

A man straddles my waist and pins me to the floor. "Remember me, you fucking bitch?"

The guard I had beat until his face swelled stares back at me. "Not really. You all look the same."

I wrap my legs around his torso and hold him tightly to my body, giving him little space to move.

His hot breath turns my stomach. "You think you can overpower me?"

"No," I tell him. I grip the collar of his standard issued shirt and tug it down, latching onto it with my other hand and creating an X with my forearms. I pull tighter, dragging him to my chest and grinning at his surprise. "I know so." With nothing but the weight of our bodies and his shirt, I strangle him until his body stops convoluting in its attempts to get free.

I shove him off me and scan the ground for my knives. Panting from the effort of such an intimate kill, I locate one of the blades and turn back to my victim. Because one can never be too sure, I plunge the knife into his chest once, twice, three times. Blood splatters onto my face and only fuels my desire to bathe in it by the time this is all said and done.

A hand appears at my side and for a split second, my first instinct is to grab it and pull the person down with me. But when my gaze trails up to the demon it's attached to, I realize that it is not the enemy, but a fellow comrade.

I permit the man with horns protruding from his forehead to assist me off the floor. "Thank you."

Something I never thought I'd offer genuinely—thanks to a demon.

"Are you injured, ma'am?" He scans my face which is now splattered with crimson.

"No." At least not any more than I already was. My entire body aches and this battle will no doubt create more wounds that will need to be healed. That is, if I make it out alive. I've evaded death all my life, but what if this is when she finally welcomes me home.

The demon's eyes go wide as he focuses on something behind me. "Watch out." He shoves me aside and steps into the line of fire, taking a knife straight to the chest.

In a flash, I circle and plunge my blade into the attacker's neck, a fountain of red pouring from in its wake. I push him aside and catch the demon before he hits the floor. "Fuck." I cradle his head and scan the black ooze seeping from around the entry wound.

"P-p-pull it out." The demon remains still but manages to spit out those few words. "Please."

Gripping the handle, I comply and free him of the knife penetrating his chest. I press my hand into it to attempt to stop the flow.

"Wren." Wes's voice seems to float toward me.

I shift my head in his direction across the room. In complete and utter chaos, I was able to locate him with ease. I watch him snap a guard's neck and toss him aside.

He nods like he's accepting that I'm okay and goes back to work killing whoever is near him.

My attention flickers through the crowd, spotting anyone I can recognize. I search frantically for Jade, pausing when my sights land on Tremont, his hands outstretched and a steady flow of magic streaming out and blasting onto the opening to the outside world. A sheer barrier in place where there should be nothing. Tremont is trying to break it so our people can finally escape. Rudy stands guard near him, blocking any threat that comes his way. His tail wraps around a man and uses the body to knock down three others before violently slamming it into the concrete floor.

"I can heal," the demon in my arms mutters. "I just need a few minutes."

I blink down at him. "Really?"

"Can you buy me some time?"

"Of course." I look to my hand blocking the wound from sprouting. "What about this?"

"Place mine on it, if you will." His gaze darts down to his arm. "I'm afraid I'm a bit paralyzed." He lets out a sigh. "Distant cousin to the scurni."

I chuckle and do as he requests. "I'm familiar." I'll never forget being pinned under that fainting ogre.

What a terrible trait to inherit.

"I won't allow anyone to harm you." I gently set his head against the floor and rise to my feet. "I promise." Taking the knife that had been sunk into his chest, and that of the one I previously had, I renew myself to the war around us.

Pippa approaches, her footsteps thunderous and booming. "We held them off as best we could."

"Thank you." I note the demon barrier around me and my injured friend. "Help Rudy defend Tremont." I motion toward the only chance of us getting out of here. If he can't take it down, then we're trapped in this prison for good. Sure, we can kill every last one of them, but if magic is holding us in place, then we need a witch to break it.

The demons protecting me follow my order and rush through the crowd to maintain a stronghold with Rudy.

The guards feign confusion for a split second at their retreat but then quickly concentrate on their target.

"Come and fucking get me," I yell at them.

One by one they attack, their arms raised with their weapons poised and ready to strike.

Oh, how foolish of them to be so careless with their offense. Didn't their trainers teach them better? Clearly, we went to two entirely different facilities to learn our skills. Or maybe I'm just naturally not a fucking idiot like these guys are.

I grin, no doubt looking like a psycho with the dried remains of their friends caked on my face. Steadying my breath, I send the first knife flying through the air and landing it with deadly accuracy into the man's throat.

His arms lower and he clutches briefly at the thing wedged into his windpipe.

I watch carefully as the next man charges at me, biding my time, waiting for the perfect opportunity to strike. I seize it, ducking to block his blow and driving the weight of my entire body into my shoulder and knocking him to the floor. I reel my leg up and kick another man in his shin, buckling his leg in the wrong direction and disarming him. I turn and thrust each of my hands to the sides, one with a blade, the other outstretched and with nothing but brute force. I slide the blade out and quickly evade those two men as they fall into each other.

Another approaches, a bit more cautious than the rest. Is he the least stupid out of the bunch?

"Fucking traitor," he spits.

I'll take that as a no.

"What are you waiting for?" I ask him while sizing him up.

He's easily a foot taller than me, triple my weight. His muscles bulge the fabric of his shirt and instead of finding them intimidating, I'm repulsed. He's either the type of guy who eats nothing but protein and hits the gym three times a day or uses enhancements to cheat the system. The vein bulging from his forehead and the sweat accompanying it tells me that he's already exhausted where I'm only just getting started.

The guard unsheathes a sword from his side and extends it toward me.

"Is that supposed to scare me?" I laugh at him.

He nods to the dead man at my foot. "Go on, I'm waiting."

I glance down, catching the glint of the sword in my sights. "Step back," I tell him.

He raises his free hand into the air and complies while lowering his weapon.

Swiftly, I drag the heavy mass of the sword out from the corpse's control and familiarize myself with the weight of it in my hand. I tend to prefer smaller blades as they offer more agility, but if he wants to test my skills, I'll gladly oblige.

The guard strikes first in an attempt to catch me in a moment of weakness. I match his blow, the blades clanging loudly. My wrist aches at the impact but I push the pain aside. I don't have time to succumb to the discomfort now.

I counter, aiming for his neck and hoping for a quick win, but he anticipates my bluntness and blocks the attack. We go back and forth like this for what feels like an eternity, swinging and blocking, blocking and swinging.

He manages to nick me with the tip of the blade, cutting through the thickness of my armor top and slicing a thin layer of my flesh.

I grow furious at the defeat of him drawing first blood and match him by advancing quickly and grazing his brow.

He brings his hand up to the wound and looks at the blood that remains on his fingers. "You're going to pay for that."

"They say women are chatty, and here you are, refusing to shut up." I use his distraction to advance him again, but he counters my attack. I turn, skimming the crowd briefly to locate Wes, my reaction time stuttering when I don't spot him.

My breath catches as the blade slashes my thigh, and for a split second, I worry that this might be the end. I shake the thought and focus on the here and now. I refuse to let *this man* be my downfall.

I plant my feet firmly onto the floor and bend my knees. I swipe the sword through the air, landing it with a loud clang against his, and immediately strike him again, and again. I've been playing this to his pace, and if I want to end this, I have to change things up. I land another strike, turning myself completely around and hitting him from a different angle. This one finds a home against his calf, spurting blood as the blade slices through his flesh.

He cries out in agony and I advance, not wanting to waste another minute with this pathetic excuse of life.

I kick him off center and point the tip of my sword at his neck. "Checkmate."

His eyes widen and the alarm of actually losing settles into his features.

Sliding the sword down further, I position it near his heart. With a grunt, I thrust the long edge into his chest and savor the gasp of horror that escapes him. I leave him there to bleed out, staining the concrete like so many others before him.

"Wes," I cry out. I shove a guard and squint through the fight to find him. "Wes!" I yell. "Where are you?" My heart aches and uncertainty takes hold. I scan the bodies lining the floor and pray to any god that might be listening that Wes isn't among them.

Pippa holds her place next to Rudy, who is still protecting Tremont as he maintains his magical connection to the wall holding us in.

Despite all of the dead around us, the number of guards doesn't seem to stop coming. It's like Parla has an endless supply of grunts at her disposal. And yet, she's nowhere to be fucking found.

If I could just kill her, maybe it would sever that idiotic and suicidal bond these guards share with her. Maybe then they would realize they cannot win this battle.

But, if it were the old me, I wouldn't have stopped until either everyone around me was dead or I had been killed. That knowledge is the one thing that assures me that death is the only option. There is no time to reason with them, not when they're determined to kill anyone that defies everything they believe in.

I gravitate toward the throng of guards that takes up one large section in the corner, fear unlike anything I've felt before boiling inside of me. What if Wes is in the center, beaten and bloodied to a point of no return? What if he's already gone? Wouldn't I know? Wouldn't I feel it? Or does our connection not work that way?

I grip onto the shirt of a guard and toss him aside, anxious to get to the core of their collective attention.

"Wes!" I shout into the space.

The guard I pushed latches onto me and drags me backward.

I elbow him in the face, crunching his nose under the force. "Don't fucking touch me." I kick him in the chest and he slams into the wall behind him with a thud.

His body slides down the hard surface and he remains motionless.

I turn to the crowd once more and watch as they take a step back.

Is this it? Are they finished? Have they inflicted all the damage they needed to?

I shake my head refusing to believe my worst fears.

Out from the center like a beacon in the night sky, Wes emerges, only he is no longer in his man form, but that of his hound. Towering over some of the men, he exposes his teeth and growls at them. In a flash, he pounces, ripping the head off one man's body and throwing it to the side. Another tries to evade him, but he latches onto his leg and drags him toward him. The man drags his fingers across the floor and screams as Wes sinks his claws across his shoulders and down his torso.

The hound's gaze meets mine and I'm met with those beautiful glowing red eyes.

I sigh and release the tension I didn't realize had built up within me.

My fated mate is alive, he's okay.

He lurches into the air but doesn't land his attack until the man has already hit me across the head.

I stumble and fall to my knees, hot liquid running down my forehead. My own blood trickles into my mouth and down the crook of my neck. My skull throbs and I struggle to blink through the stars appearing in my vision.

At least Wes is fine.

That alone is enough to keep the pain at bay.

A warm and furry head appears at my side and nudges my arm. He licks at my cheek and presses his cool nose to my face. The hound lets out a whimper.

"It's okay," I tell him while patting the top of his head. "I'm good." I rise to my feet, using Wes to help steady me.

It's then that I notice he's ripped apart at least a dozen guards in my momentary lapse.

"Good boy." I pat his head and stroke just under his ear.

He purrs and closes his eyes momentarily like he's enjoying the praise.

"We need to get out of here." I turn my attention to the rest of the room, noting how the majority of the guards are trying to penetrate the protection surrounding Tremont. We must be getting close to breaking it down if they're this determined to attack with that much force.

It must be a powerful barrier if he still hasn't broken through it yet, though.

With Wes at my side, I make my way over to the crowd, snatching a knife on the way and digging it into the back of a guard none the wiser. "Can you get me in there?" I ask Wes, watching as more soldiers flood into the room and approach our rear.

He dips his head and leans down, clenching onto a guard's ankle and dragging him from his position. He goes in for another and I use the opportunity to stab the next one.

"Pippa!" I call through the small opening. "I'm coming through."

"The hell you are," a guard blurts out when he spots me trying to get past him. He reaches for me but comes up empty-handed when Wes claims him with his inescapable grip.

I squeeze through, ducking and shoving men out of the way. At this point, it's like they're mindless robots doing whatever they can to disrupt us from continuing on our path to freedom. Their disregard for their own survival is sickening.

Pippa latches onto my forearm and tugs me the rest of the way through.

Rudy holds the line and allows us a chance to catch our breath.

"What's taking so long?" I ask her and nod to Tremont.

Pippa returns to her spot defending the attacks from the guards.

"I need more power!" he yells from his spot not too much further from me.

I step forward, doing everything I can to show a strong front despite feeling like my legs and body might actually give out from underneath me. "Take mine." I extend an arm. I might not have much to give, but I'd sacrifice every last drop if it meant getting these people their freedom.

Tremont side-eyes me and sighs. "You look worse for wear, Wren."

"This is no time for debate, sir. Whatever it takes. What do you need me to do?" I bring myself closer to him and ignore the new round of guards that have entered the confines of this room.

"It could kill you," Tremont warns.

"I don't fucking care, just tell me what to do." I grow frustrated with his lack of urgency.

"Place your hand in mine; I'll do the rest."

Without allowing him any more time to waste, I press my palm into his and mentally let down my defenses. I have no idea how this kind of transfer works, but I assume I cannot show resistance.

Tremont's entire body shakes and something electrical sparks to life between us. His stare widens, as if he's afraid of the connection that has us tethered.

I worry that it's not enough—that my power has dwindled too much and that I will not be of any help. I should have sent Wes through and had Tremont channel his power. But if this process means any chance of harm, I was the right person for it all along. I can deal with sacrificing myself, not anyone else.

"Is something wrong?" I ask him over the buzzing in my ears.

"I..." Tremont twists his free hand and a burst of white light floods out of it and pours into the barrier, shattering it with ease. He remains gripping my hand as he pulls me forward. "We must go, now."

I try to yank myself free but it's no use. I'm too weak and his hold on me is too strong. I crane my neck to peer behind me. "Everybody, run!"

Like a stampede of children on the last day of school, the demons who had been battling for their freedom turn and bolt out the opening. Wind rushes past my cheeks with each of them that escapes. I breathe in the air, noting the remnants of the explosions coating my lungs. I'll be grateful once we're away from here and can smell the freshness of the forest and appreciate the stillness of safety. Although, I'm not entirely sure that will ever come knowing what I know now.

Parla won't rest until she's brought me back here to use however she pleases.

If I stand any chance of defeating her for good, I have to get as far away from here as possible and regain my strength.

We all do.

Today's battle might be close to a win, but this war has only just started.

CHAPTER 16

Wren

"Let go of me," I demand.

"I have to get you out of here; I promised." Tremont continues to pull me over the rubble, taking me further away from where I last saw Wes in hound form.

I wince from pain all over my body taking turns assaulting me. In my ankle, my thigh, my chest, my wrist—everywhere hurts. Every single inch of my frame aches from the never-ending torment it's endured. Will the agony ever end?

"I will fucking kill you if you don't release me. Mark my words, I am not someone you want to cross."

At this, Tremont drops my hand. He turns to face me, his serious gaze meeting mine. "Wes has shifted, am I correct?"

I nod silently.

"Nothing will stop him from finding you. But if you do not get out of here, you're putting him in danger. You're putting everyone in danger."

I grit my teeth and roll my eyes. How dare this complete stranger be so damn correct?

Jade reaches my side, Everest in tow. "Are you okay?" Her gaze trails down my face and over my battle-worn body.

"I'm fine. Are you?"

"Yes, but we need to go." She goes to take a step, but I reach out and stop her.

"Have you seen Wes?" A piece of my heart breaks in anticipation of her answer.

"No, I'm sorry. He's Wes though, are you seriously worried?" She laughs it off like we didn't just escape from the worst possible place in all of Prania.

"You aren't?"

"There she is," a man calls out from the side of the building.

Tremont grips my elbow. "Come. Now."

218

I yank away from him but follow the lot of them, not because I want to, but because it's true. I'm the key to Parla's master fucking plan and in my weakened state, I'm too vulnerable to hang around and allow myself to be captured again.

We climb over the fallen remains caused by the explosions and take turns shimmying along the small gap between the debris. Everest leads the way and stops for us at every spot, making sure all four of us are through before continuing. My chest aches at the distance growing between me and Wes, but I know I cannot go back for him, that I must carry on.

A small group of demons rip a few guards to shreds as they try to subdue them. The demons hungrily look for their next target once they've completed that mission, not lingering their sights on us for long, knowing that we are not a threat.

"We're going to have to run past that tower." Everest points to the thing in the close distance. He lowers his finger to the tree line off further. "If we can make it there, we should be able to disappear."

I beg my soul to contact my mate and tell him to hurry the fuck up. He'll be trapped in this territory if he doesn't make it in time. And regardless of what he or anyone else has in mind, I refuse to leave this place without him.

"See that break in the wall?" Everest steadies his hand at the thing just past the guard tower. "That's where we'll cross."

I size up the distance between here and there and do a mental assessment of my injuries. Between those and the bit of power I lent Tremont, I'm running on fucking fumes at this point. I've been beaten and torn down, but this is almost an all-time low.

Nothing really compares to when Wes saved me from dying alone in that building.

And here I am, leaving him to the same fate.

The only difference is that he's in much better shape to fend for himself than I was back then.

"Are we ready?" Everest spares a glance at all of us. "Let's go."

We start off side by side, but fall into a formation of two by two, my weak form trailing to the rear with each step we take.

Tremont slows his pace to join me.

"Go ahead," I tell him while shifting my focus to the tower growing larger as we get closer.

Shouldn't they be stopping us? Shouldn't *something* be preventing us from escaping? Or are things really that bad that they no longer have a hold on who comes and goes from here?

Everest quickly scales the opening in the wall, pulling himself up and over the edge, and disappearing onto the other side. Jade follows suit, looking back briefly before she is no longer visible either. Tremont and I catch up to the structure.

"Go on." I look to the tower and then at the prison we just came from.

People scatter here and there, and from this distance, I can't tell if the demons remain the ones in control. Still, there is no sign of Wes, and that alone threatens to break me completely.

"Go on, damn it," I urge him again. "I'm right behind you."

Tremont latches onto my shoulder. "He made me promise that I'd get you out. Don't make me break that."

I shake him off me. "No one is breaking any promises." Although, I can't be entirely sure, because if Wes doesn't show up soon, I don't think I'll be able to withstand the visceral urge to go back for him.

Tremont climbs up and hops down onto the other side, leaving me here alone.

I hesitate, my hand positioned to follow him, my heart begging me to go the other way.

"Come on, Wes," I whisper. "Where are you?"

And like a gift from the fucking universe herself, I catch a flash of his black fur while he's running after a guard. He tackles the man to the ground and claws at his chest before dismounting him and moving on to another target.

He's not here with me, but he's safe, he's alive, and that's all that matters for now.

I tighten my hold on the wall and hike my leg up to the fractured part of it.

Looking back one last time, I'm thrown through the opening when the base of the tower to my right explodes, sending fragments flying and shattering against the stone surface. Some manage to make it through with me, little spikes of concrete impaling into the back of my legs. I gasp and clutch my chest while doing a quick scan of my body to make sure the damage is only minimal. I raise my head and count the bodies huddled together and then spot two others off in the distance. Something oddly familiar about the shape of them.

"Wren," Tremont calls out.

Ignoring him, I stand, my feet having a mind of their own, walking toward the other people. As their forms go from a blur to something more defined, my pace picks up until I'm sprinting in pain, each step a reminder of how damaged I really am.

I press the mark on my neck and blink through the tears that fill my eyes.

Like he's sensing my presence, his large figure turns in my direction, his mouth falling open at the sight of me.

Bo drops the device clung in his hand and slaps Dash on the shoulder before taking off.

Emotions spill over at seeing them, both of them, alive and well.

I've felt the connection to Bo this entire time, with moments of him getting further away and then approaching again, but he was always there. Even with Dash's phoenix nature, I still worried that something might change about his powers, and without having that same connection to him, could never grow comfortable with the uncertainty of the situation.

Bo takes the final step in front of me and lifts me into his arms, pulling me from the ground and spinning me in a circle. "Oh, Birdie."

I wrap myself around his neck and breathe in his musky scent, allowing my shape to melt into his and savoring the comfort he brings. How fucking strange that we started out absolutely hating each other and now I'm at home in his embrace.

He gently lowers me onto the ground and holds me at an arm's length. "You look like shit."

I laugh and punch his shoulder, wincing at the pain it causes my wrist. "It's good to see you, too."

Dash finally approaches, his strides much shorter than Bo's.

I sigh and take in the sight of his beautiful features while I come to terms with the fact that he's real. That he's actually standing in front of me.

He pauses and does the same, his eyes glistening.

Extending my arms, I cautiously limp over to him, no longer able to hide behind my ruse.

Carefully, he pulls me into him and hugs me. He drags in a long breath and kisses the top of my head. "We were so worried."

"You're not the only one." I rest my head against his chest and listen to the thumping of his heartbeat. A melody I could hear on repeat and never grow tired of, a steady reminder that he is still alive.

"What, no hug for me?" Jade calls out from behind me.

Bo's mouth drops open further than it did when he spotted me, and he stands there like he's stuck in place. "No fucking way."

Jade runs over to him and wraps her arms around his broad chest. "Missed you, asshole."

Bo softens his resolve and squeezes her. "I can't fucking believe it." He steadies his gaze on the other two members of our group. "Who are they? Where's Wes?"

"About that..." I rub at my neck, unsure of where to start.

"He's fucking *dead*?" Bo growls and releases Jade, shoving her behind him and squaring off to Tremont and Everest.

I step between them. "No, you irrational fool. He's just...occupied." I point to the guys. "This is Everest, he's..." I glance at Jade but decide to keep my mouth shut about that one. Another secret that isn't mine to tell. "He's been kind to us, and I expect you to show him the same respect." I point to Tremont. "This is Tremont, he broke the barrier keeping us locked in there."

Bo shakes hands with both. "A hunter and a witch, interesting." He narrows his gaze at them and then at me. "I don't trust them."

I smack his shoulder. "You didn't trust me either, and look where that got us." I place my hand on Dash's back. "This is Dash. Dash, Tremont and Everest."

Dash nods his head politely and leans into my touch.

Jade takes us in, noting the closeness and comfort we bring each other. "Are you two a thing, too?" She raises her brow at me and Dash.

"We're...not *not* a thing."

"Interesting." Jade doesn't add anything else.

Everest reverts to the current, more pressing, situation. "We need to get under cover." He motions to the tree line in the near distance. "That should do."

I wave at Bo to get his attention and lower my voice. "What was that thing in your hand back there?"

Bo blinks a few times like he's trying to recall a memory. "Detonator," he grins.

I smile, too. "That was you two blowing shit up?"

Dash wraps his arm around my shoulder. "Had to get you and Wes out of there somehow."

Speaking of, it would be fucking great if he would hurry up and meet us already. The relief of seeing him still alive was only temporary and it becomes more fleeting with each moment that passes.

Everest leads us away from the prison encampment and toward the forest surrounding the place. My heart stays put, begging with my feet to stop moving and go back for Wes. It's not right to leave him. I guess now that his hound has returned, he's not exactly alone. But that arrogant little shit has led me astray before, what if he does the same to Wes?

Bo places his large hand on the small of my back and glances down at me while Dash stays at my other side and the rest walk ahead. "Don't do that to me ever again." His stare is so intense a chill floats up my spine. "You could have died."

"I thought you wanted me dead." I swallow the lump that forms in my throat.

"Not anymore, Birdie."

He moves his hand up to the side of my face where he tucks my hair behind my ear.

It's strange to see him this...soft.

Bo is cruel, callous, and arrogant as hell. Our time apart must have really done a number on him if it's cracked that hard exterior.

His demeanor shifts from worry to curiosity. "Was there a woman...an older woman, with Wes?"

"Um, no. Why? Should there have been?"

Bo raises a brow at me. "Not with Jade?"

It's then that I realize who he's referring to, despite not having any clue who the person was. "No. I overheard Jade tell him they didn't make it." I glance at Jade walking ahead, her body gravitating toward Everest. Does Bo notice that the two of them like each other?

His jaw tenses and he nods stiffly.

"Who was it?" I ask him.

Bo sighs and rubs at his neck. "Essentially...Wes's mother."

I stop dead in my tracks, dropping Dash's hand. "We can't just leave him."

The group turns toward me and Tremont is the first to speak.

"I promised him I'd get you to safety. We aren't quite there yet."

"This *safety* you speak of," I quip. "Doesn't exist. Not in here, not out there, it's a hopeless cause."

"Birdie." Bo steps toward me with a gentle approach, his voice low. "The weird man is right."

"I'm standing right here, you know." Tremont folds his arms over his chest. "I'm only trying to help."

"I don't care," Bo tells him without turning around. He keeps his eyes on me. "We have to go; Wes will join us when he's done."

A group of demons hop the wall where we had come from not too long ago and runs toward us.

Bo exposes his teeth, and a low growl escapes him. He steps in front of me and points his arm to the ground, his razor-sharp talons appearing on the tips of his fingers.

I manage to wiggle past his defenses. "They're no threat to us," I tell him.

The herd of creatures jogs in our direction and slow their pace when they approach, each of their eyes going wide when they spot Bo. They crane their necks to look up at him but then quickly avert direct eye contact.

"Sorry, sir. Permission to speak, sir?"

Bo narrows his gaze at them and I elbow him.

"Yes," he spits out.

"It's with great urgency that you must go. They're vacating the premises, sir."

"And what's so terrible about that?"

The rest of our group steps a little closer to get in better range of the conversation at hand.

"I overheard the guards speaking that they're going to unleash a toxic poison on any remaining person left within the vicinity. Since we cannot escape the territory on our own, it's their way of ensuring we never do." The young demon's voice shakes with each word spoken.

I skim the faces of his friends, a look of terror on all of them.

Another round of demons crosses over the border and runs toward the tree line we're headed to. They divert their route and head over to us, stopping behind the first group like they're here for guidance.

Soon, there are nearly thirty creatures of various shapes and sizes looking to Bo for help.

"You don't need me," I turn to my people. "Everest can get you out. I can go back for Wes."

"In that condition?" Bo runs his hand through his dark hair and grunts. "Damn it, Wes." He glances to the place we just escaped. "I'll retrieve the little shit." He stares directly into the crowd of demons. "Go with them, they will set you free."

A collective murmur sounds from the demons.

"You won't be able to find him," I blurt out.

Bo has never seen Wes in his hound form, at least to my knowledge. I'm pretty sure Wes shifted for the first time in the prison after we marked one another.

"What aren't you telling me?" Bo stares down at me.

"I..."

Tremont clears his throat, bringing Bo's attention from me to him. "Wes would want you all to get out while you can. He wouldn't wish for any of you to attempt to retrieve him."

Bo widens his shoulders. "And what do you know about what he wants?"

Tremont stands his ground. "I know that he cares about her very much."

Everest joins Tremont at his side. "I've seen firsthand what Wes is capable of, and I have no doubt that he can take care of himself. You'd be putting yourself at risk if you leave. And these people..." He motions to the crowd growing around us. "Need you."

Dash steps forward. "I'll go."

"No," at least a few of us say at the same time.

Dash lowers his head and returns to where he was previously standing.

I extend my arm and latch onto his hand. "No offense."

Tremont twirls his wrist and throws a burst of magic in between us and the wall we climbed over. "There, none of you will go back."

"What the hell did you just do?" I release Dash once again and yell at Tremont.

"It's for your own good, for everyone's own good. Now, we need to go."

A flashing light goes off in the distance, and an eruption of something shimmering rains down on the area it had exploded over.

"It's begun, sir," the demon speaking for the rest tells Bo.

Bo presses his eyes shut and rubs his temple. When he opens them, it's like a final decision has been made. He bends at the waist and swoops his arm around my legs, hoisting me into the air and over his shoulder. "Sorry, Birdie."

I pound on his back and try to wiggle my way free. "Let me down, you big buffoon." I continue hitting him until my face tingles from being upside down.

"It's better this way," Jade adds once I stop demanding to be released.

"If something happens to Wes," I mumble. "I will kill every single one of you." Except maybe Dash—he didn't exactly do anything wrong here. And it's not as though he could overpower Bo. I can't blame him for something he has no control over.

I lift the hem of Bo's shirt and press the soft skin on his lower back between my fingers.

Bo grips my thigh and maintains a hold on me with one arm. "Stop pinching me, Birdie."

"I will if you let me down." My body aches from the position he has me in, each step is a jab to every bit of pain I was already experiencing.

"Not until we're on the other side of the barrier."

"You're hurting me," I tell him, painting the guilt on thickly.

In a flash, he maneuvers me from over his shoulder and into his arms. He cradles me to his chest and continues walking without faltering. "Better?"

I poke the side of his face. "I can walk, you know."

He glances down at me. "I didn't. But that's great, you should be really proud of yourself."

I prod at his cheek again. "Bo...this is fucked up."

This time he doesn't look at me when he speaks. "What's fucked up is you putting yourself in danger over and over again for no fucking reason."

"You really care that little of Wes that you'd leave him behind?"

"I care enough that I'm letting him do what he needs to do."

"What's that supposed to mean?"

Bo sighs. "Think about it, Birdie. Wes lost his mother. What do you think he's doing?"

Killing any and every one that could have possibly had something to do with it.

I cross my arms over my chest but don't respond. I don't dare tell Bo that he might be right.

When I saw Wes for that split second, his hound was ripping guards apart.

Is it possible that Wes could sense that I was in good hands and that's why he chose to separate himself from me to go on his murder spree? Am I the only one who is suffering from the distance between us? Like there's a hole forming in my chest and can only be remedied by my fated mate. There were once two gaping pits formed from being torn from Dash and Bo, but now those have been patched, and another has opened in Wes's absence.

What if we're never reunited? What if Wes is taken down by the poison and is never seen again? What if I could have saved him but Bo wouldn't let me? Would I ever be capable of forgiving him if I lose Wes forever?

I wipe a tear that rolls down my cheek.

"I'm sorry, Birdie."

CHAPTER 17

Wren

The cluster of freckles on the side of Bo's face begins to blur the more I stare at it. It's bittersweet to be in his arms. Partly because I'm exhausted and the comfort he brings is a welcomed change to the recent chaos, but given the circumstances, I'd rather it not be so he could hold me captive from going back for Wes.

My entire body aches, inside and out. From old wounds and new, and from internal scars that won't seem to mend. Yet, they're ripped open, the freshness of them feeling like they happened just yesterday.

The silence of this journey into the woods has left me alone with my thoughts and angry at Bo. I'm aware I shouldn't be, but it's difficult when he's the one quite literally stopping me. Wes would want it this way, hell, he made Tremont promise it into action. None of this makes it any easier to stomach that Wes is out there, alone, dealing with his own physical and mental struggles.

I've never been the type to sacrifice myself for another, yet somehow, it's all my soul drives me to do. Perhaps I'm overcompensating for the lifetime of torment I've plagued this world with. A little voice in my head tells me no amount of selflessness will ever be enough to erase what I've done.

But that won't stop me from trying.

It's hard to believe that I was the real monster after all.

"Up ahead." Tremont motions through the dense forest. "Can you hear the buzzing?"

Bo clenches his jaw before looking down at me through his thick lashes. "Birdie." He tries a gentle approach, but it comes out rough. He clears his throat and speaks again. "Think I can set you down now or are you going to make a run for it?"

"Are you going to let me go if I do?" I ask him while considering my options.

"No."

I exhale dramatically. "Fine."

"Fine, what?"

"I won't run." Because the efforts would be wasted and only continue to add to the drama and danger, and we all need a lot less of that around here. Bo's strides easily triple the length of mine, along with his supernatural speed and the fact that he's not beaten and bruised. I wouldn't make it out of his arm's reach without him catching me.

"Good girl," he tells me.

"That doesn't mean I won't be thinking about it though."

Bo gently sets me onto the ground but remains firmly in place like he's assessing whether I'll actually take off or not.

I step forward to our small, original group, my footing wobbly at the pain shooting up my leg.

Dash reaches out and steadies me, his warm touch a comfort to my soul.

Damn did I miss this red-headed man. What I wouldn't give for uninterrupted time with both Dash and Bo, just to stare at their faces and hug them over and over. I'd be lying if I said I hadn't been worried I would never see either one of them again. Up until today, the rumors of Rock Bridge had proven true. No one had ever made it out of there alive. And now, here we all are, a testament that sometimes, things change. I shouldn't assume either of them would want the same though, just like I shouldn't have marked Wes without his consent. A moment that will continue to haunt me.

Something deep within me told me to act, to latch onto his neck the same way he had done mine. I needed to taste his blood on my tongue, to feel his flesh break under the weight of my bite. I'd never had those urges in my entire life, and in the moment, they completely consumed me. It wasn't until I saw the shock and terror on his face that I realized I made a mistake, that I had disgusted him with such a repulsive act.

Whether it was him marking me, or a combination of the both of us, it brought his hound side fully to the surface, and at the very least, I am grateful for that.

I recall Wes, in the moments after shifting into his man form, reaching out to me. He held my hand and pulled me to him. Would he have done that if he didn't want me anymore?

"Wren." Everest snaps his fingers in front of my face. "You in there?"

I blink and nod. "Yeah, sorry. What's up?"

"As you know," he says. "The barrier will only take one through at a time. Since we both hold the key to granting access, we should work in tandem."

"Of course, yeah." I reach out and waft my hand through the air to feel the forcefield in question. The electricity of it tickles my fingertips like a sort of *hello*.

"We should get started." A burst sounds off in the distance, another dose of poison being spread across the confines of the prison. It's only a matter of time until we're dosed, too, killing whatever remaining creatures are trapped within the barrier. I squint my eyes to see where we just came from, not a single black tuft of fur in sight. My soul pleads with him to appear, to be okay.

Everest looks up to Bo. "Can you assemble them in two single-file lines?"

Bo laughs, almost like he's imagining order among a massive group of frantic demons.

One of them pushes through to the front, shoving whoever he can to make space. "What's fucking taking so long?" He's scared, but this is no way of getting things done.

The polite demon who spoke for the rest gets pushed down onto the ground.

Bo snatches the aggressor, snapping his neck and tossing him aside. "Would anyone else like to die today?" His voice carries over the now silent crowd. "No? Then make two fucking lines. And if one of you so much as sneezes on the person in front of you, I will personally rip the flesh from your skin and pluck your eyeballs from their sockets. Do you understand?"

A collective murmur fills the space as the demons agree with the terms of their arrangement.

Bo reaches to help the fallen demon up and swats some of the dirt caked to his side away.

"Th-thank you, sir."

Dash assists me closer to the barrier, holding me steady as I place my hand on its nearly invisible surface.

Everest approaches a few feet away and repeats the same movement. He calls out to the demons that are waiting impatiently patient, "One at a time from each line, please."

The first of both step through the border and turn back briefly. As if suddenly realizing they're finally free, they nod their heads and take off, their bodies disappearing within seconds.

"Next!" I yell into the crowd.

With each demon that passes through and the time that keeps seeming to tick by, my concern for Wes only grows. Three more blasts have gone off in the sky, only making the window of breathable air in this place smaller and smaller. What if he's trapped somewhere and needs help? What if the poison has already taken him from this world?

He promised he'd find me in our next life, but what if I'm still alive in this one? I trail my gaze to the beautiful man at my side, holding me from collapsing, and the arrogant alpha standing guard at the base of the assembly. How could I leave these two to be with Wes, but how could I ever be happy if I stayed? Both options tear my heart apart, and I'm not sure which is better—which is worse.

"He'll be here," Tremont leans in and whispers.

I glance over at him. "How can you be so sure?"

"A connection like that is impossible to sever."

I crane my head to assess how much longer the lines are, but the more demons that go through, the more that seem to appear. A fog creeps through the forest, alerting me that our time is running out.

Steadying my gaze on Everest, I nod toward the impending doom. He takes it in and motions for the next demon to step through.

"Jade, Tremont, we need to send you over." I do a poor job hiding the urgency in my voice.

"We aren't going without you," she tells me.

"You don't have a choice." I look to Dash. "That goes for you, too."

Dash shakes his head. "Not happening. I'm not leaving you behind again."

Tremont chimes in, "I made a promise."

"Fuck your promise," I blurt out.

Bo slides his shirt over his head and rips at the fabric. He approaches and shows me the section in his hand. "I'm going to secure this over your mouth and nose, okay?"

I tip my head toward the crowd much further in the danger zone than I am. "Help them first."

"No." Bo ties the thing around my head, covering my airway. He breaks off another section and gives it to Jade, then the rest to Dash, leaving himself empty-handed.

I breathe in his scent and it weirdly calms the chaos raging within. It's a temporary fix, but I welcome it all the same.

"Everybody, listen up." Bo walks over to the demons. "If you can, remove your shirt and fasten it over your face, or whatever you breathe through. Move the lines horizontally instead of vertically to get everyone out of the line of the fog. Do not panic, I repeat, do not panic. If I witness anyone forcing their way up the line, I will make your death much more painful than that of the poison." He scans the crowd. "Are there any sick, elderly, or children?"

A little girl steps out of the throng of people and stands in place, not daring to move any more than she already has.

Bo spots her and immediately stalks to her. He kneels in front of her, saying something I cannot make out from this far. The two exchange a few words and he extends his hands. She steps forward, allowing him to pick her up and hold her at his side.

She wraps her small arms around his neck and holds on tightly while he carries her over.

"You." Bo points to a woman with rainbow-colored hair a few people back in the line. "Come here." He sets the little girl gently on the ground near me and motions over to Everest. "You go through over there. Make sure she gets somewhere safe."

The woman nods without another word, complying with the order given by this alpha.

I pull a knife out of my waistband and hand it to the child. "Here." An offering that, no doubt, must look out of place, but in this world, might be the one thing that helps keep her alive.

"Thank you," she whispers before stepping across the barrier.

Bo turns back to the crowd, scanning for anyone else that might need to go through with more urgency than the rest.

"Next," I tell the demon waiting near me.

Tremont drags his already tattered shirt over his head and grips the fabric, ripping it apart. He hands it to Jade, who secures it around Everest's face, and uses the rest for himself.

"Can't you magic this away?" I ask him, unsure of the restraints of his skills. Can't he magic this all away? The barrier? The poison rain? The fucking administration of this place?

"I am no longer as powerful as I once was." His words seem to have an underlying meaning he isn't quite saying.

This isn't the time or place for me to question him, though. Perhaps if we make it through this, I will learn more about this mysterious man.

The line of demons finally starts to shorten, but the fog approaching is moving quicker than we can get through. A few on the end cough and choke and bury their faces further into their pathetic coverings.

If it's this bad for them, Wes must be trapped in it somewhere.

I urge them through the opening and look at my friends. "Jade, you need to go next. We're running out of time." I glance at the man holding me steady. "You, too, Dash."

Bo rushes over with a limp body in his grasp.

I can't make out who or what it is, but I know the person needs to get to fresh air soon if they're going to make it.

"Can you stand?" Bo positions the person upright near Everest, steadying them with a gentleness that is so unlike his natural behavior. He cranes his neck over to my side and focuses on the man about to step through. "Get her after you go over."

The man hurries across and rushes over to grab onto her hand. The two stay with each other until both of them are out of sight, no longer a concern of ours.

Ten demons on each side turn into nine, then eight.

The thick fog creeps further in, the remaining demons holding their breath and plugging their airways.

It's not until the last of them are through that Jade and Tremont enter the line.

Tremont stares directly at me. "You better be right behind me or I'm coming back for you."

"Dash, Bo." I urge the two of them to go through, leaving only me and Everest in the danger zone. I cough as the poison teases my lungs with its deadliness.

"We aren't going through until you do." Bo stands firmly in place, his jaw tight and his body rigid.

I swallow and shift my focus to him, to Dash, to Everest. If Dash and Bo don't go through, that means Everest can't either, because there's no way he's going to cross without granting them access first. My gaze skims the forest beyond, my eyes stinging from whatever they unleashed in the sky.

No Wes in sight.

How can I put three other lives in danger because of one person? One person who happens to be my fated mate. How can I prioritize his life over theirs, over my own? Especially when every single part of me is screaming to find him, to save him, and at worst, die with him.

"Mother fucker," I blurt out, furiously stepping through the barrier. I suck in a fresh breath of air and blink through the tears I can no longer control.

Jade holds onto my shoulders, rubbing them with what I assume she thinks is a comforting touch.

Dash joins us a moment later, his own lifeforce desperate for the freshness this side brings.

The fog grows thicker and I can barely make out the shape of Bo until he's crossed over. Despite his headstrong persona, I can tell how relieved he is once he's joined us.

I step closer, squinting to find Everest through the all-consuming haze.

Jade drops her hands from my shoulders and moves toward the wall of white that has formed. "Where is he? Why hasn't he come yet?"

Her worry for Everest is something similar to what I've felt this whole time for Wes, only she's just now understanding what I've been experiencing.

If I weren't freaking out myself, I'd probably say something snarky about her finally grasping what I've been saying all along.

But with each passing second, I become more concerned with not just Wes, but Everest, too. The goal was for us all to make it out of here alive, not lose some of us in the final hours.

My heart pounds harder, my stomach turning at the possibility that Jade and I might both lose someone we love today.

"I'm going back." Bo steps forward but I reach out and grab onto his arm.

"The hell you are." I place myself in front of him. "If he's dead you'll be trapped." Before any of them can stop me, I burst through the barrier and onto the other side.

"Wren, is that you?" Everest stands with his hand still firmly pushed against the wall.

"What the fuck are you doing?" I yell at him.

He coughs and holds the shirt tightly on his face. "I saw something."

A flicker of hope sparks inside of me. Could it be true? Or is Everest going crazy from the poison flowing within him?

"You need to save yourself." I tilt my head toward freedom. "Hold them off, please."

"You know I can't do that," he barely chokes out.

I use his moment of weakness to approach him, and with the little bit of strength I can muster, I shove him to the other side.

I turn my attention back to the blinding fog and pray for a miracle or a swift death. My throat tightens and I know I should follow him, but I refuse to accept anything other than those two options.

CHAPTER 18

Dash

I've only just gotten her back and she's gone again.

I expect to see her face cross over, but instead, it's that of Everest, the guy who is fixated on Jade.

Bo snatches him by the collar of his plain white T-shirt and lifts him off the ground. "What the fuck did you do?"

"I...I saw something."

"What do you mean *you saw something*?" Bo spits out through his gritted teeth.

"Let go of him," Jade cries out, scratching at Bo's arm. "You're hurting him."

"He's going to wish he was fucking dead when I get through with him if she doesn't..."

"A flash of red," Everest interrupts. "I thought—I thought it was Wes."

Tremont presses his hand to the wall of white and closes his eyes. A second later, he opens his mouth. "She's alive. I can sense her."

Bo drops Everest onto the ground with a thud. "I'm going in."

I step in front of him. "If anyone's going after her, it's me. If I die, it doesn't matter."

"The hell it does," Jade blurts out from her spot next to Everest.

"No." I shake my head. "You don't understand...I'm..." I pause, unsure if I should actually say it out loud. Is it supposed to be a secret? Will it put these people in danger if they know? Aren't we all in as much peril as we possibly can be? I find the words slipping out anyway. "A phoenix."

Jade stares at me like I grew a horn out of the center of my forehead. "What?"

"So, if I die, I'll come back. No big deal."

Bo steps around me. "You don't know if there's an expiration on that Dash. You can't just volunteer to die whenever the opportunity presents itself."

232

"Oh, and you can?" I shove his solid chest. "What are the chances you resurrect, huh? Zero. At least with me, there's hope."

"No one is dying, today." Tremont keeps his palm against the wall. "There's a secondary presence."

"That's it." Bo takes off toward the barrier. "They could have sent someone to finish her off."

Tremont uses his free hand to throw a blast of magic at Bo, holding him firmly in place. "I could do without the threats that are no doubt coming."

Bo starts to mouth off but stops at being called out for it. His pleading gaze locks onto mine.

"Don't make me restrain you, too, Dash." Tremont closes his eyes and tilts his head back toward the wall. Slowly, he steps away, but keeps his blasting energy pointed at Bo to keep him from going after Wren.

A flash of white, not dull and drab like the fog consuming the other side, but bright and comforting, momentarily explodes before us. Flames replace the light and once I'm able to blink through the chaos, a large shape appears.

Giant and standing on all fours with onyx fur and sharp, exposed fangs, rises from the burst of color. The fog that made it through dissipates, and a small body remains on the ground.

I rush over, skidding to a stop beside her.

The massive hound growls at me but I go to her anyway.

"Wren," I mutter while positioning her head off the ground and into my lap.

"If you don't let me go," Bo wrangles with the forcefield Tremont is using to hold him in place. "I have to get her away from that..."

The creature rubs at Wren's ankle with his snout and then peers up at me.

My mouth falls open. The creature is no stranger at all. Those eyes staring back at me belong to none other than...

"Wes?" Jade clutches her chest as she takes in the sight of him.

"No fucking way," Bo adds. He shrugs off the last of Tremont's magic and runs over to Wren's other side.

She opens her beautiful eyes and brings her hand up to her face, tugging down the fabric and drawing in a deep breath. "I see the dogs out of the bag." Wren pats the fur on the top of Wes's head. "Help me up." She extends her hand toward me and uses the other to press off the ground and rise to her feet. "Took you fucking long enough," she tells Wes.

He whimpers and nudges his head against her leg again.

"I'm sure we're all stunned by the recent events, but we should put as much distance as we can between us and this place." Wren flits her attention at the fog blasting the barrier around the prison.

Everest rises to his feet and runs his hand through his hair. "I have a place not too far from here. We can regroup and go from there."

"Is it warded?" Wren asks him.

He nods.

We make it to Everest's safehouse within an hour, just in time for the protective barrier Tremont projected around us to wear off once we stepped inside.

Tremont stumbles and catches himself on the wall. "That took a lot out of me, I apologize."

Bo sets Wren down on the floor, only now allowing her out of his grasp, like he's been afraid she might disappear on him this whole time.

I can't be certain, but I wouldn't be surprised if there's a fated bond there, too. In all my time in this realm with Bo, I've never witnessed him so...captivated by another. Stale bread and killing—yes. But a person, definitely not.

"Nice place," I tell Everest while I scan the vast modernness of this home. It's nothing like the shanty the guys and I rest our heads at, and it's even a step up from what Wren had shown us.

"Thanks." Everest nervously rubs his neck. "It was my brother's."

The past tense word choice doesn't evade me.

"And he's where?" Bo chimes in.

"Dead." Everest steps further into the front area and points down a long hall-way. "There are bedrooms down the hall, bathrooms in both. The water should be hot, and if you check the closets, there should be spare clothes." He pauses on Wren and Jade. "Although they may be a little big for the both of you."

"I'm fine with this," Wren skims her hand along the side of her body.

"I'm going to get cleaned up. I suggest you all do the same." Everest stalks back over to the door and turns the lock to the fastened position. "I'll put food on once I'm finished."

Tremont offers his thanks and follows the path Everest had instructed, disap-pearing into the room on the left.

"Come on," Wren says as she limps in the direction Tremont had gone. "You said there's another bedroom?" She glances over her shoulder at Everest.

"Last one on the right."

Bo locks his sights on Jade when she gravitates toward Everest. "Where the fuck do you think you're going?"

"I'm not a child anymore, Bocephus." Jade keeps her arms folded over her chest, unmoving to her brother's dominance.

Wren sighs and backtracks, latching onto Bo's hand and dragging him away from his sister. "I said come on." She meets my gaze and tilts her head, insinuating that I should follow, too. "Wes, Dash."

Wes swishes his tail from side to side as he trails behind her. His stature barely fits through the opening, but he makes it work.

I thought he would have shifted into his man form by now, but he remains in full transition. From what I recall, he spoke of his hound side like it was a separate entity, a beast that lived within him. Could it be possible that this creature has taken over and refuses to grant him access back to his body? There's so much about this world I've yet to learn and part of me wonders if I'll ever have the answers to most of the questions that keep me awake at night. And then there's the other half that makes me consider if I want to know them at all.

Just when I start to make sense of something, everything changes. Is it even worth figuring out anymore? One thing is certain—we narrowly escaped death and I'm not confident it won't come creeping back in when we least expect it.

If the people who ran Rock Bridge resorted to killing every last demon that remained trapped within their walls, there's no telling the lengths they will go to ensure that all of the demons that got away meet that same fate, too.

"Dash," Wren's soft voice calls out to me.

I follow her into the large bathroom and nearly gasp at the sight of the massive shower.

She reaches inside and turns the dial. Water sprouts out from two different spots in the ceiling and then secondary streams flow out from about waist height. Steam immediately fogs the glass up.

"Can you help me?" She fumbles with the top of her shirt, refusing to use her other hand.

I step toward her and notice the bruising on her wrist. "Are you okay?"

She looks up at me, fresh tears welling in her eyes. "Not really."

How could I expect anyone to be okay after all that she's been through? All that I don't even know but can only assume. Rock Bridge is a terrible place, and the stories that float through the demon taverns only allude to the awful things that are done there.

Wren was no exception to that rule.

"I'm sorry," I tell her, because I'm not sure what else to possibly say. My heart thuds at the unknowns, the words I've wanted to tell her since she was taken that dreadful day. I begged the universe for this moment, to have her in front of me, and now I'm at a fucking loss.

"It's not your fault."

I swipe the hair off her shoulder and spot the fresh set of teeth marks near where Bo had marked her before. "Are those from Wes?"

Because if they were from anyone else, I may have to burn this entire realm to the fucking ground.

She nods faintly. "Dash?"

I slide her thick leather armored top over her shoulder, exposing her dirt-covered skin.

She slithers out of it not bothering to cover her now bare breast.

Still, I look away to give her as much privacy as possible in this vulnerable moment. "Yeah?" I slither the rest of the shirt over her other arm and lay it on the tiled ledge of the shower. I kneel before her and unbutton her pants, carefully dragging them over her ass.

"Do you still like me?"

Her question catches me off guard. "What?" Now it's my turn to look up at her. I steady her hands so she can step out of her pants and then stand.

"I just didn't know...if what happened...if it changed things between us."

"You can't be serious."

Wren averts her gaze momentarily, almost like she's embarrassed by the conversation. "I'd understand if it did."

I gently cup her battered cheek in my hand. "It only solidified the fact that I cannot live without you."

"Really?" A single teardrop rolls down her cheek.

I wipe it away with my thumb and kiss the spot where it had landed. "Really."

How could she possibly think anything else? Have I not made her feel secure in the way I feel about her? Have I grown so numb to things that my reactions have convinced her that I want nothing more than to be by her side until she will no longer allow it?

"You remained in every single thought of mine while you were gone. I begged the universe, the gods, the angels, anyone who might be listening to ensure your safety. Bo and I would have stopped at nothing to free you from that place."

"You two made it possible." Wren closes her eyes and leans into my touch. "We couldn't have done it without you."

I guide her backward and into the shower. "Here. I'll be waiting when you're done."

Her bright blue eyes meet mine. "Join me." She pauses and adds, "Please."

"Are you sure?" I ask her. There are no doubts in my mind about showering with her, especially after how the first time went, but I don't want to take advantage of a single moment if she isn't ready to be that close again. After all that's happened, she deserves some time to herself, too.

"Yes." She reaches for the hem of my shirt and tugs it upward with her good hand.

I drag the thing the rest of the way and toss it aside. I watch her step under the water and let it cascade down her face and over each delicate curve of her body while I remove the rest of my clothes. My cock throbs in response but is quickly hindered by the bruises and cuts scattering her precious form.

I thought Wes would have been able to heal her, to keep her out of harm's way, but I was sorely mistaken.

I join her in the stream of water and pull her to my chest, savoring the contact of our skin together. "I'm so sorry." I pat her hair out of her face and press my lips to her forehead.

"Will you kiss me?" She tilts her head up toward me.

How could I ever say no to her? I do as she wishes and melt my mouth onto hers, using the softest pressure I can possibly manage. I skim my tongue over hers and sigh in relief at being able to do this with her once again. I worried I had lost her forever, and here she is, in my arms.

Her hand trails down my shoulder, my arm, landing on my waist. She melts into me and picks up the intensity, her palm finding my shaft and gripping it in her small grasp.

My body betrays me and reacts immediately. "Wren..." I hold her face in between my hands and catch my breath.

"I want to feel anything else other than pain, Dash, please. I need this." Her gaze darts to something behind me. "You can come in here."

"Don't let me interrupt," Bo says from his spot in the doorway, not a hint of jealousy in his voice. He strolls over and puts his arm on the side of the shower opening. "But if you don't give the girl what she wants, I'll come in and do it for you."

Wren extends her hand out toward him. "Come on."

Bo exhales and remains in place. "You don't know what you're asking for, Birdie."

"I think I do." She motions for him to step inside with us. "Take your clothes off."

My heart increases its tempo as Bo complies. He kicks his pants off and walks under the other stream, letting it wash over his face. He runs his fingers through his long black hair and rings the water out.

Wren stands taller to kiss me, a new longing in each movement that wasn't there before.

I tug her body toward me and run my hands over the arch of her back and settle them on her plump ass. Dragging her off the floor, I lift her up and wrap her legs around my waist.

She reaches down and positions me at her entrance, stroking me with enough finesse that I'm surprised I haven't come undone yet.

"Are you sure?" I ask her.

"Just give her your cock already, Dash," Bo quips from his spot under the stream, his own cock gripped in his hand.

I try not to stare, but the sheer size of it makes me feel a bit lacking. I shift Wren slightly and settle her tight pussy over my shaft, penetrating her carefully. I moan and throb in a way I wasn't sure I'd get to experience when she was taken from us.

"You feel so good." Wren wraps her arms around my neck and glides her body up and down as best she can given her feeble condition.

I hold on under her thighs and move her gently.

She stops her motion and pulls away slightly. "Wes, is that you?"

I step backward and walk her over to the glass with my cock still buried inside her.

She wipes at the steam covering the partition and narrows her gaze. "Hey," she keeps her voice low.

"Plenty of room in here for all of us," Bo calls out from his spot.

I catch the darkness of Wes's fur out of the corner of my eye and grow curious as to whether he will join us in his current form.

His hound whimpers and a moment later, the black coat is replaced by that of flesh.

I meet his gaze and worry for a second that he's going to rip my throat out for actively having sex with his fated mate, but if he hadn't done it while as a hound, chances are I'm probably safe from his immediate murder. I lower Wren onto the wet floor, allowing her to change her mind since Wes has joined us.

"Don't stop on my account." Wes steps into the shower, walking over to the open stream and tilting his head up toward it. The water pelts his face and chest.

I lean against the glass and wait for Wren to decide on what, or who, she wants to continue with.

She steps toward me and drags my face down onto hers, pressing her lips onto mine. She whimpers and drags her fingers up into my hair, tugging it in her fist.

When I open my eyes, Wes is behind her leaving a trail of kisses over her shoulder. He moves her hair aside and nips at her neck.

Wren lingers her own mouth down my jaw, onto my chest, and makes her way onto the tip of my cock. She licks the length and swirls her tongue over the end, dipping it under and taking me into her mouth.

I rest my head on the wall behind me and bask in the pleasure of being inside her in any capacity.

Wes enters her from behind, causing her lips to vibrate around my throbbing cock when she moans for him. He latches onto her hips and thrusts in and out of her, sending her rocking over my own shaft.

Wren tilts her head to the side, looking toward Bo. She reaches her good arm out and snaps her fingers, commanding him over to her.

He hesitates but complies, sauntering over with a lust-filled gaze.

Once he's within reach, she slides her mouth off me and spits into her hand. She takes me back inside her but uses the lubrication to grip onto Bo's enormousness.

Bo steadies himself on the wall next to him and focuses his attention on the tiny hand wrapped around his cock. He doesn't touch her, doesn't take anything more than she's willing to give. He could easily shove me out of the way and take my place, but instead, he's patient. Something that is so very unlike Bo.

I stop assessing the situation and concentrate on my own pleasure and experience with her. I bundle her hair off her face and hold it back, watching with bated breath as she consumes me. I feel myself heighten and like she senses it, her lips tighten and her tongue cups the bottom of my shaft.

She increases her suction and moans against me.

I explode in her mouth, not ready to be done but desperate for the release.

Wren doesn't pull away, yet she stays for the duration of my orgasm, sucking up every last drop I have to give her. Once she's satisfied I've reached completion, she hovers her mouth up my torso and returns to my lips, kissing me while Wes is inside her from behind and Bo is in her hand.

I reach between us and slide my fingers to her clit, applying gentle but firm pressure.

Her body quivers under the touch. She moans again and grazes her teeth over my bottom lip.

"Come for me," Wes whispers into her ear, sending her spiraling off the edge of bliss.

Wren falls into me, her lips still on mine, while Wes thrusts his own climax into her.

The two of them ride the wave together while I savor the up-close spectator's view of her pleasure.

Bo grunts and finishes right behind them.

Wren manages to continue stroking him through his orgasm while she comes down from hers.

She lays her head against my chest and continues to press her weight into me. I wrap my arms around her and cherish this moment, knowing that there's a chance it won't happen again. We may have escaped the clutches of Rock Bridge, but we haven't won this war.

CHAPTER 19

Wren

I sit on the edge of the bed while Wes kneels at my feet and studies the wounds littering my body.

"What took you so long?" I ask him.

"To shift back?"

"That...and back at Rock Bridge. I thought you were dead."

He sighs and lowers his head. "I don't expect you to understand."

I place my finger under his chin and tilt it up to me. "It's hard if you don't talk to me."

Wes nods. "We have a lot to discuss."

I steady my wild nerves and say the thing I've needed to say since the moment it happened. "I'm sorry, that I..." I trace the remnants of the mark I left on his shoulder. "I shouldn't have done that."

His eyes light up, doing that glowing thing that sets my soul at ease and lights it on fire at the same time. "Don't you apologize for that."

"You didn't consent to it, and I'll never forgive myself for doing it against your will."

"Against *my* will? Wren, I never wanted any of this for you. I didn't want you to feel obligated to be something you weren't. The mate bond that my hound formed with you, you never asked for that."

"Wes..."

He cuts me off. "It was wrong of me to pursue you. To put you in danger. To give in to my desires. To mark you."

"Wes..." I rest my palm along his cheek. "Wes," I say a little louder to get his attention. "You don't get it, do you?"

His jaw tenses and he blinks up at me. "What?"

"Why do you think I faltered that day in the warehouse? You've seen me fight;

you know I'm not that sloppy. It was our bond latching into place and you can't convince me otherwise. I felt you before I saw you. But that moment my eyes locked on to you it was like waking from a deep sleep. I denied it. Damn, did I try. You and I both know there's no escaping what fate has in store for us. This connection that you're so convinced is one-sided...I feel every bit of it."

"That's not...possible." He stares at me, his eyes darting back and forth like he's trying to make sense of what I just told him.

I shrug and smile. "At this point, I'm convinced anything is possible."

"But you're a hunter." His statement comes across a bit questioning.

"Not anymore. Not the way I used to be. Never again."

Wes rests his head on my knees and kisses them. "Can I please heal you?"

Sighing, I consider his request. "Only a few things, because you need to stay strong for us, and if I'm being honest, I feel like shit."

"What hurts the most?" he asks me, his gaze expectant.

I hold out my wrist and turn it over. "This is more frustrating than all of them."

He brings it to his lips and mutters a few words I cannot decipher, the ache and pain dulling until it disappears completely. "Better?"

I twirl it around and bask in how fucking quickly that worked. "And how do *you* feel?"

"Totally fine, what else can I fix?"

I point down at my thigh, where I had Wes melt the wound shut to stop the bleeding.

"Lay back," he tells me.

I comply, relaxing my head on the plush comforter and savoring the touch of his lips on my skin. The pain temporarily increases, but then disappears completely. I prop myself up on my elbows. "Do you feel anything?"

He kisses the inside of my leg and trails his lips down to another wound. "Not at all. And I should remind you, I cannot lie to you."

I flop back all the way and throw my arms out to the side. "Have at it then." Because frankly, I could use this kind of relief after the chaotic last few weeks.

Wes goes to work whispering sweet nothings to my body, healing the countless injuries I've sustained lately. With every wound mended, I feel my strength returning. A part of me wondered if I'd ever recover from the torment I'd experienced, but with Wes at my side, and Dash and Bo nearby, I have hope that maybe things won't always be bad.

He manages to cover the brunt of the wounds by the time Everest bursts through our bedroom door. "The house is on fire."

Bo and Dash both jump from their spots sprawled out on various pieces of furniture in the room.

"Are you fucking serious?" I ask him while hopping out of bed and rushing over to slide out of the sleep shorts I found in the closet and step into my armored pants.

"It's not hunters. It's demons." He rushes out and across the hall to pound on Tremont's door. "Sir, the house is on fire."

Tremont appears on the other side, his hair in a mess and his eyes half open. "What?"

"I repeat," Everest raises his voice loud enough for the entire place to hear. "We are under attack. The house is on fire!"

Bo steps behind me and tucks my hair behind my ear. "What's going on?"

Everest throws his hands in the air. "Oh, forget it, let's just all die."

"I'm just kidding." Bo ruffles the hair on Everest's head. "Where are your weapons?"

"Follow me." Everest takes off down the hall and into the front room, disappearing from our line of sight.

"It's got to be the wendigo army." I buckle the straps on my shirt and tuck the few knives I still had in my possession into various places on my body. "I'm not sure which is worse."

Dash tugs his shirt over his head and glances in the mirror. He walks over and kisses my cheek. "At least we're together this time." He points his finger at me. "No splitting up."

"Just try not to get killed."

Dash smirks. "I'll do my best."

We meet Everest, Bo, and Jade at the end of the hall.

"What's the plan?" I ask them, hoping someone has an answer. The last time I was in charge of something, it put all of us in danger.

Tremont lets out a breath. "Are we close to Folly?"

Everest nods. "Why?"

"There's a weak spot in the fold there. I assume it's under heavy guard, but if we can get there..." Tremont glances over at me briefly, it's not long, but long enough to send a chill down my spine. "We can cross-realm travel."

"That's not possible," I tell him. "The realms have been shut off for decades."

"And I've only been here a few years."

I stare at him, unsure of how he could be telling the truth. I recall Wes telling me this very thing, but to hear it directly from Tremont is a whole different story.

Wes speaks up. "It's our only shot, we have to take it."

"We don't have enough power to make it happen. Not for all of us." I count the bodies and note the juice that kind of travel would entail. From the minimal details I've read about the barrier put on our realm, this is simply inconceivable.

"What other choice do we have?" Tremont blinks around the group. "If it's not today, when? You can't run forever."

"Where will we go?"

"Wherever the angels send us." Tremont ducks as a flaming bottle bursts through the window in the kitchen.

It explodes, sending shards of glass flying by us.

Wes shields me with his body and pulls me toward him.

"We have to run, now." Everest latches onto Jade's hand. "If the hunters haven't caught onto our whereabouts yet, this could be our only chance out."

Even if we do make it to the vulnerable spot in the fold, we all won't be able to make it through. Someone is going to have to stay behind. Tremont is the magical creator of this plan so it's a given that he will go through. None of us will put Jade in harm's way, and there's no way Everest will leave her side. And after everything terrible I've done in my life, there's not a chance I'm willing to put myself above any of these three men I'm drawn to. It has to be me.

"I can't do a protective barrier this time. I have to save my power for the fold." Tremont clutches the knife Everest had given him.

Bo and Wes exchange a look.

Wes speaks for both of them, "We'll provide cover."

"I can help." I'm more than capable now that Wes healed many of my injuries. Not that having them would have stopped me either way.

"No." Bo grabs my hand and places it in Dash's on our way to the door. "You two stay together, do you hear me?"

"Don't you dare look at me with those goodbye eyes."

Bo scoffs. "There's no such thing."

"I'll clear a path, Everest, you lead the way." Wes grips the handle and turns to us. "Everyone ready?" He doesn't wait for an answer.

I kick off the floor and run behind Wes, being cautious of the flames that flicker off his body. I keep hold of Dash, mainly because I worry for his safety more than I do my own.

Wes remains in man form, but his beastly abilities surface. He blasts an orb of fire at an oncoming demon and sends them flying off into the bushes. Another approaches in front of him and he tosses a fireball their way, too.

I glance over my shoulder, Everest and Jade are on our heels, waiting for their opportunity to go around us.

Wes readies his arms to his side and lets out a ferocious roar, a wave of fire flowing out of his mouth and hands. The ground in front of him bursts into flames, killing anything in his path. The fire dies down and leaves nothing but a lingering smoke in its wake.

Everest uses the violent outburst to run ahead, leaving Jade near Tremont.

Dash glances over at me. "Do you trust him?" He tilts his head back at the man we know almost nothing about.

"Not really. Do you?"

Tremont could easily be running us straight into a trap right now and honestly, I wouldn't at all be surprised. Pissed, most definitely, but considering how things typically go for us, I wouldn't rule out that he isn't working for the enemy.

Not too long ago I thought these people around me were the enemy, and here I am, falling for three of them and fighting for the rest.

We leap over logs, run through briar bushes, and skid down a long slope.

My heart pounds so loud I can feel it in my ears, and a doom like no other creeps in. It's strange to be this out of control—to have nowhere safe to go. Every inch of this realm is plagued with vicious creatures that want nothing more than to kill us or steal our power.

Everest falls back, letting Wes take over, and joins Tremont at his side. "This is it, where to now?"

Tremont raises his hand and scans the air, running along the edge of the barrier keeping us trapped within Prania.

I swallow the thick lump that forms in my throat and look back in the direction we came. If the wendigo army catches up to us, we're stuck between them and an impossible boundary.

"I can't fucking find it." Tremont continues to investigate the integrity of the fold.

"Get behind me, Miss Oliver." Dash steps in front of me, a noble and kind gesture, but misplaced.

My fighting skills far outweigh his, and if anyone should be protecting anyone, I should be on the front line with Wes and Bo.

I didn't become *Furla Ain* for no reason. I earned that title—even if that role means nothing to me now.

"What did he call you?" Tremont steps in front of me and places his hand on my shoulder.

I shrug him off me. "What?"

"I was just teasing her," Dash says in what I assume is his way of trying to mediate the weirdness brought on by Tremont.

Tremont steadies his gaze, something wild and disturbing about the way he's looking at me. "What is your full name?"

A battle cry sounds in the distance; a blaring alarm that our time is nearly up.

I reach to unsheathe two of my knives but Tremont insists.

"Your name, please. I'm begging you."

"Wren Oliver, why?"

His face turns white as a sheet and his mouth falls open. "Angels." Tremont latches onto my forearm and pulls me over to the fold. "We don't need a weak spot if we have you."

I yank at my arm. "Let go of me."

"I'm not trying to hurt you, Wren, I swear." He holds out his other hand to stop Bo and Wes from advancing on him, a flicker of magic sizzling across his palm. "Either everyone hold on or this train is leaving without you."

The screams of the army grow closer, and I figure, if I'm going to die, I'd rather it not be by some creature I accidentally embarrassed.

I grab onto Dash, linking his fingers around mine. "Come on."

Dash takes Everest's hand, who takes Jade's. Jade reaches for her brother, and finally Wes leads up the rear.

He blasts a steady current of fire at the ground to buy us a little more time from attack and turns to the rest of us. "This better fucking work."

"Hold on tight." Tremont steps to the barrier and hovers his palm against it. "Grant me access to your magic."

"My magic?" I stare at him. "I hope this whole thing doesn't depend on something that doesn't fucking exist."

But with the words I speak, something strange rattles in my core. The same thing I've felt numerous times in my life but have disregarded. The thing that blasted that magical device off my chest in Rock Bridge when Parla was trying to torture me. The thing that got me and Wes through the barrier when I went back for him and consumed too much of that poisonous fog. The thing that's kept me alive more times than I can count. A piece of me that I've never acknowledged until now, simmering just under the surface.

Tremont presses on the barrier keeping us trapped in this realm. A glaring light appears, beaming brighter and brighter until we're completely consumed by it. "Don't let go," he tells me over the deafening screams of the white energy.

Don't let go, I repeat to myself over and over, praying the rest of them can hear me.

Find out where Wren went in the final installment of her epic adventure in *Fated to Monsters*, book three in the *Falling for the Enemy* series.

Fated to Monsters

FALLING FOR THE ENEMY (BOOK THREE)

Don't give up.

CHAPTER 1
Wren

My head throbs with a force that makes my vision blur more than it already was.

I scrape my fingers along the ground, desperate for any indication of my location. The air is cool and fresh as I suck in each gasping lungful, and despite it making no sense at all, gravity itself seems to have changed, too.

I blink once, twice, three times. My chest heaves, matching the same frantic energy as every other ounce of myself.

"Wes!" I call out into the abyss. "Bo!" I pause. "Dash!"

Slowly, I rise to my feet with my hands out.

"Where the fuck am I?" I whisper into the nothingness around me.

So, help me Angels, I will murder Tremont if he betrayed us.

The last thing I remember is holding on for dear life while being shoved into a vacuum of darkness. I'm not certain how much time has passed, or if we all made it out alive, let alone to the same place.

I close my eyes and steady my breath before opening them again. This time, my surroundings come into focus, and the ringing in my ears fades to a dull murmur.

A writhing body draws my attention from a few feet away, and I rush over to it without another thought.

"Wr-Wren, is that you?" Jade squints at me and sits upright. "Where's—" She glances around and I watch as her eyes widen. If I had to guess the same panic I'm feeling is now coursing through her. "Everest?" She scrambles to her feet. "Where are we?"

Clenching my jaw, I scan the vicinity and try to make an educated guess. But it's too dark. Too different. Too unfamiliar to state a conclusion.

"I don't know." I swallow harshly and beg the Angels help me locate any of the men we came here with.

"There." Jade points ahead and takes off toward another lump of a person littered in this desolate forest.

I run past her and skid to a halt beside the body. Gripping the collars of his shirt, I shake him harder than I probably should. "What the fuck have you done?"

Tremont snaps his gaze up at me. "It worked."

Within a split second, I slide a small knife out of my waistband and press it to his throat. "Where are they? Tell me what you did to them or I'll gut you right here and now."

He wiggles under my grasp but it's no use, not when I've already made up my mind.

"You have five fucking seconds...four..." I push the blade deeper into his skin without fully penetrating the soft flesh.

Jade reaches for my shoulder, but I shrug her off.

"Where are they?" I yell at him. "Where are *we*?"

A sly grin eases its way across his face.

"Arthlia." But it isn't Tremont's voice, instead, it's that of my fated mate.

My sights dart from the man I was poised to kill and up at the man who appears from the shadows ahead.

"Wes." His name is barely a whisper lingering on my lips. I drop Tremont with a thud, and rise to my feet once again, rushing over to throw my arms around Wes.

His strong grip catches and drags me toward him. "My girl." Wes inhales deeply and hugs me tighter. "We did it."

It's then that Dash and Bo come into my line of sight behind Wes, and Everest follows up the rear.

"Did I hear you threaten to kill someone, Birdie?" Bo says as he approaches. "Not going to wait for me?"

Wes sets me on the ground, and I pull Bo and Dash in for a group embrace.

"Aw." Bo pats my head. "You missed us."

I release him and punch him in the shoulder. "I thought you guys were goners."

Dash kisses the top of my head. "Going to have to try harder than that."

I exhale and bask in knowing that all three of these men are safe, but the overwhelming realization that we did the impossible punches me in the gut.

"Wait a minute." I point toward Wes. "You said we're in Arthlia. How?" I train my focus on the man responsible for our escape. "Is that true?"

Tremont rubs at the spot on his neck where the blade nicked him and pushes up onto his feet, dusting his legs off and glancing around. "Well, like I said, there was a weak spot in the fold."

"No." I shake my head. "You..." I desperately try to recall our last moments in Prania. "You said you didn't need it because..." I shift my gaze to the ground but struggle to recall the memory of the time not too long ago.

"We're here now," Jade tells us. "We're safe. And that's a win in my book." She clings to Everest's arm, and he seems to gravitate toward her with equal force.

"It's darker than I thought it would be." Wes cranes his head toward the sky.

"It must be a new moon," Tremont announces. "See that bright star right there? That's Polaris, the North Star. We can follow that and head north until we find somewhere to stay."

"Together?" I ask him.

The older man nods. "I didn't anticipate stranding you in unfamiliar territory."

"Why?" I narrow my gaze at him.

"Because that's not who I am. Not anymore. You're the reason I'm free of that place. The least I could do is give you some advice before parting ways."

"Advice?" I cross my arms over my chest.

"Yes, Wren, advice. For starters, humans don't take kindly to being threatened within an inch of their life."

"How else am I supposed to get information out of them?"

"Like this. With your words." He motions between us. "You communicate."

I sigh and roll my eyes. "Seems ineffective."

The throbbing in my skull picks up its tempo, my body tilting off balance as I struggle to regain composure.

"Wren." Dash steadies me with his soft but strong hands.

Wes appears in front of me. "What's wrong?"

"I'm fine, really." I swallow down the aching in my head and take a few steps toward Tremont. "This North Star, where is it leading us?"

"Hopefully someplace where we can find food and shelter."

"Are we in danger here?"

He glances over at me like he's about to spill a secret but decides to keep it to himself. "No. You have nothing to fear from the humans, so long as you don't give them a reason to cause trouble. They're rather ignorant and oblivious."

"But." I flit my gaze behind me at Wes temporarily. "Humans aren't the only creatures in this realm, correct?"

Tremont continues his trek forward. "That's right. Many supernatural beings reside on Earth."

Supernaturals can't even get along amongst themselves, how are they able to with a whole other species?

"The supernaturals keep their existence a secret. Ensuring the humans stay in the dark is what allows peace between them."

"But how? That doesn't make sense. How is it possible for them to fly so far under the radar that they are undetected? No one sees the horns or claws or fangs or the magic?"

"The supernatural living on earth make it a part of their life's mission to keep the truth a secret. Because if the humans were ever to learn that truth, there's no telling what they would do. It's safer this way, for everyone involved."

I walk next to him without any real idea of where we are going. A million questions fill my head faster than they can be answered. Supernaturals are just allowed to exist in this realm without consequence? Safely and peacefully? While we've been fighting for our lives in a neighboring realm and knowing no sense of freedom.

Guilt flows its way up my back and sends a chill down my spine. My stomach tightens at the thought of all the monsters I left behind to rot and never escape the hell hole I once called home.

"And it's not like they go around with their claws and fangs and horns out in the open. Those with non-human-like traits avoid those things ever being seen. Most of the supernaturals here blend in with the rest of humanity. The witches don't use their magic out in the open. The vampires feast discreetly. The werewolves go deep into the forest during a full moon. The others find homes in sleepy towns or long-forgotten cities where they can go undetected and live their lives without concern for being found out. Not everyone is as cautious but the majority of them are. Because they know what's at stake if their secret comes out into the open."

I let his words simmer before asking another question. Surely things can't be this simple in this realm. There must be a catch. Something he isn't telling me.

Tremont looks back at the hodgepodge group following closely behind him. "You can all pass as humans if you don't let your magic rise to the surface and give you away." His gaze lingers on me. "Although you may want to find some different clothing. Something that fits this realm and doesn't make you look like you came out of a fantasy movie."

"Movie?" I pinch my brows together.

"Mmhm. A motion picture." He sighs and continues on his way. "You have much to learn about Earth."

But Tremont stops after a few steps and holds out his arms to stop us, too.

Instinctually, I press the hilt of a blade into each of my hands and ready myself for the threat. "What is it?" I whisper to the man and attempt to locate the source of his concern.

"It...It can't be."

My sights settle on a large building in the distance. Its shape is massive, and it's barely visible with the minimal illumination from the night sky. "What is this place?" I ask the man leading us through this uncharted territory. "Have you been here before?"

I study the way his shoulders tense, and he harshly swallows the lump in his throat.

"Yes," he mutters. "A lifetime ago."

"Is it safe?" Jade says softly from behind us.

"I'm fucking starving," Bo tells us as he shoves his way forward. "This place better have some fucking food. I could eat twelve loaves of bread."

"What an oddly specific number." I follow behind him and hope there's no danger ahead. We've already been through hell and back; we could use a little break from the chaos.

I want to believe things will be better but a voice in my head reminds me that the worst is yet to come.

CHAPTER 2

Bo

I'd be lying if I said Arthlia wasn't way fucking better than Prania.

Fuck Prania. That place sucks in every single regard.

The food sucks. The water sucks. The people suck. The fucking atmosphere sucks.

I don't know what they put in the air here, but my lungs are grateful to not have to breathe in that garbage from back home.

And whoever it was that decided to invent something called a Hot Pocket, I'd love to give them a big wet kiss on the lips. It is quite literally a hot pocket of bread filled with gooey cheese and various ingredients. I am on my fifth, and I don't see myself stopping anytime soon. There's nothing like it in Prania. Sure, we have bread and we have cheese, and something could maybe be fashioned over an open fire but they have these things called microwaves here that blast frozen food with electricity until it's hot and ready to eat.

Who needs hunters and gatherers when you have access to places like Costco?

"And this Costco," I say to Tremont. "They have cases upon cases of these frozen treats?"

"Yes," he responds. "But that's not all. They have a whole bread aisle. All the types of cheeses you could imagine. Frozen and fresh meat. Vegetables. Fruit. Cakes. Ice cream. You name it, they probably have it."

"I..." I get lost in thought as I imagine an endless supply of food at my fingertips. "I must go there."

Tremont holds out his hand when I stand. "Perhaps another time. Not tonight."

Despite wanting to snap his neck I comply and sit back down. We've only just got here; Costco can wait for another day. There's so much to learn of this world before I foolishly step out into it. I've never been one to shy away from danger but it's not just me who is affected now.

I shift my stare across the room at my long-lost sister who is no longer the little girl that was taken from me all those years ago. Now she is grown. She has seen things, and the world has treated her with such cruelty. And if it weren't for the fact that this Everest fellow brings a smile to her face, I would rip the skin from his flesh and gouge out his eye sockets.

"Here, try this." Dash hands me a plate with a strange-looking goo on it.

"What is this?" I ask him while shoveling a forkful of it into my mouth. "Mmm," I mumble.

"Peanut butter pie. I had trouble getting it out of the pan, that's why it looks like that."

I scrape every last bit of it off the plate and lick the fork clean. "Is there more?"

Dash grins and nods. "Yeah." He walks through the large, but dimly lit kitchen to retrieve said pie from the counter. "Does anyone want any more?"

When no one takes him up on his offering, he comes back over and sets the thing in front of me.

I blink at it, and then at him. "Did you want some?"

He shakes his head and nudges it toward me. "It's all you."

"This building," Wren says while looking right at Tremont. "Who does it belong to?"

Tremont pats the corners of his lips with his napkin. "An old friend." But when his gaze doesn't meet hers until after the words are spoken, I grow suspicious.

"And where is this friend?" She takes a cautious look around the big, open space. "Is he human? Or supernatural?"

"He is long from this world." Tremont pushes his plate forward and puts his elbows on the table. "As is his wife. Although, I would assume the house was inherited by their son. They had a rather difficult relationship, so I'm not at all surprised to see the house unoccupied."

"Who would abandon such a place?" Jade trails her finger along the stone countertop and walks from one end of the kitchen to the other.

"Given the provisions stocked in the freezer and refrigerator, I would assume it hasn't been abandoned completely. It just isn't his main residence. Which means our time here is limited. I advise we keep a low profile. Recover from the cross-realm travel and depart at sunup. Now that I know where we are, I can navigate us from here."

Damn, just when I was thinking we could finally stop for more than a few hours, we'll soon be on the run again.

"Feel free to find a room to sleep in and a bathroom to freshen up but do so by candlelight, and try to stay away from the windows. We don't need to bring any unwanted attention to us."

"I thought you said they were friends." Wren stares across at him through her lashes.

"*Were.* Past tense. Things were different then, and I've been gone for years. There's no telling how a homecoming will go, especially with having many guests."

"You didn't say what they were," I add. "Human or supernatural?"

Tremont breathes through his nose sharply before exhaling. "They were witches."

"And their son? Is he a witch, too?"

Tremont nods.

One measly witch is nothing I haven't handled in the past. Sure, they have some tricks up their sleeves, but they aren't a major threat.

My focus moves to Wren as she presses her fingers gently along her neck where I had marked her. I'm not entirely sure if she knows she's doing it, or if it's simply an unconscious reaction. Either way, it completely entrances me.

"If anyone needs me, I'll be in the first room on the right at the top of the stairs." Tremont latches onto one of the candles lighting up the space and takes it with him. "And this should go without saying, but please don't break anything." His gaze lingers on me far longer than it does on anyone else.

Once the door to his room creaks shut, I'm the first to break the silence. "Should we make a run for it?"

Wren runs her hand through her hair and sighs. "If we knew anything of this world, I would say yes, but we don't, Bo. We don't know what's out there."

"I'm with Wren," Wes chimes in.

Of course, he and his stupid mutt are with her.

Dash scoots in closer. "He's lying about something, isn't he?"

"Definitely," Everest adds. "But I agree about staying until morning. We're in no shape to go wandering around a new realm right now."

Jade reaches across the table and places her hand on top of mine. "Promise me we'll stick together this time?"

I clench my jaw. "Fine."

"We'll figure this out tomorrow, okay?" Wren stands from the table. "In the meantime, I think we could all use some rest." She extends her arm toward me. "Come on, grumpy."

I roll my eyes but rise to my feet, too. "I'm picking the room." Plucking a candle from the table, I go in the direction Tremont went, turn, and go up the winding staircase to the upper level of this large house.

The floorboards creak under my steps despite doing what I can to be quiet.

The landing opens up to a long corridor that seems to go on and on. Six doors are easily visible, and given that Tremont has chosen the first one on the right, I select the first one on the left. That way, we can be near if he tries to pull anything while we're waiting out the night.

I grip the cold metal door handle and open the door, shoving the candle through to illuminate the space.

It's large, like one would expect considering the size of the rest of the house.

Dust particles float around the flickering flame, and a chill drifts out to greet me.

"Don't go too far," I tell Jade as she and Everest pass us in search of another room.

"I missed this overprotective brother thing." She stops at the door just past the bedroom I chose and disappears inside without another word.

I step fully into the bedroom and peruse the contents, noting the squeak of a faucet being shut off in the near distance. Tremont must have finished washing up.

"This is nice," Wren says as she plops onto the bed with four giant wooden things coming out of each end.

"What are these for?" I grip one of them and shake it.

"Decoration, I think." She pokes the intricate design and reclines onto her back. "I wonder what it's like to be this wealthy."

I raise a brow at her. "You weren't exactly living in squalor, Birdie."

Wren props herself up onto her elbows. "This is different and you know it."

"Yeah."

"There's a bathroom through this door." Dash clears his throat. "It's equally extravagant."

Wes opens another door. "There's a closet here." He goes in, his entire body vanishing into the space. "Looks like it's men's clothing," he calls out from inside.

I spot a lounge chair near the front of the room when I do a full circle. That will do for keeping post while the others rest their little heads. No fucking way I'm getting a second of sleep when Mr. Secrets is just across the hall, scheming Angels know what.

Wren hops off the bed and fumbles with the fasteners on her top. She pulls and yanks and tugs until she breaks free of its confines and discards it onto the floor.

Wes walks over like an obedient puppy and picks her shirt off the floor, folds it neatly, and sets it on top of the nearby dresser.

I lean against the bedpost and watch her performance.

"What?" She looks up at me as she leans down to drag her bottoms over her bare body.

I shrug and grin. "Just watching."

"That's your thing, isn't it?" Wren stands there, completely naked, waiting for my response.

I swallow and do everything I can not to gawk at every inch of her.

Would I rather march over there, throw her onto the bed, and spend the rest of the night learning where every freckle and scar marks her porcelain skin? *Absolutely.*

But this whole situation is more complicated than that, and I cannot be that reckless. Not when it comes to her. Not when everything is already more complicated than it should be.

She is a hunter. She is my enemy. She is fated mates with Wes, a hellhound with more power than me. And she's clearly in love with Dash, too, a creature we thought was only real in fairytales—a phoenix.

"Well, are you going to just stand there or do I have to drag you over here?" Wren snaps her fingers in front of my face.

"What?" I focus on the angelic features of her face.

"Come on." She latches onto my hand and pulls, but when I don't budge, she turns around and glares at me. "I will not ask again. *Come on.*"

And because there isn't anything I wouldn't do for her, I move in her direction.

I would follow her to the ends of the world and back, and given that we're quite literally in another realm, it's safe to say I'm a man of my word.

For now, I will submit to her requests, but there will be a point in time I have to resist her if I stand any chance of keeping her in my life.

CHAPTER 3

Wren

"This shower is nicer than the one at Everest's safe house." I adjust the knobs on the wall and watch the stream of water as it changes. "Does the one over there do that?"

"Yeah, Birdie. But you're going to break it if you keep fucking with it." Bo stands under the other showerhead with his face fully submerged. He runs his fingers through his long black hair and then wipes the droplets off his eyes before settling his sights on me. "Look who's staring now."

I roll my eyes but turn to hide my blushing cheeks. Scanning the labels of the bottles tucked into the shelf in the wall, I locate the one labeled *shampoo* and squirt some into my hand. I work the substance into my hair and bask in how damn good it smells. Upon rinsing the suds from my locks I note how clean they feel. I'm going to have to get a bottle or twelve of that shampoo whenever we settle into a place of our own.

My stomach knots. *A place of our own.* What if none of these men intend on sticking together once we learn the ways of this world? They always have in the past but that was when they were running for their lives and trying to survive. Without that threat here what if they choose to go their separate ways? What if they choose to start their lives over, and I am not a part of that? I can't assume that they would want me to be in their new normal just because of our short time together. But I also can't imagine any future without them. I never meant for the feelings to start but now that they have there's no turning back. Not for me.

Being with them is the only certainty that I actually have in my life. Everything up until this point has been a fucking lie. I devoted my entire existence to fighting on the side of a war that was unjust. And now that I know the truth, what else do I have? I used to wake up every day with one single thing on my mind—killing as many demons as possible. Without that my life has no meaning, no purpose, no drive. The only silver lining was that I found them. Or well, they found me. They saved me. Not only from death but from a worthless existence.

But things haven't really changed for them. Hunters still want them dead. Parla is still out there plotting her revenge, and it's no doubt because of my interference. They may be safe temporarily but until Parla is gone and the soldiers that still wish to carry out her mission, the clock will continue ticking like a time bomb.

We were able to escape Prania but what will happen once she figures it out too? Her desire to kill all demons will no longer be confined to one realm but to potentially all of them. At what point will it be enough for her? She will stop at nothing until she has killed every last one of them.

Wes and Dash and Bo included.

How can I sit back and let that happen? I've already done too much to enable her and her sadistic plan to take over the world, I refuse to not use every resource I have to take her the fuck down.

I can't expect any of these men to want a future with me if they can't even expect to have a future for themselves. What kind of person would I be to even ask that of them without ensuring their safety?

"You okay in there?" Dash's gentle hands cup my cheeks and pull me out from under the water. "I thought you were trying to drown yourself for a second."

I blink through the droplets still trickling down my face. "Yeah."

"You okay?" Concern hides in the soft corners around his eyes.

"I will be once you kiss me." Because if this world has taught me anything it's that we must take advantage of the little downtime we get. It never fails to be gone before we least expect it, and there's no telling when we will ever get it back again.

"Are you sure?" Dash glances behind him at Bo who has both hands resting against the shower wall and his face down as the stream pelts his back.

Bo might be one grumpy son of a devil but damn is he a fucking masterpiece. Every sinewy piece of muscle is highlighted by the shimmer of the water.

"I'm sure," I tell him while grabbing his hand and placing it around my waist. "Don't worry about him."

Dash steps forward, his naked body meeting mine underneath the stream of water, reminding me of our very first time together. It seems like a lifetime ago when all of us were enemies, and I was held captive by the men I was supposed to execute. There was no telling how much longer I had until they killed me, so I did the unthinkable; I slept with one of them.

I hadn't admitted to myself at that point that I already had feelings for Wes. I knew *something* had blossomed between us, I just assumed it was a new form of hatred. Is it possible to hate someone so much that you end up falling for them? I guess there is a very thin line between love and hate.

But with Dash, things were completely different.

I didn't instinctually hate him the way I had Bo and Wes. Dash showed me kindness. And there was always this innocent part of him—a wholesome harmless-ness that I had never experienced. I knew Dash wouldn't hurt me, not in the tradi-tional sense. And my attraction to him was without question. Maybe that was because he didn't remind me of all the other men I had interacted with in the past. Whatever it was, I felt confident enough to act on it and satiate that hunger I felt toward him.

The same hunger I still feel, that has yet to dissipate in any capacity.

With Wes, I assumed it was the fated mate bond making my feelings for him so fucking strong. And with Bo, I chalked it up to the alpha marking he left on my neck.

Dash has none of those supernatural ties to my soul, and still, I feel for him the way I do with Wes and Bo.

Is it possible that what we share is as simple as an honest connection?

How could I have gone my entire existence and felt nothing resembling what I do for them, and now all of a sudden, I'm drawn to three drastically different men?

A hellhound. An alpha of alphas. And a phoenix.

The fiercest demon assassin of all falling for the three most enigmatic monsters.

Maybe it's not a coincidence—maybe it's something else entirely. There's so much I have yet to uncover about my past, and maybe once I do, it will uncover our future.

I'm brought back to reality by Dash's tongue dancing with mine. He runs his hand up into my hair and digs his fingers in, pulling me toward him. I melt into his embrace and savor every fucking second of this, afraid it will be gone too soon.

His erection grows between us and presses to my stomach. He moans into my mouth when I wrap my hand around his girth.

I want nothing more than for him to take me here, right this instant. But Dash doesn't give in as easily to the frenzied passion. Instead, he creates distance between us and breaks away from my kiss.

"Let me take you to bed," Dash says while staring into my eyes. "I want to take my time."

Without needing any convincing, I reach for the lever of the shower.

"Leave it on," Wes tells me when he enters the large bathroom. "I'm right behind you." He grabs two towels from the counter and holds them out for me and Dash.

"Thanks." Dash takes one and gives it to me before taking the other and blotting his face with it.

Wes tugs his shirt over his head and puts it neatly onto the counter. He reaches for the buttons of his pants.

I swallow and dry myself off, the memory of Bo watching me bringing a grin to my face as I do the same thing to Wes. I look over my shoulder to Bo, who's still in the same position he was in minutes ago. "You coming, big boy?"

Out of all these men, I never expected Bo to be the one who needs to be persuaded into following a naked woman. I've practically spread myself open and begged for it, and he still won't have sex with me. Sure, he's let me tease and stroke him, but he doesn't take things all the way.

Is it something I've done? Is it because he really doesn't want to?

He jokes around like he does, but when it comes down to it, he's the most reserved in that department. Maybe he's not attracted to me the way I am to him. Maybe the feelings are only one-sided, and the alpha mark is the only thing keeping him from finishing what he started.

My chest aches at the idea of my feelings not being reciprocated, but I cannot force myself on him if that isn't what he wants.

"We'll meet you in there." Wes brings my hand to his mouth and kisses my knuckles. He releases me and steps into the steamy shower with the man who still hasn't responded to me.

I sigh and follow Dash into the bedroom.

"He's always in a bad mood, don't take offense to it." Dash guides me over to the bed and nudges me onto the mattress.

"You don't think I did something to piss him off, do you?" I scoot onto the newly changed blanket—one that doesn't produce dust particles with each movement.

"There's no telling what's going through his thick skull." He trails his lips up my leg, starting from my ankle and ending near my center. Dash glances up at me. "Is this okay?"

I swallow and nod, the anticipation of where he's going to touch me next killing me.

Dash dips his tongue along my slit and grips both of my thighs with his hands.

"He didn't say anything?" I ask him.

"Wren." Dash doesn't look up as he continues teasing me. "You have nothing to worry"—he twirls his tongue again—"about. Nothing to be insecure about." He slows his pace. "Not now, not ever."

Insecure. Worry. Those are two things that I have never experienced, so why am I feeling them now? Not too long ago I was a strong, independent woman who gave zero fucks about men. And here I am concerned about three of them.

Wes, I don't worry about. Fate has already made that decision for us, and I find a strange comfort in that. In knowing that no matter what the thread connecting us is permanent and binding. Is it terrible of me that I revel in no longer having a choice in the matter? I've always been a fan of free will, but I also love certainty. And what's more certain than a fated mate bond?

When have I ever been in my head this much over something that isn't life or death?

A sexy, red-headed man is going down on me, and I'm questioning whether another man is into me or not. What the fuck is wrong with me?

I sit up on my elbows. "I'm sorry."

Dash kisses my inner thigh and up my stomach, stopping at my chest to give attention to each of my nipples.

I drop my head back and become lost in him. In his warm mouth on my eager body. On his patience despite my lack thereof.

He drags his lips over my neck, nibbling but not biting the soft flesh. Just on the other side are marks from Bo and Wes. They are reminders of the commanding and dominant nature of both men. The contrast between Dash's delicate and gentle personality is a beautiful contradiction. Together, we are four people who shouldn't make sense.

"You have nothing to apologize for." Dash brings his face to rest just against mine. His skin on my skin. His breath mingling with my breath. "You've been through hell and back," he whispers into me. "I can't expect to understand that, but your feelings are valid either way."

"How are you so perfect?" I stare into his baby blue eyes.

"I'm not." He softly presses his lips on mine. "But I know what it's like to have more questions than answers. To wonder and worry and not be able to make sense of things."

"You're perfect to me," I tell him without really comprehending it myself. There isn't much I'm certain of, but there's one thing I know for sure: Dash is too good for all of us.

Dash positions himself between my legs and climbs on top of me. He reaches for my hands and tracks them over my head, pinning them down. He glides his cock over my entrance and draws in a breath before positioning himself into place.

"You're already hard." I blink up at him.

"I've been hard since the moment I laid eyes on you, Wren." He grins bashfully. "I'm a little obsessed with you, if you haven't already noticed."

With his sights still set on me, he slowly pushes inside of me, his eyes flickering shut momentarily.

"Fuck," he whispers. "You feel so fucking good."

I stifle a giggle at hearing this sweet as sugar man curse twice in a row. "Yeah?"

He moves deeper. "Oh, yeah."

I bask in the fullness and tighten around him.

The weight of his body presses down onto mine, and he picks up his pace.

"I dreamed of this, being this near to you, over and over again when you were taken away." Dash kisses me and thrusts himself harder.

I rock myself with him and pump against his movements. Freeing one of my hands, I wrap it around the base of his neck and weave it into his hair to pull him closer and intensify the kiss. I break away for only a second to say, "Show me how badly you missed me."

Dash takes his free hand to wrap it around my waist and lift me toward him, the new angle sends pleasure through me in a whole other way. He fucks me harsher, our bodies crashing into each other in pure bliss. He's never been this rough, and I love every fucking second of it.

My core tightens, my breath catching as my climax rises to the surface.

Like he's fully aware, Dash moans into my mouth and grips the hand above my head tighter, his cock hardening inside of me with each thrust.

I dig my nails into his back and inch him farther, deeper, harder until I cry out into him and pleasure ripples through my entire body.

He pumps into me and slows his pace, his ragged breath matching mine. "Fuck, that was intense." Dash rests his forehead on mine as he comes down from the high.

He softly kisses me while pulling out and collapses onto the bed next to me, his arm flopping over his sweat-lined forehead.

I smile triumphantly at seeing this side of him—his take charge side. Somehow he's still very Dash-like, but at the same time...he's more possessive.

My gaze shoots across the room to the man standing in the doorway, his body pressed into the frame, his arms crossed over his broad chest.

"Always such a lurker."

Bo remains firmly in place without saying anything.

"Afraid I might bite?" It's a phrase humans throw out as a joke but the possibility of that happening in a room full of supernatural creatures is pretty high.

Bo finally breaks from his stone-cold stare. "I wish you would."

"Come here and I will."

"You don't know what you're asking for, Birdie." Bo drags his hand over his solid jaw.

"That's not the first time you've said that, Bo."

"And it won't be the last." He shoves off the wall and stalks over slowly. "What is it you want from me?"

"Isn't it obvious?" I inch my legs apart without overly exposing myself any more than I already am.

The towel around his waist barely covers his wide frame, and with each step, the corner where it's bunched together loosens little by little.

But Bo reaches down in time and secures it back into place. His sights return to me. "Did you kill him?" He darts his attention briefly to Dash.

I side-eye the beautiful man who's quietly snoring next to me. "That could be you."

Bo latches onto my ankle, the heat of his skin sending a wave of pleasure up my entire body. He slides me to the edge of the bed, and my ass nearly hangs off the end. He holds one of my legs in the air and the other cups his body. "Is this what you want, Birdie?"

He leaves my leg leaning against his shoulder and skims his rough palm down.

I shiver at his touch.

"You want this..." Bo keeps his dark gaze on me as he swirls his fingers over my center and teases my clit. "You're throbbing, Birdie."

I rock my hips toward him in a desperate attempt to feel any friction against my aching desire.

"What about this..." Bo circles my entrance, and just when I'm certain he's playing one sadistic game, he shoves two fingers into me.

I bring my hand up to cover the gasp that escapes my mouth and clench my pussy around his long fingers.

"Or what about..." He drops to his knees at the foot of the bed and hooks his hand over my thigh to drag me closer while keeping my leg still propped on his shoulder. Bo leans in and takes in a deep breath. "Angels, you smell..." Finally, after what can only seem like an eternity, he presses his lips to mine, his tongue darting out and joining the party. "And taste"—he whispers into my pussy—"like heaven."

My chest heaves and I grip the bed sheets to ground me in this magical experience. This is the first time Bo has truly touched me, and damn if it isn't everything and more than I thought it would be.

I want him inside of me, on top of me, all over me, but fuck if this isn't glorious, too.

He thrusts his fingers in deeper, the force moving my body back and forth as he glides his tongue and lips over my most sensitive areas. Bo grips my thigh tighter and the pain from his touch only intensifies this whole experience.

I reach down and rake my hand through his hair and grab a fistful.

He moans against me, the vibration sending me further into paradise.

Bo surprises me by filling me with another finger, the width of all of them spreading me wider. He heaves them deep and pinches my clit between his lips.

"Fuck," I whimper and tug his hair tighter.

It only takes one more thrust of his hand and I come undone around him, my whole body quivering with pleasure.

Bo slows his torment but continues to lick and suck me. He glides his fingers out, spreading me open for him to get a better access point with his mouth. His tongue slips inside of me, going further than I imagined it could. He softens his hold on my leg.

I spasm on his tongue and release my hand from his head, dropping it to the side and melting into the bed.

After another minute of exploration, he concludes his tour by leaving the gentlest kiss on my pussy lips. He runs his fingers down my thigh as he stands. Still licking my desire off his lips, he says, "Is that what you wanted, Birdie?"

I stare up at him through my lashes. "That...and more."

He shakes his head. "You can't handle more."

"You don't know that." I push down the anger that instinctually rises to the surface.

Bo tips his head toward the bathroom. "Hound boy is finishing up. He can have you next."

"Excuse me?" I rise up onto my elbows. "What do you think I am, some whore you can all have your way with?"

"That's not what I said." Bo takes a step back as I push onto my feet in front of him.

"Sounded like that's what you meant."

"It isn't what I meant and you know it."

"That's the thing, Bo." I glare up at him. "I don't know. Because you won't fucking tell me. You're full of arrogance and banter but refuse to say anything real."

Bo remains standing there, his mouth pinched in a hard line.

"See." I shove his chest. "Nobody is forcing you to be here, Bo. Leave if that's what you want." But before he can see the tears welling in my eyes, I turn away from him and march to the bathroom, and shut the door.

"What's wrong?" Wes asks the second I'm in the closed-off space. He comes over from his spot at the counter.

"Nothing," I lie. "What were you doing over there?"

Wes glances back and then focuses on me. "Just being nosey and looking at all the stuff in the cabinet. This human world fascinates me." He sighs and pulls me to his chest. "Tell me what happened."

I close my eyes and savor the comfort of his body, his truth, his unfaltering loyalty to me.

"Bo being Bo," I finally mutter into him.

Wes pats my back gently. "Want me to kill him?"

I peel myself off him. "Kind of." I force a laugh. "Just kidding. Don't actually." My fingers trace the outline of the alpha mark on my neck. "Especially while I'm still connected to him."

Maybe that's why Bo sticks around; he feels bad about the alpha mark. If he leaves, it will ignite the beacon and alert demons to my whereabouts. But, if that's the case, why doesn't he just remove it and be done if being around us is so fucking terrible?

"Did he tell you how to remove it?" I ask Wes.

"No, just that my hound wouldn't like whatever it is."

"And I asked if any of you had to die, and he said no. What else could it be?"

Wes shrugs. "I have no idea."

Whatever it is, it's bad enough that he's keeping it from us.

CHAPTER 4

Wes

I wait in the bathroom for Wren while she rinses off in the shower.

When she's finished, I stand there, my arms outstretched with another clean and soft towel to wrap her up in it.

"You sure are a gentleman, you know that?" She grins up at me from her spot tucked close to my chest.

"I've been waiting my whole life for this. There isn't anything I wouldn't do for you."

And that doesn't just apply to me, it goes for my hound, too.

He's constantly foaming at the mouth to break free and murder anyone who dares to look at her cross. Her happiness is his main priority, and I couldn't be any more relieved that we're at least on the same page about that.

"You know it's the same for me, too, right?" Wren stares into my eyes, her gaze intense.

I swallow and tuck her damp hair behind her ear. "Is it?"

"Yes."

I told you, my hound declares.

"Let's get you to bed." I kiss her forehead and with my arm still wrapped around her shoulder, I lead her toward the door.

Only once we're in the bedroom, her body goes rigid upon the absence of Bo.

"Bo's a night owl, he's probably just exploring the property."

"I thought you couldn't lie."

"I'm not lying. Bo is weird. Nothing he does makes sense."

Wren hugs her body tightly.

"How about some clean clothes?" I guide her over to the side of the bed. "Give me a second."

Helplessness cascades through me at not being able to mend what is happening between her and Bo. I never thought that I would accept my mate being with another but I also never thought I would fall for a hunter. My hound doesn't prefer it, but her happiness supersedes his. Nor could I have anticipated being here, having escaped Prania. I've always dreamt of Arthlia and what it might be like to flee the confines of our homeland. Freedom, autonomy, safety. It was a pipe dream, and now it's real.

In the past, when I thought about my future, there was always this void. This emptiness I thought I would never be able to fill. I imagined a life outside of Prania, but I was alone—or alone with Bo and Dash.

No matter the scenario...I was alone.

It wasn't until she came to kill me that I realized she was what I was missing all along. My soul had locked onto her with a force unlike anything I had ever known. I suppressed it. I tried to hide it. I attempted to resist every bit of the pull she had on me. But there was no denying what was already there. Fate had decided it long ago. And I have never been more grateful for anything in my entire life.

I wasn't lying when I said I would do anything for her. I would kill for her. I would die for her. And when Parla tried to tear us apart, I chose to live for her.

I fumble through the clothes in the closet and locate the smallest T-shirt I can find. I settle on a pair of sweatpants in one of the drawers and grab something for myself, too. Luckily, whoever lived here in the past left their belongings behind. Only the pit in my gut tells me they haven't abandoned this place completely. And with Tremont being as cryptic as he is, there's no telling what's in store for us. Tomorrow we will get answers and figure out how to move on in this world. How to start over.

I exit the large closet to find Wren lying along the edge of the bed with the towel still clung around her delicate body, and her eyes closed. My chest flutters at the sight of her, and a smile creeps its way across my face. It's amazing how such an angelic creature can be so fucking deadly. But maybe that's what makes me love her even more, that she is not what she seems. She is fierce and strong and intelligent, but she is also kind, compassionate, and sensitive. She tries to act tough but she cares more than she lets on. I see it come through in the way she treats others. How she refused to leave people behind at Rockbridge. For a woman who was born in blood and violence, she still has a way of radiating such light.

With great caution, I slide the legs of the pants over her dainty feet and up her legs, tying the string around her waist tight enough so they won't fall completely off.

She stirs, her eyes fluttering open to meet mine. "I fell asleep."

"Here," I tell her while she's awake. "Put this on." I help her up, tug the shirt over her head, and pop her arms through each hole. "There. That's better."

Wren grins with her eyes closed and yawns. "I'm tired."

I untuck her hair from inside her shirt and scoop her into my arms, carefully gliding her under the covers and closer to Dash, who remains completely zonked out with his arm resting over his head and his mouth agape.

Once I've dressed, I walk across the room to shut off the lights and climb in next to her.

I settle into the plush mattress and wonder where this level of support has been all my life. No hard lumps. No lack of pillow. No thin blanket. And to top it off, a beautiful girl nestled into the crook of my neck and intertwining her body with mine.

Is it possible I've died and gone to heaven? Because I can't imagine anything fucking else that could be better.

<hr>

I sleep better than I ever have in my entire life, only, it's cut short by about fifty-seven hours when we're woken by the sound of an argument.

I shoot out of bed and rush to the door.

"Where are my knives?" Wren shows the same level of concern that I do.

I blindly point to where I put her armored clothing and slowly turn the door handle. I peek through the thin gap and see Tremont standing at the end of the hall and another man, easily half his age, a few feet in front of him.

This newcomer has his hands in his dark, curly hair, and he seems distraught but has no visible weapons and he hasn't done any harm to Tremont. Maybe this threat is not as severe as it appears.

I hold out my hand to Wren to hopefully stop her from going into full defense mode.

"We can talk about this," Tremont says to this other man.

"What is there to talk about?" The man draws in a breath and shakes his head. "You shouldn't be here. This ended years ago."

Tremont nods. "I can assure you, I am a changed man, Sydney."

Sydney—the man has a name.

"If she finds out you're here, she'll kill you herself. Tell me why I shouldn't do it right here and now." Sydney remains in place a few feet from Tremont, and Tremont makes no effort to evade him.

"What's happening?" Wren whispers as she tries to see through into the hallway.

Dash stretches and yawns.

Wren and I turn and shush him at the same time.

He offers a quiet, "Sorry."

"I have..." Tremont pauses to find the right words. "Information."

"About what?" Sydney rubs his chin. "What information could you possibly have that she doesn't already? You have no idea the power she wields now. You're a nobody."

"I know." Tremont doesn't dare argue with this other man, yet he tries to plead his case. "I mean no harm, Sydney. I am ashamed of what happened and the role I played in it. I wouldn't have come here so foolishly if I didn't mean that."

"Why did you come here? Huh? This is the worst possible place you could have chosen."

"Because I'm telling you the truth. I was going to find you, or Silas, or anyone. I needed to give my travel companions time to rest. They are not from this world."

Sydney's eyes go wider. "What kind of evil did you bring here, Tremont?"

My hound overpowers my arm and forces the door open, exposing myself and Wren to this random man assuming the worst of us. And if my hound continues to call the shots, he's going to be proven right.

Sydney doesn't jump, he doesn't falter, he simply turns his attention on me. "Who are you?"

Tremont steps between us. "This is Wes, he's from another realm. He and his family have sought refuge here on Earth."

"From where?" Sydney eyes me and then Tremont.

"Prania."

"Prania?"

"Yes. There is a terrible war and a great injustice to his kind."

"His kind?" Sydney steps to the left to avoid Tremont's obstruction. "What are you?"

I clear my throat. "I'm a hellhound."

Sydney's brow rises. "You're a man."

Summoning my powers, I let them rise to the surface, only showing a fraction of my true form. The flames flicker along my skin and comfort me in a way that the luxurious bed of his never could.

"And who's behind you?" Sydney points past me.

Wren shoves her way through the door. "I'm Wren. Wren Oliver."

Sydney's mouth falls open slightly and his gaze trains itself onto Tremont. "What are you trying to pull here?"

"Nothing, I promise you. Get a truth stone, do whatever you need to do, but trust this, she is who she says she is." Tremont moves out of the way to give Sydney a better view down the hallway.

I shift to put myself in front of Wren. "She's not on show here."

"What is she?" Sydney tilts his head around to look at Wren.

Wren does her best attempt to shove me out of the way. "I'm right here, you don't have to talk about me like I'm not in the room."

Sydney runs his hand through his hair again, a nervous habit. "You're right. Sorry. I don't mean to be rude, this is just all very...unexpected." He focuses on Tremont. "Have you not told them about our past?"

Tremont shakes his head. "Not entirely."

"Perhaps they would no longer put their lives in your hands if they knew the truth."

"My life is in my hands, and no one else's," Wren says to Sydney. "We only met him briefly before fleeing our realm. Whatever past you two have together has nothing to do with us."

"And yet you're traveling with him."

"Out of necessity." Wren steps closer and I clench my hand into a fist to shield my desire to force myself in front of her again.

"You come here bearing the name Oliver, so very conveniently." Sydney crosses his arms over his chest. "I don't buy it."

"Why would I lie about that?" Wren matches his movement and folds her arms, too. "Does that name mean something?"

Sydney laughs abruptly. "Really?" He points to Tremont. "This must be hilarious to you, isn't it?"

"Care to explain the punchline?" Wren asks him.

"You show up, after all these years, out of the fucking blue, claiming you want peace, using *this house* to find refuge, and with a girl bearing Willow's last name."

"Who's Willow?" Wren speaks the question that was on my mind, too.

"Really? You're telling me you have never heard the name Willow Oliver, that Tremont doesn't have you going along with whatever game he's playing? I find this way too convenient to have a shred of truth in it."

I shove around Wren and put myself back into his line of sight. "I've had enough of you accusing her of being a liar. Get your little truth rock and do what you must, but if you so much as hint at one more bad thing toward her..."

"Ah." Sydney grins. "The violent welcome party I expected." He looks me up and down. "Why don't you try?"

He saw the flames licking my skin, and yet he's standing there completely unfazed by what I could possibly do to him. He wields no weapons and hasn't even hinted at having magic of his own. He's unmatched and unbothered, meaning only one thing, I'm underestimating him entirely.

And when I take another step forward and am met with the sturdy wall of an invisible forcefield, I realize he had the upper hand all along. I was just too stupid to see it.

CHAPTER 5

Wren

"Are you okay?" I grip Wes's shoulders as he stumbles back.

"Yeah." He regains his footing. "What is this?" Wes places his palm against seemingly nothing.

I fight the desire to lose my entire mind at being held captive *once again*. First, it was by Wes, then Rockbridge, and now, this.

Will I ever be truly free?

Even before Wes found me bleeding out in that building where I was supposed to kill him, I spent my existence in a chokehold by Parla and her merciless cause. I've never been of my own free will, why did I expect things to have ever changed? If only I had just died that day with my mother, none of this would have happened. Wes and Dash and Bo would be living much better lives without me, and so many wouldn't be dead by my hands.

"It's a barrier spell," Sydney tells him. "To keep all of you contained while I figure out what to do with you." He nods down the hallway. "How many more are there?" He raises his voice. "Show yourselves."

Dash comes out of our bedroom with his hands in the air. "Uh, hey, I'm Dash. I don't have any special skills or anything, I'm just really good at dying. I mean, not dying, but like, coming back to life. I don't know, that doesn't make sense. I'm not making sense."

I take one of his hands and lower it, weaving my fingers into his and pulling him toward me. "Everything is going to be okay, don't worry." It might be a lie, but it's what he needs to hear. The truth is, I won't let anyone hurt him, not if I have any say in it.

Sydney's brows bunch together. "Your specialty is dying?"

"Yeah, I'm a—"

Tremont cuts Dash off. "He's harmless is what he is. And until you start negotiating our release, I don't think they should have to give you any more information."

"Do you not realize how sketchy that sounds, especially coming out of your mouth?"

"It's fine, I don't mind," Dash speaks up. "I'm, I guess I'm a phoenix, whatever that means."

Sydney leans against the railing to the stairs. He trains his focus on Wes. "You're telling me that you're a hellhound." Then on Dash. "You're a phoenix." And then on me. "And you're a witch."

I shake my head and interject. "No. I'm not a witch. I'm a hunter."

"A hunter? But..."

"She's been in Prania her whole life," Tremont adds. "She was raised as a hunter. Her magic has lied dormant. Ring any bells?"

I step toward Tremont. "When are you going to realize that I don't have any magic? None of my own at least."

"What's that supposed to mean?" Sydney grows defensive.

"It's complicated." How am I supposed to explain something that doesn't make sense to me either?

"Right."

"Is this where we introduce ourselves?" Jade pokes her head out of the bedroom she and Everest share.

Sydney throws his hands up. "By all means, just keep them coming. Anyone else hiding in there?"

"Just me and Everest." She walks out with her hand tucked into his, the two of them side by side, declaring for the whole world to know that they're *together*.

If Bo saw this, he'd be foaming at the mouth.

Bo. My heart stutters from the realization that he's not here, and that he never came back last night.

My fingers trace the scar he left behind on my neck, the constant reminder of his presence in my life. It doesn't burn, doesn't run hot, but it's how it normally is when he's nearby. Which means he hasn't abandoned us completely. No, he must be lying in wait for his time to strike. Or, he's gorging on the rest of the hot pockets in the freezer downstairs. One option is just as possible as the other.

"And what might you two be?" Sydney narrows his gaze at them like he's trying to decide for himself before they answer.

"I'm..." Jade holds her hand to her chest.

"No," Wes cuts her off and turns toward Sydney. "I need to know that no harm comes to any of us." He flits an apologetic look toward Tremont. "I understand you two have history, but the rest of us have done no wrong other than eating some of your food and sleeping in your beds. I will do whatever you wish to repay you for that, but I beg of you to show mercy to the rest of us."

Sydney takes in Wes's request and chews at his bottom lip. "You two, the hellhound and the phoenix. You're with her, the *hunter*?"

"They have names," I blurt out. "Wes and Dash."

Sydney smiles. "You're more and more like an Oliver with each passing second."

"See," Tremont says. "I told you so."

"Silence." Sydney stares right at Tremont. "I've heard enough from you." He steadies his gaze on Wes. "No harm will come to you so long as the same is reciprocated. The second I find out you're lying to me, I will have no choice but to take back my word."

Wes and Sydney exchange a swift nod.

"So then you'll free us from these confines?" I ask the question that's no doubt on all our minds.

"I still don't know what those two are." Sydney motions down the hall.

Jade steps closer. "I'm a banshee, and Everest is…"

"I was born a hunter, as was Wren, but I do not associate myself as one."

"Let me get this straight." Sydney rubs his hands together and pauses momentarily. "You three are some of the rarest, if not completely obsolete supernatural beings in existence. And you." He focuses right on me. "You're a distant relative to my wife."

"I…" But no other words come out of my mouth. I have family? Living relatives? In another realm outside of Prania? Is this possible? I thought I was the last of my bloodline. That's what Parla told me when she helped me trace back my lineage. Although, when has anything that bitch has ever said or done been without some hidden fucking agenda behind it? Maybe Parla realized how powerful and significant I would be when she was pretending to be my friend, and instead of telling me the truth, she fed me more lies to keep me under her authority.

Because had she told me then that there were more of my kind, I would have done everything in my power to find them. And that alone would have ruined her carefully laid out plan.

She didn't just take my life from me, she tried to take away my future and my past, too.

Is this why Tremont was shocked when Dash had called me by my last name? Because he knows the woman who is married to Sydney? Tremont mentioned he had history with Sydney's parents, but how does that affect Sydney or his wife? It clearly does, because Sydney is labeling us all the enemy just for being in Tremont's company. What could Tremont have done that was so bad to make Sydney hate him so much?

Unless…

"Sydney." I grow worried about the question I'm about to ask. "Is your wife, this other Oliver, is she dead?"

"What?" He shakes his head. "No. She's very much alive."

"Oh." I let out a sigh of relief. "Sorry, I thought you were mad at him because he hurt her."

At least I don't have to add *dead relative* to my list today.

"You really don't know, do you?" Sydney stares at me.

But before either of us can say anything else, a dark flash darts up the stairs.

"This party is over." Bo grabs Sydney by the neck and lifts him off the ground. "This fucking spell, you take it down, *now*."

I choke on a gasp. "Bo, stop!" I rush forward, not sure where the boundary of the barrier spell is in place. But when I bolt past where I'm certain it was without being stopped, I continue pushing my feet forward until I'm latching onto Bo's arm. "Please, Bo, don't hurt him."

Bo's dark gaze meets mine and he blinks, like he's wondering how it's possible Sydney complied with his demand so quickly.

"See, I'm right here, the barrier spell is gone. You can let him go."

"Uh, Wren," Wes says from somewhere behind me.

I turn, expecting him to be closer than he is, but he's still in the hallway, where everybody else remains.

"What are you waiting for?" I ask him. "Come on."

He shakes his head and places his hand along the rippling magical edge of the boundary which is very much still intact.

"Bo, I command you this instant, release him."

Bo drops Sydney onto the hardwood floor, where he wheezes and clutches at his throat.

"Fucking psycho," Sydney spits out.

Bo squares his shoulders. "If you don't release them, I'll show you a true psycho." A growl rumbles in his chest.

Sydney scoots back and up onto his feet. "I'm not letting Tremont out."

"I don't care about him. But the rest of them, let them out, *now*."

I step in front of Bo and inch carefully toward Sydney. "What he's *trying* to say is, would you please let our people free? We have spent a lifetime in captivity." I glare over my shoulder at Bo. "He lacks the proper manners to ask politely."

Sydney rubs at his throat and flits his gaze between us. "Don't make me regret this." He snaps his fingers and a moment later, everyone except Tremont is free of the barrier.

"You can't just lock me up in here." Tremont pounds his fist on the invisible forcefield.

"I can, and I will." Sydney swallows harshly. "Could I have a word with the rest of you downstairs?"

"Yeah, of course." I shove Bo from his spot firmly in place. "Knock it off, grump ass." I wave my hands at the rest of my group. "Go ahead, I'm right behind you." I hang back to make sure they go without causing an issue and then walk down with Sydney.

Something in my gut tells me he wouldn't hurt me, not if he doesn't have a reason to. If my distant relative trusts him enough to marry him, that means I should be safe to be near him.

"Is he"—Sydney nods ahead—"one of your mates, too?"

I bite at my lip. If he had asked me yesterday, I would have said yes without hesitation, but now I'm not so sure what Bo is to me. Is he simply the alpha who left a mark on my neck? Or is he more? To me, he is one of the men I care deeply for, but I cannot force someone to want to be with me if they don't want to. And I surely won't be reduced to a piece of meat they take turns sharing. Perhaps Bo and I were always destined to remain enemies and nothing more.

I settle on responding, "It's complicated." Because that's the truth and I'm sick of lies.

"I'm familiar with complicated." Sydney matches my stride down the winding staircase. "My wife has four mates."

My eyes widen and I turn to take him in, to assess whether this is another deceit. But when he offers me a soft smile, I conclude that he's being honest, too.

I want to ask him more, to let the million questions rattling around inside my head spill, but upon reaching the bottom of the stairs, the rest of the group stands there in wait for their next command.

"Through here." Sydney motions ahead and walks past them, leading us down another long hallway and into a grand living room with a large fireplace and lavish furniture. "Have a seat while I tend to the fire."

Wes follows him over, mumbling something along the lines of, "I can help with that." I don't catch everything that's exchanged, but it seems civil to say the least.

Sydney throws a few logs onto the fire and steps back, waiting for Wes to do his magic.

Wes balls his hand into a fist, the fire of his other half rising to the surface and creating a blazing orb that he tosses onto the wood in the brick hearth. The thing ignites instantly and settles down once the wood has been engulfed.

The two of them say a few more words and make their way over to the rest of us who have chosen a seat among the many in this room.

"For the sake of clarity, could we agree to be honest with each other?" Sydney glances around the room at the faces he's only met moments prior in an equally hostile situation. "We didn't exactly get off on the right foot, and I have to admit, you being anywhere near that man upstairs makes me immediately suspicious."

"And you locking them into a wing of your house isn't doing you any favors either," Bo mouths off.

"I don't know how it works back where you're from, but there's this thing called breaking and entering here, and it's illegal." Sydney leans against the arm of the couch Jade and Everest have taken up residency on. "Human law, not even supernatural. So the fact that you're supernatural makes it that much more complicated when I show up to my childhood home to find a misfit bunch of creatures sleeping in my beds. Plus, the fact that they're shacking up with my literal enemy. Anyone else may have killed you on the spot, but you caught me on a good day."

Dash raises his hand. "I would have come back. And you'd have had to clean up all the ash and soot, and I'm not going to lie, it's pretty messy."

"Noted." Sydney crosses his arms. "Someone want to tell me what you're doing here. The truth this time."

And that's what I do. I tell him the truth. That our homeland was in a forever-long war, that demons and hunters would stop at nothing to rid each other from the realm. That up until I met these men, I was considered the most feared demon assassin of them all. That I was brainwashed into thinking they were the enemy when in reality, we were the evil plaguing our land, and I didn't learn that until it was too late. But that we found a way out, that we rallied together to escape an inescapable prison, and we banded together to outrun those that wished us dead. Our enemies turned into allies, and we chose to blindly put faith in those around us because it was the only thing to do to stay alive.

"So you didn't know Tremont long?" Sydney asks.

"He was my cellmate," Wes tells him. "He told me he knew of a way out, not of the prison, but of our realm. I had no other choice than to believe him." He draws in a breath and continues. "We've all made our fair share of mistakes, and the man I met in that prison cell showed genuine remorse."

"Did he tell you what he did?"

"No, not really. He mentioned a past he was regretful of. That he lied, and stole, and let people down. I recall him saying he was a bully, and that he went through painful withdrawals in Prania but that when it was all said and done, he was glad because he realized that he was wrong for what he had done. He said he wanted to make amends but thought it was too late. I didn't pry any of the details out, not when the most important thing on my mind was getting her out of here." Wes grips my hand tighter and rubs his thumb along mine. "I would have formed an alliance with the devil himself if it meant saving her."

"Are you going to keep tiptoeing around it or are you going to tell us what he did?" Bo folds his fingers into his palm and looks at his nails. He's never really been one for patience.

But when Sydney opens his mouth to speak, he's distracted by something else.

Dash, who was sitting on the edge of the chair being his sweet and opposite of Bo self, falls face first into the table, banging his head on the side and collapsing onto the floor.

"Angels." I rush over to him and turn him over onto his back.

Blood pools from the open wound on his forehead, and his eyes remain shut. His body starts trembling uncontrollably.

"What's wrong with him?" I say to anyone listening.

"Here." Sydney gets to my side, a small pillow from the couch in his grasp. "Put this under his head." He meets my gaze. "Has this ever happened before?"

"I..." But I haven't been with Dash long enough to know if it has or not.

"No," Wes chimes in. "Never."

"What did you do?" Bo accuses. "Did you poison him?"

Sydney lets out a gruff breath. "I'm not as cruel as you think I am." He presses his hand to Dash's chest.

"What are you doing?" I grab at his wrist a bit too hard.

"I'm trying to see if I can figure out what's wrong with him." Sydney's eyes flutter closed.

I hold my breath, hoping and waiting and praying to the Angels that Dash will be okay.

Because if he isn't, I might just become the villain that Sydney suspects is in this room.

CHAPTER 6
Dash

Darkness. Pain. Isolation.

A blast of light. A crack of a whip.

A woman yelling.

My hands dig into the dirt, and it consumes my fingers, shielding the smallest piece of me from harm.

I wish to sink deeper, go farther, until I am buried in the ground and surrounded by nothing but dirt to protect me.

Another slice across my back. Agony courses through me. Numbness. The scent of fresh blood pooling.

I tremble and will it to stop. Please stop.

Please stop.

Please stop.

Please.

Stop.

Please.

I pinch my eyes shut, convinced that if I pretend I'm not here, I'll disappear.

Maybe I can just disappear.

Disappear.

"Come back to me," a whisper floats to me.

It is kind, gentle, safe.

I focus on it, even if it is only a figment of my imagination.

Anything is better than this.

Another torrent of the whip. I am ripped open.

I shake.

Hands, warm hands, grip my shoulders.

"Dash," the voice calls out again, this time with more urgency.

Is this person in danger more than I am? Do they need me? How can I break away from my hell to save this other person? No one should be helpless, scared, afraid. I must find a way.

"Please," they say. "I need you."

I fight. I scrape. I push with every ounce of strength.

And when I open my eyes, I am no longer in hell, but in the arms of the woman who I care most about in this entire world.

"Dash," she pulls me to her. "Angels, are you okay?"

I hug her back, grateful to be gone from whatever nightmare I was just living through. It felt too...real. No dream has ever made me experience such torment.

"I'm fine. I'm sorry I worried you."

She releases me but keeps me at an arm's length. "Are you really apologizing right now?"

"Sorry."

Her cheeks turn up into a smile. "Dash."

I pinch my lips together to keep myself from saying sorry again.

Wren blots at my forehead with a towel.

Bo rises from his chair in the corner of the room and moseys over. "Thought you were a goner, bud." He pats my shoulder. "Where did you go?"

I scoot up and rest my back against the headframe of the bed we slept in last night. Someone must have brought me here when I...

"The last thing I remember was we were in a big room." I avert my gaze to attempt to recall the memory. "There was a fireplace. And I was listening to everyone talk." I glance at Wren. "Is this right?"

She nods.

"I can't really remember what they were saying. But I got hot, real hot, real fast. And woozy. I thought I was going to throw up. And then I fell." I place my hand on my forehead where a bandage covers the spot that must have made impact.

A breeze from the open window licks at my cheeks.

"Damn, that feels good." I kick my legs over the edge of the bed and stand.

Wren grips one arm while Bo holds the other.

"I'm not going to fall. I'm fine."

"Better safe than sorry." Wren doesn't let me go until I'm leaning on the windowsill.

"What happened after that?" Bo presses his shoulder into the wall and crosses his arms over his chest.

"I had this terrible nightmare. I was being tortured." I reach toward my back and replay the anguish. But when I touch a spot, it actually *feels* tender. "Uh, will one of you do me a favor?"

"What is it?" Wren comes back over with a glass of water in her grasp.

I drag my shirt up my back and turn toward them. "Do you see anything out of the ordinary?"

Wren sucks in a breath. "Angels." She extends her hand but doesn't touch me.

An indicator that my hunch was correct.

"How is that possible?" Bo asks us.

"What does it look like?" I ask them.

"Like someone just got done beating you senseless." Bo steps forward.

Wren adds, "Your scars. They're not open wounds, but they're red and swollen. Not all of them. But quite a few. Like they're fresh. Do they hurt?"

"No," I lie. "They're sore." I let my shirt fall over them and turn around to sit near the window again.

That nightmare didn't feel like a nightmare. It was more like a memory. But a memory that I don't have. And a memory that could somehow hurt me. None of that makes sense.

"Anyway," I say. "What did I miss?" Because I would do anything to change the subject and escape from the sad and pitiful stares they're giving me right now.

"Dash…" Wren places her hand on my shoulder.

I bring it to my face and kiss the soft flesh before putting my hand over it. "We have more important things to deal with than my mystery scars. We're in a different realm. In someone else's house. And traveling with a potential asshole."

Wren sighs. "Bo isn't just a *potential* asshole."

"Hey, now, that's the nicest thing you've said about me all day." Bo continues to lean against the wall.

Wren rolls her eyes. "Sydney was about to tell us what Tremont had done when you face-planted into the table. Bo carried you up here, and we've been at your side ever since. Sydney left. He said he was going to get some rock to see if you had a *glitch*, whatever that means. But we have no way of contacting him to let him know you're awake. Tremont is confined to his room, and the rest of our group is down-stairs giving us some space. That pretty much catches you up to where we are now."

"How long was I out?"

"A half hour or so." Wren glances at Bo, who nods stiffly.

I lower my voice. "And we still don't know what he did?"

She shakes her head. "Something bad enough that Sydney hates him for it."

"I don't trust him," Bo chimes in.

"You don't trust anyone." Wren faces Bo. "What is it? His enormous manor. The fact that he didn't kill us for breaking into his home? His giant freezer full of delicious food? That he was willing to go find something to help Dash?"

Bo stares right at her, expressionless. "Tremont, not Sydney."

"Oh."

Bo huffs. "I'm going to tell the others you didn't die."

"Actually," I reach out toward him. "You. Stay. Wren will inform them."

"Yeah, of course." She kisses my cheek before leaving the room.

When I'm sure her footsteps have hit the stairs, I glare at Bo. "Spill."

"I don't know what you're talking about." Bo presses his hands on the windowsill and shoves his head out the window. "The air is different here, have you noticed that?"

"Yeah, it's fresher, and it doesn't smell like soot and rotting flesh. But don't try to change the subject."

Bo sighs dramatically. "I can't change the subject if I don't know what the subject is."

"Don't play dumb with me. You're too smart to be that stupid."

"Aw, you think I'm smart." Bo brings himself back inside and returns his arms to the crossed position over his chest, shutting me out like he does everyone else.

"What's going on between you two? And before you ask me who, I'm talking about you and Wren. What happened?"

"Nothing happened."

"Something happened."

"Why are you so worried about it?"

I pinch the bridge of my nose between my fingers. "Because she's important to me, and you're important to me. I'm not an idiot. Something is clearly going on. This is a different kind of banter. I can literally *feel* the fucking tension when you're both near each other."

Bo's dark eyes widen. "Did you just say *fucking*?"

"Why does everyone get so alarmed when I cuss?"

"You're the sweet and innocent one of the bunch." Bo shrugs. "It's uncharacteristic of you."

"Maybe I'm sick of being the odd man out. And for the twenty-seventh time, stop deflecting the conversation. I'm not going to leave you alone until you tell me what it is."

"And then what, Dash, what does it matter?"

"It matters. To you, to her, to me, to all of us. You're going to tell me, and then we're going to fix it."

"What if it can't be fixed?"

"Then, you better start groveling. Sooner rather than later." I stick my arm out the window to let the breeze wash over my skin. "What did you do?"

"It's more like what *didn't* I do?"

"So you admit that you did something wrong?"

Bo runs his hand through his long hair, tugging it and letting out a breath. "I don't know. Yes. No. Kind of. Everything has been wrong from the start. And I'm..."

But he doesn't finish his sentence, not even after a full minute of silence.

"You're what, Bo? You're sorry? You're worried? You're angry? What are you feeling?"

"I'm afraid."

Two words I never expected the man in front of me to ever say. He's never been fearful of anything. He takes danger head-on with a sly grin on his face. But this... this is something different. It's not something he can beat or fight or outmaneuver. No, caring about someone is a new kind of fear that he's only known in small blips. Romantic feelings are entirely different than that of family—because family is forever, love is chosen, it's all or nothing, and quite literally the fiercest competitor he's ever had.

"Hey," I say softly and place my hand on his shoulder. "You're going to get through this." I bob my head up and down. "You will."

Wren comes back into the room, her warm presence a welcome comfort. "They made some food if you guys are hungry."

Bo shrugs me off and leaves me behind at the window, marching past Wren and disappearing in the direction she just came.

"Good talk," she mutters on her way over to me.

"Don't worry about him."

"Oh, I'm not." Wren sits across from me in the window and stares outside. "Not one bit."

I hide the way my lips turn up. "Uh-huh. Okay."

"What?" She glances over at me. "I'm not!"

"What did he do?" I ask, despite knowing both of them are equally hot and cold on whether they're willing to talk about things.

"What didn't he do?"

Her response, so similar to his, makes me laugh.

"Sorry," I tell her while covering my mouth and regaining my composure. "Is there something specific this time?"

She inhales and looks outside prior to exhaling and focusing back on me. "Promise you won't say anything?"

"I promise."

"Last night, he basically implied I was some piece of meat you guys pass around."

My jaw clenches and without realizing it, I'm standing, both of my fists balled tightly. "I'll kill him."

Wren stands, too, to block me from going any further. "You said you wouldn't say anything."

"I did, didn't I?" I force myself to sit back down.

It's no wonder Bo is worried about things, he fucked up. Never should anyone feel the way that Wren most likely does since he said that. Regardless of the context or the tone or whatever was going through his thick skull, he should have kept his mouth shut. Wren is so much more than that to us—to me, at least—and if I have to be celibate with her to prove that, I'll do it in a heartbeat.

"On behalf of men," I say to her. "I apologize." I take her hand in mine. "And I'm sorry if us being together last night brought this on."

"You didn't do anything wrong, Dash. You're perfect, really." She returns to her spot next to me. "I just don't understand Bo. He's into me one minute, and not the next. He shows he cares, or is worried, but then he's so distant and reserved. I never know what he's actually feeling or thinking. And if the only thing connecting us is this stupid mark, I'd rather it be gone so he could go his separate ways."

Tears well in her eyes but she blinks them away and stares out the window.

"I'm sorry," she tells me, her focus returning. "You just went through hell and here I am blabbing about boy trouble."

"Shh." I hold her hand tighter. "You brought me back, okay? I'd do anything to make you feel better."

"Don't worry about me, I'm fine, really. That stuff isn't important."

"You're important," I remind her.

"Well, so are you, Dash. And you're probably hungry, aren't you?" She stands and tugs me up with her. "Come on, you should eat before Bo wipes the entire house of all its food."

"Now that, that wouldn't surprise me." I weave my fingers through hers and walk the length of the room by her side.

Oh what I would do to make this our every day. The problems we face are that of arrogant men who don't know how to share their feelings and nothing of wars and revenge and running for our lives.

I want that with her. A human life. Or at the very least, a human-adjacent life here, where the air is fresh and we can stop looking over our shoulders in fear of what's coming next. That's what I will fight for because it's what we all deserve.

And although I don't want to break my promise to her, it's going to be difficult to not confront Bo and make him pay for the hurt he's caused her.

"**G**lad to see you're back on your feet," Sydney tells Dash when we file into the large kitchen. "I was worried we'd have a mess to clean up for a minute there."

Dash forces a smile. "Just keeping everyone on their toes."

We settle into two empty chairs at the end of the table where everyone else is sitting. Well, everyone aside from Bo. No, Bo chooses to scarf down his food while standing in the farthest corner of the room like the rest of us might give him the plague if he comes too close.

Whatever.

"Here, give me your plate." Wes takes the shiny white dish in front of me and scoops some food onto it, along with a hunk of bread. "Pass that over to Dash." He hands it to me, and I'm wafted by the heavenly aroma as it crosses in front of me and over to Dash.

"Damn, that smells amazing." My stomach growls and reminds me that eating more should move up on the list of priorities.

During our stint in Rockbridge, there was no telling when our next meal would be. Not to mention, whether it would be edible. Usually, it was some sort of greyish sludge that could have been borderline toxic waste. Sometimes there would be a cup with a small amount of water, and rarely, a moldy piece of what resembled bread. We were only there for a short period, and yet the experience isn't something I wish to ever go through again.

My gaze darts across the table to land on Jade, who spent, from my understanding, years in that horrid place. How is it possible she survived that long on scraps of nearly nothing? But when I see Everest push his plate toward her, I realize the answer to that question.

He was the light in the darkness that kept her going. Her lifeline when all hope was lost.

And he was more than likely a huge catalyst in not just her survival, but ours, too.

I thought I was the only hunter who fought against our kind, but maybe Everest and I aren't the only ones who see the errors of our ways.

"There's cheese on this." Wes picks up the piece of bread on my plate and points to a gooey substance on top. "And this." He latches onto a peculiar tube and pops the top. "You can sprinkle on the pasta."

"It's called parmesan cheese," Sydney says from down the table. "Try it."

I reluctantly take the thing from Wes and sprinkle some on top of the pile of food on my plate. Taking the fork from beside my plate, I swirl some of the pasta and shove it into my mouth. My eyes instinctually close and a moan escapes me. "This is," I say with a mouthful. "So fucking good."

Wes grins and sets the bread back onto my plate, but I snatch it up and bite off a chunk, chewing it with the pasta.

I practically drown the noodles with more cheese and mumble through each bite.

"I didn't have any breakfast foods stocked in the house." Sydney walks over to the large refrigerator, which is apparently powered by electricity, not magic.

To me, they're one and the same.

An entire home with running water and lights and heating, that sounds magical.

"Is this not *breakfast*?" I pat my mouth with my napkin and reach for the glass of water in front of me. "Because I could eat this for every meal."

Sydney chuckles. "Usually humans eat eggs or meat, pastries, pancakes, fruit, things like that, for breakfast. With coffee or juice."

"I could go for some ale." I point to the tray of bread in the middle of the table and whisper to Wes, "Can I have another?"

"Ale? Hmm." Sydney continues browsing the contents of his fridge. "I have this spiked cider." He pulls out a bottle and brings it over to me. "Deghan got a six-pack the last time he visited."

"Deghan?" I take the thing from him. "Will they mind if I have this?"

He shakes his head. "He probably forgot all about them."

What a luxury to have so much that you forget about things. I may lose track of an apple here or there, but I would know if someone took something like this from one of my safe houses.

"And who is this Deghan? A friend?" I fumble with the thing covering the end of the bottle.

"Here, let me help you." Sydney twists the cap off and tosses it onto the table.

I sniff the end. "It's kind of fruity."

"Yeah, it's fermented apples."

Everyone except Bo and Sydney stares at me in what I can only assume is anticipation of my response to the drink.

I bring the bottle to my lips, the cool fizzy liquid pooling into my mouth. I swallow it down and shrug. "It's not bad." I hold it out to Wes. "Want to try it?"

"Sure." He takes it from me, then passes it to Dash. "Not bad at all."

"I can get more, if you'd like." Sydney opens a drawer and pulls out a notepad. "And to answer your question, Deghan is one of my wife's husbands."

"Wife plural or husband plural?" I ask him to clarify.

"Husband, sorry, I should have been clearer. I have one wife, she has four husbands. And each of us are married to only her."

"Is that common here on Earth?" Because it's not something I'm super familiar with.

"Um, yes and no." Sydney makes a note on the pad of paper. "Relationships with multiple partners are becoming more widely normalized and accepted. Legally speaking, no, you can't technically marry multiple partners. Our ceremony wasn't traditional in the sense, and more so to connect us on a spiritual level. It meant more to us than having a legally binding arrangement."

It's comforting to know that I'm not the only one who finds being with more than one person appealing. It isn't that I want to collect men until the end of time, but there's no denying that I have a connection to each of my guys, and if forced to choose between them, I don't think I could. Each of them makes me feel a different way and imagining a life without any single one of them seems dull and void. Even Bo, who drives me completely fucking insane.

I'm not open, available, or interested in any other suitors—I just want my three demons.

"It's more common in the supernatural world," Sydney adds.

Jade speaks up from her spot at the end of the table with Everest. "What are you going to do about Tremont?"

A question no doubt on all our minds. I don't particularly care either way what happens to him, but I am curious.

Sydney draws in a long breath and leans against the countertop. "I haven't made a decision." He runs his hand through his shaggy hair. "If I'm being honest, this entire situation has thrown me. Between him, you, being back here—I'm unsure what to do about any of it."

I sip more of the cider. "Are you going to tell us what he did?"

"It's...complicated." Sydney glances down at the floor and back up. "And kind of a long, twisted story." He shakes his head. "One that I thought was behind us."

"Maybe just give us the highlights, or well, the low lights. His worst offenses." I understand where he's coming from, because if someone asked me to explain things with Parla, I'd be lost at where to begin, too.

"The worst?" Sydney drinks from his cup, the condensation trickling down the side and dripping onto his shirt. "He hurt my wife." He nods. "That's something I'll never forgive him for, no matter what amends he tries to make."

"Is she okay?" I ask.

"Yeah, she's better than ever, growing in strength every day, no thanks to him."

He must care a great deal for his wife if he's *this* mad at someone for harming her.

"What does she say about him, and us, being here?" I can't help but wonder what she must be like—this distant relative of mine. I wonder what features we share, what things we have in common.

"I haven't told her, not yet, not until I know more. I don't want to burden her, she already has too much going on as it is."

A part of me grows worried that he never will, and we will remain locked away in this house, in this other realm, without any hope of a real future.

But I push that intrusive thought away. It's only been a day; I need to not jump to conclusions. I've spent a lifetime in captivity, what's a little longer?

"Here's the deal. Tremont hurt her in more ways than one. He hurt you, too." He looks directly at me when he says this. "He's the reason your magic was suppressed for all those years. He conspired with my parents to steal magic from an entire bloodline in some sadistic power-hungry rampage. Up until not too long ago, the Oliver name was cursed, and he played a huge role in making that happen."

Rage boils within me at each word he speaks. It's no wonder he was shocked when he found Tremont shacking up in his house and threw together that barrier spell. Hell, I would have killed him on the spot if I were him. Sydney has more willpower than me, or maybe he's not accustomed to that kind of violence. Or is it that things aren't handled that way here on Earth?

"I say we kill him." Bo finally breaks his silence.

Leave it to Bo to say the thing on my very mind.

I flit my attention at him briefly before settling my gaze back on Sydney. "You really believe I have hidden magic somewhere within me?"

"Without a doubt."

I thought Parla took everything from me, but it seems Tremont was a key component in trying to ruin my life, too. What if I came into my powers sooner? Could I have stopped the war in Prania earlier? Could I have saved myself a lifetime of serving that heartless bitch? Would I have been strong enough to prevent my mother from being murdered when I was a child? I'll never know, and it's his fault I'll never find out.

"I think he knew." I recall the memory of him taking my *magic* to break the barrier spell at Rockbridge, the one that was keeping us confined inside the building.

He acted shocked, like my power was somehow alarming. I passed it off as him getting a jolt of all the demon essence I harnessed, but in reality, he was getting a taste of what he already knew. *Oliver magic.* He gave himself away again when he questioned my last name, and insisted I would be capable of cross-realm travel without a weakness in the fold. He knew the whole time, and never once thought to tell me who I was, who I am. And because I was blind to the truth, I never truly picked up on any of it. My biggest concern was getting my people to safety, and in that, I overlooked the enemy right at my side.

But if he truly meant ill, would he have brought us to the very place where those secrets would no doubt come to light? He had to have known how dangerous it would be here, and that it would only be a matter of time before I learned what he had done.

The entire situation makes no sense from his perspective if he had some nefarious plan.

Regardless of whether his intentions were good or evil, it still makes me want to kill him no less.

He may not have known he was hurting me when he suppressed the Oliver magic, but the impact of what he did runs deep. His actions very well could be the catalyst that set my entire life on the path that it took.

Would my path have crossed with Wes's if he hadn't, though?

Or what if we had met sooner, under different circumstances?

"Oh, he did, for sure," Sydney confirms. "I'm guessing he brought you here as a bargaining chip, for his freedom."

How dare someone use me for anything, especially for forgiveness of such heinous acts.

"Wait." I play the details of what he said back in my mind. "Your parents, what became of them?"

Sydney's jaw tenses. "They got what they deserved. And now they're serving out the rest of their days in Balial's hell dimension." He puts his arms up. "This was their home, the one I grew up in. I can't bring myself to part with it but being here is a constant reminder of a childhood I don't wish on anyone else."

That makes two of us with a screwed-up adolescence.

Wes grips my hand under the table.

None of us have had it easy, that's for sure. But if I have any say in our future, it's one that isn't plagued with memories we beg to forget.

"I'm guessing you didn't share your parent's ambition?" Dash stands from the table, taking his empty plate and the one in front of me.

"No, my parents and I had nothing in common. They hated me and what I stood for—what I was."

"How could a parent hate their child?" The question leaves my mouth without me really meaning to say it out loud.

"I was a reminder of what they would never have. True angel given power." Sydney glances around. "I don't know how much you know of your ancestry, but we all have some level of light and dark magic coursing through our veins. Every supernatural being does. The lighter, the more powerful. That isn't to say darker can't be potent, too, but lighter is purer, a more direct link to the Angels. My parents, with the help of Tremont and many others, going back centuries, had been suppressing and harnessing the Oliver line, because it was stronger than anything they could have naturally."

The comparison of what Parla had me doing to the demons of Prania is so eerily similar to what Sydney's parents were doing to my bloodline.

At the end of the day, what makes me any different than him?

What if he was manipulated and convinced that what he was doing was the right thing?

How can I hate him for doing exactly what I had been doing?

I didn't just steal their source of power, I killed them in order to take it.

If anything, what I did was fucking worse.

I swallow down a lump that forms in my throat and grow ill from the damage that I had caused.

I knew I was taking their essence, and I had no reservations about ending their lives. I thought I was doing my realm a service to free us from the creatures that plagued our lands. But all they were trying to do was survive. Sure, they fought back and caused their fair share of mayhem, but they were doing what they had to do to stay alive—and with me out there, fueled by nothing but vengeance, they stood no chance. None of them did. The only thing stopping me from making sure Wes had met that same fate, was fate itself. If the curse hadn't been lifted, would I have even known who Wes was when I locked eyes with him? Would I have killed him without knowing he was my fated mate? When would it have ever registered in my mind, in my soul, that I was responsible for his death?

Suddenly, I find myself grateful for whoever, or whatever freed the Oliver bloodline of their curse.

"How? How were we set free?" I hold Wes's hand tighter and silently thank the Angels that he's here with me today.

"It wasn't easy," Sydney tells me. "There was a series of obstacles, but ultimately, it came down to Willow, my wife. She went through hell and back, quite literally, multiple times even. There were a few times I didn't think she'd make it, that any of us would, but somehow, she overcame the impossible." Sydney smiles softly. "I'm not sure there isn't anything she can't do once she sets her mind to it."

The love he has for her radiates through each word he speaks of her. He's protective, proud, supportive. It's a beautiful thing to see despite all the ugly I'm familiar with.

"I'd love to meet her." I would settle for anything to help me wrap my head around the information that's been thrown at me.

Nothing about my life is what I thought it was. And every day, something else seems to change. What else do I not know about who I am, who I was, or who I could be?

"I need to process things before bringing her into this." He lets out a breath. "I hope you understand. This is rather unexpected, and my primary concern is her well-being. I don't know how she'll react to any of this. I want to tread lightly, be cautious."

And given I'm the worst monster of them all, I don't blame him for wanting to shield her from me.

CHAPTER 8

Wren

Tremont stays tucked away inside his room.

I don't bother knocking, or paying much attention to him aside from imagining him bursting into flames and experiencing a painful demise.

I shower again, doing what I can to rid myself of the lingering remains of his touch. He didn't hurt me, but I can't help being repulsed by the idea of him having access to my power.

Let me in, he had said.

I gave him entry to my magic without realizing the severity of the situation. But if he was going to abuse that gateway, wouldn't he have taken more? Taken so much that it rendered me completely powerless.

Nothing of this makes sense, and the more I try to rationalize what has happened, the more confused I become.

So instead, I sit in the large expanse of the shower and let the water wash over me, the heat reddening my pale flesh.

How much longer will we remain in this house? What will happen to us once Sydney makes up his mind? We're at a standstill on how to move forward, especially considering Tremont was going to be the go-between for teaching us the ways of this world.

Without that, we pose too many risks to be set loose on Earth. One hour of Bo being free and he'd probably eat an entire town for lunch and out the supernatural world by the end of the day.

These beings have spent their entire lives maintaining the secret of their existence, what kind of people would we be if we fucked that up our first week?

They have peace here, or at least, some form of it. They get to exist and live without fear of someone like me or Parla coming after them to take what is theirs.

Granted, that's my understanding of how it is here with the minimal information I've gathered from talking with Sydney.

There's always the possibility of him lying and feeding us a line of bullshit to keep us from leaving this house but what would he gain from that? I'm sure he wants us out of here just as much as we do.

"Hey." Dash pokes his head into the steamy shower. "You okay in there?"

I blink through the water covering my face and wipe at my eyes. "I'm good."

"Those clothes Sydney brought for you are clean. You wouldn't believe the machines they use. It makes doing laundry so simple once you figure out which buttons to push. Although, I do warn you to use caution when filling the cup with soap. There's a line on there for a reason."

I stand and turn the faucet off, not yet growing tired of the endless hot water supply this house has. What a plethora of wonders this world has and we've only just visited one place.

"And Bo," Dash adds. "He found something called *Netflix* on this large thing on the wall. I thought it was a black piece of artwork but he found this other little black thing with buttons and started pushing them. The artwork lit up so he kept clicking and found this thing that apparently has motion pictures inside of it that you can watch."

"Tremont said something about a fantasy movie." I towel dry my hair and wrap the soft fabric around my body, focusing on the man in front of me. "How are you feeling?"

Dash shrugs. "Totally fine. How are *you* feeling?"

I tilt my head at him. "Dash."

"Wren." He mimics my movement.

I roll my eyes. "Would you tell me if something was wrong?"

He sighs dramatically. "If I thought it was a big enough deal."

"What if what we think is a big deal are two different things?" I slip into the shirt sitting on the dresser, noting how it fits tighter than the other clothes I've been borrowing since being here.

Sydney was kind enough to locate some women's clothing since most of what's in this house is either men's, or weird fancy clothing left behind by his mothers.

It's like the woman never wore sweatpants or T-shirts.

Don't get me wrong, I appreciate her commitment to the look she was going for, but it's too stiff and swanky for me. And I'd be lying if I said it didn't remind me of the way Parla dressed.

My gaze falls on the armored clothing I was wearing when I got to this realm. My fingers itch to reach out to touch it, but I restrain myself. I'm safe here; I don't need to hide behind the thick layers. Running for my life and constantly fighting battles is a thing of the past.

But I'd also be lying if I said I didn't miss it.

And maybe because it's all I've ever known, or maybe because it's a part of who I am.

Either way, I must come to terms with the fact that it is not my future.

Dash settles his hands on my shoulders. "You don't need to worry about me, okay?"

"I could say the same to you." I raise a brow knowing that he's aware that what he's asking is easier said than done.

"Not fair."

"I'm a skilled assassin, Dash."

"And I'm an immortal phoenix. That has to count for something."

I reach up and cup his face in my hand. "You might not be able to die, but you can still get hurt."

And the fact that it can happen in his nightmares is even more alarming.

How can I protect him when I can't even see the threat until it's already sunken its claws into him?

"This is proof." I skim the bandage on his forehead where he split his head open on the table in the living room.

"I'll heal." Dash's bright blue eyes look back and forth between mine. "So, what do you think, want to watch a Netflix?"

I breathe in, separating myself from this beautiful man and finish putting my borrowed clothes on. "I don't know."

"Because of Bo?"

I shrug and sit on the edge of the bed. "Kind of. He pisses me off."

Dash smiles. "He pisses us all off."

"That's the truth."

"You have enough going on, don't let him ruin your day. You should get to enjoy your time in this new place, too."

"And how are you liking it here? Well, with the limited exposure to this realm."

Dash leans against the bedpost. "I love it. It's nice not to be constantly running for your life. And the food, well, that speaks for itself."

"It really does, doesn't it?" I imagine that warm, cheesy bread melting in my mouth.

"The bed." Dash pushes his hand down onto the mattress. "I don't think I've ever rested that soundly in my life."

It sure beats the measly thing they had shoved in a corner of their tiny house.

I thought things were bad for me in Prania, but everyone I came here with was struggling in ways I'll never imagine. It's no wonder they're settling in with ease.

Still, I can't ignore the itch in my core telling me not to get too comfortable.

"Can I ask you a question?" I chew the inside of my lip.

"You just did." Dash chuckles. "Sorry." He brushes my shoulder playfully. "What's up?"

"Does it bother you, you know, that I'm *with* other people?"

"Honestly..." He pauses for what feels like an eternity. "Not at all. Maybe if it was anyone else than who it is, but I'm still not sure I would be *bothered*. I trust your judgment. My only concern is that you're happy and cared for. Other than that, I'm thrilled to be involved."

How did I get lucky enough to find someone so kind and understanding?

"I don't plan on adding anyone else," I tell him, just to make sure he knows.

"And that's a bridge we can cross if it comes up. I would never hold you back from living the life you desired." He stands from his post. "But, for the record, you're the only woman for me."

Dash holds out his hand toward me. "Now come on, let's see what this Netflix thing is all about."

Apparently, this giant home has more than one living room. The one we talked to Sydney in is technically considered a *sitting* room, while this one has a *television* and is somehow different than the other. Elaborate furniture fills both, along with dark paint and large windows, covered by decadent drapery. Someone took great concern while decorating this house, and it shows in the finest of details.

What a different world to find myself in after having spent my life ignoring and being completely oblivious to those types of things. It's not that I didn't appreciate it, it just wasn't on my radar in any capacity.

With Dash and Wes at my sides, Dash leans his head on my shoulder while Wes drapes his arm around me, resting his hand on Dash. The comfort of their presence almost drowns out the magnetic and negative energy Bo radiates.

"So, you're telling me," Bo says loudly. "This guy can stalk and murder people and it's considered romance, but when I do it, it's bad?"

Jade presses a button on the remote, pausing the show. "Bo. I love you like a brother, you know this, but if you don't keep it down, I'm going to be the one murdering you. I want to know if he's going to kill her boyfriend or not and I can't hear over your outbursts."

Sydney comes in from behind us. "Ah, you're watching *You*, that's a good one. But hey, let me see that." He points toward the button clicker thing in Jade's hand. "If you push this." He does as he says and pokes the thing a few more times. "You can get subtitles on the screen, so you can read what's being said, too." He hesitates before handing it back to Jade. "That is, if you can read English. I only assumed since you speak it."

"We don't call it that back home, but yes, it's the same." Jade takes it from him and turns the show back on.

"Wren," Sydney says. "Can I have a word with you? Privately."

I nod and scoot myself up from the depths of the comfortable couch and the warm bodies I'm pressed between. "Of course, yeah."

He tips his head, a signal for me to follow him.

"I'll be back, guys." I glance over at Jade. "And gal."

Bo does a poor job hiding his stare when I get up and leave the room, but I don't bother giving him a blip of satisfaction by acknowledging him.

I follow Sydney down the long hallway with dusty artwork and doors that lead to unknown places. We end up in the kitchen, where Sydney goes straight to the counter and points to a seat for me to take.

"Would you like some coffee?"

"Sure." I've grown to like the bitter hot liquid and besides, it would give me something to do with my nervous hands. Usually, they're filled with knives or chains or whatever weapon of choice for the day.

It's going to take me a hell of a lot longer than a couple days before I grow used to not knowing what to do with all this idle time. Even when I had breaks between cases, I would spend the time training or preparing for my next battle. Here I have nothing to worry about other than what type of snack I'd like between meals.

Is this all humans do? Or Earth folk in general? Is life this mundane that it revolves around eating, shitting, and watching television shows?

It could be worse, that's for sure, but it's nothing at all like what I'm familiar with.

But that could simply be because we're confined to Sydney's parent's estate, and we haven't ventured out into the *real* world.

"I never properly asked, but you're a witch, right?" The hunter radar within me that typically alerts me to these things hasn't really worked properly since I was taken captive by Wes. None of my skills ever really came back fully.

"Yes, that's correct." Sydney fills two mugs with coffee and nudges one across the counter to me. "There are many like us here, and with the curse finally being lifted, more and more come into their powers each day." Sydney blows on the steaming drink. "Although with time it has slowed a bit, the first initial wave was intense. A multitude of new witches that had no idea they had magic suddenly started presenting signs of magical use. It took the majority of our resources to get it under control and get everyone the assistance they needed."

"What do you mean? What do you do for people like that?"

"Well, aside from explaining what was happening to them, we had to open new schools across the world to accommodate the teachings of magic. We couldn't run the risk of being exposed so we had to act quickly to get everything in order. It was so overwhelming that Willow had to temporarily step down from her position on the supernatural council to make sure everyone was taken care of. She still advises, and has recently regained some of the responsibilities, but her main concern is of the people, not the power. She's less about politics but the two go hand in hand, unfortunately."

I put my palms around the mug to warm them. "She sounds...incredible."

The kind of woman I aspire to be.

But I'm aware the things I have done will make that nearly impossible. My mistakes won't be so easily forgotten and it will take many lifetimes to offset the damage I have done. I must atone for my sins if I wish to seek redemption.

"She is." Sydney stares off blankly. "From the moment I laid my eyes on her, I knew she was special, and every day, she continues to amaze me." He blinks to center himself. "Anyway, I wanted to talk to you. We have much to discuss, and so much to learn of this world, but I was curious, what are your intentions here?"

I tilt my head and take a cautious sip of my drink. "What do you mean?"

"You came here, to Earth, or Arthlia as some refer to it, to seek refuge. Are you planning on staying long-term, short-term?"

"I..." I find myself unsure what to say considering we've only just arrived.

"I only ask because it will impact how I handle our approach. Obviously, the choice is up to you, and those you've traveled with, but if it's meant to be a short visit, I'm not convinced we should spend our time focused on the insignificant details."

"We, uh, we don't really have anywhere else to go." When we fled Prania, I had no idea we would land here, in Arthlia. This place was always considered a fever dream, something talked about in drunken conversations at the bar. A paradise of sorts that none of us had ever been to, but hoped to visit someday. We all knew it was impossible, that's why we talked about it the way we did.

But now, now that I'm quite literally standing on the other side, I can't help but feel like someone should pinch me and wake me up from this dream.

"Did you intend on coming here when you traveled between the realms?" Sydney leans his butt against the counter and crosses one arm over his torso while he keeps his mug out in front of him.

"No." I shake my head and try to recall the moment everything changed. "We were there. A wendigo army was closing in on us, we had nowhere to go. We were pressed between the border and countless demons that wanted us dead. Tremont latched onto me, told us all to hold on tight, and the next thing I knew, there was a bright flash of light and we were waking up in the darkness."

"Why hadn't you ever left before if things were that bad?"

"We couldn't. Prania had been closed off for realm travel long ago. Centuries maybe. I'm not keen on the actual origin date."

"If my research is accurate, and that's the case, the power Tremont harnessed from you was what granted you access, and that was because of your bloodline. And if I take it one step further, the realm that you ended up in is the one that the angels decided you should be in."

"You're telling me the angels transported me here?"

Sydney nods. "In theory. But that goes both ways. Tremont was no doubt sent to Prania because it was inescapable. His ultimate punishment."

"Then why would they let him out?"

"That is the million-dollar question." Sydney exhales. "This is all speculation based on what I've gathered. We have a past with cross-realm travel because of our experience with hell dimensions but never with a realm that doesn't exist on paper. I scoured textbooks and couldn't find anything on Prania. It's almost like it doesn't exist."

"But it does," I tell him. "I spent my entire life there."

"I know. I believe you. But it does beg the question, why was it completely erased from history?"

CHAPTER 9

Bo

I stand just outside the kitchen, leaning against the wall, and eavesdrop on Wren and Sydney's *private* conversation.

How dare he think that he can whisk her away to chat without involving the rest of us?

It's nothing that juicy either, only some minor details about our entire home-land pretty much being completely unknown to the world outside of Prania.

But I'm no stranger to my past being erased completely.

Us demons did what we could to preserve the buildings that housed the litera-ture and recordings of our existence, but hunters did everything they could to make sure not even an ounce of us remained.

They killed us, and then removed any trace of what we may have left behind.

Our legacy disappeared out of sight like dust in the wind.

So the information leaving Sydney's mouth is no surprise at all.

The hunters want us gone in every way possible.

And they have stopped at nothing to make that happen. Only, Wren threw a big fucking wrench in their scheduled programming when she turned on them and got herself a fated mate that was one of the most powerful demons of all.

It's kind of funny, really, if you think about it.

The one major component in their plan for world domination ended up being the very person that brought it to a staggering halt.

Sure, Wren may have evaded Parla's grasp, but Parla is still in Prania, slaugh-tering innocent demons and following through with whatever eradication she can.

Wren being gone isn't going to stop Parla from being a conniving bitch.

Maybe *innocent* was a bit of a stretch but still, they're unjustly killing people that don't deserve to die. I don't know what could be more innocent than that.

Wren has taken her fair share of demon lives, but so have I. Not only demons, but hunters, too. Anyone who threatened me—or Dash and Wes—met the fate that I decided was best fit for them.

It's a shame I didn't get a chance to end that wendigo before we were thrown into another realm. It's no surprise that we desperately needed out, but it would have been nice to have a bit less unfinished business in a realm that I have no clue how to get back to.

Parla and that wendigo need to die, and it won't sit right with me until they do.

Although, they would be doing me a solid if they went ahead and offed each other since they're enemies anyway.

But then that would deprive me of the gratification of doing it myself, and I don't think I'm ready to give that up.

Wren shoves her head around the corner and into the hallway. "You're not being subtle, Bo. I can hear you all the way in here. Either stop breathing or get in here."

"Birdie, I was just..." I run my hand through my hair and pretend she didn't give me a slight start.

"Chop chop, big boy." She snaps her fingers, and it's like every fucking fiber in my stupid body responds to her command.

I hate the control she has over me.

She could say *sit, Bo* and I'd sit.

Roll over, Bo, and I'd roll over.

I'd do anything for her, other than what's right, because all I seem to know how to do is the wrong thing.

Every word that leaves my mouth is interpreted an entirely different way than intended, and despite my best attempts, I fuck up left and right.

She'd be better off if I disappeared and never came back.

But I can't. Not when she bears the mark of my bite on her neck, and my distance means the flesh-hungry demons of Earth would be able to track her down and kill her.

I made a mistake marking her. I just didn't realize the severity of it until after my feelings developed. Hatred was replaced by something I didn't and still don't recognize. I do, however, get glimpses of what it should be when I see her with Wes and Dash.

We could have that, but I won't allow it. Not when I'm no good for her and her main attraction toward me is a result of the stupid fucking mark I gave her without her consent.

And ridding her of the beacon my mark exudes would be a worse fate than she's already met, and I can't bring myself to do that to her either.

Instead, I have to be around her with this ache in my chest and the knowledge that she will never be mine—not truly.

"I'm coming," I tell her, my trail hot on hers. I breathe her in, her scent lingering in the air with each step she takes.

The soaps in this world do nothing to mask her true, delectable scent.

I can even catch whiffs of the blood pulsing through her veins and causing my throat to burn with a lust unlike anything I've ever felt.

I want so badly to sink my fangs into her neck and taste her once again, but if I do, there's no telling if I'll have the self-control to stop this time.

She tastes better than I ever could have imagined, and just the thought of my mouth pooling with her blood makes my cock throb in my pants.

Her desire rivals the decadence of her blood, and if I had my choice, I would drown in both and die a happy fucking man.

My dick pulses at the thought of pleasing her while she's on her moon cycle, my two favorite things paired with the idea of bringing her to climax.

"Actually, on second thought. I have to go." I throw my thumb up and point behind me.

"What?" She turns on her heels. "Where?"

"I, uh, I have somewhere to be." I glance at my wrist despite not wearing a watch. "Yeah, the time." I take a few steps back, and once I'm out of the room, I dart down the hall and disappear out of sight.

"Bo," she calls out but it's too late, I'm already gone.

I rush up the stairs, ignoring the usual appeal I have to tear down Tremont's door and rip his limbs from his body, and go into the bedroom Wren has claimed as hers. I drag my shirt over my head, toss it onto the floor, and step out of my pants on the way to the bathroom. I close the door and lock it behind me. With a deep breath, I step into the shower and yank the faucet on, turning it to its coldest setting.

I stand under it for a full minute, my hand pressed into the wall and my head down, the water rolling over my face. It does nothing to rid my mind of the image of her soaking wet and spread in front of me. I lick my lips, the taste of her so fresh in my memory that I can still smell her delicious lust.

With my free hand, I grip my cock and stroke its full length, hoping that will be enough to stave off my hunger. But when my eyes close, and the thought of her pussy clenching around my fingers fills my head, I grow even harder in my grasp.

"Angels," I whisper.

I want her so badly it hurts.

I change the water from freezing cold to scalding hot and return my palm to my dick. I rock it up and down, squeezing tighter and deciding that the only thing I can do now is find a release. Maybe if I come, I won't be so fucking tense and ready to kill anyone. Who am I kidding though? That's how I always am regardless of whether I'm horny or not.

Imagining her hand in place of mine, I stroke myself faster, wanting this whole experience to be behind me. It's not that I don't enjoy a good self-pleasuring moment, but when it's to stop yourself from making bad decisions, the fun kind of goes out the window.

"Did you really come in here to jerk off?" Her voice fills the entire bathroom and rattles through my entire core.

"Maybe," I tell her. "But if you don't mind, I'd like to finish, so either stay and watch or get out."

"How about I do you one better?"

I glance over my shoulder to find her undressing.

Fuck. I can't be *this* horny and near her naked body at the same time. It's one thing to be around her when I have a bit more self-control, but now I worry I won't have the same level of restraint.

Wren strolls over, the water sprinkling her as she approaches, the droplets beading on her breasts and running down her perfect fucking body. Taut, petite, subtle round edges. Her dark eyes meet mine, her lust-filled gaze fueling my erection that much more.

"What are you doing?" I ask her, my jaw tense.

"Whatever I want." She reaches for my cock, sliding her hand beside mine.

"Wren," I breathe.

"Do you want me?"

I swallow and fight every carnal desire I have to throw her against the wall and fuck her with a force that might kill us both.

"You know I do," I tell her the truth.

"Then if a climax is what you so desperately need, allow me to give it to you." She drops down onto her knees, her doe eyes staring up at me through her thick lashes.

Fuck, I'm a goner.

She licks her lips, her gaze leaving mine and settling on my cock that's only inches from her pretty little mouth. Wren strokes my length and positions it at the edge of her lips, the heat from her breath alone sends a wave of pleasure through me.

"Angels, Birdie." I grip the base of my shaft and shove into her, the warmth consuming me instantly.

Wren widens herself for me, cupping her tongue and allowing me to go deeper. Water pelts her face but she doesn't seem bothered as she focuses solely on my cock in her mouth. She grabs the backs of my legs, pulling me toward her, a silent permission to give her more.

I try to hold back, to control myself, but it becomes more difficult with every second I'm inside of her.

My hand weaves its way through her hair, gripping her skull and holding her in place. I rock my hips, fucking her harder.

Wren digs her hands in and pushes back to free herself, and I fear that I may have taken things too far. My erection softens at the immediate and unfamiliar concern.

She looks up at me. "Plug my nose."

"What?" I blink at her.

"Plug my fucking nose. Water keeps splashing me and it's distracting." She strokes my cock.

"You won't be able to breathe."

"I'd rather die from asphyxiation than drown." She latches onto me tighter and pulls me toward her. "Do it, Bo."

I comply, pinching her nose between my fingers as she takes me into her hungry mouth.

"Fuck," I moan and slide myself deeper until I hit the back of her throat.

She keeps me there, in the depths of what she's able to take of me, and meets my gaze. Wren bobs her head in her attempt to consume more, not daring to come up for a breath, yet her lifeforce becomes swallowing every inch of me she can muster.

I grow harder and my inhibitions lower as a side of me that I beg to keep hidden rises to the surface. Releasing her nose for a second, I return my hold and use my other hand to grab the back of her head and fuck her gorgeous face.

Her moans vibrate against my shaft, and my climax builds.

I blow deep inside of her throat, refusing to pull out and allow her the breath I'm sure she desperately needs. I grunt through the pleasure and accidentally shift, my demon side taking over my more human-like nature—my cock included. Small barbs poke out, sinking their way into her mouth like a bunch of tiny bee stings, only the stingers stay in place and keep her there, her blood rolling down her throat with my orgasm. I thrust one last time and force my demon side to return to its hidden capacity and pull out of her.

She gasps and wipes at her bottom lip, not at all fazed by what just happened.

"Are you okay?" I ask her, tilting her head up toward me.

Wren nods. "Yeah, what the hell was that?"

"I...I didn't mean to." Because showing her that side of me, truly exposing who I am, was never what I wanted to happen and part of the reason why I can't *be* with her.

"Bo," Wren rises to her feet but still has to look up at me. "I'm not afraid of you." She stands taller and presses her body closer to mine. "You're not going to hurt me."

But haven't I already? Both physically and emotionally?

She slides her finger down my arm and latches onto my hand, slowly moving it between us and tracing it over her clit and down her vulva. "I want you, Bo. All of you." She continues moving me as she spreads her legs slightly. Wren lifts her leg and holds it against my side, and without thinking and simply letting myself do what it wants, I thrust two fingers into her.

Her head tilts back. "That's it."

And in a sheer millisecond, I shove her into the wall, lower myself in front of her, and with her leg over my shoulder, I taste her once more. I'm more aggressive this time than last, my tongue morphing into my demonic tongue, the end splitting and touching both sides of her clit before diving down and lapping up her juices. I fuck her harder, giving her another finger to fill her fuller while dragging my other hand up her body and pinching her nipple between my fingers. I cup her breast in my hand and return to her nipple, squeezing harder when she moans louder.

Her pussy tightens around my fingers, and I thrust them in deeper and harder, my knuckles hitting her pelvic bone. I suck on her clit and bare my teeth, my fangs slicing her ever so softly. Considering how ravenous I am, I remain in control, only allowing myself the smallest indulgences.

But when the taste of her blood tempts me, I nearly lose it all.

I breathe in, desperate to not tear her apart right here and now, and center myself on the subtle movements of her body. I focus on her heartbeat, her ragged breaths, and the pulsing of her pussy on me.

Wren whimpers and comes undone, her pleasure satisfying me in an entirely different way than I was only moments ago.

She finishes and I stand, gently lowering her leg onto the damp tile floor.

Together, we step fully back under the steaming hot water and rinse off in silence.

I grow worried with each quiet moment until finally, she speaks.

"I'm still mad at you."

I tuck her hair behind her ear and study the shape of her jaw and trail my gaze up to meet hers. "I wouldn't have it any other way."

"Why are you so difficult?" she asks me.

"Why do you expect me to be anything else?"

Wren sighs. "Touché."

I don't say anything else. Instead, I listen in a manner that only someone who's paying great attention could. Her chest rises, her heart stutters, and she swallows harshly. She's thinking about something that makes her unsteady.

"If you don't want to be with me, why don't you just tell me?" Wren avoids making direct eye contact with me.

I don't mean to, but I smirk at her shy vulnerableness. She's the most badass woman I've ever known and here she is, showing insecurity.

But who am I to judge—I'm in the same exact boat. All this boils down to my fear that once the mark is gone, she will no longer want me, and with its removal, I'll never actually know.

"That's what you think this is?" I lean against the wall of the shower and avoid gawking at her naked and wet body.

"What else would it be?"

That I'm scared, terrified really, and for the first time in my life, I have someone I want to keep but have no idea how to make that happen because from the very moment I laid my eyes on her, I've been making mistake after mistake and setting us up for nothing but failure.

I don't say that though.

Nor do I mention that I have no idea how I'll fit in, in this world. It's unfamiliar and new and different and a demon like me can never exist with humans. I get angry and kill people and take what I want when I want it. That doesn't work here, at least not in reality, only in fiction. Being a murderous psychopath is frowned upon, and I don't know how to be anything else.

If she wants to stay here, there's nothing I can do to stop her, nor would I. I might be a blatant asshole, but I do actually care about what's best for her. And if living out her days in this realm with Dash and Wes is what she wants, I will suffer from a distance without putting her in danger.

"Bo," she says, snapping her fingers in front of my face. "What else would it be?"

I shake my head and run my hand through my wet hair, the tangles catching on my fingers. "It's complicated, Birdie." Kicking away from the wall, I take a step toward leaving.

She catches my arm. "You're the one making it complicated, Bo."

Each time my name leaves her lips, my heart constricts tighter.

"This is the way it has to be." I yank free of her and leave the shower, latching onto the first semi-clean-looking towel I can find.

The faucet creaks as she turns it off and her footsteps pound on the floor behind me. "Fine, if that's the way you want it, we're done."

Her last two words cut like the sharpest blade through my heart.

I want to protest, to scream and fight and beg and plead but I can't bring myself to say a fucking word.

CHAPTER 10

Wren

"Hey," Dash says upon entering the bedroom. "Sydney's ready."

Fuck. In the chaos of things with Bo, I completely lost track of time and the plan that was already set in place.

Dash catches my shoulders and steadies me, his blue gaze meeting mine. He keeps his voice low. "You okay? What's wrong?"

I force a smile. "Nothing. I'm good." Because I refuse to let Bo hear a single word that I'm anything other than completely fucking okay about what just happened.

If he wants to keep his emotions at bay, then two can play this fucking game.

I rush over to the pile of women's clothes and rummage through until I find something to throw on. I shove my feet into my boots and go over to the mirror, smoothing down my hair and pinching my cheeks to bring some color to my otherwise pale face.

"You look beautiful," Dash tells me without even having to ask.

Always the gentleman, that one.

Bo, on the other hand, he's everything but.

I meet Dash's gaze in the mirror, ignoring Bo dressing off in the corner. "Do you want to come with us? Be good to get out of the house."

Bo perks his head up immediately. "You're leaving? Like leaving, leaving?"

"Are you sure?" Dash steps closer.

"Of course. You're the only one I don't have to worry about unleashing your powers. I can't imagine Sydney would have any issue with it either."

"Is someone going to tell me what's going on?" Bo marches over to where Dash and I are standing.

"No. It's none of your business." I cross my arms over my chest and turn toward him. "Now if you'll excuse me, we have somewhere to be."

Bo catches me in the same way I had caught him when he tried to leave the shower. "What about the mark, Wren?"

The usage of my name only means that he's doing what he can to get under my skin more than he already has.

I shrug him off. "I've been informed it isn't but more than a few miles, nothing we haven't dealt with before. The *mark* you put on me shouldn't fully engage so long as you stay here."

The mark is a burden tying us together despite the very fact that he wants to get far, far away.

Maybe if he hadn't acted like an irrational idiot, we wouldn't be stuck in this mess and he could be free of me like he desires.

"Come on," I tell Dash while sliding my hand into his.

The sun shines through the window and casts light across the room, one that I imagine will feel warm and comforting on my skin once I'm outside. I've spent all my time inside this house, only venturing out in the darker hours when I'm most comfortable.

But with Sydney as our escort, I'll get to go out during the daytime.

The sun hasn't shone in Prania in centuries, at least, that's what I'm told. There were moments the sky would be clearer than others, but the ruins of that world taint the atmosphere with a relentless cloud of smoke. It's thick and heavy and completely different than here in Arthlia.

"You can't be serious," Bo calls out after us.

I don't bother turning around, instead, I tug Dash along with me into the hallway and down the stairs of this massive house.

Sydney waits at the bottom, his attention turning from the small device in his grasp to the two of us. He clicks a button on the thing and shoves it into his pocket.

I'll have to ask him what that is later.

"You don't mind if Dash comes, do you? He's harmless, I promise." I wait for his reply, watching the way he rubs at his neck and hesitates to answer.

"Uh, I mean…" Sydney glances between us.

Wes approaches from another one of the hallways and plants one hand on my shoulder and one on Dash's. "He's practically human aside from coming back from the dead."

"Yeah, I suppose that will be okay." Sydney shrugs. "Things are already weird enough, why not bring a phoenix along for the ride?"

Wes kisses the top of my head and whispers, "Be safe, and come back to me, okay?"

My cheeks blush even more than when I pinched them.

"Thanks for not throwing a fit about me leaving." I turn to tell him, my gaze flitting to Bo, who stands at the top of the stairs like a fucking statue as he glares at me.

Maybe he could learn a thing or two from Dash and Wes about how to engage with a woman. Bo might be expertly skilled in the bedroom but he's an idiot otherwise. An infuriating and sexy idiot.

"You can explore the grounds if you'd like. It's a rather nice day today, but please don't venture beyond the tree line. I'd rather people not ask questions we can't give them answers to just yet. The less you draw attention to yourselves, the better." Sydney looks at Wes the whole time, almost like he's putting him in charge while he's gone.

He's typically the most reserved and rational of us all, so it makes total sense Sydney would gravitate toward thinking along the same lines.

I don't imagine Jade and Everest will need much convincing to keep themselves concealed, but I wouldn't put it past Bo to defy the orders just because he can. Sydney may have been better off encouraging Bo to roam as far as he pleases, and Bo would probably stay in and be a lazy bum.

Tremont is supposedly still confined to his room, so it's unlikely he'll cause any issues.

Dash and I follow Sydney down another hallway that leads to a part of the house I have yet to venture into. A strange unease rises through me at being led away by a stranger, but in these few short days, Sydney has shown me a different side of what being supernatural means.

Where I come from, everyone is filled with hatred and darkness—but Sydney has this pure aura about him that I can't help but put trust in. Like my gut knew before I did that he would be on my side.

Perhaps it's that there are no sides. Instead, a common good that the people of Earth, or at the very least, Sydney, and from the sound of it, Willow, want for everyone.

The Angels sent me here for a reason, I should put a little faith in that.

Air hits my cheeks, warming them and spreading throughout my body. I blink a few times to adjust to the light and take in a deep breath. "Angels, this is..."

"Welcome to spring," Sydney says. "We've been having unseasonably higher temperatures lately but none of us are complaining. Winter was rough and aside from Deghan, none of us are really a fan of the snow."

"Is Deghan a witch, too?" I ask him since he's mentioned him enough that it seems an appropriate question to have.

"Deghan is a werewolf." Sydney points toward a shiny-looking thing with wheels. "My car."

"Car," I say, getting a feel for the word on my tongue. "Does it operate on magic?"

Sydney chuckles "No, it uses fuel to function. Gasoline."

Fuel. Gasoline. Car. Not magic. Got it.

"Interesting."

"You don't have cars where you come from?" Sydney opens a door on the side of the car and motions for me to enter. "You can sit in here. Dash, you okay sitting in the back?" He points across from my seat. "I have to drive otherwise you could sit up there with her."

"Yeah, no problem at all. I'm just happy to be here." Dash reaches for the handle the same way that Sydney had and slides into the seat behind mine.

I climb in, unsure what I'm supposed to do with my hands, and sit there, waiting for my next instruction.

Sydney shuts my door, closing me into this metal contraption, and walks around the front to get in the other side. He shoves a key into a slot and turns it, the death trap roaring to life and rumbling my entire body gently.

"What is that?" I fight the urge to panic. I am safe here, with Dash, with Sydney, in this foreign place.

"The motor." Sydney pats the *car* and reaches toward the door to retrieve a belt-like thing. "This is a seat belt. It keeps you from flying out of the car."

"I'm going to fly out of the car if I don't put it on?" My heart picks up its pace. I thought my old world was threatening, but this is an entirely new kind of concern.

"Only in emergencies, like if we were to crash. It's unlikely, but a precaution that I suggest taking." Sydney latches his into a hook that seems to keep it in place.

I glance in the back. "Does Dash have one to keep him inside the car, too?"

Dash has his in his hand and secures it in the holder, leaving me the only one not belted in. "Got it." His smile warms my heart more than the sun did my skin.

"So yeah, seat belt for the car that is fueled by gasoline. It's not magic but it might as well be. I never really understood mechanics at all." Sydney grips a stick with a ball on the end of it and moves it, causing a clunking of sorts to take place before the entire thing we're in moves.

"We have wagons," I say to distract myself. "They're powered by magic, but usually only the wealthiest hunters can afford them. I've ridden in a few in the past. It was nothing like this. This is..." I run my hand over the door and the fabric of the seat. "More sophisticated."

I push a button on the door, and the glass of the door lowers. I gasp. "Angels, I didn't mean to do that. Did I break it?"

Sydney laughs again, his humor at my expense somehow making me feel less concerned. If I broke something, he probably wouldn't find it funny.

"No, that's the window. They go up and down. You can keep it down if you'd like."

Dash pushes the button on his, too, lowering it and shoving his arm out of it, his fingers spreading and waving about delicately.

"Is he allowed to do that?" I turn toward Sydney.

"Absolutely. You can, too. Here, look." Sydney follows suit and once his window is down, he puts his arm out, and weaves it about. "It won't hurt you."

Is that what I'm afraid of? Something hurting me? Haven't I already been through enough in the past to not be fearful? Maybe it's not fear of being hurt, but more-so fear of the unknown. I've always been in control of every aspect of my life. Down to the way I handled killing demons. I had a protocol and a specific method, and that all changed when I was tasked with the assassination of Wes.

I lost control, and since then, I've fought to regain my footing in life.

Nothing makes sense, and the more I try to figure it out, the more that unravels.

I've always been more of a loner, going through the motions of life on my own and dealing with problems myself when they arose. It worked that way. There wasn't anything I couldn't handle. No demon too strong, no task too big. There was no teamwork, no concern for anyone else's safety. I researched things, I paid attention, the risk was mine and mine alone.

Now, I worry about other people constantly and grow terrified that if I make the wrong decision or don't do things correctly, they will suffer—or worse.

What if it's my fault they get hurt or die? What if I don't know all the variables, and I'm the reason for our demise? Things were different when it was just me, and that terrifies me worse than any monster ever could.

"Try it," Sydney tells me with one hand out the window.

Carefully, I lift my arm, inching it toward the opening, the air whipping by my fingers. I push it through, somewhat expecting there to be pain or discomfort, but instead, a rush of adrenaline courses through me. I move my wrist, spread my fingers, and become one with the air cascading by.

"One of the simple pleasures of life." Sydney glances over and looks back at the road.

"What do you mean?" I ask him with my hand still waving about like I'm attempting to catch the wind in my grasp.

"This, for instance." Sydney holds his hand up higher and then swoops it down. "The sun on your face after a long winter. The first sip of your morning coffee. Canceled plans when you really wanted to stay in. Finishing a good book. Freshly baked cookies. Making someone you love smile."

Hearing him rattle off examples makes me wonder what it would be like to live somewhere those things could actually happen. He doesn't appear much older than me, but he speaks as though he's lived such a grand life. I want that for myself one day, only, I'm not certain it's possible, not after everything I've done. Do I really deserve any of it considering what I've put so many through?

Still, I can't help but imagine the endless possibilities.

Would any of the guys want that? How do people like us transition to a life unlike anything we've ever known?

Even Dash, the sweetest and most innocent of us, has grown familiar with the violence and turmoil of our homeland.

Yet, it hasn't broken him, not entirely. He remains optimistic and ready to try new things. This new world doesn't have the same impact on him as it does on the rest of us.

And with my constant paranoia, can I get used to not constantly assuming anything I don't know is a danger to me and those around me?

How will I differentiate between a threat and something harmless when everything seems so foreign?

"That sounds nice," I tell Sydney.

"There's much to enjoy in this world, if you'll give it a chance." Sydney pushes a button on the console of this car, and noise quietly fills the space. "Music is another simple pleasure. You won't like all of it, but you'll end up preferring some styles over others."

"This one is nice." I lean back in the seat and allow myself to relax with my arm resting on the windowsill. Trees whip by, blurring into one indistinguishable shade of dark green.

"I like it, too," Dash says from behind me. He reaches through and gives my shoulder a gentle squeeze. "I think we'll be happy here."

I have zero doubts that Dash will fit in nicely in Arthlia. Calm and peaceful is kind of his thing. But will I be able to abandon my violent tendencies and resort to a life of domesticity?

How can I come to terms with my past and accept that I abandoned Prania and left it in the hands of Parla?

"What are you going to do about Tremont?" I tilt my head toward Sydney.

His hair wafts in the wind like slow-moving clouds, and his gaze darts down and then onto the road again. "What do you think I should do?"

I chuckle. "I don't think I'm the right person to be asking. In my homeland, things like this usually ended in violence."

Sydney nods his head. "That's what I'm trying to avoid, but I can't ignore the fact that he nearly ruined everything for me—and for so many others, too."

"But he didn't. You were able to stop him."

"That doesn't change what he did."

I chew at the inside of my lip, his words stinging worse than he intended. "What are your options?"

"That's the thing, I'm not sure. I guess I could kill him, that's the obvious one. But that doesn't sit right with me, not with who I am now. Not to mention, it's super illegal."

Does that mean that's who he was in the past? Maybe we aren't that different after all.

"Releasing him is another option," he continues. "But what if he's lying and he has wicked reasons for being here? What if he causes more chaos and hurts people? I'd be responsible for any harm he inflicts if I let him go."

"So you can't kill him, and you can't free him." I scratch at my chin.

"You could imprison him," Dash suggests.

My stomach clenches at the sudden recollection of my time spent in Rockbridge with Wes. Surely their prisons are nothing like Prania, but still, wouldn't that be a worse fate than ending his life?

"In theory, holding him hostage and imprisoning him is also illegal." Sydney flips a lever and a faint clicking sound appears. He turns us onto another road, and then the sound goes away.

"What does that mean though? What are the consequences?" I scan the new road in total amazement over how lavish this land is.

"Well, the humans, the people living on Earth, have these groups of higher-level officials called the government. They have them at all levels. Cities. Counties. States. Countries. We live in Harper County which is located in the United States." Sydney runs his hand through his hair. "I'll have to teach you about geography sometime. Or maybe there's a crash course I could have the academy put together for you. We school new supernatural creatures; I don't know why they couldn't make an exception for your situation."

My mind struggles to catch up with the fresh information.

"The government is in charge of making laws and there are law enforcement officers who, well, enforce them. There's a justice system, so when someone breaks a law, they go through a set process and they're either proven guilty or not, and then depending on the crime, there are different punishments. Something simple like a parking ticket is not punishable by jail time, but simply a fee that has to be paid. More severe crimes, like murder, that's going to get you locked up for a very long time. There are instances of accidental murder, or self-defense, which are taken into account when the decisions are made. Basically, bad things are off-limits here. No killing." He takes a second to look over at me. "No drugs. Most violence is a no-no. Weapons are pretty much off the table, too, unless you have a license for them. And one of the most sure-fire ways to get in trouble with the government is tax evasion."

I blink and come to terms with the fact that Arthlia is sounding less and less fun by the minute. But with these strict rules, the burden of being constantly in a state of worry reduces. If Prania had these types of laws, maybe things wouldn't have been in total anarchy.

"What's tax evasion?" Dash asks.

"Citizens of the United States have a duty to pay taxes on the income they make. Some people try to avoid doing so, for various reasons. But if the government finds out, you can be charged with tax evasion."

"What do they do with the taxes? The government?" Dash leans forward a bit in his seat.

"It depends on which level. There are taxes at the city level, all the way up to the federal. A lot of it goes to funding public services for things like health care, education, and transportation. They spend it on our military, um, what else, I don't know, there's probably a website I could find with more information if you're really invested in the topic."

"No, I was just curious. It's fascinating." Dash smiles softly.

Sydney turns the car again, but this time, we pull onto a one-lane road with no yellow or white lines like the rest. He drives slower, barely moving us down the long lane. "This is where we live, Willow and the rest of us."

My mouth goes dry, and my hands sweat within seconds of hearing the words leave his mouth.

A house that rivals the size of Sydney's comes into view. The lane circles around the front, making a perfect loop in front of the massive structure. Greenery weaves its way up the sides of the building, and perfectly sculpted shrubs line the entryway.

"You guys are *rich* rich." Dash says the thing that was on my mind, too.

Sydney laughs. "We inherited this home shortly after Willow became head of the supernatural council. We're fortunate for the resources that were provided for us. Not everyone is so lucky."

I had safe houses back in Prania, but none of them were *mine*. They were property of Parla and the hunter's organization. I only got them when I advanced through the ranks and proved what I could do for them. Other hunters weren't living the way I did because they weren't as skilled as me. I got preferential treatment because I worked my ass off for it. I vetted the witches that spelled the houses, but I only had access to them through my position working for Parla.

Witches. That reminds me of what Parla had been angry about at Rockbridge. She claimed I was working with a witch to stop her from harvesting the demonic power I had been harnessing from those that I killed and consumed. What if that had something to do with what Sydney had told me—of my bloodline being connected to Willows? Was it *my* powers that stopped her from taking what was mine? How strange that Willow fought a war to regain the magic that was stolen from her, and here I was, doing the same fucking thing to demons? The similarities are chilling.

I'd love to know the truth that Parla was asking for, but I'd have to confess to my crimes, and I don't think I'm ready to face the ghosts of those demons just yet.

The punishment of losing the people I care for is far worse than anything a *government* could do to me.

CHAPTER 11

Wren

I hold my breath upon crossing the threshold into Willow's home.

Dash slides his fingers through mine, and it's like I can breathe again, the comfort of his touch holding me together. He always has a way of settling my soul in times of disarray.

He smiles and my heart warms to his presence.

"This way," Sydney says, guiding us through the entry.

Two staircases hug the walls on both sides, curving and leading up to a second story with an open walkway. The floor is made up of something hard and shiny, like a polished rock that had been cut into perfectly sized squares and laid with such ease that not a piece is out of place. A mirror hangs on a wall we pass, the gold frame of it beautiful in a peculiar kind of manner.

Our footsteps patter on a hard surface, then on a long rug, winding us through the labyrinth of this home before Sydney brings us to a halt.

"Wait here." Sydney points toward a sitting area. "I'll be right back for you."

He disappears through a door, the thing almost closing but not quite latching all the way shut.

Dash settles into one of the seats without question, his palms rubbing the arms of the chair. "This is nice."

I appreciate the carelessness in his demeanor and how he's not bothered by the unknowns of this world. He goes with the flow and despite having a nightmare that quite literally hurt him, he doesn't seem impacted by it.

Or, he's just really good at masking what's wrong.

I hate to think something could upset him and I wouldn't know about it. Out of the three men in my life, he's the one I want to shield the most from harm. Bo and Wes are supernaturally strong and capable of fighting their own battles, and it's not that Dash isn't, but he isn't as equipped as the rest of us; naturally, my concern falls mostly to him.

Dash is pure, and he deserves more than this world has to offer.

And I'm convinced that anyone who ever meets him would think the same thing.

I pace the space Sydney left us in but pause when I hear faint conversation from inside.

"Can you send them through processing, Syd? I don't really have time today." Her sweet voice floats out toward me.

I swallow down the unease at her not wanting to see us.

"This one's different Wills."

The nickname he has for her brings the corners of my lips up faintly.

Papers shuffle and she sighs. "How so?"

"Just let me introduce you to her, and then we can go from there. Five minutes, that's all I'm asking."

"This is very unlike you, Syd." She pauses for a brief second. "Come here, I want a kiss first, then I'll meet this mystery girl of yours."

I wait patiently outside the room for them to do what they need to do, my stomach growing wild with the realization that I'm seconds away from seeing her face-to-face.

My relative. My kin. My blood.

The door swings open, and I take a hurried step back.

Sydney's face greets me. "Come on in." He motions for me to enter. "Dash, you can come, too."

Willow, at least who I assume is Willow, stands from behind a large desk, her smile soft and her features delicate but somehow also sharp and etched like the angels themselves took extra caution bringing her to life. Her nearly white hair, with a long strip of black down one side, billows in subtle curls over her shoulders and falls the length of her elbow.

Automatically, I'm drawn to her, my chest pulling and tugging me toward this woman I've only just laid eyes on.

She raises her brow and shifts her focus on Sydney before focusing back on me. "Willow Oliver," she steps around her desk, walks toward me like she's gliding across the floor, and extends her hand. "And you are?"

I blink and blink again, my heart stuttering but my arm inching up and sliding my hand into hers. "Wren...Wren Oliver."

The second our skin touches, a sort of current zaps me, but not painfully. I suck in a breath and meet her gaze. "Is that normal?"

Willow releases me and reaches toward Dash. "Only sometimes."

"I'm Dash," he says. "Just Dash."

She shakes hands with him, too. Willow holds on a bit longer and narrows her gaze. "It's kind of my job to know what type of supernatural creature people are but I'm drawing a blank with you. You're not human."

"No, ma'am." Dash plasters on his typical Dash politeness. "I'm a phoenix."

"A phoenix," she repeats. "Interesting." Willow shifts her attention between us.

"I told you," Sydney says from his spot off to the side.

Willow grins at him. "Such the know it all." She nods toward the far corner of the room. "Perhaps our guests would like something to drink."

Sydney goes over without question. "Coffee, tea, water?" He pauses before adding. "I could run to the main kitchen if you'd like juice or something else."

"Coffee is fine," I mutter and look at Dash.

"Same."

Willow motions toward a sitting area in her large office. A long couch lines the wall with two plush chairs opposite of it. A table with a few books rests on top, along with a pot filled with flowers with tiny petals.

I settle onto the couch with Dash at my side.

He rests his hand on my knee, and I thank the Angels that I asked him to come along today. Does Dash know how much support he's providing by simply being near me?

Willow takes the chair closest to me and props her elbow on the armrest. "Where are you from?"

Such an innocent question that harbors more than she's bargaining for.

"Prania," I tell her.

Willow tilts her head, another display of her beauty shining through with each movement she makes. "I'm not familiar with Prania. What state is that in?"

A lump forms in my throat and multiplies in my stomach. Why am I so fucking nervous about speaking to her and telling her my truth? Maybe it's because if I talk too freely I will ruin this for all of us.

Sydney comes over with a tray in his grasp. He carefully sets it on the table and distributes the steaming mugs. "Prania is another realm, dear." Sydney lowers himself onto the other seat and joins our conversation fully. "They traveled across the fold."

"I've never heard of Prania, though, in our time researching other realms." Willow presses her palms around the mug like she's warming her hands, the same thing I do; it's one of the reasons I love coffee.

"I hadn't either until they told me about it." Sydney sips his drink. "Could ask the headmaster about it. You have a meeting with him later today."

"Who's that?" I ask her while suddenly realizing there are probably a lot more people in this realm that I'm unaware of and will come across. When we were confined to Sydney's house, our interactions were limited, but now we're out in the world, there's no telling how many I'll encounter. How will I know if they're supernatural or human? What if I say the wrong thing to the wrong person? How is she able to determine someone's species just by shaking their hand? Is that something she could teach me?

Too many questions and not enough breath to speak them all.

Willow interrupts my rampant thoughts. "He's in charge of the local shadow academy Sydney and I both attended. Headmaster Walker. He's highly knowledge-able of the supernatural world and the academy itself houses an expansive library full of supernatural literature. Surely there's something between him and the books that would shine some light on Prania." Willow speaks with such confidence and elegance that it makes me sit up a little straighter in my seat.

"I'm sorry, did you say *shadow* academy?"

"Mmhm." She sips her coffee. "Much like a regular undergraduate college, except half the students are supernatural and attend their magical classes without the human faction having any idea of their powers."

"That seems...dangerous."

Willow shrugs. "Existing in their world has its risks, but this way, students learn how to balance the two and navigate keeping their abilities concealed. Of course, there are times when that is tested, but for the most part, it works well without issues."

Humans and supernaturals living in tandem, going to college together, peace-fully. What a strange place Arthlia is. And how incredibly fascinating.

"And what of your parents?" she asks me.

"My mother," I chew my lip. "She died when I was young, and my father left before that."

Willow nods like she somehow understands what I'm saying. "That makes sense." She reaches out her hand and her tone shifts. "Not about your mother dying, for that I am so terribly sorry, but your father, that is a common Oliver situa-tion. It was part of the curse." She turns to Sydney. "How much of this did you already tell them?"

Sydney shrugs. "Some of it. It's a lot of information."

"It really is." She glances down at her watch. "Listen, I don't mean to cut this short, but I have another pressing matter to attend to." Her mesmerizing gaze meets mine. "Would you walk with me for a moment?"

"Yeah." I rise to my feet without question because what other option do I have? I'd do anything she asked if it meant taking one step closer to finding out the truth of my continuously mysterious life.

"Syd, keep Dash company while I steal her for a few minutes?" Willow gives Sydney's shoulder a gentle squeeze and offers Dash a kind smile.

"You okay?" Dash mouths to me.

With a nod, I confirm that I am, despite the aversion to leaving him behind. It's not me that I worry about, but Sydney has been considerate enough to allow us to get away with breaking into his home and using his amenities. It wouldn't be farfetched to assume he wouldn't keep Dash alive for a few more minutes.

My footsteps patter quietly along the floor behind Willow's. Once we're outside her office, she slows her pace to fall beside me, walking in unison like equals.

"I apologize for my shortness," she tells me. "It's not at all uncommon that we have new witches, but one actually bearing the Oliver name...that's a surprise."

"You don't have any direct relatives?" I match her strides but give her the lead since I'm not exactly sure where she's taking me.

"Mother and father, yes. My uncle isn't a blood relative." She leads us through a swinging door, the aroma of berries and warm bread greets us with a warm embrace.

A man with honey-colored hair looks up from his spot at the counter, his eyes beaming once they settle on her. His cheeks turn up and he exposes his teeth. "You're just in time." He dusts his hands off over a doughy mixture and wipes them on the towel tucked into his apron.

Willow continues toward him. "Cam, I have someone I want you to meet."

A buzzer goes off. "Hold that thought." Cam presses one finger up into the air and turns on his heel. He slides a mitten onto his hand and reaches into the oven to pull out a batch of whatever he must be baking.

My mouth waters at the sheer scent of it but I restrain myself from latching onto the hot pan and running out of here like my life depends on it. Food is not a scarcity here, not like it is back home. I may not have lived like a demon on the run, but even as a hunter, things like substance and shelter weren't always easily accessible. And considering only the elite had the best of what our world had to offer, the provisions we got weren't anything compared to what Cam just placed on the counter between us.

"You didn't have to." Willow walks around and throws her arms around his torso and presses her lips to his.

He returns her kiss and hugs her tightly before releasing her. "I knew you had a busy day ahead of you." Cam brings her hand to his face and kisses that, too. "Anything for you."

Willow blushes and gives her attention back to me. "Wren, this is Cameron, my husband. Cam, this is Wren Oliver."

Cam's brows perk up. "An Oliver, ey?" He extends his arm. "Always nice to meet family."

Family. Is that what this is? I shake his hand, noting how nothing sparks at our touch the way it had with Willow. Does that mean he's not supernatural? Or is it possible that the reaction I had with her was only because we share the same blood? Either way, I'm grateful for the connection even if it doesn't have the same *spark*.

A week ago, I had no one, and now I have Willow and her husbands.

"Can I offer you a blueberry muffin?" Cameron plucks napkins out of a square wooden holder before taking two warm muffins out of the tray and setting them on the counter.

"Thank you," I tell him. "That's mighty nice of you."

What did I do to deserve the kindness that these folks have had to offer? Sydney has been gracious in introducing me to Willow and giving us a place to stay. And Cameron is willing to part with one of his delicious concoctions.

"Cam is the best baker in the state." She elbows him gently. "Angels, maybe the whole world. Can't say I've had a blueberry muffin that tastes better than this." She takes one from the counter and hands it to me, then keeps the other for herself.

"I think *world* might be an overstatement, babe," he tells her.

"Doubtful." Willow kisses Cam's reddened cheek. "I'll try to be back for dinner, but don't wait around on me. You know how Deghan gets if he misses a meal."

"Speaking of, have you seen him? He was gone before I got up." Cam scratches at his scruffy chin and leaves behind some of the white debris that was still on his hand.

Willow pats him with her napkin. "He's out with the wolves doing wolf stuff."

"Oh, right, that new pack is in town. I forgot he's training them." Cam nods as if he's just had a realization. "That explains why two pans of brownies were missing this morning."

"Are you surprised?" Willow chuckles.

"Not even a little bit." Cam steadies his baby blue gaze on me. There's something so soft and innocent about him—wholesome, really. He reminds me of Dash with his genuine and caring nature. He lacks the overbearing masculinity that I've grown familiar with in my lifetime. Most men make it a mission to assert their dominance and be seen as the top alpha in the room. Cam and Dash are both okay with their position in the ranks and seem to thrive in the truth of who they are. It's calm, endearing, and a welcome breath of fresh air in a sea of men and their pissing matches.

I don't need a man to protect me—I need respect.

Dash has given me that from the start. He's been on my side even when I wasn't and continues to stand by and support my desires. Bo could learn a thing or two from Dash. My relationship with Wes hasn't always been easy, but given our complicated attachment to each other, it makes sense that it wouldn't be smooth sailing. What relationship ever really is? Maybe I'm being too demanding for thinking that the situation with Bo should be anything less than difficult? He and I are exact opposites. We were brought up to hate each other. And not too long ago, we were enemies.

I shouldn't compare Bo to Dash, nor should I compare any of the guys. Every one of them is different, along with my connection to them. I should accept that some may come easier than others, and some might take a lot more work. But what if I'm the only one willing to put in the work, and Bo doesn't even feel the same way at all? I guess my biggest issue with the entire situation is not knowing whether he actually wants me. I could handle his bad attitude, temper, and short-fused nature if I was certain of his feelings for me.

He's so hot and cold I can never get a good read on what's going through his thick skull.

Maybe that's something I can talk to Willow about if I ever get the opportunity to meet with her again. She does have four husbands after all, and I'm confident things weren't always this simple.

Sydney speaks of Deghan in a good nature, and Cameron does the same. There doesn't appear to be any bad blood between them—but there's another husband I haven't heard anyone refer to. Is he the troublesome one of the bunch or is it happenstance that he hasn't been brought up yet?

"Don't be a stranger," Cameron adds. "You're an Oliver, which means you're one of us."

My heart clenches in my chest. Does he realize how much of an impact his words have on me?

"Thank you," I tell him. "I appreciate that more than you could know." I hold the muffin out toward him. "And for this, thank you. It smells divine."

"My pleasure." Cam places his hand over his chest and looks at Willow. "My love." Another buzzer rings through the air and captures his attention.

Willow tilts her head, nodding toward the opposite side of the kitchen. "This way," she says while peeling back the paper on her muffin and taking a bite.

No longer wanting to hold back from devouring this warm thing in my hand, I do the same and follow her out. I suppress a moan and swallow the soft decadence he created. "I can't imagine this tasting better."

Willow grins. "He really is an incredible baker. Cam may create some wild concoctions from time to time but there isn't anything that man makes that isn't delicious."

It's sweet to hear her speak of him so highly but she's not exactly lying, and this muffin is proof.

We go down another hall that is almost identical to the other ones weaving their way around this expansive house. Any other person might have lost sense of direction, but this kind of thing has always come naturally to me. That's a surefire way to get yourself into unnecessary danger. One can never be too sure if they're being led to their death, even if it's by a newfound family member.

"Sydney tells me you're staying at the old estate?" Willow keeps her strides matching mine and bites off another bit of her muffin.

"Yeah, we sort of stumbled upon it and didn't really know where else to go."

"Well." She glances over at me briefly. "I believe sometimes we find ourselves in places we're supposed to be without understanding how. I can't imagine how my life would have turned out had I not gone to Harper Academy."

"You weren't always planning on going there?"

"Honestly, I was at a crossroads. I had been caring for my mother most of my life and didn't think I could take the time away to do something that would mean abandoning the role of caretaker. It was hard allowing myself that chance to stretch my proverbial wings, but it was something I felt called to do. I knew I wouldn't be far, and my uncle agreed to step in temporarily while I figured things out. Had he not pushed me, I don't think I would have. From the second I stepped foot in that academy, my entire life changed. Nothing was ever the same, and as difficult as the next few years of my life would be, I'm grateful for every second of it."

"The curse, that's right. Sydney mentioned you had great obstacles to overcome to break it."

Willow nods, rounds a corner, and continues walking. "Yes, to say the least. But in doing so, not only did I liberate myself, but so many others. And had I not, I wouldn't know the true nature of who I am. Every struggle, painful and traumatic as they may have been, brought me here today; I wouldn't have stepped into my power, met my mates, my friends, my family, or been able to help others without everything unfolding the way it did. It may have been a simpler life, but us Oliver's..." She nudges me with her elbow. "We're not much for taking the easy way out."

Every word she says speaks directly to my soul. My life has been chaotic from the start. Ripped from my mother at an early age, I spent every day after training to become the best at what I do—killing. I harnessed and tapped into my anger to unleash the ultimate soldier who fought in a war that never should have been waged.

Willow reclaimed her power and fought a similar evil.

I'm not convinced she'd still want me as her family if she knew the truth about who I was and what I had done.

Would I still have become that person if my mother wasn't brutally slain? If my father had been involved? What if Prania had never been overrun by hunters who wanted to eradicate every demonic creature in existence? The plethora of possibilities and what-ifs do nothing to change the fact that I am the person I am, and that I have done the things that I've done.

But as Willow said, each painful reality is what made her who she is today. Had I not gone through every single thing I did, would I be standing here with her? Maybe this is all part of the plan that brings me to whatever purpose I'm supposed to have. Maybe I have more suffering to endure before I can step into the next chapter of my life.

I cling to the hope that one day, perhaps my life will be as grand as hers.

And if it isn't, I'll die trying to make it happen.

"I'd love to talk to you more sometime," she says to me while slowing her pace. "I'm afraid my schedule is rather full at the moment, but in the coming months, I may be able to carve some time out."

I swallow down the lump in my throat. *Months.* I can't wait that long for answers. I didn't expect every one of my questions answered today, but matters are still pressing, and I don't have the luxury of time on my side.

"I do hope that Sydney can give you a warm welcome in my absence though, and as Cam said, don't be a stranger." Willow lingers near a door which I'm guessing leads to wherever she must be off to. Given the circumstances, it could be the outside world or a whole other realm entirely.

"I...I need your help," I blurt out. "I wouldn't ask if it weren't necessary." Requesting aid from anyone has never really been my strong suit, and the sinking pit in my stomach is a reminder of why I'd like to never do it ever again.

"Sydney is a master scholar, if there's any research you need done, he's the most equipped for the job."

"He said he already did and couldn't find anything." I grow angry at the weakness in my voice—at the hopelessness blooming in my chest.

"I understand how frustrating it can be to struggle to find the answers you're looking for." Willow breathes in deeply and exhales. "I have a meeting with Headmaster Walker later. I'll see what I can figure out..." She seems to lose track of where her sentence was going.

I wait for her focus to return and plead with the Angels to bring with it good news.

"Have Sydney bring you by the academy around 7:00 p.m. I have an idea."

An idea—that's surely better than nothing at all, and regardless of how vague it may be, I cling to the prospect of its possibilities.

Willow pushes the door open but doesn't leave just yet.

"Thank you," I tell her.

"Don't get your hopes up, it's a long shot, but back when I was searching for answers, it was something I did that helped me." She shrugs. "Maybe it will work for you, too."

And if it doesn't, at least I'll get some more time with her—my family.

"I'll try anything," I say truthfully. Whatever might help uncover the secrets of Prania and potentially provide a solution to save those that were left behind.

I can't stay in Arthlia and pretend my entire homeland isn't falling completely apart.

"Can you find your way back?" She nods in the direction we just came.

"Two lefts, a right, through the kitchen with these." I hold up what's left of my muffin.

"A sucker for details." Willow nudges me. "We're more alike than you may think." She smiles softly. "If you ever get lost, here or out there. Just close your eyes, ground yourself to the universe, and ask for the way. You'd be surprised what answers are waiting if you remain patient."

How can I stay patient when so many are dying back home because Parla still rules over Prania? I must find a way back to avenge those lives I've taken and put a stop to any further damage she may cause.

"I'll see you this evening." Willow slips through the door and it latches shut behind her, leaving me here at the end of this corridor with nothing but my thoughts.

Taking a second to let out a breath and relax my tense shoulders, I shove the rest of the muffin in my mouth and quickly savor the taste of such a creation. Bo would lose his mind if he could get his arrogant lips around one of those muffins. Maybe on my way back I could barter with Cameron to bring one back to him.

Perhaps bribing Bo with something edible will convince him to drop his guard and let me in enough to figure out what's going on in his head. And even if it doesn't, the look of satisfaction that will no doubt be on his face will be enough of a reward.

Turning toward the open hallway, I'm brought to an abrupt halt. I nearly slam into another body, and my feet instinctually move to take a step from this person suddenly appearing.

"Angels," I gasp while clutching my chest.

His sort of purple gaze stares down at mine, his jaw clenched and his shoulders broad. A white T-shirt does a half-ass job of covering his tattooed body and ink spills over the exposed parts of his wrists that his black leather jacket doesn't cover.

He's...beautiful, in an almost too-perfect kind of way.

"Willow?" His lips part only slightly to mutter the one word.

I tilt my head in the direction she went, and when I blink, he disappears from in front of me and darts through that same door.

With an exhale, I shake off the awkward interaction. "I guess that would be her *other* husband," I whisper to myself. "Either freakishly fast or definitely super-natural."

CHAPTER 12

Wes

I don't hate it here.

There's damn good food. Comfortable lodging. And much less danger than where we came from.

It's not that I don't enjoy a battle or two here or there, but the constant fighting for our lives thing was a bit exhausting.

Not to mention, Wren being in a safer place is a huge perk, too.

My hound worries a lot less, and so do I.

She's tough, to say the least, and without enemies looming around every corner, I have fewer doubts that she can and will remain unharmed.

"You're really okay with this?" Bo mouths off from his spot leaning against the counter. He throws his arms toward the door exaggeratedly. "She's Angels knows where and you're fine playing house."

Shut him up, my hound tells me.

I sigh and shake my head. "You're overreacting."

Bo's dark gaze widens. "You're *under*reacting."

"What's this really about?" I ask him while drinking my third glass of orange juice. I'm not sure what they put in this stuff, but it sure is tasty.

Simple pleasures, Sydney calls it.

Whatever it is, it's reason enough to want to stay in Arthlia for as long as I live.

"It must be nice." Bo folds his arms over his chest. "Knowing that no matter what, she's coming back to you."

"What?" I lower the glass and stare at him.

"The fated mate bond. It's like a fucking guarantee that you two will always find each other."

"You're jealous?" I try my hardest not to laugh.

Bo's jaw tenses and the vein in his forehead bulges. "No."

I let out a chuckle. "You're jealous."

"Well, at least I gave her a choice in the matter. Who's to say she isn't with you just because of the stupid bond? She may be your mate but at what cost? Her free will? No." Bo kicks off from the counter. "No, I'd rather die than force her to be with me."

He storms out of the kitchen, leaving me behind with the unraveling thought I do my best to keep concealed.

Bo might be an arrogant asshole, but he's right.

The mate bond that Wren and I share is unbreakable. Our connection will overcome any obstacle. It is sure and steadfast, and nothing could hinder our loyalty to one another. There isn't anything me or my hound wouldn't do for her, and if I had to take my best guess, I'd say that she feels the same.

But as certain and secure as it may be, is that really the best thing for her? A love she cannot choose to escape. A love that would chase her to the ends of the universe and not once stop until it found her again. I would traverse hell and back to worship at her feet. Even in death, I would come for her. I would die a thousand deaths just to be near her.

I knew it from the very moment I laid my sights on her.

My hound growled deep within my chest, claiming her as his—as *ours*.

I did what I could to resist the carnal desire to be with her but I was no match for what fate had in store for us.

Would my love be that powerful without the magical bind that ties us together?

Would she still choose me if given the chance?

I thought I was doing the right thing in allowing the bond to tether us, but was I a fool for following through with allowing her to link herself to me permanently? I wanted it—Angels, I needed it. Perhaps I was blinded by the visceral plea my soul had been screaming out to make her mine.

Have I doomed her to a worse fate because I couldn't defy what was already written in the stars?

Jade waltzes into the kitchen and plucks an apple from the bowl on the counter. "What's got Bo's panties in a bunch?"

"You know, typical Bo." I drain the rest of my juice and rinse the glass out in the sink. "I've been meaning to ask you." I turn toward her once I've placed the glass in the dishwasher. Another mysterious and magical creation of this realm.

"Oh Angels, what is it?" She bites into the crisp apple and wipes at her mouth.

Fruit from back home doesn't even remotely compare to that of Arthlia.

"Do you and Everest have plans for the future?" I rest against the wall and do my best to come off as less overprotective brother as I can.

Still, I can't help but want the best for her, especially now that she's gone through what she has. I'll never begin to understand what it was like to be held captive in Rockbridge for such a long period, but if my short stint there was any indication, Jade deserves the best life has to offer. And what kind of person would I be if I tried to prevent that from happening?

Do I want her to go off on her own with some random man? No, absolutely not. But he was one, if not the main reason for her survival, and if he's what brings her joy, I support that.

Any good brother would.

"Um, I mean, not really." Jade presses her hands behind her on the counter and scoots back until she's sitting on the hard surface. "Do you?"

I draw in a breath and exhale slowly. "I'd like to stay here, in Arthlia. I don't know what that entails, but I don't want to leave."

Jade bobs her head up and down while chewing another bite. "Me either. Ev and I want to stay, too."

Her face lights up and her gaze shifts to Everest as he walks into the kitchen and joins us.

"What about you?" I ask him. "You going along with whatever she has to say or do you actually want to stay?"

Everest strolls over to Jade's side, kissing her cheek and gripping her thigh. "I'm all in wherever she is."

I grin. "Didn't answer my question."

"I don't have anything anywhere else." He glances up at her before focusing back on me. "She's it for me. I'd be an idiot if I left her now. And the thought of ever going back to Prania—I'll pass. There's nothing left for any of us there. It's a wasteland."

It turns my stomach to think about what we escaped from, but he's right. There's no going back. What remains of our homeland will burn to ashes in time and if it doesn't, it will be overcome by hunters and the entire demon population will be eliminated. Why return there when it's a hopeless cause?

"You mentioned your brother is no longer with us."

"Wes," Jade snaps at me.

"No, it's okay," Everest reassures her. "He died a few years ago."

"I'm sorry for your loss." I shouldn't press, but I can't ignore the nagging that he isn't divulging the whole story. "Casualty of the war?"

Everest nods and his gaze falls to the floor. "Yeah. You could say that." Just when I'm sure he won't say anything else, he opens his mouth again. "It was random, his death. No explanation. Only a letter that came to his house stating if next of kin wanted to pick up his body, they could show up at Rockbridge to get it."

Hunters paint a picture that demons are cruel, but that lack of consideration is cold-hearted and unforgiving.

"Of course, I did," he continues. "I showed up demanding answers, but when they had none to provide, I infiltrated their operation in an attempt to figure it out for myself." Everest laughs dryly. "They never expected me to not be on their side. Few non-demons ever go against the natural way. Because my brother was respected and had made a name for himself, I got preferential treatment. I refused to work in the field so they gave me a higher-ranking guard position. I thought I could lay low and uncover the truth."

"Did you?" I ask him.

Everest averts his gaze again. "Only took about a month to learn what had happened."

"A month? And yet you stayed there for years?" That's when it hits me, he went there for the truth of his brother's death, but he stayed for something else entirely.

"I was assigned sector eighteen." He grips Jade's thigh, and she wraps her fingers over his. "I found what I was looking for and then some."

"You saved me," she mutters to him.

"We saved each other," he whispers back to her.

"I'm grateful you found her, Everest." I can't fathom the possibilities had he not been there for her when she needed him the most.

We may have lost Mother, but thank the Angels that Jade was spared.

"I am, too." Everest forces a smile.

"I hadn't spoken to anyone since Mother." Jade's eyes glisten with each word spoken. "It was Everest who finally broke through to me. I was a shell of a person left there to rot, and somehow he saw something in me that I thought I had lost forever. He was kind, and patient, and eventually, I started to trust him. He's the one who insisted I use a fake name. He didn't want me to lose anything else to that place than I already had."

"And so, Franny was born," he says.

"I never lost hope," I tell her. "I never quit trying to get you two back. I'm so sorry for all that wasted time. I should have come sooner."

"It wasn't all wasted." She tugs Everest toward her, positioning his back to her chest, between her legs. Jade hugs him close, kissing the top of his head and resting her chin on it.

"And what of your brother? You said you uncovered the truth." My heart swells at seeing the two of them find comfort in the darkness together.

Maybe powerful love can come not just in fated mates.

"I discovered that the hunters, the true hunters, were somehow harvesting demonic power after their kills. And they were ordered to return to Rockbridge for some kind of ritual to extract that power. Most hunters only made it through one or two of these rituals before their life force gave out, my brother included. He was the last to die before they put a stop to it. They expanded the prison and changed the orders. Instead of being told to kill the demons on sight, they were informed they must bring them in alive. I think they were biding time until they could figure out how to start extracting again without losing hunters in the process. They couldn't afford for their numbers to keep dwindling so they had to do something."

How is it even possible for a hunter to harvest demonic power from a kill? Does Wren know anything about this? What would they do with that power? Both the hunter *and* the organization calling the shots? I thought eliminating us was their sole mission, but apparently, it was something more complex. Was she participating in said rituals and stealing the power of those she killed? She would have been doing the same thing that had been done to her bloodline for centuries. Stealing and suppressing someone else for unjust reasons. Would there even be a *just* reason at all? Surely, she wouldn't do something *that* unbelievably wrong.

But when my thoughts bring me back to that room, that day I thought everything was going to end, isn't that what Parla was trying to get Wren to do to me? She wanted Wren to kill me and said if she did, she would allow Wren to live. Is it possible that Wren, and whatever magic she holds, can do the ritual without meeting the same fate the other hunters did?

Because Wren isn't a hunter at all, she's a witch—one descended from the Angels themselves.

I want to question more, to learn what else Everest knows of this heinous act, only the second my mind slows down long enough to ask, the door opens and Wren walks in.

Her smile distracts me, something bright and beaming about her that wasn't there a few hours ago. It tugs at my heart, and without meaning to, I gravitate toward her, my soul being called to hers.

"Oh, what do you have there?" Jade hops off the counter and goes toward Wren.

"The most incredible muffins in the entire world." Wren sets a box on the counter and flips the lid open. She pulls one out and gives it to Jade. "You have to try, seriously." She raises a brow but gives me no choice to say no. She shoves one toward me, too, and then takes another.

I kiss her cheek and bask in how her sheer presence alone can soothe me.

"Where's Bo?" she asks with a muffin still in her grasp. "He has to eat one of these."

I crane my thumb in the direction he stormed off not too long ago. "That way somewhere."

Sydney enters through the same door Wren had come from. "I have another box of them, so feel free to have as many as you want."

My attention flits to him, and in that split second, Wren moves out of the room in her pursuit of Bo. Her absence leaves a chill in her wake and grants the space for my concerning questions to rise back to the surface.

CHAPTER 13

Wren

Taking the stairs two at a time, I rush up to the second floor of Sydney's home to locate Bo.

Certainty that I'm on the right path fills me with each step closer to him. Is it the mark on my neck that allows me to sense him? Maybe the hunter nature in me kicking in? Or perhaps it's something else entirely that makes me sure he's nearby.

I bolt through the door to our shared bedroom, and my heart drops when I don't see him.

Was I wrong in thinking what he and I share is anything more than nothing?

"What's the rush, Birdie? House on fire again?" His gruff voice calms my aching soul.

"You," I say while spinning on my heel. "Have to try this."

"What is it?" He raises a dark brow but doesn't move from his seat in the corner of the room. Instead of sleeping in the bed with the rest of us, he slumbers uncomfortably upright in a chair. And that's if he sleeps at all, knowing him, he probably lurks in those dark hours.

"It's a muffin." I stalk toward him. "Blueberry."

"Did you poison it?"

"What?" No. Why would I do that?"

"You're entirely too excited. You must admit, it's rather suspicious."

"Fine," I pout. "Don't eat it." I peel back the paper surrounding the still-warm muffin and bite off a huge chunk of it, way more than I normally would have.

But I'm brought to a halt when Bo grabs my waist and tugs me toward him. He positions me between his legs and grips my chin. "Open up." He tilts his head to where his lips are just a breath away from mine.

I do as he says, the muffin falling from my mouth and into his. Heat swells between my legs.

How is it possible to be turned on by such an act?

Bo's eyes widen. "Damn birdie." He keeps his one hand around my waist and says, "More."

I break off a chunk and plop it into his mouth; my fingers grazing his lips only heightens my desire for him. I continue until there's nothing left for me to give him.

"Tasted better straight from your mouth." He relaxes into the chair but doesn't take his hand off me.

And because I can't miss the open opportunity, I plop myself onto his lap. "Was that so hard?"

"You keep pressing your ass up against me and I'll show you what's hard."

I wiggle on him and laugh. "You wouldn't."

He pokes me in the side. "Keep messing around, Birdie. You're going to be sorry."

Why can't he be like this all the time? Fun, playful, cocky. This side of him is temporary and fleeting and makes me wonder which version of him is actually real.

Bo slides my legs sideways over his and keeps his arm draped over them while his other remains wrapped around my torso. He leans back and stares over at me, his resolve softening. "You really brought that up here for me?"

"What?" I settle into him and rest my head on the high back of the chair.

"The muffin. You got that for me?"

But there's something about the way he says *me* that tugs at my heart.

"Of course, I did." This time it's my finger that jabs him in the ribs. "I believe my exact thought was *Damn this is delicious. I have to get one for Bo.*"

"Really? You thought about me?"

"Are you serious?" I melt into him a bit more. "Aside from wondering what the fuck we're doing here, you're on my mind a lot, you big idiot."

"Why?" His dark gaze steadies itself on mine.

I swallow down the intensity of his stare. "Because...I...care...about...you."

"Why?"

"Did you hit your head or something?" I pinch my brows together. "I know the concept is foreign to you, the whole *caring* thing, but it's not just me. Wes and Dash and Jade care about you, too."

"Oh," he says.

"And do you care about them?"

Bo blinks, his attention faltering as if I asked him to solve the hardest riddle. "I mean, I don't want them to die."

"That's not the same, Bo, and you know it."

"I don't know what you want from me." His palm tenses on my thigh.

"Do you care about me?" I shouldn't ask, but I do anyway.

"It's complicated, Birdie."

"You've said that before. It's a simple yes or no."

"It's not simple, Wren, and you know it."

"Are you mocking me?"

"No."

"You can answer that, but you can't admit whether or not you care about me." I scoot away but he keeps his hold tight on me.

His jaw constricts and his nostrils flare. He lets out a breath. "Is that what you want? For me to say I do?"

I shake my head. "Not if you don't mean it."

"It's just words, Birdie." Bo skims his hand along my leg. "This," he whispers and continues moving his touch up until his rough palm is resting against my cheek. "This is..." His fingers spread, encapsulating my entire cheek and dipping into my hair. Bo swirls his thumb gently, so very unlike who he typically is. Bo is harsh, violent, and commanding. The man touching me is everything but.

"What is it, Bo?" I mutter, practically begging him to finish his train of thought.

But as quickly as he became this soft version of himself, he blinks and it's gone.

"I can't do this." He stands and in one swift motion, drops me onto the chair he was in and rushes out the door.

I pinch my eyes shut and bring my hand up to rub my temple. "Great, that went great," I mutter to no one but myself. The warmth from his body on the chair does nothing to replace what it felt like being that near him.

He was so fucking close to saying *something*. What stopped him? Why is he so resistant to letting me in? If he truly didn't want me, surely, he would just say it. I can't imagine Bo ever doing *anything* he didn't want. If it were a no, he would admit it. Unless the only reason it feels like a yes is because of this stupid fucking mark on my neck. What if Bo truly isn't interested but the mark is what ties him to me?

More reason to remove the thing and free himself for good.

Am I forcing an issue on something he doesn't want at all?

"You okay in here?" Wes pokes his head into the room. "Saw Bo leave in typical Bo fashion."

"Yeah," I lie. "I'm good." Leaving the chair Bo and I intimately sat in together behind, I stroll over to the edge of the bed and plop down onto the mattress, patting the spot beside me for Wes.

"Those muffins were to die for." Wes comes over, his body filling the void Bo just created.

I've never been the type to need anyone near, but now that I've gotten a taste of what it's like, I can't stand being without any of these three men for long. Even simply having Dash with me today was a comfort I didn't realize I desired until I had it.

"They were, weren't they?" I only meant to bring the one home for Bo, but Cameron was kind enough to send me with a whole batch of them. I offered to repay him somehow, and yet he insisted I take them without anything in return. This world is strange, and with each interaction, it becomes even more bizarre.

Back home, nothing is given without something being taken. It's a familiar exchange and something I could rely on. Unless it was stolen, there was always a swap of some capacity.

A favor for a favor. A barter of sorts. Everything had a balance.

Here, people do things for others without the need for them to be reciprocal, even if it costs them time, energy, or money. Or at least, that's what it seems—there very well could be a price down the line that one party is unaware of until it comes due.

"What are you thinking about?" Wes asks me.

"This place," I say. "It's too good to be true. Don't you agree?"

Wes drags his bottom lip into his mouth and rakes his teeth over it. "Perhaps we're used to things being harder than they need to be."

"A lifetime in Prania and you're so willing to accept that things can really be this good?"

He shrugs. "Why not? What do we have to lose?"

"What does he think?" I press my hand to his chest.

Wes's hellhound hasn't come out since we've been in Arthlia. Is it possible he has abandoned us again?

But when Wes's irises glow, I'm reminded that he's very much here with us now.

Wes pushes his palm into my hand. "He said he likes it wherever you are."

"He *said*?" I tilt my head.

"Mmhm."

"What does he think about this?" I climb onto his lap and straddle him.

Wes hides a grin. "He wants you to continue."

"Does he?" I slide my hands up his chiseled chest, his muscles bulging the fabric of his shirt. "What about this?" I rock my hips and weave my fingers through his hair, tugging on it gently.

Wes latches onto my waist, his eyes igniting that familiar red that has me completely captivated. He pushes down and pivots himself upward. "He wants you."

I swallow and gently move over his growing erection pushing the space between us. "And what about you? Do you want me, too?"

His fiery gaze stares up at me. "More than anything." Wes finds my lips with his, kissing me with an intensity that sets my soul ablaze.

I moan and dig my fingers in deeper, desperate for every bit of him I can get a hold of.

He tugs me tighter and spreads his hands over my back, my waist, my hips, my ass.

I barely notice when he stands, my body not daring to separate from his.

How had I been so fucking oblivious to how badly I wanted him until this very moment?

With my legs wrapped around his torso and my arms on his neck, Wes grips the waistband of my bottoms and rips them off me, the fabric shredding along with my panties as they fall away from me. He unbuttons his pants and frees his cock, gliding it over my soaked entrance before lining himself into place.

Wes sits on the bed and shoves me down onto him, my pussy spreading around him.

"Fuck," I whimper. "You're so big, I can barely take you."

He draws my lip into his mouth and looks into my eyes. "You were made for me, Wren." Wes thrusts deeper. "Every inch of me was made for you."

I shove the weight of my body down and revel in the pain that mixes with pleasure.

"That's it," he whispers as he holds onto my hips. "You're taking me like such a good girl." Wes lies back on the bed but moves his hands to the nape of my shirt, ripping it down the center and exposing my bare breasts.

I adjust to fit this new angle of him and sigh at the fullness.

He squeezes my tits before trailing one hand back to my waist. Wes brings his thumb to his mouth, licking it and returning it to my center. Pushing it against my clit, he swirls it with the perfect amount of pressure.

"Angels," I sigh.

"That's it," he says. "Come for me."

I climax around him, reaching back to grip his thighs as pleasure consumes me.

He slows his hips but moves his thumb through my orgasm, not stopping when I've finished. Instead, in one swift movement, he stands, throws me onto the mattress, and continues rubbing my clit while pumping into me once again.

I bring my knees up, spreading myself wide for him to give me everything he has.

He complies, fucking me harder and wrecking my pussy in the most beautiful way. Wes pinches my clit and sends me over the edge, his cock still thrusting into me through the second orgasm. Shoving both my legs to one side, he keeps his pace while deepening his strokes.

The new sensation heightens my pleasure even more.

I drag my hair out of my sweat-lined face and take in just how fucking beautiful this man is. I barely make it from his chiseled jawline to his perfectly plush lips before I get distracted by his grin.

He licks his lips and lowers himself down, scooting me up onto the mattress to climb more on top of me. Wes slows his movements and stares into my eyes.

I want to open my mouth, to say something, but nothing could ever be said to make him realize just how much he means to me. He was the catalyst that set my entire world on a different course. The person who finally made me feel alive for the first time in my life. He is one half of my soul, and not a single thing could ever make me love him any less.

Love.

My heart stutters at the thought.

I've never *loved* anything, let alone *anyone*.

Cheese is probably the only thing that comes close, but that doesn't count.

We haven't been together long, and most of our time has been spent running for our lives. Is it possible to love someone that soon? How else would I explain the feeling that courses through me when I look into his blazing eyes? We're fated mates, doesn't that give us a free pass to fall deeply and fast?

I plant my hands on his cheeks and study the man that stares back at me.

His lip twitches, and his mouth parts slightly. "I love you, Wren."

A smile breaks across my face and a laugh bubbles out of my chest.

"You think it's funny that I love you?" Wes frowns but keeps pumping himself into me, his desire to continue having sex with me stronger than his pride at thinking I'm laughing at him.

"I think it's funny that you said the very thing that was on my own mind." I drag him closer to me, my lips a hair from his. "I love you, too, Wes." I press my mouth onto his before he can say another word and kiss him with a renewed passion.

He matches my force and dances his tongue along mine.

My core tightens and his cock throbs in response, filling me even more.

We orgasm in tandem, both of us crying out into each other in a wave of pure bliss.

Another moment passes, our bodies not quite ready to be apart just yet.

Wes stays inside of me but collapses beside my shuddering form. He presses a kiss to my forehead, my nose, and finally, my lips, while dragging my leg over his to lay atop him. "I mean it, Wren. I love you."

I prop myself onto my elbow and drag my fingertip along his forehead. "I meant it, too, Wes. With everything in me." I smile at him. "Plus, I know you can't lie."

"Right. How could I forget?" He lets his head fall back but then quickly returns his attention. "I didn't hurt you, did I? I was rough, I'm sorry."

I bask in the soreness and appreciate the fullness he still provides even though his erection has softened inside me. There's something incredibly intimate about staying this close even after we've both finished. If only there was a way to get nearer without cutting our bodies open and sewing them together.

What a morbidly romantic and disturbing thought.

"No," I tell him. "It was perfect, really."

"If only you couldn't lie either." He rolls his eyes but doesn't push the issue more.

"How can you not see how completely content I am?"

"Content. Hmm. I should really strive for something better than content."

"I am supremely satisfied." I bring my leg off him and kick at the loose fabric still clinging to my ankle. "Although, I owe Sydney some new clothes."

"I could set them on fire, and we could pretend they never existed."

"Good plan. Maybe we could do that with all the food Bo has eaten, too." What was meant to be a lighthearted remark somehow feels like a swift kick in the gut. I should have known better than to bring Bo up so soon. Leave it to him to always get under my skin, literally and figuratively.

As if Wes can sense the shift, he pushes up onto his elbow to face me. "He'll come around. Don't worry."

I chew at the inside of my lip. "And you're not mad about that?"

He narrows his gaze. "What would I be mad about?"

"I don't know. For starters, the whole sharing me thing. Being a possessive hellhound and all, you're both sure taking that pretty well."

"We would never do anything to hurt you. Not intentionally. And making you choose, that would hurt, wouldn't it?"

I let the thought run through my head, it only needing about half a millisecond to rip a hole through my chest.

"See," he says. "That right there, it goes against our very nature." Wes sighs. "Do we want to share you? No. But will we do everything in our power to make you happy and keep you safe? Absolutely."

"Because of the mate bond."

"Because you are our person. Is it the bond? Maybe. I don't know, I don't care. All I know is this." He grazes his hand over my cheek. "Us." He leans in closer. "You're my world, Wren. My entire universe." His lips caress mine. "I'd die to prove that to you."

"Can you not die? That would be great." I kiss him and smile against his mouth when his cock hardens inside of me again.

My entire life might be up in the air right now, but at least I have this, I have us.

And that counts for something.

CHAPTER 14

Wren

Twirling my finger through the hair on Wes's chest, I lose myself in the comfort of him.

"What are you thinking about?" I ask the burly man.

His eyes flutter open, that familiar shade of glowing red flashing through as he settles his sights on me. He smiles softly. "You."

I rest my chin on his stomach and look up at him. "I'm right here, doofus."

"I like to consume myself in you. Bathe in all things Wren, if I may. It's simply not enough to be near you, I want my every waking thought to revolve around…" He pokes me on the tip of the nose. "You."

"Obsessive much?" I tease.

He shrugs. "Guilty as charged."

"How do you feel about Everest?" I change the subject.

"Well, he's not nearly as good-looking as you."

I let out a laugh. "Ha. Ha. Very funny."

Wes drags his arm behind his head to prop him up and rubs the other over my bare shoulders. "He's a nice guy, from what I've gathered. Was there for Jade when I wasn't."

"That's not your fault," I tell him. "It was out of your control."

"Doesn't make it any easier to stomach. I should have tried getting to her sooner. Maybe I could have—"

"Wes," I cut him off. "It's not your fault."

"Yeah." He lets out a breath.

"He does seem like a good guy. I guess I'm just confused about why he was at Rockbridge."

"Oh." Wes repositions himself slightly. "He was there to investigate his brother's death. And after he figured it out, he stayed for Jade. Said he didn't want to leave her behind and was biding his time until he could figure out how to free her. I'm glad someone was there to give her hope."

"What was the cause of death?"

"Everest was certain that hunters were harnessing demonic power after their kills, and when it was harvested from them, it killed them in the process. Few hunters made it past a couple sessions before it would end their lives."

My heart stutters and I wish there was a way to turn back the clock and guarantee none of this ever happened. The killings, the theft of magic, the curses. So many died for a hopeless cause on both sides of this pointless war.

And for what? For the power-hungry bitch named Parla to gain some kind of advantage over the demons. She's never going to win. It's been centuries and Prania is still descending into the abyss. If only hell would swallow her whole and rid us of her reprehensible ways.

No one else has to die and if I have to kill her myself to make that happen, I will.

"Did you know anything about this?" Wes stares right into my eyes, his focus intense.

"I…"

But I don't get a chance to answer him, and even if I did, I'm not sure what I would have said. The truth? Parts of it? How do I tell him that I was doing the very thing he's referring to? Would he forgive me if he knew how much I hated myself for it? If I told him that I wasn't aware, not fully, of why I was doing what I was doing? I was going off orders—doing what was commanded of me, but that doesn't make what I did any less wrong.

I'll never forgive my actions and that burden alone is a weight I carry through each day. Can I handle the pressure of his judgment, too?

Dash comes into the room, not at all bothered by me and Wes lying here intimately. "Hey," he says. "Sorry to interrupt, but Sydney is downstairs waiting for you."

"Oh shit." I jump up from my spot on the bed and point to a pile of clothes on top of the dresser. "Throw me something to wear, please."

Wes props himself onto his elbows. "Where are you off to? And should I be concerned about this *alone* time you're spending with another man?"

I roll my eyes, rushing around the bed to press a quick kiss to his lips. "Jealousy looks cute on you."

"Here." Dash hands me a few items from the stack—all shades of black or dark grey.

I toss the sweater over my head and step into the leggings.

"Sit," Dash says, kneeling in front of me with a pair of socks in his grasp.

"You don't have to—"

Wes grabs my waist and tugs me onto the edge of the mattress. "Listen to the guy." He nuzzles his head against my side while Dash slides a sock onto each of my feet.

"Thank you," I tell Dash.

It's strange to allow someone to do such a simple task, but it doesn't fail to warm my heart at the thoughtful gesture. This isn't the first time they've made it a point to do little things for me. Even in Bo's frustrating way, he does, too. Like when he serves my rations first instead of just helping himself, or when he steps aside to let me walk through a doorway in front of him. Maybe it's so he can get a better look at my ass, but I choose to believe it's for something else entirely. Bo is more subtle than Wes and Dash are in their displays of affection, yet still, I feel his consideration whether he refuses to admit it's there or not.

And maybe that's something that I'll have to get used to—how Bo chooses to give himself only in longing stares and those soft fleeting moments. Or even in the smile of a victory won together after a brutal battle. I could learn to love him in the manner he prefers, because isn't that what love is about? Give *and* take, not just take. I can't expect him to change for me but perhaps I could change for him. Or at the very least, meet him somewhere in the middle.

I slide into my boots and give Wes one last kiss, leaving him lying there like he was sent here by the angels themselves with his hair wafting onto his forehead. His sleepy gaze follows me out of the room.

"You coming?" I call out to Dash, taking a departing glance at the closed door across the hall from ours.

Tremont. Another one of life's mysteries that has yet to be solved.

He hasn't made a commotion or tried to escape. Sometimes I expect him to be gone, but he remains imprisoned in the room of his enemy. Is it possible that he's familiar enough with captivity that he doesn't desire being set free? Or have his wrongdoings finally caught up to him and made him realize that he deserves the punishment? Either way, I'm no better than him. I killed without question and stole power that was not mine for the taking.

I even enjoyed doing it and took great pleasure in becoming the most lethal of my kind.

I should be locked away the same as him.

Dash catches up to me on the stairs and distracts my mind from imploding.

"You're coming with me, right?" I take in his gentle but masculine features and try not to lose my footing and fall down the stairs.

"You want me to?" He does a poor job hiding the grin that forms on his handsome face.

"Obviously." I cup my hand around his biceps and continue descending.

My relationship with Dash hasn't always been easy, but it's never been challenging either. There have been times when I worried or had doubts or grew frustrated. He's been a constant support and goes above and beyond to show his fondness of me. Even when I didn't deserve it. He has been kind and optimistic despite having everything taken from him. He never gave up hope that there was something better out there, and I adore his persistence to persevere. Part of me wishes I could be more like him, but I'm not foolish enough to think my darkness wouldn't immediately drown out that light.

Maybe that's why Bo and I can't seem to get things right—because we're too much alike. Both of us forged in the depths of our despair and fueled by the continued rage pumping through our veins.

Sydney glances up from his spot in the kitchen and shoves that tiny device of his into his pocket. "You ready?"

"What is that?" I ask him. "That thing you're on all the time."

He slides it back out and holds it in front of him. "This? It's a cell phone."

"Oh," I say, moving in his direction. "What's so special about it?"

"Um, well, nothing and everything, I suppose." He pokes the front of it, and it lights up. "You can call people, text them, email. Um, there are social media apps. The weather. Games. News. Pretty much any information that you could possibly want is at your fingertips." He pushes it another few times and points it at me. "It has a camera." Sydney turns it around to show me the picture.

"Ew, I look like that?"

"What are you talking about?" Dash gawks at me. "You're beautiful."

I pat the sides of my head to tame my hair. "I look like I fell off a wagon and got sat on by a scruni."

"Do not." Dash elbows me in the ribs.

Sydney touches the screen again. "Here, I deleted it. That better?"

"Yeah," I tell him. "Thanks."

"I'm sure you'll all get one of your own at some point once you've established yourselves in our realm. It's easier to stay connected that way. I was just talking to Silas about upcoming plans." Sydney snatches his keys off the counter and makes his way toward the door.

"Silas." The memory of that attractive man popping up out of nowhere at Willow's house comes back to me. "Is that another one of Willow's husbands?"

"Yep." Sydney continues down the hall and opens the door to the outside world.

"He's, uh, interesting." I breathe in deeply and savor the freshness of the air.

"You two met?" Dash stays close to my side without being overly into my personal space.

I urge to yank him toward me but refrain from the intrusive thought.

"He sort of appeared out of thin air. Right after I shoved half a muffin in my mouth, too. I probably frightened him."

"There isn't much that can scare him. He's been to hell and back."

"Haven't we all?" I reach for the handle on the car door, my body already falling in line with the ways of this world.

"No," Sydney says from the driver's side. "Literally."

"Oh." I climb into the passenger seat and buckle myself in before I'm told to. "That explains why he's so broody."

Sydney chuckles. "He was like that prior, actually. That's just how he is." He turns the key in the ignition and backs us out of the parking spot. "We've had our differences, we still do, but he's a good man."

"So you two didn't always get along?" I glance over at him, wondering how much I'm allowed to ask without coming across too overbearing. I can't help but want to learn everything I can about Willow and her men. *My family.*

"Not for a great while, really. We hated each other." Sydney turns onto the main road and accelerates to get ahead of the car he pulled out in front of.

It grows smaller in the mirror behind us.

"Was it because of her? Like you were fighting over Willow?"

Sydney shakes his head. "No, not really. Although, that didn't make the beginning of our relationships any easier." He puts the blinker thing on and switches lanes. "Witches and vampires are natural born enemies."

Silas was freakishly fast and able to sneak up on me without drawing attention to himself.

"He's a vampire," I say out loud, confirming what Sydney already said. "So you and Willow are witches, Deghan is a werewolf, and Silas is a vampire. What's Cameron?"

The one I haven't quite figured out yet. I had a hunch that Silas was *something* in line with vampires or dhampirs but Cameron leaves me with a big ol' blank in the supernatural department.

"That's a great question." Sydney reaches for the bottle of water in his cup holder, takes a swig, and then puts it back in its place. "Cam is Cam. He's no one thing."

"That's..."

"Not the answer you wanted?" Sydney glances over at me.

I snort. "Something like that."

"Cameron's kind of the glue, if that makes sense. Which I'm guessing it doesn't. It will over time, the more you learn of your ancestry and how your partners play a role in your magic."

"You keep mentioning my magic, and I keep doubting it exists." I swirl my index finger over my thumbnail and consider that maybe we have this all wrong. Maybe I'm not really an Oliver. Maybe I don't have magic. Maybe I'm an imposter who is clinging to the hope that she's something that she isn't.

"You've had hidden magic your entire life. It may take some time for it to come to fruition. I wouldn't worry."

I pray to the Angels that he's right, that there's more to me than a washed-up assassin.

"What did you mean about her partners and her magic?" Dash asks from the back seat.

Sydney briefly meets his gaze in the rear-view mirror. "The Olivers are fueled by love. Their magic made more powerful by it, which is no surprise that Olivers are drawn to have multiple mates."

"Willow mentioned a mother and father. Does she only have one partner?" I cross and uncross my legs, unsure of what to do with them. Why am I suddenly so fidgety?

"Yes, but that was from before. Ancient textbooks linked back to the early days suggest that the original Olivers had many partners prior to the curse. It was the cursed magic that put a stop to Oliver's being with their love. A fail-safe of sorts. If the Olivers are powered by love, they are weaker without it, meaning those that wish to steal their magic have a greater probability of doing so."

"That's fucked up," I blurt out.

"It is," Sydney confirms. "And it will never happen again. Willow made sure of that."

We turn down another long lane, this one narrower than the last. It takes a minute before a structure comes into view, but when it does, my eyes widen.

"What is this place?" I inch forward in my seat to study the beautiful architecture of the building. Stone walls with vines wrapped up and down them. The circled pathway out front leads to a lush garden that's concealed by an iron gate.

"This is Harper Academy, or as the supernaturals know it, Harper Shadow Academy." Sydney pulls his car out of the way and puts it into park. "Most of the human faction is on spring break, but there are some that remain." He pivots his body toward us and glances between us. "I'm taking a risk bringing you here. Please don't make me regret it."

I press my hand to my chest. "I promise, I won't."

Dash puts his palms into the air in front of him. "I don't have any magical powers, I'm just weird."

"Aren't we all?" Sydney smiles and reaches for the door handle. "Let's do this."

Carefully, I follow suit, stepping out of the car and stepping onto the gravel. It crunches beneath my feet and distracts me temporarily from my racing heart. I don't move any farther until Sydney approaches and waves us over.

"This way." He strolls through the gated area at a much quicker pace than I prefer.

I want to take my time and consume every detail of this astonishing place. Maybe if things go well, this won't be my last visit to the Harper Shadow Academy.

The door to the massive building creaks when Sydney opens it.

I go through the threshold, something tingling within me at the atmosphere of this place. My eyes desperately scan the contents in their attempt to take it all in. They stop and widen, my head tilting up to admire the enclosed garden smack dab in the middle of the open area. A tree grows right in the center with lavish shrubbery and flowers surrounding it. I step closer, cautiously and wonder how such a thing is possible. Upon further inspection, the roof to the garden seems to also be glass, and doubles as the floor to the second level of the building.

"This is...magical," I whisper. That would be the only explanation of how it would work.

Sydney appears at my side. "It is, actually." He winks and turns around. "This is sort of the main floor common area." He points in the direction we came where extravagant furniture speckles the grand area. "People hang out here between classes. There are stairs to the dorms there and there." He continues to move his hand around to signal to new things. "Down that hallway is the west wing, this is the east, and I'm sure you can guess the north and south are that way."

Sydney waves us over like he doesn't realize how incredibly amazed and entranced I am. "Infirmary is through there." He taps gently on a door that he walks by. "Women's restrooms are there, along with stairs that take you to their dorm." He shifts his body. "Headmaster's office that way and this is..." He leads us away from that grand display in the main area into a large room filled with empty tables. "The dining hall."

The space is vast and open, with windows that line the far wall and allow copious amounts of natural light to rush in. Orange and red echo off the floor from the sunset.

I spin in a slow circle and consider what it might be like when the students are here. Who sits at what table? What kind of food do they eat? Is it loud with chatter or quiet as they keep to themselves? Do the humans and supernaturals co-mingle? How can the supernaturals be so close yet remain hidden? Are humans that oblivious? Or are the supernaturals just that good?

Dash smiles and stays by my side.

"What are they doing out there?" I ask when I spot Willow and someone else out through the windows.

They're standing against the rail of a large patio attached to the back of the school. There are a few empty tables scattered about, and it leads to a grassy area that's encased by a tree line in the distance.

Willow rests her head on a person nearly half a foot taller than her, and from a simple process of elimination, I assume it's her other husband, Deghan. The only one I haven't met yet.

The sun dips out of view in the distance, and the sky changes into a darker shade of orange with pink swirls cascading through it.

"Watching the sunset." Sydney comes near me, his arms crossed over his chest but not in a closed-off kind of way. More like he's admiring the view, too. The one of two people he deeply cares about. "It's kind of his thing." He glances over at me. "That's Deghan, by the way."

I nod and watch Deghan stand from his bent-over position at the rails, his height growing even more. He snatches Willow into his arms and twirls her into a circle before slowly lowering her to the ground. Both of their faces beam with happiness and somehow it warms my heart to witness such a simple, yet intimate interaction.

They share a brief kiss and lock hands, turning and stalking toward us together.

I feel like we should look away, do anything other than stare at them, but Sydney remains in wait, so I do, too.

"Syd, my man," Deghan says the second he walks through the door. "How was your day?"

"Eventful, to say the least. And the pup training?"

Deghan laughs sharply. "Kept me busy, that's for sure." His gaze trails from Sydney to me, to Dash, then back to me. "And who do we have here?"

"Deghan," Willow begins. "This is Wren, Wren Oliver."

His brows curve up as he continues toward me. He releases Willow, and before I can react, he's wrapped his arms around me into a body-crushing embrace. He lets go, holding me at an arm's length, his gaze scanning my face. "Oliver, ey? I think I see the family resemblance."

I force a smile.

"Pleasure to meet an extension of the family." Deghan turns his focus to the red-headed man beside me.

"And this"—Willow steps close—"is Dash."

"Dash," Deghan tries out on his tongue. He spares no expense, wrapping Dash into his arms and pulling him to his chest. He slaps his back and Dash seems to do the same, not bothered by the smothering affection this stranger is giving him.

"Nice to meet you," Dash says under Deghan's stronghold.

"Deghan's a bit of a hugger, if you can't tell," Sydney mentions all too late.

Willow chuckles and tugs Deghan away from Dash. "You're going to scare them away, Deg."

"It's fine, really," Dash reassures them. "It's a heck of a lot better of a welcome than what I'm used to back home."

"Where is home?" Deghan asks him.

"Prania," Dash says.

I tilt my head in the direction we came from and grow suspicious of how much information we should be confessing so publicly. Are there humans nearby that might hear and question what we're discussing?

"Never heard of it." Deghan flits his gaze to Sydney.

Sydney shrugs. "Me either."

"Weird." Deghan scratches at his scruffy beard. "Have you asked Walker?"

"That's the plan." Willow tilts her wrist toward her to check the time. "He should be back shortly." She looks at me. "In the meantime, I have a theory I want to test. You in?"

I point to my chest. "Me?"

"Yes, you. Mind if I borrow her for a minute?" Willow asks Dash.

"Uh, sure, yeah. As long as she stays safe."

His misplaced concern warms my chest. If anything, I'm the one worried about him going off on his own.

"Without question," she tells him. "We won't be far, just going to go down to the library."

"I'm starving," Deghan announces and latches onto Dash's shoulder. "You hungry? We can raid the kitchen." He tilts his head toward a set of closed doors at the far side of the dining area.

"I could eat." Dash shoots me a wary look.

"I'll be fine," I tell him. "You be careful though." I don't enjoy the idea of leaving him behind, but I won't be gone long, and Deghan doesn't exactly come across as a threat. If anything, he's the nicest out of Willow's husbands, and that's saying a lot considering Sydney has been nothing but gracious—outside of his initial interaction when he found us crashing at his place. And Cameron gave us two boxes of those delicious muffins and offered to bring us more.

Silas isn't in the running, with the whole one word he spoke to me, but even still, I can't imagine he would harm any of us either. Not unless we posed some threat to Willow, and that is something I would never do. She's my family. My *only* family. I would die for her.

Sydney reaches out to gently grasp Willow's arm. "I'll let you know when Walker arrives."

"Thanks, Syd." She steps toward him, standing a bit taller and pressing her lips to his cheek. "And you." She turns toward Deghan. "Stay out of trouble."

Deghan averts his gaze and feigns innocence. "I don't know what you're talking about." He throws his arm around Dash's back and moves him toward the kitchen. He mumbles something to Dash, but I can't quite make it out.

Dash laughs and I know with certainty that everything is going to be okay.

At least, right now, in the short term, it will.

"Follow me," Willow says as she heads in the original direction we came.

Sydney comes with us, but takes a seat in the common area, pulling out his phone and poking the screen to life. "I have some emails to answer."

"Evening, Professor," a round-faced girl mumbles with her face buried in a book as she walks.

"Clara," Sydney acknowledges.

Willow continues forward and walks us down a set of concrete stairs. "That's Clara. Second-year witch."

"Interesting."

"She's a bit of an overachiever, but I can't say I blame her."

We go through a doorway into a room that lights up upon our entry.

"Was that magic?" I whisper, unsure if there's anyone else around.

Willow shakes her head. "No, just a motion sensor. It's to preserve electricity."

"Sounds like magic."

"So, what you see here." Willow extends her arm and motions to the shelves full of books lining the walls and the tables in the open area. "Is the human side of the library." She continues through the space, walking around more tables and past a few rows of shelves. "But this..." She steps through a threshold that appears to be a dead-end to nowhere.

I trail her, but once I'm on the other side, a long, seemingly endless hallway with doors on both sides appears.

"This is magic." She winks at me and goes in a bit farther. "This is the supernatural library, which houses a plethora of ancient and new text covering all things supernatural. There are sections for basic witchcraft, the origins of werewolves, history of most creatures, whatever you can think of, there is probably a book in here *somewhere* covering the topic."

My heart constricts in my chest at the idea that the answers I've been searching for my entire life are under one giant roof.

"It's...incredible," I whisper and press my fingers to the mark on my neck that seems to warm with the growing distance between me and Bo.

Does he feel that distance, too?

"I want you to try something." Willow turns toward me. "I want you to close your eyes, take a deep breath, and allow the angels to guide you."

"The Angels?"

"I know it sounds silly, but just trust me, please."

"What's the worst that could happen?" I say, not expecting an answer. I drop my arms to the side and shake my fingers, releasing the tension within me. Drawing in a lungful of air, I let it out slowly and pinch my eyes shut.

A quiet humming plays a backdrop to the steady thumping of my pulse.

I stand there and consider whether Willow has this all wrong. Has me all wrong.

Am I wasting her time when she clearly has more important things she needs to attend to?

It's selfish of me to demand her help, especially the more I learn how important she is to this world. I should give up, let her go, and stop bothering her and her mates with my woes.

"Do you feel that?" I ask her with my eyes still shut.

"Let it guide you," she says softly like she understands this strange tugging in my core.

I take a cautious step forward, a sense of relief gently washing over me like a reassurance that I'm going in the right direction. Blindly, I walk foot by foot with my hands out in front of me. Turning down a corner, and then another, I must go for two whole minutes before I feel called to stop.

Blinking myself back to reality, I open my eyes to find a doorway in front of me.

"I believe this is Angel archives," Willow says while stepping into the room.

Why would I be drawn to this room? What information is waiting for me here?

Willow strolls the wall, her fingertip grazing the shelf as she goes by. "I think I studied here years ago when I first came to the academy." She pauses at a shelf, skims the spines, and then latches onto an old dusty book. "This one, yes." She blows on the front, exposing the faded letters, and cracks it open.

I examine the shelf opposite of where she's standing, my gaze trailing the old tomes. Nothing sticks out any more than the last. They're all interesting and my gut begs for me to scour them each, but not in a magical kind of way. More general curiosity than anything else.

That is, until I find my hand hovering along the spine of a larger text, my fingers itching to pick it up. I swallow harshly and give in to the craving, sliding the book carefully out of its home tucked among many others.

With great caution, I walk the thing over to a nearby table and set it on the surface.

"What did you find?" Willow shuts the book in her grasp, returns it to its spot on the shelf, and comes over beside me.

"I don't know," I tell her honestly. "I don't see a title."

"Hmm." She wipes at the cover but doesn't reveal anything other than the leather encasement. "Well." Willow tilts her head toward me. "Ready to find out what's inside?"

My jaw clenches and I grow increasingly unsteady. I've never both wanted and feared something so much in my life. What if this book holds information that will make things worse? What if it uncovers a truth that I'm not prepared to face? What if I really am the monster I believe myself to be, and Willow is there when I find out? What if she rejects me and I lose everything I've gained here in Arthlia?

I've already lost my home, what if even more loss is yet to come?

But before I can choose to succumb or overcome my fears, a figure appears in the doorway. Large, older, and masculine but with a sort of non-threatening aura.

"Headmaster Walker." Willow immediately greets him, rushing around the table to wrap her arms around him.

"Willow." He hugs her back and steadies his inquisitive attention on me.

"Walker." She releases him. "I have someone I want you to meet." Willow points toward me. "This is Wren Oliver. Wren, this is Headmaster Walker."

I nod politely. What are the formalities in this world? Everyone sure does hug a lot, but that isn't exactly how I've grown used to greeting strangers. Do I bow? Shake hands? Offer him something? I don't want to offend him, but I have no idea what I'm supposed to do. I shall make a mental note to ask Sydney once I've departed this magical place.

"Oliver?" The headmaster rubs Willow's shoulder before leaving her side. He glances down at the book in front of me. "Arcane Angelic text."

"You're familiar?" I ask him, my interest getting the best of me.

"May I?" He approaches and points to the book.

"By all means, it's kind of yours anyway." I scoot it toward him.

He flips over the thick cover, exposing a pale beige page with faded, unreadable text. And not because of the condition, but because it's in another language.

"I've never had it translated." Walker fingers through a few pages.

Of course, I would be led to the one book in the room that no one can read. How is that supposed to help answer any of my questions? Including why this book is even of any relevance to me.

"Was there something specific you were after?" He side-eyes me while continuing to move through some of the pages.

I shrug. "I don't know." Glancing at Willow, I silently pray for her to have some input.

Like she could read my mind, she opens her mouth to speak. "Remember when I was struggling at the beginning of my magical journey?"

Walker gives her his attention.

"I came down here, and I was guided toward various texts. I believe it was the Angels leading me toward what I needed to find. That's how I learned more about the Oliver curse, the Harlow curse, the hell dimensions." Willow dips her head to the book none of us can read. "This is where Wren was led. There must be something in there for her."

Walker takes a breath in and runs his hand through his dark but speckled grey hair. "I see." He rubs his chin. "I can see about having it translated, but it may take some time."

Time. Something I both do and do not have.

I am no longer running for my life, but how can I remain here when I know the truth about what's happening in my homeland? There is no luxury of time regarding Parla and her mission to kill every demon she can get her manicured hands on.

"I would very much appreciate that," I tell him. Because even if it takes forever, it's something he's willing to do. "How can I repay you?"

He shakes his head. "Not necessary. I'm happy to help."

"Speaking of help," Willow says. "I wanted to ask you something."

"Shoot." Walker closes the book and focuses on her.

"Are you familiar with a realm called Prania?"

Walker blinks stiffly. "Why?"

"That's where Wren is from. And Sydney can't find any literature on it. He's scoured the archives, and he came up empty. We figured it's worth a shot to see if you know anything about it."

I chew at the inside of my lip in anticipation of what could be another dead-end.

"That's impossible." Walker's serious gaze rakes over me.

"Do you know something?" Willow questions him.

"I know enough to tell you who you need to talk to." He hesitates before saying, "But you're not going to like it."

"Why?" Willow and I say at the same time.

"Because Prania is a demon realm." Walker stares at Willow as if that should be enough.

"What does that have to do with anything?" I shift my gaze between them, desperate to read something on their faces that would give me more insight.

Willow's body goes tense. "No."

"Yes," Walker answers her.

"Someone please tell me what's going on." I grip the edge of the table.

"If you want answers about Prania," Walker says. "You're going to need to talk to Balial."

Willow cringes at the very mention of his name but I don't quite understand.

Balial is one of the princes of Hell. What does that have to do with Willow? Why is she so turned off by the idea of speaking to him?

She shakes her head. "No. Not happening."

"I can do it, you don't have to," I suggest. "I wouldn't want to put you out."

"I doubt he would willingly give you information, Wren." Walker adds, "No offense. He's just not the most communicable person in existence."

"And what makes you so sure he would for Willow?"

"They have...history."

Willow grimaces again at that last word. "I'm sorry, Wren. I can't help you."

I get one step closer, and another obstacle is thrown in my direction.

"There must be some other way. I'll go myself and see if he will. How do I get there? I don't know how to realm travel." I'll get down on my knees and beg if that's what I have to do. If there's even a slight chance I can learn about Prania enough to free it from the hold Parla has on it, I'll do anything.

Walker raises a brow. "Then how did you leave Prania to begin with?"

"I, uh." I shift from putting all my weight on one leg to the other. "I had help."

"Help?" he presses.

"Before you freak out, I assure you, the situation is contained." My heart pounds so loudly that I swear it's going to leap out of my ears.

"Who helped you?" Walker asks and Willow stares, both waiting for my answer.

"Tremont." I don't know which one of them to focus on.

Willow folds her arms over her chest. Walker takes a step back.

"I didn't know what he was to you," I insist. "Not until we were already here. Sydney is the one who told me."

"Sydney knows about this?" Willow tightens the hold she has on her body, her voice growing more frustrated.

"He spelled him to a room in the house. He can't come out. I swear, he seems harmless, really," I spit out every bit of the truth I can to convince them.

"No. You don't know what he's capable of," Willow tells me. "He's a monster."

But if that's how she feels about him, there's no doubt she'll have the same reaction when she finds out what I've done.

Tears well in my eyes, and I blink them away. "I'm sorry. I didn't mean to upset you. I'm not with him. Or on his side. You have every right to be upset. I shouldn't have said anything."

Walker sighs. "You told the truth, Wren, and that means something in my book." He reaches toward Willow, his hand lingering in the air between them. "There has to be some reason Sydney didn't tell us yet. If he thought it were an immediate threat, he would have. We have to trust that he has the situation contained like Wren says he does." He looks over at me like an idea just struck him. "He's confined to a room where?"

"Sydney's estate," I answer without hesitation.

"That means the barrier spell wore off." Walker picks up the angelic book and tucks it under his arm. "I should have stayed up on ensuring it was in place. I'll double-check the wards but it'll require your help." He looks to Willow.

She nods. "Yeah, of course. Whatever you need to keep the academy safe." Willow avoids my wandering gaze. "As far as Balial goes. I'm sorry, but I can't help you."

Her declaration is heavier than being crushed under a passed-out scruni.

"I don't expect you to do this out of the goodness of your heart," I tell her. "I will pay whatever the cost. And I'm willing to do it myself if someone would just teach me how."

Willow lets out a long breath. "This has nothing to do with my heart, Wren. I *want* to help. Probably too much. That's why I'm spread so thin as it is. It's simply a matter of impossibility. There are only so many places I can be at one time, and I'm already overextended on my list of obligations. Unless I can figure out how to clone myself, there isn't enough of me to go around." She pauses and reaches out to grab onto my hand. "I promise you, I'd love to help if I could. Even as much as I loathe that man, I would. But it would require an immense amount of my power to travel there, and I wouldn't be able to fulfill my obligations here."

"What if..." I rack my brain to figure out a solution. "What if I help you? With your *obligations*? There has to be something I can do for you."

"I'm sorry, these are things that only I can do. I can't..."

"Wait—I have an idea." Walker cuts Willow off. "Wren is of the Oliver bloodline."

"And?" Willow says as if she doesn't understand his train of thought.

Although, it's not like I do either.

"Your tasks, while some of them are truly only things that *you* can do. Some are things that require an *Oliver witch*, not necessarily *you*," Walker explains.

"So what you're saying is I *can* help?" Even if it was to simply repay the kindness they have shown me since being in Arthlia, I would do anything.

"If your blood is a close enough match, then yes, it's possible." Walker looks to Willow. "It's worth testing, and honestly, might take some pressure off of you in the meantime."

"I don't know. I..." Willow rubs her hands together and cracks her knuckles. "I'll need to think about it."

It might not be the answer I was hoping for, but it wasn't the one I was dreading. And for now, that will have to be enough.

CHAPTER 15

Bo

I sit outside by myself on a hard wooden chair not nearly big enough for me to rest comfortably.

Being uncomfortable is something I've grown used to, though.

It's my normal.

The human world is vast, but everything is built for small creatures. Their furniture, their ceilings, their fucking food portions. I have to consume at least five times the *suggested* serving size to feel remotely satiated.

Not that I should complain. Especially when Prania is set up to favor anyone but demons.

No place has ever felt warm or inviting or remotely like home. But Prania is all I know. It's what I was used to. And despite it massively fucking sucking, I can't help but yearn to be back there.

Because in Prania, at least I knew where I stood. I was the hunted. But in that, I hunted the hunters, and in a way, I enjoyed the sick little game of cat and mouse. The roles reversing each day made my time there a bit more interesting—especially when compared to sitting here and doing nothing.

The chair creaks when I adjust myself, and I worry for a moment that the whole thing will collapse out from under me.

"What are you doing out here?" Wren asks with her arms tucked tightly across her chest.

"Admiring the view." I stare out into the dark abyss of the forest beyond Sydney's house.

"It's pitch black."

"I have night vision."

"What's that like?"

"I'm guessing where you see black, I see shades of grey."

"That's cool." Wren kneels beside my chair and puts her hands on the armrest. "Can we talk?"

"About what?" I don't look at her because if I do, I may lose the ability to restrain myself from taking exactly what I want.

"I need a favor."

I cave and turn toward her. "What?" Can she sense how desperate I am to do anything I can for her?

"I need you to come with me somewhere."

"Where?"

"Balial's hell realm."

"Have you lost your mind?"

"He has answers, Bo. About Prania."

My hand tightens into a fist, but I refuse to let my anger unleash itself. "You don't know that."

"Neither do you," she spits out. "You hate it here. Why wouldn't you jump at the opportunity to go somewhere else?"

"I don't hate it here."

"You're miserable. More so than usual."

"Am not."

She sighs. "Whatever. Fine." Wren stands. "I'll go without you."

I latch onto her wrist. "No, you won't."

Wren tries to yank herself free. "I'm going one way or another, Bo. You can either go or don't, but you can't stop me."

"Let me rephrase then. You're not going without me." The mark on her neck would surely light up if she were *that* far away from me. The distance between here and the academy today was enough to flicker it to life. There's no fucking way I'm allowing her to go to a realm filled with demons with that marker blaring on her neck.

"Was that so difficult?"

"When do we leave?" I ask her while ignoring her own question.

"Tomorrow morning." She pulls herself from my loosened grip and turns to walk away.

"Birdie?"

Wren stops in her tracks. "Yes?"

"Did you ask me because of the mark or because you want me to go?"

"Does it matter?"

"No," I lie. It matters more than anything, but I won't tell her that.

"Then you can decide for yourself what the answer is." She marches away, leaving me here where I began—alone with my thoughts.

I stand in a classroom at Harper Shadow Academy with Willow, Wren, and Sydney.

Willow was strangely nice considering I'm a demon living in her husband's parents' estate. She's prettier than I thought she would be, too. There's something familiar about her, like there are pieces of Wren inside of her because of their bloodline connection. Her presence isn't threatening, but it is powerful. I can sense the magic rippling through her veins at a sheer volume, unlike any other witch I have ever come across.

The witches from Prania were weak compared to the strength of this vibrant woman standing before me. Is that what's in store for Wren when she comes into whatever magic Sydney keeps claiming she has? I don't doubt that there's something hidden under the surface, but I'd be surprised if it's as vast as Willow's.

I could taste the heavenly power upon sinking my fangs into Wren's flesh. There was nothing as sweet as her blood on my lips, but within a split second, I knew the gravity of the situation and that if I didn't restrain myself, I would suck her dry.

I've craved her every moment after but have done everything I can to withstand that hunger. Yet with it, I have deprived myself of blood altogether. Since I tasted her, I have not been drawn to consume another even though it's in my very nature. If I can't have her, I don't want it. I'm not so sure that I could. The thought of draining someone else repulses me.

Biting Wren changed me, and I don't know how I'll ever recover.

It's like her blood in my system somehow altered my entire DNA.

"Are you ready?" Sydney glances at each of us.

I nod while Wren says, "Yes."

"You sure you want to do this?" Sydney asks Willow. "I can come with you."

"I'll be fine. He won't hurt me. It will be better for me to go alone."

He's the prince of hell, how is she so sure he won't harm her?

I've been told that this little mission is harmless, that we aren't actually traveling through the fold the same way we did to get to Arthlia, but we're doing a sort of astral projection that will send us there while our corporal forms remain without putting us in danger. It doesn't really make sense, the whole being in two places at once, but they assured me it's the less strenuous of ways to get there and back quicker. If we fully traveled there, it would require more power and put us all at a greater risk.

Sydney remains rooted in place in the classroom and will be our anchor to Arthlia.

When we wish to return to our bodies, we either say the phrase, *"Copeth trebum,"* or push this little button that all of us got. A failsafe in case we're not able to speak for whatever reason.

"Okay," Sydney speaks. "I need all of you to lie down and hold hands."

"Does it matter who is where?" Wren asks.

"You should be in the middle since you have a strong tether to both Willow and Bo."

We lower to our respective areas, and I reach for Wren.

She weaves her fingers between mine, my entire world rocking despite everything being so incredibly still.

It's just her fucking hand, you idiot.

But when I've deprived myself of her for this long, it's that much more. I want to be fully consumed by her. I want to hold on and never let go and force her to realize just how much she means to me.

I'll never do that though, because it wouldn't be fair to her.

Wes might be able to be selfish enough to allow his hound to claim her, but I care enough to allow her to keep her free will.

Even if it fucking kills me.

"Close your eyes," Sydney tells us. "And don't let go until you're there. If possible, come back at the same time, too." He mumbles something I can't make out. A blur of words that don't sound anything like our language.

My body feels heavier, and then lighter. I keep my eyes shut, noticing the brightness that's quickly replaced with darkness. Heat swells around me, and all I can seem to truly focus on is the small hand wrapped tightly around mine.

"We're here," Willow says from her spot on the other side of Wren.

I blink a few times, allowing my vision to adjust to this new place. It's dark but somehow light at the same time, flames flickering over the barren land. Lava flows like a creek near us, and steam rises from crevices scattered about.

I stand, keeping Wren's hand in mine, not yet ready to let go of her.

She doesn't bother releasing me, either. "It's warm here."

Sweat beads on her brow, and I salivate at the idea of stepping toward her and licking it from her forehead. Anything to taste her sweet essence. Against my growing desire, I restrain myself.

"I've tried getting him to turn the temperature down, but he's rather persistent on keeping things hot." Willow looks around her. "This way."

"You two are like friends or something?" I ask her.

"We aren't friends," she says.

"Or something. Got it." I guess I shouldn't be surprised that a powerful witch has even more powerful connections with people from the underworld.

My boots crumble against the rocky ground, and if I didn't know better, I'd never expect my entire being to actually be here, in this Angel-forsaken place. I *feel* here. The heat covers my body like a cloak, and the stench of rotting flesh and charred ashes greets me. The desolate expanse calls to me—almost welcoming me home.

We follow Willow in a single-file line over an embankment and across a thin walkway surrounded by flowing lava.

Wren moves with ease behind her, never once faltering along the sketchy terrain. She is elegant and covert and if I had to guess, this is a result of her many years of being a hunter.

I do what I can to not stare at her plump ass as she walks, but it grows impossible when it's right in front of me.

"You okay back there?" Wren calls out to me over my shoulder.

"Yep." I give her a thumbs up and look anywhere but her rear end.

My shoe slips and I lose my footing. I slide toward a steep cliff overlooking a seemingly bottomless pit.

But instead of falling, Wren catches my arm and prevents me from tumbling over the edge.

"What the fuck, Bo?" She yanks me onto solid ground. "Did you do that on purpose?" Wren plants her hands on my shoulders and stares up at me. "Bo. Answer me."

Raising my hand, I skim it across her cheek and tuck her hair behind her ear.

"You two good?" Willow pauses to ask us.

"Yeah, we're fine," Wren tells her then focuses on me. "Don't you dare throw yourself off a cliff to get away from me. I can handle you being an asshole, but I can't handle you being gone forever. Okay?"

My attention falls to her lips, soft and plush and begging to be taken.

"Do you hear me?" She shakes me.

"I hear you, Birdie. Loud and clear."

"Good." Wren releases me. "Now go ahead of me so I can keep an eye on you."

My cheeks turn up. "Not a chance."

"Then promise me you won't mess up again." She narrows her gaze.

How can I make that promise when that's all I seem to be capable of doing?

Not just here, but in every facet of our relationship. If it's not one thing, it's another, and everything I do only drives her away from me.

But if that were true, would she be standing here before me asking me not to die? Maybe I haven't lost her after all. Maybe there's still hope that I can fix this. Maybe I should tell her why I am the way I am, and then she could understand why I push her away every chance I get. Why I can't get too close. Why I can't be what she wants me to be.

In doing so, I would have to confess things that I've never told anyone before. And I'm not so sure I'm ready to admit, even to myself, what I keep locked inside.

Instead of giving her the response she wants, I say, "I'll try."

Her chest rises and she lets out a breath. "I can work with that."

Wren returns to her spot in front of me, and Willow and I exchange a nod to signal that we can keep moving forward.

It's only another minute until we step into a foggy clearing. Through the haze, a throne sits in the distance, covered in skulls and bones.

A man rises from the throne, standing tall and peering in our direction. He comes closer, his entire form gliding over the ground like he's hovering about an inch above it. His all-black outfit matches his fully black eyes.

Without meaning to, I kneel and bow my head.

"You may stand," he declares once he's right in front of me. He crosses his arms over his brawny chest and steadies his intense gaze on Willow. "My love. Have you come back to haunt me? Or have you realized you cannot live without me?"

"You wish," Willow says.

"Then you're back for another attempt at torture."

"I'll figure it out one way or another."

"My love, not being with you is torture enough, don't you see?"

"I'll never be with you." Willow shakes her head. "This isn't a social visit, Balial."

"Ah, they never are, are they?" He floats near her and then turns his attention to Wren. "And what do we have here?" Balial closes his eyes and breathes her in deeply. "Another Oliver." He licks his lips. "Bring me a consolation prize?"

A growl leaves my chest, and I step between Wren and Balial.

Balial grins, his extremely white teeth bared. "I see this one is claimed, too." He points to his neck. "Still an alpha mark though." He focuses on me. "What are you waiting for?"

"Bal." Willow steps forward and presses her hand to his chest, immediately snapping him out of his trance on me.

"What can I do for you, my love?"

Screams sound in the distance, followed by the sound of dogs barking.

Wren takes a step forward, her body gravitating closer to mine. "We came to ask you about Prania."

"Prania. Hm." He presses his long finger to his chin. "Doesn't ring a bell."

"Tell the truth." Willow stares at him, her gaze unwavering despite him being who he is.

My demonic nature kicked in the second I saw him, my body betraying me and submitting before him. I might be at the top of the food chain in any other realm, but here, he is superior.

It's not something I'm quite fond of. Although, unlike Arthlia, I know where I stand here.

This hell dimension is much more a home than Arthlia ever could be.

"And what do I get in return?" Balial tilts his head to the side.

"Nothing," Willow retorts without hesitating. "You owe me a lifetime of favors. Don't act like you don't."

What could he have possibly done to get this type of response out of her? The prince of hell owing someone else something? And a multiple something?

"Please," Wren adds.

"Fine," the big bad king of darkness huffs. He hovers back and with his hands out in front of him, he begins. "Once upon a time, there was a great war. One that spread millennia. Sides were chosen, lives were lost. Magic was stolen." He looks to Willow. "I'm sure you're familiar." He pauses for effect and continues. "Realms fought each other, until one day, things got out of hand. The..." He scratches his chin. "Hunters, I believe they called themselves, vowed to eliminate all demonic creatures."

Wren tenses and hangs on his every word.

"This one immortal bitch spearheaded the whole thing. And so, the Angels and some of the princes got together and closed her off into her homeland. The end."

"The end?" Wren blurts out. "That's it? Really? You left an entire realm to fend for themselves even knowing what she was capable of."

Balial turns his hand over and studies his nails boringly. "Mmhm."

Willow shoves him. "Why? Why would you do that?"

"She needed to be contained. This was the only way to make that happen."

"You could have just, I don't know, killed her?" Wren grows angrier and steps around me, but I put my arm out to stop her from going any farther.

"We tried. She kept evading us, and the threat to other realms was too great." Balial shrugs. "You should be thanking me."

"Why not open the realm, give the demons a chance to escape? You left them there to die." Wren shoves my arm. "Don't touch me right now, Bo."

"Prania cannot be opened until Parla is dead. What happens to those demons is no concern of mine, not in the grand scheme of things. Eventually, she will run out of demons to feed on and her immortality will fail. It's only a matter of time until there is nothing left of both Parla and Prania."

"And if I kill her? Then you'll lower the barrier?"

Balial hovers toward her. "You know." He takes another breath. "I thought I caught a whiff of something else on you."

Wren holds her ground, not moving with his advance.

"You're an Oliver...but you're also a...hunter." Balial latches onto her neck and yanks her toward him.

I lurch forward and am met with a powerful forcefield keeping me glued to the ground. "Let her go," I yell at him.

Willow plants her arm to the side, a ball of magic forming in her fist. "Don't make me hurt you, Balial. Release her." She readies herself to throw it at him.

But Balial complies and drops Wren from his grip.

She clutches at her neck and gasps for air. "What the hell," she mutters.

Willow rushes to her side, holding her shoulders. "Are you okay?"

I remain stuck in place.

"There are many secrets between you. Ones that will tear you apart. You cannot withstand neither the truth or the lies. Both will be your demise." Balial looks directly at me. "You are not fit for that world, son. You have a place here." He motions to the vast expanse around him. "An endless supply of flesh to feed on. Whatever you want is yours for the taking. Under my command, obviously."

"No one wants to join you here, Balial. Give it a rest." Willow stands. "Why do you think you're alone? You're a bully."

"My love, what sweet words your delectable lips mutter."

"You're an asshole."

Balial grins. "Like music to my ears."

Willow glances back at me. "We're done here."

"Ah, yes," Balial says. "Such a short visit." He snaps his fingers and Willow and Wren disappear, leaving me here with the prince of hell. "Now that it's just us boys, we should chat."

"I have nothing to say to you," I tell him.

What's the phrase I'm supposed to say to get home? If I could break the hold he has on me, I could reach into my pocket to press the button on the device.

"That's very well." Balial hovers closer. "You know, that marking was quite clever."

"Where did you send them?"

"Your concern is misplaced. I would never harm a hair on Willow's beautiful head. Not again, at least."

"That doesn't answer my question. Where are they?" I grit my teeth.

"Back with the witch that cast the spell to send them here, I suppose. Sydney? Unless they've already abandoned you and moved on from casting another to retrieve you. That's the sinking pit in your gut right now, am I correct?" Balial exhales. "You sure are insecure for such an influential creature."

"You know nothing about me."

"No?" he taunts. "Not even that you're afraid she will no longer desire you if you remove the mark? But that if you do rid her of it, you'd ensure she'd be yours forever. What a predicament."

I swallow harshly. How can he be aware of such things? The things I keep hidden deep within me.

"You'll never have her. Not the way you want her. You're too much like me. And despite her darkness, she'd never accept you for yours. Need I mention, she's marked by a hellhound. That mate bond is already forged and cannot be reversed. Perhaps it was one of mine. I'll leave that to determine later."

Wes never should have succumbed to the pressure of the bond. He should have been stronger and let her go. She deserves much better than what he and I have to offer. She deserves someone like Dash—who is kind and patient and does not pose a threat to her.

"There's another way." Balial touches my chin with his finger. "A way to remove the mark without doing the very thing you fear. She would never forgive you for putting her through that."

"What is it?"

"I would gladly remove it for you."

"At what cost?"

"No cost you wouldn't benefit from."

"Tell me."

"You'd remain here, with me. You'd get the life you always wanted. And you'd free both yourself and her of that heinous alpha marker on her neck. At this very moment, the thing is lighting up brighter than ever before. The distance between the two of you is greater than ever. Any demon near the academy will surely be racing toward her, to end her life with great haste. All you have to do is say the word, and I will eliminate the threat you pose to her."

Wren is at a school for supernaturals, where there are no doubt creatures of the demonic variety. Hell, even Deghan and Silas have enough demonic blood to send them into a frenzy to kill her. And depending on Sydney's origins, he might feel that desire, too. The only one capable of withstanding that urge is Willow, and there's no way she would put herself between one of her mates and some girl she's only just met.

Every second I'm away, the danger rises to an unbearable level.

"Let me go," I yell at him and strain against the magic holding me in place.

Why can't I just remember the stupid fucking words that get me out of here?

"This worry of yours, you wouldn't have it if the mark weren't there."

"I swear to the Angels, I'm going to—"

"You're going to what?" Balial laughs. "I am more powerful than you'll ever be. Where do you think you get your strength?" He comes closer. "It's that demonic blood coursing through your veins." He lowers his voice. "The same that Wren harbors inside of her."

I stop craning against the magic keeping me secured in place. "What?"

Balial covers his mouth. "Oops. I wasn't supposed to say that, was I?"

"You're lying."

"The truth is much more entertaining in this case."

"She's descended from the Angels. I've tasted her, she's pure."

"Yes, you are correct, Wren is very much an Oliver at her core, but you fail to see what's right in front of you. She was a hunter. The most feared of Parla's assassins. She has strength unlike any other yet has never come into her true power. Why do you think that is? Because of her good looks and tenacity?" He shakes his head. "No."

If what he's saying is true, and Wren really does have demonic power inside of her, there's only one way she could have obtained it.

And if that's the case, she's no better than the witches who cursed the Oliver bloodline, or the sadistic bitch who plagues Prania to this day.

"It can't be true. She wouldn't," I tell him.

"Then maybe you don't know Wren Oliver as well as you think you do."

CHAPTER 16
Wren

"Where is he?" I yell and jerk Bo's limp shoulders. "He was right there with us, why isn't he back?"

Sydney leans against the wall.

Willow rushes over to him. "Are you okay?"

He nods. "Took more out of me than I thought it would. I underestimated the power it would take to send all three of you."

Willow grabs a chair and drags it over to Sydney. "Here. Sit."

"What's taking so long?" I take in Bo's rugged features and smooth the hair from his face. "Come back to me, Bo," I whisper.

"I'm sorry," Sydney says. "I can't send you back. Not yet."

"Tell me how to do it," I demand. "I can do the spell. I'm a witch, right?"

Sydney shakes his head. "It's too advanced. If you get the slightest pronunciation wrong, there's no telling where you'll end up."

I shift my attention to Willow. "You can do it, can't you?"

"I'm sorry, Wren." Her sad doe eyes don't make it hurt any less.

"Fuck," I blurt out. "Bo." I continue to move his large body. "Can you hear me?"

"What happened?" Sydney asks.

"He attacked her," Willow tells him. "Then started on about secrets." She looks at me. "Do you know what he was talking about?"

"No," I lie. Is it possible Balial can sense the demonic power coursing through me? Is he aware that I'm the worst monster of them all? Is that why he kept Bo behind? To tell him about what I had done and convince him to end my life before I can continue killing demons for Parla.

"Clara." Willow jumps up from her spot next to Sydney and rushes toward the door. "Nothing you need to see in here."

But Clara doesn't listen. Instead, she pushes through into the room and steadies her gaze on me. Dark, threatening, and determined. She heaves her arm in front of her, a blast of green magic flowing from her fingertips and shoving me away from Bo.

I slam into the wall and gasp for breath. An invisible hand wraps around my throat, tightening and constricting my airway. I scrape my fingers against it but there's nothing there for me to grab onto.

"Clara!" Willow yells as she rushes over to her. She throws herself in the line of the attack but it's no use, the spell is already latched onto me.

My vision blurs and I struggle through the fog to stare at Bo's lifeless body still lying on the floor. Tears well in my eyes. "Bo," I mutter.

In my final moment, I swear I witness him rising to his feet, and with that, I slide comfortably into the darkness.

But instead of death, I'm caught by a stronghold.

"I've got you, Birdie." Bo scoops me into his arms.

"I'm..." Clara's voice fills my ears. "I'm so sorry. I don't know what came over me."

"Is it really you?" I weakly reach up to touch his face.

"I'm here." Bo holds me closer to his broad chest. "I'm here."

"The infirmary," Sydney says. "Down the hall to the right. I'll be right behind you."

"It's not her fault," Bo tells them. "As long as I'm near, she won't have that urge again." He walks us through the room. "Just means she has demon blood in her veins."

Someone gasps but I'm not sure who. If I had to guess, it was probably the sweet and innocent second-year witch who just tried to murder me for no reason other than the demonic pull this stupid marker on my neck has when the alpha who bit me gets too far.

I had a hunch that would happen when visiting Balial's hell, but I was hoping given the nature of our travel, that those same laws wouldn't apply. Now we know astral projection is off the table unless I want any demon around to be alerted to kill me.

"I have to remove this mark from your neck, Birdie. I can't keep putting you at risk." Bo carries me out of the room.

"I can walk," I mutter through my tender windpipe.

"Good for you."

This isn't the first time he's insisted on carrying me when I told him I was fine. And I'm sure it won't be the last. He might pretend he doesn't care, but this is just another instance of him proving himself wrong.

Bo continues around the corner and opens another door, nudging it shut behind him. He flips on a light switch with me still in his grasp and brings me over to a table covered in a thin layer of paper. "If Wes were here, he could fix this for you."

I sit up and scoot myself to the edge of the table while rubbing at my neck. "I'm fine." Between the hold Balial had and then the one Clara did, I am rather sore. "You got back in the nick of time."

"Had I been a moment later, she may have succeeded." Bo lowers his head.

"Don't act like this is your fault. You couldn't have known Balial would keep you there. It's just as much my fault."

Bo slams his fist into his chest. "I'm the one who marked you, Wren. *Me.* I'm the only one to blame here."

Sydney comes into the room like he promised and makes his way over to us. "I have something that should help." He fumbles with a few vials in a large glass cabinet and plucks two of them out. "Here. Drink this." He hands me one of them and consumes the other himself.

The color returns to his cheeks within seconds and the energy he had lost seems to return.

I drain the one he gave me, the taste bitter on my tongue. Warmth spreads through me, and despite really understanding how, the pressure on my neck subsides. It's still there, but not half as bad as it was seconds prior.

"It will take some time to take full effect, but it should take the edge off." Sydney glances at Bo and then at me. "I'll give you two a minute. I'm going to find something for you to eat."

"I'm not hungry," I tell him.

"It's a witchy thing. You should always replenish after a spell that big to counteract the impact it has." Sydney doesn't bother waiting for my protest. He strolls back the way he came and leaves Bo and me behind.

"Bo." I press my palm on his shoulder. "Will you talk to me, please?"

He clenches his jaw. "I should see if he needs any help." Bo makes his way across the room but stops when he turns the door handle and it doesn't budge. He tugs and twists it. "It's locked."

I hop off the table. "From the outside?"

"That bastard locked us in here." Bo slams his fist against the door but it doesn't flex in the slightest.

"Let me try." I shove him out of the way.

"Yeah, like you're going to be able to get it if I can't."

I narrow my gaze at him. "Rude." I close my eyes and latch onto the handle, willing whatever power I have within me to rise to the surface.

But no amount of strength will get us through this door.

Sydney didn't *just* lock us in this room together, he sealed us in with magic.

"Well, I guess you can't run away like you always do." I stalk back over to the table and sit back on the crumbled paper.

"I don't run away." Bo crosses his arms over his chest.

"You do, too. Every time you almost say something that might actually let me know what's going through your thick skull, you bolt." I scoot farther onto the table and let my legs dangle over the edge. "What are you so afraid of?"

"I'm not afraid of anything." Bo stays near the door. "You don't know what you're talking about."

"Oh? I don't?" I let out a laugh. "At least Wes can't lie to me, and Dash has enough respect for me that he chooses not to."

"Is that what you want? Me to be more like Wes and Dash?" Bo throws up his arms. "That's never going to happen."

"I'm aware." I huff. "Angels forbid you have a shred of decency in you."

"Whatever."

"Whatever," I repeat.

We sit there in silence, my heart pattering in my chest the only sound I can make out.

I lie down on the table and stare at the ceiling of this unfamiliar yet sterile room.

How long will Sydney keep us in here? I can only imagine he did it on purpose, but why? Did he know something was going on between me and Bo? Or maybe it was Willow that could sense our tension based on what happened when we visited Balial's hell?

I recall the fear that coursed through me when I woke up and Bo wasn't in that room. He was there, his body, but not him, his soul. The part of him that matters the most. I had no way to get back to him and I was terrified that something had happened in those fleeting moments.

"I was worried about you," I admit.

"When?"

I chuckle. "Always. But I'm referring to when you stayed behind."

"Oh."

"What took you so long?"

Bo sighs. "Balial propositioned me."

I rise onto my elbows. "Sounds kinky."

"Pretty sure he's into Willow, not me."

"Pretty sure he's *obsessed* with Willow. But what did he want with you?"

Bo walks over, drags a chair across the floor, and sits in it backward, facing me. "He offered to remove the mark on your neck."

I sit completely up and return my legs over the edge of the table. "What?"

"Yep." Bo nods.

"I don't get it. Why do you act like that's a bad thing?" That's when it hits me. "What did he want in return?"

"My eternal allegiance."

"What does that mean?"

"He said he would do it in exchange for me staying in his realm. Permanently."

"That's not fucking happening," I tell him.

"It would get the beacon off your neck."

"And what good would that do me if you're stuck in fucking hell? I said no. It's my body, my choice. I'd rather keep the dreaded thing. Besides, didn't you say you can remove it yourself?"

Bo rubs his hand over his jaw. "It's worse than me being in hell, Birdie."

"I'll be the judge of that."

"No."

"Bo, so help me, Angels,...if you don't tell me what it is." I climb off the table and stand in front of him. "How bad could it be? No one has to die. You don't have to spend eternity with that creep of a man. And I wouldn't have the beacon anymore. I see zero downsides."

Bo looks up at me, his lip quivering in the slightest. "I won't do it to you, Birdie."

I grab his face and force him to keep his gaze on mine. "Tell me what it is, Bo. Tell me what you're afraid of."

"I can't."

I lean in closer, my breath mingling with his. Our noses graze and I realize this is the closest our faces have ever been. Despite our few intimate times together, he's never once kissed me.

"Please," I beg him. "What are you feeling right now?"

His intense stare bores into me. "I'm scared. Is that what you want to hear?"

"Bo," I whisper. "Why?"

"For the first time in my life, I feel vulnerable, torn apart at the seams. I finally have something, some*one* to lose that I cannot recover from." His voice is the quietest he's ever spoken. "I'm afraid that the only thing I'm good at is making you hate me, and I'd rather have you hate me than feel nothing at all. If you won't love me, at least you could hate me. I could live with that."

"Why would you ever think I couldn't love you when that's all I've been trying to do?"

"You don't mean it, not really." He reaches up to cup my face in his hand. "It's just the mark."

"I don't believe that." Tears fill my eyes. "This is why you keep pushing me away, because you think the only reason I like you is the mark connecting us?" I let out a laugh. "I was starting to think you actually hated me."

"Oh, Birdie." Bo grazes my cheek. "I could never hate you, not in any lifetime."

"Remove the mark then, please. And then I can show you that it has nothing to do with my feelings for you. Let me at least try to prove it to you."

Bo softly rocks his head back and forth. "The only way for me to rid you of that mark, is to..." His sullen gaze tugs at my heartstrings.

"What is it, Bo? What do we have to do? I'll do anything. Just tell me what it is."

"That's the thing, Birdie. I know you would. And so would I, that's why I can't."

"You have to help me understand, Bo. You're killing me. Is that what you want? To hurt me?"

"Never."

"Please, I need to know."

"I have to replace it."

"I don't understand. Replace it with what?" I scan his features, desperate to find the answer he keeps hidden from me.

"With a fated mate mark."

I blink and register his words. "I..."

"I won't do that to you," he tells me. "I won't take away your right to choose."

"My right to choose? Isn't that what you're doing now?" A single tear rolls down my cheek. "You dislike me so much that you refuse to be with me? You'd rather go be in hell with Balial than be stuck with me because of some mark?"

"That isn't what I said." Bo rises from his seat, his stature towering over me.

"Then explain it to me." I wipe my face and sniffle. "Why won't you do it?"

"Because Wren, don't you get it? There's no going back from a fated mate mark. Ask yourself this, could you walk away from Wes?"

"Well, no. I wouldn't do that."

"Wouldn't, or couldn't? There's a difference there. It's one thing to be with a person because you *want* to, and it's another to be forced to be with someone because of the mark. I don't want you to be with me because you have no choice in the matter. How do you not realize that I can't be selfish with you? As much as it fucking kills me. As much as I want nothing more than to give in to every fucking desire I have to make you mine, I withstand that urge because it's not fair to you. Wes may not have had the willpower to withstand it, but I do. And I won't do that to you."

"You think...you think the only reason Wes and I are together is because of the mate bond?"

"Can you honestly tell me otherwise?"

"I...I'm not fated to Dash, and I want to be with him."

Bo sighs. "It's Dash. He's the perfect guy. He's the one you should be with. Not me. Not Wes."

"You want me to choose?"

Bo puts his large hands on my shoulders. "I want you to *have* the choice, Wren."

"Then I choose all of you."

"You don't get it. Not when your head is clouded with the marks. And the only way I can make you see what it's doing to you is to take Balial up on his offer."

I take a step back. "You're going to say yes?"

"I have no other choice, Birdie."

"So you get to make the decision for me, under the pretense that you're doing what's best for me? That's not fair and you know it."

"This is the only way."

"No. I refuse to accept that."

"I already told you...I can live with you hating me."

"If you leave me, you can guarantee that I will."

"If that's what it takes, Birdie. I'd give you that."

"That's not what I want, Bo." My shoulders tense and my hands ball into fists. "You'd rather leave me than face the possibility that we might have actually had a chance." I turn on my heel and march away from him and toward the door. I grip the handle and yank with all my might. It's strong and the hold is firm but it's no match to how fucking determined I am to get away from him.

CHAPTER 17

Wren

Bo ignores me more than I ignore him.

He sleeps in the chair in our bedroom but doesn't come in until he's convinced I'm already asleep.

I'm not.

No, I stay up all night, unable to fall into a slumber, and I consider what I could have done to make him prefer spending eternity in a hell dimension instead of staying here as my mate.

He says he's doing it to give me a choice in the matter, but what actual choice has he allowed me?

Is life in Balial's realm more appealing to him than staying in Arthlia? I wouldn't be surprised if that would be the case, but is he really ready to give Wes, Dash, and Jade up, too?

Jade will remain with Everest, wherever they end up—that much is given.

Wes and I won't leave each other, and Dash doesn't seem like he's wanting to go off on his own. The only person hanging in the balance is Bo, and he's made his decision to accept Balial's offer.

The thought of him leaving cuts like a hot knife through my chest. How did I go from wanting to end his life when we first met to not being able to imagine a world without him?

Is leaving that easy for him?

Wes and Dash sleep soundly at both of my sides. Wes with his arm thrown over my stomach, and Dash with his freckled face buried in his pillow.

Carefully, I peel Wes off me and sit up.

He stirs but goes right back into his peaceful slumber.

Without making a sound, I scoot from under the covers and inch to the foot of the bed. Then, I hop over and onto the floor.

I hug the loose sweater around my chest and tiptoe through the room, the door creaking on my way out and almost giving me up. The hall is quiet and desolate, and it welcomes me with its solitude. My footsteps silently descend the stairs, and once I'm at the bottom, I release the breath I had been holding. Sydney's house is vast and has an eerie ambiance to it that only comes with the memories of something terrible.

Growing up the way that I did, I'm familiar with tragedy.

Every single person in this house has their own trauma.

Maybe that's why we get along, because we share in the agony of what our past has dealt us. The real test is what we choose to do with our suffering. We can inflict that same pain on others in an attempt to settle the score, or we can overcome the hardships we've experienced.

Dash is a perfect example of someone who perseveres despite everything that's happened to him. And Bo and I are the opposite, we have taken our past and allowed it to shape us into the murderous psychopaths we are today.

I want to do better. Be better. But it's hard when that innate desire to kill still remains.

At least now I've channeled it into wanting to end Parla and free Prania from her hold.

But how will I be successful if I'm here, in Arthlia?

My entire life, I've never thought it was possible to escape Prania. People talked about it in hushed conversations or drunken moments. It was a fever dream that could never come true. Yet I am living proof that there is more out there than the forsaken remnants of my homeland.

"Couldn't sleep?" His deep voice nearly makes me jump out of my skin.

"No." I shut the fridge, empty-handed, and consider snatching a banana off the counter. I don't. "You?"

Bo leans there in the doorway, his arms crossed over his chest. The grey sweatpants he's wearing leave little to the imagination. "No."

I stalk toward him with every intention to go right by and back up the stairs.

"Can we talk?" he says when I'm inches from him.

I pause in the doorway but don't look up at his ruggedly handsome face. "Now you want to talk?"

"Yes."

"What's left to say, Bo?"

He slams his hand up on the doorframe, caging me between it and him. Bo takes his other hand to grip my jaw and tilt my head toward him. His dark gaze darts between mine like he's trying to say something without words.

But doesn't he know I can't read his fucking mind?

"You don't get it, do you?" he whispers.

I swallow at his nearness—his breath that kisses my cheek. "Explain it to me."

His thumb grazes my bottom lip. He leans in closer and inhales, his eyes widening. "You're bleeding."

"What? No, I'm not." I turn my hands over in front of me and examine my arms. "I'm fine."

Bo drops to his knees, his hands on my hips. He drags his nose over my crotch. "Birdie." He stares at me through his thick, dark lashes. "I want to taste you." Bo clutches the sides of my bottoms. "I need you to stop me."

But how can I do that when it goes against every desire consuming me?

"No," I tell him. "I won't."

"You're giving me permission?" The defiant alpha doesn't move, not even when I nod. "I need you to say it, Birdie."

"You have permission."

His chest rises and falls dramatically, and he yanks my sweats over my ass, along with my panties, exposing me to anyone who might walk by. Bo inches closer and grinds his nose against me, only this time, I'm no longer covered by clothing. "Fuck," he moans.

My body gravitates toward him, a traitor to the early version of me who was trying to avoid the man who would rather abandon me. But it's the furthest thing on my mind when he's swirling his long, split tongue over my clit and dipping it into me.

I've never been one to shy away from a little action while on my cycle, but no one has ever practically begged to go down on me while I was actively bleeding.

And never in a million years did I think I would be *this* turned on by it.

Bo grips the back of my legs and digs his fingers in. His claws prickle but do not quite penetrate my flesh. Only a small taste of the pain heightens my already rising pleasure.

I shouldn't give in to him, but it's hard when he's this fucking tempting.

"Birdie," he breathes against me. "I don't think I can..." With my fingers weaved through his hair, he glances up at me in the dimly lit space. "I want you so fucking bad."

"Then what are you waiting for?" I nearly pant in anticipation for him to keep going.

"I'm afraid I won't be able to restrain myself." He licks at his lips. "You taste... divine."

"I trust you," I tell him, the words surprising me probably more than they do him.

"You shouldn't."

"That isn't going to stop me."

Just when I think he might actually end things, he moves forward and presses his lips to mine. His tongue darts out, coating and swirling and tasting every drop of me. His fangs gently scrape my skin, and I do everything I can to remain upright and not melt into a puddle on the fucking floor.

"Angels," I moan and spread myself wider to give him better access.

He slides my leg over his shoulder and cups my ass with his large hand, pulling me closer. Bo takes his hand and slides his finger along my soaked entrance.

With no warning, I climax the second he pushes into me, my orgasm rattling through me and shattering on his hungry mouth. I bite down on my lip to suppress my moans as he laps me up.

He keeps going, long after the tremors have stopped. Bo shoves another finger inside of me, the width of him spreading me open. My core tightens and my pleasure builds under his influence again.

He rocks himself deeper inside of me and tilts his grasp up, hitting me in just the right spot to send sparks flying in my eyes. I whimper and thrust my hips against him.

Heat swells between my legs, and I can no longer withstand the sudden urge to come yet another time. It's no surprise that I'm hornier than usual when I'm on my cycle, but Bo seems to know his way around my body better than I do.

Better than anyone else ever has.

How infuriating that it's him, though, when he would rather leave than be with me.

Bo slows his movement and draws out his hand. He licks every bit of me off his fingers before rising to his feet, pulling my bottoms up on his way. He towers over me, his dark gaze melting into mine.

"I'm still mad at you," I say.

"I know."

"This doesn't change anything."

"I know."

I want to yank him by the collar, pull him toward me, and kiss him, while also wanting to slap his face and shove him away. Both equally vying for my attention. But I do neither. Instead, I stand here, desperately wishing for things to be different. For him to see me for who I am and what I have to offer and accept that maybe the possibility of a future together is something worth fighting for. That will never happen though, and if I've learned anything from Bo, it's that changing his mind once he's made it is an impossible feat.

But considering we started out as complete enemies, maybe hope isn't entirely lost.

"You didn't kill me," I announce.

"I guess I have more control than I thought I did." His tongue glides across his lips. "That doesn't mean I didn't want more, though."

I recall the first moment we met. Bo had rushed toward me and sank his fangs into my neck, marking and solidifying our connection. I was lightheaded but a euphoric feeling coursed through me, and I'd be lying if I said I hadn't missed that strange and unfamiliar sensation. There was something incredibly intimate about his fangs penetrating my flesh and my blood pooling in his mouth. I never understood the appeal of the blood sharing we were taught about in our training, but now, the attraction is very much there.

I want Bo to drink from me.

No, I *need* Bo to drink from me. The desire is far too visceral to be a simple want.

Does he have any idea just how badly I want to be entangled in him? Body and soul.

Maybe it's the mark making me crave him that much more, but whatever it is, no amount of hate for him will deter me from not giving up. I have every reason to put that final boundary between us and call the death of our relationship before it's even begun, but I can't bring myself to stop chasing after something that I think, deep down, he really wants, too.

I skim my fingers over the scar on my neck. "Do you want to bite me?"

"No."

"Are you lying?" I move my hair off my shoulder and expose the area to him.

He clenches his jaw. "No."

I tilt toward him. "You know you want to."

"Wren." He uses my name like a threat but it doesn't have the impact he wants.

No, it only tells me just how badly I'm getting under his skin.

I grab his hand and force his fingertips over the mark. "Just a little taste."

Bo snarls, his fangs showing. His gaze flits to my neck, to my eyes, and back down. "I can't." He pauses and adds, "I shouldn't."

I stand a bit taller and tug him toward me. "What's the worst that could happen?"

"I could kill you."

I shrug. "I'm not scared." At this point, I'd say anything to get him to follow through.

"You should be." A low growl leaves Bo before he leans down and presses his lips around the scar. He hesitates for what feels like an eternity, and my flesh snaps as he sinks his teeth into my neck.

Ecstasy cascades through me, and immediately, I feel faint.

His strong hold keeps me upright as my blood flows into his mouth. There is no agony, just sheer pleasure of his intimate nearness. I melt into him and bask in this moment for fear that it will end too quickly. That maybe *I* will end too quickly. But death isn't what scares me. No. What I fear is losing this moment with him. Not experiencing it fully. I'm overwhelmed with wanting it to last, to slow time and be here, in this temporary heaven with him.

Bo bites down harder, his teeth penetrating me deeper.

I grow cold despite his warm embrace. I need to feel him. To be enveloped by his entire existence and allow him to swallow me fucking whole.

Both literally and meta-fucking-phorically

I don't want him to stop, not now, not ever. If this is what it takes to be close to him, I'll take whatever I can get. Even if it results in my death. Because what is love without a little sacrifice?

Bo releases me quickly, his gaze frantic as it scans my face. "Birdie," he breathes, the scent of my blood lingering. "Oh Angels, what have I done?"

My body, still and paralyzed, remains in his grasp. I part my lips but nothing comes out.

I am weak, tired, but so content.

"Fuck," he blurts out. "What have I done?" Bo scoops me into his arms, lifting me from the floor. He rushes out of the room and up the stairs.

His jaw tenses, his face so fucking beautiful from this angle. He holds me tighter than he ever has.

Bo darts through the doorway of our shared bedroom and rushes over to the bed.

My heavy eyes close, and there isn't anything I can do to keep them open. Here, I am home in his embrace.

"What's wrong?" Wes mumbles, his presence growing near, too. "What the fuck did you do to her?"

"I...I..." Bo lowers me onto the mattress where Wes must have just risen from.

I tuck into myself and lie there, still and blissful.

Don't they see that their concern is misplaced? There is nothing wrong.

Wes leans in. "Wren, baby. Can you hear me?"

"Mmhm," I mumble.

His voice grows quiet but more intense. "I'm going to fucking murder you."

"I didn't mean to," Bo responds with a hint of concern unlike I've ever known from him.

"Stop arguing," I manage to spit out. "I asked for it."

"What's going on?" Dash says sleepily.

"Be quiet," Wes snaps.

I try to sit up but my body won't seem to cooperate with any of my normal commands. Everything is somehow heavy and light, all at once, and no matter what I do, I can't get anything to function properly. What I'd really like is to fall asleep— to drift off into the abyss and savor this decadent release from reality I'm consumed by.

Wes comes toward me, his lips hovering next to my face. He moves lower, mumbling something I cannot make out, and then comes closer again. "Come back to me." He lets out a soft breath. "Give me your pain. I accept your suffering. Allow me to carry that burden."

But what he doesn't understand is I'm not in pain. And the suffering I'm experiencing isn't physical. It's something internal I can't quite get my hands on. It's discouragement mixed with helplessness at not knowing how to fix everything I've broken.

If I could end Parla, maybe I could make things right. But until then, how can I play pretend that anything is okay? People are dying and it's my fault. I gave her too much power, and she ate up every bit of it.

Even with Bo's euphoric venom coursing through me, I can't ignore the truth of what's really happening. That I must kill her if I stand a chance at ever moving forward in this life. No matter the distance between Prania and Arthlia, I cannot escape or forget what she's doing.

And when I regain the strength to control my bodily functions, I open my eyes and declare the one thing I cannot get off my mind, "I must murder Parla."

"You're okay." Wes tucks my hair behind my ear, his eyes glowing softly as he watches me intensely. "You're going to be okay."

"I have to kill her, Wes. There's no other way."

"Shh." He's soft and gentle despite his dominating exterior. "You should rest."

I sit up in my attempt to convince him that I'm fine. "I'm not joking, Wes," I say with a bit more conviction. I shift my focus to Bo, who remains like a statue, secured in place with a concern still lining his brow. "I'm going back, I have to go back."

"To Prania?" Bo speaks, his voice strained.

"You're not going back there," Wes says.

But I don't look at him, I keep my gaze on Bo, because he might be the only other one in this room that truly understands how fucking badly I hate Parla. Regardless of our differences, at least we have a common enemy.

"I'm with you, Birdie." Bo takes a small step forward, almost like he's testing the distance between us.

"This is not up for discussion tonight." Wes turns toward Bo. "You need to watch your mouth."

Bo crosses his arms over his chest, the one that I had been pressed against not too long ago. "Don't tell me what to do."

"I shouldn't have to, Bo. You're a fucking adult. But here I am, cleaning up yet another one of your messes. You're a child and you must be stopped." Wes stands from the bed and positions himself between me and Bo.

"Guys, come on." Dash yawns and pushes himself onto his butt. "Is this really necessary?"

"Yes," Wes and Bo mouth off at the same time.

I scoot off the bed, throwing my legs over the side, the weight of them heavier than I remember them being. With Bo's venom no doubt still in my body, the effects of his bite linger.

Bo reaches toward me, but Wes shoves his arms away.

"Don't touch her." Wes's hound side surfaces, his entire body glowing. "You have no self-control."

Bo laughs loudly. "Are you fucking serious? I don't? Who's the asshole who fucking marked her because he couldn't keep it in his pants?" He steps dangerously close to Wes, not daring to back down from him. "You're a coward. You couldn't fathom the idea of her not choosing you so you took that choice away from her."

"Did not." Wes pushes his torso against Bo's.

Bo shoves into Wes. "Selfish prick."

Wes burns brighter, his fiery self becoming more present.

"I'm not afraid of you." Bo stares directly at Wes. "You want to burn me, burn me. Doesn't change what you did."

I slide off the bed, wedging my weak body between them. "Both of you"—I look briefly at each of them—"need to grow up." I push past them and march toward the door, not bothering to look behind and witness whether they've decided to murder each other.

Crossing the threshold, a chill washes over me, and my attention locks onto the small opening in the doorway across the hall. A shadow appears in the illuminated space, his body moving around the door to come into view. "My apologies," he says. "I was having trouble sleeping and heard the commotion."

"It's fine." I fold my arms over my chest and stand there, a few feet away from him.

He remains in his room because that's his only option. Tremont cannot escape the confines of that small space—not until Sydney decides what he's going to do with him.

Tremont doesn't seem bothered by it. Mostly, it's as though he's accepted his fate and realized there's nothing that can be done to rid him of this confinement. He hasn't begged for his release or tried to convince anyone to let him out. He takes the food Sydney brings him and leaves the empty plates in the doorway. The room he's in has a bathroom and more accommodations than Rockbridge, so he hasn't exactly lacked in comfort at all.

After having endured what he has, I'm not convinced I would put up much of a fight either. Especially knowing how similar our paths were. He's not in the wrong for feeling defeated. There's a part of me that pities him, but I recognize that's the same part of me that wishes there was a way to make amends for what I have done. Perhaps I wouldn't sympathize with him as much had I not realized that my heroic acts only turned me into the villain in someone else's story.

"I don't blame you for wanting to go back," he says.

"How much did you hear?" I ask him.

"Enough."

I nod and avert my gaze while remembering the conversation. My head is still fuzzy, and I'm going to need to sleep off the venom high, but one thing is certain, I wasn't lying when I said I needed to kill Parla. It's the only scenario where contentment remotely finds me. Every other alternative leaves me with a sinking pit in my stomach.

"I don't know how I'll get there," I admit. Cross-realm travel wasn't in the teachings during my hunter training, and until recently, I had no knowledge of the hidden magic within me. I'll have to consult Sydney and see if he is willing to assist me on my final assassination mission.

Dash joins me in the hallway, his body gently pressed behind me. He rubs gentle circles on my shoulders, and it melts away some of the tension overwhelming me. "Hey, you." He kisses the side of my face.

"Evening." Tremont nods to Dash.

"Sir." Dash's manners have no bounds.

Tremont focuses back on me, his gaze strangely more serious than before. "When you're ready, I can help you." He pauses only slightly and then disappears back into his prison.

"What was that all about?" Dash continues skimming his arms over my biceps.

"Nothing," I lie and weave my fingers through his. "I'm going downstairs. Want to come?"

"Duh." He yawns and swoops the hair off his brow with his free hand. "You know I'd go anywhere with you."

I don't respond, not when my mind runs wild at the possibility that maybe Dash could come with me to Prania. It's not that I want to put him in danger, but if he *is* a phoenix, what's the harm in having someone who supports me there? I'm not particularly sold on inviting either Wes or Bo, and after everything that's happened to Jade, I would never ask her to return to such a place. Sydney and his family have been gracious, but I could never put them in danger, not in the way that Prania would. It's not their fight and it would be careless of me to involve them any more than I already have.

Dash and I walk down the stairs, the creaking of his steps a bit louder than mine.

It isn't until we're in the large living room some distance from the kitchen that I finally speak. "Would you ever go back to Prania?" Relaxing into the couch, I turn toward Dash, who settles in, too, opposite of me.

Dash sucks in a breath and exhales. "I mean, I can't say it sounds very enticing. I didn't exactly fit in, but I'd be lying if I said I felt like I fit in anywhere. Why? Is that why you've been on edge lately? You want to return to your homeland?"

"I've been on edge? How so?"

"I don't know." Dash extends his arm over the back of the couch and finds my hand. He swirls his finger along my skin. "Nothing major. I've just felt it. Something different. A shift. A sort of unspoken internal struggle. Whatever it is, you can tell me. Or you don't have to. That's okay, too."

"Dash..."

"I hope you don't think that's weird. I care about you, so I notice things."

My heart constricts. "It's not weird. It's...unfamiliar. I've never had someone look out for me before. Not the way you do."

Dash forces a smile. "I don't plan on stopping, so get used to it."

"How are you, Dash?" It's my turn to focus on him for a chance. He's been going through his own things lately, and I've been consumed with my own bullshit that I haven't checked in. "How's your back?"

"It's fine. I'm fine. Don't worry about me."

I narrow my gaze. "Look at you being all evasive."

Dash chuckles and his eyes sparkle with that beautiful Dash-like twinkle. "I'm good, sweetheart." He leans in closer and kisses my hand. "When are we leaving?"

I blink at him. "What?"

"You want to go back. When are we leaving?"

"To Prania?"

He nods stiffly.

"Oh. I—I would never ask that of you." Even though having him there with me would be equal parts great and terrible. I don't want to put him in danger, but there is a silver lining to his phoenix abilities. Perhaps I'm being selfish for desiring his presence.

"You're not asking, I'm offering. I want to go with you. I want to be there.

Whatever you need. I'll be there for you." He pauses and adds, "Do you plan to stay, or is it something more short-term?"

I let out a breath I hadn't realized I had been holding. "I have to kill her," I whisper, the declaration barely audible.

"I understand," he says.

"You do?"

"What she did to you, to Wes, to Jade, to everyone in that realm—it was wrong. She deserves to be punished. Death is too kind for what she deserves."

I would love to torture her. To make her pay with every ounce of pain I could potentially inflict. But the only sure way to stop Parla from hurting anyone else is to slide a blade straight through her cold heart.

"Tremont said he could help," I admit.

"Do you trust him?"

"Not really. But he got us here, didn't he?"

"Why not ask Sydney or Willow?"

I shake my head. "I don't want to bother them any more than I already have. They've done enough. More than enough, really. This isn't their battle."

"Well, I support whatever decision you make." He sighs and leans back, extending his arm to invite me toward him. "In the meantime."

I smile softly and scoot into his embrace, the warmth of him swallowing me whole and encasing me in a sea of comfort.

He drags the blanket off the back of the couch and covers us up. Dash kisses my forehead. "Get some rest, we'll come up with a plan in the morning."

Everything might be up in the air, but at least I can count on Dash to be with me to see things through.

I just hope going back to Prania, especially with Dash, isn't a grave mistake.

I would never forgive myself if something happened to him.

CHAPTER 18
Dash

"And you're sure we'll be back by tonight? I told Willow I would help her." Wren asks Tremont from her spot leaning against the wall in Tremont's bedroom.

According to the information Wren gave me, she did some kind of test to determine that her blood was a close enough match to Willow's to ensure that she could act as Willow to help take some things that only Willow could do off her plate. Supposedly they are not threatening in any capacity, just time-consuming when Willow has many obligations to maintain. Wren was eager and willing to help.

"Yes," Tremont tells her. "If you haven't returned on your own, I will pull you out myself."

"I don't like this," Bo announces.

But Bo doesn't exactly ever like anything, so it comes as no surprise he's not thrilled about me and Wren taking a quick trip to Prania without him.

Wren side-eyes him briefly but doesn't give him any more attention than that. "What do you need me to do?"

"You and Dash need to lie down and hold hands. You'll have to open yourself up to me again. Do you remember what that was like back in Prania? It gives me access to your magic. I won't need much since this is simply astral projection, but it will make penetrating the barrier into Prania easier than with my magic alone."

She nods. "Okay, yeah. I can do that." Wren tilts her head in my direction. "You ready for this?"

"I am if you are."

Wren makes her way over to Wes, who has remained quiet through this whole interaction. She stands taller and presses a kiss to his cheek. "I'll see you soon."

Wes wraps his arms around her and tugs her toward him. "I'm not a huge fan of this either," he whispers to her. "So hurry back."

Wren didn't want Bo to come, mostly because she wants the alpha beacon to engage. I'm sure it had something to do with their constant disagreements, too. And with Wes's immense authority, it was too much for Tremont to manage, leaving me as the most viable choice. I kept it to myself that I had already asked Wren about coming with her in my attempt to not make them feel any less important than they really are to her.

I might be aware that she's capable of caring for us all, but that doesn't mean they've wrapped their heads around it yet.

Bo exhales dramatically and storms out of the room.

Wes points to Tremont. "I'll make you suffer if something happens to her."

Tremont nods. "I'd expect nothing less."

"Keep an eye on him," Wren tells Wes.

"I will." He pecks her lips quickly with his and leaves in the same direction Bo had gone in just moments prior.

Wren makes her way toward the center of the room, lowers herself onto the rug on the floor, and pats the spot next to her. "Let's do this."

I follow her over, repeating the same movement, and lie next to her. Weaving my fingers through hers, I close my eyes and wait for what comes next.

"Just relax," Tremont says. He mumbles a few words under his breath, the language unknown.

Wren holds me tighter and rubs her thumb along my hand.

Tremont continues chanting and within another few seconds, it's like I'm being sucked into a vacuum and spit out.

The air is thicker, heavier, and filled with a stench I had hoped I'd never smell again.

"We made it," Wren declares while rising to a sitting position.

I blink through the dense fog and take in my surroundings. It's familiar and foreign all at once. Most of Prania looks the same with its murky atmosphere and lack of lighting. It's nothing like Arthlia.

"What's the plan again?" I ask her, the details of it blurring in my head now that we're actually here.

"Everest said there's a group of insurgents in the north that we could rally. The goal is to make contact with them." Wren pulls a compass out of her pocket. The little dial moves and rocks, but then settles itself into position. "This way." She rises to her feet and reaches down.

I latch onto her and allow her to help me up. "Thanks."

"Of course." She presses her fingers to the wound on her neck. The one that was reopened last night. "It's hot so I'm guessing it's on."

"Are you in pain?" I hadn't considered what else that mark entailed outside of it alerting demons to her whereabouts. Perhaps I would have been more hesitant about Bo not coming along had I known it would cause her pain.

"No," she says. "It's fine."

The same thing I had said to her when she asked me how I was yesterday.

I wasn't lying, but I wasn't telling the truth either.

Is that what she's doing now?

I couldn't have answered her truthfully even if I wanted to. I don't know how to explain how I am. Nothing is technically wrong. But I keep having these vivid nightmares that feel more like long-forgotten memories than dreams. Some of them cause actual physical discomfort, and some tear at my heartstrings more than others. They've made me question reality a bit more, but overall, it isn't anything I can't handle on my own. Wren has enough going on, and my bad night's sleep is nothing she should concern herself with.

"You still have the button Tremont made for you, right?" Wren dusts her legs off and examines the compass again.

"Yeah, do you?"

She pats her pocket and nods. "This way." Wren navigates us through the wooded area we're surrounded by.

A chill creeps up my back at how strangely eerie and quiet it is here.

Prania has never been a place of much commotion, but generally, there are other demons or hunters making some kind of noise.

We walk side by side for a few minutes, our footsteps crinkling against the ground. Wren's are softer than mine—her stealth hunter nature doing what it can to conceal her presence.

I do what I can to match her movements, but I'd need years of training to be as sly as her.

"What if we come across demons first?" I whisper.

"We reason with them." She continues forward. "There will be no more demon bloodshed."

I never thought I'd see the day when a hunter as fierce as Wren would put a stop to the unjust killings. This life is all I've known and for my entire time in Prania, there wasn't a single hunter that didn't want to kill either of my friends. And they would have done the same to me the second they found out I wasn't on their side. There was no reasoning with them. The only thing they were capable of was ending demons and nothing else.

Wren throws her arm out in front of me, stopping dead in her tracks. Her intense gaze meets mine, a silent warning to not make a sound. She looks past me, turns her head, and stares behind her. "Something is coming," she mutters enough for me to hear.

I barely have time to blink when a blur flashes across my vision, tackling Wren to the ground many feet away from where she just was.

Her scream pierces through my chest, and I can't possibly move fast enough to get to her.

A large, off-white wolf-like creature pins her to the ground, its teeth snapping at her neck as she holds it off the best she can. She keeps her arms extended and her head to the side to avoid its ferocious bite.

I run toward her and do the only thing I can think of—I leap toward it, hoping the weight of my blow will knock it off her and give her a chance to escape. The beast can tear me to shreds but I refuse to allow it to hurt another hair on her beautiful head.

I throw my arms around the wolf's torso and pull with all my might.

The two of us spin and hit the ground hard, dust flying up around us.

"Run!" I yell at Wren before the thing tosses me aside and sets its sights back on her.

It bears down, scraping at the dirt with its claws as it snarls at her, its mouth salivating.

Wren throws up her arms. "I'm not here to harm you. Please see that."

But this creature does not care; it wants to end her life.

I gasp for breath and rise to my feet, scurrying quickly to position myself between her and the animal. But it's no use, the thing leaps toward her at a rate faster than I could ever manage.

I watch in horror, her arms lowering and shielding herself from impact. But the impact never comes.

Seconds before the thing makes contact, another creature barrels through the clearing and slams into the wolf's side, tossing it away. Just when I think the worst has yet to come, Wren's savior turns toward her and releases a heavy breath.

"What are you doing here?" the familiar person asks.

Wren takes her in, her eyes scanning the dull-blue woman standing in front of her. "Pippa," Wren sighs and throws her arms around the person. "You're alive."

Pippa hugs Wren back, her trunk wrapping around Wren's small torso. "Barely."

Wren releases her and holds her at an arm's length. "Where's Lo?" She scans the direction Pippa just came.

Pippa slowly shakes her head. "He didn't make it."

The wolf that Pippa tackled whimpers and struggles to get to its feet.

I rush over, my sights settling on the claw marks on Wren's arm. "You're hurt."

Wren shrugs, not at all bothered by the bleeding wound. "It's fine."

No doubt another lie. But because things could have been a lot worse, I decide to let it go for now.

I rip at the bottom of my shirt until I've pulled off a long, thin strip of fabric. Without Wren's consent, I secure it around her biceps to stop the continued bleeding. Wes can tend to it once we have returned home.

"I'm so sorry, Pippa," Wren tells her but glances over at the wolf. "Who's the mutt?"

"That's Gary. He's a bit of a hot head." Pippa points to her neck but looks at Wren's. "That thing is sending out a massive signal."

Wren grazes her fingers over it briefly. "Yeah. That was kind of the point. I guess I just didn't think it through fully." She scans Pippa's dirty face. "What's stopping you from tearing me apart?"

Pippa forces a smile and reaches out to touch Wren's shoulder. "I know you're not the enemy."

Wren puts her hand on top of Pippa's. "I just need to convince the rest of the demonic population of that, too."

Pippa steps in front of Wren when Gary saunters over. "I'll snap your neck if you touch her again." Pippa glances behind her. "I owe Wren my life, and if you're going to make me cash that in today," she turns back toward the wolf. "Then so be it."

Gary whimpers and lowers his fur-covered head in submission.

"Fill me in," Wren tells Pippa. "What's happened since I saw you last?" Wren glances down at her compass. "Mind if we walk this way while we talk?"

"Sure." Pippa steps past Gary but remains at Wren's side.

I lead up the rear, keeping myself between Wren and her attacker. I won't be too much of a diversion, but maybe it'll be enough to allow Pippa to save Wren if Gary decides to go after her again.

"Things have worsened," Pippa says. "Many demons were killed in that poison fog at Rockbridge. Those of us that escaped sought refuge together, but it wasn't long until Parla and her soldiers sniffed us out. It was like she could track us somehow."

"I wonder if she put trackers in the prisoners without their knowledge. Or slipped something into the food. We had to eat at some point, so it would almost guarantee that she could slip it into our system."

"There's no telling but I wouldn't be surprised." Pippa steps over a log and continues walking. "They keep taking us out. One by one. It won't be long before they've won." She laughs dryly and puts her hands out in front of her. "What a prize."

Wren lets out a breath. "She's sick and twisted. Parla won't stop until she's killed every last person who disagrees with her way of life." She glances over at Pippa. "Speaking of, where can I find her?"

Pippa's shoulders rise and fall. "Beats me. I tend to try to avoid her. You know, the whole self-preservation thing."

"Understandable."

"Where have you been hiding out?"

Wren flits her attention back at me before opening her mouth to speak. "Arthlia."

Pippa stops and I nearly run into her. "That's impossible."

Wren pauses, too. "It's not. We left the day after Rockbridge. We've been there about a week."

"A week? Honey, the last I saw you was over a month ago."

"A month?" Wren meets my gaze.

Pippa points to the compass. "Where are you heading?"

"North. I was told there's a group of rebels hiding out that we could align with."

"There isn't much left of the north. It's a wasteland."

I swallow the lump that forms in my throat. There's already been so much loss, when will it ever stop?

"I have to try." Wren continues moving in the direction we came here for. "If we can get help, maybe some intel, we can eliminate her."

"Is that why you came back? To kill her?"

Wren nods. "I never meant to abandon you." She moves a branch out of the way and walks past it, holding it long enough for me to latch on before it snaps me in the face. "I would have come sooner if I could have."

"If it's been a month, there's no telling when he'll pull us back. We may have more time than we think," I tell her.

"What do you mean?" Pippa asks.

"We're not actually here," Wren explains. "We're astral projecting. Our physical bodies are on Arthlia. This was an impromptu recon mission."

"You appear here."

"Yeah, I don't really understand how it works. I didn't think I could get hurt, either, and well..." Wren holds out her arm. "This blood is very much mine."

"And that alpha beacon is very much engaged, too."

"That I knew would happen. When I traveled to Balial's hell dimension, it went off."

"You went where?" Pippa's footsteps thunder against the ground.

I thought I was the loud one, but mine are whispers compared to hers. Gary doesn't seem to make much noise but I'm not that thrilled about that considering I can't tell how far or near he is to me at any given time unless I'm looking right at him.

"According to Balial, Prania was sealed off ages ago to keep Parla contained. If I can kill her, maybe they'll reopen the realm and those that remain can be set free."

"Why didn't they just kill her themselves if they were capable of sealing off a whole realm?" Pippa asks the same question we all wondered, too.

"She kept evading them. It made the most sense for them to do what they did. Can't say I agree with their methods, but apparently, it was for the greater good. She had planned on eliminating all demonic creatures, no matter how big or small their demonic nature was."

"Sick bitch," Pippa says.

"She has to be stopped." Wren pauses and puts out her arm before pressing her index finger to her lips. Her gaze flits to each one of us, even the wolf that attacked her. "This way," she mouths.

We follow her slowly into a bit of overgrown shrubbery. She kneels on the ground and peers through an opening.

I step closer to her and look for myself, noting the smoking structure ahead of us.

A group of at least six soldiers surveys the place. All wearing identical outfits with matching buzz cuts. I recall walking into hunter territory and stealing those provisions, not entirely sure if I would make it out of there alive. I escaped with more than my life and almost lost it again moments later. Bo and I struggled to stay alive while trapped in Rockbridge's territory, but we did everything we could to rescue Wes and Wren from that hellish prison. Even if that meant bombing the place until we could locate them.

Nothing felt as good as seeing her across that field, and the second I wrapped my arms around her, I knew I never wanted to lose her again. Bo experienced it, too, and even though he denies his feelings for her every chance he gets, I'm certain he was just as concerned about her as I was when she was locked away.

My sights adjust to another person that walks out of the building ahead. A woman, middle-aged, with clothing unlike anything other women wear. It's too formal, too rigid, and too uncomfortable looking. Something in my chest tugs, and my stomach turns over.

"That fucking bitch," Wren whispers but doesn't move toward her. She might be hot-headed, but she's rational, and marching herself up there right now would not be the safest thing to do. Wren wants to make sure she succeeds in her mission, not fail before she even gets started.

"I'd love to…" Pippa doesn't continue her sentence but leaves the rest to our imagination. There's no denying what it is she'd like to have said.

Gary growls low and his furry shoulder rubs against me.

I glance down at him, the strange urge to pat his fluffy head is strong. But I deny my urge in fear that he'll bite my entire arm off. I might be a phoenix who can be reborn in death, but I'm not sold on my limbs regenerating. If I'm not mistaken, my body does no supernatural healing aside from bringing me back from the dead. Which explains the scars on my back that are only visible to me when I look in the mirror. I would have never known they existed had Wes and Bo not seen them. They don't hurt, at least, they didn't, not until recently. Lately, though, they've been aching like they're fresh. It makes no sense at all.

But as I stare through the haze at the woman in the distance, something inside me tugs at the seams.

"Leave no survivors," she orders the soldiers around her. "And then clear out."

Her voice floats back to me, smacking me dead in the chest.

I avert my gaze and try to recall a memory that's been hidden from me.

It's right there, but just out of reach. That outfit. That voice. That cruel demeanor.

"What's she doing?" Pippa whispers, drawing my attention to the unfamiliar yet familiar woman.

"Knowing Parla…something nefarious." Wren sighs and waits for the scene to unfold.

I can only imagine how hard it is for her to not run out there and drive a knife straight through her heart. Or maybe she would snap her neck in one swift movement. Regardless, Wren came here to see Parla's death through, and being this close to her without acting on it is a difficulty that is not lost on me. I press my palm against her shoulder in an attempt to reassure her that I understand and that I am here for her.

And when the time is right, I will stand by her side to see this through.

A portal appears in front of Parla, green and blue with hints of shimmering orange.

In my state of distraction, I don't notice the figure that towers over me from behind, the one that latches its grimy hand over my mouth and yanks me a few feet away. I gasp but it's no use, the sound is muffled under the clutch of this thing holding me hostage.

Wren spins on her heel and crouches down, her mesmerizing eyes going wide. She's frozen in place, like her mind is trying to run possible scenarios through her head and decide which of them has the best outcome.

I try to shake my head, to tell her not to act, but I can barely move.

I'm brought back to when the wendigo had taken me from her once before. Sheer panic coursed through me at the idea of never seeing her again. I'm not sure who was more surprised upon my rising from those ashes, me or my loved ones. Either way, I was thankful that I wasn't a complete anomaly of this world. That finally, I fit in. Even if my only magical trait is dying.

I recall the rancid smell of his grasp, the one matching that of the thing holding onto me now.

It groans, the sound matching that of the wendigo from once before.

It isn't just some random creature who has found me, it's the wendigo.

"Do you want to be caught?" Wren whisper-shouts at him and throws her thumb toward Parla and her cronies. "Because if she doesn't kill you today, it will be tomorrow. Or the next day. You're never going to make it out of here alive. Not without me." Her gaze flashes to mine but darts back to the wendigo.

She's attempting to appeal to his desire to survive. Instead of threatening him, she's telling him the truth.

"I always finish what I start," the wendigo says, his voice deep and gravely.

I stare through the small gap in the brush at Parla. She glances around, and for a split second, I swear she's glaring in our direction. But instead of coming toward us, she steps into the magical thing and disappears. Her men follow her through, and within a few short moments, they're all gone.

"This one doesn't want to stay dead." He tightens his hold and moves back a few inches, dragging me farther away from my love.

Pippa remains with her hands sort of in the air in front of her, almost like she's waiting for Wren to make a move. Gary has taken his spot next to Pippa.

If he would just hurry up and kill me, Wren could attack him and end his life. Then she wouldn't have to worry about me getting *hurt* in the crossfire. I can heal myself from death, but not from being injured. That much she's aware of, too. If I had a knife on me, I would drive it straight into my heart. With his hand over my mouth and his suffocating grasp, I can't say the word to bring me to Arthlia, and I can't reach for the button, either. Both fail safes fail epically. Who could have prepared us for me losing my ability to speak and move all at the same time?

Part of me wishes I could tell her to run, to use the means to get back to Arthlia, and that I would be right behind her. But I can't even do that. No, I'm stuck at the mercy of this arrogant and idiotic asshole who refuses to let go of some random vendetta.

If he kills me, surely the three of them can end one wendigo. Suddenly, the thought of being dead while Wren must fight for her life unsettles me. What if she's unable to escape? What if I'm burning into ashes while she dies her own, very permanent, death? I thought it was a good idea for me to be here, but perhaps I was wrong. Wes would have been the better person, because at least then, if she got hurt, he could heal her. Not to mention, his natural ability to kick ass is a major bonus, too. They probably wouldn't even be in this position if he were here.

But I can't change that now, and being mad at myself for making a poor decision won't serve me in this moment.

I mumble under his strong hold and wiggle in his grasp. If I can get him to release his hand on my mouth, I can blurt out the magic word to bring me home, and Wren could follow suit. Both of us finding safety in Arthlia and leaving Pippa and Gary behind.

The battle with the wendigo is between us, surely, he would leave those two alone, wouldn't he?

And on the off chance that he wouldn't, there's no way that Wren would leave knowing those two would be in danger.

Fuck.

"You don't need to hurt him," Wren says, her gaze pleading with the cautious step she takes toward us.

He matches her in the opposite direction. "Now, now."

"Fine." She throws her arms up like a white flag. "What do I need to do to convince you we're on the same side here? This war, it doesn't have to be between us. We have a common enemy."

The wendigo laughs sharply. "You are a hunter marked by an alpha, my dear. You are ripe for the taking."

Wren shakes her head slowly. "He's my partner," she explains. "I came here without him to engage the beacon. I wanted demons to find me. I wanted to convince them that we should be fighting together, not against each other."

"There are not many that remain."

"Then what better reason to join me, to join us." Wren motions to Pippa and Gary.

"I don't believe you." The wendigo grips my face tighter, his rough fingers digging into my flesh.

Pippa stands taller. "Then believe me. I am with her." She shoots her stare at Gary.

He hesitates but bows his head down in submission.

"You've convinced a couple demons, so what?" The wendigo leans in closer and breathes deeply. "And whatever this is."

Wren puts her hand to her chest. "I have made mistakes, okay? More than I'm proud to admit, but my pride doesn't prevent me from knowing that something must be done if Prania stands any chance of being saved."

"What makes you the hero of this story?"

"Someone has to do it." Wren swallows harshly. "I don't want to be labeled as the good guy. I just want to do the right thing for once in my life."

"And I want to escape this realm, but we can't always get what we want now can we?"

"What if I could make that happen?" Wren's chest heaves. She extends her arm toward me again like if she reaches just a bit farther, she'd snatch me from his vicious embrace.

My vision blurs from his hold, and I wish nothing more than to be out of here, to be with her in the safety of Arthlia once again. But like the wendigo just said, we don't always get what we desire.

"You wouldn't be here if you could." The wendigo wastes not another moment when he moves swiftly and snaps my neck for the second time.

It only hurts for the shortest second, the pain of leaving her worse than that of death.

CHAPTER 19

Wren

"What is taking so long?" I pace around the living room.

Dash's body lies on the floor in the center of the large space, unmoving, unbreathing, lifeless.

Was I wrong to bring him back here?

We weren't supposed to be able to get hurt in astral projection, and yet I have gash marks on my arm, and Dash is quite literally fucking dead.

I should have listened to my original instincts and charged the wendigo the second I saw him, but I thought I could try a new tactic and convince him that we should align.

I did, ultimately, convince him, but it was too late.

As I crouched to the ground with Dash in my grasp, tears welled in my eyes and I told him that in seconds, I would confirm to him that cross-realm travel was possible. I pleaded with him and made him promise that if I were speaking the truth, he would leave Pippa and Gary alone.

He assured me the feud was with me and my mates, not with them, so either way, I felt somewhat sure that their safety would remain. At least, there would be no threat from him—I couldn't stop the wrath that Parla insisted on inflicting on them.

I explained that I had traveled to Arthlia and found refuge there with others. I went on to confess what I had learned from Balial, and that the only way Prania would be a free realm is if Parla was eliminated. I vowed to return, to see things through, and despite him laughing at me, he gave his word that he would fight on our side if given the opportunity. He claims he would rally those that remained in my absence and await my beacon once I have returned.

But how can I go back there when Dash still hasn't resurrected?

Have my worst nightmares come to life with the final death of this beautiful and broken man?

"According to this text"—Sydney says from his spot on the couch with that ancient book from the library at Harper Shadow Academy in his grasp—"the phoenix is made from the death of two very specific angels. Their DNA, and theirs alone, combined, is what created the phoenix. Their death would result in them rising from the ashes to be reborn again, a result of the potent angelic blood running through their veins. They are said to be a myth, and that they do not exist."

I stare at him, blink, look at Dash, then back to Sydney. "Are you telling me Dash isn't a phoenix?"

He shakes his head. "No. I'm telling you Dash is *the* phoenix. The only one in existence. There are no others like him. There is limited information on the subject, at least from what I have gathered."

"Does it say anything in there about their resurrection?" I stalk over to him and attempt to read the foreign text on the page. "A limit? Something that kills him? How can I protect him if I don't know what his weaknesses are?"

Sydney shrugs and lets out a sigh. "I don't know. I wish I could be of more assistance. This is all new information to me. I'll try to continue to decode the text and fill you in every step of the way."

Wes enters the room and walks right over to me. He grabs my shoulders, steadies me, and looks into my eyes. "He's going to be fine. It's Dash."

I glance behind him. "Where's Bo?"

He infuriates the ever-loving shit out of me but I crave for him to be near, especially in times like this, when so much is uncertain.

"Off stewing." Wes slides my hair off my face and tucks it behind my ear. "He was fuming about the mate bond."

"Right, yeah. He'd rather go live in hell with Balial than be with me."

Sydney perks up from his textbook. "Wait, what?"

I lean into Wes's embrace but turn toward Sydney. "Yeah, Balial told him he'd eliminate the alpha mark on my neck if he pledged his allegiance to him."

"I thought you were with all three of them." Sydney flits his attention between Wes and Dash.

"Bo claims the alpha mark is the only reason I like him and said the only way he can prove that to me is to remove it. Because apparently if he does it himself, the removal, he must mark me as his fated mate, and he'd rather die than be stuck with me." I ignore the tugging of my heart at saying this all out loud.

It's no secret that Bo and I have a futile relationship. What's the point in hiding the truth that he would rather run away than be fated to me?

"Balial is so desperate for company he'd do anything to procure it." Sydney runs his hand through his hair, the pencil he was holding, still in his grasp. "So let me get this straight. Bo marked you, and because he's an alpha, it became an alpha mark. Bo thinks you only like him because of the mark, and refuses to replace it with a fated mate mark, because he thinks you both would have no control over your feelings for each other?"

I nod and point to Wes. "He thinks the same about me and Wes, too. That the only reason we love each other is because of the mate bond."

Wes stares down at me, his eyes glowing a bit redder than they were. "You love me?"

I smile up at him. "Duh."

Not being bothered that Sydney is right here, or that Dash is still lying motionless on the floor, Wes presses his lips to mine.

He breaks away, resting our foreheads together. "I love you, too."

I knew it, for a long time, really, perhaps even that first moment I locked eyes with him across that building. He changed the entire course of my life that day, and despite its tumultuous nature, I am grateful for where it brought us.

Although, having this war behind us and finding true safety might be an even better outcome.

"I hate to break up such a sweet moment, but it's worth sharing that mate bonds don't work that way." Sydney positions himself toward us. "There is a definite pull toward your fated mate, but that's not all that factors in. It can be rejected."

I stare at him and let his words wash over me. Could what he's saying be true? That I was right and my feelings for Bo really are mine and mine alone, not forced upon me by the mark he left on my neck.

"There are obvious magical influencers of lust and desire. That is not what you're experiencing though. Trust me, I went down a very deep rabbit hole when I found out the love of my life had four love interests of her own. I wanted to understand it, to figure out its complexities. And back when Silas and I hated each other, a strong part of me wished that their fated mate bond was the only thing that drew her to him."

"And it wasn't?" I ask him with bated breath.

"As a matter of fact, no. It's what brought them together, but it isn't what sealed their fate. Ultimately, it was their decision, their choice, their own free will, that secured their love for one another." Sydney takes a sip of his coffee. "There are things that come with the fated mate bond, supernatural things, but those are merely perks or extras, not the whole package. Willow and Silas share another supernatural bond, too, although it's far too complex to get into today. As do her and Cameron."

I want to ask him more questions, to find out every last detail about the mate bond and revel in how very wrong Bo was in thinking that what we shared wasn't real, but when Dash *finally* starts to molt, my every waking thought falls to him.

"This is so interesting," Sydney says from the couch.

Dash does his thing, molting and burning and his entire form becomes encased in a hard shell of ash. It's a beautiful process once it's started, but the moments leading up to it are brutally painful. To think that it's ever his last life drives a serrated blade straight through my heart.

After a small eternity, Dash shoves his fist through the center and emerges from the rubble. He blinks a few times, the debris falling over his long lashes, and settles his sights on me.

I rush over to him, my hands finding his face, my thumbs rubbing circles on his renewed flesh. "Took you long enough."

The corners of his lips turn up. "Sorry to keep you waiting."

Wes walks over and reaches down. "Glad to have you back."

Dash latches onto him and allows him to pull him onto his feet. Dash dusts off his body and steps out of the remains of his process. "I remembered something."

"What is it?" I ask him.

"That woman." Dash pats his arm. "Parla."

"Yeah?" The very being I can't wait to end.

"She's the one who tortured me." Dash reaches back to slap his back. "My scars. They're from her. I don't remember all of it, but there are fragments that keep coming to me. I think my mind was trying to uncover it with those nightmares. To show me the truth of what happened."

My blood boils—my hatred for that evil bitch growing with each passing second. I thought I couldn't hate her anymore, but I was wrong. It's one thing to fuck with me, and something else entirely to hurt any of my men.

I will make her pay for what she's done, one way or another.

And the sooner I can return to Prania, the better.

Time moves much quicker in Prania than it does in Arthlia. Tremont said we hadn't been gone long before we abruptly came back. And if that's any indication, there's no telling what else Parla has done in her extended time in Prania.

I promised Pippa and Gary that I would return, I gave my word to that wendigo.

What kind of person would I be if I went back on that now?

"I will make her pay." I plant my hand on Dash's shoulder.

"We both will," Wes chimes in. He glances over at me. "I'm not letting you go without me."

Sydney sighs. "If you're both going, I'm going to have to help Tremont with the spell. It's the only way to ensure enough power to send you."

"You'll help us?" I turn toward him, not quite believing how easily he volunteered.

"If I've learned anything from being married to an Oliver, there isn't any convincing her of something she's set her mind to. I'd rather assist and greater your chances of survival than let you go off on your own. She'd say the same thing."

"I...I don't know how to thank you." My eyes glisten.

"Try not to get yourself killed, that would be a start. Willow will be pissed if I let someone die."

I study the ticking clock at the far side of the room. "In theory, I still have enough time to get there and back before she needs my assistance later." Letting her down is not a part of this plan.

Neither is losing.

Bo's heavy presence makes itself known as he comes into the room and leans in the doorway. He takes in the most current version of Dash. "You're alive."

Dash chuckles. "Don't sound so disappointed."

Bo keeps his attention on Dash. "How was it?"

"Death? Kind of boring, really. A lot of darkness until I catch on fire."

"Prania. How was Prania?"

"Devastating." I interrupt Dash before he can begin. "We're going back immediately."

"What?" Bo stops leaning and stands up straight. "I'm coming this time."

I shake my head. "Can't."

"Why the hell not?" Bo looks to Wes.

"I need the beacon to engage," I tell him. "The plan doesn't work without it."

"And how did that work out for you last time? You got hurt and Dash died."

"I am very much fine, and so is Dash." I pause and consider my next words carefully, deciding that there is no gentle way in telling him the truth. "Plus, Wes is coming."

"You're kidding me." Bo rakes his hand over his face. "Everyone gets to go except me?"

Sydney clears his throat. "I'm, uh, going to get Tremont." He slips out of the room, and I wish I could follow him out and avoid Bo's seething glare.

"Not everyone," Wes says. "Jade and Everest are staying here. As are Sydney and Tremont. You'll barely even know we're gone."

"They don't count and you know it." Bo tightens his hand into a fist. "This is bullshit."

I step toward him, my head tilted up at the tall, broody man in front of me. "You know what's bullshit? You trying to leave because you don't want to be with me."

"It's the only way," Bo mutters through a clenched jaw.

"It's not actually, and when I get back, we need to talk."

"Talk?"

But before I can continue, Sydney and Tremont come into the room.

"I've extended the barrier for Tremont to the entire house, this will allow him to assist in the spell." Sydney walks to the center of the open space, near the spot Dash and his phoenix powers were activated.

I follow him over and stand at his side. "Thank you," I whisper.

He nods. "I must warn you, astral travel this frequent comes with risks. If you notice any uncomfortable side effects, you need to return immediately."

I had a feeling this type of thing didn't come without a cost but that isn't going to stop me from completing what I said I would do.

Parla must die.

Not tomorrow. Not next week. Today. Right now. As soon as fucking possible.

"What should I be on the lookout for?" I ask him.

"Headaches, fatigue, nose bleeds, nausea. Those are all precursors to worsening symptoms."

"How worse?"

"Death." Sydney sighs. "It's incredibly uncommon, but I've read cases in which the soul of the astral traveler was stuck in the in-between, unable to reunite with its body." He looks to Dash. "Because of your regenerative abilities, you should be fine for immediate travel. And Wes, you haven't yet, so you're good to go, too."

Relief washes over me at not putting Dash or Wes at any more risk than they already are.

"Are you sure you want to go through with this?" Wes's fiery gaze meets mine.

"Without a doubt." I lower myself onto the floor and wait for my direction from the witches sending me to Prania.

Dash lies next to me, weaving our hands together, and Wes settles on the other side.

"I can't fucking believe this," Bo blurts out. "Absolutely ridiculous."

"Tell us how you really feel," I mumble.

Dash squeezes my hand and Wes rubs his thumb along mine. Having two out of three of my men being supportive will have to do, at least, for now. I'll deal with Bo when I return from hopefully what will be my final assassination mission.

With a few daggers tucked along my leather gear, I close my eyes and brace myself for what's to come. Ever since I stepped foot in Arthlia, I haven't been able to shake the thought that my work in Prania was not over. I hurt many. I made bad decisions. I was a close-minded fool doing errands for a woman who manipulates and controls anyone she possibly can. She is pure evil, and she must be stopped. And who better to do it than the person that was trained to do her bidding?

The room spins, that familiar vacuum-type thing happening as Sydney and Tremont mutter the incantation necessary to send us to Prania. I should have pushed for Dash to stay behind, but after hearing what Parla had done to him, I knew with certainty that if he wanted to come, I would be selfish for not allowing it. He deserves to watch her die just as much as the rest of us. I'll do the honors of holding her down and letting him rip into her the same way she had done to him.

Any death, no matter how brutal it could be, would still not be enough punishment for the terrible things she has done.

Once everything has stopped moving, I open my eyes and blink through the thick haze of Prania's sky. Sitting up, I notice a trickle run down my nose. I wipe at it, the crimson staining my hand. As quick as I can, I sniffle the rest of it up and drag my hand against the ground to rid myself of the evidence. I've only just got here and already the symptoms that Sydney mentioned are present.

"You guys good?" I rise to my feet and dust off my legs. There is no time like the present to get this show on the road. I refuse to leave here without following through, and I can't exactly do that if I die in the process.

"Yep," Dash joins me at my side.

Wes huffs and comes closer, too. "Can't say I'm thrilled to be back here." His eyes glow and his skin radiates heat like his hound side is already on high alert. I don't blame him for being proactive, I would probably do the same if I had those types of abilities.

I unsheathe a blade and shove the handle into Dash's hand. "If it's not a demon, kill it. And if it's a demon trying to kill you, kill it. Do not hesitate. Just because you're a phoenix doesn't mean I'm okay with you dying."

Dash nods. "Yes, ma'am."

I roll my eyes and scan the vicinity, unsure of where we landed. There's no telling where Pippa, Gary, and the wendigo went, but if my beacon is doing what it's supposed to be doing, they should be alerted to our whereabouts if they're nearby. I just hope they get here before any other bloodthirsty demon does.

I don't want to have to kill, but I will if it's what stands between us and our survival.

"Let's stick to the plan," I tell them while pulling the compass from my pocket. The dial swivels and then settles on its direction. "This way."

We take a few steps and I stop, holding out both of my arms to prevent them from going any farther.

"What's wrong?" Wes asks immediately.

"Do you see that?" I point to the ground.

"No."

"What are we supposed to be seeing?" Dash glances over my shoulder.

"That. Right there." I kneel and get a closer look at the faint but illuminated petals on the ground. They brighten, only to dim out and be replaced by another set a bit farther away.

"Are those...flowers?" Wes reaches toward them, but I grab his arm.

"Don't touch them." Something visceral within me wants to protect them, to keep them out of harm's way. I don't quite understand how I know, but I'm certain I'm supposed to follow them. Despite following a trail north, I step in between the glowing things and walk in the direction it guides me.

"Are you sure?" Wes asks skeptically.

"Yeah." I meet his gaze. "Just don't step on them." Shifting my focus to Dash, I add, "Please."

I shove the compass back into its home and put my faith in whatever magical miracle is leading me away from the north. Is it possible that I'm chasing a false hope that will get us killed? Definitely. But could this be the same divination that brought me to that book in the library at Harper Shadow Academy? I guess I'll find out.

We walk silently through the wooded area for at least ten minutes, my heart slowing its pace with each step. I shouldn't feel this comfortable in wartime, but my body is strangely at ease. This is what I was trained for. What I'm known for. What I'm good at.

I am the furla ain, and soon, I will make Parla regret the day she ever came into my life.

The illuminating ground dies out completely, as do my steps.

"Where did they go?" Dash whispers from behind me.

"I don't know," I tell him, a strange unease trickling up my spine. "Over here," I rush over to a nearby bush and cower beside it.

They join me a second later, almost entirely too late, as a group of half a dozen soldiers march by, their formation eerily perfect and orderly. The soldiers don't look our way as they march past us like they don't see or notice us at all.

"That was creepy," Dash says the very thing going through my head.

"It's like they're mind controlled." I shift my weight and watch them disappear into the distance.

"I think they are." Wes leans in closer. "I mean, how else would she get full compliance from them? It has to be some magical mind control. Remember when…"

But he doesn't have to finish his sentence for me to recall the memory of Parla using mind control to get me to kill Wes.

"I do," I tell him, not needing the details repeated out loud. I am ashamed I allowed her to take control and almost succeed in forcing me to murder my beloved.

"How did you break it?" he asks me.

I hadn't put too much thought into that part. "I don't know, I just did."

But that couldn't be all of it, there had to be something I did to rid myself of that influence.

"Think, Wren," Wes encourages. "You had the knife in your hand poised to my chest. I told you I'd find you in any life."

I shiver at the image of the fear that had consumed me. I was terrified, quite possibly, for the very first time in my life—truly and utterly terrified.

"It was something she said," I tell him. "She commanded me to kill the monster. But I never saw you as one. She was, at least, in my eyes. And then…" It was similar to what I felt when that magical torture device had been embedded in my skin. A flash of bright light, a welcoming and protective presence. Could that have been my hidden magic rising to the surface to save me? What else could explain what had happened?

"Wren." Dash reaches across and catches the blood that trickles out of my nose. "You're bleeding."

I rise to my feet and wipe my face. "I'm fine."

Dash looks to Wes, who steps toward me.

"Come here." Wes pulls me to his chest and mutters into my hair. He hugs me with a firm gentleness and kisses my forehead. "I need you to tell me if you're feeling bad." Wes releases me and stares into my eyes, his glowing orbs something that would have made me want to kill him in my past life, but now, all I want to do is spend every moment at his side.

"You have to promise me you won't do that again. You must preserve your energy, Wes. I'm fine, really." I avoid their pitying glances and step from around the bush that was concealing us. "We should get going. We're running out of time."

But when I take a few more strides, I smack into a large body I never saw coming.

His rough hands latch onto my shoulders and hold me firmly in place. Standing at least twice my height with antlers protruding from his bare skeleton skull, he growls. "You."

Wes immediately ignites his entire body, his flames licking everything within a few inches of him. "Let her go or I'll burn—"

"It's okay," I tell him and shake off the creepy hands of the wendigo. "He's on our side."

Dash comes into the wendigo's view. "I'd appreciate it if you refrained from killing me for the third time."

The wendigo raises its hands. "A promise is a promise. I am a man of my word."

"Where's Pippa?" I look past him and swallow down the fear that I may have been too late in my return.

What is minutes at home is much longer here.

"Waiting." He tilts his head in the direction he just came. "I gathered what I could, but there aren't many of us that remain. And those that do are in hiding. It wasn't easy to convince them of something I was skeptical of myself."

How bittersweet that my friend is alive, but so many others are not. We have all lost someone, and hopefully soon, after one final battle, the violence will stop.

"I understand," I say while following this demonic creature through the woods.

Wes hurries to join me at my side and Dash takes up the rear.

I flit my attention to Wes and dart my gaze to the semi-helpless phoenix behind me.

Wes sighs but falls back, knowing damn well that Dash shouldn't be the one left exposed.

I reach toward Dash and tug him closer to me. He's safest at my side where I can protect him from anything that may come his way. It's risky having someone else to keep my eyes on, but it's a risk I'm willing to take to give him a front-row seat to Parla's execution.

"I've never come across a phoenix before," the wendigo says over his shoulder. "Assuming that's what you are."

"The one and only," I confirm. "Sydney translated some of that text when you were taking your good ol' time molting. According to that book, you're the only phoenix in existence."

Dash's eyes widen. "Whoa. I don't know if I should be proud or sad."

I nudge him with my shoulder. "You're allowed to be both."

"We're coming up on a group of hunters." The wendigo motions to a large boulder off to the side. "We can wait it out here."

"How many are there?" I ask him, a theory popping into my head.

"Three," he says, his voice harsh.

"There's four of us." I settle my sights on Dash. "Three. You can stay here."

He frowns but doesn't protest.

"Honestly, I can take them all if you'd rather—"

The wendigo holds up his hand to stop me. "Like taking bread from a baby."

If only he knew the kind of bread they had in Arthlia. He would surely lose his creepy little mind.

"Leave one of them alive." I slide a dagger out of my pants and turn it around in my hand, familiarizing myself with the blade. It's been too long since I properly held one, and yet it feels completely at home in my grasp. Taking a steadying breath, I look at each of the men standing here with me.

The three unsuspecting soldiers march right near us, the same way the others had done. Their postures are stiff and rigid, their movements almost identical to one another. Before I can even fully step into their line of sight, the wendigo rushes toward them. He snatches two of them and bashes their heads together before tossing their lifeless bodies aside. He clutches the other by the neck and drags him over to us.

"Um." I shove my dagger back into its sheathed position. "That works, too."

Wild-eyed and panting, the remaining soldier kicks his feet to try to free himself. He opens his mouth, but the wendigo shoves his hand over it and silences his cries for help.

"What's this all about?" Wes steps toward me. "What do you want with him?"

I exhale. "I'm not sure. I want to try something."

The wendigo brings the man closer, stopping just a foot in front of me. "Haste; we must not keep the others waiting."

Rubbing my thumbs against my fingers, I suck in a breath and summon whatever power is within me. I close my eyes and will it to the surface, knowing damn well just how foolish what I'm doing must look from their point of view. That doesn't stop me from trying, from testing this possible theory that might change everything.

When nothing happens—no stirring in my chest or magical lights appearing—I bridge the space between me and this bewildered man.

"I don't want to hurt you," I reassure him. "But you're being manipulated." I close my hands into fists. "I think you're mind controlled, actually."

He tries to shake his head but the wendigo keeps him firmly in place. I ignore the similarities of how he did the same thing to Dash, not only once, but twice.

Sometimes you have to align with your enemies if you wish to take out the even greater threat.

Extending my arm, I press my palm against the man. His heart beats aggressively in his chest, thudding so aggressively it rumbles up my forearm.

I pinch my eyes shut. "Angels," I whisper, barely audible, and pray to anyone listening to hear my call for help. If that's who saved me when I needed to be rescued, can't they assist me today, too? I push my palm into his chest and thrust any magic that may lie dormant within me to rise to the surface. My fingers tingle, my arm growing warmer and cooler all at once. I peek through my lids to witness a strange silver glow faintly illuminating my skin.

Am I losing it or is this really working?

I lock sights with the man, his gaze terrified, no doubt from the wendigo holding him hostage, but also the crazy woman in front of him.

"Wren, you're..." Dash mutters.

But I ignore him. I ignore everything except the sensation bubbling up inside of me.

I shove it forward with no real direction of how this is supposed to work and hope with everything in me that I'm doing this right.

A blast of rippling power slams the man in the chest, his eyes widening before shutting completely. His body goes limp in the wendigo's grasp.

"I didn't mean to kill him." My chest aches from the loss of a man I was only trying to help.

"He's not dead," the wendigo tells me while lowering the man's weight onto the dirt.

I kneel at the soldier's side and press my fingers to his neck, finding his slow but steady pulse. "He's not." My sights lock on Wes temporarily. "I didn't kill him."

What a strange thing to get excited about, considering my past as a trained murderer.

The man gasps for breath, his sudden movement knocking me onto my ass. He clutches his chest at the spot I blasted him and stares directly at me.

My fingers inch toward the blade at my side, ready to yank it out and throw it into his throat at a second's notice.

None of us move, like we're all waiting for the other to decide how this is going to go.

Finally, he opens his mouth. "Furla ain?"

I swallow and nod. "Yes."

"I..." His gaze trails off. "I think I've made a mistake." That distant, empty look is no longer. His shoulders are stiff but nothing of the way they were moments ago. The mind-control that Parla had been dominating him with has disappeared, along with his immediate murderous tendencies.

I did it. I broke his compulsion. And with it, it brings me hope that maybe, just maybe, we can win this war.

I had come here with the sole mission of killing Parla, not exactly working out any of the other details. I would eliminate anyone that stood in the way but would do my best to save as many innocent lives as possible. I wasn't sure if her death would be enough to break the hold she had on the hunters, but with this new ability I've discovered, maybe I can turn her own against her.

"We both have." I rise to my feet and extend my arm to him. "But it's not too late."

The soldier locks onto me and I pull him onto his feet. We stand there, at an arm's length, a heavy silence filling the space between us. I nod, and then he does.

"Very well," I say and break away from him.

"Great work," the wendigo tells me as he slaps my back, the impact rattling my entire body.

Does he think that we are friends now that we've come to a truce? It wouldn't be the worst thing to happen, although I cannot overlook that he murdered my sweet Dash on two separate occasions. I may be in my forgiving era, but that isn't easily forgotten.

Wes eyes me like he's trying to decide if I'm injured, and I do everything in my power to convince him otherwise. He doesn't need to know that my head throbs and my vision keeps blurring in and out of focus. He'd try to heal me, to convince me to return to Arthlia. Both options that I refuse to take. His strength as a hell-hound is better served fighting to protect those that remain than absorbing my ailments. Not to mention, when he whispered those words to me earlier, there was no positive effect the way his healing power usually works. Typically, I feel better within seconds, but then, I felt nothing. And returning to Arthlia would be giving up on Prania completely. The amount of time it would take for me to properly recover would grant Parla the ability to eradicate the rest of the demon population.

This is our only shot and I won't waste it.

The solider stumbles, his hands darting out in front to steady himself.

I reach for him all too late.

He goes down hard with a thud. He doesn't move, he doesn't make another sound. Not a wisp of air filling his lungs, not a single heartbeat thudding in his chest.

He is simply *dead*.

"What the fuck?" I crouch next to him, grip his shoulders, and turn him face up.

Dash grabs my elbow and pulls me to my feet. "He's gone," he says with such a gentle tone.

"We must go," the wendigo tells us. "We're losing time."

"I don't know what I did wrong," I mutter despite knowing damn well that I have no understanding of how magic works. What was I thinking in blasting him with my power? It may have broken the compulsion, but it killed him in the process.

How are we going to win this war with minimal casualties if I can't stop Parla's mind control? Her soldiers don't deserve to die just because they're held captive by her mind tricks.

CHAPTER 20

Wren

We make it to where the rest of the demons are hiding. An old, dilapidated building similar to the one where Wes and I first met.

The wendigo was not lying. There are not many survivors, at least that are able-bodied and willing to show up to fight.

I stand in front of them, a lump forming in my throat as they look at me with rage-filled stares. I'm not entirely sure if it's from the marker signaling them to kill me blaring off my neck, or the fact that Parla has done nothing but make their lives completely miserable.

Miserable doesn't even cut it.

She's threatened by their very existence; she hates them so much that she vowed to kill every last one of them despite not truly knowing any of them. I'm the first to admit that the stigma associated with being a demon is nothing but a harmful stereotype that serves only one person. How can someone hate something they don't even understand? But how can I blame her when I did the very same thing?

I blamed the demons for the death of my parents and took that same oath to rid our realm of the demons and their bringers.

"Is it true?" one of the smaller demons calls out from the front of the crowd. "You came from Arthlia?"

"I did." I nod and look her straight in the eyes. "We all did." I glance over at Wes and Dash, who stand supportively at my side. Inhaling, I scan the crowd and raise my voice. "After the bombing at Rockbridge, we were able to flee and seek refuge in Arthlia. I, personally, spoke to Balial, who told me that Prania was sealed off to prevent Parla from escaping. It was not her that created the border like she has led us to believe, yet the angels and demons who collectively decided this was for the greater good. One realm as opposed to her wreaking havoc on all of them. Until she is eliminated, none of us are safe. It doesn't matter if you have a spec of demonic blood in your veins, nothing protects you from her wrath. Anyone who opposes her is as good as dead, and those on her side, she sees them only as disposable pawns."

Wes places his hand on my lower back, almost like he could sense I needed the support.

"Today"—I stand taller with his touch still on me—"that tyranny ends."

The crowd claps their hands, their energy fueling me despite my already weakened state.

"Today—"I repeat—"we take back what is ours."

They roar louder.

"Today, we will kill Parla."

A collective bellow sounds this otherwise quiet and abandoned section of Prania.

"Think that will be loud enough?" I turn to the wendigo as the few dozen demons cheer and go wild.

"I don't doubt they could have found us without it." His gaze floats past me into the distance. "They're already approaching."

I breathe in deeply. "How many?"

The wendigo looks down at me, his solemn expression is more dire than ever. "At least a hundred. Maybe more."

We're outnumbered and there's no telling what kind of magical powers Parla and her goonies will possess. I knew this would be a challenge, but I hadn't realized the magnitude of it until this very instant. And when I look out at the last of the demons, I grow concerned of the death toll that will no doubt rise. There will be casualties on both sides, but at what point will enough be enough?

Parla won't rest until we're all dead, and we won't stop until she is.

I latch onto Dash's hands and pull him toward me. "You need to go into that building and hide. Okay? Do not come out until this is all said and done. Neither the hunters nor the demons can sense you, and we must use that to our advantage."

His gaze darts back and forth between mine. "I don't want to leave you."

"You aren't." I force a smile and shake my head. Worrying about Dash's safety will only bring more harm to me and Wes. He needs to stay tucked away, safe and sound, if we stand any chance of keeping our heads clear during battle. And I'm already struggling to do that without adding Dash into the mix. "I'll find you when it's over."

Dash kisses my cheek briefly and takes a final look into my eyes. "I'm holding you to that."

"I would expect nothing less." I unsheathe one of my blades. "You still have yours, right?"

Dash pats his side where his own knife is tucked away.

"Don't be afraid to use it," I tell him as he disappears through the chaos of the demons that swell around me.

"You ready for this?" I ask Wes, who stays silently at my side.

"You sure that you're okay?"

"I am." The energy of the coming fight rumbles through me, temporarily overriding any reservations I may have. I don't worry about Wes. He and his hound can overcome any obstacle. He can fully engulf himself in flames and catch fire to anyone who dares threaten him. He can shift into his hound form and move around this battlefield quicker than any other creature standing here today, ripping out throats and tearing off limbs. Now that he has unlocked his full form, he is unstoppable.

I've only just scratched the surface of what I'm capable of, and so far, my magic has done me almost no good. I stepped foot into Prania in a weakened state, and with each passing moment, my health declines even more. It's going to take everything I have to simply survive an extended stay, let alone fight to the death.

But luckily for me, the mate bond does not insist that *I* tell *him* the truth.

Hunters emerge from the near fog, their boisterous footsteps pelting the ground as they charge us, armed with knives and swords and magic and unrecognizable devices.

"This is it," I say to no one in particular.

As one solid group, we rush toward the hunters, erupting total chaos in the clearing in front of the building the demons were previously hiding out in.

I duck to avoid a flying knife and slice my own through the exposed flesh of a hunter as he reaches over his head to throw another blade.

His insides spill out as he hits the ground with a thud. One down, so many more to go.

Kicking my next target, I spin and drive the sharp end of my knife into the throat of the man, who clutches at the gushing wound. The air becomes thick with the stench of death and gore. I rub at my nose, more blood trickling down despite not being hit in the face.

The minor distraction allows a hunter to charge at me, his sword slicing a thin section of my armored top as I dive out of his way.

"Fucking bitch!" he screams at me.

I roll my eyes. "At least I'm not a mind-controlled puppet." I turn toward him and steady my footing. "Are you even able to wipe your ass without permission from your master?"

"At least I'm not sleeping with the enemy," he barks back.

I laugh. "At least I'm actually getting laid." I run toward him, letting him think he knows exactly where I'm going to strike, but at the last second, I slide past him and slice through his biceps. Blood splatters onto my face and provides a nice camouflage from my own dripping out of my nose.

Shoving onto my feet, I reel back my arm and slam the blade into the soft spot between his shoulder and spine. And with everything I have, I grunt and force all my weight down, cutting him wide open.

Should I have tried to save him? Probably. But this early in the battle, I don't have time to waste on something that's already failed me once.

My vision blurs and I struggle to remain upright, bodies running past and sending me spiraling. I slap my face and regain my footing. "Get it together, Wren."

After a few blinks, the image of destruction comes into focus and I narrowly avoid an oncoming attack. Only this time, it's a demon, not a hunter.

"Angels, man!" I yell at him. "I'm on your side, remember?" Steadying my blade toward the wild-eyed guy with small horns protruding from his forehead, I watch him intently and hope that he will change his mind.

"I forgot, sorry." He points his dagger toward me. "That fucking beacon makes me want to kill you."

"I know," I tell him. "It makes me want to kill me too." Coming here without Bo was a great idea at first, but now it seems more of a risk than I bargained for. It helped me find the wendigo and the rest of the demon army, that much is certain. Perhaps I could have found them without it, though. Was it my magic or something else altogether that lit those leaves up on the ground and led me toward them?

Now, the alpha mark does nothing but confuse those on my side, allowing the threat to my life to continue to rise. In a way, Parla has an advantage she's not even aware of.

Not that I will allow that to stop me from following through with my mission.

That isn't to say that I wouldn't prefer Bo here, fighting alongside me like lovers dancing to their song. It's one of the few moments he lets down his guard long enough for me to see him. We come together in an unusual way and despite it being twisted, those are some of my fondest memories with him. It's as though the only time he recognizes me as an equal is on the battlefield.

I scan the crowd, locating Wes who is currently melting another man's throat with just his grasp. Pippa slams her hoof-like hand into a hunter, knocking him to the ground before stomping on his skull and smashing it with ease. The wendigo is surrounded by six hunters, but he doesn't seem at all discouraged by the number.

"Where are you?" I whisper, my sights frantically searching for the entire reason I came here today.

"On your left," Pippa screams across the way to me.

I drop to my knees and through the air soars, Gary, the wolf that had attacked me once before, only this time, he lands the weight of his blow on a hunter who flanked me.

Gary latches his razor-sharp teeth around the man's throat and rips the flesh right off him. He tilts his furry head toward me as blood dribbles out of his mouth. He growls, but this time, it isn't meant to intimidate me. Gary rushes off and snatches another random hunter that goes after that small demon who had asked me about Arthlia.

I continue to search the crowd, taking short breaks to duck, to spin, to kill.

That's when I spot her, my heart completely skipping a beat.

Parla.

She's surrounded by at least two dozen hunters and a witch at her side that's casting a glowing orb around her. Leave it to her to not be willing to fight her own battle.

Her sadistic gaze locks onto mine, and I want nothing more than to teleport into that magical bubble and slit her fucking throat.

Parla's stupid cheeks turn up into a grin and she winks at me before pointing in my direction and saying something I cannot make out from this far away.

Another person appears from behind her and casts a wand toward me.

Within split seconds, I drop to my knees, the weight of the world feeling heavier than ever. Is this from the side effects or what Parla's other witch is doing?

Wes screams and we lock eyes as his entire form bursts into flames. He takes off into a sprint, his footsteps leaving a trail of fire in his wake. But he doesn't get much farther when something flies through the air toward him and secures itself around his throat. The fire dies out immediately and he clutches the device with all his might, yanking and trying to free himself.

It's no use—whatever has attached to him is suppressing his powers, and if it's anything like what we dealt with at Rockbridge, there's no telling whether Wes will be able to overcome it without his hound side.

I try to move, to push up onto my feet. My body is too heavy, too weak, too defeated.

"No," I mutter. "This is not how I die." Not when I'm *this* fucking close to snapping her neck.

Parla and her horde inch closer, my stomach dropping with every bit of ground she covers without being able to regain my strength.

The faint whistling of a knife calls my attention, and I duck as it whizzes by, the blade slicing into my cheek but not securing itself into my skull where it was aimed. Hot blood coats my chin and drips onto the ground.

I clench my jaw and summon whatever may lie dormant within me.

This battle may have been a lot different had I learned how to use my magic like a proper witch. Although, I was not afforded the luxury of time, considering I have already wasted too much and cost too many their lives.

A strong hand wraps around my biceps, and I come to the sudden realization that this is it, this is where my story ends. Not at the hands of Parla, but some random stranger who got to me first.

But when I draw in a breath, the familiar scent of musk and rain washes over me. My eyes fill with tears and my heart swells.

"Bo," I mutter without even having laid my sights on him.

He drags me to my feet. "What are you doing down there, Birdie?"

I turn toward him, my body already feeling lighter and less under her authority. "Just hanging out."

He steadies my shoulders and studies my exterior. "You look like shit."

"Thanks." This forces a smile out of me. "What are you doing here?"

Chaos continues to erupt around us but for a second it feels like it's only the two of us standing here.

"Sorry to disappoint. Just couldn't let you have all the fun." His dark stare doesn't leave mine. "I came the second your nose started bleeding."

"That was hours ago."

"Seconds ago, in Arthlia." He releases and shoves me behind him, grabbing the knife that soars through the air toward us. Bo sends it back in the direction it came, landing straight into the chest of a hunter. He skims his attention over the dwindling crowd. "You guys are getting your asses kicked."

My lip quivers despite everything I'm doing to hold myself from falling apart.

Bo returns to face me, his hand coming up to rest against my non-injured cheek. "Hey, if we go down, we go down together."

"I'm glad you came," I tell him, because this might be my last chance to tell him the truth.

"I don't know how much longer Sydney and Tremont can hold us. Five is too many."

"Five? Who else came?" I do the math in my head.

Me. Dash. Wes. Bo. Who's the fifth?

"Everest." He points off in the distance.

Bo slams his elbow into a hunter that runs by, stopping him completely in his tracks and using the knife the man was holding against him to jab it into his throat.

Never in my wildest dreams would I have assumed Everest would return to Prania, especially when that meant leaving Jade behind. Those two have been inseparable since Rockbridge, and if I was a betting woman, I would have wagered all the cheese in the world that he'd never part from her.

"He came to help me find you. Insisted I didn't come alone." Bo wipes the blade he just killed a man with on his leg, only to drive it into another hunter that approaches. He repeats the same motion. "Angels, there sure are a lot of them."

"They're mind controlled, Bo. They don't know what they're doing." I exhale. "I was able to break the compulsion on one of them."

"Why can't you do it to the rest of them?" He motions toward the throng of people around us.

"I killed him." I keep Wes in my line of sight while talking with Bo. Despite the restraints suppressing Wes's hound side from rising to the surface, he does not lack in the combat department. He's killed a minimum of three hunters since I started watching him. Defending himself enough to lessen the worry that overtook me seeing him fall to one of Parla's magical defenses.

"Probably easier that way." Bo glances down at me. "Is that why your nose started bleeding?"

"No, it happened as soon as I got here." What's the point in lying when the chance of our survival is decreasing with each demon slaughtered?

"Where's Dash?" Bo latches onto me and spins me out of the way of an attack.

"Hiding."

"Good."

"Directly behind you," I say while picking up the knife I lost when Parla grabbed a hold of me with her magic.

"You, too."

Bo and I turn, both of us seamlessly moving in unison and forcefully implanting our knives into the people who attempted to threaten us.

"That's my girl," Bo says while a shit-eating grin forms on his handsome face. He drags his hair out of his eyes and winks at me.

Just like that, all the tension that was between us is erased, and what remains is a friendship that has grown through the strangest of ways. Bo has seen me at my worst, hated me, and wanted me dead. I have never sugar-coated the version of myself that he has seen, and despite being at odds, a relationship formed whether we wanted it to or not. Bo has always been attractive, but I didn't *truly* start to notice it until I saw more pieces of him that were uncovered. He is brutal, irrational, and a pain in the ass, but he is as broken as the rest of us. He is a lover of bread and violence, and he would do anything for the people he cares about. Bo might not let people in so easily, but when he does, he will go to the ends of the universe for them.

Literally.

And as he hovers behind me, our forms back-to-back, our knives poised to kill, I realize, I am one of those very lucky people.

He could have stayed in Arthlia. He didn't have to come. But the second he saw that something was wrong, he risked himself to be here with us.

We fall quickly into a rhythm and use the shield each other provides to slaughter anyone who dares to come our way.

I ignore the fatigue that sets in and focus on the adrenaline coursing through me.

Panting, I shove my blade into the thigh of a hunter. His screams pierce my ears and do nothing to stop me from yanking out the knife and driving it into his neck. Blood speckles my face, coating me with yet another layer of red.

Bo throws his weapon into the chest of an oncoming hunter, and reaches for another, tilting his head and sinking his fangs into his throat. He jerks back, his vicious teeth ripping a huge chunk of his flesh off. Bo spits it out and rushes over to snatch his knife from the other man's deceased torso.

"They just keep coming," he calls out to me. "Where's the bitch?"

"I..." I slam my fist across the face of one hunter and spin, extending my leg and kicking another right in the chest. "Don't know." Quickly ducking, I swipe my blade at the ankle of another unsuspecting victim. "I lost her when you showed up. I've been searching ever since."

My gaze continues to skim the crowd between every kill, but aside from being able to locate Wes and my friends, I haven't found Parla. Did she retreat when Bo arrived? Or is she planning something for him, too? There's no telling what kind of magical defense she has up her sleeve.

Most of the hunters look alike, just varying heights and weights. They're all dressed in the same attire, making them easy targets. But because of this, it's difficult to differentiate the ones that belong to Parla's personal guard. Just when I think I've homed in on them, they disperse and go their separate ways into battle. Is this a purposeful distraction or simply another advantage she doesn't even realize she has?

Four rather large hunters charge at me at once, one of them landing a blow across my jaw.

Stars dot my vision, and I lose my footing. My hands scrape against the ground as they catch the brunt of my weight. "Fuck!" I cry out.

Someone kicks me square in the back, knocking the wind out of me and cracking my spine.

I dig my fingers into the dirt and spit out the blood that's filled my mouth. "Is that all you've got?" Pushing onto my feet, I'm met with another blow, this one turning me over and onto my ass. I stare up at the endless hunters that surround me, my gaze darting to Bo, who has at least twice the number of hunters to tend to. I locate Wes, grateful to see him still standing, but that hope is dimmed quickly at noticing how many are attacking him, too. Pippa struggles with the man in front of her, and even the wendigo seems surrounded, only his antlered head poking out above the throng of hunters.

Is this it? The end? I thought I would have met my maker numerous times before, but I don't think things have ever been quite as hopeless as they have right now.

I wanted to die that day in the warehouse when Wes saved me. I thought he was going to torture me and make my final days worse than any death imaginable. But who would have thought that this, witnessing the people I care about losing a war that was never meant for them, would be more painful than the most brutal of torture? I would spend an eternity in Rockbridge to rid them of this.

My head throbs and I cough, blood spewing from my lips. The men close in, their knives and swords pointed toward me. Eyeing my empty ankle holster, hopelessness continues to hit me like a ton of bricks. My sights fall on my dagger, lying discarded in the dirt a few feet away.

It's too far.

I am weaponless and injured.

In my peak form, maybe I could have taken the lot of them on, but here, now, beaten and bloodied, I'm not so sure.

That doesn't mean I will give in without a fight, though. I size them up and quickly analyze any potential weaknesses and opportunities. Three of the men are easily twice my size. One holds a long sword, but his grip is loose, a bit unsure, as though this might be the first time he's held a weapon that massive. He's the biggest of the bunch, and somehow, the most unsteady on his feet. The littlest man's hands shake as he clutches a dagger. The other two, a tinge more confident than the others, poise their knives in my direction.

It's only been a few seconds since they knocked me onto my ass and already, I've learned more about them than their comrades probably know.

Spreading my fingers into the cold dirt, I make the decision that I'm hoping is the correct one. I shove the brunt of my weight onto my hand and force myself up, moving as quickly as I can to rush the largest of the guys and thrust the brunt of my boot into his knee.

It buckles just as I'd wanted it to, and he lets the sword slip from his grasp. It clanks onto the ground, but I leave it. It's far too heavy for either of us to use effectively and his concern is no longer on me as much as it is on his broken leg.

He whimpers and moans and clutches the awkward-shaped thing on the ground like a baby.

The two moderate fighters run toward me, their knives aimed in my direction. The little guy follows up the rear and manages to drive his blade through the flesh on my arm on his way by. Pain, hot and steady, just like the blood gushing from my wound.

"Bleed, bitch," one of the two says.

My vision grows fuzzy again, making me miss the knife that punctures my armor top and shoves its way through my stomach.

I latch onto the person the knife is clutched by and pull them toward me, keeping the blade still buried in my body. Without even truly being able to see, I dig my nails into the soft skin on top of his hand and don't stop until his grip has released the hilt, leaving the knife up for grabs. I yank it out with a grunt and clasp the handle so hard my fingers ache. Pointing it at them, or at least, the blurry shapes in my line of sight, I press my palm to my side to apply pressure to my new wound.

"Who's next?" I scream. "Take your best fucking shot." I keep blinking and hope that will clear up my sights and allow me to finish them off.

But I'm not as lucky as I thought I was. Especially when three more blobs turn their attention toward me. Spewing blood and inching back, I keep the knife out in front of my body.

Another shape rushes over, this one tackling one of my assailants and pinning him to the ground.

"Wren, are you okay?" Everest calls out toward me.

"Yeah," I cough. "I'm good." I swing through the air, somehow landing the sharp edge of the blade across one of my targets. My sights sharpen enough for me to charge the man I hit, and I use the momentary clarity to rush toward him and slam the knife into his chest.

One, two, three blows, and his body falls to the ground.

I spin and aim for another, my hand still pressed to my side.

This man kicks me in the shin, but instead of buckling to the blow the same way the other did, I grit my teeth and fight through it. A scream bubbles up and out of my chest as I allow the pain to flow through and power me forward. Everything aches. Dull and sharp and throbbing, all at once. Between the blood of the fallen and that of my own, I can't seem to tell who's is who's.

I kill, once more, my hunter nature rising to the surface and refusing to succumb to those that try to eliminate me. *This* is why I am furla ain. No amount of pain or suffering can break me. If they want me dead, they're going to have to take the bleeding heart from my chest.

A renewed sense of vigor flows through my veins, but when I turn toward the man who rushed over to save me, my mouth falls open and another scream forces its way between my lips.

Everest takes a sword straight through the stomach, his kind eyes going wide and meeting my frantic gaze.

"No!" I yell and dig my feet into the ground to run toward him. Without hesitating, I throw the man off him and slide my own knife into his attacker's chest, aimed directly at his heart. His life ends in one fell swoop and I turn my attention to Everest, the man who is the reason I'm here today. Not only did he save me moments ago, but back at Rockbridge, too. In more ways than one, really. If it weren't for his assistance, there's no telling if we would have been able to escape that place, let alone make it out alive.

Tears well in my eyes and my hands hover at the sword, still embedded in his torso.

"I...I..." If I remove it, he could bleed out within seconds, but if I leave it in, it could continue to do more damage.

"Pu-pull it out," he mutters.

And because I would do anything to make these final moments tolerable, I comply, slowly withdrawing the sword and tossing the blood-soaked thing aside.

"I'm so sorry," I tell him. "I never meant for you to get hurt."

Everest forces a smile. "Don't be sorry." He hacks up blood, his lips coated in crimson red. "Tell Jade..." He coughs again. "That I..."

"No," I shake my head and the tears scatter around us. "You're going to make it. You're going to tell her yourself." I push my hand to his gushing wound and will him to make it. I plead and beg with anyone who might be listening to spare his innocent life. He doesn't deserve this. None of them do.

My hand grows warm, and I wonder how much blood he can lose before he's gone for good. I sniffle and dig into my pocket and pull out the device that Sydney had sent me in with. I shove it into his palm and close his fingers around it.

"I'm going to let go, Everest. And when I do, I need you to push that button. Can you do that for me? Push the button and go home. Be with your love." I stare into his deep blue eyes. "Do not die here, do you hear me?" I rise to my feet and chew at the inside of my lip to stop the tears from coming. "Go home, Everest. Be free."

With whatever strength he's able to muster, his entire body disappears before my eyes, leaving behind not a shred of proof that he was here other than his blood that stains the ground and covers my hands.

I swallow down the sadness threatening to take hold, and channel the pain to bring me back to this reality. Everest is gone. One more lost to the twisted war that Parla waged.

I turn toward the continued chaos, scanning the crowd to find the rest of my people.

"Where are you?" I yell into the battlefield. "Come out and play, you fucking bitch." I latch onto two knives and secure them in my grasp as I run toward Bo, the closest of my friends. I fight my way to his side, returning to my position at his rear. Each footstep rattles the wound that has stopped bleeding on my stomach, but I ignore it; I ignore the exhaustion that wants to drag me under.

"Was worried about you for a second, Birdie," Bo shouts over his shoulder.

"Never been better," I tell him while gripping onto a hunter's shoulder with one hand, holding him in place, and shoving the knife in my grasp into his chest. I push him aside and settle my sights on my fated mate in the near distance. "Let's get to Wes."

Bo and I move as a solid unit, beating and kicking and slicing our path to Wes, one dead body at a time. It doesn't take us long, working better together, to make it to him.

"You good?" I ask Wes.

He grips the collar on his neck. "Could do without this, if I'm being honest."

From the blood coating his handsome face, he has claimed many victims, and without that fucking device, there's no telling how much more damage he could be inflicting. Parla was smart in launching that counterattack because if she hadn't, we might actually have the upper hand for a change.

Wes skims his gaze over my feeble frame. "You need to go back, Wren. Before it's too late."

"You know damn well I'm not leaving, not without finishing what I came here to do." If I go now, Parla will have won for good, and won't stop until she eliminates the last of the demons on this battlefield. They will not die while I run back to safety in Arthlia with my tail between my legs.

"I can't heal you." Wes tugs at the magical device again. "Not while I still have this on."

"I wouldn't let you even if you could. You need to preserve your energy for battle." I turn my back to him and wait for the next wave of hunters to attack.

"My energy"—he yells over the chaos erupting around us—"is pointless without you."

The wendigo that was once our enemy runs full speed ahead toward us, carrying two smaller swords in his grasp, slicing through the bellies of hunters on his journey toward us.

"Not this guy," Bo huffs.

"He's on our side, remember?" I give the wendigo space to join us in our growing little kill circle.

"The numbers keep rising," he shouts. "No matter how many we kill, they keep coming."

I breathe in deeply and scan the vicinity. "We have to take out Parla or this will never stop. She must be cloning them or something. I don't fucking know. But unless we get to her, we're fighting a losing battle."

Even if I were able to use my powers to break the compulsion, I don't have enough strength to do it with an endless supply of grunts at her disposal.

"Or"—Bo chimes in—"we kill the witch that's helping her."

I think back to the old man that she was using to torture me at Rockbridge. He didn't want to be used as a pawn, but he had no choice. I'm sure this new witch is in the same situation, too. If we kill them, who's to say she doesn't have another in her pocket to pull out as a replacement? How many witches must die before her arsenal runs dry?

Even if I wanted to retreat and save what's left of Prania's demonic population, I'm not capable of doing the spell to send them to Arthlia. The only reason I'm here is because of an astral projection spell that is performed by another, more powerful witch. The single path forward is the one where Parla's head is on the end of my sword.

One of us has to die—that's the only way this ends.

And as more hunters fill the gaps where their fallen have perished and surround the few of us that remain, I realize, this battle might finally be coming to an end once and for all.

CHAPTER 21

Wes

There is no greater desire coursing through me than to heal Wren.

But I can't.

Not with the device around my neck suppressing my powers.

She's stubborn. Too stubborn. And refuses to return to the safety of Arthlia.

How can I blame her when her determination and her dedication to follow through is one of the things I love most about her?

Wren is fierce.

I knew it from the first moment I saw her.

My hound locked its sights on her, and from that day forward, my life has forever been changed.

If only my hound would show the fuck up and unleash itself on every single person that stands in the way of what my beloved wants most—to free Prania of its cruel leader.

And without him, I'm not certain any of us will make it out of here alive.

There's no way Bo will leave her, not when he's more afraid to lose her than death itself.

It's a feeling both of us share, along with the phoenix who, hopefully, remains concealed in the darkness of the building near us.

This war is far from over and Wren gave him specific orders to not come out until then.

He knows better than to risk his, and her life, by exposing and putting himself in danger. Wren would easily become more distracted than she already is and potentially falter at the wrong moment in the same manner she had that fateful day at the warehouse.

Our mate bond flickered to life, causing us both to waver. I hadn't realized that's what had happened, but later, Wren confirmed she felt it, too, and that's why she was overcome by the demons that almost brought her to her death.

Love is often more disruptive than the visceral urge to stay alive.

"What's the plan?" Bo yells over his shoulder at our small group.

"Where's Pippa?" Wren calls out. "We should stick together."

We've been fighting these battles on our own, it couldn't hurt to try a group effort if we want to make it out of this alive. Individually, we've held our own, but our defenses are weakening, and there's no telling how much time we have left.

"This way," I tell them.

Gritting my teeth, I plead with my hound to return, to blast through the device clamped around my neck, and end this war once and for all. With him, I'm confident our chances of survival would greatly increase, but without him, I'm not so certain.

I slam my fist into a hunter and latch onto his shoulders, steadying him and giving Bo the chance to drive a knife straight through his chest. Discarding his lifeless body on the ground, I continue on my path toward Pippa, who is battling two hunters by herself.

If the hunters didn't continue to spawn out of nowhere, victory would have already been ours, but it seems Parla has a never-ending supply of men at her disposal.

"Are you okay?" Wren shouts overtop the chaos to Pippa.

Pippa wipes at her brow, her chest heaving. "Yeah. You?" Her gaze trails to Wren's blood-soaked body, no doubt wondering what is hers and what's her victims.

Not very convincingly, Wren nods. "We need to find and eliminate Parla, otherwise they're going to just keep coming."

"I say we take out the witch," Bo suggests before ripping the throat out of a hunter that charged him.

"No," Wren protests. "She'll only find another and then another. We have to kill her. That's the only way this stops."

From all directions, hunters appear, knives and swords locked in their grasps, blank stares on their faces.

Our small but mighty group tightens, all our backs facing each other in a kill circle. Collectively, we rotate and wait for our attackers to close in.

I glance over my shoulder at Wren, who despite being severely injured, is powering through. My heart aches at not being able to heal her, to save her from this nightmare, to win this war for her, and take her back to Arthlia where she will remain safe.

A large part of me wants to shove the device that Tremont had given us into Wren's hand and force her to return to safety, but she would never forgive me. Her being mad sounds better than losing her forever, though.

My thoughts return to battle, my body reacting automatically to the men that charge at us. I punch, I kick, I drag my nails across throats and rip them out. I kill without hesitation, my only desire is to eliminate anyone who stands in the way between Wren and what she came here to do.

But the numbers continue to grow. One hunter turns into two. Then three. Four. Ten.

I end a life and more come—this battle endless, and the damage we inflict on them not seeming to make a dent at all.

Wren gets farther away from me, but I keep a watchful eye on her every chance I get between my own kills. She can handle herself, but with the injuries she's sustained and the fatigue hitting her harder than ever, I need to be aware of when she's hit the threshold of what she can no longer take. I want to give her the freedom and space to continue in battle, but I refuse to let her become yet another casualty in this war.

A stout hunter lands a blow across my face, snapping me back to reality.

He drives a blade forward and I jump sideways, barely evading the blade. It slices through the outer flesh of my stomach but doesn't penetrate any deeper.

The wendigo that has caused so much turmoil lurches forward and grips my attacker's head, ripping it clean off the attached body, and tosses it carelessly to the ground.

"Thanks," I blurt out, never having expected I would thank the man who killed Dash twice.

Two hunters storm him, one of them shoving a sword straight through the torso of the antlered man. The wendigo's eyes go wide, and he steels his gaze down at the blade piercing through him. He looks up at me and says, "Pull it out," before spinning his back toward me.

Trying not to inflict any more damage, I slide the knife out of him and watch in amazement as he palms both of his attacker's heads and smashes them together.

I use the darkly coated sword to slice through the next hunter that runs toward me, cutting his head clean off his body. The thud of his remains hitting the ground echoes through me somehow louder than the anarchy happening around us.

"Are you okay?" I yell out at the wendigo.

But he doesn't answer me, he just continues fighting anyone that comes within arm's reach. Black blood oozes out of the wound in his torso and makes me wonder how much longer he has left—how much longer any of us have left.

And as more and more hunters close in around us, worry overtakes me that all hope might be lost.

I once told Wren that I would find her in the next life, and I've never meant anything more. I don't know what that entails, but deep within me, I'm certain that this lifetime wasn't our first together. And it won't be our last. There's something eerily familiar about being near her. Even her scent unlocks memories I can't quite locate. Like a gentle whisper of the past to remind me that she truly is my fated mate. That no matter what, we will return to one another.

Perhaps that's the only thing bringing me any fragment of comfort as I stare down a death sentence that seems impossible to escape.

"We're outnumbered," Pippa calls out from our kill circle.

"Keep fighting!" Wren shouts.

She has the ability to leave. All she has to do is mutter the word Tremont gave us. Bo and I have the same option. Neither of us will return without her. Pippa and the wendigo don't have that luxury, and if they did, I'm certain Wren would insist they flee. She would grant freedom to any of the demons remaining in this realm if she could. Maybe then she would return to Arthlia, if she knew they would be safe from Parla's wrath. That is not an option though, and the only way Wren will leave this wretched place is if Parla dies.

Hunters attack us from all sides, charging us at easily triple the rate. But despite their numbers, they lack the same tenacity for survival that we do. They're mindless, where we are overcome by the need to free this realm from their unfair torment.

Still, I can't help but wonder if our determination will be enough to see this through.

I yank at my collar, hoping there will be a weakness in its hold on me. But it's no use, this thing is magically bound, and my hound is not here to put up a fight. Doesn't he realize the severity of the situation? Doesn't he see that if he remains suppressed, it might be the difference between any of us making it out of here alive?

"Come on, you bastard," I mutter. "Where are you?" I skim my gaze across the foggy terrain and pray to the Angels that my sights will land upon Parla. If I could find her, then maybe this could end.

But instead of locating that ignorant bitch, I blink and do a double take on the man who shouldn't be here.

A fist lands across my face, and I quickly regain my footing to snap the neck of the hunter who attacked me.

"Tremont," I blurt out and settle my sights on him as he runs toward us, a faint transparent orb around him and the beautiful woman at his side.

Her almost white hair flows in waves around her shoulders and for the slightest second, I'm mesmerized by the strange resemblance she has to Wren. Her features are the opposite of Wren's yet somehow similar. Wren's rugged exterior conceals the soft lines of her femininity but that doesn't mean it isn't there, hidden just under the surface.

"Willow?" Wren appears at my side, her stance wide and ready for another attack. "What are you doing here?"

Willow and Tremont come into our circle, and it isn't lost on me how Willow remains stiff at Tremont's side. She doesn't trust him, and I don't blame her. From what I've heard of their past, I'm surprised she hasn't already killed him just to rid him of her life.

"I came as soon as I could," Willow tells us, her eyes darting over the few of us that remain.

Other demons are fighting around us, but the numbers keep dwindling the more the hunters respawn in the arena.

"If you're here, who's holding the spell?" Wren narrows in on Tremont.

"Sydney," Willow tells her. She side-eyes Tremont briefly before continuing. "I didn't want him to be in charge of sending me in."

Pippa and the wendigo battle the hunters and keep most of them from us as we catch up with the newcomers.

"Where's Everest?" Tremont asks, finally breaking his silence.

"I sent him back," Wren says. "He was in rough shape. You must have missed him."

Willow steals a glance around us. "There's too many of them. You're fighting a losing battle."

"They're mind controlled." Wren steps toward Willow. "I was able to break the compulsion, but I killed the person on accident."

Willow tucks her hair behind her ears and exhales. "Take my hand." She holds her arm out between her and Wren. "I have an idea."

Without hesitation, Wren plants her palm in Willow's. "What do you need me to do?"

"Whatever it was that broke the compulsion." Willow's gaze trails up, lingering on the device around my neck, to meet mine. "Hold them off, okay?"

I nod and put my body between the two Oliver witches and the endless hunters, turning to keep one eye on them while I do everything I can to keep them from harm's way. I snap another neck with ease, the guilt of these deaths piling up on top of each other. I shouldn't care about ending their lives, but if they truly are under Parla's spell, why do they deserve to die pointlessly? If only she would stop being a coward and face us herself.

My stomach lurches when I spot that familiar red hair across the battlefield. Stepping over the rubble of the building he was supposed to remain concealed in, Dash emerges into plain sight. I swallow and dart my attention to Wren, who remains attached to Willow, a powerful energy radiating off them. With her eyes pinched shut, she doesn't see one of the men she loves walking right into the line of fire.

I want to tell her and run as fast as I can over the dead bodies that litter this land and shove him back to safety, but I can't, not when doing so would put her in danger. I must wait it out and hope like hell that Dash has a damn good reason for going against Wren's wishes.

His gaze momentarily locks onto mine and I shake my head, a warning that he shouldn't be doing what he is. Dash remains steadfast as he cautiously, but foolishly, surfaces from the safety of that building. I'm grateful he's alive, only I'm unsure how much longer that will last now that he is no longer concealed.

"It's not working," Wren tells Willow. "Something's wrong."

Tremont steps toward them. "You need an amplifier."

Willow narrows her gaze at him. "That won't work."

Tremont nods. "Yes, it will." But there's something solemn written across his face I can't quite make out. What could he be hiding? His betrayal? His next move? The reason he was drawn to us all along? The final moment when he shows us who he really is?

"It could kill you," Willow adds.

"Wren," Tremont says, ignoring what Willow just told him. "The demonic power you yield is getting in the way."

"What?" I finish killing the man in my grasp and turn my head toward them. "You said she was..."

Tremont doesn't indulge me yet remains focused on my mate. "You know what I'm talking about."

Wren swallows and dips her head slightly in acknowledgment.

"What is he talking about?" Willow asks her.

But when the tears form in Wren's eyes, I understand exactly what he means. I had worried that Wren was involved in stealing demon magic, but I hoped that she would never stoop that low and do such a dreadful thing.

Wren hasn't just been killing every demon she was sent out to eliminate, she's been stealing their essence and harnessing it within her so Parla could harvest it and grow in power. The same thing that had been happening to Willow's family, was the very thing that she has been doing to demons. Is she aware of how wrong that is? How similar to what had been happening to her ancestral line? Did she know what she was doing or was she only another pawn in Parla's twisted game? There's no way she hadn't figured this out by now, and considering how hell-bent she was on returning here to eliminate Parla, I wouldn't be surprised if she thought killing her would somehow redeem the treachery that she has done.

But getting herself killed isn't going to erase or make right any of her actions.

Wren's lips part. "I..."

I step forward and interrupt her. "There's no time," I tell them. "Whatever it is, it can wait."

Wren's wavering gaze meets mine and I've never wanted to pull her to my chest more than I do at this very moment. To reassure her that although what she did was wrong, that I understand—that I forgive her, that she shouldn't punish herself for the sins someone else manipulated her into doing. And perhaps, that's why she's gone easy on Tremont, because he was under someone else's influence when he stole the Oliver power. His crimes were not much different than hers, and with the years he spent in Rockbridge, he seemed to have learned that what he did was wrong.

"Allow me." Tremont holds out his hand toward Wren. "Please." His stare pleads with her and for the first time in a long while, I believe he means well. I've always been skeptical of him, but if my gut is right, he really does want to make amends.

"It's okay," I say. "If he hurts you, I'll snap his neck."

Wren reluctantly slides her hand into his. "What do I need to do?"

"Just let me in, I'll do the rest." Tremont flits his attention to Willow. "I know it doesn't mean much to you, but I'm sorry. For lying to you, hurting you, everything I did that played a part in the suppression of the Oliver's magical bloodline." He shakes his head. "It was wrong. I see that now. I have for a while. I should have never done the things I did. I don't expect you to forgive me, but you must know how sorry I am."

Willow glares at him through her lashes. "I don't forgive you."

"That's fine. I'm not asking for your forgiveness." Tremont, with his greying hair and tired face, focuses on Wren. "It was a pleasure meeting you."

His last statement feels more like a goodbye than anything else, and it makes me question whether I should have offered my approval.

But before I can say anything, four hunters attack, and I'm forced to react. I duck and avoid one man's punch, spinning and kicking at the same time, knocking another of the men down. I shove the sword through the chest of the tallest man, quickly withdrawing it and slamming the brunt edge of the handle into the other's face. Blood splatters and adds to the already gory atmosphere.

I catch Wren out of the corner of my eye, her body trembling under Tremont's authority. He shudders even more as a current of dark magic floats out of her and into him. Is he absorbing the demonic magic? Should I stop him from continuing whatever it is he's doing? Or should I risk the life of my mate in hopes that he's actually trying to help?

Wren's eyes pop open and she glows in a way that I've never quite experienced from her before. She's still injured and exhausted but there's something different about her.

"Now," Tremont calls out to her. "Try again."

Willow and Wren lock hands while Tremont still keeps hold of Wren.

A crackle of white light blasts out from the womens' embrace that's surely enough to temporarily blind anyone who might be looking their way.

Tremont holds his other hand toward the sky, the power leaving the girls and flowing out of him. His body stiffens and for the longest moment, a sharp and glaring brightness pours into the grim area.

The light increases its luster until all that can be seen is white.

I blink through the illumination as it fades and watch the man who was holding onto Wren collapse onto the ground.

Every single hunter on the battlefield stops their advances, some of their arms hovering in the air between them and their target.

"Stop," I scream at everyone. "Stop fighting."

For the first time in the history of my life in Prania, the hunters and demons exist in a space without immediately killing one another. Every person, hunter and demon alike, seems dazed and confused, but none of them continue with their previous attempt at murdering one another.

"What are you waiting for?" a voice calls out, this one feminine and familiar.

I locate the source a distance away, unmoving hunters circled around her.

"Kill them," Parla commands.

I skim my attention across the many people that remain, waiting and wondering which one is going to make the first move. Have Wren and Willow really broken the compulsion or is this some fleeting moment before we lose it all?

Dash comes into my line of sight, his body inching toward the woman we came here to kill.

"Dash," Wren mumbles, her own vision locking onto him.

But when she releases Willow's hand and takes a step forward, she doesn't make it any farther. Her body collapses onto the ground next to Tremont's.

I'm at her side in a flash, and Bo joins me as we turn her lifeless body over. Blood coats her face, and I can't quite determine if it belongs to her or someone else. My hand presses softly against the wound on her stomach and tears uncontrollably well in my eyes.

"Wren," I whisper.

Bo clenches his jaw and breathes in deeply. "She's still alive. I can hear her pulse. It's faint, but she's still in there." He meets my gaze. "It's fading fast."

I shove the person I care most about in this world into another man's arms. "Take her back. I'll be right behind you." As much as it kills me to leave her, Bo is better suited for the job. With the mark still remaining on her neck, it has to be him that returns her to Arthlia, otherwise, there's no telling the amount of danger she would face when the beacon activates, and she isn't able to protect herself.

What kind of mate would I be if I force her to return without following through with why she came here? I must finish her mission and return Dash to her unharmed. With him stepping closer and closer to Parla, I grow unsure of how much time he has left.

Latching onto Willow's wrist, I steady her attention on me. "Save her, please. I'll do whatever it takes. Just don't let her die."

Willow nods stiffly and lowers herself to the ground next to Wren. She exchanges a glance with Bo, and a moment later, the three of them disappear; my heart and soul leaves with them. Rage, unlike anything I've felt in the past, builds within me. Greater than when Mother and Jade were taken from me. More than when I found out Mother was killed. More than the time I spent in Rockbridge knowing that they were torturing my mate.

No, this is different. This feels final. Absolute. There's an undiluted fury at being this close to the finish line and coming up short.

But I refuse to allow Wren to succumb without avenging her.

My nostrils flare and that familiar sense of warmth courses through me. I press both hands around the device still clamped around my neck. I exhale and grip it tighter, not caring at all about how it digs into my flesh as I tug each side away from the other. The metal cracks under my pressure until finally, I snap the thing clean off and toss it onto the ground.

Fire, quick and hot, licks at my flesh, my hound rising to the surface.

"About damn time," I mutter.

I could say the same to you, he growls in my mind.

I narrow my gaze across the way at the woman who is responsible for this bloodbath.

She takes a step back, stumbling over the corpse of one of her soldiers. Her arms go wide to catch herself but the phoenix is there, gripping her shoulders and holding her in place.

"You're not going anywhere," he tells her.

"For ages, Prania has been plagued," I say loud enough for anyone near to hear.

"We were told that it was a feud with demons and hunters, but..." I glance to my left, then to my right. "In reality, we have one common enemy." I point a fiery finger toward Parla. "Her."

The few remaining demons follow behind me, while some of the hunters march in my wake, too.

"This stops today." I continue forward until I'm only a few feet from where Dash has Parla hostage. "Someone else hold her." I make eye contact with the wendigo and he immediately walks over to take Dash's place.

"You won't get away with this," she blurts out, desperate to say anything to attempt to threaten me. "I'm not the only one. If you kill me, you'll never find out who's next."

I laugh. "I've had enough of your fear tactics."

The mob of people stands in wait, no longer attacking each other but coming together to witness the end of an era.

I step toward her, my hand creeping closer, the fire burning a bit brighter.

Parla wiggles in the wendigo's grasp but is no match for his strength.

Wrapping my hand around her throat, I unleash some of my power. "How does it feel?"

Her skin melts under my grasp. Her scream pierces my ears. And I wish there was a way to bottle up this agony so I could gift it to Wren in the afterlife. To show her that in the end, Parla suffered.

She doesn't deserve a quick death, yet a long and antagonizing one. If I had it my way, I would imprison her in Rockbridge and expose her to the same torment she did to us, only dragging it out over decades until she withered away to nothing. I would peel every inch of flesh from her body but make sure she lived through every tortured moment just to experience that same pain over and over. I would have a witch take away her free will and force her to hurt herself and then sit back and watch her anguish and attempt to withstand the control. I would revel in the bliss of certainty that she would never hurt another person, hunter or demon, ever again.

But if I had it my way, the barrier trapping the citizens of Prania within its confines would never cease to exist. The only way to free them is to kill Parla once and for all.

I release her from my fiery grip and bask in the tears streaming down her cheeks and the sticky flesh that remains on my hand. I shake it to my side, ridding myself of her skin, and turn toward the horde that's formed behind me.

"Your entire life is a lie. You have been under the influence of this pathetic excuse of a woman right here. She convinced us that we were enemies so we would kill each other without question." I press my hand to my chest. "I have been to Arthlia. I have seen the coexistence of creatures. We do not have to hate one another. We can live in peace."

Parla spits blood onto the ground near me and chuckles. "You know nothing of peace."

I spin on my heel and face her. "You used my mate. You convinced her that I was the enemy, and you made her kill for you."

A chilling smile creeps across her face. "That's not all I made her do."

Stepping forward, I peer down at her. "You think I don't know?" I shake my head. "You should be ashamed of yourself."

Dash comes closer and I move to give him space. "Remember me?"

Parla glares up at him. "How could I forget?"

"You killed me. Over and over again. And when you were done with me, you beat me until I had no memory of who I was."

"My only regret," she says. "Was not finding a way to kill you for good."

Dash's jaw tenses and I expect him to snap at her, to follow through with his innate desire to end her life that I don't doubt is coursing through him right now. But he doesn't. No, he remains planted in place in front of her, his form fixed to the ground.

"I thought I wanted to kill you," he tells her. "But that would be too easy. Too kind for you." Dash glances over his shoulder. "So instead, I'm going to watch as they rip you apart. *You* Parla, are the evil that must be purged from this world."

"Wh-what?" Parla's evil eyes widen.

Dash grins. "You heard me." He pops his fingers into his mouth and whistles loudly. He raises his voice and faces the crowd. "If anyone would like to have a piece of her, now is your chance."

Murmurs fill the space and without another moment passing, bodies approach from all directions, only this time, they're trained on the true villain, not us.

Dash and I take a cautious step back, leaving Parla there, secured by the wendigo who once wanted nothing more than to kill us.

"Are you sure about this?" I ask Dash.

If anyone deserves to get their pound of flesh, it's Dash. After everything he's been through, he should be able to feel the satisfaction of taking her life.

It's a shame she doesn't have resurrection abilities so we could each get a shot at ending her life repeatedly.

"I just want to go home." Dash keeps his attention focused on Parla as the crowd springs toward her.

She screams out but it's no use.

A demon claws at her back, a hunter jabs his knife through her stomach. Another demon sinks its fangs into her neck while the wendigo keeps her upright, his razor-sharp fingers impaled into her shoulders.

Parla disappears but her cries remain until eventually, they fade out among the cheers of the lasting victors. And with her departure, another burst of bright light fills the entire realm, followed by something I have never seen in all my years of living in Prania.

The sky. Blue and hazy with fluffy clouds.

"I can't believe it." I blink twice and steady my squinted eyes.

The crowd roars louder and dissipates from the woman they were descending upon. Only pieces of her remain. A twitching hand, a mutilated leg, part of her torso. The few demons that stay near her continue munching on her corpse until nothing is left of her.

I breathe in deeply, the air in this realm already seeming fresher than it ever has been.

"We did it," I say out loud to no one in particular. "Prania is free."

But with that declaration, my heart constricts, the uncertainty of whether my mate will live to learn the outcome of this war eating me alive.

Pippa appears at my side, her face covered in blood but seeming otherwise unharmed. "Is she going to make it?" Her serious gaze darts back and forth between me and Dash.

"I don't know," I tell her, because truth be told, my hound and I are terrified that Parla isn't the only one that lost this battle today.

CHAPTER 22

Wren

I'm sitting at the table, patiently waiting for my mother to cut off a chunk of cheese and pass it to me.

"Cheese was always your father's favorite, too." She smiles warmly at me, but I can't quite make out her whole face. "I prefer bread…"

I take the piece she offers me, glancing down at my small hands.

This doesn't make sense, none of it does.

Where am I? Why am I here?

Is this a dream, a memory, or maybe a nightmare?

Commotion sounds in the distance but grows closer to our home.

My mother sighs. "Take the cheese and go hide. Don't come out until I find you. Okay, my sweet Birdie?"

A pang shoots through my heart. How could I forget that Mother called me Birdie? What else have I possibly forgotten?

I loved my mother, adored her more than anyone—how could that memory have escaped me? Seeing her now and feeling the emotions flood through me, I recognize that clear as day.

I grip the salty chunk and climb under the floorboards like we had done countless times before. My little heart patters away in my chest but I go along with my mother's orders. I would have done anything to make her happy.

Since Father left, there wasn't anything I wouldn't have done for her. I never made a fuss. Never told her when she burnt or undercooked a meal. Never mentioned when she braided my hair too tight or forgot to read me a bedtime story. I picked up after myself—and her when I could—and never asked for anything she wasn't already offering me. I could sense the sorrow, and I knew the only thing I could do for her was stay out of her hair—be a good girl.

I'm not sure when I realized Mother was sad, but perhaps I always knew.

She didn't speak of Father often, and those few times she did, it was a blessing.

So, when she asked me to hide, I did so without question. Anything for Mother.

I don't bother eating the cheese, not when Mother will soon come and tell me it's safe to come out. I wish to savor it with her because she is my favorite person.

But little did I know, that day would be different than all the rest.

And every day after would forever be changed.

Because instead of the commotion passing our shack like it had those other times, the door flings open, and men step inside.

I peer through the cracks in the floor, my breath catching as they come farther in, closer to Mother. I want to scream, to shout, to draw their attention away from her, but I can't, not when she told me time and time again that I must remain quiet until she comes for me.

"No matter what, Birdie, you must not come out," she had said.

I hug the piece of cheese to my chest and do everything I can to steady my thudding heart. My eyes dart from person to person through the tiny cracks in the floor, and I wonder how long it'll be until they leave. I don't care if they take all the cheese, I just really want to be with Mother.

I'm frightened but I must obey her orders.

"Where's the girl?" one of the men asks her.

"I don't know what you're talking about," Mother tells him. "I live here alone."

Why would Mother lie about me being here? Is she ashamed of me?

Familiar clicking sounds across the floor but I can't quite place it.

The man presses a dagger against Mother's throat, a faint speckling of red kisses the tip of the blade. I clamp my hand over my mouth to suppress any noise that may arise.

"I'm going to ask you one more time...where is the girl?" He pushes the blade deeper, and I want nothing more than to jump through the floor and kick him in the shins. But I can't move. Not yet. Not when Mother told me to stay put.

"Kill her," a woman says.

Her voice is just as familiar as that clicking across the floor.

She comes into my line of sight, and the cheese falls from my hand, thudding onto the dirt beneath me.

The woman slowly turns in my direction but doesn't look directly at me. Instead, she continues glancing around until she's facing Mother again.

"What are you waiting for? I said kill her."

The man grabs the back of Mother's neck before she can move and slices the blade across her throat. Blood pools out and Mother drops to her knees. Her body falls forward and collapses on top of the floorboard above me, her once bright blue eyes dimming and filling with tears as she peers through at me.

"I'm sorry," she whispers, those two words meant for just me.

The scarlet pooling around her trickles down and speckles my small face, coating the piece of cheese I had dropped into the dirt.

"Burn the house down and find the girl." The woman crosses her arms over her

chest, so unbothered about everything she's just ordered. "Then wipe her memory. Make her think demons did this. Then, she'll have no choice but to join our side."

"Yes, ma'am," another one of the men says.

I remain there, silent tears running down my cheeks as I stare into the eyes of my dead mother. How will I know when it's safe to come out if she doesn't tell me?

But when the bad people leave and many minutes pass, I wonder if I could stay down here forever?

Only, the fire that consumes my home and the smoke that fills my lungs makes it difficult to remain any longer. If I don't want to find out what happens when the flames find me and the smoke fills my lungs, I must do something.

I push on the boards above me, but they won't budge.

"Mommy, you're too heavy," I say to my dead mother. "I can't get out." I push harder and wipe at the sweat and tears on my face. Coughing, I fall to my knees and beg the universe for an ounce of fresh air. "There has to be another way."

I dig my fingers into the dirt, clawing my way under the house in a desperate attempt to escape. I don't want to leave Mother behind, but if I don't, I won't make it out either. Maybe it would be better that way. If I stay with Mother so she doesn't go into the afterlife alone. What if Daddy isn't there to help her find her way? Who will guide Mommy if I don't?

I stop digging and look back at where Mommy once was, but the smoke makes it too hard to see exactly. What if I'm too late and Mother already went without me? I don't want to be alone, there or here.

"What do I do?" I ask no one but myself.

But when a slight flickering of light appears near my fingers, my gut tells me that I must continue forward. I scrape my nails into the ground and rake out what dirt I can, frantic to find an exit from this hell.

I continue scraping away the dirt, throwing it behind me and going back for more.

Until finally, the cool night air greets me, and I squeeze through the small gap to free myself from under our burning house. I gasp for breath and wipe my nose on my shoulder as I take in the sight of the flames engulfing the house. Dirt cakes my face, and I scoot away from the fire, unsure of what I'm supposed to do.

Mother told me to wait. But now that she's gone, what do I do?

I crawl away from the house and into a shrub, hiding from anyone who might wander by. I allow the tears to fall and pull my legs to my chest. I cry until there is nothing left that remains, the waterworks disappearing just like Mother does in the rubble of what was once home.

I fall into a dreamless sleep and hope that I never wake.

But the darkness is soon replaced by a faint white light and a glowing, but beautiful creature that hovers in the distance.

It speaks to me. "You must wake up, Wren."

I rub my eyes, still in my dream, and shake my head. "I don't want to."

"Sometimes, we must do things we don't want to."

"I'm scared," I tell the creature.

"You're allowed to be afraid, but you mustn't give up."

"Mother is gone. I have no one." I sniffle. "Who are you?"

"I cannot stay." The creature flutters in and out of sight. "I'm already being pulled from this realm. But Wren, you must wake up. Wake up. Wake up."

I shoot my eyes open, gasping for breath, and find strong hands that latch onto each side of me.

"Wren," Bo blurts out. He tugs me to his chest and practically smothers me. "Angels, I thought you were a goner."

I catch my breath and recall the terrible dream I had just had. One that felt too damn real.

No, it couldn't have been a dream, it must have been a memory.

But that isn't what I remember from that fateful day.

The version I've always known is of demons coming into my home and killing Mother.

My stomach sinks at hearing Parla tell the men to find and alter my memory.

Is that what really happened? Parla manipulated my recollection of that day in order to brainwash me into being on her side of the war? What other choice did she have? There's no way I would have joined her if I knew she was the reason my mother was dead.

I didn't think it was possible to hate Parla any more, and somehow, here I am, seething with the insatiable desire to wrap my hands around her throat until her eyes bulge from their sockets.

"Birdie, talk to me." Bo smooths the hair from my cheek and stares into my eyes. His touch is soft and gentle and unlike how he normally is.

Am I still dreaming?

Taking in the room, I recognize that I'm in Sydney's home—not in Prania.

My heart picks up its pace as I frantically put the pieces together.

"Wh-where's Dash and Wes? Did they make it out?"

"They're alive and well. They ran out of matches downstairs, so Wes went to light the fire. Dash is checking in on Jade."

Uncontrollable tears tumble down my cheeks. "Everest," I whisper, neither a question nor a statement.

"Don't worry about him. He's going to be fine."

My eyes widen and my mouth drops open. "Fine? He survived?"

Bo's cheeks turn up into the faintest smile. "They don't know what you did, or how you did it, but he was partially healed when he came back. You saved him, Birdie."

"We saved each other," I mutter the same words that he and Jade had shared once before.

"Are you okay?" Bo runs his rough palm over my shoulder and down my arm. "Are you in any pain?"

"I'm fine." I reposition myself, ignoring the aches in my body. They're nothing compared to the thought that I had lost any of my people.

My people. Is that what they are?

But how can I celebrate their lives when I never freed Prania of its tyrant, Parla?

Disappointment fills me anyway. How many more has she killed in the time I've spent unconscious?

"What's with the face, Birdie? What is it?"

"I...I have to go back," I tell him. "I have to finish what I started. Even if it's too late." I scoot out from under the covers and swing my legs off the side of the bed, noting that I'm no longer wearing my armor. Someone must have undressed and cleaned me prior to putting me here.

Bo doesn't stop me, but he says, "It's done, Wren. It's over."

I meet his dark stare. "What do you mean?"

Footsteps patter on the stairs outside our room, drawing our attention temporarily.

Dash rounds the corner first, his face breaking out into a contagious smile the second he's through the door. Wes is on his heels, the sheer sight of him calming my raging nerves. Bo might have said that they were fine, but seeing them in the flesh is something else entirely.

"You're awake," Dash says while rushing toward me. "Do you need anything? Water? Food? I could get you some cheese."

I wrap my arms around his torso and breathe him in. "This is all I need," I mutter into his chest.

He releases me and presses a soft kiss on my forehead. "You had us worried."

I shift my sights on Wes and hop off the edge of the bed, doing my best to walk normally over to him. My body throbs but it isn't anything a couple days won't mend. My injuries were much more severe when I was in Prania, meaning only one thing—Wes healed me.

"You should get back in bed." Wes cups both sides of my face between his hands and runs his thumbs over my cheeks. He pulls me closer and kisses the tip of my nose before dragging me toward him. "I thank the Angels that you're okay."

I allow myself one full minute of his embrace, my body melting into his and reveling in the reality that all four of us made it out alive. But once that minute is up, I break away and stand on my own. "Bo said it was done. What did he mean?" I glance around at my men, waiting for one of them to answer me.

Bo reaches for my hand and tugs me back to the bed. I comply and sit along the edge, grateful for the ability to get off my feet again. I've been worn out after battle before, but this is something else entirely. It's almost like my insides were taken out, thrown in a blender, and put back in without any consideration of where they belong.

Wes looks to Dash, the two of them making eye contact for an unbearably long moment.

"Someone tell me what's going on or I'm going to go back there and find out for myself," I say to them.

"She's gone, Wren," Wes finally spits out.

"Gone like, she got away?" My stomach turns at the idea of her possibly escaping and continuing to wreak havoc on demons wherever she is.

"No," Dash confirms. "Gone like her body was ripped apart into so many pieces that when it was all said and done there was nothing left of her."

My lips part but I find myself unable to speak words.

"It's true," Wes says. "Dash and I witnessed it."

I tilt my head toward Bo, but he just shrugs.

"I was here with you, Birdie." He rubs his hand over my back.

"You didn't stay?" I ask him. "And continue to fight?"

He shakes his head. "My fight is where you are."

Has hell frozen over and Bo been body swapped with someone else? How long until he runs out of the room to avoid his emotions?

I don't push him, not yet. I don't have the energy to chase after him if he decides to flee.

"So you're saying Parla is dead. We all made it out alive. And Everest survived, too?" That's when it hits me, we weren't the only ones there. "Willow?"

"She's fine," Wes is the first to say. "Silas was waiting here for her, pissed that she went without him. But other than that, she's okay. Everyone made it except…"

"Tremont," Bo finishes where Wes left off. "Whatever magical bullshit you guys did, it killed him. He went down first, then you did shortly after. You had so much blood covering you I could barely tell what was yours."

"Pippa? The wendigo?" I hold my breath because there's no way we got *this* lucky.

"They were alive when we left Prania. They were celebrating. The hunters and demons were celebrating together." Wes folds his arms over his broad chest. "I wish you could have seen it, Wren. The sky, it was bright blue, the air, it was nothing like here in Arthlia, but it was fresher than it ever had been."

"I don't understand," I admit.

"When Parla died, the barrier disappeared," Dash says from his spot leaning against the bedpost.

"You did it, you really did it," I choke on the words as more tears threaten to break free. I've never cried this much in my entire life. Well, except…

"No," Bo places his large hand on top of mine. "You did it, Birdie. None of this would have been possible without you."

"She killed my mom," I blurt out. "And then she altered my memory to make me think demons did it."

Bo removes his hand and wraps it around my shoulder, pulling me toward him. "It's over now. She can't hurt anyone else."

"I'm so sorry," I tell them. "I can't believe how easily she manipulated me. I…" This is the part where I tell them the truth, where I admit that I was the reason Parla had as much power as she did. The part where they grow disgusted with what I had done and decide that they no longer want to be with me. I'd rather keep the truth concealed, never allowing anyone to know how terrible of a person I am, but how can I lie to the people I love and not give them the chance to make that decision for themselves?

"Don't be so hard on yourself." Dash lowers himself onto the bed next to me, sandwiching me between him and Bo.

Wes kneels at my feet and puts his hands on my thighs. "You did what anyone else would have. We don't blame you for that."

I sniffle and brace myself for the moment when I ruin everything. "That isn't it," I say. "There's more. And I understand if you change your mind about me. But I can't continue to keep this from you."

Wes grips my legs tighter and forces my gaze on him. "We know, Wren. We know and we understand."

I shake my head. "You can't possibly."

Dash puts his hand on my back and rubs gentle circles. "That's why she wanted you so badly, because you could take the power without dying."

Bo sighs. "We kind of put it together on our own, Birdie. But we don't fault you for following orders. Whether you knew what you were doing or not, that isn't who you are anymore. You've shown us, and anyone who meets you, what kind of person you are."

"You don't hate me?" I hate the way my voice cracks when I ask such a simple question.

Each of them holds onto me a bit firmer, telling me everything I need to know. That they aren't going anywhere. Not now, not ever.

I don't know what I did to deserve them, but damn do I feel like the luckiest girl alive.

CHAPTER 23

Wren

"Are you sure you want to do this?" Willow asks me. "It's only been a week since you got back."

"I would have done it the night I woke up if you would have let me," I tell her. "I don't enjoy not sticking to my word."

"Who could have blamed you? You were off saving the world."

I laugh. "One realm is not the whole world."

She smirks at me. "It is to some people."

We step through the threshold to the Harper Shadow Academy, students passing us by without a second look in our direction.

It's strange being this near both humans and supernaturals, but I'm growing used to the weirdness of this realm—how very non-threatening it is.

When you've run to and from danger your entire life, it takes some getting used to not assuming every single person that crosses your path is a threat.

"This way," Willow tells me as she leads me down a hallway off the right of the entryway. "I was able to buy some time on the other obligations, but I wanted to guide you through assisting in the barrier spell."

"Is it difficult?" I step into an empty classroom and immediately, I focus on the far corner where a sort of ripple in the seam crackles. "What is that?"

"That would be a shadow realm." She holds the door open long enough for Headmaster Walker to come in behind us, and then latches it shut. "Morning," she says to him.

He extends a cup in both of our directions. "Good morning, ladies. Coffee?"

Headmaster Walker has always been kind, especially to Willow. It's almost like he's a father figure in her life. If I didn't know better, I would assume he *was* her father. But Willow has told me of her biological father and the great lengths it took to locate him. Another one of the many mysterious and dangerous adventures she went on in her journey to free the Olivers of their curse. Still, that doesn't make the relationship she has with the Headmaster any less important. He was there for her through the darkest of times and that alone forged an intense bond between them.

"Thanks," Willow says to him while taking one of the cups.

"Thank you." I do the same.

"Sydney's been teaching me, so hopefully it doesn't taste horrible." He rubs his hands together and points to the ceiling. "We're overdue for reinforcing the barrier."

"I'm sure it's great." Willow takes a cautious sip and nods. "It's great."

Walker smiles triumphantly. "I can do advanced spells and somehow manage running a covert supernatural academy, but damn if making a good cup of coffee isn't the most challenging thing I've ever had to do."

"Sometimes the hardest things are those we cannot use magic for." Willow steps farther into the room and glances up at the ceiling. "I see the breakage here."

Walker follows her over. "I suspended all shadow classes the second I spotted it. Wouldn't want a repeat of your first semester here."

"No, we wouldn't." Willow sets her coffee on a nearby table and focuses on me. "That's a story for another day."

I take a quick drink from my cup, savoring the rich warmth of the coffee. "You're right, this is good."

"I went with mocha today," Walker adds.

Setting my cup next to hers, I join the two of them under the glistening magical forcefield. "What is that thing?"

"It's an opening to a realm very near to ours where students do a lot of their supernatural training. It's one of the ways we're able to conduct magical classes without the other students having any knowledge of it. It's only visible to the supernatural eye. But, if not maintained, it can grant direct access to anyone trying to enter our dimension. Good or bad," Walker explains.

"Wouldn't want that to happen." I study the hazy purple as it floats near the corner of the ceiling. "What do you need me to do?"

"Take my hand, like we did back in Prania." Willow steps toward me.

Without question, I slide my palm in line with hers. I haven't known her long, but I'm not sure there isn't anything I wouldn't do for her. She's not just family, she's a damn good person. She didn't have to come to Prania and fight a battle that wasn't hers, but she did it anyway, and for that, I will be forever grateful.

If it weren't for her, I may not have made it out of there alive. Willow might be the very reason *any* of us lived to see another day.

And surprisingly enough, Tremont sacrificed himself to make that happen, too. He gave his life to prove that he had changed. And I'll spend the rest of mine doing that same thing.

"Now take your other hand and hold it up like this." She points her palm to the ceiling, her magic already dancing along her flawless skin. Soft purple mixed with a faint pink flutter on her hand, and for a second, I'm completely mesmerized by how beautiful it is.

I do as she says, hoping that the movements are similar enough to hers to do whatever it is that needs to be done.

"Good." Walker opens a small leather-bound book and traces his finger along the text. He mumbles a few of the words but I can't quite make out what they are.

I focus my attention on my arm and grow amazed when a reddish hue appears in the same way the pinkish purple did for Willow.

Expecting discomfort, I wait for whatever Walker is saying to do what it's supposed to do. But instead of pain or distress, he simply snaps the book shut and says, "All done."

I blink a few times and hesitantly lower my arm. "That's it?" I rub at where the magic was only moments prior.

"That was easier than I thought it was going to be," Willow chimes in.

"I'm not surprised." Walker leans his butt against the nearby desk. "Willow, you alone made this tedious task tremendously simple, but add the both of you, it's a cakewalk."

"Speaking of cake. I'm kind of hungry." I ate a banana before leaving the house, but I find myself suddenly famished.

"That's normal," Willow tells me with a kind smile. "Doing any kind of magic will typically leave you feeling a bit ravenous." She pats my shoulder. "You'll learn what to expect the more you practice. Some spells will take more out of you than others. That's why I have to be careful about where I spend my energy."

"Well, now that we know I can be of assistance, maybe I could pick up some of that slack." If I'm going to be living in her husband's house and eating their food, the least I could do is help. She's already done so much for me.

"Yeah." She nods and glances over to Walker. "That would be nice."

After saying our goodbyes to Walker, Willow and I exit the academy and make our way to her car. It's a bit nicer than Sydney's, with sleek edges and more comfortable seats.

I buckle in and wait for the death mobile to roar to life.

"Thank you," I say. "For trusting me with today."

Willow pushes a button that turns the car on, unlike Sydney's where you must insert a key. Does this one not require such things? I would ask but it seems too silly to bring up.

She pivots her body toward me. "It's what family does."

I breathe in her words, grateful for how welcoming she and her men have been. They could have easily dismissed us and thrown us aside. Instead, they've been more gracious than I probably deserve.

"I know you didn't want to get involved with the Prania thing. But I hope you know how grateful I am for that. For the talk with Balial, for coming to my rescue. I...I couldn't have done it without you." It's strange to admit that for once in my life, I couldn't handle things just on my own.

Freeing Prania was a group effort. It took everyone coming together as one to defeat that evil bitch. Me. Dash. Bo. Wes. Everest. Willow. Sydney. Tremont. Pippa. The wendigo. Heck, even Gary. And finally, the remaining demons and hunters that had enough of her tyranny.

"I'm grateful it had a happy ending. Not all stories have one of those." Willow stares past me like she's recalling a memory of a time when things didn't go well.

"And I'm sorry if I uncovered any old trauma from being with Tremont." I can't imagine how Willow must have felt when she found out he was shacking up in Sydney's house.

Willow sighs. "Our relationship was complicated. But it's been long enough that I've healed, at least partially, from what he had done. And if I'm being honest, I forgave him a while ago. I just didn't want him to know that."

"Really?" I ask her.

She bobs her head up and down. "It doesn't serve me to hold onto all that anger. Hanging on to grudges is like poisoning yourself over and over. Eventually, you have to be the one to stop, move on, and recognize that you can't control anything other than how you react to situations. Did I hate him for what he did? Absolutely. But I had to stop giving him that power over me long after he was gone. I defeated him. I was strong enough to withstand any attack if he came back. There was no chance he would ever have the upper hand on me again. And with that, I finally gave myself permission to let go. I forgave him, but I would never forget. That was enough for me."

"You are a wise woman, Willow."

She chuckles. "When you've been through the shit I have, you learn a thing or two." Willow puts the car into gear and pulls us out of the parking lot in front of the school. "Maybe one day I'll tell you all about it."

I press the button to lower my window and shove my arm out. "That would be nice."

***

We step into the kitchen of Sydney's house to find everyone gathered around. Jade sits on the counter with Everest standing between her legs. Just the sight of him warms my heart, something I wasn't sure I would experience again when he was brutally injured in Prania. Somehow, I had shoved healing magic into him before forcing him to return home. I still don't understand how I did it, but Sydney and Willow have told me that magic doesn't always make sense, and you have to come to terms with not knowing the hows or whys.

If only I could figure it out though, because then I would have the ability to help those in need. Until then, I'll keep trying to uncover whatever lies hidden inside of me that allowed me to heal him.

Bo leans against the wall in the far corner with his arms folded over his chest. He's been more present lately, but still stays just on the edge like he's ready to leave at any moment. Either way, I'm grateful that he runs away a heck of a lot less lately.

Dash sits on a stool at the counter with Sydney standing opposite of him. Wes shuts the refrigerator door and pops the top on something called cherry cola. It's too fizzy for my liking, but Wes can't get enough of the bubbly drink.

Willow walks directly over to Sydney and wraps her arm around his waist. He slings his arm over her shoulder and pulls her close, pressing a kiss to her forehead.

"Missed you," he whispers.

She tugs him tighter. "Missed you more."

The love they share flows out in heaps.

"How did it go?" Dash asks us.

"Really well," I tell him as I approach and climb into the stool next to him.

"She's a natural," Willow adds.

"Sounds a little like you, Mrs. I-didn't-know-I-was-a-witch," Sydney teases Willow.

She giggles and pokes him in the ribs. "I can't help that I was a late bloomer."

Dash drags the hair from my face and tucks it behind my ear. "I'm glad it went well."

I look across the way at Everest. "You feeling okay?"

He rubs Jade's legs and nods. "Better each day."

"I was doing some thinking," Sydney says as he shifts from light-hearted to serious mode. "This house...prior to you all coming here. It was just sitting empty." He glances at each of us before continuing. "I don't know why I ever hung on to it, really, but maybe this is why. Maybe I knew someone would come along that needed it. So, here's me formally offering it to you. If you'd like to stay, it's yours for the taking."

"You're not serious," I say in disbelief.

Sydney chuckles. "I am."

"I don't know how we would ever afford it," I tell him. It's not like any of us have Earth money or Earth jobs. I can't imagine living in a place like this would be cheap, and I don't know the first thing about owning a home.

"We would work those details out if you say yes. The house is paid off, the only real cost would be utilities, taxes, and upkeep." He looks at Willow briefly. "You don't need to make a decision now. You can think about it. The house isn't going anywhere." Sydney slides his hand down Willow's arm and weaves his fingers through hers. "We'll get out of your hair and let you talk it over. No hard feelings either way."

Willow walks over and latches onto my hand with her free one. She gives it a gentle squeeze. "I hope you'll stay." She releases me and the two of them disappear in the direction she and I had come from only moments ago.

The door shuts behind them, sealing us in here with the gracious proposal they gave us and the silence of everyone being lost in their own thoughts.

"I wouldn't mind living here a bit longer until we figure out our next move," Jade is the first to speak. "It would be nice to catch our breath for once."

Everest tilts his head up toward her. "I'm in if you are."

"I do really enjoy how comfortable the mattresses are." Dash shrugs. "And we don't exactly have any better options on the table."

I look at Wes and wonder what's going through his head.

"Couldn't hurt to stick around." Wes takes another drink of his cherry cola.

So far, every vote has been to stay, which leaves things up to me and Bo.

Bo's intense gaze meets mine. "Can we talk? Privately."

My heart stutters and I worry that this is when he finally tells me the truth, that he's leaving for good. That he's going to take Balial up on his offer and spend the rest of eternity in hell being Balial's bitch. The idea of life without Bo weighs heavier than any scruni collapsing on top of me ever could. Still, I slide myself off the stool and follow him out of the room.

Once I'm at his side, he ascends the stairs and makes his way into the bedroom that we have claimed as our own.

He points to the bed. "Sit down."

I comply even though my chest aches with every second he waits to say whatever it is he needs to say.

Bo paces in front of me. "Birdie..."

When he doesn't continue, I say, "My mother used to call me that."

He pauses and looks at me. "Really?"

I draw in a breath and exhale. "I must have suppressed the memory, but yeah. When I dreamt of Parla having her killed, I remembered the moments prior. She told me that my father was as obsessed with cheese as I was...and that she preferred bread." I force a smile. "Like you."

Bo's shoulders relax and his resolve softens. He drops himself to his knees in front of me, taking my hands into his. "I'm sorry."

I pinch my brows together. "For what?"

"For everything. For how I've treated you. For that damned mark on your neck." His gaze flits to the scar he left behind. "For not being honest with you. For not being the man you needed me to be."

I cup his face in my hand and tilt his head up toward me. "I forgive you."

"You shouldn't."

"Good thing it's not up to you."

"I never wanted to be selfish with you, Wren. But I don't think I'm strong enough to withstand my feelings anymore."

"What do you feel, Bo?" I bite at the inside of my lip and hope he doesn't do the thing he always does—leave.

"I'm scared. Scared that you might not actually want to be with me if it weren't for that mark on your neck. Scared that if you do, I might keep letting you down. I've never been more conflicted in my entire life but all I do know is that I worship you. I am honored to be in your presence, and I am terrified that I have ruined things between us."

"Bo..."

"I never want to be apart from you. Not in this lifetime or the next. I can't explain it, Wren, but you need to know, you own me. Body and soul. My heart, my love, you can have it all. It's yours. Whether you choose to accept it or not, I will spend eternity worshipping at your feet and be forever grateful I'm privileged to breathe in the same air as you. I'm yours."

The heavy weight I was carrying dissipates with each word he mutters.

I run my fingers through his dark hair and hold onto the base of his neck. "I love you, too, Bo."

He blinks up at me, his dark gaze glistening. "You love me?"

I break out into a grin. "Yeah, you idiot."

Bo rises to his feet, swooping me into his arms and lifting me from the bed. He presses his forehead against mine and squeezes me so tight I could possibly break in half if he applied any more pressure.

With my hands wrapped around his neck, I graze my lips along his. "Are you going to kiss me, or what?"

Bo crashes his mouth onto mine, his touch cool and warm and soft and intense all at the same time. His tongue spreads my lips and cascades itself passionately. My heart skips a beat, and I die in the best way in his arms.

He breaks away, resting his head on mine again as he catches his breath.

"That's the first time you've ever kissed me," I tell him.

Bo presses a quick one on my lips and smiles. "It won't be the last."

Someone clears their throat at the door. "Are we interrupting?" Wes asks with a hint of *about damn time* lingering in his tone.

"She loves me," Bo tells him while lowering me onto the floor. "Can you believe it?"

Wes and Dash file into the room and Dash shuts the door behind him.

"You're only just now realizing this?" Wes strolls over, plants his hand on the bedpost, and shakes his head.

"Took you long enough," Dash adds.

I shove Bo playfully in the chest. "He can't help that he's a little slow."

Bo snatches my hand and kisses the top of it. "Better slow than never."

I stare up at the man who has finally given me a piece of him that I wasn't sure he ever would. "Can we finally get rid of this alpha mark or are you going to keep teasing me about it?"

Bo's nostrils flare. "I don't think you know what you're asking for, Birdie."

"You love to repeat yourself don't you." I wink at him.

He glances at Dash and Wes. "I'm going to need your help."

I tilt my head and cross my arms. "You think I can't get you hard?"

Bo chuckles and it's the most beautiful sound I've ever heard. "You're going to wish I wasn't hard when I fill you so full you can't take any more." He runs his tongue along his teeth and rakes his hand over his face.

"What do you need us to do?" Dash walks over and plops himself onto the edge of the bed. He scoots back and settles his head into his hand, laying sideways towards us.

"If this is what you really want, Birdie, I think you should let the guys warm you up first."

I narrow my gaze. "Why, so you can make another comment about passing me around to whoever wants a go?"

Bo growls and steps toward me quicker than I can react. He grips my chin and peers down at me. "No one, other than the men in this room, will get to be with you," he mutters. Do you hear me?"

I swallow and fight the urge to latch myself onto him right this instant. "I hear you, loud and clear."

It took him a couple months to finally come to his senses, and now that he has, his possessiveness drives me completely wild. Is this what he's been hiding this whole time?

"Good girl," he says while staring into my eyes.

Wes pushes off from the bedpost and stalks over to place himself between me and Bo. He causes Bo to take a step back and grazes his hand over my cheek. "You sure you want to do this?"

"Is it okay with you?" I ask him, unsure if he and his hound are willing to share me with yet another man. It was one thing when Bo was playing hard to get, but now the reality of me being intimate with one more guy is upon us. I don't know what I would say or do if Wes refused, but I find myself asking for his approval either way. We've had a couple intimate encounters with the four of us, and Wes has been aware of my feelings for Bo, but we've never gone all the way.

Wes leans down toward me, his lips just a breath from mine. "I want what you want, my love."

I stand taller and kiss him, our mouths hungrier than they ever have been before.

He wraps his arm around my torso and lifts me off the floor with ease, backing me closer to the bed. Wes lowers me carefully onto the mattress, his tongue dancing with mine.

Dash repositions himself behind me, his hands finding the bottom of my shirt and dragging it over my head, forcing me and Wes to break apart for the split moment my top is removed.

I meet Bo's fierce gaze in that sheer second and continue kissing Wes.

Wes moans into my mouth and my arousal builds.

Someone, who I assume is Dash, glides his hand over my back, skimming it around the front, and slithers it into my pants. His gentle touch grazes my clit, and he dips his fingers along my wetness.

I arch toward him and all but beg for his fingers to penetrate me.

"Take her pants off," Bo commands whoever might be listening.

Wes breaks from my kiss long enough to drag my bottoms down and over my ass, discarding them onto the floor. He's usually the tidy one, but right now, that must be the last thing on his mind.

Completely nude in a room of fully clothed men, I spread my legs and wait for whatever it is they're about to do to me.

Starting at my ankle, Wes moves his way up slowly, his eyes glowing and locked onto mine. He skims his tongue over my flesh until he halts at my core.

"Please," I beg while leaning back onto my elbows.

Dash comes around my side and lowers himself closer, his mouth landing on mine for a heated kiss. Our tongues swirl together as Wes does his own exploration of my center.

I moan into Dash and whimper when Wes trails his finger over my clit before shoving it inside of me.

He turns his palm upward and slides another finger in, rocking them gently but firmly.

Dash weaves his hand under my neck, supporting the back of my head, and uses his other hand to skate over my bare breasts. He stops at my nipple, pinching it between his fingers, and I nearly come undone.

"That's it," Bo breathes, his presence closer than it was moments ago.

My core tightens and I find myself unable to withstand the pleasure any longer. I climax hard, biting down on Dash's lip and shuddering around Wes. My entire body shivers with bliss, and all too soon, Wes withdraws himself from me.

A second later, I hear the brief hissing of a zipper and feel the weight of Wes crawling onto the bed, on top of me. With no other warning and my mouth still melting with Dash's, Wes glides the tip of his cock over my entrance and pushes himself slowly in, stretching me with gentle ease. He fills me gradually and hooks his arm under my frame to lift me toward him.

Still trembling from my first orgasm, I tense around Wes's shaft, his hardness filling me so fucking full that I grow concerned about Bo's warning. There's no way he's bigger than Wes...but when I think back to having his cock in my mouth, he might actually be. Especially if he shifts into his demonic side. Those barbs that penetrated me were only just the beginning of what Bo has in store for me.

"You're doing good, Birdie." Bo exhales and from the sound of his footsteps, he must come closer.

Wes slides into me deeper, his girth and length spreading me open.

I reach my hand and search for Dash's groin, finally landing on his hardened cock concealed in his pants.

He moans against my touch but doesn't take his mouth off mine.

Wiggling my palm under his waistband, I secure myself around his shaft, gripping and tugging him. I stroke Dash as Wes fucks me and Bo watches from his close distance. Having the attention of all three of them is overwhelming to the senses and makes me crave them that much more.

If only Bo would stop biding his time and join in on the fun instead of being a voyeur.

Wes grips my waist and pulls me upward, the change in position sending a newfound spike of pleasure through me. A thumb finds my clit, and when I briefly peek through my lids, it's Bo that's touching me. With one of his hands bracing himself on the bedframe, he uses the other to apply steady pressure on my most sensitive area. His muscles bulge the plain dark T-shirt he's wearing, and just the sight of him heightens my arousal.

I keep my eyes on Bo, my mouth and hand on Dash, and rock my hips to allow

Wes to fuck me. My center tightens and my breath catches as my climax builds. Wes's cock hardens inside of me and alerts me to his near orgasm, too.

Sweat glistens on Wes's brow and accentuates his already gorgeous features. His gaze darts between his cock pumping in and out of me and my eyes. He doesn't seem at all bothered that two other men are touching me.

Bo pinches my clit, and I cry out into Dash as Wes pumps inside of me, both of us falling over the edge into bliss together.

Wes groans, his face contorting, and somehow, it's the sexiest sight I've ever witnessed.

I grip Dash's shaft and ride out the orgasm with Wes, this one lasting much longer than the first. My pussy quivers around him, and he thrusts inside of me, each one slower than the last, until he's fucked me all the way through.

With even more caution, he gently pulls out, leans down to kiss my cheek, and steps away with a slight smirk on his face.

Bo dips his fingers into his mouth, making no attempt to fill the space that Wes just vacated.

And because I'm still hungry for more, I nudge Dash into the empty spot, breaking my mouth away from his, and saying, "I want you to fuck me, Dash."

"Are you sure?" he mutters as he climbs into position anyway.

He hooks his hands under his waistband and shoves his pants down, allowing his cock to spring out.

I sit up and grip his shaft, spreading the precum over his tip before lining it up to my mouth and swirling my tongue around the edge. We both moan when I slide him inside, and his dick twitches.

Dash pulls the hair from my shoulders and holds it behind my head.

I glide his girth in and out and bounce the tip of his cock against the back of my throat.

"Angels," he moans.

Squeezing the base of his shaft, I stare up into his eyes and continue to suck him until I almost bring him to the brink. I slow down, smiling as I slide him out, and flip over onto my stomach, bringing myself up onto my knees, leaning down, and arching my ass toward him.

"I don't think I can last with you looking this damn good, Wren." Dash cups my ass with one hand and steers his dick to my entrance with the other. He skates it over onto my throbbing clit before entering me carefully.

Immediately, I tense around him, grateful for the penetration. I gather two fistfuls of the bedsheets and back my ass onto him; the motion fills me full of Dash's thick cock. He isn't nearly as long as Wes, but he is wider.

Bo strolls around the bed and stops in front of me, his intense gaze boring down onto me. He takes my chin between his fingers and tilts my head up toward him. "You almost ready for me, Birdie?"

"Mmhm." I nod and lick at my lips, wondering how it's possible to want more. Maybe it's the thrill of Bo's warning that drives my excitement, or maybe it's the immense love I have for each one of these men.

Dash picks up his pace, and I buck against him to match his intensity and give him silent approval to keep going. "Fuck," he sighs with both hands hooked at my thighs and dragging me back onto him.

I release one fist from the sheets and latch onto Bo's waistband, my eyes on his as I pull him closer and unbutton his pants. He doesn't stop me, so I continue unzipping. His cock bulges against his pants, dying to be set free, and because he isn't wearing any underwear, the second the zipper goes down all the way, he pops out.

"You want a taste?" Bo asks me.

I answer by latching onto and tugging him closer, not caring at all how rough I'm being. If his warning was any indication, things are going to get even more intense than they already are. My sights trail to the cock in my grasp, my mouth watering at the sheer size of him. He's bigger than I remember, and we're only just getting started. Still, the thought of him ruining me sends a jolt of heat straight between my legs where Dash is currently fucking me.

"Tell me," Bo says, his voice gruff.

"I want you," I whimper and open for him.

Bo skims his juicy cock over my lips, taunting me.

I graze my teeth gently along his sensitive flesh and widen my mouth to fit the tip of him.

"Fuck," Dash moans again. "I'm going to..."

Pushing the weight of my body back onto Dash, I manage to fit as much of Bo in me as I can, my eyes watering from the size of him. My arousal heightens and I stifle a moan on Bo's cock.

Dash explodes inside of me, my orgasm following his and pulsating my pussy around him. I fight through the tears and choke on Bo as Dash fucks us through completion. Dash is gentle but firm, both with his thrusts and his hands gripping my hips. He leans forward, his body pressing onto mine, and kisses my shoulder.

Dash whispers into my ear, "That was fucking divine." He pulls out, his absence allowing cool air to wash over my ravished pussy.

Keeping Bo still in my hand, I remove my mouth and sit up on my knees, daring a glance around to see where Dash and Wes have gone.

Wes sits at the front of the bed, one knee brought up and his elbow resting on it with his head in his hand, watching us intently. He winks at me, and it's enough of a confirmation that everything is still okay. His irises glow and tell me his hound is good with this, too.

Dash repositions his cock inside his pants and pulls them back over his waist.

Still, I'm the only naked person in the room.

"Where do you want me?" I ask Bo, turning my attention back to the only man remaining who hasn't fucked me yet.

Bo steps away, freeing himself from my grasp, and shimmies out of his bottoms. He climbs onto the bed, claiming the spot next to Wes, and puts his back against the pillows at the headboard, with his legs straight out and his cock on full display. He takes the base of it into his hand, standing it upright.

I swallow down the lump in my throat and eye him.

"Crawl to me, Birdie."

And because I'm apparently a newfound obedient little thing, I drop down onto my hands and knees and crawl the short distance over to him, our eyes locked onto each other the whole time.

He reaches underneath of me, grazing his palm over my dangling breasts, giving both an equal amount of attention.

I kiss the tip of his shaft and span my lips over his hardness.

He uses this new closeness to drag his hand over my body until he reaches my center. Bo tangles one hand in my hair and uses the other to glide his fingers over my clit and onto my soaked vulva. Dipping a few of his fingers into my hole, he doesn't penetrate me any deeper; instead, he teases my entrance and spreads the wetness all over, coating me with the remains of Dash and Wes.

"It's too big," I tell him. Bigger than I thought it was going to be.

"You have to want this," he growls.

"I do."

"Climb on top, Birdie," Bo commands and drags me toward him. "If this doesn't kill you, you're going to be dying for more."

"Cocky much?"

"Not cocky. Confident."

I straddle his legs, his hands resting on my hips, his cock positioned between my pussy lips. I drag myself along his shaft and wonder how it's possible that he's going to fit inside of me.

"I need you to talk to me, Birdie. Tell me if it's too much." Bo glances at Wes and then Dash. "I need you two to keep her comfortable and relaxed. Can we do that?"

We collectively murmur, "Yes."

Wes rises from his seat and kneels beside me, stroking my hair out of my face. "If you want to stop, all you have to do is say so, okay?"

I nod and lean toward him, kissing his lips. "Okay."

Dash comes over to my other side. "Whatever you need, we're here for you." He plants a soft kiss on my cheek.

"I'm ready," I tell them, because if I'm being completely honest, the anticipation is fucking killing me, and if I don't do this soon, I might back out. It isn't that I don't want to be with Bo or remove the mark, it's the not knowing every little detail it entails that drives my control-freak mind insane.

What if I'm bad? What if he regrets marking me? What if the guys get upset and realize they're not okay with sharing me? What if Bo's giant monster cock rips me in half?

Whatever the outcome may be, I'm surely going to find out soon enough.

I've cross-realm traveled, won a war against an evil tyrant, and survived near-death experiences numerous times—I can handle sex with Bo, right?

"Fuck I can't do this."

"Do you want to stop?" Bo pauses.

"No. Give me all of you."

"Easy, Birdie." Bo guides my hips up and releases one hand to hold onto his shaft. He lines it up with my dripping entrance and looks into my eyes. "Is this okay?"

I lower myself onto him, his girth spreading me wider than I ever have been. "Yes." Carefully, I continue down his cock.

"You're so fucking tight," Bo whispers.

"Does it feel okay?" I ask him.

He narrows his bushy brows. "Are you serious?" Bo shakes his head. "It's like I've died and gone to heaven, Birdie. Don't worry about me. The focus is on you."

At this, Wes draws my attention, pulling my face toward him and distracting me with his fiery kiss. His tongue darts into my mouth and seductively grazes over mine.

My body relaxes and slides farther down onto Bo's cock as he spreads me so fucking wide.

Bo cups my tits in his hands and keeps his body still, allowing me to be in control of how far he penetrates me.

Dash moves from his spot at my side and comes around between Bo's legs, behind me. He trails his fingers over the back of my thighs and squeezes my ass gently. Having so many hands on me at once, it really does sort of distract me from the massive cock inside my pussy.

"You're doing so well, Birdie." Bo pinches my nipples harder. "Tell me if you want to stop."

I drag one hand up his chest and settle it along the crook of his neck, digging my fingers into his flesh, my other hand weaving along the base of Wes's skull, tugging his face closer to me to intensify our kiss.

Dash surprises me by gliding his tongue over my inner thigh and spreading my ass. He blows cool air on the back of me and glides his tongue over my stretched-out pussy.

Moaning into Wes, I arch slightly toward Dash but not enough that it causes me any pain.

"Grip the base of my cock, Dash," Bo says. "That way she won't go too deep."

Dash complies, his hand sliding under to settle his fist against the base of Bo's shaft and my pussy. The friction from his hand dances along my clit in the best way possible. He wiggles his thumb to tease my asshole and then inches himself closer to lick it. Dash swirls his tongue across, and up and down.

I push myself lower onto Bo, surprising myself at how much of him I can take. Maybe this won't be as bad as he warned after all. Dash's hand prevents me from going much farther but I'm grateful that he's there to act as a buffer against what might be too much. Each time I get closer, he uses his thumb and index finger to tease my clit and asshole.

Wes breaks away from my kiss to grip my face. "Are you still okay?"

"Yes," I breathe and rest my forehead against his.

"Are you ready for more?" Bo tweaks my nipple harder, the pain shooting straight to my pussy.

I focus on him. "I'm ready for more."

"This is going to hurt," Bo tells me. "Are you sure?"

"Have you ever done this before?" I stare into his dark eyes.

"Not like this, Birdie. And I've never meant it."

I swallow and bask in Dash's mouth still exploring my ass. "I'm ready."

Wes roams his hands over my body while Bo breathes in deeply, like he's giving everything he has to concentrate on what comes next.

My gaze widens as Bo's cock grows inside of me, the sides of it morphing into ridged edges. He widens me even more, and I gasp at the fullness.

"Fuck," I blurt out.

Bo halts but I cut him off from saying anything. Dark, thick scales appear on his arms, and his teeth sharpen into pointy fangs.

"Keep going," I tell him. "Keep fucking going." I inch my legs apart and grant him more room to ruin me.

Dash keeps his hand locked around the base of Bo's cock, no doubt feeling the changes himself as Bo shifts into his demonic side. Dash laps at my ass and continues to lick at the back of my pussy, his tongue gliding over Bo's shaft on his exploration of my rear.

"Hold her hair back," Bo tells Wes, who immediately gathers all my hair into his fist, wrapping it around his hand. The tautness heightens my pleasure.

Bo looks into my eyes, his gaze darting back and forth between mine. "I'm going to bite you, Birdie. Is that okay? I have to reopen the mark."

I nod and tilt my neck toward him.

"I need you to say it."

"Bite me, Bo."

A sly grin forms on his rugged yet handsome face. "Good girl."

I lean closer to Bo, exposing the soft flesh of my neck to him.

His cock continues to contort inside of me, but I remain focused on seeing this through.

If we stand any chance of being together, we must complete this ceremony.

At the same moment his fangs graze over the scar, Bo rocks his hips up, giving into his desires for the first time since we started. He sinks his teeth in and digs his fingers into my sides, dragging me closer. He doesn't stop there, he pivots his hips harder, crashing his monster cock into me. If it weren't for Dash's hand gripping the base of Bo's shaft, Bo might actually tear me apart.

I lean into him, my face resting against Bo's shoulder as he drinks from my vein and his cock swirls and swells inside of me. I breathe in, the scent of him mixed with all this sex sending me into sensory overload. Without processing my next move, I latch my own mouth onto Bo, kissing his skin at first, but the second he moans, I drag my own teeth over his flesh and drive them down until I break through, his blood pooling in my mouth.

Warm decadence pours into me, and I suck harder, no longer recognizing my carnal desires but succumbing to them either way.

I grow lightheaded and hot all at once, but I don't care—not about anything other than Bo finally giving in to being with me. I thrust down onto Bo and moan against his neck as he plunges into me and drinks the blood gushing from my neck.

All at once, Bo breaks away and drags my face toward his, our mouths melding into one another, our essence mixing together as one.

I lean forward and brace myself on the headboard with one hand while Wes takes my other hand and drags it to his rock-hard shaft. I grip it tighter and stroke him with his hand on top of mine guiding me through my distracted state.

"Come for me, Birdie," Bo mutters. "Come *with* me."

With our breaths ragged, my pussy tightens around his enormous, bulbous cock, my orgasm hitting me like a brick wall.

I scream out but, luckily, the sound is muffled on Bo's lips as he thrusts deeper and finishes inside of me.

He releases me, his hand finding my cheek, his gaze meeting mine. "Are you okay?"

"I'm okay," I pant, my hand still stroking Wes's shaft even though Wes finished, too, his climax lost in the chaos of the entire situation.

Dash plants soft kisses over my thigh and lower back.

"It's not over yet," Bo warns.

"It's not?"

"Don't move, Birdie." The barbs on Bo's shaft pierce my pussy, the pain fierce and hot on my completely sensitive and still throbbing area.

I stay still for a moment but grow curious about the sensation and shift my weight slightly. The barbs penetrate deeper like they're trying to keep me in place, and I push against them, allowing the pain to consume me.

"Are you fucking crazy?" Bo pants, his hands on my sweat-soaked cheeks.

"Maybe," I grin.

He latches his palms onto my thighs to steady me from moving any more. "It'll be over soon."

But what if I don't want it to be?

I've never been much of a masochist, but damn am I enjoying this torment.

Bo's cock shifts again, the barbs piercing harder before withdrawing themselves. At first, I wince, but the second they're gone, I'm numb to the pain. Only, a moment later, his shaft swells and swirls, sending equal parts pleasure and anguish before cutting me deeper than it has yet.

My head spins and I fall forward, Bo catching me with his strong arms.

"Birdie," he says, his voice layered with concern. "Fucking heal her."

I lie there, still and pressed against his chest, my entire body radiating with sheer bliss despite being utterly ravished. I want to move, to reassure them that I'm fine, but I can't bring myself to move a single muscle. It's like I'm paralyzed by the pleasure and stunned by the pain.

Dash and Wes shuffle around, the two of them acting fast like they're worried I might actually die as a result of sex with Bo.

But I just sigh and melt into Bo and revel in the possibility that eventually I'll be able to have control over my body again.

The mark on my neck tingles, but different than when we started. It no longer radiates the same sensation, yet now it's altered into something else entirely.

Does that mean that it worked? That Bo was able to successfully change it from an alpha mark into a fated mate's mark?

Bo raises me off his shaft but keeps me tightly to his chest. A cooling sensation washes over my pussy as words are whispered by who I can only assume is Wes.

A split second later, my eyes flutter open and strength is replenished in my entire form, the fatigue being replaced by pure fucking ecstasy.

I push off Bo's broad shoulders and exhale. "Did we do it?"

Bo leans back onto the headboard and looks me over. "We did it."

Lowering myself down, I press my lips onto his for a quick kiss. "We did it," I repeat and collapse willingly at his side. "We did it," I tell the two other beautiful men who are mine.

Bo scoops me into his arms and manages to climb off the bed. He glances over his shoulder on his way to the bathroom, "You guys coming?"

I scoot higher in his embrace and smile as Wes and Dash hop off the bed and follow us in, a look of contentment on both of their faces.

"I love you, guys."

Dash rushes ahead and turns on the shower before Bo can get me there.

Wes comes to Bo's side as he lowers me onto the tiled floor, careful to give me an extra hand to ease me down as gently as possible. "We love you, more."

Dash takes my hand and leads me into the steamy oversized shower, pulling my hand up to his lips to kiss. "Yep, so much more."

I'm overcome by emotions, tears welling in my eyes at how far we've come.

I once thought I hated these men and everything they stood for—never would I have imagined I would feel the way I do today.

First, I was stolen by monsters.

Then I was fighting for them.

Now, I'm fated to monsters.

And I couldn't be any happier that I've fallen for the enemy.

Epilogue – Wren

"Wait, tell me again, which beats which, a straight or a flush?" I glance at the cards in Bo's hand and those laying out on the felt-lined table.

Bo narrows his gaze at me and presses his cards down to conceal them. "If I lose because of you I'm going to…"

But I cut him off. "If you lose it's because you're bad at poker."

Deghan laughs and reaches for his soda, tipping it back and taking a healthy swig. "A flush beats a straight. But a straight flush beats both."

I sigh. How could I retain enough information to successfully assassinate any target, minus Wes, but I can't remember which set of cards triumphs over the other? Maybe poker isn't for me.

"All in," Dash says from his spot across from Silas.

Silas looks at Dash, and if I wasn't certain of his character by now, I'd grow concerned about the intensity of his stare. That's how Silas is. He's mean and broody and a bit too serious for his own good. But he's harmless, at least, unless you cross Willow or the rest of his family.

Silas pushes a stack of chips in, which I think means he calls Dash's bet.

Bo tosses his cards onto the table. "I'm out."

Sydney glances around at the remaining card holders.

Wes discards his, and Cameron follows behind.

"Turn 'em up, boys," Sydney tells Silas and Dash.

Silas flips his cards over, not saying a word.

Sydney scans them and slides three of the other cards from the five on the table up higher than the other two. "Flush, queen high." He turns his attention to Dash, who lays his cards carefully down in front of him.

A grin breaks across Sydney's face as he takes Dash's cards. "Flush, king high.

Dash wins." He shoves the chips toward Dash, who had gone completely all-in on that hand, taking quite a chunk from Silas's pile.

Silas lets out the faintest sigh and folds his arms across his leather jacket-covered chest.

"Aw, don't be a sore loser." Willow plants her hands on his shoulders and kisses his cheek.

His resolve softens and he turns to plant one right on her lips. "He's just having beginner's luck."

Bo eyes me. "You keep looking that good and I'm going to put a baby in you."

"Ew, no you aren't." I giggle and shove him. "You're too much of a baby yourself to have one."

"Doesn't mean I won't do it." He pokes me in the side and latches onto my waist, pulling me into his lap. "One of these days, one of us is going to."

"Gross," Jade says from her spot near the door. She plugs her ears. "You're going to scar your sister for life."

I weasel my way out of Bo's grasp to rise from his lap and walk over to where she stands.

"No offense," she says.

I laugh. "None taken." I lean against the doorframe and take in the sight in front of us. So many various people and creatures coming together for something as simple as a game of poker in one of the many rooms in Sydney's childhood estate we now call home. "Think you can handle things around here while we're gone?"

"And get a little peace and quiet from Bo tormenting me all the time?" Jade side-eyes me. "I think I can handle that."

Willow strolls over and stands next to me. "How long will you be gone?"

"Not sure, but I can't imagine it'll be much in Arthlia time. A week or two? Long enough to help Pippa and Diego rebuild."

"Diego's the wendigo, right?" Jade asks me.

I nod. "Yep. I finally got tired of calling him *the wendigo* so I asked his name. Kind of felt bad after all we'd been through."

"I'm sure he'd been called worse things," Willow adds.

"Bullshit," Bo calls out before slamming his hand against the table, chips splattering from various piles. The rest of the guys, minus Silas, burst into laughter. Bo shakes his head and leans back in his chair, the two legs barely supporting his large frame.

"I keep telling him he's going to fall if he continues doing that." I stare at the legs and wonder how much longer they'll last.

Willow sighs. "You'll have to let him learn the hard way." She turns toward me. "Speaking of, when you return, how about you enroll in some classes at the academy? I could really use your help around here and I'd love for you to learn proper magic."

"Yeah?" I say, my heart nearly bursting with the idea that I might finally come into my powers fully.

A gentle knock sounds on the front door, and a second later, it opens, and a dark-haired girl comes through.

Willow immediately rushes over, throwing her arms around the new person. "Lills," she squeals. "I've missed you." Willow releases her and grips her hand, dragging her over to us. "Lillian, this is Jade."

Jade and Lillian shake hands as I wait for my introduction.

"And this is Wren, Wren Oliver." Willow nearly dances with excitement.

I fit my palm into hers, noticing the spark of energy that pulses between us. "It's so nice to meet you," I tell her.

"Likewise," she replies. "I've heard a lot about you. All good things."

A smile creeps across my face and I tuck my hair behind my ear nervously as I wonder what Willow could have said.

Willow points into the room where the rest of the group is. "The guys are in there. The big one with long, dark hair is Bo. The red-headed one is Dash, and the other guy is Wes—all of which are Wren's mates."

Lillian raises a brow at me. "I see the Oliver likeness. Good for you, girlfriend."

I chuckle and my cheeks turn red, my attention turning to the men who have stolen my heart.

Lillian leaves Willow's side and walks into the room, hugging each of Willow's men briefly before shaking hands with each of mine.

"Who's that?" I whisper to Willow, who remains at my side.

"Family," she says. "You have family all over." Willow turns toward me, "You never have to be alone again, Wren."

Suddenly, it dawns on me that Willow was right.

As I look around at this space, so full of family and love, I realize something.

All the pain in the world was worth it to get here today.

Thank you for reading Fated to Monsters! If you want more from this magical universe, check out Willow's 5-book completed paranormal academy series: Harper Shadow Academy.

All caught up with both series? Make sure to join us to chat books in Luna Pierce's Gritty Romance Squad on Facebook!

Or sign up for the exclusive newsletter so you get details on upcoming releases and sales! www.lunapierce.com/subscribe

About the Author

Luna Pierce is a paranormal and contemporary romance author who loves getting lost in her stories. She brings you tough characters that love fiercely and fight for what's right, even if that means burning the city down for the ones they love. Luna adores all things gritty, and even supernatural.

When she's not writing, you'll find her consuming way too much coffee, making endless to-do lists, and spending time with her daughter and cats in small-town Ohio.

Join the exclusive reader group: Luna Pierce's Gritty Romance Squad

Join Luna's newsletter to receive updates at:
www.lunapierce.com/subscribe

Also by Luna Pierce

Sinners and Angels Universe

(Dark romance with MF, RH, and MFM)

Broken Like You (Standalone MF)

Untamed Vixen (RH Part One)

Villain Era (RH Part Two)

Wings of a Devil (MFM Standalone novella)

Ruin My Life (RH Standalone)

Brothers of Sin Series

(MF billionaire romance)

Dangerous Haven (Standalone)

Book two (Standalone)

Book three (Standalone)

Book four (Standalone)

The Harper Shadow Academy Series

(Paranormal academy reverse harem)

Hidden Magic

Cursed Magic

Wicked Magic

Ancient Magic

Sacred Magic

Harper Shadow Academy: Complete Box Set

Falling for the Enemy Series

(Paranormal reverse harem)

Stolen by Monsters

Fighting for Monsters

Fated to Monsters

www.ingramcontent.com/pod-product-compliance
Lightning Source LLC
Chambersburg PA
CBHW061541190726
48289CB00004B/1122